PROMISES

PROMISES

CATHERINE GASKIN

DOUBLEDAY & COMPANY, INC.
GARDEN CITY, NEW YORK
1982

Library of Congress Cataloging in Publication Data

Gaskin, Catherine.
    Promises.

    I. Title.
PR6057.A75P7   1982   813'.914   AACR2
ISBN: 0-385-15989-7
Library of Congress Catalog Number 81-43631

Grateful acknowledgement is made to the following for permission to reprint their copyrighted material:

"Keep the Home Fires Burning"
By Lena Guilbert Ford and Ivor Novello
Copyright © 1915 by Chappell & Co., Ltd. Copyright Renewed.
Published in the U.S.A. by Chappell & Co., Inc.
International Copyright Secured. All Rights Reserved. Used by Permission.

"Moonlight and Roses"
By Ben Black, Neil Moret, and Edwin H. Lemare
Used by permission of Chappell & Co., Inc. (Intersong, Music Publisher).

"Over There"
By George M. Cohan
Copyright © 1917. Renewed 1945, LEO FEIST, INC.
All Rights Reserved. Used by Permission.

"The Darktown Strutters' Ball"
By Shelton Brooks
Copyright © 1917. Renewed 1945, LEO FEIST, INC.
All Rights Reserved. Used by Permission.

"The Rose of No-man's Land"
Music by James A. Brennan
Printed by permission of copyright owner, Jerry Vogel Music Company, Inc.,
58 West Forty-fifth Street, New York, NY 10036.

"Ain't We Got Fun"
By Raymond Egan, Guy Kahn, and Richard Whiting
© 1929 (Renewed) WARNER BROS. INC.
All Rights Reserved. Used by Permission.

"There's a Long, Long Trail"
Music by W. Stoddard King, Lyrics by Zo Elliot
© 1914 (Renewed) WARNER BROS. INC.
All Rights Reserved. Used by Permission.

"First Fig" by Edna St. Vincent Millay, from the book, Collected Poems, published by Harper & Row Publishers, Inc. Copyright 1922, 1950 by Edna St. Vincent Millay. Reprinted by permission of Norma Millay Ellis.

"Show Me the Way to Go Home"
Lyrics by Reg Connally and Irving King
Copyright: Edward B. Marks Music Corporation
Used by Permission.

*To Robert and Stephanie Harben
with thanks for so many years
of friendship and encouragement*

PROMISES

❦ PART I ❧

1900

CHAPTER 1

I

The child seemed to fall from nowhere almost under the horses' hoofs on that snowy gray twilight. Black Jack Pollock, as big and dark and handsome as the horses he owned, liked to drive himself, while his man sat in dignified disapproval on the box beside him, and so the reins were in Black Jack's hands as the small figure, which had been part of the hurrying throng outside the Corn Exchange in Leeds, suddenly detached itself like a top spinning out of control. The jerk on the horses' mouths had been cruel, and a loud, ripe curse fell from Pollock's lips. Instantly the coachman had been down from the box and had his hands on the bridle of the nearest of the pair. Black Jack himself hardly dared to look at the bundle that lay on the cobbles. He found he was shaking as he climbed down and flung the reins to his man.

The bundle was ominously still, but there was no obvious blood, and no mark he could see made by the iron-shod hoofs. The blanket which covered the creature was dirty and wet with snow; bare, thin legs stuck out sticklike as a dead bird's; the black hair was matted. The crowd gathered, as it always does.

For a moment Black Jack hesitated to touch that heap of rags; then the raw strength that was his temperament overcame the fastidiousness which life had laid upon it. He turned the dirty, wet-streaked face upward to the darkening sky, felt the thin chest for the heart that fluttered. Once again the image of a wounded bird came to him. He looked up at the circle of curious faces about him.

"Whose child is this?"

A negative murmur greeted him. "Dead, ain't it?" someone asked, curious rather than concerned. The bird's heart still fluttered under Black Jack's hand, but now he could see blood in the dark, matted hair.

"Alive," he answered. He thought, though, that if the blow to the head had not killed the child, it might soon have perished from hunger and cold. In his mind he called the child "it"; the face under the flaring gaslight was sexless, the drawn lines across it making it appear both pitifully young and still unbelievably old.

"It'll croak pretty soon, mister," someone offered. "Better take it t'Infirmary. Get it off thy hands. 'Tweren't your fault. See'd it meself. Right out in front of t'horses . . ."

"Will you say that?" Black Jack Pollock demanded. "Will you witness that . . ." He stared as the crowd suddenly dissolved, faded back into the growing darkness; whatever witnesses there might have been were gone. The passers-by now looked quickly and averted their gaze; it was no business of theirs. They saw a handsome carriage, a splendidly matched pair of horses, a big, well-dressed man kneeling by a dirty bundle of rags. He could take care of himself and whatever problem that bundle represented.

The child's eyes opened briefly, the lids fluttered to the beat of the small heart. It had dark eyes, this child, like its hair. The lids closed over them again. It was then Black Jack saw the paper pinned to the blanket. The wet snow had made the one scrawled word almost indecipherable. He bent closer and with difficulty read it. *Lily*. The child was a girl, and he knew that the piece of paper marked her as abandoned.

"Best take it to the Infirmary, like the man said, master. Or maybe the Foundling Hospital," his coachman offered. He looked distastefully at the thing his master bent over; it meant delay; it was a nuisance. They had miles of uphill pull to get out of Leeds and home. The horses wanted their stable, their oats. He wanted his supper.

Only momentarily Black Jack hesitated. To take this unwanted, penniless fledgling who had dropped, broken, to the ground, to either of those places might amount to no more than giving it a place in which to die. He gathered up the child called Lily. "We'll take her home, Kitson."

"She could die on you, master, and that's trouble—"

"We'll take her home." Black Jack waited until his man opened the carriage door, paying no attention to his continued protests, his unwanted advice. Pollock took advice from very few. He climbed in and settled back against the soft upholstery, holding the sour-smelling bundle close to him, desperately trying to give it warmth. The blood had congealed, but the child did not again open her eyes. He wrapped the carriage rug about her, and with his big hand Pollock kneaded the frozen bare feet, cursing what life had flung at him. If he could help it, she would not die. Two deaths in two weeks was more than he should be asked to bear.

* * *

Mechanically he continued to rub the sticklike body as the dusk gave way to complete darkness, and the outskirts of Leeds were left behind. They skirted Bradford, and headed along the Aire Valley to the high country where his home was, and the wind struck down from the moors. He did not think much about the future of the bundle in his arms, what he should do with it; all he thought was that it was alive, and his wife, the woman whose beauty had inspired his pet name for her, Lily, was dead. Latitia had been her given name, and her family had also bestowed on her a string of other names that went with her aristocratic background. But it was big Black Jack Pollock she had married, in defiance of her parents' wishes. She had given him two beautiful children, as graceful, as lightning-swift as she. He had been at the mills all that day, two weeks ago, when she had gone against the custom of the hunting field and outpaced the huntsman. She had not seen the newly placed wire on the fence; the mare's hoofs had fatally grazed it. Secretly, Pollock had been glad when they had told him it had been necessary to destroy the mare. It did not seem right that the instrument of his wife's death should be allowed to live. The fact that it had been his own horses, with the reins in his own hands, which had run down this starveling waif to whom chance had given the name Lily was a bitter irony. He did not want what chance had flung under his horses' hoofs and which felt like a piece of garbage. But he willed her to live. Her name was Lily, and there was a spark of life left in her, unlike that pale, lifeless beauty brought back from the hunting field.

II

Pellham Langley, to which they drove, was the many-turreted house that Black Jack's father had built as, some said, a *folie de grandeur*. "A residence for a gentleman" the architect called it, but everyone had known that James Pollock was not what anyone would recognize as a gentleman. He was the son of a much more colorful man who was known on all the racecourses in Yorkshire and as far as Newmarket as "Gentleman Jack"—a man who lived for cards and horses and women, a man who never married but acknowledged as his son a boy born to a milliner in Leeds. He had earned his nickname because of his dandyish style of dressing, his courtly manner with women of any class, and the grace with which he could concede defeat when he lost a bet. Some said he won more often than he lost, and that there was another, more careful side to that flamboyant character. It happened that his bank balance was considerable when he died on the Doncaster racecourse as his hundred-to-one-chance horse streaked ahead and won the classic St. Leger by a nose. His son was eleven years old, and already an ardent student of figures; he scrutinized the contents of his father's bank account and the winnings from the St. Leger with an eagerness he managed to disguise. He put away his father's gold watch as being too ostentatious, and vowed that the day would come when what his father had left would look like a pittance.

To this end, when he was fourteen, he had himself apprenticed to a solicitor, his theory being that those who knew the law, and handled the estates of the rich, could hardly help picking up some of those riches themselves. He surveyed the great textile industry of Yorkshire, saw how its millowners had prospered, and he maneuvered for every small opening he could find. He watched the mills of which the management was poor or lax, and was ready, through others, to put pressure on for debts which would throw the owners into bankruptcy. He studied the vast coal fields of Yorkshire, picked up information about the small mines that were underfinanced, and waited for the time when they would be ripe for plucking. By the time he was twenty-four he was asked to leave his law firm. Clients had complained that young James Pollock was to be trusted with no information because he would use it to his own account. He left the firm cheerfully and set up on his own. He had no clients but himself, and he wanted none. James Pollock's own enterprises took all of his time. He installed his mother in genteel shabbiness in a small terrace house in Bradford, and forgot her, except to pay her small allowance. He continued to live at the same modest boardinghouse, and he never put his foot on a racetrack. He reckoned he was gambling for bigger odds than ever his father had. He was good-looking enough in a sharp, thin fashion, but his father's friends, if they happened to remember he existed, always declared "Gentleman Jack wouldn't have put a shilling on the nose of a ferret like that." Like a ferret, he clawed and nosed his way toward fortune, pursuing it with a single-mindedness which left many of his victims gasping and helpless. He made a life study of Yorkshire. He knew who held title to its land, its mines, its mills. He was aware of who owed money, and who needed money. He lent money to those whose weakness made them vulnerable. He owned pieces of mills and mines, and he strove for full ownership. By the time he was forty he owned outright six mills and two mines. By his middle forties he looked around and realized he had no heir for the fortune he had amassed.

He set about righting that condition. He had long ago left the Methodist Church, which was traditional with his class, and joined the Anglican Church, which was the church of the gentry. That the gentry did not accept him, he hardly noticed. He set about, with considerable confidence, wooing the widow of a Sheffield steel manufacturer, who had herself come of a Manchester cotton family and brought her own inheritance. The latent residual of Gentleman Jack's way with women won over this meek and plain little woman. She was like a rabbit mesmerized by the attention of a snake. She married him and was just young enough to conceive and bear him one son, her only child, and she died from the effort. James Pollock deplored the weakness of women, looked at his bawling, lusty son, and decided to make him into a real gentleman. To this end, he had acquired, very cheaply, in the valley next to the one where he was building his biggest mill—one whose looms were the most modern, the fastest, the thriftiest of labor—the estate which was known as Pellham Langley. It had been in the Pellham family since it had been recorded in the Domesday Book, and its last owner held an ancient baronetcy. Bankrupt, the man had sold gladly to James Pollock, and had turned away from his fine but crumbling Jacobean mansion. He had left behind a famous garden, running to seed, and gates which boasted his crest and which had rusted off their hinges. For once, none of this downhill slide had been assisted by James Pollock. Pellham Langley, with its garden and small park, with its tenant farms and great shooting moorland, with its own village, which boasted the Pellham arms above the sign on the public house, came into James Pollock's possession just after the birth of his son. He had gone with the architect to survey the house he had just bought. "It's naw't but a load of old rubbish," he had declared, dismissing the fine Jacobean linenfold paneling, the elaborately worked ceilings. "Falling down. Build me a proper house. A fine big house. Keep the garden—though it needs more than a pair of clippers put to it." Enough land had gone with the transaction to qualify this new house as the residence of a gentleman, which he had vowed his son would be. It was an untypical thing for a millowner to do. They had their own place in society, a powerful and comfortable place, and for the most part they were content to see their rise through wealth take them naturally to whatever level society would accept. But they did not buy ancient manors and baronial arms.

If people shook their heads and talked of James Pollock having gone soft in the head, he cared not at all. He was not interested in the opinions of others. He had observed, when he had time to spare from the preoccupations of business, that the gentry of Yorkshire invited their friends to shooting parties in August, and the grouse fell by the thousand. James Pollock had no friends, but that fact did not trouble him. When his son was a man, he would have friends, or at least acquaintances, among the right people. In anticipation of that day, Pellham Langley rose with all the ebullience of the Victorian era; that it was a tasteless horror never occurred to James Pollock. It and its furnishings had cost a great deal of money. He looked with satisfaction at its great granite bulk, viewed its rich Turkish carpets, its plush curtains, its wonderfully solid mahogany furnishings, the heavy brass of its door handles, even the shining copper pots of its vast kitchen, and thought a gentleman could desire no more. Money continued to roll in from his mills and his mines, from the stainless steel of which Sheffield was the instigator and home, from the heavy steelworks in Wales, and a cotton mill in Lancashire, which was another legacy from his wife.

His son was admitted, not without some pressure in the right quarters, to a respectable prep school. To his everlasting surprise and anger, no matter how thick he spread his contracts and benefices or his charitable contributions, James Pollock could not achieve the admission of his son to Eton or Harrow or Marlborough—or to any of the few other schools he had been told were the forging grounds of the leaders of England. His son, however, did attend one of the minor "public" schools—a term which always irritated James Pollock when he came to pay the substantial fees demanded by this very private school. But he was assured it was among the best of the second rank, there being only a few of the first. Its system of flogging and fagging was equally as barbarous as that of any other school of its time, but James Pollock wanted no milksop for a son, and he was pleased that his son never complained. "Black" Jack Pollock, as he was called from his great mass of dark hair and black hooked eyebrows, learned Latin and Greek, learned to become a gentleman, played rugby with knockdown brutality that was reassuring to his father; what was far closer to the heart of a Yorkshireman was that he played cricket with skill and style. When the summer holidays came, he was sent to work in the offices of the textile and the steel mills. Greek and Latin were all very well in James Pollock's opinion, but a man had to know how and where the brass was made.

To his great satisfaction, his son, who was no fool, gained admittance to Oxford. James Pollock thought that three years there might be considered a waste of time, except that it provided that extra social cachet he desired. He lavished uncharacteristic praise on his son when Black Jack achieved his Blue by playing cricket for Oxford. It mattered not at all to James Pollock that his tutors predicted only a very meager Third when it came to the final degree examinations. Black Jack had learned how to ride and shoot, to fish and play tennis, all the legitimate pursuits of a gentleman. But James Pollock's office accountants had also told him that Black Jack had a keen head for business, and had already made suggestions for a few transactions that had proved profitable but were of a slightly questionable nature. This was more accolade in James Pollock's opinion than any university could confer.

The final accolade came when Black Jack was called, at the last moment, to fill in as eleventh man on the Yorkshire County cricket team to play against Lancashire. Rivalry between the two counties had always been intense—the War of the Roses was still being fought on the cricket pitch some said—and Black Jack was fielding as the light faded on the last day of the match. Lancashire needed only one run to win. The ball came toward him; the crowd saw the figure in white flannels spin and turn in the air, reaching . . . He crashed down on his back with a force that almost crippled him for the next few weeks. But the hand that grasped the ball was held high and upright. The ball had not touched the ground, and Lancashire was all out. The crowd exploded with cheers and curses. Black Jack Pollock never played in first-class cricket again, but he had become, with that one great catch, a minor local legend.

Black Jack did not have the three full years at Oxford necessary to take his final examinations. In the first term of his final year his father suffered a stroke and died two weeks later. The young man had come home to Pellham Langley, and to a much larger fortune than he had known existed. He looked at the loveliness of the garden and park spread about that monstrous house, at the famous topiary garden, at the wild beauty of the moors rising above and about it, and he pondered the mills and the mines which had built it, the money they brought, the brass so esteemed by the hardheaded businessmen of the North. He sat with his father's solicitors and discovered that he was a very "warm" man indeed. He learned that his unknown grandmother had died some years before in the same shabby terraced house in which James Pollock had placed her when he had set out to make his fortune.

He listened to the frightening clamor of the mills, saw the pale faces of the women operatives who worked there; he watched the stream of grimy, weary men who poured from the mines, and knew he could do nothing to change the conditions which caused the "black lung." He was a creature of his times and of the industrial revolution which had created this prosperous Victorian England. He was a man of considerable compassion, but he knew it would be no compassion to take from these men and women the jobs on which they depended. If he walked away from this grubby industrial commitment, sold it all to cleanse his hands of its grime, some other man would only take it over, and conditions might be even worse. It was his inheritance and he would take it, with whatever pains and pleasures it involved. Alone, he listened to the silence of his great, empty house, and did not know how to fill it. He did not realize that, at twenty-one, he had never loved, nor known love. That was something James Pollock could not give him, and something the school and university could not teach him. He was not even aware of its absence.

So he attended to his business at the mills and the mines, in Leeds and Sheffield, and journeyed regularly to his mill in Wales. He invited acquaintances from Oxford to shoot the moors in August. He entertained the mayor and aldermen of Leeds and Bradford, he paid extravagant but meaningless compliments to their wives and their hopeful daughters. He looked at the faces of the prettiest of those daughters and none moved him. In time, as his social standing was observed, he was invited to join one of the Yorkshire hunts, and he rented a small hunting box over in the Wolds, and tried to hunt at least once a week in winter. He had the right clothes tailored in London, and he stocked only the best wines. He knew that by the standards of the aristocracy he had only the trappings of a gentleman, but those of his own social standing and slightly lower were prepared to accept him at face value. That face had become decidedly handsome, in a dark fashion; his manner could be charming. There was no need to examine his money value; it spoke for itself. Those who observed Black Jack acknowledged that it took a generation or two to make a gentleman, but with the blatantly money-grubbing James Pollock off the scene, his son might safely be admitted to the company of that select band who called themselves gentlemen. It would be unfair, given that fortune, to hold a man's father against him forever. With the help of two Oxford friends who sponsored him, he was admitted to a good London club. The fact that he had been an Oxford Blue, that he had made that one, magical, impossible catch for Yorkshire was remembered, and it carried some social cachet. It was decided by the ladies of the county who were, in the end, arbiters of such things, that Black Jack Pollock could be considered highly eligible. These ladies, however, did not include the aristocracy, who were a breed unto themselves. For them, Black Jack barely existed. If he had been told this, Black Jack would have shrugged and said the existence of the aristocracy meant nothing to him. He would marry where and when he chose.

He did not choose for some years, and then it was rather that he was chosen, so little say did he have in the matter. He flirted, as was his nature, with the young ladies he continued to meet at social functions, and his heart was still quite untouched. Physical comfort he found with high-class prostitutes in Leeds and London. Because he was fastidious, for a time he supported a mistress in Leeds so that he might have her bed and her attention all to himself. He knew he would never marry her, and so did she. To the murmured suggestion of his solicitors that a man should not wait too long before establishing a family, when a family meant the heirs his fortune demanded, he merely laughed. "Plenty of time. Plenty of time."

There was not plenty of time. It seemed no time at all once he had laid eyes on the beautiful and slightly wild Lady Latitia Stafford. He saw her one day in the hunting field, and his heart gave an unfamiliar lurch. He did not recognize the symptom at all; no woman had ever touched or moved him in that fashion. She was fair, with a glint of red in her hair where it was gathered into a knot at the back of her tall hat; she had wonderfully white skin, a perfect profile that went oddly with her crooked little smile, and there was the flashing, half-humorous, half-wise look of a vixen in her amber eyes. She put her hunter at a ditch with a recklessness that appalled and thrilled him. She laughed at him, and challenged him, and managed to lose him at the end of the hunt.

Refusing the invitation of friends, he hacked his way back moodily to the hunting box. All the time he thought of the vixen smile; he thought of Pellham Langley and it occurred to him to wonder, as he never had before, if the place could possibly be good enough for this laughing daredevil of a girl whose name he did not even know.

He knew it soon enough because he asked about her the next day at the Leeds Conservative Club; he asked carefully, discreetly, and what he heard dismayed him. She was one of the three daughters of Viscount Bletchley, to whose great house at Witfell Black Jack had never received an invitation. There was, he was told, something slightly wrong with Lady Latitia, something in her young past which had frightened Lord Bletchley enough to cause him to send her, in the company of an aunt and a governess, to France two years ago—something to do with her falling head over heels in love with a totally unsuitable boy. A boy, not even a man. The aunt, exhausted by the stormy period of trying to hold this fledgling beauty in check in cities all across the Continent, where the sight of her caused men to stop in the street and stare, had given up and returned her to her parents. At eighteen she was ripe for marriage; no one could be sure if she was still a virgin. That made her a slightly doubtful runner in the marriage stakes, when such a condition was not only prized but necessary in any well-bred young woman. She taunted and teased, they said, and even the formidable Bletchley could do little with her. If she did not care for her own reputation, where would she end, they asked, and shook their heads. It was difficult to lock up a young woman of eighteen. Black Jack listened to it all, discounted half of it, and still his heart beat with that unfamiliar intensity. The lovely vixen face was before his eyes as he labored pointlessly over his desk that afternoon. He went back to Pellham Langley early; it was a sweet, fresh afternoon at the end of winter. Even Yorkshire would soon give way to spring. There would be no more hunting, and when would he ever see her again?

She was there, in his vast, ugly crimson drawing room, standing before the mantel, her riding habit still hitched up, her polished boots splashed with fresh mud. She had taken off her tall hat, and the gold-red hair glowed in the firelight. The tea tray, with its heavy silver and dainty sandwiches which his housekeeper had set out, was untouched.

"They tell me you *work*, Mr. Pollock. You work at your mills." She smiled her crooked little smile. "I've been waiting some time."

"And you shouldn't be here—you know that, Lady Latitia."

She paid no attention. "I had a little difficulty in finding you, Mr. Pollock. My parents don't know you."

"That's true," he said. "No more than they know the farmers who hunt with the pack. I'm not their kind, Lady Latitia. I'll send for the carriage, and you must leave. The groom will take your horse back tomorrow."

She touched the fringed velvet which draped the mantel. Her hands were beautiful. "You haven't asked me why I came."

"No—I haven't. Tell me, then. Why *did* you come?"

The smile was mocking, taunting. It could all have been a mad, wild, cruel joke. "I thought I'd better begin to know you a little. I think I want to marry you."

* * *

In the end her parents gave way, not because they wanted to, but because Latitia would have it no other way. They might even, Black Jack thought, be glad, secretly, to get her off their hands. He wasn't the husband they would have chosen for her, but he was generally accepted as a gentleman, and he could support her, indulge her, even. That dark, firm face of his, with which their daughter seemed infatuated, might even promise the strength to keep and bind her, as long as her infatuation lasted. Once married, the responsibility of holding her would be his. They preferred to look away from that shadowy figure of Black Jack's father, were thankful that he was dead. Lord Bletchley gave away his daughter at the altar of the Witfell Manor church, where the Staffords had worshiped for more than four hundred years. The cynics among the gathering on that late April day, when the radiant light of spring flooded the Yorkshire dale in its particularly luminous fashion, wondered if the haste with which the marriage and the wedding ceremony had been arranged did not indicate that the bride was already with child, and that the child might not be Black Jack's.

In an ecstasy of physical happiness and emotional tenderness he had never experienced before, Black Jack found that night that his wife was a virgin. As he felt her respond to his body he knew that the love he had never believed in was truly his. The unfillable void was filled.

"Why, Lily," he said, "did you choose me? Why?"

She was softly washed in the morning light; she had insisted on the windows being open and the curtains drawn back. The sweet, pungent air of the moors filled the room. "I feel as if I must surely be a hundred years old, and I have been looking for you all my life. I knew—when I saw you. When you have been struck by lightning, you know it, Jack."

His life changed in ways he had not foreseen. He grew somewhat mellow. "Gone soft," some said, while they regarded his happiness with envy. His wife bore him first a son, and then a daughter. Pellham Langley changed, and not only because there were children. Some of the ugliness softened, some was banished, as Latitia seemed to soften the edges of everything she touched. The bright Turkish carpets gave way to subtle Persian silks, the harsh reds and greens were changed to gold and silver-gray and faint blues. The stark outlines of the gardens seemed to change also, as flowers and shrubs were allowed to drip over the lawns. His wife remained what she had always been to him—mocking, fascinating, alluring. He loved her totally and passionately, and he knew his love was returned.

It could be said that they lived happily ever after—for as long as after was permitted to them in their brief married life.

III

Afterward Black Jack could remember very clearly the disdainful shock which had registered on the face of Margaret's nanny when he had carried the bundle of rags into the nursery. The door to the day nursery was open, and Jon sat with his governess, Miss Trimble, before the fire. All looked at him, and Jon, with his usual curiosity, raced toward him, his face alight and questioning.

"What's that, Father? What have you got there?" They were used to the arrival of presents from an indulgent parent, these children of his, but they were not used to him arriving with something carried in a dirty blanket.

Black Jack trusted his young son's instincts. At six years old he was very sure of himself, of what he thought about the world. "Had a bit of bad luck, son. This . . . this little girl got under the horses' feet. I rather think she's so hungry she just fainted and fell there. I picked her up."

"Want to see," his daughter demanded. Margaret at three years old was so incredibly like his adored wife—the little pointed vixen face, the amber eyes—that until Latitia's death she had given special delight to Black Jack. He tried now to be very careful not to let her see that her appearance caused him intense pain, a wound rubbed raw with each sighting. So he carefully lowered the little body so that Margaret and Jon could gaze at the pinched, wizened face. They crowded together, his two children, gazing with unshocked, unsentimental curiosity.

"Why, Mr. Pollock," Nanny said, using all the strength of her disapproving voice, "whatever do you mean, bringing that—that creature in here? It's certain she's got . . . things. Looks to me as if she's about to die. Suppose Master Jon or Miss Margaret caught something . . . ?"

He looked at the healthy faces of his children. "I doubt that will happen, Nanny. Now don't crowd too close. You'll frighten her. And we must feed her very carefully. Can't stuff her. Nanny, heat some milk, please."

"Mr. Pollock, this is *my* nursery. I say who shall come in here."

"Nanny, this is my house." For perhaps thirty seconds they stared each other down over the bundle in the blanket. Few people could withstand the blast of determination from Black Jack's eyes. With a crackle of her starched apron, Nanny turned away, and rang for the young maid who attended on the nursery floor. Her manner clearly indicated that Mr. Pollock might get above himself by bringing in this piece of dereliction from the streets, but Nanny would not demean herself by actually waiting on it herself.

Miss Trimble stood in the doorway. She was a slender, soft-voiced creature whose drab brown dresses seemed to blend into the color of her hair. Black Jack felt vaguely sorry for her whenever he remembered her presence. But he knew that she was kind to his children, cared about them, and he had decided that she would stay on to teach Margaret when he soon must engage a tutor for Jon. He did not care to keep his son too long in this entirely feminine atmosphere.

She said hesitantly, "Is this wise, Mr. Pollock?—I mean, what shall you do with her?"

"Tell me what is wisdom, Miss Trimble, and I'll tell you what would be right to do."

She edged nearer. "Shall I take her, Mr. Pollock?"

She was braver than he had thought. She would incur Nanny's wrath and scorn. She would soil her hands. "Look—I do believe she's starting to stir. Why yes . . . look, Jon. Have you ever seen such strange black eyes? She's had a bad blow on her head, Mr. Pollock, but she seems rather more in need of food than anything else. No doubt, poor thing, she's dizzy. We must try not to frighten her. I'll feed her, if you like, Mr. Pollock. Warm milk, with a little bread in it, I think."

"And a bath," Nanny said. "A bath. And those filthy rags must be burned immediately. Her head must be shaved. I cannot—I *cannot*, Mr. Pollock, have Miss Margaret infected."

"What is her name?" Jon demanded.

"Her name is Lily."

His daughter could not quite get her tongue around the word, even though she had heard her father call her mother by it. "L . . . Lally," she came out with. "Lally." She was satisfied that she had got it.

"What's her other name?" Jon said.

Black Jack answered quickly, the first word that came to mind. "Leeds. Her name is Lally Leeds."

I V

Between them, Black Jack and Miss Trimble began the battle to save Lally's life. It was more than a matter of bread and warm milk. After Miss Trimble had managed to coax her to swallow a little food, after they had washed her—Black Jack in an unprecedented switch from his male role had actually taken off his coat and held the tiny body upright in the bath while Miss Trimble bathed it; after the black hair had been clipped off to reveal the wound on the skull onto which the skin had seem to shrink—they were joined together as allies in a battle to keep the fitful spark of life alive. Miss Trimble put Lally into her own room, into her own bed, because Nanny had resolutely refused the nursery to this sick stranger.

"Surprised at you, I am, Miss Trimble," Nanny remarked, uncaring that Black Jack heard her. "I thought you were a lady."

For the first time, when he carried Lally to Miss Trimble's bed, Black Jack saw the interior of the room his son's governess occupied. Large enough, but rather sparsely furnished. One degree more of comfort than his younger servants had, but not so much as his housekeeper or his butler. Educated, penniless, unmarried women came cheap—cheaper by far than a good cook. There was a fire burning in the grate, but it would not last the night. He rang urgently and demanded more fuel. He realized that Miss Trimble had been given her ration, probably on the housekeeper's orders, and would have had to make do; the mornings in Miss Trimble's room would be cold.

"Where will you sleep?" he asked.

She pointed to the horsehair sofa. "There. I'll be watching her during the night, so just a blanket will do." He rang again, and this time his housekeeper appeared. A full, florid woman, she indicated that she did not like this irregular disruption of a very regular household—moreover, a household which was in deep mourning for a woman just two weeks dead. In contrast to her face, her tone was icy. "Mr. Pollock, I must advise against this. You are bringing more trouble on your head than you know. The correct thing would have been to take the . . . the unfortunate . . . to the Infirmary."

"The correct thing at this moment, Mrs. Plaidstow, is to keep the child alive. And to keep this room—and Miss Trimble—warm. We need several more scuttles of coal, and more blankets. And a pillow. Several hot-water bottles. Send Billings with a brandy for me. One for Miss Trimble, too. Tell Cook to shake herself and send me up something on a tray. Have you had your meal, Miss Trimble?"

"I've had my tea, Mr. Pollock, as always with Master Jon."

He didn't know quite what that meant. Did she have the polite drawing-room tea that Latitia had served at four o'clock, or was it the high tea of the workers—bacon, eggs, fish, perhaps? "And I don't drink spirits, Mr. Pollock," she added.

He lost patience with all the rules of protocol which seemed to hem in these people and had nothing to do with the child in the bed. "For God's sake, Mrs. Plaidstow, tell Billings to bring me the brandy. Send up some cold beef and bread and butter. And send a good burgundy. And two glasses. Miss Trimble will have some wine. And . . ." To reinforce the fact that he did not fear the house-keeper's scorn of such low tastes, he deliberately added the last item: "Some pickles."

"Mr. Pollock, this is very irregular. I don't know what Mr. Billings . . . well, the servants are not accustomed—"

For the second time that evening he found himself in conflict with the class structure he had hardly noticed existed. The servants, she was clearly saying, were there to serve him, as in a small degree they served Miss Trimble. They were certainly not there to serve this nameless nothing from the slums. Before he had married, his house had been run by the butler, and none of this had troubled him. After he married, his commanding, willful wife had overridden every such objection which might even have been raised. Servants, she had said, tried to gain the upper hand only where they suspected weakness or uncertainty. Lady Latitia had never shown either of those things.

He strove to check his impatience. "Mrs. Plaidstow—I am tired and I am hungry. I wish a glass of brandy. I want some food. And a good fire. If necessary, I shall go and get those things myself. I intend, if I can, to keep this child alive, with or without your approval. And if you—or Billings—or anyone else does not approve, you may pack your bags. Now!"

Mrs. Plaidstow folded her hands implacably on her lace apron. "You could be without help in this house, Mr. Pollock."

Black Jack witnessed the stupid, mindless rebellion in the woman's face. "I'm sure Miss Trimble and I could manage for one night." He was tired of servants—his coachman, Nanny, Mrs. Plaidstow—who expressed disapproval of his actions, and all because of the little creature who lay in the bed. He knew as well as the housekeeper that he and Miss Trimble would have to last more than one night in the unlikely event that the whole staff should accept his invitation to pack. It was a huge house, and its kitchen regions were almost unknown to him. He couldn't count how many fires he might have to keep going in that time. He continued to stare at Mrs. Plaidstow and they both assessed the other's relative strengths and weaknesses. At last her eyes wavered, and she turned. "I'll tell Mr. Billings, Mr.

Pollock." The one knowledge they shared, as well as a knowledge of his comparative helplessness in his own house, was that servants, high and low, were easily replaced in those days of 1900.

* * *

The young maid, Nell, heaped coals on the fire; she had been instructed, she said, by Mrs. Plaidstow, to see to it through the night. "You need your rest, Nell," Miss Trimble said. "I'll see to it."

The lids fluttered over the tired eyes with gratitude. She had to be in the kitchen at six sharp every morning. It was she who brought Nanny her early morning tea, she who carried the hot water to the nursery. But she lingered as Miss Trimble placed the hot-water bottles, wrapped in blankets, near the pale, sticklike body of the child. Some color had begun to come into the sharp little face, but it was an ominous flush. Miss Trimble felt the forehead under the damp, shorn hair. "I think she has a fever . . ."

Billings and a footman appeared with the brandy, the burgundy, and a heaped tray of beef, ham, and mutton. There was cold lobster and a white wine to go with it, an apple pie with only one portion removed. Looking at the lobster, Black Jack couldn't help wondering if this overturning of all the rules hadn't shocked his butler into adding to the spread the delicacy he had set aside for his own supper. A table was produced and laid with a starched cloth; silver and glasses carefully set. Billings spoke not one word, except when he brought the wine for Black Jack's approval. "I trust this will suffice, sir?" It was, Black Jack saw, taken from the best bin his cellar could boast. Billings' tone clearly indicated that if Mr. Pollock was bound on folly —the folly of sheltering the unknown, unwanted child, if he were so mad as to commit the supreme folly of actually dining in the governess's room—then he might as well be damned in the best style. Billings stayed to wait on them himself; let it never be said that he, Billings, did not know how to respond to the most unusual circumstances.

There was a visit from Jon, who came to bid his father good night, and to catch another glimpse of the dramatic stranger with the bandaged head in Miss Trimble's bed. "Margaret was angry that Nanny made her go to bed. She wanted to come too." Jon had been bathed, was wearing his flannel nightshirt with a padded robe that was a duplicate of the one he admired on his father. He knew he looked like his father, though the planes of his face had some of the delicacy of his mother's, and he was fair, not dark. He was proud of his height and his strength. Everyone said he was a fine boy. He had only now, after the strangeness and solemnity of the funeral, after the overpowering impression made on him by the black-plumed horses, the black-draped tall hats of the men, the veils of the women, begun to realize that his mother would not return from that dark pomp. He felt lonely, and he did not want to relinquish the familiar companionship of Miss Trimble, the security of his father's presence. Alone at night sometimes he wept, trying to understand the finality of what his father had told him of his mother's death. Latitia had held him in thrall, as she had her husband and her small daughter. Jon did not quite believe that when his father had said she would not come back to them it had been the whole truth. Something of this must have shown in his young, beautiful face.

"Come here, son," Black Jack said. "Here, this'll help you get settled down nicely in bed. It's snowing out, did you know?" He poured more burgundy into his own glass, and added a dash of water. "Take it easy, old man. Like it?"

Miss Trimble clamped her mouth on the conventional protest which she should have voiced. It would do Jon no harm—a sip or two. What mattered was the affection, the warmth in his father's voice. Miss Trimble, in her thirty-three years, had been a governess in enough houses to know how rare such a gesture was. Life at Pellham Langley had been better than anything she had known since, to take a position as governess, she had left the modest cottage of her mother, the widow of a naval officer. Lady Latitia had been capricious, demanding, but never unkind. Miss Trimble had recognized a free and generous nature. She had witnessed, with a little envy, the tumultuous love affair that had continued between Lady Latitia and Black Jack long after most marriages had settled into bland and bored domesticity. If that highly strung, volatile creature, Lady Latitia, had bequeathed too much of her own temperament to her children, particularly to Margaret, then she had also given them her laughing generosity. She had even treated her son's governess as if she were a human being, almost a woman like herself. Miss Trimble had been overlooked, ignored, even gratuitously insulted often enough by her former employers to know what a rarity that was. For Lady Latitia's sake, as well as her own, Miss Trimble loved the children, Jon and Margaret—as dangerous as love was for a governess who might be fated to be sent away as the children grew up. But she couldn't help her love. Nor could she help the pity she felt for the tiny creature in her bed. These emotions, she knew, must be expunged from her face. Governesses were not expected to have emotions; they should not love or hate, only do their duty. She saw Black Jack's arm go around his son's shoulders. Here also was a man who did not perfectly observe the rules.

Eventually Jon was persuaded to go to bed, and Billings and the footman removed the food. Black Jack gave orders that one of the stable boys was to be sent for the doctor first thing in the morning. Only by the faintest twitching of his lips did Billings indicate his disapproval; his manner proclaimed that he was past being shocked.

"If that will be all, sir . . . ?"

"That will be all, Billings."

They were alone with the sleeping child. Her breathing seemed labored and difficult. "I should have sent the carriage for the doctor this evening . . ." Miss Trimble turned her eyes toward the window, where the wind thrust with mighty force. Black Jack nodded. "Yes, I know. He could have refused to come . . . for that . . ." He nodded to indicate the child. Then he looked directly at Miss Trimble. For a moment he studied her as he sipped his replenished glass of brandy. "You do understand I had to bring her here?" He didn't attempt to explain why.

She nodded. Even in the dim light from the fire, with the lamp behind her head, her face seemed ordinary—almost plain; but her skin had a translucent sheen, and her eyes were deeper, more warmly brown than he had ever noticed before. Miss Trimble was not a woman one made such observations about in the normal course of events. "Yes," she said. "I understand." Her voice was both sweet and mellow. If she had been a beautiful woman he might have thought it sensuous. But Miss Trimble would never be a beautiful woman.

* * *

The wind had died, and he went to the curtains and partially drew them back. In the first light of dawn he saw that snow covered all of Pellham Langley's formal gardens, cloaked the wider beauty of the moors. The wind had dropped, and the world was infinitely still. He had spent the night dozing in the chair by the fire. Miss Trimble had lain under a blanket on the sofa. The fire now had died almost to nothing. The lamp had burned out. But Miss Trimble was no longer on the sofa. He moved to the bed, and for a time stood and watched the two figures there. Fully clothed, Miss Trimble had slipped under the bedcovers, and she cradled the thin body of the child against her as she slept. Her prim knot of brown hair had come undone, and Black Jack was surprised at its luxuriant length and thickness; beside the cropped fuzz on the little skull of the child, it shone like a cascade of water in one of the little brown becks which tumbled between the heather on the moors. As he watched, the eyes of the child opened, darting around frantically, bright with fear and burning with fever. But she had courage, this Lally Leeds, Black Jack thought, or she had learned that silence was safer. Her lips trembled, but she did not cry.

*   *   *

Black Jack did not go to the mills for the next four days. It was as if he lived his wife's death all over again as he witnessed the child's struggle for life. The doctor had come and diagnosed acute congestion of the lungs and diphtheria, and ordered strict isolation from Jon and Margaret. The nursery maid, Nell, was detailed to serve only the sickroom. Black Jack himself helped to hold the child over a pan of coals, whose fumes caused her to choke and writhe in his strong hands. This was a desperate suggestion of Nanny, who had heard of it from her grandmother. It was intended to cause her to cough up the deadly phlegm which threatened to cut off her breathing. It might have killed or cured the child, but whichever event, Nanny wanted the stranger either well or dead, and no further threat to her charges. It was Black Jack who sent for ice to form a collar around the swollen neck glands, which gave the shrunken cropped head a monstrous appearance. The doctor was distressed that Black Jack should have been present in the room at all; it was no place for a man. By day, a nurse came from the village to assist Miss Trimble. In the doctor's opinion, Black Jack had done far more than anyone could have expected in giving the child a comfortable place in which to die, much less undertaking to help in the forlorn attempt to restore her to life. But he insisted on staying there. He kept himself away from his own children to help with this dying stranger. It was inexplicable. It gave such a bad example to the servants, the doctor thought. Neither did he understand Miss Trimble's determination, her lack of fear in handling the child, although she was inexperienced. It was as if two strong bodies willed life into the frail one. And one morning it seemed as if that was exactly what they had done. The doctor made his usual call, the first on his morning round. After all, despite the dubious origin of the child, Black Jack Pollock paid his bills promptly, and without complaint. The doctor found two exhausted figures slumped in the big chairs that had now become part of the furnishings of the room. Miss Trimble's hair was untidy; the white sheet she wore as an apron was stained; she looked, the doctor thought, decidedly unattractive—or at least not the neat figure of the governess he had known. Black Jack snored gently. The maid, Nell, stood by the bed. She smiled shyly as the doctor entered, bobbed a curtsy, and, as neither of the others spoke, she ventured to address him. "It seemed to come to a head during the night, sir. Something terrible, it was. I thought she would surely die—she was choking to death. Mr. Pollock, he just took her up, held her in his arms, and stuck his fingers down her throat. She vomited a lot. Maybe he broke a passage for her to breathe. She was easier then. She seems less feverish now . . ." Her voice trailed away nervously. She had no business to address such a personage as the doctor in the presence of her master and Miss Trimble.

The doctor looked down at his tiny patient. The pulse felt stronger. The face was still wan and lined, but the breathing was far less strained. Her eyes no longer burned so brightly with fever. He looked into their enormous gray darkness; he was not a man given to flights of fancy, but he could not help himself when he compared them to the swirling sky over the moors when a storm was brewing. He wondered then what Black Jack had brought upon himself.

* * *

The convalescence was slow, mainly, the doctor said, because the child had been so weak before she fell ill, and had used what strength remained in her fight for live. He warned Black Jack of possible heart damage, of the possibility that the condition could recur if she exerted herself in any way. Only gradually did the shadowed hollows of her face fill out as she learned to take the invalid foods presented to her. She ate everything on her tray, did not reject anything, but indicated no particular preference. In fact, she rarely spoke at all. Certainly, she never complained. She lay in the bed, blankets piled upon her, the fire built high, and did not seem to know what to do with the toys Black Jack brought to her. She touched them curiously, but shyly, as if a furry rabbit was something she did not comprehend.

She never acted toward them as if they were her own. "It's very simple," Miss Trimble said. "She has never had anything to play with before. She doesn't know what they're for."

Black Jack returned to his desk at the mills, his visits to the mines, his lunches at the Leeds Club, but his pattern of visits to Miss Trimble's room to monitor the progress of the child continued. Sometimes it was late in the evening before he came; if the child were still awake, the beginning of a smile might flicker across her face, quickly wiped away, as if she feared to express any emotion. More often she was asleep. She slept long, long hours, Miss Trimble said; the small body seemed to crave the rest, the forgetfulness of that oblivion. He would often bring his after-dinner brandy when he made this visit, and stand at the bottom of the bed, staring thoughtfully at the child as he sipped it.

Fifteen days after he had brought her to Pellham Langley he stood there, watching her as she slept, and he said, "I think we've saved her, Miss Trimble—this Lally Leeds. What do we do with her?"

"Ah . . ." It was half a sigh, half a question. "What, indeed, Mr. Pollock? The practical would say you had done more than your Christian duty, and she should now go to where you should have taken her in the first place, and where she almost certainly would have died—the Foundling Hospital."

"And what would *you* say, Miss Trimble?"

Her gaze flickered toward him, and then back to the child. Her face betrayed weariness, but the eyes still had that unexpected warmth he had found in them on the night they had started their struggle together. "I'm not very practical in these matters, Mr. Pollock, nor, I suspect, very wise, as you reminded me when you brought her here. She is like some little creature blown in from the moors. Half wild. Afraid, I think. Docile only because she hasn't the strength to be otherwise. Myself, I think . . ." She paused.

"You think, Miss Trimble? What do you think?"

"I think if she were well she would have run from here to something more familiar. She's not used to food on plates, to sheets, to a fire. This truly is a piece of dereliction you have picked up, Mr. Pollock. I say you must return her at once to the sort of place you found her, or you must be responsible for what she will become. What do you intend to make of her? Will she grow up in the nursery —or the kitchen? Will she be a servant to your children, or a companion? You cannot hesitate, Mr. Pollock. This child has her own wisdom, and she will very quickly know what you intend."

He turned and looked at her fully. The lamp was low, the light of the fire washed softly, flickeringly, across the room. The woman's translucent skin caught the light of the fire, as did her hair. He remembered how it had rippled about her shoulders and over the child as they had lain sleeping. Now her eyes were fixed on him steadily, questioningly, and they also reflected the moving light. He felt drawn, compelled, bound. It was as if some unbreakable triangle had been forged between himself, this woman, and the unknown child. His hand moved slowly along the tall brass bed rail until it lay on hers.

"I promise you, Miss Trimble, that Lally will never be my children's servant."

"Does that mean you will send her away?"

"I could not send her away—no more, now, than I could send you away."

They moved to the fire, their hands still lightly touching. He stood looking at her for a few moments. Then, quietly, steadily, as if he were afraid she might start back from him, he took the first of the pins from her hair. "I want to see it as it was. All around you—so beautiful." As the pins came out they fell to the hearthrug. The wash of heavy, silken hair seemed to transform her face. It came close to her eyes, and all he could see was the whiteness of her skin, the heavy hair, and the depth of her eyes. He seemed to see himself reflected there. He saw his hand go to the simple cameo brooch at the neck of the plain brown dress. Her own hand helped him, without haste, to unbutton her bodice. It slipped off her, revealing the totally unexpected beauty of her shoulders, the magnificence of the swelling breasts above her corset. Who could have imagined such beauty hidden beneath the plain brown dress? As the corset was unlaced, the chemise dropped, he said, "I loved my wife very much."

"I know that. I don't expect that sort of love. Just . . . just to have you hold me." They knelt before the fire as the rest of her clothes came off. And then they lay on the hearthrug, he stroking the mounds of her breasts and buttocks, exclaiming, placing his lips to her eyelids and lips. "I shouldn't do this . . ."

"Yes," she urged. "Yes. I love you."

As unexpected as the beauty hidden by the brown dress was the deep sensuality of her lovemaking. He knew she was a virgin as he attempted to penetrate her, but there was only one short exclamation of pain. After that, joy, pleasure, the sounds of love, endearments muffled against his shoulder. Afterward he held her tenderly, stroking her again. "What have I done?—what have I done to you?"

"Made me what I wished to be," she said. "If I have nothing else, I'll have had this one time. I love you. Everything is worth this one time. Just to possess you—this once." It occurred to him that she had as effectively seduced him as he had seduced her. He had never thought of the woman who took care of his children as more than an upper servant whose feelings, if she had any, must always be rigidly and properly no more than a spinster in her thirties was entitled to. That she had had stifled longings, a depth of sensuality which could not have been feigned by the most skillful courtesan, was shocking— and yet a source of delight and wonder to him. He thought of his wife, Latitia, so recently dead. He had loved her fanatically, passion- ately, wholeheartedly. No other would take her place. But this woman did not seek to; she seemed indeed content with just this one possession of him.

"I will go away," she said. "I cannot stay here now."

"I will not let you go away. I told you that. No more than I can let Lally go away. In time . . . in a little time . . ."

She put her fingers over his lips. "Do not say it. I want no prom- ises. I want only to be with you for as long as you wish it. A day—a year. Whatever it is, it is a life. A life I never hoped for. We will never marry. I cannot take her place. Your wife's. I don't look for it."

"You will stay," he repeated gently. "You and Lally."

Then he thought of something. "I don't even know your name." She was as nameless to him as the child he had brought half-dead to his house.

"Alice."

"Alice," he repeated. It had a sweet and gentle sound, but this was not an altogether gentle woman, not when her passion had been aroused. He was still surprised by the love he had inspired in a crea- ture whose existence he had hardly been aware of, as remote, imper- sonal, sexless as his children's nanny. Beside the bright flame of his wife, she had not even been a spark. And yet she had burned within herself, a hungry fire which had seemed to want to consume him in this joyous coupling. He knew that there would be many problems ahead with this woman newly called Alice; but he would meet them.

He would meet those problems as he would meet the ones posed by the child Lally. The two had come into his life as if to counterbalance his grief over Latitia. He thought, looking into the brown eyes, of the amber vixen eyes of his dead wife. The generous, laughing eyes. Latitia would not have begrudged him either this woman on the rug beside him or the child in the bed. She had always known she would remain first with him.

In time he eased himself away from that warm body, marveling at the beauty of it stretched naked in the firelight. He went to the washstand to bring water and towels, and as he turned back he was aware that, from the shadows of the bed, the dark eyes of the child were open, wide awake and staring at his nakedness and the nakedness of the woman on the hearthrug. The unabashed, unblinking stare told Black Jack that she had seen such things before. He did not feel ashamed before her.

❧ CHAPTER 2 ❧

I

Life changed after that at Pellham Langley. It had been bound to change with the death of Latitia, but the coming of Lally Leeds, and the alteration in the relationship between Black Jack Pollock and his children's governess, made the change more fundamental, though more subtly felt. Before the world Black Jack continued to be a man deeply in mourning for his wife, which indeed he was. He was bewildered and half ashamed that he should so swiftly have seemed to find comfort in the body of Alice Trimble. He hated the fact that theirs was a clandestine relationship, something he could not proclaim before the world. "When a year is up . . ." he said to her. "It seems such an insult to Latitia to marry before then."

She insisted quietly, as she always did, "I will never marry you, Jack. I can't take her place. I don't want to try. I'll take care of your children . . . and of Lally. I'll serve you in every way I can. But I'll never marry you."

Looking at her calm face, he saw a determined nature almost as strong as his own. He perceived her fears about trying to assume the role of mistress of Pellham Langley. But time would alter that, he thought. Time changed everything. He would observe the conventions, and wait.

The child Lally returned to health. She left Alice Trimble's bed and room, and actually shared a room at night with Margaret, while Jon was promoted to a room of his own. He enjoyed the change. He was masculine enough to enjoy the authority he assumed over his sister and the stranger his father had brought among them, the waif with those incredible dark eyes, and the jagged, spiky hair which the cap Alice Trimble had crocheted for her covered only about half the time. Only half the time because it became clear that such things as caps and conventional clothing were not in Lally Leeds' experience. "Like a little savage," Nanny complained. "Am I supposed to teach her everything in a day? How to behave herself? Not to eat her food with her hands? Not to wipe her hands on her skirts? How to keep herself clean? Such a bad example for Miss Margaret. And just when I had everything going so nicely. Mr. Pollock . . ." She raised her head so that the several chins seemed firmer. "I've come to the conclusion that if that child stays—if she is going to stay with Miss Margaret and Master Jon this way, I must give my notice. I am used to more *class* than this." She folded her hands and waited for Black Jack's protestations, his persuasions, for his final submission.

"Well, then, Nanny, I am sorry you must go. It's a pity. It's sad that Miss Margaret must lose you when she's so recently lost her mother. So much change so suddenly in the life of a small child."

The woman's face flushed dully. "You can't mean that you really intend to keep her *here,* Mr. Pollock. To bring her up with your own children. Why—it's unheard of. There's many a woman in the village who'd be glad to foster her for a few shillings a week. Be glad to. She'd grow up with her own kind. Better than her own kind, if I'm any judge of it. This is gutter scum, Mr. Pollock, I warn you. You'll rue the day—"

"Nanny," he said patiently, quite gently, but with the emphasis of inevitability. "I wish you would stay, but if you must go, then you must. The child stays here."

She put her hand to her face, just for the moment breaking the rigid facade of her ingrained sense of what was right and proper. "Oh, Mr. Pollock—what will happen to Miss Margaret? I can't answer to that."

"I shall answer to it, Nanny. Margaret will have a companion of her own age, Jon another little sister. They will be great friends—"

"Excuse me, Mr. Pollock." For a moment the offended expression gave way to one of real concern, telling Black Jack at once that this starched, authoritarian woman had a genuine affection for his son and daughter, something that showed through her snobbish disdain of Lally. "No doubt, sir, you're a lot cleverer than I am. But I've

been with a number of families. I know something about children.
I've watched them. She's a deep one, this—this Lally. How do you
know what she won't take away from Miss Margaret? Miss Margaret
should have all your attention, your affection. This Lally is already
spoiled with all the fuss that you and Miss Trimble have made of
her. Miss Margaret feels that she's been neglected. By you and Miss
Trimble . . ."

A smile broke on Black Jack's face. He knew he had won, and
that Nanny, although she grumbled, would not leave. "Then you'll
stay and see that there's no favoritism, Nanny. You'll have to watch
out for Miss Margaret's interests. See that she doesn't miss out on
anything. Then there's the challenge of teaching Lally. Think of the
good you'll be doing for a nameless child . . ." He had laid it on too
much, he knew. But the thought of his demanding, imperious little
daughter allowing herself to be second to anyone amused him vastly.
Quite suddenly he knew the depth of his gratitude for the unexpected
arrival of this changeling, and the dynamic bond that had been
forged between Alice Trimble and himself because of her. He could
look at Lally and it eased the hurt of always looking at Margaret and
seeing his dead wife's face. He could lie with the tender comfort of
Alice Trimble's body, hear her quiet, loving tones, and for a time forget the ache of his devastating loss. He knew he was a coward to so
use these two female, helpless creatures to form a crutch for his own
life. But he could not stop himself. They had come his way, as Latitia had. He had to grasp at them to save himself. It was selfish, probably very wrong. But he would go on with it; he had not the strength
to do without either of them.

"Well, Mr. Pollock," Nanny conceded. "I hope I know my Christian duty. No doubt it's very good of you to give this child a home. I
will try to play my part, as you would expect of me . . ."

"Thank you, Nanny. I'm sure your charity will be rewarded."

It was rewarded swiftly, and in a tangible fashion. Nanny's salary
was raised by thirty pounds a year. It imparted to her an immense
sense of prestige and importance. But it had not been hinted at as a
bribe to entice her to stay. She was also given a new young nursery
maid, Agnes, to help Nell. The little kingdom she ruled had swelled.
She comforted herself, as she looked at the uninviting little morsel
she was expected to teach how to "behave," that her stature now was
no less than that of any nanny in the whole county. No one had a
better-appointed nursery, more staff, was better paid. She knew now

that all she had to do was ask Black Jack for what she wanted, and it would be hers. There was power in that, and Nanny was not the only member of the household at Pellham Langley who enjoyed the taste of power.

* * *

In many senses the child Lally seemed to bloom. She ate every scrap that was put on her plate, but never asked for more unless Nanny offered it. She seemed to strive desperately to imitate the way Margaret ate, the dainty mouthfuls, sometimes even the rebellious refusal of what Nanny said was good for her. But she never succeeded in repressing the appetite which seemed to grow as it was fed. She would take a few small bites, and then suddenly start to cram the food into her mouth, like a hungry animal uncertain of the next meal. Alice Trimble noted this with dismay, and tried gently to assuage the fear. She succeeded in some degree, but not completely. It became clear that Nanny would have no trouble in getting Lally to eat.

If the child felt any shame it was only when Jon good-naturedly teased her. "You'll get as fat as Billings, Lally. You'll get like a jam roly-poly. Then I won't be able to have you on my cricket team because you'll be too fat to run."

After such teasing the child would make real efforts to control her eating, but they crumbled in the face of the food piled on the nursery table. Nanny herself did not check her. It had become a point of pride to demonstrate to Black Jack how well she fed and cared for the child. There should be no cause for complaint, as there would be no evidence of favoritism. It wasn't possible that this common little waif from the streets of Leeds could ever rival the beauty and breeding of her Miss Margaret. She could afford to be magnanimous.

Other things Lally learned quickly. At first she thought the little kid boots on her feet too precious to wear, and took them off. Then she saw that Margaret would not even put a foot out of bed without a slipper on it, and she copied that. She copied everything she saw. "As quick as a monkey," Nanny once remarked, injudiciously. Jon seized on the name, and it became a sort of teasing pet name he used for Lally. "Monkey." He also could afford to be magnanimous because Lally was as devotedly his slave as she was Margaret's. Before she had even the confidence to utter more than a few words, she was following Jon about, whenever he would permit it. She listened to him even more carefully than she listened to Margaret, to Nanny, or Miss Trimble. She listened, did as she was told, and uttered no more words than were barely necessary.

Black Jack remarked on her long silence to Alice Trimble. "She seems quick enough, but she hardly says a word. I hope she's not going to turn out a fool. *That* would be a disaster for Margaret. She needs a challenge, not a stupid little follower."

"I think she's just defending herself," Alice Trimble replied. "Like most of the things here, the way everyone speaks is almost unknown to her. Another language. She's learning it, and she's terrified of making mistakes. I think she's so little a fool that she won't talk until she's able to."

"That's very unnatural for a child. After all, Margaret's vocabulary isn't much."

"Lally's an unusual child—unnatural, if you want to put it that way. And it's Jon she's trying to speak like. She obviously worships him. I would guess that when she's ready to speak she will use the words Jon uses. She may be well ahead of Margaret."

"I hope so. It would do my spoiled little daughter good to have to make a run for her money." He used the words carelessly. He had become so used to money that he was hardly aware anymore that there was, in the opinion of the outside world, a good deal of money to make a run for.

* * *

For the child Black Jack Pollock had called Lally Leeds there was the ever-present fear that it would all end. She had opened her eyes on a place of light and warmth and food; sometimes she dreamed that she was back in the other place. The other place she could now only indistinctly remember—cold and hunger being the strongest memory. When such dreams came she would sometimes cry out, and then the figure they called Nanny, robed and nightcapped, hair in a single plait, would come and soothe her, hush her and the little girl, Margaret, back to sleep. Sometimes she would just lie awake in the dark—or rather in the dimness of the night-light Margaret demanded —and unbelievingly try to absorb the change. Life in the other place had been filled with rough voices and very often blows or kicks when she got in the way. There had been a dark and damp room, sour- and evil-smelling, where many people slept. She would then finger the white linen of the things they called sheets, and wonder why the change had come about, wonder, also, if quite as suddenly she would be returned to the other place. The wisdom learned from those kicks and curses told her that she should do nothing to offend—hardly even let them notice her, lest, in remembering, they would send her back.

She strove to master all the intricacies of the unfamiliar things. Hardest of all to comprehend was the established order of it all. At precisely the same time each morning Nanny would appear and they, she and Margaret, would get up. They sat down to the same meal each morning; sat down—they did not eat it standing up, nor did they snatch at the food. There was more food than she had ever seen at one time before on the table, and she had to hold herself back from grabbing for everything that was left over, even though she was already full. After breakfast, she and Margaret walked with Nanny in the garden, while Jon went to lessons with Miss Trimble. Sometimes, if it was fine, they ventured a short distance on the moors, escorted by one of the men who took care of this new world. The gardens were huge and varied—more often than not now wreathed in snow, with swept paths where they could walk.

In the afternoons they were joined on another walk by Jon and Miss Trimble. There was something Miss Trimble called a topiary garden, hedges cut into shapes Lally did not recognize, but she had her first lessons in spelling from them. "Dog," Margaret would call, and yes, there was the shape of a dog, though it didn't much resemble the half-starved mongrels Lally remembered. "C-A-T," Miss Trimble would pronounce. "Rabbit!" Margaret would cry, though she couldn't spell the word. Mouse was another inhabitant of this world. There were no rats. Perhaps here the fearsome, loathed rats of Lally's memory did not exist. Lally had no idea what had happened to the cobbled streets, the noise and confusion of the carriages and carts, the ring of the horses' hoofs, the crowded pavements, the shouts, the cries. This place was eerily quiet. There was little sound except the wind and the birds.

The strangest, most frightening experience occurred during a brief thaw when the snow vanished almost completely. Nanny was kept indoors by a cold, and Miss Trimble took them on their morning walk, and Jon came also. Jon's headlong rush was barely restrained by the presence of a man called a gamekeeper, wearing a sort of uniform. The only uniforms Lally had ever seen before were those worn by soldiers and the police, which she feared, and those worn by the servants at Pellham Langley, which she also feared, but in a lesser way.

Jon ran on and on, Miss Trimble running after him, calling good-humoredly, not really trying to bring him back, as if she enjoyed the run herself. Before anyone could stop him, Jon had reached the place he sought, the place where the moorland path met the steep down-ward plunge of the moorland beck, freed by the thaw from its shroud of ice. On each side it was intersected by jagged rocks. "Our water-fall," Jon cried, and started to scramble up its side. Only half-heart-edly Miss Trimble tried to call him back. "Now then, Master Jon—" The gamekeeper's warning was ignored as Miss Trimble hitched her skirts and started to climb after Jon. "Help them, Hughes," she com-manded. So the gamekeeper took the hand of each little girl and half pulled them, sometimes nearly slipping himself, to the top, where the beck seemed to spring magically from the earth. Lally felt as if a band of fear and panic had tightened about her chest, but she dared say nothing. She scrambled on, as Margaret did, and when they reached the place where Jon and Miss Trimble stood, a wide flat rock, it was a new world revealed to her.

She had never imagined such distances, such a vast sky. From here they could look down on the mass of Pellham Langley, its chimneys comfortingly smoking, telling Lally that it still existed, and its warmth still waited for her. From here the shapes of Dog and Cat, Rabbit and Mouse merged with the rest of the greenery, and no longer overawed her. Then she looked in the other direction from this ridge. There were tall, tall chimneys rising from long lines of high buildings, and steep streets of tiny houses merging into them. "The mills," Jon said. "Father's mills. And that's Pellham Langley." But he did not point toward the great house, but to a small huddle of houses nestled in the fold of the moor, a plain steeple rising among them. "That's the manor of Pellham Langley." Lally had no idea what a manor was, but it was something Jon spoke of as if he owned it.

Then they scrambled down the rocks beside the waterfall, Miss Trimble and the gamekeeper going first, ready to catch them if they should slip. To Lally it seemed a long way down, and she was afraid to look. She was glad when they got back to the familiar, safe gar-den. Even the carved animals in the evergreen hedges did not now look so frightening. They returned to the nursery and Nanny's scold-ing. "I'm surprised, Miss Trimble—you letting them climb up there. Slippery at this time of year. And the wind up there—"

"A little adventure, Nanny—and they'll sleep better for the exercise."

At midday there was another meal, and then a rest in bed. A rest from what, Lally didn't know, because there had been no work, no task set her. The only task was to acquire as quickly as possible the skills and knowledge of this world so that Jon would not tease her, nor Margaret laugh at her clumsiness. She played willingly with Margaret—"play" was something they did together. Perhaps that was the work demanded of her, Lally thought. They played with dolls and a dollhouse that was a miniature of the great house in which they lived. They played with blocks which had letters on them. Sometimes Jon allowed them to play, under his supervision, with his great army of lead soldiers. Lally watched Margaret scribbling with colored pencils, and so she did the same. It was all very bewildering. But no one hit her, and there was plenty to eat, and she was warm. The dark dream was of when it might suddenly end. Sometimes she struggled against sleep so that the dream would not come. She thought of the visits to the nursery of the big, dark man Jon and Margaret called "Father." Lally couldn't remember a father in her other world. Margaret told her, with some air of importance, that her mother had died. Been killed. Lally could remember dead people, cold thin people who died in the damp, dark room. She could not remember someone called a mother. There had been no one in that other world like this woman here, with the gentle voice, who always wore a brown dress. The first morning she had wakened in this new world the woman had been lying on the bed holding her. Lally remembered the sweet smell of her, the warm curve of her breast. The woman's face had come and gone through a mist of raging heat and choking for breath. She had felt the strong but not cruel hands of the dark man. They had seemed pleased with her just for making the effort to be rid of the choking phlegm. They seemed pleased with each other, also. Lally remembered how they had lain together before the huge fire. She remembered the sheen of their white bodies.

They had names for her here. Lally and Monkey. She didn't mind what they called her; she didn't mind anything, just so long as they didn't send her back. She was determined she would do everything exactly as they wanted, so that she would never be sent back.

II

There was no way to stop the knowledge spreading to the rest of the household. There were some emotions which Alice Trimble could not discipline out of her face and her voice. The woman, formerly as quiet and demure as a little brown bird, was suddenly gifted with a magnificent confidence. She laughed often with Jon, her skin and her eyes glowed. There was no masking the attitude of a woman in love; there was no disguising the ripeness of a body fulfilled.

Black Jack's valet noticed certain things, and he murmured them to Billings, who advised him to mind his own business. Nell, the little maid who cleaned Miss Trimble's room and brought her coal and water, also noticed things, but said nothing. She liked Miss Trimble. Inevitably, though, Mrs. Plaidstow, the housekeeper, came to notice things for herself. Hear things. Her relationship with Black Jack had been icily formal since the night he had insisted on bringing Lally Leeds into his house. She could not forgive herself or him for the indignity of her backdown. She hated the child Lally. She missed no opportunity, in conversation with Billings, or by implication when she spoke with Black Jack, to criticize or disparage. She saw the child with the dark eyes in the face that grew steadily rounder, with the dark hair growing into a thick, straight fall which Miss Trimble kept neatly trimmed, as the instrument of her humiliation. Everyone knew that governesses were worth nothing. Housekeepers, good housekeepers like herself who had trained in a ducal household, were hard to find. But still, she looked at her comfortable sitting room, the heaped fire in her bedroom, she saw the loaded table in the servants' hall and the room where she and Billings ate apart from the other servants, and she was loath to disturb any of it. But she was also a staunch, churchgoing Methodist. Was she to stay here, eat and sleep under the same roof as a whore?—take the money of a whore's master? She thought in those terms. Finally she spoke to Black Jack.

"It is a scandal, Mr. Pollock. Before the eyes of your innocent children. Your wife hardly cold—"

"Mrs. Plaidstow, I'll thank you not to mention my wife's name."

"Then someone else should. Perhaps her parents—the grandparents of those innocent children. What example is this to give them? You must send her away, Mr. Pollock. No doubt she has played upon your weakness in your time of grief. There are wicked women who do that."

He openly laughed at her. "Wicked? Mrs. Plaidstow, you have a strange taste in jokes."

"Indeed I wasn't joking, Mr. Pollock. I'll not have it, I tell you. I will not live under the same roof as that woman."

"Then you, Mrs. Plaidstow, must change your roof. For Miss Trimble shall not."

She was outraged by the sheer brazenness of it all. "That Jezebel! I give you a month's notice. Either she or I will go."

"Then you may take an extra month's salary in lieu of a month's notice, Mrs. Plaidstow. You may go, I would not wish you to stay in a position you find distasteful."

"Distasteful?" she echoed. *"Disgusting!* Lady Latitia—" She stopped, because something in Black Jack's expression reminded her that he was, as some maintained, only one generation removed from the gutter which had spawned his father. No doubt that was why he had brought in the child. That was why he could so lightly take as a mistress that timid mouse of a woman. She began to fear the anger she saw growing in his face. She knew that this time there would be no backdown on either side. He would not forgive the words she had spoken. She would not ask his pardon. Her time at Pellham Langley had ended. She packed her bags that same day, received the money due her, spurned the extra which was offered, and left. But her tongue could not leave Black Jack or Alice Trimble in peace. Her conscience told her that she should not.

The next day Lord Bletchley stood in Black Jack's drawing room. He drank the other man's brandy and felt uncomfortable about the errand on which his wife had sent him. Through the years of his daughter's marriage to someone his wife had called a social climber, he had come to like and even give a measure of respect to his son-in-law. Black Jack Pollock had had the qualities which his daughter, Latitia, had needed. Bletchley, against all odds, witnessed a happy marriage. The man was strong enough—Bletchley shied away from the word "loving," but that was included in his thought—to hold together the quicksilver temperament of his daughter. She had been an admirable and even envied wife and mother. She had been loved by husband and children, and in her turn gave love. Bletchley had known Black Jack's real anguish at her death. He was as certain as he could be of anything that this unfortunate affair with the brown mouse governess had not begun until after Latitia's death. Even that admission had been wrung from Mrs. Plaidstow when she had come with her story to Lady Bletchley.

"It's too bad, Jack," he said now to his son-in-law. "I'm sure I know how you feel. But it won't do, you know . . . not in your own house. Really, no one would blame you for taking a bit of comfort where you can find it. But outside. Discreetly. No need to involve your household here. The children . . ." He privately thought that perhaps grief had temporarily unhinged Black Jack. Why on earth had he committed the madness of bringing a nameless brat from the slums into his house, placing her on equal footing with his own children? There was madness in that, all right. No self-respecting York-shireman would fling his money about that way, or give a waif what belonged to his children solely. Just for a moment Bletchley wondered if what Mrs. Plaidstow had suggested could be true. What if this child were Black Jack's own? No, impossible. Whatever he did not know about his son-in-law, he was certain that no child of Black Jack's, legitimate or otherwise, would have been allowed to descend into the state Mrs. Plaidstow had described.

"I'm sorry, Lord Bletchley. You must take back those words. Miss Trimble is not 'a bit of comfort.' "

It went against the grain for Bletchley to take back any of his words, but his feeling for Black Jack forced him into conciliation. "Sorry, old man. Careless of me. Naturally I didn't mean it that way. But it's the look of the thing, don't you see, Jack. I mean—well, she's the children's governess. It's all wrong."

"I can't help what she is. She is staying here." The face that Black Jack turned to Bletchley was disturbed, but uncompromising.

"You don't surely mean to marry her? I mean—to put her in Latitia's place?"

"No one will ever be in Lily's place. No one. As for marriage, ask Miss Trimble yourself. She says she will never marry me."

Bletchley choked on his brandy. "You mean you've *asked* her? The governess? It won't do, Jack. The governess to be mistress of this house? Stepmother to Latitia's children? It won't do."

"That is exactly what she says."

Bletchley stayed for a little more ineffectual argument. How did one reason with a madman? And was the governess more cunning than anyone could believe in this refusal? Did it make her seem a woman of high principle?—endear her even more to this man, upset, slightly maddened, by his wife's death? It was beyond Bletchley's comprehension. It was not done. He retreated, and the next day his place was taken by Lady Bletchley.

"I feel it is my duty, Pollock"—her cold voice addressed him as if he were an upper servant—"to remove my grandchildren from an immoral environment. It is sad that they should lose both mother and father, and I am past the time of life when I care to undertake such responsibility." Just for a moment she remembered the tumultuous years when Latitia had been growing up. She privately thought that Margaret was far too like her mother for comfort. It would have suited better if she had inherited just a trace of the sturdy—her mind would not let her use the word plebeian—stock of Black Jack's father. No, she really did not care to take on another Latitia. But she said what she had to say. "But I consider it my duty to do so unless you promise that that woman will not remain here a day longer. And as for the child . . . Most unsuitable. I haven't a doubt she was planted on you. You'll have all kinds of undesirable characters coming to make claims on you. No, the woman and the child must go, or my grandchildren must leave with me."

Black Jack rang the bell by the mantel, and waited until Billings, who had been hovering in the hall, appeared. "Please order Lady Bletchley's carriage, Billings."

The woman looked at the ferocity of her son-in-law's face. "Am I to take it then that you will do as I say? The children will remain with you. And the—the others will go."

"The children will remain with me, Lady Bletchley. And so will Miss Trimble and Lally." He shook his head, as if he were weary of repeating the words. Weary of the battle. "This is my house—they are my children. I will fight you in every court of the land before you will take them from me. Or force any of them from me. They are all I have in the world. The four of them. I intend to keep them."

She rose. She was a slightly built woman, but she had immense dignity, and was aware of the power of her position. "You will be shunned, Pollock. No one will come to this house. You are condemning your children to isolation and ostracism. They will grow up friendless. They will have no place in society." She made it sound like the black fate she truly believed it to be. "Do you want to see Margaret unmarriageable?"

He gave a wild laugh, a release of his pent-up feelings. "Now I know how ridiculous it all is. Margaret is three years old!" Billings appeared again at the door. "Let me see you to your carriage, Lady Bletchley."

"Don't trouble." At the doorway the stiff figure turned. "It may be a long way off, Pollock, but gels do grow up." He followed her politely to the hall, stood by the carriage as she prepared to ascend. She shunned the hand he offered. He watched the carriage start down the avenue, and for a moment was weak enough to fear the words of the angry woman. Then he laughed again, aloud, wildly, as before. He laughed as he raced up the flights of stairs to the nursery floor. He laughed so that he should not weep. Weep for lovely, lost Latitia. Weep for all the future that had been taken away. Why had she had to put the mare at the damned fence? Why had she had to die? She had no right . . . His thoughts stopped there. She had been what she had been—loving, generous, reckless always. They had had their years together. And time had run out on them. Now there were these others.

He shouted as he ran down the corridor. "Jon! Margaret! Miss Trimble—are you there?" He remembered the last one, the one whose coming had seemed to symbolize the rekindling of the spark of life in his own self. "Lally!"

Jon opened the schoolroom door. "That was grandmother's carriage," he said with a faint note of accusation. "I saw it. Didn't she want to see us?"

"Your grandmother wasn't very well, son. A little tired. She sent her love. She has a cold coming on . . ."

"Margaret has a cold coming on, Mr. Pollock." Nanny's voice sounded just as accusing as Jon's. Was Black Jack to blame for everything? he wondered.

"A cold? Well, it's because spring is late. We all need some warm weather." He bent to his daughter, as if he pleaded for her approval. "That would be nice, wouldn't it, Margaret?"

"Can you make it warm?"

"No—but I can take you all where it *is* warm. We'll go to Italy. All of us. Spring in Florence. All the flowers . . . think of it!" He caught up Margaret and swung her high. "Lally shall learn Italian."

"Lally," Jon said, "can't speak English."

"She will, son. She will." His eyes went to the quiet figure in the brown dress, and he longed then for the time when they would be together, the time when her voice soothed him, her body warmed him, assuaged his hunger and loneliness. "Miss Trimble, we must all pack.

Nanny, you're coming, of course, and so will Seath—" Seath was his valet. "And Nell, to help with things. Perhaps Agnes also."

"How long shall we be gone?" Jon had a practical turn of mind. "I've been promised I shall play cricket with the Brodstons this summer. They are going to get up a team of boys from the village—"

"We'll be back in time, son. We'll be back by the time the meadow pipits fly up on the moors. When it's warm."

He knew he was flying precipitately from this house of mourning, and he didn't care. He was taking his family to a mythical place. Latitia and he had been there on their honeymoon trip. It was not a disloyalty to her memory, but a tribute. The house would be closed for weeks—perhaps months. He wondered if he had made a false promise to Jon about the time of their return. He was trying to run away from the ostracism Lady Bletchley had threatened. He could not bear to see his son hurt. If a little time passed . . . It would also, he thought, for the moment, put in abeyance the problem of finding a new housekeeper.

"You'll like that, won't you, Jon? Florence—Venice—Rome?" Margaret didn't know what he was talking about. He looked beyond her to the dark child, Lally. For a moment he felt sorry for her. She had barely come into one strange world when she was being moved to another. And Alice Trimble . . . His resolve tightened. He would take them all. And no one would threaten him—or them. Hadn't he said they were all he had?

❧ CHAPTER 3 ❧

I

Pellham Langley remained closed for more than two months. The swift tide of the Yorkshire spring had given way to the deep green of summer on the moors before they returned. The great, many-turreted monstrosity of a house seemed almost graceful as they approached it along the drive whose trees were now in full leaf. Black Jack craned forward to get the first glimpse of the house; he had grown up to recognize what an ugly thing it was, but it had also seen his happiest years with Latitia. In the weeks after she had died he felt he hated the place. Now, as he saw it, in the carriage with Alice Trimble, Jon, Margaret, and Lally, he experienced a strange sensation. He was glad to be back. "It's good to be back," he said. He looked around at the four faces. His son and daughter expressed excitement; only in Lally's face was there a trace of an emotion he could not quite understand. Alice Trimble also leaned forward. Her eyes were questioning, clouded with a shadow of apprehension. Then she realized he was studying her, and a quick smile came to her lips. "Yes—yes, it's good to be back."

He wondered truly how good it seemed to her. The brown dresses had given way to a quiet but becoming lavender gray, sometimes, daringly, in the evening, a rich blue. But she still dressed in the role of governess, even though now a somewhat stylish governess. In public she played the role of governess. She still continued to insist that she would never become his wife.

The weeks in Italy had worked on them all. Jon had taken to it ex-uberantly, learning a few words of Italian, letting himself be a little spoiled by the Italians, who loved all children but who talked of a Botticelli angel when they looked at him. Margaret had displayed all the bright and dark sides of her nature, smiling when she was pleased and everything around her was pleasing, weeping and storming when she was tired or things did not go well. She complained a lot. The food was different; she didn't like so much sun, why couldn't they go home? She didn't like "abroad." Then the storm would pass, her mood was as sunny as the day. She ate ice cream and chocolate, and said to Nanny that they must have the same at home. She would never again eat rice pudding. She wore her white lawn dresses trimmed with lace as if she had lived in nothing else. She was de-manding, and often enchanting, Black Jack thought. And Lally had to be with her constantly. It was as if Margaret already knew that she had found the complete slave in Lally. The other little girl, solemn, dark, looking not quite comfortable in the lawn and lace dresses, was her companion during every waking moment. If Margaret had a headache, complaining of the heat, Lally would lie on the bed with her, refusing to go out with Jon. If Margaret wished to play in the parks, Lally was at her side, obeying her, being her foil in everything. Unlike Margaret, she made no complaints about the food. She ate whatever was put before her, and Italian waiters, seeing that enthusi-asm, piled her plates high. She showed a surprising dexterity with spaghetti. She was compliant and obliging, and still said almost noth-ing. "Will that child ever talk?" Black Jack wondered aloud.

It amused Black Jack to take his family shopping. There were piles of silks and gloves and straw hats; there was a gold Florentine chain for each of the little girls. Jon got straw boaters and silk shirts. When they were alone he took Alice Trimble shopping. She kept insisting that her clothes in public conform to the image of the gov-erness. She was helpless before his insistence on giving her things that she might wear only in private. She found herself with night-gowns of silk and lace, and a double string of pearls. There was a flame-colored silk robe, and a dark-green velvet one, trimmed with fur. When she put them on she saw herself transformed; the colors brought out the shimmering tones of her skin, the pearls threw light into her face. She began to see herself as she might have been if all the years of poverty and work had not been there. Unconsciously she began to wear her new straw hats at a more jaunty angle; she permitted herself some pretty parasols. The orders she gave to servants came in a more assured voice. She would never be pretty, much less beautiful, but the sumptuous lines of her body, displayed in the new dresses of delicate tones, began to cause some men to look twice at her. It became difficult to keep the mold of governess from cracking. She felt a little intoxicated by the events of these last months. She began to wish herself back at Pellham Langley so that she might draw breath, so that the quiet might wash over her, so that there might be time to think. So she also craned for a view of the ugly pile rising against the sky, which was a threatening gray. The languid blue of the Italianate sky was gone; they had come home. She was suddenly afraid. All the dreamlike quality of the Italian months might now be shattered.

Billings was waiting on the steps. Footmen were hurrying toward the carriage, ready to help the passengers down, ready to unload the second carriage, which had been sent for their piles of luggage—a much larger load than that with which they had left.

"Welcome home, sir. Welcome home, Master Jon. Miss Margaret." For just a few seconds even Billings' aplomb was shaken at the sight of the governess. It wasn't that she looked all that different —she simply *was* different. "Miss . . . Miss Trimble." The dark little foundling from the slums was last from the carriage, almost tumbling out because no one even remembered she was there and needed assistance. She was wearing identical clothes to Margaret's. The hair, now grown much longer, was thick and black, silken but straight. The dark eyes seemed smaller because the face had grown much rounder. Billings barely recognized the then still-thin child who had left Pellham Langley. Lally took Margaret's hand in hers, because Margaret, tired from the train journey, looked as if she might be on the verge of tears.

Almost against his will, Billings said the words "Miss Lally." But the little girl seemed not to hear him. She was leading Margaret up the steps past the servants. She said nothing.

*   *   *

Margaret was immediately made ready for bed, but for once Lally did not attend her every movement. Nanny was distracted by the fuss of unpacking essential items, she herself tired from the long train journey. Lally never gave her trouble, so she didn't think about Lally. At nursery tea, Nanny concentrated solely on Margaret. Pouts and then tears came; Margaret rejected the solid English food and demanded Italian pastries. Nell and Agnes rushed to get hot water for the hip bath in front of the fire. Nanny undressed Margaret, and Lally slipped away into the day nursery.

It was still all there, just as she had imagined it on every day of the Italian journey. The tea table had been set with the same white cloth; they had been given the same food. She went to examine the dollhouse, opened it, and looked at all the familiar and, to her, beloved little pieces of furniture. Then she went to the tall cupboards, and, stretching, managed to open them. There were the toys they had played with, the beautiful dolls all neatly laid or seated on shelves. She touched the stuff of their dresses. All the same.

Silently she slipped from the nursery. The same number of stairs led to the floor below, where Jon and Margaret's father slept all alone—alone in a corridor of countless rooms. She hesitated only fractionally before beginning down the much grander staircase that led to the great marble and mahogany hall. She lingered for a moment in the shadow of the massive banister, fearing that Billings or one of the footmen might be about, might send her back, might be angry with her. There was no one. The light of the summer evening flooded the hall, though when she made the effort to reach and turn the massive brass knob of the front door and it swung open on perfectly balanced brass hinges, the same gray sky threatened her. But she could not wait. She ran down the steps and along the terrace which led to the topiary garden. It was all still there—the immaculate hedges, the pool in the center. There was the Rabbit fashioned from yew, there the Cat, there the Dog. There was Mouse. All the names she had learned from Margaret. She whispered the names to herself. Then she ran all the way along the highest terrace to the gate which opened to the wilderness of the moors. She discovered she was no longer afraid of them. She could hear the tumble of the beck where she and Margaret were forbidden to go alone, lest they should fall in. There was no one about, so she went. It was the first act of disobedience she had committed since she had come to Pellham Langley. But she had to satisfy herself that it was all the same. She looked back at the great bulk of the house. That was the same, unchanging. She had returned to the same safe world she had begun to fear was lost. As they had traveled from place to place she had begun to think they never would stop; they would never come back to the massive, comfortable enduring world onto which she had opened her eyes from a dark dream. Until the touchable reality was restored to her, she had not felt safe.

She climbed among the boulders at the side of the beck, reached down and touched the icy water, scooping it up, letting it fly from her fingers. She didn't notice that her dress got wet, nor that the water came over her smart little boots. She did things she had never done before. She found and threw small stones to see if she could make them reach the other side of the beck. She wondered if there was a place shallow enough for her to wade across. Suddenly she was free of all her anxieties and fears; she wanted to see the wider world up there at the top. She wanted to reach the crag, to look down on Pellham Langley, to sigh with happiness at its great solid mass. She wanted to see the mill chimneys in the valley beyond. She started scrambling upward, hardly noticing that the first raindrops were falling. Once she fell and grazed her knee and tore her stocking. Her boots were sodden. She was about to stop and take them off, returning to the barefootedness she had always known, when the voice reached her.

"Lally! Lally—don't move. Stay just as you are. I'm coming for you."

She looked back and down, and was instantly terrified to see what a drop lay below her, how cold and ferocious the white tumble of water seemed from above. And there, so far below, scrambling among the boulders, was Black Jack. He waved at her. "Lally, stand still. I'm coming."

It took him some time to reach her. She closed her eyes, afraid now to look at the cold depths beneath her. The rain grew heavier. At last she heard Black Jack's hard breathing close beside her, and dared to open her eyes. All at once she realized the seriousness of her crime. She had disobeyed. She had given trouble. She had not stayed to help soothe Margaret's tantrum. She would be sent away. Almost unconsciously she shrank from the blow she was certain would fall on her. Instead she felt herself swept up in Black Jack's arms. For an instant a memory from a far-off past returned to her. Once before this man had lifted her in his arms. He had not cursed her, but carried her to a fairy-tale world.

"Oh, Lally! You're all right." For a time he stood there rocking her, on top of their high world, rocking and comforting her. "Lally— Lally! We searched the house. And then I found the garden gate open. Oh, Lally . . . you could have fallen. You could have been killed. Why, Lally? . . . why? Why did you want to run away? Was anyone unkind to you?"

She rubbed her round young cheek against his rougher one. She loved the smell of Black Jack, the smell of his cigars and his soap. She loved the feel of his tweed suit. His thick mustache tickled her face, and suddenly she laughed. The fear was gone, and with the laughter, she found her tongue.

"I wanted to see it was the same. Everything. Rabbit and Cat and Dog. No one took it away. I wanted to get up here all by myself." She pointed to Pellham Langley below them. "The house . . . just the same. My house."

He stared at her in amazement. "You didn't think it would be the same, Lally?"

"I thought I would never come back . . . or it would be . . ." She struggled for, and found the word: "Different. Not so good. But it is good." She reached into her memory for a grammar lesson she had heard Miss Trimble give to Jon. "It is better."

"Lally, you sound just like Jon!"

She laughed, immensely pleased. "I love Jon. I love Margaret. And Father. And Miss Trimble." She threw out her arm, indicating the wide world about them. "I love it."

"You've been learning to talk, you little monkey, and you never told us. You've been learning to talk just like Jon."

It was true. Now that she uttered more than monosyllables, her voice was strangely deep and mellow for a young child, for a little girl. It had a dark timbre to it. But it was free of the accent of the slums. It had Jon's rhythm and inflection. It had some of Alice Trimble's richness. It had none of the babyish charm of Margaret.

He carried her down carefully among the boulders, which were becoming slippery with the rain. She felt safe with him, held him tightly around the neck. When they were back at the garden gate he did not set her down, but ran all the way back to the house, to the open front door. Alice Trimble waited anxiously there. She went to take the little girl from Black Jack's arms, but he had already begun to race up the stairs.

"No, we'll have to let Margaret know quickly that her playmate isn't dead. And that she's found her tongue. And I doubt anyone else in the house will get a word in until she's said everything she means to say." He bounced her happily as he took the stairs two at a time, called ahead of him, "Lally lost her tongue, and now she's found it again. Beware, everyone!"

*   *   *

After that, she expanded like a flower opening to the sun. It was as though she stretched to capture and contain everything they could give her. The words came tumbling out, as unstoppable as the flow of the beck. She laughed, she sang nursery rhymes with Margaret; if she was not smiling, her forehead was drawn in a frown of concentration as she strove to understand the meaning of the words in the story-books. Suddenly she raced ahead of Margaret in comprehension. She begged Jon and Alice Trimble to teach her what Nanny deemed was too advanced for Margaret. Jon obliged with good-natured conde-scension. "Well, Monkey, what have you learned today?" She wrote in a big childish scrawl the words he taught her. Simple words, but they were magical to Lally. The doors of a kingdom had been opened. She no longer feared that they would be slammed shut.

Never again did she disobey a command, never again did she wan-der off by herself to taste the delights of the garden and the moors. It had been her biggest adventure, but she had learned that Black Jack had been truly frightened. She had caused him worry and anxiety. She would never do so again.

She was as devoted as ever to Margaret's comfort and entertain-ment. But now she had the words to speak to her, the relationship became less one-sided. She was able to teach as well as to learn.

Alice Trimble wondered aloud to Black Jack, "It may be that she's older than we thought. She was such a starved scrap of a thing when you brought her here she looked less developed than Margaret. Now she's growing up as well as out." She laughed. "If I didn't remember how miserably thin she was then, I'd say she's too fat now. It's . . . it's a sort of miracle to see her respond." She smiled quietly, remembering how the struggle to save Lally's life had brought such richness to her own. She sat in the rose-colored embroidered silk robe, and smiled at Black Jack, and knew her own life had expanded exactly as Lally's had.

II

But to the outside world, their lives at Pellham Langley appeared to contract. There was no stopping the word that Mrs. Plaidstow and

Lady Bletchley had spread about. The governess, Alice Trimble, was Black Jack's mistress. Heads were shaken in wonderment. At the Leeds Conservative Club the opinion was that Black Jack was entitled to anyone he desired, but he should have been more discreet, more tactful than to have formed a liaison with someone who was entrusted with the care of his children. "A right messy situation that lad's in," was the verdict. But in the male world of the club, he was greeted and talked to as always. Men understood such things. There was a tacit acknowledgment that until a year after Lady Latitia's death Black Jack would not have been entertaining in any case, and would have refused all invitations. It remained to be seen what would happen after that. If the governess was clever she would become Mrs. Pollock. There was doubt, though, that she would ever be received in the drawing rooms of the wives of the other members of the club. "Aye, a right mess that is," they said.

No new housekeeper came to preside over Pellham Langley. Black Jack interviewed some applicants, and found them wanting. There was something in their attitude that he construed as condescension, as if they fully knew the situation of Alice Trimble, and they behaved as if conferring a favor on Black Jack by consenting to come into such a household. Those were the more desirable types. There were others he suspected of having less glowing pasts than they claimed, whose references were dated years earlier, who were vague about their recent employment. The last of them, a woman in her sixties whose slightly untidy dress and hair, added to the red, broken-veined cheeks, made him suspect that she would regularly raid his wine cellar, was outspoken when he declined to arrange a second interview.

"Well, Mr. Pollock, it's my opinion that beggars can't be choosers, can they?"

"And what do you mean by that?"

"Well, you'll not get many as'll want to come to a place where you keep your fancy woman. Respectable, I am—"

He rang the bell for Billings, and prayed that Alice Trimble or his children did not hear the stream of curses that fell from the woman's lips as she was shown out. After she had gone he sent for Billings.

"Well, Billings, what is your decision? Are you leaving or staying?"

The thin eyebrows of the man jerked upward. "I beg your pardon, sir?"

"You know what the situation is. Don't pretend you're blind and deaf. If that . . . that creature knows, then everyone knows. If you wish to leave, I'll, of course, give you excellent references . . ."

Billings had made up his mind on the day Black Jack, the children, and Alice Trimble had returned from Italy. He didn't approve of the situation; he didn't, in fact, understand it. Black Jack, if he wanted a mistress, could have found someone a good deal more enticing than Alice Trimble, younger, pretty. He could have kept her discreetly, in Leeds or Bradford, and no scandal would have attached itself to Pellham Langley. For the life of him, Billings couldn't grasp what anyone would see in a creature like Alice Trimble. But then, there was no accounting for other people's tastes. Perhaps Black Jack had been trapped into a situation, unwittingly, too soon after his wife's death, and didn't know how to extricate himself. But Billings could see no signs in Alice Trimble that she wished to exploit the change in her situation. She gave herself no airs; she gave no orders in the household. She just looked . . . in his unimaginative mind Billings groped for the word. She just looked a happy woman. The happiness had transformed her so that sometimes, seen in the right light, she looked almost pretty.

But Alice Trimble's happiness or unhappiness was no concern of Billings'. He was forty-six years old. He had come to Pellham Langley in answer to an advertisement placed by Black Jack. He had been trained under a martinet of a butler in the service of a baronet with wide holdings in Wiltshire, and who also had dealings in the City, so that a footman in his employ could expect to receive a varied experience. Billings had had no intention of remaining a footman all his life, and to that end he had studied wine lists and menus, had eradicated every trace of his native Cockney from his speech, and had waited for the time when he would be old and experienced enough to apply for a post as butler. Women did not interest him very much. His occasional need was satisfied discreetly, and he had seen no need to saddle himself with a wife and children. Security and comfort were his goals, and he knew he would better find them with such a person as Black Jack than in a more aristocratic household. He implied a sophistication and a knowledge to Black Jack that he did not, at the time he was hired, quite possess. He had liked the idea of having a young bachelor to mold to his own liking. It turned out that Black Jack had his own ideas on that, but they had got along well, and Billings was at Pellham Langley when Black Jack had married. Billings had striven in every way to please Lady Latitia. She had joked about him with Black Jack. "He's such a dreadful snob. But then—most butlers are. It's part of their stock in trade." But he had served her well, and she, in her turn, had taught him things he had not known. He had been deeply attached to Lady Latitia, and had dreaded the woman who might one day take her place. That it might be this mild, quiet creature, Alice Trimble, was a surprise and a disappointment both. Billings would have preferred a more outstanding woman, even if she had been both more demanding and imperious, than this lowly governess. But he never forgot his first concern in life, his own comfort. He could, like Mrs. Plaidstow, have taken a moral stand and found himself dismissed from Pellham Langley. He now knew that Alice Trimble would not be dismissed. Black Jack had always been a generous man. He had never questioned the food bills in his bachelor days; he consulted with Billings over the purchase of wines, but turned a blind eye to what was missing from the cellar. Billings thought of his comfortable quarters, the endless supply of coal for his fire, the delectable dishes that Cook provided for all the staff. Cook had sniffed at the scandal that brewed about Pellham Langley. "What happens upstairs is naught to me. As long as they don't interfere in my kitchen, and don't tell me to scrimp, I'm staying. Reckon I'll have a better do here than starting some place afresh. Better this —no *real* mistress in the house—than some mealymouthed thing as'll ask me to account for every pound of sugar. . . . No, none of my business, so long as they leave me in peace."

As so, Billings thought, it was with himself. Leave him in charge of the household. With no housekeeper, he would, without interference, rule the household. His comfort would be undisturbed. He was a greedy man; he liked his food and he liked Black Jack's cellar. He could squeeze Black Jack for a regular rise in wages. There were many worse situations.

"I'm afraid, Mr. Pollock, I don't understand what you're referring to. I have never contemplated leaving Pellham Langley. Unless, of course, you have reason for dissatisfaction with my services."

Black Jack laughed. "Go to hell, Billings! You're such an old hypocrite. So you'll stay—and we'll work it out."

Gravely, Billings backed toward the door. "I assume everything will run as smoothly as before, sir. One endeavors to give satisfaction."

* * *

Very quietly, Alice Trimble then slipped into the role of unofficial housekeeper at Pellham Langley. Billings had the supervision of the staff; Cook continued to order as she pleased, but she sent menus up for Alice Trimble's approval. They were always approved. Billings consulted with the governess over any household matter which he deemed needed a woman's touch, or in which it would be politic to be seen to be seeking Alice Trimble's advice. Secretly he thought he could have done it all himself, with no fuss, and that the position of housekeeper had never been necessary; but he did not say so. Alice Trimble had mysteriously gained some ascendancy over Black Jack. Billings did not mean to quarrel with her. If, in the end, Black Jack committed the folly of marrying her, then Billings wanted no enmity between them. He settled into the comfortable niche he had chosen for himself, and prepared to await developments.

One of the developments was that Alice Trimble came to occupy a bedroom and sitting room on the same floor as Black Jack, and Black Jack himself moved from the room which had connected with Latitia's and into the wing which housed Alice Trimble. None of the servants missed the significance of this, but the children seemed oblivious. Margaret and Lally still slept in the room adjoining Nanny's, and Jon relished the independence of his own room opposite the night nursery. Since Alice Trimble had always taken her meals alone—had spent her evenings alone, after she had handed Jon back into Nanny's charge—on the surface there was little change. It meant, though, that there was little use of the big formal rooms downstairs. Black Jack ate his evening meal alone in the dining room, which was capable of seating fifty, and instead of retiring to the library, where a fire was always kept burning for him, he went upstairs to Alice Trimble's room. The austerity associated with a governess's room had given way to a kind of bower of feminine delights. Carpets and curtains were rose-colored, to match the Florentine silk robe; there were flowers brought freshly each day by the gardeners. Dresden ornaments stood on the mantel, and a Florentine silver-gilt framed mirror gave back the reflections of the cut-crystal perfume bottles ranged on the dressing table, which itself wore a skirt of frilled silk. It was as if all of Alice Trimble's sensuous nature had found expression in these rooms; feelings long pent up had been released in a flood. When the servant had taken away her tray of food, she put gold slippers on her shapely feet, let down the silken luxuriance of her hair, and wore the pearls. She waited patiently, happily, for Black Jack.

There were few visitors to Pellham Langley to disrupt this routine. Cook, recalling the days when Latitia had entertained frequently and lavishly, sighed before the fire in the quiet room which adjoined the kitchen, sharing a glass of port with Billings. "Ah, them was great days . . ." She seemed to have forgotten that then she had complained of overwork.

They were hardly back from Italy with Black Jack was seized with a fit of building mania. "It's all so old-fashioned," he declared. "We should have bathrooms. A lot, and have hot-water heating piped through the whole house. It's only civilized. . . . All this carrying of water could be done away with. In the end it would be an economy."

Pellham Langley had been somewhat ahead of its time in that it possessed several water closets, but Black Jack now decreed great marble-lined rooms such as he had seen in the best of the new hotels on their travels. He ordered huge marble tubs and basins. The architects were aghast when he decreed that even the servants' quarters should be supplied, even though more modestly. Washbasins were to go into all the bedrooms. "My father was thinking only a little way ahead. When Jon and Margaret and Lally have done with the nursery floor, they'll want better accommodation on this floor." Looking at the huge rooms, he added, "Heaven knows, there's space enough to fit them in."

Alice Trimble did not try to disguise from herself that the orgy of rebuilding would also encompass new arrangements as to her own accommodation. Since she still refused to marry Black Jack, some way had to be achieved of giving her a suite of rooms which actually adjoined his. He finally acknowledged this himself. "Damn it, Alice, I'm sick of this scurrying back and forth. In my own house . . . If you love me, as you say you do, you'll marry me."

For the hundredth time she repeated her argument. "I'll not have it said that I tricked you into marriage."

"Do I seem such a fool—to be tricked?"

"I cannot try to take her place—Lady Latitia's. She was so beautiful . . . brilliant. What sort of a figure would I cut in the drawing room? After a time you'd despise me. I'll go when I must . . . not before. But I'll go."

"I can't let you go, Alice. I need you." She was well aware that he had never said, "I love you." That love, the only love, had gone to Latitia.

But one day, after a visit to Leeds, Alice Trimble did pack her bags and she left Pellham Langley. Billings brought the news to Black Jack on his return from the mills.

"In God's name, where has she gone?"

"She refused to say, sir. Kitson took her in the trap to Leeds station. She called a porter to take her luggage, and Kitson doesn't know where she bought a ticket for."

"You fool!" It was one of the few times Black Jack had been seriously angry with his butler. "You should have sent a message to the mills at once!"

"I'm very sorry, sir . . ." Billings backed away. "I thought perhaps you already knew . . ."

Black Jack called for the carriage again, and set off for Leeds station. He questioned every porter on duty; none remembered the lady. After he had spread a few sovereigns around, he was promised that every porter would have his memory jogged when he reported for work the next day. Black Jack spent the rest of the evening going through the jumble of papers in his wife's desk. Latitia had never been a tidy woman; he had thought it a charming fault. Now he cursed it. Somewhere there should have been the address of the place where Alice Trimble had grown up, the cottage which belonged to her widowed mother. Some seaport, he thought. But which? How little he had asked her; how much he'd taken her for granted. Why, for example, had he never said he loved her? It had seemed such a betrayal of Latitia's memory. Now he knew he loved her and had only just discovered it. His bed felt cold and empty that night without Alice.

Next day at Leeds all they could report to him was that the lady had taken a train to London. From London she could have taken a train to anywhere in England. He searched Latitia's desk again, and questioned Billings. "Doesn't *anyone* in the house know where she lived—where her mother lived?"

Billings shook his head. "Perhaps Mrs. Plaidstow . . ." he suggested.

Mrs. Plaidstow had taken a post as housekeeper to an elderly Methodist minister in a district near Bradford. Black Jack thought the place a considerable comedown from Mrs. Plaidstow's previous situation, and he was prepared for the hostility with which she greeted him. "I know nothing of *Miss* Trimble's whereabouts. It is none of my concern."

"You left Pellham Langley because of what you call your Christian principles. I would ask you to show a little charity . . . to search your memory carefully. You were at Pellham when Miss Trimble was engaged as a governess. You may have seen letters she addressed to her mother . . . the postmark on letters she received." Without subtlety he showed her the sum of money in his hand. It would have amounted to several years' wages in her present circumstances. He saw the struggle clearly pictured in her face.

"I'll consult my notebooks . . . perhaps there's something." She returned a few minutes later. "I see I made a note . . . in case she was ill and her mother had to be sent for. A place called Fowey—in Cornwall. On a river near the sea, I think. She *said* her father was a naval officer. I doubted that myself . . ." Her opinion fell on empty air. The money was in her hands, and Black Jack was gone.

He reached London just in time to take the long, overnight train journey to Cornwall. Fowey was a small place rising steeply on both banks of the river estuary. It did not take long to discover where the widowed Mrs. Trimble lived. It was one of a row of cottages, pretty, neat, very modest. The woman who opened the door to his knock was aging, had the remnants of a sweet prettiness still about her. She wore black with white lace at her throat. "Mrs. Trimble, I'm Jack Pollock."

The pale lips trembled. "Thank God," she whispered. She held the door wide.

Alice sat in a back sitting room which looked onto a tiny enclosed garden. She wore the old plain brown dress. Her hair and eyes seemed to have lost their luster.

"I had to go," she said. "I'm going to have a child. I did everything I knew not to have a child. I never wanted you to know."

"You fool! You blasted little fool. Did you think you could keep me from finding out?"

"If I'd had more strength I would have gone further. I should have been strong enough to go where I knew you couldn't find me. It was weak to come here—where you could follow. I have enough savings to take me to America. I thought of selling the pearls, but I couldn't bear to do that. Not yet. Not until the baby . . ."

He bent and took her hands, and pulled her from the chair. "Alice, I've asked you to marry me often enough. Now I'm saying that I love you. Do you understand? I've been in hell since you went away. I love you, Alice."

A slow flush spread on her face; a radiance dawned in her eyes. "And I have always loved you. You know that."

"Then we must end this madness, and be married."

"It's not a year yet," she said. "It's not usual—"

"Damn what's usual. Do you think Latitia would have cared for the conventions? You will bear my child as my wife. That's that!"

III

They were married in Fowey, and returned to Pellham Langley immediately afterward. "Miss Trimble is now Mrs. Pollock," Black Jack announced briefly to Billings. When Billings took the news to the kitchen, Cook paused at her work and gave a snort. "That's what he may *say*. But is it the truth?"

The news sent a little shock wave through the household. Jon was silent when his father came to tell him. Lally looked from one child to the other, and then at Black Jack, glad to see that at least he looked happy. Whether Miss Trimble was known by her old name or as Mrs. Pollock was of little significance to her. She waited for a reaction, and it came as a kind of explosion from Margaret.

"Is she my new *mother*? I don't want a new mother! She's a governess. Why couldn't she stay a governess? I want my own mother!"

Her small, intense face crumpled in a way Lally had come to dread. The voice, which had been pitched too high, now became a shriek. "I don't want her! I don't want her!"

"Hush, Miss Margaret. Hush . . ." Nanny caught her up in her arms. "If you please, sir, I think it's better . . ."

Black Jack nodded. "She'll understand in time. Mrs. Pollock has no intention of trying to take her mother's place."

"Of course, sir." But Nanny's own expression was grim.

"Come, Jon. Come down and have tea with us. Your—Mrs. Pollock is in the drawing room."

"Me too, please," Lally said. She had missed Alice Trimble.

"No!" Margaret shrieked. "No! Lally must stay with me. I want Lally!"

Black Jack's eyes pleaded with Lally. She nodded, instantly wiser in that she understood his need, but did not quite understand the situation. "I'll stay. I'll stay." Anything that Black Jack wanted would be done.

"Good girl. I'll tell you—if it's fine tomorrow we'll take the trap and we'll go for a picnic on the moors. You'll like that." Since the day he had found her perilously poised at the top of the beck, he had known her love of those strange, wild places. By tomorrow Margaret would be calmer, sleep would bring some forgetfulness, some acceptance. In her mind Alice might slip back to her old position. But Nanny's face told him that there were many who would never accept Alice in her new, her real position. He sighed, and found other things to talk to Jon about on the way downstairs. They entered the drawing room to see Alice seated behind the steaming silver kettle, acting for the first time as mistress of Pellham Langley.

Suddenly he knew that this brief absence had affected Jon; the boy stopped at the sight of the former governess in this new role, and then he raced toward her. "Miss Trimble!—Miss Trimble, where have you been? I've had no lessons, and Margaret has been such a bore. Miss Trimble . . ."

"It isn't Miss Trimble anymore, Jon. It's Mrs. Pollock," Black Jack said gently.

"Am I to call you Mrs. Pollock?"

She shook her head. "No. That does sound funny, doesn't it?" It was understood that she would never be called "Mother" or "Mama." "Why don't you just call me Alice? Now that we're related in a sort of a way."

It was unheard of for a child to call an adult by a given name. But Alice Trimble had broken more than one rule.

*   *   *

Black Jack hurried the builders on, fearful that the noise and dust would disturb Alice. She appeared not to mind. She was too easy to please, he thought. All she appeared to want was his presence. He gave as much as he could of it, often leaving details at the mills and the mines to subordinates which he knew he should have attended to himself. She made light of the difficulties of her pregnancy, and of any other difficulties which arose. Margaret seemed to be the chief of them. She had stubbornly turned her face away from the former governess, refusing the little bribes by which Black Jack attempted to bring them together. And she was jealous of any attention Lally gave to Alice. "Lally is mine! Mine!"

"Lally does not belong to you, Margaret." But Black Jack strove for patience, hoping that time would reconcile the little girl. He could not force her; he could not punish her. Something of her mother was always there in her face, something of Latitia's temperament which, if pushed or distorted, could turn to a strange ugliness. But he was beginning to realize that Latitia, in her wildest moments, had never been as extreme as this child of theirs. Patience, he counseled himself. And time.

Time brought heaviness and languor to Alice. She still smiled, but her movements were slow and tired. She had had to give up the effort of teaching Jon. Black Jack found a young man to come out from Bradford during the week to tutor him. It had been arranged that Jon would go to his father's prep school when he was eight years old, at the end of next summer. "I'll be grown up then," he said, and believed it. They celebrated Christmas quietly. The huge hall was decorated with fir and holly, and the carolers came from the village to sing, receive money, and eat mince pies. But that was the extent of the festivities. No one talked of the fact that people did not call at Pellham Langley. It was to be expected that they would consider Alice's condition, and not intrude. Lord and Lady Bletchley sent Christmas presents to their grandchildren, but no greeting to Black Jack. Black Jack rather desperately filled the house with lavish presents so that the absence of other things would seem less.

The baby was to have been born in May. But Alice's labor began on a March night when the wind blew the snow straight from the Russian steppes, and the doctor, hastily summoned when the midwife found the complications of the birth beyond her, had to struggle the last half mile to Pellham Langley on foot through the drifts. It was useless to hope that the famous specialist whom they had expected to call in case of need would be able to make the journey from Leeds, though a message had been sent in the hope that he could arrive in time. During the night the storm blew itself out. By the morning light —a rosy, innocent-looking dawn which belied the ferocity and cruelty of the night—the moors above Pellham Langley lay in deep snow, the stone walls obliterated. Standing at one of the turret windows, Black Jack thought he had never seen a clearer, more sparkling morning. But under that snow he knew that sheep lay buried. His farmers were struggling to try to reach the ewes in lamb, to save those they could. And his own child struggled to be born.

The doctor shook his head. "Mrs. Pollock's age is against her. It is late to be having a first child, and it is going to be a breech birth. I cannot turn the child." They stared out at the snow together, gloomily. Nothing would move by road or rail for days. The specialist would not arrive.

It would hardly have mattered, the doctor thought, if he had arrived. A tiny, puny, though pretty girl was born stressfully into the bright winter glow of the late afternoon. And Alice died. Black Jack put his face against those loved breasts, clad now in their clean white lawn and lace, but which were already cold, and wept without shame. "What have I done to you, Alice?—Alice . . . ?"

Lally slipped away from the nursery and found him there. She was not surprised or frightened by the storm of weeping. She had memories of a time when she had seen them together, when they had cared for her, and they had loved each other. She had opened her eyes upon the love they had for each other. She put her face against Black Jack's and found that he clutched her desperately.

"Have you seen the little baby? She has a lot of fair hair. What shall we call her?"

He just kept repeating Alice's name, and so when Lally finally led him away, and she returned to the nursery, she told them all that the new baby's name was Alice.

Few people gathered when, for the second time in less than two years, Black Jack buried a wife. Few people were sure she had been his legal wife. Mrs. Trimble could not travel in the winter weather all the way from Cornwall to be present. She sent a small bundle of knitted things to her only grandchild.

Black Jack sat alone that night in the library. He hardly dared mount the stairs to the room he and Alice had occupied; he could not return to the room that had been Latitia's. He stared into the fire and drank too much brandy and hoped for merciful sleep. He could hear the hall clock striking—what hour he didn't know—when the plump little figure of Lally, clad in a flannel nightgown, appeared at the door; she closed it carefully behind her.

"Lally, you should be asleep."

She sighed; it was a strange sound from a little girl. Her round face stared up at Black Jack's with concern. "We got Margaret to sleep." It sounded like a task she had had to perform. "I heard

Nanny tell Nell you haven't been properly to sleep since . . . well, for a long time. I thought I'd come and sit with you."

"Nanny doesn't know you're here?"

She gave an impatient shrug. "Do you think Nanny would let me come down?" She leaned against his knees and stared up at him with her round, dimpled face. "Are you worrying about the baby? I'll take care of her. I'll take care of Alice just the way I do of Margaret."

He felt a twist of conscience. The dark eyes were very serious, intent. Had he unconsciously let this child assume too much of the burden of Margaret's difficult nature? Although he knew Lally took as much delight as anyone in the sunnier moments.

He smiled tiredly at her. "Yes, I know you'll take care of Alice, Lally. I know you'll help me take care of her." Then he lifted her and placed her in the big chair beside him. "Perhaps we could both go to sleep now."

She snuggled contentedly against him, like a fat, warm puppy. When she was asleep he carried her to the room where Margaret lay, covered her, and left. In the room along the corridor, the wet nurse sat rocking the cradle of the new baby. He stood watching the soft light play on the face of this newest child of his. "She's right sweet and good-tempered, Mr. Pollock. Hardly a cry out of her. And she seems to ber putting on a bit of flesh. I think she's going to live, Mr. Pollock. Look how sweetly she smiles . . ."

She continued to smile sweetly. She gave no trouble. She gained weight, and she lived, as the wet nurse had predicted. She was an unusually beautiful little girl, even when seen by the side of her half sister, Margaret. "A little angel," Nanny called her. "As good as gold. A perfect innocent."

She was almost three years old before they were finally forced to admit what had happened. The mind of this sweet-tempered child had been damaged in that too-lengthy, rather bungled struggle to save her life. She remained the perfect innocent.

❧ PART II ❧

1914

❧ CHAPTER 4 ❧

I

Black Jack sat with his panama pulled forward over his eyes, sprawled in a deck chair. The sun of the August afternoon was hot, the regular plop of the tennis balls lulled him; sometimes he dozed and his head fell forward, and then he would be jerked awake, and wonder what the score was, and if he had missed anything. Usually he hadn't. It was a mixed doubles. It would probably be the last set before Billings headed the string of servants who would bring tea things to the pagodalike building which overlooked the tennis courts, and which was backed by the high clipped hedges of the topiary garden.

Margaret and Lally were partnering two of Jon's friends who were at Oxford with him—were they from Oxford, Black Jack wondered, or had they been friends at Eton who then went to Cambridge? Two of those who lounged on the grass watching the play were brother officers at Sandhurst. He kept getting them mixed up, forgot their names half the time. Some of them seemed extraordinarily alike. They called him "sir," and when he couldn't remember a name, he simply called them "dear boy." He hoped they didn't think him patronizing. Most of all he hoped they didn't think him an old bore. It had, altogether, been an exhausting summer. He had met so many new young people he might be forgiven for forgetting a face or two.

The two girls played in their usual form—Margaret lithe and swift, but lacking concentration, sometimes allowing her annoyance at missing a shot to deteriorate into bad temper—Lally strong, with amazing power behind her shots which made the men respect her, playing a steady, determined game, just a little too slow at times. She always knew, though, when to leave the shot to her partner. A dependable, predictable player, Lally, but never displaying Margaret's occasional touch of brilliance. At the moment that Black Jack woke from a few seconds' doze, Margaret returned an almost impossible shot from the back line and placed it just beyond Lally's reach. The game went to Margaret and her partner. A little splatter of applause came from the group of young people, wearing white dresses and flannels, seated in deck chairs and sprawled elegantly on the grass. Margaret tossed her hair, which was gold with Latitia's touch of red in it, permitted herself a smile, and went back to take Lally's service. Her pleasure in that last effort ruined her seriousness. Lally's balls came with devastating accuracy, always just inside the line, as if it were a drill. Every time Margaret had to face Lally's service she lost her nerve. Lally's partner, who, Black Jack reckoned, must be only one of half a dozen of the young men present who appeared to be desperately in love with Margaret, could not summon the heart to press the advantage against her. He weakly allowed the shots to fall where Margaret could return them. The game went back and forth with a boring predictability. Black Jack dozed off again.

He woke at the touch of a hand. Alice was on the grass beside his chair. She offered him the head of a rose, and smiled. She was thirteen, and so beautiful that sometimes it hurt Black Jack just to look at her. The long fair hair flowed about her perfect oval face; she was all the things that the perfect fairy princess was supposed to be. She was slender and tall for her age, gifted with an enchanting grace of movement; her mouth was curved and tender, her skin had the translucence he remembered in her mother. But instead of the blue eyes of the fairy princess, she had inherited the deep brown of her mother. She had his own dark brows and lashes. But the eyes that looked at him were not the eyes of Alice Trimble, alive with intelligence. These eyes looked at him with innocence and trust, and little comprehension. She offered both the head of the rose, and her bloodied hand, where she had unthinkingly grasped the thorns. She smiled as he took his handkerchief to wipe away the blood, and when he tied it about her palm she regarded it with an air of pleasure, like some trophy won.

He glanced at all the young people around him, in their attitudes of careless grace, of young beauty. He looked at his beautiful daughter Alice, and he thought his heart would break for them all. All the pleasures and the pains of the thirteen summers since Alice Trimble had died seemed to wash across him as the shadows lengthened on that hot August afternoon. He looked at his children, and he wished he could hold everything still for them, have them caught in some spell which would freeze them in time so they should hold these golden moments of youth forever. But as surely as the guns would sound over his shooting moors later that month, so he was perfectly convinced that the guns of August, the big guns of the German Army, would sound over the fields of Belgium. The young men would fall, as the birds fell.

II

Life had flowed on in a steady rhythm at Pellham Langley after Alice Trimble had died. Black Jack did what he could to ensure that his children should not feel this second loss too much. They had, after all, been barely used to Alice as a stepmother before she was gone, leaving them a sweet, frail half sister. Lally seemed a more permanent legacy of Alice Trimble's time. It was she who was most affected by that death, because she had seen Alice Trimble as the woman who had saved her, who had brought her to life. But in a stolid, enduring sort of way she sensed that she had to be of service, both to Black Jack and to his children, and she stifled her grief. It was a luxury not much indulged in in the place she had come from.

A new governess, Miss Godson, came to Pellham Langley—an unexceptional woman in her forties who roused no memories either of her predecessor, Alice Trimble, or of Latitia. No new housekeeper ever came because Billings insisted that he could run the household to everyone's satisfaction, as well as his own. Black Jack was too numbed from the losses he had suffered to try to argue. He endured his solitary meals, he visited his children on the nursery floor, and he wondered what he would do with the rest of his life.

Jon passed out of the hands of his young tutor, and went to prep school. Black Jack almost kept him at home, but thought better of it. It was, in the usual English fashion, a casually brutal place to which his son was going; but it was what was done to prepare a boy for life. Jon seemed suddenly very vulnerable in his new school cap and blazer. But he had no qualms about going. There was no last-minute hanging back as Black Jack put him into the train at Leeds, and paid the conductor to keep an eye on him.

Jon shook his father's hand as if he were already a man. "It's too bad you'll be all alone with the girls, Father. But it won't be long until the holidays. Perhaps we could get up a scratch cricket team from the village? You'd let me play, wouldn't you?" He had grown up with the legend of his father's moment of glory when he had caught out the Lancashire side.

"You'll be playing rugger, old son, by the time you're due home."

The fair, still-childish face beamed at him. "A lot of things to learn, Father. I expect I'll still like cricket best." He waved exuberantly as the train steamed out. Black Jack behaved as if a piece of soot had gotten into his eye; he blew his nose fiercely.

The girls, Margaret and Lally, waited for him at home. They were well turned out, wearing identical dresses and holland pinafores. Lally, knowing nothing when she had come to Pellham Langley, had streaked past Margaret in learning. She wrote industriously, a vigorous but correct hand, always taking time, Black Jack observed, to turn back to help Margaret over something that defeated her understanding. Perhaps Alice had been right, Black Jack thought. Perhaps she really was older than they thought. It was as if an intelligence, like a dry piece of wood, had been touched by a flame. He marveled at her patience as she stopped her headward rush to backtrack and support Margaret.

The governess, Miss Godson, had something of the same attitude toward Lally as all the others at Pellham Langley, save Black Jack and Jon. She was a fair-minded woman, he judged, and she strove to be absolutely impartial in her dealings with both her charges. But she could not help a slight shade of favoritism creeping in as she handled Margaret. It could be argued that Margaret demanded more of her attention because Lally did what she was told without fuss, and seemed to absorb whatever came her way without effort. Margaret was often difficult of temper, and then tantalizingly sweet and obedient, so that it was easy to forget what she had done half an hour before. What was undeniable, as was reported by so many, was that Margaret had her mother's lovely little vixen face, her wonderful hair, almost her voice and manner. Beside her, Lally's darkness sometimes seemed thick and clumsy, although her mind was so quick. And Margaret was Black Jack's daughter; she had her place in this house by right, not by chance, as Lally had. Miss Godson never voiced an objection to teaching this nameless waif from the slums of Leeds, but Black Jack often wondered if she didn't feel it.

It would be good for both of them, Margaret and Lally, he thought, if they could be sent to school when they were older. And his heart ached even more at the thought of the appalling loneliness of the great house.

But it didn't happen that way. As Margaret grew it became clearer that it might be unwise to send her away. She clung to her home and her familiar surroundings, and Black Jack doubted that she could have survived, even with Lally's support, the buffetings of everyday school life. Could she survive the competition, the exams? Could she play games and behave in a sporting fashion, losing without display-ing anger or temper, as would be expected of her? He knew she should be made more aware of how the world functioned, and that she was not the center of it. But the experiment could be dangerous if she did not survive it. He felt helpless in the face of the decision to be made. It was so much easier to leave things as they were. Just to hope Margaret would grow up normally and marry someone safe. Memories of Latitia haunted him; memories of the way she and he had met and married. What if Margaret did the same? He turned more and more to Lally as the counterbalance of good sense and solidity to that mercurial temperament.

"Oh, Lally, Lally . . ." he murmured to himself as he sat over his brandy in the library. "Am I sacrificing you so that Margaret can have a playmate, a keeper, someone to pace her? To offer her a little challenge but be kind enough not to beat her too badly into second place?" He knew, unhappily, that left to herself Lally might have gone far beyond what would be her portion in the schoolroom of Pellham Langley. When he voiced this thought to Miss Godson, he got a sharp reply.

"Nonsense, Mr. Pollock! What can you be thinking of? Why, the child must be everlastingly grateful for your generosity. Where would she be without it? If not dead, then almost ready to take her place in the mills . . ." He winced at the thought, but it carried more than a grain of truth.

"Lally is perfectly happy to stay with Margaret." Black Jack was conscious that the governess was groping for words of praise to find for her other pupil. "She's a good little girl. She's very fond of Mar-garet. I never hear her complain."

And no one ever would hear her complain, Black Jack thought.
That was the trouble.

* * *

At a far younger age than they would have in any other household, the girls were dressed and came down to dinner in the dining
room with Black Jack on the evenings he was at home. He would return early from the mills so that they could go to bed at the usual
hour. But very early in life Lally learned what it was to be dressed in
silk and velvet, to sit at the long table with the tip of her toes not yet
able to touch the floor, a table set with silver and finger bowls. She
was waited on by a butler and a footman, and never quite got over
the wonder of it. She thought Black Jack and Margaret looked marvelously handsome in the soft light of the candles. She wished she
could look like Margaret just to please Black Jack; to try to compensate she began taking the newspaper from the library in the mornings, after he had finished with it, and trying to read and understand
some of the smaller items so as to have something to talk to him
about. Some things were difficult to understand; she often asked him
to explain. He seemed to delight in trying to do so. He beamed at
both of them with pride. "And how are my two ladies tonight?" Margaret's chatter amused him; Lally's struggle to stretch ahead of herself awed him. He was overjoyed. The mealtimes were no longer solitary. He stayed away less often for dinner. The lady, Mrs. Campion,
whose small, discreet house he paid for, complained. "What can I
do?" He shrugged. "The girls have got to be brought up."

"As if there aren't plenty to do it for you," she retorted. She knew
she had no hope of marrying Black Jack. Nor, after what had happened to his two marriages, did he seem inclined to marry anyone
else. She had to be content with the gifts he gave her, the style in
which he kept her. And she spent many lonely, boring nights by her
own fireside, thinking of Pellham Langley, of which she had heard
much, but had never visited. Black Jack Pollock, she thought with
some bitterness, was never going to risk contaminating his two precious pets by contact with his mistress. And yet she knew, as everyone in the county seemed to know, the scandal of the mistress he had
kept at Pellham Langley and had finally married. And if the story
were correct, that woman had been far from a beauty, and not
young. Where was the sense of it?—where the justice? But Black Jack
paid the piper, and he called the tune.

Gradually, over the years, a semblance of normal social life began to return to Pellham Langley. The affair of Alice Trimble could be glossed over, now that she was gone. People shook their heads over the tales that the beautiful daughter she had left was said to be a little "soft." Not at all difficult, but simple-minded. Well, Black Jack could afford to have her properly cared for. It seemed he had no intention of shutting her away from the rest of the family. In fact, he insisted that they should make every effort to include her in all their doings. But she had her own special nursemaid, Nell, and her own teacher, Miss Garner, because the time of the governess could not be taken from the other two girls. It was kind, and a little pathetic of Black Jack, they said, to hope the child could be taught anything at all. She was, they all said, a perfect innocent. No harm in her, a beautiful child who smiled when she was petted, and had hardly ever shed a tear. Her body grew, but her mind did not. The only echo of her mother was her sweet name, Alice.

Black Jack began to give dinner parties at Pellham Langley at which there was no hostess. The merchants of Leeds and Bradford came gladly, putting up with the long drive because Black Jack's dinners were something to remember. Their wives came because Black Jack, in the social scale, was a cut above their husbands. He managed to mix, with perfect ease it seemed, the town merchants, the textile magnates, the mineowners, and the county gentry. He had never been hunting since the accident which had taken his first wife, the lovely, laughing Lady Latitia they all remembered so vividly. But he kept up with his hunting friends. He even rented again the hunting box where he had been staying when he had met Lady Latitia so that his children should meet their social equals in the field. He took the two girls, and Jon when he was home from school, to the point-to-point races. The girls were often to be seen, turned out in riding clothes of impeccable cut, accompanied by a groom, on their ponies on the moorland roads. It was said, a little maliciously by some, that there was no difficulty in spotting which one was Latitia's daughter. The dumpy little black-haired thing looked uneasy in the saddle and seemed to bounce around, while the golden-haired charmer appeared to have been born there. And yet it was remarked, when the children entered the riding events of the local farmers' shows, that the dark, fat little one put her pony at the jumps with a surprising steadiness and courage; that she seemed to impart this to the animal itself, so that there were some who secretly admired her. She learned through sheer determination how to gather up the little creature to face the jumps the best way. Margaret could sail over them; she could jump a perfect round. But, if at the first fence the pony's hoofs grazed the bar she would be so shaken that the round became a shambles of falling bars, and the pony unwilling to face the next one. "That dark little pudding has the temperament of an elephant," someone in the crowd on the stand behind Black Jack said rather too loudly. "And she looks rather like one, too."

Black Jack glanced back quickly, his feelings for Lally as outraged as if she herself had heard the words. He recognized one of his rich, well-connected neighbors, and fumed inwardly. He privately considered the man an idiot, condescending in his manners, rough with his own horses, one who obviously didn't know that the temperament of an elephant was one of the most intense devotion and loyalty to the herd, especially the small offspring of the cows. They were also renowned for their intelligence. It was sad, Black Jack thought, that Lally was too often considered Margaret's pet elephant. And like the jolly, amusing, good-humored elephant at the zoo, Lally continued to eat up whatever was put before her. But she would have defended Margaret as jealously and courageously as would any of the cow elephants of the herd have defended the newest of the newborn. In so many ways, consciously and unconsciously, Lally was fulfilling the promise whispered to him that night years ago when she had come to him in the library. "I'll look after Alice, just the way I do Margaret." Even with grim determination just scraping around the jumps of the ring, Lally was fulfilling that promise. She trailed after Margaret as if she meant to be near her in case she fell.

But as Black Jack watched his first daughter grow up, he knew that not even Lally could be there often enough to catch her when she fell.

*   *   *

Jon finished at prep school, still loving cricket more than rugby. He went to Eton, where James Pollock had not been able to place Black Jack. This could be, Black Jack acknowledged, as much due to the fact that his grandfather was a member of the House of Lords as to the fact that his father had been educated as a gentleman. It only needed three generations, they said. But they also had a saying in Yorkshire—"clogs to clogs in three generations"—and Black Jack did not forget it. In the same form at Eton, in the same house, was Jon's first cousin, the Honorable Patrick Kimble. Against all the odds of cousins liking each other, the two became friends. Patrick was the younger son of one of Latitia's sisters, Elspeth. They had never met before that first term when the two were suffering the miseries of their lowly state in the school's hierarchy, suffering the indignities of fagging for the sixth formers, the casual cruelties inflicted on them. They commiserated with each other when either was beaten, which was fairly often, complained to each other, but never to anyone else, lent each other pocket money, and shared the food hampers which came from home. It was inevitable that Patrick would be invited to Pellham Langley, and that Jon would be invited to Patrick's home on the borders of Wales. It was inevitable that, while in Yorkshire, Patrick would go to visit his grandparents at Witfell. It would have seemed the height of bad manners if Jon had been excluded from that invitation. Contact between Pellham Langley and Witfell began again.

Lady Bletchley came to tea. Margaret and Lally wore their best afternoon dresses, and handed around the plates. Lady Bletchley observed them closely, questioned them, but did not ask to see Margaret's half sister, Alice. When they had returned to the schoolroom she said to Black Jack, "I have been unfair."

He knew what it must have cost a woman of her nature to say such a thing, but it was a measure of her fairness that she did say it.

"I thought it would be a total disaster. You should have married again after that . . . that unfortunate woman died. I thought you owed it to your children. But you've done well. Jon is a credit to you. I found I liked him rather better than Patrick—he's not so full of himself. Margaret will always be a handful. She reminds me of Latitia . . . not just the way she looks. But I think Latitia was never so . . . so extreme. Margaret will be very beautiful. You'll have your hands full. And as for the other one—the Lally child. Strange little thing, isn't she? Not so little, unfortunately. You really must stop her eating so much, Jack. She could be quite presentable if she weren't so plump. But she has nice manners, I'll grant you that, and she seems intelligent. It's obvious that she's devoted to Margaret. Yes, I have to admit I was unfair—and mistaken. Margaret is lucky to have had her for a companion and a friend. Heaven knows where she's sprung from, and from the look of her, there's no breeding there, but she's turned out well. You must bring them over to Witfell at Christmas when Margaret's cousins are visiting. It's time she got to know them."

Lady Bletchley looked at the portrait of Latitia in a ball gown, painted by John Singer Sargent, hanging over the mantel of the drawing room. "She used to give me more worry than all the others, but I have to confess I cared the most for her—which wasn't fair, either." She turned back to Black Jack and a slight, wintry smile touched her lips. "I must be getting old—confessing all my faults this way." She got rather stiffly to her feet, leaning on her silk parasol. "We'll have to see Margaret properly launched in society. *That* can't be left entirely to a man. Perhaps I'll be of some use yet."

Black Jack rose and pulled the bell for Billings to order Lady Bletchley's carriage, remembering how it had been between them when last he had done the same thing. "Margaret and Lally are only eleven yet, Lady Bletchley. They've a few years to go yet before we need worry."

"You surely don't expect to *launch* the Lally girl into society, Jack. After all, she's nobody."

"We'll see, Lady Bletchley . . . we'll see." He escorted her to the carriage and stood to watch it disappear among the trees of the avenue. "You'll have both of them, or neither, you old bitch," he murmured softly.

* * *

Apart from Patrick, Jon regularly brought other friends from school home at the holidays. Pellham Langley became known as a good place to stay. Pollock's father, they said, was very indulgent. The food was superb, the house supremely comfortable. It was noted for the number of bathrooms it possessed. One could do almost as one wanted. There were tennis courts and a cricket pitch, horses to ride, fishing in the river that wound through the valley, boats to ride on the canals that served the mills. There was a billiard room with two tables. That almost took Pellham Langley to the height of vulgarity, but everyone enjoyed it. There was, of course, the shooting in August. And there was Pollock's sister, Margaret, who was very pretty, and another girl called Lally, who wasn't much to look at, but was reckoned a jolly good sport, and who played the piano in the evenings while the boys waited their turn to dance with Margaret. All in all, invitations to Pellham Langley were sought after. It was, Black Jack knew, exactly what his own father had dreamed of when he had built his monstrous house. Black Jack knew exactly why Jon's young friends came, and it amused him to play the indulgent father to the hilt. It pleased him to see the young faces gathered around his table; he willingly organized visits to the theater in Leeds when something suitable offered, he organized the pony treks on the moors. He saw that the pantries were loaded with the kind of food that young people seem to be able to eat without end. When the days were fine he stayed away from the mills to accompany the picnic parties to the famous beauty spots of the area. He had acquired two motor cars, and a chauffeur to take care of them, since they were such unpredictable machines. He still maintained his stables and on the picnic jaunts a trap would follow them in case of a breakdown. Jon had taken to cars with all the enthusiasm of his youth, and soon was driving skillfully. What dismayed Black Jack was Margaret's demand that she also be taught to drive. She learned with amazing speed because she loved it. Black Jack would permit her to drive only on the roads of the Pellham Langley estate; she was too young and exuberant to allow on the public roads. She always drove with the chauffeur, who nervously confessed to Black Jack that he would have preferred not to drive with Miss Margaret. "Now Miss Lally, sir—she's something different. Steady as a rock. Miss Margaret seems to want to win races."

Everything was done to encourage the life that suddenly flowed through the house. Margaret and Lally never did lessons while Jon had his holidays. Black Jack encouraged Jon's friends and the two girls to mix as much as possible, though he himself was as quietly, watchfully present as many times as he could manage. The girls were learning their first social lessons. Margaret was forgiven much because she couldn't help pleasing the eyes and the senses. Lally was liked because the boys felt comfortable with her, and she studied their preferences so diligently. But Black Jack couldn't help thinking that for all her seeming willingness to please, in the traditional fashion of the girl who knows she is not pretty, Lally was secretly laughing at these young lords of creation. He listened as she earnestly discussed whatever it was a boy wanted to talk about—butterflies or fishing, Latin or the War of the Roses. There was still a part of her reserved for herself alone; it was as if a central, inextinguishable memory of a night years ago when she had suddenly come to warmth and care removed her forever from these young saplings of England's ruling class. She knew how to play their games, talk their talk, act as if she had always belonged. But she had not belonged, and she remembered. Sometimes, meeting her eyes in the midst of this mixed, sometimes boisterous company, Black Jack was devastated to see the dark eyes retained just a hint of the weary, ageless wisdom of the tiny, starving waif. Not all the years had removed it. The fat, friendly, rather plain little girl who chatted amiably in the approved upper-class accent with the sometimes awkward boys who came home with Jon, who appeared to be absorbed in whatever interested them, still had that dash of shrewd cynicism he observed in the slum brats of Leeds and Bradford. He knew that Lally's heart lay utterly with him and Margaret, with Jon and the sweet-looking innocent, Alice. But occasionally he saw in the flicker of her eyes a dark knowledge he could not explain.

* * *

Margaret only grew more beautiful as she grew toward maturity. "A handful," Lady Bletchley had prophesied. Her moods of warmth and generosity redeemed her. She was spoiled but not unkind, thoughtless but not cruel. And for Lally the years only stoked the hunger for learning that seemed to have been bred into her when she came to Pellham Langley. Black Jack often wondered, amid all the time she gave to doing whatever it was Margaret wanted to do, where Lally found opportunity to read as much as she did. When James Pollock had built and furnished Pellham Langley, he had bought, at the architect's decree, all the approved classics bound in the approved colors of leather. Black Jack realized that Lally must have been the only one ever to have opened many of them. But to his delight she had discovered and shared his own passion for the works of the Brontë sisters. Her favorite outing was a drive across the moors to stand and gaze at the parsonage at Haworth. But she avoided the reputation of a "blue stocking"; she talked of books only if someone else was keen to; it seemed to be a private world she kept to herself.

Once Jon, in a thoughtful moment with his father before the fire in the library, when the girls had gone upstairs, ventured to speculate about Lally. It was not long after he had progressed from Eton to Oxford. "You know, Father—in a way it seems a shame she's being kept back by Margaret. She's really very clever, even though she doesn't care to show it. One hears of girls going to university these days. Not many—and they're usually not the sort the chaps much take to. But Lally could make it, if she were given the chance. After all, what's there for her in life? It's not as if she's pretty, or got money, or anything . . ." He looked at his father hopefully, the idea seeming to burst upon him. "Well, of course, she'd just love to stay here with you and take care of the place. She'd be very good at it . . ."

Black Jack smiled, and was surprised at how much pain he felt at the idea of Lally's life being just what Jon had described, however much he might have wanted the comfort of her presence for himself. "I think Lally will find something for herself, Jon. We'll wait until Margaret . . ." He didn't finish. It was taken for granted that Margaret would marry young, and make a brilliant marriage. Everyone said so, and her grandmother, Lady Bletchley, was actively working toward it. She came to see Black Jack one day in the autumn of the year before Margaret's seventeenth birthday. No one knew Lally's birthday. When asked what day she would like to have as a birthday to celebrate, she had asked Black Jack if he could remember the date she had been brought in his arms to Pellham Langley. So Lally's birthday was in November, and she was assumed to be that many months older than Margaret. But it was not Lally whom Lady Bletchley had come to talk about. "You have left it late, Jack. I don't know how it came to slip my mind, but a letter from Elspeth the other day reminded me. Her Julia's going to be seventeen next year, and she's having a London season. Naturally she'll be presented at Court. You must start making arrangements at once. There's the Lord Chamberlain's office to contact, and a London house to rent, and all the other arrangements to make. The coming-out ball. I expect Elspeth would be willing to present her, though I doubt if she'd want all the trouble of looking after her—chaperoning her, and so on, for the season." She sighed as she sipped her tea. "If she isn't willing to present Margaret at Court, I suppose I could do it myself. Though, really, I don't feel quite up to arraying myself in those ridiculous white feathers again, and my joints are a touch stiff to be going down in a full court curtsy. Though Their Majesties don't expect too much from an old gel like me." It was only possible, Black Jack knew, to be presented at Court by some lady who had herself been presented. And what were the other requirements? Unimpeachable reputation? Latitia had been presented, and would have presented her own daughter. She had had her London season before she had begun her wild fling which had called her reputation into question.

Perhaps it would be better to get the presentation over before Margaret started exhibiting any more of her mother's characteristics. He too sighed. She would be soon lost to him, his beautiful, willful, vixen-girl.

"And Lally," he said softly. "Of course she must have a season with Margaret."

Lady Bletchley drew herself up in utter disbelief. "Oh, Jack . . ." Her tone was quite kindly. "I'm sure Lally is a good girl, and Margaret has been fortunate to have her as a companion. But it is now the ways must part. You surely don't imagine . . . ?" But she read his expression. "You *can't* be thinking . . . Jack! It's out of the question. Why, the girl's . . . Who *is* she? She hasn't a name, much less a position. You can't present a girl like that at Court. They wouldn't stand for it. She would just be humiliated and miserable. Jack . . . think!"

"What I thought was that any lady of unimpeachable reputation had the right of presentation to the Queen. Lally has been brought up as a lady. I would swear on my life that she's of unimpeachable reputation."

"You're mad, Jack," was all Lady Bletchley said. She departed, subdued but unshakable. "It can never happen."

What Lady Bletchley had not counted upon, nor had Black Jack really hoped for, was Margaret's stand of absolute loyalty to Lally. She made a special visit to Witfell to confront her grandmother. "Do you imagine I'm going to go through all that without Lally?" she demanded. "Why, we've been together every moment since we were . . . well, forever. If you leave Lally out of this, then you must leave me out. Who wants a season? From all I've heard it's a great bore. At any rate, I'll not do it without Lally. How could I look her in the face?" Black Jack had never been so proud of Margaret, nor loved her more. He saw Latitia's free, generous spirit in her bright, steadfast gaze, and was thankful.

There were hurried telephone calls to Elspeth, the Honorable Patrick's mother, but she declined to present anyone except her daughter, Julia, and, as a favor, Margaret. "You really can't expect me, Jack"—the voice was shrill on the phone—"to take a nameless slum brat to Buckingham Palace."

He had to accept her refusal, but he did not accept the situation. He went to London, stayed at his club, listened carefully, asked some discreet questions. Then he paid a visit to the house of the Dowager

Marchioness of Ross in Belgravia; the house bore a FOR SALE sign. The Marchioness had been widowed a year ago, and it was well known that her husband had shot himself because he had had no way to satisfy the demands of his creditors. His mania for gambling had eroded his estate to the point where it barely existed; the couple had been childless, and the title and the few assets of the estate had gone to a distant cousin, who regarded trying to pay off his relative's debts, provide a small pension for his widow, and run the diminished estate as a thankless burden. The knowledge of all this imparted a certain bitterness to the rather severely handsome, slim woman in her thirties who received Black Jack. He spoke frankly, and she listened. They agreed on a price. She would present Lally at Court, and would be her chaperone for the season. She would be the official hostess when Black Jack gave a coming-out ball for Margaret and Lally. They then concocted a story of an acquaintanceship between her husband and Black Jack in the past; they had indeed belonged to the same club. The price they had agreed to was a very generous one. It would enable the Marchioness to settle the claims of some of her creditors, debts incurred before she knew the true state of her husband's affairs. It was a mutually satisfactory arrangement, and one which was not altogether a novelty.

One other detail of forgotten business was attended to. Black Jack formally adopted Lally. She became legally Lillian Pollock.

When Black Jack returned to Pellham Langley with the news, Margaret's face glowed with pleasure; he had not mentioned the fact that the Marchioness was being paid for her favor. Margaret flung her arms around her father's neck. "Oh, you *have* been clever! We'll have such fun."

Only Lally looked doubtful. But she tried to seem pleased. She knew if she refused the plan, Margaret would also refuse to go through the season. She muttered darkly, "I shall look an utter fool. Like a cart horse dressed up in white feathers."

II

In the spring of 1914 Black Jack and the two girls went to the rented house in Wilton Crescent. The girls started on the round of tea parties which would introduce them to all the other girls coming out that season. "It's really silly," Margaret remarked. "We're all going to be seeing exactly the same people at every ball and dinner party, and exactly the same young men will be asked. We'll all troop to Henley and Ascot and the Fourth of June at Eton hoping our hats are a bit different from one another's . . ."

Black Jack pressed Jon into service to find partners for Lally. Most of them, he suspected, accepted the invitations because they wanted to be near Margaret, even if not her official partner. "Clever of you to put them together like that," the Marchioness said. "Your golden swan is bait for the ugly duckling."

"I wish you wouldn't call Lally that, Lady Ross."

She spread her hands. "I don't do it to her face. But it seems foolish not to recognize the obvious." But she played her part, as she had contracted to do, and she did it wholeheartedly. Something in her began to respond to the dark, heavy-set girl; a kind of respect was dawning. She drilled her mercilessly in the court curtsy, making her wear several heavy towels tacked together to simulate the train. "Chin up, eyes down, back perfectly straight."

The day came when the carriage provided by Black Jack for the Marchioness joined the long, slow line wending its way up the Mall toward the Palace. Lally wore the white dress and train; the regulation three white feathers dressed her hair. She didn't look as bad as the Marchioness had expected, but she would cause no heads to turn —a plain, dark, rather fat girl dressed up in strange clothes. She held her hands, wearing the long white-kid gloves, perfectly still in her lap. The pearls Black Jack had given her, the Marchioness thought, were beautiful. She might not be a credit to her, but she would do nothing incorrectly. She would not let overwrought nerves spoil the curtsy; she would not put a foot wrong. Somewhere behind them in the line of carriages was Lady Kimble with her daughter, the Honorable Julia, and her niece, Margaret Pollock. The Marchioness had noticed, when she had come to the Pollock house in Wilton Crescent to supervise Lally's dressing, that Margaret had quivered, and was deadly pale. She had looked quite exquisitely beautiful in her long dress and train; the three feathers looked as if they belonged naturally in her wonderful golden hair; the pearls, which were identical to Lally's, only made her face more translucent. But Black Jack looked anxiously at her, for all his pride. She appeared as though she might faint. Lady Kimble had ready a tiny phial of sal volatile.

Lady Ross and Lally waited on the little gilt chairs with the whisperings of the girls and their mothers or aunts, or whoever was presenting them, all about them. Some looked bored after the long wait in the carriages, some looked as nervous as Margaret. At last a tall, splendidly handsome young guardsman called:

"The Dowager Marchioness of Ross. Miss Lillian Pollock."

Lally was before the thrones. She made her curtsy as if by clockwork, expertly kicked the train out of the way, and made the backward steps. She was not aware of seeing Their Majesties. It was a matter of getting in and out of that terrible room without disgracing herself—more important, without disgracing Black Jack. She did it perfectly, mechanically, and was aware that only slightly burning cheeks betrayed her emotion.

"Well done, child," the Marchioness said. They were some of the sweetest words Lally had ever heard. They returned to the house in Wilton Crescent to await Margaret's return; Black Jack plied them with champagne. Lally started to take off the headdress. "No, don't," he begged. "I just want to see the two of you in them together again." As if, Lally thought, she could possibly look anything like Margaret.

Margaret returned, her eyes red, her features distorted from weeping. "I wobbled!" she cried, snatching off the headdress and flinging herself into her father's arms. "I thought I was going to fall, and I had to put one hand down on the floor to steady myself. I was a disgrace!" Black Jack held her trembling hand while she put the champagne glass to her lips.

"Nonsense!" her aunt snapped. "It was only the slightest little mishap. Hardly noticeable at all. All this fuss about nothing. Why, the Queen actually smiled at her. *That* is a great compliment!"

After a time, Margaret stopped crying. She drank the champagne with more enthusiasm than caution. "Well, for better or worse, it's over. Perhaps we can start to enjoy ourselves now."

The next day they dressed up again in the white court gowns, the feathers and pearls, to have a photograph taken. The result made Lally acutely miserable.

The season itself was a kind of torture for Lally. She went through all the motions because Black Jack wanted her to do so, but she suffered. The great coming-out ball Black Jack gave for them both was a triumph for Margaret, a nightmare for her. She stood woodenly in the receiving line, knowing that people pitied her her plainness, especially compared with Margaret's vibrant beauty. She felt dull and fat and unlovely; the young men who danced with her did so from a sense of duty to their friend Jon, to Black Jack as the splendid host he had been to them, and with the hope of finding favor with Margaret. The boys who had considered Lally a jolly good sport when they had holidayed at Pellham Langley regarded her now with a kind of pity. "Cheer up, old girl," one of them said to her as she sat gloomily over the supper of cold salmon and meats, strawberries and cream, the huge array of confections to which she turned as a consolation for the misery she felt. "It'll soon be over. I always feel sorry for you poor debs. It's really a bit like being thrown to the lions. But you'll soon be back at Pellham Langley. Did you know that Black—that Mr. Pollock has invited me for the shooting in August? I'll be seeing you then. You'll be the old Lally then, with all this nonsense behind you."

She hung hopefully on the thought as she ate. She always spun out the suppers at these interminable balls as long as she could, bringing up all her resources of conversation for the benefit of whatever young man the Marchioness had bullied into taking her in to supper. She knew she ate too much, but it was a reason for staying. To be returned to the Marchioness' side, to sit there as a wallflower, was unbearable. She was glad that she had a separate chaperone in the Marchioness, and Black Jack had put a carriage at their disposal. Margaret always stayed until the last dance, and often had to split them to accommodate her partners. She crept up the stairs at Wilton Crescent as the early summer dawn was breaking, to sleep, exhausted, happy, until noon. Lally and the Marchioness were seldom late home. "At least I'm not losing any sleep," the Marchioness was heard to sigh.

They went for the ritual four days to Ascot, where Black Jack had taken a box, and the champagne was unlimited. Lally thought she looked ridiculous and already middle-aged in the huge hats she wore. From the back, she decided, she definitely did look middle-aged. She gazed wistfully at Margaret's slender radiance. Margaret had quite forgotten the anguish of nearly falling at Their Majesties' feet. She now preferred to remember the Queen's smile. She knew she was spoken of as the debutante of the season. Amid the crowded ball cards, and the invitations, the faces of young men swam before her eyes, and she hardly bothered to distinguish one from the other. She had received several proposals of marriage. She talked of them lightly to Lally, and laughed. "If any of them thinks I'm going to get married just after my first season, and settle down to having babies, they're as stupid as they look. I intend to have fun."

Lally had an unexpected success at Ascot. Not even the clothes from the best dressmakers could transform her, but the word went around their small circle. "Lally Pollock's winning! She is betting on every race, and winning." The young men liked that. They began to ask for introductions; her friends of the holiday times at Pellham Langley had precedence. They buzzed around her, asking for tips on winners.

Black Jack was delighted, and amused, by her small triumph. He guessed what a heartbreak the season had been for her. He admired the stoic fashion with which she had endured it. "How on earth did you do it, Lally?"

She raised her head from *The Times* at the breakfast table. Margaret was upstairs, asleep, and would not appear before noon. "It's easy. I read *The Sporting Life*. I study the form. The law of averages just seemed to favor me at Ascot. I knew it couldn't last, but studying the form is a bit better than sticking a pin in the race card, which is what all the others seem to do."

The interminable weeks of June and July spun themselves out at last. Now it was only days that Lally counted until August would release them to Pellham Langley. So many of the newly acquired friends of the season, and the old friends of Jon's school and Oxford days, had been invited for the start of the grouse-shooting season on August 12 that even the resources of Pellham Langley would be strained to accommodate them, and specially hired servants would have to be imported from London to help cater for their needs. Black Jack remembered, when he had started on his orgy of new plumbing and putting electricity throughout Pellham Langley, that these weeks ahead had been a vague thought. Long after he had built it, the house was at last serving the purpose for which his father, James Pollock, had intended it. To his surprise the Marchioness had indicated, not too subtly, that she also would like to visit Pellham Langley in August. Black Jack was pleased. It would put a seal of authenticity on the relationship, taking away some of the taint of his having bought the Marchioness' services for Lally. "I've grown quite fond of the child," she observed dryly. "There's good stuff in her."

But the Marchioness did not reach Pellham Langley that August. All through the summer, as the young girls and their partners had danced until each night turned into a pale summer dawn, the armies of Europe had begun to make ready. The Germans had been ready far too long, and any excuse would be seized on. The British press talked of "trouble in the Balkans" over the assassination of the heir to the Austro-Hungarian Empire. Many people had never heard of the Balkans; they looked to their great navy, and felt the comfort of security. Britain was safe in her island state; she rested on her empire. They cared little about interlocking treaties. Only the serious newspapers drew attention to them.

"Will there be war?" Lally had said one morning to Black Jack as she read *The Times*. A terrible fear caught in her heart as she thought of Jon. Her tone was one of appeal to Black Jack to dispel it.

He tried to dismiss the idea from her mind. Why let her worry? But there was a certain war fever among the young men. They talked of it lightly, as if it were some other form of sport. At the beginning of August, Britain was suddenly caught by the clauses of the treaty guaranteeing the neutrality of Belgium. Surely, everyone said, they would not go to war over another country's neutrality? As Black Jack sat watching the tennis his mind turned over the events of the day before when Sir Edward Grey, the Foreign Secretary, had addressed a packed House of Commons. This morning, August 4, they learned that the Germans had crossed the frontier into Belgium.

As he watched the last of the match, the bright summer day seemed to darken for Black Jack. All the things he loved in the world were here about him—his son, Jon, his daughters, Margaret and Lally, and this precious but flawed sprite beside him. The free clean air of the moors stirred beyond the garden walls. He noticed that the shadows had begun to edge along the tennis court. The figure of Billings appeared on the terrace. It was a little early, Black Jack thought, for tea. And Billings was not followed by the expected retinue of servants. He hurried straight to his master, and bent to speak softly to him.

"I thought you would want to know, sir. The Marchioness has just telephoned the news. The Prime Minister has announced in the House a message from His Majesty. The Mobilization Proclamation has been read. An ultimatum has been sent to Germany. It expires at midnight."

Black Jack looked at the young faces around him. "Thank you, Billings," he said quietly. "I'll tell them . . . and perhaps we'd better have tea in the dining room. Everyone will want to be near the telephone."

"Very good, sir."

Slowly, Black Jack rose. He put on his blazer, and took Alice's bandaged hand in his. "We'll go and wash it, my darling." And then he approached the nearest of the young men, who was lying on his back on the grass, not watching the game but the cloudless blue sky above.

❧ CHAPTER 5 ❧

I

Lally slipped from the great tower room which was officially Margaret's bedroom, but which she insisted on Lally sharing. "I hate to wake in the dark alone," she had said. Lally went through the connecting bathroom—one of Black Jack's great areas of marble and shining taps, to a smaller room, which had been intended as a dressing room, but which also held a bed which Lally regarded as her own, though she seldom slept there. She had used it during the years as a room of retreat, a place where she could read through the hours of the night without disturbing Margaret. It had a writing table placed before the long window; she sat down there and looked over the beloved and familiar landscape of the crags above, with the summer dawn just touching the eastern ridges, before the light slipped down to the valleys.

There had been a sort of frantic gaiety at the long dining table last night. But already the ranks of the house party had been thinned by the departure of the two young officers to get the evening train to return to Sandhurst. Everyone had waited together in the drawing room until the expiration of the ultimatum, which had been eleven o'clock British time. "That's it, then," Jon said. "We're at war."

Someone gave a cheer. Black Jack couldn't remember having given the order, but Billings was there, handing around a tray of champagne. It was an unlikely party. They talked of war as if it were a game, and one or two expressed disappointment because they would hardly be through their training in time to see some action. "It'll all be over by Christmas" was the common sentiment. The girls looked disturbed because it seemed, from what they said, that every young man would leave Pellham Langley first thing in the morning, and every single one of them was going to join up. There would only be a houseful of women, and no shooting party on the moors.

Margaret had tossed restlessly when at last they had gone to bed. "It's spoiled it all, hasn't it, Lally? Damn! Who would have thought of a war coming along just when I was all set to have a good time. I was so looking forward to that weekend at Harewood. It'll be next year before things get back to normal." It was a long time before she slept.

Lally sat and watched the light grow steadily on the ridge, watched one familiar feature after the other begin to be touched by it. She had not slept, even after she heard Margaret's soft, regular breathing. She had drunk the champagne, but she had been unable to toast the future with any sense of confidence. Across the room she had seen Black Jack's gaze fixed on his son, and she had shared his agony of apprehension. Her face, she knew, was perfectly composed, but her stomach had twisted with fear. None of them, these gilded, beautiful young people, seemed to comprehend what might happen, so she kept her own fears to herself.

But here alone some dark memory of a time long past came back to her. It was a shadow which often touched her, and which all of Black Jack's love had been unable to dispel. Fear, to Lally, also had a tangible smell. It was there, a persistent, haunting recollection of a time before she had come to Pellham Langley, as if she could remember what it was like to have lived before she had been truly born. The smell was rank and sour. It came to her at times in the strangest places—even with the window open to the scents of the garden, or seated close to the cut flowers on the dining-room table. It was associated with a dark and crowded place, many bodies—the smell of filth and sickness. And with it came that gnawing emptiness in her stomach that not all the good food in the world seemed able to fill. She had experienced it the night before as the minutes to the ultimatum had run out.

Her fear, because her mind was not able to comprehend the magnitude of what might be before them, focused on one object, Jon. She had always been a willing servant—she could even face the fact that she might have been called by some people a slave—to Black

Jack's children. She had grown up as Jon Pollock's sister, but her mind and her body both knew that she was not his sister. She dared, sometimes, to whisper to herself, as she did now, that she loved him as intensely as any woman could love a man. She knew she was different from every young woman about her. She had lived a hideous, sickening existence in that other life, and it had aged her. So that what she gave Jon was a love far more mature than whatever number of years she was reckoned to have lived. And Jon treated her affectionately, trusting her with much that he could not trust Margaret with, trusting her to take care of Margaret. She knew his eyes did not see a woman when he looked at her; she was his sister—his plump, dependable, clever, obliging Lally. He did not know the way she loved him. She could never show it. But the war was here, and Jon would be in danger. The smell of fear was acrid and strong. Her stomach lurched. She endured the fear, the smell, and the hunger as long as she could. Then she went quietly downstairs and through to the kitchens. She sat in the huge pantry and began to eat slices of a bacon, egg, and onion pie. She was still there when the first kitchen maid came sleepily to poke the still-hot coals in the kitchen range. She put her head around the open door of the pantry.

"Oh, it's you, Miss Lally." She betrayed no surprise. She just reached out and accepted the slice of pie that Lally cut. "Terrible about the war, isn't it, miss?" She had often encountered Lally there early in the morning.

* * *

Black Jack also greeted the dawn wakefully. He sat at one of the long windows of the room he and Alice had shared in the few months of their married life. In the opposite wing of the house the room he had shared with Latitia was still undisturbed; it was dusted daily and fresh flowers were placed there. The scent evaporated slowly in the cut-crystal bottles. Her dresses, in the style of the grand Edwardian period, still hung in huge presses. Her riding boots stood polished and bright in their wooden trees. Alice Trimble had never sought to drive away the memory of Latitia.

But now Black Jack's thoughts were with neither woman. If he had known of it, he would have crept downstairs to share the bacon and egg pie with Lally, because he shared her fear. His heart seemed numb as he remembered the talk of the night before. He dared say no word to hold Jon back from the headlong rush to enlist. He was a fit young man, and he would go, as they were all clamoring to do. He tried, in an effort to turn his thoughts from Jon, to think what would be happening in his mines and his mills.

Far more closely than even Lally suspected, he had followed the events of the last years. He had read the transcribed speeches of the Kaiser, watched the count of the German Army grow, watched the building of the German Navy. He had refused to believe what was said of Russia—that her great population, her vast spaces, made her impregnable. He had seen the coming war, and had made his plans. Now, as he thought of his only son, his beloved, amiable, handsome Jon, he wished that every plan he had made had gone awry. He would more gladly have faced bankruptcy than the prospect of his son engulfed in the holocaust he had predicted, and which now seemed to be upon them.

In the last year he had borrowed heavily to finance his purchases. No one, during that splendid season he had given Margaret and Lally, no one, drinking his champagne at their coming-out ball or at Ascot, could have suspected how deeply into debt he had gone. The Marchioness, who had been given a free hand to spend as she pleased, just so long as she made Lally's ordeal bearable, had not suspected, and she was a shrewd woman about money. Only his bankers shook their heads as they accepted the title deeds of Pellham Langley and its moorlands, as they accepted the deeds of the farms in the dales, of the streets of little terraced houses he owned in Leeds and Bradford and Sheffield. They had accepted them as collateral because they were men of money, and what Black Jack presented was money—money and the interest on the debts he had incurred. And to the managers of his mills, the textile and the steel mills, the managers of the mines, he had given the order to stockpile every scrap of raw material his borrowed money would purchase. There were new mountains of coal piled at the tipheads he owned; he bought the iron it needed to rest beside it, waiting until it could be turned into steel. The precious wool was baled in warehouses, unwoven yet, strong with the oily smell of sheep. He signed contracts with the cotton spinners of Manchester, and owned the product they produced. Warehouses, some of them almost derelict, from the Mersey to the Humber, bulged with the goods he bought. "Mad," the managers had said. "Surely he's gone beyond the limits," the bankers said. But they said it without emotion. They were receiving their interest. They looked at the mills, the mines, warehouses, and rows of streets, Pell-

ham Langley and its acres, the dales and their farms; the collateral
was sound. If they should one day own them because of Black Jack's
recklessness, they would have a bargain.

And now Black Jack sat in the dawning light of that August day
and knew, with agony, that all his guesses had been right. His mills
would turn the wool into khaki uniforms, the cotton from Manchester would make sheets and bandages. The coal and the iron
would make the steel for the guns. He had not joined the youthful,
lighthearted sentiments expressed the night before. The war would
not be over by Christmas. He had gambled on a long struggle. His
father had left him a rich man. He knew that if this war took the
course he believed it would, he would end it as a very much richer
man. And now, with the vision of his son's face before him, Jon's
smiling, excited face, he would have handed it all back if he could
have prevented the ordeal of the young men he saw as the natural
outcome of his own grim and prophetic visions.

II

More quickly than most people expected, they were plunged
deeply into war. The sweep of the German Army through Belgium
was breathtaking to those who had not studied the preparations for
just such an event. "Let the German soldier on the furthest right
flank brush the Channel with his sleeve," had been von Moltke's
strategy for years, and now his directive. This the German Army pro-
ceeded to do with frightening efficiency. Too many, free of war for a
generation, thought of it as a high and liberating adventure, some
grand gesture for which a young man might gladly die. Sadly, much
later, Black Jack came across the poems of Rupert Brooke—*1914*.
They spoke, an unconscious blasphemy of a world cleansed and
nationalism glorified. *Now, God be thanked. Who has matched us
with His hour . . . we have come into our heritage.*

Lally set up maps in the library at Pellham Langley. "The Battle
of the Frontiers" they afterward called it, as France and Germany
fought, invaded, and counterinvaded. August was not even finished
before the British and the Germans first made contact at Mons, and
to the astonishment of the nation, the British were obliged to fall
back with the French. By September the Battle of the Marne had
begun. Lally looked at Black Jack wonderingly. "How? How can we

have let them do this—get so far? Weren't we supposed to be ready?" He shook his head. "Not ready enough." He was seldom at Pellham Langley these days. The mills and the mines absorbed all his time. The young men were going, his young managers, his salesmen. "Though God knows," he said to Lally, "I don't need any salesmen these days. Every scrap of cloth, every ton of steel is spoken for by the government. I only wish I knew where to turn for more."

He stayed almost every night in Leeds or else went to Sheffield, or on to Wales. He had only one customer, the military. He saw his stockpiles eroded with frightening speed. He sought desperately for more supplies. He paid up his interest with the banks, he repaid the loans. The deeds of the mills and the mines, of the farms, of Pellham Langley and its acres were returned to him. The money flowed in, and he could not find enough avenues through which to rechannel it. Even a small shoe factory he had bought in Bradford years ago, and almost forgotten because it barely paid its way, was suddenly profitable, sickeningly profitable. "It has switched to making soldiers' boots," he said to Lally. Sometimes he said more than he should to Lally—knowing he sought to ease the burden of his suddenly long days, the burden of a conscience which now saw the money he had planned as a profit being tainted. Jon was drilling at Catterick, a cadet officer. By the end of October the battle of Ypres had begun, and no one talked any more of it all being over by Christmas.

Lally moved restlessly through the empty days in which there was not enough to do; the books which had lured her before now seemed a waste of time—but how to use the time? Margaret sulked, and fretted. "It was going to be the best time of my life," she wailed to Lally. "And look at what's happened. There's no society. Nothing to do."

"There are no young men," Black Jack finished for her. Margaret went over to visit her grandfather's home at Witfell, and returned, disgruntled. "It's just the same there," she complained. "Nothing but war . . . war. Nothing's going on but Granny organizing the Red Cross. The ladies have tea parties and roll bandages. We had some first-aid classes. One of the maids . . ." She tried to repress the wicked laughter, and failed. "One of the maids was supposed to have a broken leg, and all of us were being taught how to put it in a splint. As a grand finale, we were carrying her away on a stretcher to an imaginary ambulance, and one of those idiots dropped her end, and the poor girl fell out and *really* broke her leg. It put everyone in their place, I'll tell you."

"Why," Lally said, "don't we go and learn how to be real nurses?"

They both looked at her; Margaret's mouth fell open a little. Black Jack drew heavily on his cigarette. He was now smoking more of them than he could count.

"Do you mean it?" Margaret demanded.

"Why not? What use are we to ourselves or anyone else just passing the days here at Pellham? We're not married. There are no children. There are plenty of other women to roll bandages."

Still no one spoke. Black Jack lighted another cigarette from the butt of the one he was finishing before he could frame any reply. "Aren't you rushing things a bit, Lally? I mean—girls like you and Margaret . . . surely they don't need you yet?"

Unstated was the truth that the hospitals were not designed, their staffs not structured to cope with young volunteers like Margaret and Lally. Some "ladies" might have taken up nursing as a vocation when no marriage had been offered to them. They were regarded as saints, martyrs, or beyond hope. The gently bred and nurtured young girls, especially if they were pretty, were regarded as a liability, a nuisance. At that stage the matrons of hospitals did not welcome their presence. If they were there only to arrange flowers, they were in the way. The thought had begun to sink in that there might be many more months of casualties. There was no room, no time for training amateurs.

"Why—do you think I'd drop the end of the stretcher?"

Black Jack shook his head. "No, Lally—not you."

Margaret flushed. "Well, *I* didn't drop the end of the stretcher. I was just telling you . . . I thought it was funny!"

"Not for the poor maid, I'm sure."

"Lally, you can be so superior at times." Margaret looked as if she wanted to weep. The idea of being in a real hospital was both attractive and frightening. Lally touched her arm, gently.

"You know I didn't mean it that way. I'm just trying . . ." She looked around at Black Jack. "We might be doing something *useful*. We might be accepted in the Voluntary Aid Detachments. Of course, it would mean going into a hospital in Leeds or Bradford. Not living in, or anything . . . but helping."

"How could we live here, and be in a hospital in Leeds? We couldn't use a carriage for the journey every day—it wouldn't be patriotic to use the petrol for a car." A sudden hope lighted in Margaret's amber eyes. "Of course, if we had a *house* in Leeds . . .

Why, Father, we could all have a house in Leeds. We could live with you there. So much more convenient for you. We could close Pellham . . ." Her thoughts were racing on. "We could—"

"Gently, Margaret. Gently. We'll just take one thing at a time." He knew well enough what she meant. In Leeds, they were on the main railway line. Young officers coming to and fro would call. There might be visits to London. Society was possible again, in a limited way, without seeming to be unpatriotic. He suddenly realized that Pellham Langley, its wide acres and splendid isolation, purchased at such cost, might now seem a prison to this fledgling daughter who had so recently shone in London society. Lally fretted only because she felt useless at a time when everyone was being pressed into service of some kind. Margaret fretted because she was without her admirers, without the come and go of her life these last months. They were out of the schoolroom, these girls; there was no longer a governess to set them tasks. There was no mother to advise, to keep house, to manufacture the activities. Black Jack, tired after a strenuous week at the mills, when the deficiencies of his suddenly diminished work force had become evident, was lost for a solution.

He said only one thing. "I don't think we can close Pellham, Margaret. There's Alice. She's used to it here. I wouldn't . . . I wouldn't want to disturb her."

Margaret's fondness for Alice warred with her desire to be away from the place, to be active in something. "Of course we won't desert her. I didn't mean really to close the place completely. But if the war lasts as long as they're beginning to say it could, we will have to manage with much less than we have now. I heard two of the maids talking the other day. War work, they call it now. Some of the factories are beginning to offer high wages. It isn't as strict as being in service. They'd like to go to the towns . . ." For a moment her tone faltered. Black Jack thought it might be the first time in her life she had ever thought of herself as being in any way like the young creatures who moved busily around Pellham Langley in their caps and aprons, having similar hopes, wishes, desires. "Billings could run the house. We could leave Alice . . . undisturbed. She'd have Nell with her, and Miss Garner. And we would all come and visit whenever we could." She looked at Lally for information. "I suppose they do give you . . . leave, or some such thing, from these hospitals?"

* * *

Black Jack rented a Georgian house on the outskirts of Leeds in an area which had once been well outside the city, surrounded by its own farm acres. Now it stood in spacious gardens, but the Victorian villas of the prosperous merchants of Leeds crowded its boundaries. Its name was Grangewick—a beautifully proportioned but small house for those who had been used to the vast spaces of Pellham Langley. "Pokey," Margaret pronounced it. "But we shall be comfortable enough here. It needs hardly any staff . . ." She was happily settling herself in the room she had chosen, looking down over the growing sprawl of Leeds, the city whose chimney smoke belched so that it seemed to live within a gray cloud of its own. Soot lay on the windowsills at Grangewick, but at the bottom of the hill a tram line ran, so that it was possible to think of coming and going to the city as one pleased. And if they could come and go as they wanted, so could visitors. Margaret and Lally quickly selected what furniture they wanted from Pellham Langley, and Lally gave directions about closing most of the rooms. Billings stubbornly refused to remain at Pellham Langley. "The Master will need me, Miss Lally . . . especially if you and Miss Margaret go on with this silliness about entering this nursing business." Billings had reached the age and status with the household when he was privileged to air his views. "Quite honestly, Miss Lally, can you see Miss Margaret . . . ?" He raised his eyebrows. "Most indelicate, I call it." He didn't, Lally noticed, seem to think it would be an indelicate occupation for her. But then, looking at her sturdy, thick body, her strong hands, knowing her reputation for steady nerves, who could think any situation would be indelicate for her? Whereas Margaret . . . Already Lally could visualize that golden hair somehow partially escaping from the Voluntary Aid Detachments' veil, that arresting, mobile face twisting with sympathy and pain as she smoothed the sheets of wounded officers; the little vixen mask would mirror every emotion she witnessed around her. Privately Lally agreed with Billings. Margaret was not ideal material for a nurse.

While they were still settling into Grangewick, Black Jack arrived with Alice. He drove the Rolls himself. The chauffeur had enlisted, and the second car was permanently laid up in the stables. "I've been out to Pellham. We just can't leave her there. Not just with Nell and Miss Garner." Alice's lovely face was still blotched from the tears she had shed. "She thought she'd been left behind." He looked appealingly at Lally.

Lally rushed to her, conscience-stricken. Hadn't she promised she
would take care of Alice as well as Margaret? It wasn't enough to
make sure that Alice was well cared for. She needed more than that.
Lally swept the delicate little body up in her strong arms, holding her
high, as she knew Alice loved to be held, as if she were still a child.
"Dearest . . . we'll never leave you alone again. I promise. Father
and Margaret and I . . ."

"And Jon?" Alice rarely questioned anything; they always listened
when she did. "I heard them say they would send Jon away somewhere. Where is Jon?"

"Jon's just doing some special exercises, dearest," Lally answered.
"You know how he trains for his cricket—and for rugger. It's a game,
Alice. A special sort of game. He'll be back with us soon. For a
while. And then he has to go out and play the game. Do you understand, dearest . . . ?" She had set Alice down, and taken her hand.
"Now you must have a look at where we've put the furniture. We
have a new piano . . . the one from Pellham wouldn't fit here."
They moved toward the drawing room. Alice held the worn rabbit
which had been her favorite toy since Black Jack had given it to her
many years ago. The late winter sunlight, diffused through the layers
of Leeds's smoke, fell softly on her as she walked with Lally, her
hand trustingly placed in her sister's. Soon after, Black Jack and
Margaret, still standing in the hall, heard Lally's strong, true, surprisingly good voice singing Alice's favorite song, as her hands, rather
woodenly, played the melody.

> *"Oh, don't you remember sweet Alice, Ben Bolt?*
> *Sweet Alice whose hair was so brown,*
> *Who wept with delight when you gave her a smile,*
> *And trembled with fear at your frown?*

Margaret moved restlessly. Black Jack sighed.

III

Occasionally the wind carried flurries of snow, but between the
gusts it was possible to see the lights of Leeds down below. More
lights than there should have been. There was much talk of zeppelin
raids, but no one, that first wartime Christmas, seemed to understand

the necessity for precautions. The fighting was fierce, but it was on
the other side of the Channel.

Christmas had come and gone quietly at Grangewick. Since Jon
could not get leave, it was not thought worthwhile to open up Pellham Langley. Black Jack worked long hours; Margaret and Lally
had begun, the lowliest of the new VADs at the Infirmary. The
wounded were being brought back from France and, since the military hospitals were swamped, they spilled over into the general hospitals. But they seemed a world apart from Margaret and Lally, who
were seldom allowed near them. Black Jack still looked askance at
what he considered a caprice on Lally's part, of which she would
soon tire. He worried more about Margaret, who would return home
with stories of the frightful injuries she had seen—or thought she had
seen. She lived too much with the sight and memories of things she
had never imagined existed. Black Jack had been glad when a summons had come from her grandmother, Lady Bletchley, to spend
Christmas at Witfell. "I can't come, Granny," Margaret had said on
the telephone. "I have duty during Christmas week."

"Nonsense! You're run-down and need a rest. I'll speak to the matron."

Whether it was what Lady Bletchley had said, or her standing in
the Red Cross, or Black Jack's contributions to the hospital which
swayed the matron, no one knew. But it was suggested to Margaret,
after only six weeks' service at the hospital, that she was looking too
thin, and needed country air. The matron saw her go thankfully. The
hospital was crowded; she needed more staff, but what she didn't
want was the beautiful, highly strung daughter of a man with too
much local influence. She was pleased that Lady Bletchley's demands
had not included the stolid, enduring Lally. Lally Pollock could fetch
and carry endless hours without showing fatigue; she was not given
to attacks of nerves. Privately the matron thought that without her
ever-present appendage of Margaret, Lally might, in time, make an
excellent nurse. Lally stayed on duty through Christmas week. She
had helped trim the wards with Christmas decorations; on Christmas Day she had scrubbed out the floor of the sluice room, and
handed around the Christmas dinners. She cut up goose for a soldier
whose eyes were still bandaged, and who would probably never see
again. "Thee's a right pretty lass, I just know it," the matron had
heard him say to Lally as she had made the round of the wards during the festive dinner. That was one thing Lally Pollock would never

be, the matron thought. But she was capable and calm; her hands were red and cracked.

"Miss Pollock," she said crisply, with Sister by her side, "you may take New Year's Eve and the next day off." She was aware of Lally Pollock's history. She was aware of Black Jack's feeling for this nameless child. She also was aware that neither Lally nor Black Jack would ever ask for favors, and she failed to see why the other one, Margaret, should have all the treats. So she directly ordered Lally to take New Year's Eve off, without knowing if there would be anyone to celebrate it with her.

Lally, sitting at the drawing-room fire at Grangewick, began to think that she would see in the New Year alone. Alice by now was asleep upstairs. Nell had gone with her, as always. When the decision had been made to close Pellham Langley, Miss Garner had given her notice. "I've taught Alice everything I think she is capable of learning, Mr. Pollock. I could have—I should have liked to continue to help, as a sort of companion, but in view of the war, I think my services are needed elsewhere. I intend to join the Queen Alexandra's Nursing Service. I shall miss you all—most of all I shall miss Alice. A sweet child . . ." So she had gone, and the household had diminished even more.

Lally had hoped that Black Jack might return to Grangewick early that evening, but he had telephoned Billings to say he would not be in to dinner. That probably meant, Lally thought, that he would be visiting the house, not so far from Grangewick, where Mrs. Campion lived alone. She and Margaret and Black Jack kept up a pretense among themselves that Mrs. Campion did not exist. He made sure that Mrs. Campion did not impinge on them, but there must have been times, Lally thought, when Mrs. Campion and the pleasure of her bed exerted the usual pull on Black Jack. He had never been meant to live as a monk, she reminded herself. But they did not fear Mrs. Campion; there would be no other Latitia or Alice Trimble in his life.

Her attention wandered from *Sons and Lovers,* which was considered daring reading for a young, unmarried woman. Sometimes the almost painful intensity of D. H. Lawrence's writing was too much like what she experienced herself, but had no way to express. She knew very well what an impression she gave to the world—stolid, dependable Lally, not given to passion or storms. She stared into the fire and thought of Jon, and a storm that was not quiet or small raged in her heart. She wrote dutiful, sisterly letters to him, and got back scribbled replies. Unless something happened to overturn their universe, unless they were changed by events she could not foresee, there would be no other relationship between them. She could love Jon with all her heart, but he would never see her as other than a reliable, jolly friend who was also an adopted sister. People like herself did not inspire passion, no matter if they felt it. In the quiet warmth of the room, she shivered violently. She leaned toward the fire; the book slid from her lap.

The clock was chiming eleven when she heard the sound of the motor outside. With a sigh of pleasure she thought that, after all, Black Jack had returned, and they would see in the New Year together. But the horn was honked loudly, and she heard voices, and then Billings' hurrying footsteps in the hall. She reached the drawing-room door and flung it open just as Billings opened the front door to the cold air of the night.

Jon came in, and with him another young man, wearing an officer's greatcoat, and a young woman in a long fur coat and a scarf, sprinkled with snow, wrapped around her head.

"Lally!" Jon rushed to her, and held her briefly in his arms, placing a kiss on her cheek. "Good to see you, old girl. Got a spot of unexpected leave, and I thought I'd surprise you all."

"You're staying . . . ?" She didn't try to keep the delight from her voice. Surely that much was permitted her?

"Only a few minutes. Just time to drink a glass of champagne and say 'Happy New Year.' Where's Father—and Margaret? Is Alice in bed?"

She told him about Margaret's visit to Witfell, and made the usual excuse about Black Jack being delayed at the mill, and eating at the club. It was their way of referring to Mrs. Campion.

"Lally." Jon put his arm around her and drew her toward the other young people. "This is Alexandra—Sandy—and her brother, Richard. Richard West. Richard's in my regiment. My sister, Lally."

"How do you do?" Lally saw that the girl called Sandy was not at all like her name. She was fair, but vibrantly pretty, with high cheekbones and deeply set, aquamarine eyes like a Siamese cat. She flung off the scarf to reveal golden hair. When Billings took her coat Lally saw that she was slim, and dressed with a simple, expensive elegance. Lally could not help noting the kind of proprietary pride Jon took in her.

"Do . . . do come in, please. Father will be so disappointed not to be here. Are you sure you're not staying?"

"Can't, old girl. Richard and I got leave, and Sandy provided the car in Catterick. We're on our way to their place over beyond York."

"You've driven from Catterick?" She tried to keep the note of disapproval out of her voice. It was wartime; one was not supposed to make unnecessary journeys, or to use petrol on pleasure.

"It's leave, Miss Pollock. It's leave," Richard West said. "We suspect it might even be embarkation leave. A time to bend the rules a little . . ."

"Not embarkation—" No one seemed to hear the fear and shock in her voice; no one seemed to hear her at all.

"Billings," Jon said, "could you manage to fix up something to eat? We're frozen and hungry. It was a bit of a detour to come here, but we just did it on the off-chance that you'd all be here . . ."

"At once, Master Jon," Billings said. "I don't think Cook's retired yet. Waiting to see the New Year in, like most of us."

"Good show, Billings. But don't have her cook anything. There isn't time. A sandwich would be the thing . . ." He was leading them to the fire in the drawing room. "Great to see you, Lally. How are things at the hospital?"

She mumbled some answer, and heard, as if far off, the talk of the others, chatter almost. It meant nothing. It meant nothing at all beside the fact that Jon might soon be going to France. Did they talk to hide their own tension? It was no longer the confident, rather simplistic talk of last August, when they were going to win a war swiftly, and it was regarded as a high adventure. Too many battles had been fought, and lost; too many casualty figures released— downplayed, but released nonetheless. These two young men had to know now what they were going to. Billings had come back, a bottle of champagne wrapped in a napkin, four glasses on a silver tray. "Cook says, 'Welcome home,' sir, and conveys her good wishes for the New Year."

"I'll slip down and see her before I go," Jon promised. "Father still keeps a good cellar, Billings."

"We have stocks, sir, to see us through the present emergency. I pride myself that Mr. Pollock laid down some excellent wines years ago on my advice, and the cellar at Pellham Langley is like owning the Royal Mint." Lally was beginning to wonder if Billings hadn't

been celebrating the New Year lavishly before it began. Jon appeared
not to notice. He raised his glass.

"To victory!"

"Victory!" they echoed. Why did they not, Lally thought, toast
peace? She would have liked to have made a point of it; but they
would have thought her too deadly earnest. They were all in a nervously frivolous mood; the talk ranged widely, but superficially, over
many things. Their training, when they guessed they might be sent to
France, Sandy's work with the Red Cross. She had taken a flat with
two other girls in London, and they all worked at a canteen at Victoria Station, where the troops departed for, and arrived back from,
France. She spoke lightly of the marvelous spirit of the troops leaving, and said nothing at all about the casualties returning. Nothing
must discourage or dishearten her brother or Jon. In a little time Jon
had the gramophone wound up. They listened to, and swayed to, a
record which Sandy had brought with her, a tune called "Watch
Your Step" by a composer called Irving Berlin. Billings, and the
young parlor maid, Molly, who had volunteered for the task now
that Billings had no footman to help him, appeared with big silver
trays bearing ham and beef, salmon, apple pie, cherry pie, butter and
brown bread, and cream puffs. Less and less did it seem to Lally that
there was a war on. They still ate well in the kitchen at Grangewick.

Billings brought more champagne. "Oh, I'm starving," Sandy said.
To Lally she looked as if she must always be starving, or that the
beautifully slim figure was given to her by nature. Lally herself kept
away from the food. She hated to be seen eating too much, even
when every instinct urged her toward it. Instead she drank rather a
lot of champagne, trying to blot out the fact that, once he had
greeted her, Jon had eyes for no one but Sandy West.

"We'll have to be on our way," he finally declared. "Tell Father
I'll try to look in on the way back. But it's only two days' leave."
Two days' leave, and he was spending it with Sandy West.

"If you'd telephoned, Father would have been here," Lally ventured. Then she realized her mistake. Young men like Jon and Richard West, when they were close to going to France, didn't want to
spend their last days dully sitting by their family's fire. They wanted
something like the mad caprice of driving from Catterick, in uncertain weather, to spend only a few rollicking hours in the company of
someone they thought they had fallen in love with. Perhaps truly

were in love with. Lally wished she wasn't so logical as to see the sense of it.

They were putting on their coats. Jon slipped downstairs to wish Cook a "Happy New Year." He came up with a package wrapped in brown paper, and a bottle of brandy Billings had brought from the cellar. "Cook thinks we may get stuck in a snow drift between here and York. We may freeze to death, but we won't starve. . . . Thanks, Billings. Good show. Happy New Year."

He was kissing Lally, but his mind was elsewhere. "Happy New Year . . ." Their voices were lost in the roar of the engine as Richard swung the crank of the motor and it finally started. It went off, sliding a little on the thin layer of snow which was beginning to ice over. Standing in the doorway, Lally held up her hand in a farewell gesture, but she didn't know if any of them had turned their heads to see.

Then she and Billings were back in the hall, staring at each other. "Well, Miss Lally—short and sweet."

"Yes, Billings. Father will be sorry to have missed him."

"Mr. Pollock will understand, miss. Youth must have its fling." Lally thought he might have been talking to someone of his own age. The grandfather clock opposite the fireplace showed that it was only three minutes to twelve.

"Is that clock right, Billings?"

"Miss Lally, I pride myself—"

"They might have waited." She turned and marched back into the drawing room. She picked up one of the used glasses. "You don't really mind, do you, Billings? We're taught at the hospital that alcohol is entirely antiseptic." She filled two glasses with a haste that sent the bubbles to the top of the glass, and brought a pained frown to Billings' brow. She handed one to him.

"Happy New Year, Billings."

"Happy New Year, Miss Lally."

She tossed the champagne back as if it were a glass of water, and she had filled her glass again before the little clock on the mantel and the grandfather clock in the hall both began to chime the hour. As they did so, Lally went to the window and parted the curtain, not caring that it was against the regulations. Below, the lights of Leeds, the city where she had been born, nameless, and had had her rebirth in Black Jack Pollock's arms, was a misty smudge of light under the softly falling snow. All around she heard the chimes of the church clocks, and the bells of church towers ringing in the New Year. Wasn't that also against the regulations? she wondered. They rang still with hope; the rituals of the days of peace had still not gone. She let the curtain fall, and walked back to the bottle of champagne.

"Another, Billings?" It was highly irregular. But it was wartime, and it was a new year.

"A trifle, Miss Lally." She poured a full measure for them both. Silently, then, they raised their glasses to each other.

"Shall I clear away the trays, Miss Lally?"

She looked at the food, which she had longed to eat when Jon was present, but would not permit herself. But Jon was gone, and his mind was on Sandy West. She, Lally, was alone.

"Not yet, Billings. I'll . . . I'll just have a peck or two."

"Very good, Miss Lally."

When he had gone, she went to the trays and began loading up a plate with the ham and beef and cheese on the slices of brown bread. She ate them, and her eyes went to the pies, hardly touched. She thought of the way Jon had looked at Sandy West. She poured herself another glass of champagne before helping herself to the cherry pie.

⚜ CHAPTER 6 ⚜

I

Lally was almost certain she knew the moment the young soldier died. She was alone in a large military ward of the Infirmary, the night sister having left her to tidy up after they had applied a dressing to try to stem bleeding in an amputee. "If it gets worse I must call a doctor," the sister had whispered as she left to continue her rounds. Lally had collected the soiled dressings, plumped the pillows while disturbing the patient as little as possible, given him the water he asked for, stayed a moment to murmur a few words to him in the dimness of the ward with the neat but too crowded rows of beds. She would have liked to have stayed, because he seemed frail and somehow lonely, but she had to follow Sister's progress, and assist with any task she could. She knew she was often given duties which were beyond the prescribed range of a VAD, but as the casualties grew heavier the lines of demarkation became blurred. So she moved swiftly, but quietly, down the long room. It was near to dawn on a May morning in 1915. Already, outside, she could hear the first faint chirps of the birds that would soon swell to the full dawn chorus in the trees around the hospital.

Some movement caught her attention. The head of another young soldier turned on the pillow. She heard the rasp of breath in his tortured lungs. She went and bent over him. A night-light on a central long table flickered and showed his face, pale even against the pillowcases. She put her ear close to his lips, trying to understand the words he attempted to speak. Whatever they were, they were said, and gone, in one last sigh. She had caught none of them. But his suddenly staring eyes alarmed her; she felt for the pulse. The tiny spark of life that had remained in him seemed to have fled. He had breathed, and was gone. Lally stood a moment, awed. It was as if a spirit had visibly passed from him. The first glimmer of light showed at the long window; a bird announced his presence. She kept her fingers to the pulse, hoping, but with little hope. He had been engaged in the second battle of Ypres in April, and had been one of those to receive the first dose of chlorine gas used by the Germans. It had been conceded, when he had been returned to Leeds, that there was little chance he would survive. Lally, like others, had continued to hope. A second bird began to dispute the territory of the first who had spoken. Lally picked up the dressing tray and hurried to find Sister. They were not yet so desperate for staff that death was entirely the province of an inexperienced VAD.

There were many other tasks to do before the night shift was finished, but Lally was in the ward when the mortuary staff came to take away the body. She helped slide it onto the trolley, covered the face gently with the sheet. She would never see him again, he who had struggled mightily these last two weeks for his life. Humbly she had watched the doctors try what limited treatment they had. His death affected her in a more subtle way than the others that had happened around her. He had borne no wound upon his body. It had been a beautiful young body, clean now that it was out of the pervasive filth of the trenches. Lally had washed him, and changed his pajamas. She was no longer embarrassed by handling a man's body. And the men, accepting her ministrations more readily than if she had been one of the pretty VADs whose movements about the ward their eyes followed, were not embarrassed either. She might have been the sister, in age, she thought, for all the difference it made to them. They liked her, they thanked her; they did not flirt with her. She watched the young soldier go. He had been in the First Yorkshire Light Infantry, Jon's regiment. For that, as well as for other reasons, his life had been special to her.

She watched him go, and then turned swiftly to all the other tasks that must be completed before the day staff came on. There was no time to stand and mourn.

* * *

But despite her weariness she lingered over her mug of cocoa and bread and marmalade when she came off duty. She must go and try to sleep through the bright spring day. She thought of the soaring larks above the moors at Pellham Langley; she could almost feel the fragrant toughness of the heather under her body as she had so often lain and stared up into the sky. She remembered the picnics of the years past; she heard Jon's voice, Margaret's, Black Jack's. She heard Alice hum a tune. It was a world away from this austere room with its long table, where the spring sunlight did not come.

It was a world away in time, also. The innocence was gone. No one joked about the war anymore. The young men had gone in their waves, and been swallowed up. They had fallen, wounded, into the now eternal mud of Flanders, and been drowned. They had died, obscenely, hanging on the wire, sometimes raving in their agony for half a day or more before they died. Some lay unburied, except for the mud that merely cloaked them. Letters coming back from the front did not talk of this; they were phlegmatic, these young soldiers. The generals did not speak of it; they did not speak of their failure. But sometimes Lally had listened to the words spoken during the nightmares; sometimes a man would utter something he had not meant to when changing a dressing caused great pain. They would curse, almost under their breath, curse the uselessness of what they had seen, curse the General Staff, who apparently did not see. She could remember a soldier whose arm had been shot away; he had been amazingly cheerful.

"Well, I'm lucky, lass, I am that. I got a Blighty." "A Blighty" was the term they used for a wound serious enough to send them back to England. "Someone pulled me back into the trench, and I was passed back to the dressing station. Surgeon made a right fine job of it. Clean as a whistle. And I'm never going back to that hellhole again. I made it, you see, lass. I'm right sorry for them poor buggers who have to stay over there and die."

Lally thought of Jon. He had been over there since late January. His letters were determinedly cheerful. It was as if he were writing something that his own men could read for encouragement. He complained little, only asked for parcels, for the socks he and his men so constantly needed, for soap and cigarettes, anything that might relieve the boredom of the biscuits and bully beef which was all they ever got when they were in the front lines. Lally wondered if, secretly, he would have understood this soldier who laughed at the loss of an arm because it had saved his life. Would Jon have given up his dream that one day he might play cricket for Yorkshire for the certain knowledge that he would live merely to watch cricket on a summer's evening?

In so many ways the war had brought change to their own lives. After the move to Grangewick, when it appeared certain—though it was never officially admitted in high places—that the war would drag on, Black Jack had offered Pellham Langley to the Royal Army Medical Corps as a convalescent hospital. Wounded officers, as many as possible drawn from the county so that their relatives could easily visit them, were sent there to regain strength, and either be returned to France or invalided out. Privately, Lally thought the officers were no different from the soldier who had been cheerful over the loss of an arm because it meant he would never go back to the trenches; but of course they did not say such a thing.

She was in contact with them only because Black Jack had been allowed to keep a few rooms over the empty stables where they all went when there was time off from the hospital and the mills. They were the quarters once occupied by the grooms and stable lads, and it was an occasion to remember and bless Black Jack's generosity with bathrooms for the staff. He had fitted out a rudimentary kitchen-sitting room. It quickly became a more intimate home than any of them had ever known. Lally cooked, Black Jack smoked and read, and Alice played with her dolls and worked patiently and persistently on a ragged piece of knitting which was intended as a muffler for Jon; of an evening, when she was sure Alice was asleep, Lally ripped out the poor, mutilated rows of stitches Alice had contrived and re-knitted them, so that the child should see some evidence of progress. Lally doubted the scarf would ever be finished. But Alice was strangely happy at Pellham Langley, even in the changed circumstances. Nell was still with her, and took care of her, but Alice was a real favorite among the convalescent officers, whom she visited regularly. The sheer beauty of the girl was an undeniable attraction, but Lally sensed that Alice's own particular simplicity and directness had a true appeal. She was able, with all the innocence of a child, to face the most appalling mutilations without flinching. She would gravely show her doll or her knitting to a man with half a face blown away; she would walk in the garden with her hand holding the empty sleeve of a man who had lost an arm and seem to find nothing strange or awkward in doing so. She shared the fruit on their bedside tables, they read to her from the childish books she brought to them. The most completely shattered and disillusioned of them could do no less than answer the radiant smile she gave them. It was possible to believe in innocence again when one looked at Alice.

Margaret was mostly absent from these small excursions to Pellham Langley, and though they never admitted it, they all knew the peace was more complete for that reason. It had been a time of restless bafflement for Margaret. She had lasted no longer than a month at the hospital after her Christmas leave. The matron was apologetic to Black Jack, but quite firm. "She is not nursing material, Mr. Pollock—even for the few nursing duties that VADs are allowed to perform. We really cannot have someone who looks as if she is about to faint or have hysterics each time she as much as comes near a seriously ill patient. It's bad for the morale of the men—and I may say, bad for your daughter. She is willing enough, anxious to help. But a hospital is no place for the highly strung. Miss Pollock will never develop a professional detachment. She cannot learn to sympathize without coddling. All she sees is the pain, not the hope of recovery. Now Lal—" The name had almost slipped out, proving that the matron was not quite as professionally detached as she would like to have appeared. "The older Miss Pollock is quite different temperamentally. She has enormous stamina and endurance. She remains very calm. I am aware that for these young girls it is often a difficult life, something quite different from what they imagined it was going to be when everyone was signing on in a patriotic fervor. I am sorry for Miss Pollock, but she will find other ways to serve." It had been final.

Margaret had wept when she had heard the news, but Black Jack sensed that they were more tears of relief than disappointment. Then she packed her bags and swept off to spend some weeks at Witfell with her grandparents. "Granny will think of something," she said.

Lady Bletchley did produce a solution of sorts. She spoke to Black Jack on the telephone. "It's no use to think of trying to bury Margaret here in the country. She'll get so bored I'm afraid she'll go and do something wild . . ." What that might be, she left unsaid. Black Jack remembered, as he so often did when Margaret was discussed, the reputation her mother had earned, most of it unjustified. Lady Bletchley did not want another Latitia on her hands. "Elspeth's friend, Mrs. Ponsonby-Williams, is forming a Red Cross group which will be comprised only of drivers. Initially they will be taking a train-

ing course at Camberley. They'd have to learn—what is it called?—to
strip down an engine, or something of the sort. Of course, Margaret
is a marvelous driver, and I suppose she could make herself understand how an engine works—she's not stupid, after all. But after Margaret's unfortunate experience at the Infirmary—I never *did* approve
of her going there, Jack—I've made it clear to Elspeth that Margaret
must never be assigned to ambulance duties. She will eventually be
assigned to drive staff cars. It's quite a responsible job, and a necessary one. But she will not have to face what she did in the wards.
Naturally, the girls will live in a dormitory, and be heavily chap-
eroned there—"

"But not when they're working," Black Jack pointed out. "Margaret is just eighteen."

"This is wartime, Jack. The young are anxious to do their bit."
She added, with a touch of wry desperation, "Can you keep her idle
at Grangewick? Will she sit out the war here with an old woman?
Things are changing, Jack . . ." Her sigh was audible on the line. "If
only she were married and had children to absorb her. But I don't
approve of wartime marriages. Too chancy."

Everything with Margaret would be a chance, Black Jack thought.
But as he had nothing else to suggest, he agreed. Margaret went happily to her training course. It was true what her grandmother had
said: she was a good driver, skillful and unafraid. But Black Jack
doubted that she would ever understand what went on under the
hood of a motor car. Yet no doubt there were always some willing
male mechanics around who would indulge her helplessness.

She had giggled at the thought of it. "You'd know how to do it,
Lally. I'll just have to bluff my way through." Then her voice had
grown softer, almost wistful. "But I'd like to make a go of this. I feel
such an idiot—being turned out of the hospital."

Lally had said, "Not everyone's meant to be a nurse. You'll make
a marvelous driver, though. I've looked up a place in Savile Row
that will tailor your uniform. You'll be driving officers. We'll want
you to be a credit to us."

As always, Margaret had brightened at the thought of clothes, of
men—even if they would be men of an age to be colonels and upward. All of them would have aides of lesser ranks, and presumably
younger. She had applied herself with unusual diligence to the
course, and managed to learn enough to scrape through the test. She
complained of the accommodation. ". . . cold and drafty," she

wrote, "and the food's pretty terrible. The C.O.'s a dragon. We have
to be tightly locked up by ten at night. But I do manage to get to
London on my days off. It's not too bad . . ."

Black Jack privately thought that even those restraints were hardly
enough, but in wartime they would have to suffice. All the old order
was breaking down. He had no notion of how he might begin to con-
struct new walls around his daughters, or even if he wanted to try.
When the war was over there would be a major change—almost a
revolution. The votes that militant women had been demanding for
so long would have to be acknowledged as having been earned. In so
many ways they were breaking out of the old confines. He doubted
that they could ever be put back within them again. His experiences
with Latitia and Alice Trimble had made him deeply aware of the
hypocrisies which surrounded women. He knew that his own relationship with Mrs. Campion was one that suited his own convenience
rather than her feelings. But Mrs. Campion would never volunteer
for war work, and was content, or seemed to be content, to live off
his money. All his life women had been a conundrum to Black Jack—
saying one thing, meaning another. They could not be dealt with or
treated like men. Which was the reason, he acknowledged, he found
them so delightful, as well as so aggravating. His three daughters,
wayward, beautiful Margaret, his solid, dependable Lally, fragile,
sweet-natured Alice, who looked like an angel, were a constant
source of happiness to him. Mrs. Campion gave him comfort, allowed the expression of his sensuality. On his infrequent visits to
London he dined with the Marchioness. She had managed to sell the
Belgravia house and had retreated, gratefully, to the much smaller
space of a flat near the Royal Albert Hall. She lived carefully, thrift-
ily, and gave all her time to the Red Cross. Black Jack enjoyed her
company, her pungent, often witty conversation; he glossed over her
sometimes scathing remarks on the way the generals were conducting
the war. "Women would have had it settled long ago." He was uncomfortable with the new role of women as critics. He had always
loved women, but they, like the times, were changing. He hoped he
would be past caring before they changed beyond his recognition.

But as the months of the war ground on, as he knew Jon's regiment to be in action, he had also to acknowledge that the fullest extent of his feeling was with his son. He recognized a large part of his
own father's nature in himself; his father had sought an heir. Now he,
Black Jack, looked to his only son to inherit. He cursed this ele-

mental force in himself, but could not deny it. Three daughters were placed in the balance with one son.

But Black Jack had little time to ponder these new thoughts and emotions which the war had brought. His only son was in mortal danger, but life went on. The mines and the mills had to satisfy the needs of war. They worked around the clock, and could not produce enough. Black Jack saw the stockpiles down to almost vanishing point; he desperately sought replenishments. It seemed almost obscene that his bank balances grew so bloated on the spoils of war. He invested heavily in War Loan stock. It did not seem enough. But what was he to do—stand on a corner in Bradford and hand pound notes to each figure in uniform? He gave heavily to charities; there was still more money than even his avaricious father had ever dreamed of. He wondered what he would do with it all when the war was done, and there would be time to think about spending it. When the war was done . . . His thoughts always stopped there, lest he permit himself to think the unthinkable. The armies of Germany, France, and Britain, battalions from the Empire, had fought futilely over a few miles of wretched, blasted earth. The despised Turks had inflicted slaughter at Gallipoli. It was whispered that Sir John Arbuthnot Fisher, First Sea Lord of the Admiralty when he had resigned, had said, "Damn the Dardanelles—they will be our grave." The victory they had so confidently expected within a few months had receded almost out of sight. Black Jack, who had felt the conflict coming, and gambled his all on it, dared not now to think that victory might not, in the end, be theirs. To have uttered the thought aloud would have been treason.

II

It was August again. To Black Jack it seemed extraordinary that the Glorious Twelfth had come and gone and he had barely remembered that it was the opening of the grouse-shooting season. Last year they had gathered at Pellham Langley just for that purpose; he remembered the young people in their white tennis clothes and Billings pouring champagne to mark the beginning of war. They were at Pellham Langley now—two precious days of leave for Lally, and he had decided she should spend it away from the city. They occupied their cramped rooms over the stables, and Black Jack cleaned a gun in a desultory fashion, thinking that he and Lally might take a walk on the moors that afternoon, and if a brace or two of grouse conveniently got up almost under his gun, it would make a nice contribution to the larder back at Grangewick. When he recalled the elaborate ceremonial of former years—the shooting parties, the huge organization of the beaters overseen by the gamekeepers—it seemed a world utterly lost and, in a sense, trivial. The beaters had been mainly young men—most of them would be in uniform now, some dead. He had one gamekeeper left, who now worked in the kitchen garden of Pellham Langley to help stock the pantry of the hospital with vegetables, and with whatever game he could either shoot or snare. The gamekeeper had almost become the poacher, and everything was forgiven in the name of war.

The day was fair, and he and Lally did walk on the moors that afternoon. Alice, in the charge of Nell, was playing her favorite role of visiting all the convalescent officers. Each visit to Pellham Langley she gravely made a round of the wards and the recreation rooms, greeting each man in turn. Sometimes she remembered a particular man from the last visit, and claimed him joyfully as a friend. Others she approached with her fearless, smiling face. Never having suffered a rebuff in her life, she expected none. None, Lally knew, was ever offered by the sick and convalescent at Pellham Langley; who could turn away from Alice when she smiled?

So Black Jack and Lally walked alone on the moors, going their favorite way, which caused them to scramble up by the waterfall and come out on top, where they could look down on the big house, and over to the next valley, with the distant chimney stacks of the mills. Black Jack had bagged a brace of grouse, but his heart wasn't in the exercise. They dropped down on the heather to rest at the top of the waterfall, the sun warm on their faces. A golden day in August, and across the Channel in Belgium the Germans had arrested the British Red Cross nurse Edith Cavell on charges of assisting Allied prisoners to escape; Warsaw had fallen to the Germans on the Eastern Front; Italy had declared war on Turkey. They had talked of these things so much, they had talked of Jon until the topic was exhausted because they could not speak of their fear for him. They had talked of Margaret, that the Red Cross driver's life seemed to suit her, and they discussed Lady Bletchley's assurances that Margaret would never be sent to France, although Margaret herself wrote of wanting to go. "No woman under twenty-three is allowed overseas. And it will be long over before she reaches that age," Lady Bletchley had said to Black Jack. But now they knew they were mired in the war. Each day Jon survived at the front seemed a miracle, but they did not want to chase the miracle by giving it a name. So as they lay in the heather, which wore its purple August bloom, faces turned to the sun, they talked of the day Black Jack had come scrambling up here after Lally, the day they had returned from Italy, the day she had found her tongue. These were safe memories to talk of; they carried no pain.

They did not see him; they heard his almost tuneless whistle carried on the light wind—different from the cries of the birds who flew high above them. It was indeed almost tuneless, a shrill, nearly hard sound in which the notes did not seem to have any sequence. Lally sat up.

"Someone's coming."

Together they watched him as he negotiated the rocks by the side of the waterfall—and knew he was a stranger. His dress proclaimed that clearly, but there was also something in his movements—he climbed with ease, the tuneless whistle never breaking for extra breath—but he had never been in this place before, and he sought the footholds and the narrow little path with care. He was wearing tweeds which were a trifle too new, too stylish, as if some Savile Row tailor had told him that was what he must wear in Yorkshire. They were both gazing at him expectantly as he reached their level. He removed his cap.

"Good day, sir. Mr. Pollock, I believe. Miss Pollock."

"Yes," Black Jack said, and Lally recognized the coolness in his tone. Black Jack had always granted the freedom of his moors for anyone to walk—though no one could shoot without his permission— but he expected only local people to take advantage of that right. Strangers were another thing.

"Forgive me, sir. They told me down at the house that you were walking, and the path up by the waterfall was your favorite walk. It is too good a day to be sitting still, waiting, so I thought I'd try this way, and if I missed you, well, I'd have had a little exercise, at least." He added, and his voice now gained a certain edge, as if he hoped Black Jack would break the silence, but was prepared to hold his own if he did not, "Do you mind if I sit down?"

Black Jack shrugged. "Help yourself. You seem to know your way around. For a stranger."

Lally realized that the accent was American; she had met very few Americans. The only ones she remembered were those whom she had encountered during that one London season—a time of fantasy now, which could hardly be believed. And this man, in his new, correct tweeds, seemed part of that fantasy, something like the dance cards left over from the end of the season.

"Thank you." The man dropped down lightly, legs crossed, knees high. He reached into the pocket of his Norfolk jacket and produced a cigarette case. It was a dull, burnished gold. But instead of extending it to Black Jack, he held it toward Lally. "Do you smoke, Miss Pollock?"

Lally felt herself blush. "No—no, I don't." Why was it oddly flattering that this strange man should have thought she might be among those modern young women who smoked? But at least he had not condemned her immediately to belonging to those who would be outraged at the suggestion. She watched as Black Jack took a cigarette, and the stranger lighted it, and then his own. He was dark, like Black Jack, but his face was narrower, and there were hollows slashed across his cheeks, almost lines, which seemed deeper than they should be for his age. But what was his age? A little over thirty—no, she thought, older than that. He was tall and very lean; he could almost have been described as gangling if he had not also carried an indisputable air of certainty. He had brown eyes—not soft or warm, just dark. His lips were a firm, straight line. She remembered he had not smiled as he had reached them. He looked as if he seldom smiled.

"You have the advantage of me, sir," Black Jack said. "I don't know your name."

The man's hair was almost too perfectly groomed; it looked as if he brushed it hard every morning, and directed it to stay in place. The wind did not ruffle it.

"My name?—oh, yes. I'm Brock Weymouth."

"Am I supposed to know you?"

For the first time the lips relaxed slightly; it might have been intended as a smile. "I know I'm trespassing, Mr. Pollock. You are the master of all the land I can see, and of the mills over in the next valley. This is your kingdom, and one of your precious days off. And I have intruded. No, you're not supposed to know me. I just hoped to do some business with you."

"And you come *here*—to do business? I usually see people in my office."

"I know." Brock Weymouth gestured as if in apology. "I've done the unforgivable by breaking into an Englishman's privacy. Into his castle, in fact." A jerk of his head indicated the turreted mansion below. "But I heard your name mentioned in London, and a weekend was too long to wait. I thought I'd just come up to Yorkshire and chance seeing you."

"It was so urgent?"

Weymouth drew on his cigarette. "In wartime, everything's urgent, isn't it, Mr. Pollock? I thought we might be able to do some business."

"My business hours, Mr. Weymouth—"

"If I came in business hours, you'd never remember me. I'd be just one more faceless, nameless man in and out of your office. I had the weekend to spare. Before I had to show up in other people's offices. I thought I'd take a chance. Besides, I've never been to Yorkshire before." He gestured with what seemed a rather uncharacteristic exaggeration; Lally had the impression that he reserved such gestures for the right moment. "I expected rain and a howling wind, and at least the ghost of Emily Brontë and her dog, Keeper. But I have sunshine and the birds singing."

"You know the name of Emily Brontë's dog," Black Jack observed.

"Yes." Weymouth did not expand, but he had, perhaps innocently, but also possibly, Lally thought, with infinite guile, touched on one of Black Jack's passions. Did this Brock Weymouth somehow know that Black Jack was hopelessly, romantically in love with the Brontë legend? But Black Jack was not drawn into a discussion of his love; no more would he have discussed with a stranger the memory of Alice Trimble. No one spoke for a few minutes; the two men contemplated the wide world set about them—the valley below, the great house, the vast amplitude of the moors, which vanished on the horizon in the rare heat haze of this August day.

Finally Black Jack spoke. "Then what brings you?" His tone was slightly more easy.

"I think I may have something to sell you, Mr. Pollock."

There was another silence. Salesmen came to the mills, waited patiently until Black Jack summoned them; they did not seek him out in his own house or, worse, follow him into this realm of his privacy.

The American looked fully at Black Jack. "Gentlemen are not salesmen, you're saying, aren't you? They would never invade your privacy. And those who are not gentlemen would never dare invade your world at all. So, where do I belong—and how do I dare come up here?" He drew on his cigarette, and in those moments his eyes met Lally's; it was she who looked away, not he. "Well, I figure, in wartime, a man doesn't have time for the niceties of the game. I can't hang around London waiting for the right introduction. You need raw materials, and I may be able to get them for you. Are you interested?"

"What would I want that my own agents are not able to get for me?"

"You're short, Mr. Pollock. Everyone in England is short of things, these days. I can't sell you coal or iron, because it would cost too much to get it here to you. That's up to your own miners—your own government. But wool and cotton I can get. You have your own suppliers of wool from Australia, but I also have sources. Cotton I have a ready access to, and every mill in England is crying out for it. Just the spare parts for your mills and your mines, the grease that keeps the wheels turning, the wheels themselves. You've heard of Yankee 'know-how'? I have it. I can get you what you need. We're in for a long war, and you're one of the few men who realized it quite a long time ago."

"And where did you hear that?"

"One hears, Mr. Pollock—one hears. I've made my fortune by keeping my ears open. I came to England to get orders. I figured you were one of the men who wouldn't give me the old patriotic shuffle about 'muddling through,' and the Empire, and all that garbage." He broke off. "I'm sorry if I seem to offend you, but anyone who made the sort of preparations for the war that you did didn't entirely believe in the readiness of Country and Empire. You aren't exactly surprised that the Allies are in a worse position now than they were a year ago. Last August it was all going to be over by Christmas. What would you bet now about how many more Christmases we've got to go through before it really is all over? There's a certain length of time before America will be forced to come in. In that time I'm allowed to supply you. After that, I'll have to supply our own war effort."

"So you think America will come in, do you?"

Weymouth stubbed out his cigarette, ground it carefully into the earth until not a wisp of smoke trailed up between the heather. "I'm certain of it, Mr. Pollock. Can anyone doubt it since the *Lusitania* was sunk? There will be more sinkings. America will come in, later rather than sooner, and it may be by accident. Then I won't be any use to you. Now I can be. Call me a procurement agent. Call me anything. I can get what you need."

"A war profiteer, Mr. . . . Mr. Weymouth?"

The lean, rather hard face turned directly to Black Jack. "And aren't you, Mr. Pollock?"

Now it was Black Jack's turn to grind the stub of the cigarette into the ground beneath the heather. He looked out over the vista of the moors, his back to the distant chimney stacks. For a time Lally thought he was not going to reply, but Weymouth waited, as if he had known before he ever climbed to this crag that the answer would come. It came. "Even if it is only half the truth, Mr. Weymouth, I have to acknowledge a half-truth." He turned back to the other man. "We'll talk."

Brock Weymouth proffered his cigarette case once again. Black Jack accepted a cigarette and a light. Weymouth did not launch into talk about the things he wanted to sell Black Jack. He stared out over the sunlit moors. "What do you suppose really killed the Brontës so young? Was it their frail constitution—or the climate? Or was it their father?"

"You're a cool one, Mr. Weymouth, to call a Yorkshireman on that one. Do you expect us to do down our own?"

"Patrick Brontë was Irish, Mr. Pollock. Mrs. Brontë came from Cornwall. They were Celts. What Yorkshire gave them was space for their imagination."

Black Jack got to his feet. "We'll talk of it further, Mr. Weymouth. Come on down to the house. Lally has a bite of supper to get ready. You won't mind accepting our humble wartime English fare?"

"I'd be honored, Mr. Pollock."

*　　*　　*

They ate in their small living space over the stable. Black Jack produced whiskey; Lally boiled potatoes and poached a piece of fish, taking great care with the sauce. Alice came and sat beside Brock Weymouth; she interrupted the conversation to put the new Teddy bear she had seen in a Leeds shop at Christmas and instantly craved into the stranger's hands. He immediately focused his whole attention on her. "You're a very beautiful young lady to be carrying this odd fellow around with you. You must love him very much. Did you know he is called 'Teddy' after one of our American Presidents? Teddy Roosevelt. But Mr. Roosevelt is rather more battered than this boy." Brock Weymouth showed not the slightest surprise at the sight of a fourteen-year-old girl carrying around a bear as a beloved companion. Lally knew that Alice was delighted when someone talked to her as if she were grown up, even if she didn't quite comprehend what they were saying. She wanted attention, and from Weymouth she got it. He offered to help Lally with the preparations. "Please let me. I was taught to be useful when I was young." He made a pretense that Alice was helping to chop the parsley, but he was careful to guide the knife himself, his two arms reaching around and above her so that she seemed cradled in them. Lally saw the effort it cost Black Jack not to protest about Alice handling the knife at all, but he had been told many times that he must permit her all the independence she would ask for. Seeing Alice there with a stranger's arms about her, Lally experienced a moment of fear; they could not for very much longer pretend that she was a child. She had become an almost dangerously beautiful girl who would never understand the danger of her own beauty. Something of this knowledge shadowed Black Jack's face.

Lally herself was quiet as the meal was eaten; she had cooked a bread-and-butter pudding that morning, and she strove now to make the portion she served herself as small as possible, and still despised herself for pretending that she ate little. Weymouth dutifully nodded his appreciation. "You're a good cook, Miss Lally."

Black Jack had gone to his cellar and produced some bottles of burgundy. It made the simple meal seem festive, and it was a mark that he was enjoying the company of this stranger. Lally had not responded to Weymouth's compliment about her cooking; why bother him with the knowledge that until this last year she had never cooked, and was heavily dependent on a cookbook? She sipped her wine and listened to the talk that could not help but focus on the war, the strategy, the errors, the events that might bring in America. But for a while, warmed by the wine and the heat of the range, the war itself seemed to retreat. Listening to the firm, confident tones of the American, she could believe it would, indeed, someday come to an end. It would be over. Jon would come home. She stopped listening to the talk, and her daydreams slipped forward in time. Jon would be home . . . they would take up their lives again . . .

She roused herself to refill Weymouth's cup from the pot of precious coffee; she supposed it was a great compliment to be told by an American that she made good coffee. It was then Black Jack said, "And where in the States are you from, Mr. Weymouth?"

"I don't know."

Black Jack put down his cup. "You don't know?"

"I only know that when I was old enough to look around me I found I was in an orphan home near Boston. But no one knew if I'd been born there. I'd just been left there. There were no records, no documents. The proverbial waif literally left on the steps of the orphan home—at least, that's what they told me. I hadn't got a name, so they called me after the two handiest names. The home was about halfway between Brockton and Weymouth in Massachusetts. Brockton Weymouth. They could just as easily have arranged them the other way around. In any case they kept me until I was sixteen and then they opened the door and showed me the world. They told me to go and get a slice of it." He permitted himself a slight smile. "I got a slice of it, and I'm after more."

What he said after that Lally didn't remember. It was back with her, the smell, the taste, the shadowy form of the dark place she had come from, the damp, dark room. Despite the meal, she felt the familiar, gnawing hunger that she seemed never to be able to assuage. This man, like herself, did not know where he came from. He did not know his real name. Over and over in her mind spun the name Black Jack had given her that November night she had come to Pellham Langley—Lally Leeds. Brockton Weymouth and Lally Leeds. They were two of a kind, but which kind they did not know. Lally shifted uneasily in her chair; she did not like the sense of a bond formed with this man who also had no name. She wished he had not come. She did not want the memories of the dark place. She was suddenly fearful. This man brought with him some sort of menace, a threat to their futures. No, that was absurd. His eyes were gentle when they looked at Alice. He and Black Jack would meet at the mills tomorrow morning. They would do their business, and Brock Weymouth would return to America. She would never see him again, and the dark memories would not be stirred.

Black Jack, mellowed by the wine, was in good humor as he walked his guest around to the front of the big house where a shining, beautiful motor stood in the drive. He held Alice by the hand, and she skipped as she went. The late August evening was still bright, and a radiance spread over the moors.

"You manage to equip yourself well in wartime, Mr. Weymouth." Black Jack indicated the Hispano Suiza. "One doesn't see many of these."

"I have a few friends. This is a loan, of course, but then they borrow from me when they get to the States." It was said with such ease. The boy had truly picked up a slice of the world they had shown him when they had opened that door of the orphan home and told him that world was his if he could take it.

"I've another daughter, Margaret, who drives for the Red Cross. She'd love to drive a Hispano Suiza. Anything exotic. A good old English Rolls isn't enough for her . . ." Black Jack talked on about Margaret, and Lally wanted to call to him to stop. The bond must not become stronger; this man must not know them any better than he did now. She checked her thoughts. Fear must not push out reason. Why be afraid? He had done no more than comment politely on the other daughter who drove for the Red Cross. His whole manner indicated that someone of eighteen would never interest him, even if she was mad about fast cars. He held out his hand. "Thank you, Miss Lally. That was a fine supper. I didn't know something that sounded like bread and butter could taste so good."

He would remember her, of course, in terms of food. That was probably the only way men remembered her—the round good-natured face, the hands that seemed capable. If he ever met Margaret she would demand the Hispano Suiza to drive, and Brock Weymouth would never forget that drive.

They watched him go. "Strange fellow. Come from nothing, and from the looks of it, he's come a long way from nothing. Well, let's see what he can do for me. Any bit helps, and he seems to have connections . . ." He turned to Alice. "Come now, my darling. It's time you were getting ready for bed."

"Teddy Rose," she suddenly said. "Brock said his name was Teddy Rose." She swung the Teddy high, and laughed.

"Why, so he did. How clever of you to remember."

❧ CHAPTER 7 ❧

I

After that summer there seemed no hope. There would be no end to war; they were bogged and mired. The despondency of the troops in the trenches began to seep back across the Channel. No one talked of quick victories; no one seemed to believe in it except the generals, who still talked of "a final push." The same territory was futilely, hopelessly fought over, back and forth. The second battle of Champagne, the third battle of Artois, Loos. Lally read the names in a daze of fatigue, thinking bitterly that some time in the future they might begin to count the tenth battle of Artois. No one treated her as an inexperienced VAD anymore; they needed the experience, the valuable experience she had gained. Her feet burned and her back ached, and still her essential strength never failed her. She put away her book of Rupert Brooke's poems; she had gotten used to the idea that he was dead. He had not died in one glorious moment of battle— some said he had hoped to die that way—but of blood poisoning. The only fitting thing about his death, Lally thought, was that in the end he had been buried on a Greek island, among his heroes. She saw the wounded come in endlessly; there weren't many deaths there in the Leeds Infirmary—those who died did so in the trenches and the dressing stations and the military hospitals on the other side of the Channel. Some were healed and sent back to France; some regained just enough strength to be sent off to convalescent hospitals, and then to be invalided out. None of them talked about glorious battles. *If I should die, think only this of me* . . . was somehow already out of date. Lally had begun to realize that few wanted the honor of death in battle, though many, with a terrible resignation, expected it would come to them.

It was there, masked, in Jon's letters. She knew he found it difficult to write at all. What was there to say? He wrote to Lally once on the night before battle. *I'm afraid, Lally. And I think you're one of the few people I could confess this to and not expect scorn. In the morning I shall lead my men, as I'm supposed to, and I won't hang back. I'm even more afraid of being branded a coward than of being a coward. Will you send me some socks and soap? I think if I ask you to send something, it's like making a pledge that I will come back—will survive, even if it's just tomorrow. I think only one day at a time. To try to think of a battle—a whole series of battles—of the Germans being pushed back and finally defeated is an unimaginable stretch of time. And I'm just too damn tired to think that far ahead. Good night, dear Lally. Dear old Monkey. I've some more letters to write. Take care of Father and Alice. I know he would lean on you very hard if the worst happened to me. You'd comfort Margaret, too, wouldn't you? Poor Lally, we've always dumped so much on your shoulders. Can you take this bit more? Love, Jon.*

They were her treasures, these few, tired letters he wrote. She shared them with Black Jack and with Margaret when she came up from London, but she did not want to. But what was there in them to keep to herself? They were the letters of a brother to a sister, a member of his family. There was nothing private, nothing that could not be shared except that one admission that he, like all the others, was often afraid. What did he write to Sandy West? Lally wondered. Did he love her?—was she the golden-haired dream of a girl he remembered when the times were grimmest? He had not had leave in England since that last Christmas leave. He would not have seen Sandy West since then, but his letters were peppered with references to Richard West, her brother, and so, by inference, to her.

In September, Margaret had written one of her hasty, ill-composed letters home, letters meant for everyone because there was not time to write to individuals. *The Marchioness invited me to tea the other day, Father—I suspect you've asked her to keep an eye on me. She seems to be working terribly hard, and hasn't much time off. It was just a quick cup of tea and a frightful bun at Lyons Corner House. She's something quite high up in the Red Cross, and I felt such a use-*

less little fool just driving my colonels and brigadiers around. But she was kind and made me feel it was something important. I ran into Sandy West at the Savoy. With a Captain Gaunt and a Major Palmer, and a girl I vaguely remembered from our "Great Season." Dolly Traynor, wasn't that her name? Everyone looking very smart and having a good time. Well, why not? It's one's patriotic duty to help entertain the men when they're lucky enough to get leave. I must say I felt rather odd being at the Savoy with someone who wasn't in uniform, but anyone can see at a glance that he's an American. He let me drive the Hispano Suiza on the way up from Aldershot, but not on the way back. Wise man. He said I'd had too much champagne. Sandy said she'd just had a letter from Jon. There's a chance of home leave. Wouldn't that be wonderful? Father, who exactly is Brock Weymouth? Do you believe that story about the orphan home, and how he got his name? Can there be someone who truly has no history? He seems to have a lot of money. Perhaps that's a story too. I don't remember meeting a divorced man before. The Marchioness wasn't sure you would approve of my going to dinner with him. But he behaved perfectly—more than I can say for some of our home-grown gentlemen. I find it intriguing about him not knowing who he is. That really means he could be anybody, doesn't it?

Margaret had forgotten, Lally thought, that Lally Leeds was an invention, too.

Black Jack's mouth twisted slightly as he read the letter. "Perhaps Lady Ross is right—perhaps I don't approve of Margaret seeing a divorced man. And as to whether Mr. Brockton Weymouth is an invention or not, I wouldn't doubt that he either has a lot of money, now, or he's about to have a lot. Some of it will be Pollock money, from Pollock mills and Pollock steel. He's a procurement agent, all right, Lally, and it's on a grand scale. I've never encountered a man quite like him, so seriously intent on making money—unless it was my own father." The thought seemed not to please Black Jack. "Yes, they're alike, if you can put aside the basic difference of being a Yorkshireman and a Yankee. I think Brockton Weymouth would subscribe very heartily to that Yorkshire adage 'Where there's muck there's brass.' I wish he hadn't got in touch with Margaret. She says it was accidental, but that man has ears like a fox. The way he heard about me, and hunted me down here at home. He's too old for Margaret. And he's too worldly wise. She thinks she's such a sophisticated young woman now, but she never stops to think. . . . I'll be glad when he goes back. He has to, soon."

And when Brock Weymouth went back to America, he wrote another polite thank-you note to Lally. There had been one immediately after the Sunday he had so suddenly appeared on the moor above Pellham Langley. This second one was quite formal, as if he never expected to see her again. But oddly it broke from character in the last line. *I'm sending you a copy of a book that's causing a sensation over here—by some lawyer-fellow from Chicago. It's called* A Spoon River Anthology. *I wonder what you'll make of it.*

So Lally read the somber free-verse monologues of the Chicago lawyer-poet Edgar Lee Masters, and all around her everyone was singing Ivor Novello's song "Keep the Home Fires Burning." At the railway stations as troop trains gathered in their young men the bands of now-aging men were playing "Pack Up Your Troubles in Your Old Kit Bag and Smile, Smile, Smile." Lally hated both of them, and she reread *A Spoon River Anthology,* and stared often at the strong, back-handed script on the flyleaf: *To Miss Lally—the maker of the marvelous bread-and-butter pudding. Brock Weymouth.*

II

Lally and Lieutenant Thomas Handley trudged up the snowy hill from the tram line toward Grangewick in almost total silence. Their pace was slow because Thomas still walked with a limp, and the snow made the road slippery; he breathed a little heavily. He was still convalescent, and, out of consideration for this, Lally didn't try to make conversation. He needed all the breath he had to make the hill and carry the burden of his overnight bag. He was not now, as she was, used to being on his feet sixteen hours a day; she knew she could have run up the hill and hardly been short of breath. Somehow her own health seemed a reproach to the wounded who packed the Infirmary. But Thomas Handley was mending very well. After Christmas he would have some home leave. And then he would be sent back to France.

But even if he had been in perfect health she wondered what they would have had to say to each other. She had asked him only because it had been impossible for him to get to his family in Devon for the Christmas period. Why Thomas Handley, and not any other of

the dozens of young men she nursed? She didn't know. He had just
been there, and lonely. The shortage of hospital beds had placed him
in Leeds, where he knew no one; he had received no other invitation
for Christmas Day. Almost every other military patient who could
walk was having Christmas dinner with a local family. She had
known Thomas Handley was not, and at the last minute she had invited him to Grangewick for Christmas and Boxing Day. He had
blinked with astonishment, and his face had flushed strangely—a
handsome, though rather austere face, but a gentle face. "Why—why
thank you, Miss . . . Miss Lally. That's capital! Capital! Best thing
that's happened to me since . . . well, since I left for France."

"It'll be very quiet," she said. "On Christmas Eve my father is
having a few people in—just some friends, and some of his senior
people from the mills. There's not a lot to celebrate, is there? But
he's always liked having people around him. Are you certain Sister
will let you go?"

"I'll kill her if she doesn't. I'll tell her it's vital to the restoration of
my health. That I'm pining away for some home life—which wouldn't
be far from the truth. How did *you* manage Christmas leave?"

"I suddenly realized I hadn't had much time off in the last six
months—August was the last time I remember. Matron's—well, she's
a good stick when you know her."

"She'd better be good to you, Miss Lally. You do six times the
work of the other girls. That's why I'm surprised you're off for
Christmas. You're usually the one who volunteers to stay." She volunteered, of course, because there was no young man pressing for
her company. The other VADs knew they could always ask Lally to
fill in; Lally didn't mind. But now she tossed her head as if she had
been Margaret, pretending there were a dozen invitations to choose
from, a dozen young men she might have asked.

"For once I decided to be selfish. Besides, my father's all alone.
My sister Margaret can't get leave. She's at Aldershot."

That had seemed to exhaust what they had to say to each other. In
the tram on the way out the clanging noise had covered the lack of
conversation. They knew nothing about each other; she realized it
was the first time she had ever invited a young man to her home. She
had recognized the note of surprise in Black Jack's voice when she
had telephoned last night to say she was bringing Thomas Handley.
"Wonderful, Lally! Of course he's welcome." It had been too enthusiastic. Did Black Jack think she had found herself an admirer? It

wasn't so. Thomas Handley was just grateful, and polite. He would, for these few days, pay her all the courtesies and attention he would have given a pretty girl. He would be kind to her—and grateful. And very soon he would leave the hospital, and too soon be back in France. There would be a few letters exchanged, because all the men in the trenches loved to receive letters. After the war, if he survived, she would never hear from him again. After the war . . . an impossible phrase. The war would last forever, and it was very possible Thomas Handley would die. Their warm breath was thick on the cold air. But they were alive tonight, Lally thought. And young. But of course she didn't say it.

They finally reached the big open gates of Grangewick. In the faint light they could see some parked motor cars. There was the stamp of horses' hoofs from the stable yard. The drivers, if there were any left to drive, would be well treated in Billings' servants' hall. Cook had been stretching the increasingly scarce food supplies for months to provide for this Christmas season. Even though they knew Jon could not get leave, she persisted in believing he would. "Either Christmas or New Year," she said. "Mark my words."

A crack of light showed from the drawing room. "Billings isn't very careful about the blackout, I'm afraid," Lally said. "I don't think he understands how all these little chinks of light add up. I suppose . . ." The thought had never occurred to her before: Billings was unchangeable, immutable, forever. "I suppose Billings is getting old. He doesn't understand."

They heard the voices before Billings answered the door. He flung it open to answer their knock, forgetting about the blackout curtain behind it. "Ah, Miss Lally. Welcome home. Happy Christmas."

"Billings, this is Lieutenant Thomas Handley. Father told you—"

"Yes, certainly, Miss Lally. Always delighted to welcome a friend of the family, sir. And a serving officer. Happy Christmas, sir."

Lally pulled the blackout curtain behind her. Billings would always be the perfect snob. He believed implicitly that officers would always be gentlemen, and now he could not quite cover his surprise as he had his first good look at Lieutenant Thomas Handley. What had he expected, Lally thought—that Thomas would be ugly and squint-eyed, just because she, Lally, was fat and plain? These equations were always made. Thomas Handley would not have come if he had not felt himself perfectly safe with her; she would never impose on him, make demands of him. Only pretty girls could do that. Only girls like Margaret. And then there was the fact that she was in love with the man who was supposed to be her brother, Jon. Thomas Handley did not know that; but he must have sensed the security in her self-containment. No, she would ask nothing of him. He was safe with Lally. If he dreamed of some other girl, he could go on dreaming. Lally wasn't the kind to disturb anyone's dreams.

They left their bags, and Billings took their coats. Black Jack came into the hall to welcome them. They could see the drawing room crowded with guests; there was even the tinkle of the piano. It wouldn't be a very merry party. The guests were mostly middle-aged. But Black Jack and Billings and Cook would do their best; everyone would go home feeling the warmth of spirits and good wine in them; the Yorkshire tradition of hospitality would be well satisfied.

Black Jack kissed her. "Well, my pet. Delighted you could get away. And this is Lieutenant Handley. Welcome, sir. Good that they let you out of that place for a few days. We'll try to look after you."

Damn it, Lally thought, if only they wouldn't all look so surprised. Had they expected some freak? Or someone with half his face blasted away, someone they could feel sorry for? For one of the very few times in her life she was out of patience with Black Jack. "Of course we'll look after him, Father. After the Infirmary, this is—" Then she laughed, overcoming her petulance. It was only because Black Jack loved her, after all. "After the Infirmary, this is going to be like Christmas." She thrust her arm through Thomas's, determined to face out the stares, the repeated looks of surprise which she knew would greet her. Let them think what they liked; let them think this good-looking young officer, in his blue convalescent's suit and red tie, was her beau. "Come on, Thomas." For once she was not embarrassed to say the words. "Come on—I'm famished. I could eat a horse. And I know Cook's been saving up for six months for this."

She and Black Jack and Thomas swiftly made the round of the guests, the introductions gone through punctiliously. Some of the people she remembered well; they exchanged greetings, but it seemed that it was over the tide of a lifetime. There had been no party like this since the Christmas before her coming-out. Then they had forgiven her for her fat, her gaucheness. They had been kind, because she was still officially in the schoolroom. Now the looks were critical. They had heard she was nursing, they said. Worked very long hours, dear Jack told them. And their eyes devoured Thomas Handley and wondered who he was. Next, Lally thought, as she urged Thomas toward the buffet table in the dining room, pausing to get their glasses refilled from Billings—next they would be murmuring to themselves that this handsome young man must think he was on to a good thing. And perhaps he was. It was well known that Black Jack would stand no partiality among his daughters, the adopted one as well as the two others. No doubt there would be a nice little sum for her when she married, if she ever married. And there would be an even nicer sum for her when Black Jack died. Yorkshire always thought in those terms. Brass was respected. But then, Lally conceded, as she heaped her plate with cold ham and chicken and beef, the whole world thought that way. She looked around at the well-fed faces; as yet the shortages were not biting too badly. They still ate well, though the women might wear last year's dresses. There was Black Jack's usual mix of merchants and bankers, a sprinkling of gentry—those whose sons were away in France and who could not bear their own fireside on this Christmas Eve. Somehow, Lally thought, he always managed to do it. To get this mix. The top managers from the mills and the mines would rub shoulders with the hunting squires; the bank manager would nod affably to the man who owed him a nice round sum of money, knowing that while the times might be stringent, there was money being made through this war, and interest being piled up. Black Jack brought them all together. Always had. But he had never managed to mix them with his first wife's parents. There was the John Singer Sargent painting over the mantel, removed here from Pellham Langley. The sight of the pointed little face of that young beauty could remind the most insensitive mill manager, the iron master who had dug his hands most deeply into the muck that made the brass, that Black Jack had married into the aristocracy. She was an alien spirit among them, Lady Latitia Pollock. Free, generous, laughing, but never completely understood. They almost, Lally thought, preferred the way she looked. There was much they could forgive her for, whereas Lady Latitia appeared to be perfection. Lally looked away from the portrait, and for some quiet place to sit down and eat.

"Come out into the hall," Thomas said. She was surprised that he was still by her side. "There are a couple of chairs by the fire." He carried the two plates, and she the two glasses. She hadn't expected him to stay with her; there were two pretty girls among the older people, girls she barely remembered as children when she had last seen them—but then, she had been a child also. Why should she be

surprised that Thomas stayed by her side? He was as she had predicted—polite, and grateful.

He talked a little of his home in Devon as they ate, and she of
Pellham Langley. He had had two years at Cambridge before joining
up, reading history. He hadn't any idea of what he wanted to do
"when it was all over." None of them, Lally had observed, liked to
talk of definite plans. Did it seem to tempt fate too much? "My father would like me to read law. He's a country solicitor, and he'd just
love to pass on the practice. I thought I would once—but now . . ."
He shrugged, staring into the fire. "It's hard to say. At times I find
myself thinking that if I can just get back to turn into a country solicitor, it's all I'd ever ask of life. And then other times—well, one sees
such a lot over there. There's so much death, it makes one want to
live, if one lives at all. I'd like to do something with my life, Lally—
or else make sure I had a bloody great time of it. Live it up, you
know. Or make some sort of mark. Peace might just be too peaceful.
Do I sound mad?"

She shook her head. "No—not mad at all." But still she could not
help feeling chilled by the words "Peace might just be too peaceful."
How many of them thought like that?

"Here," he said, "your glass is empty. I'll get some more wine."
When he returned Billings followed him, carrying plates on a tray.
"Miss Lally, Cook made your special favorite, sherry trifle. And
there's Black Forest cake—though we don't call it that anymore, because of the Germans, you know. She's been saving up the chocolate
for it, and she'll be hurt if you don't at least sample it." To Lally's
shame Billings put the plate with the bigger helping into her hands.
Of course Cook knew she would more than sample the Black Forest
cake. What else had Lally done all her life?

Then Billings turned in surprise at the sudden loud hammering of
the knocker at the door. It had an exuberant, familiar sound about it.
"Who could it be at this hour? It's almost time . . ." Then he hurried to open the door, once again forgetting to arrange the blackout
curtain. The light fell fully on Jon's smiling face.

"What!—Master Jon! Of all things wonderful! Come in, sir! Come
in! The best Christmas present for us all. Wait till I get the master."

Lally sprang to her feet; the plate on her lap slipped to the marble
floor and shattered. To her it was a joyful sound. "Oh, Jon!" She
flung herself into his arms.

"Lally, love. Oh, good God, Monkey, you're not going to cry? I wasn't certain I could swing it, and I didn't want you all to be disappointed. It seems as if I've come just at the right time for a celebration party. And here's Sandy. You remember Sandy West, don't you, Lally?"

Slowly, Lally withdrew herself from Jon's arms. The chill that had come with the open door seemed to engulf her. There it was again, that strikingly pretty face above the fur coat, the marvelous golden hair piled high, and escaping in tiny, enchanting little tendrils to touch her smooth cheeks, cheeks which glowed, either from the cold or from excitement. "We've traveled up by train from London. I thought I'd have to telephone from Leeds station, but we managed to find a cabby who'd make it out here for twice the price and a pint or two. So, Billings, I've sent him round to the kitchen. Will you . . . ?"

"Certainly, sir. Of course. I'll just inform the master."

But Black Jack was there. He wrung Jon's hand, holding it, quite speechless for a time. Lally saw the tears that almost welled over. "My boy—my boy," he managed to say at last. "How wonderful! I didn't dare hope you'd get enough leave to come over." He blinked away the tears. "Well, I shall have to reward Cook with something special. She said she felt it in her bones." He couldn't now restrain himself. He caught Jon by the shoulders, and hugged him, as he used to do when his son was a child. "What a Christmas this is. The best Christmas present I ever had in my life."

"Father, you've never met Sandy West. But you know all about her. I contacted her in London. It was a toss-up about whether she'd go on to York, where her people live. But it was so late we decided we'd better get a billet here for the night."

Black Jack was frankly puzzled, but he put out his hand and smiled. "Miss West, it's a pleasure to meet you at last. Of course I know your brother, Richard. And we hear about you both in Jon's letters. I say—what a shame Margaret isn't here. It would complete the picture. I must send Nell up to bring Alice down. She wouldn't forgive me if she didn't see you tonight."

"As soon as I got to London, after meeting Sandy, I telephoned Margaret at Aldershot. She says there's just a chance she might get some leave. You know, pull the old stuff about the only brother home from the front. I have until January third."

Black Jack beamed as he helped Sandy West off with her coat. "January the third. To me, son, that sounds like a lifetime. We'll make every moment of it count. Tell me anything you'd like to do.

Of course, there's no hunting now. But I'll beg or steal petrol if you want to motor around. And there are still two fairly decent horses at Pellham . . ." Billings had appeared with a tray full of glasses.

"Sir, I hope you forgive the presumption. But I thought it was an occasion . . ."

"Certainly, Billings. Splendid idea." Black Jack just barely remembered to hand the first glass of champagne to Sandy West. "You'll attend to all our guests, Billings . . . ?"

"Of course, sir. Nell's just helping me before she goes up for Miss Alice." The word had spread through the party. People had come crowding to the doors of the drawing room and the dining room, spilling over into the hall with enthusiastic, almost joyful greetings. The return of a man from France now touched them all. They saw a thinner, more handsome Jon, his features slightly touched with the perpetual fatigue of the trenches. But to them all he represented survival, he represented the hope that one day they also would greet a son or a brother or a lover unexpectedly returned. There was a sudden welling forward. Jon and Sandy West and Black Jack were engulfed. Lally found herself back at Thomas's side.

"Wonderful, isn't it, Lally? Your father's so happy. Must be— Why, Lally, you're crying!"

"Well, what if I am?" she demanded. "Mind your own business, Thomas Handley."

Then his finger was lightly under her chin. He raised his glass to her. "It is my business, just a little, Lally. Let's drink to reunions, and no farewells."

They drank, and his eyes remained on her.

*   *   *

The party went on longer than anyone had expected. There was reason now to refill glasses, and Billings was profligate with the champagne. His attitude indicated what most people suspected; among Black Jack's other, more serious preparations for the war, he had undertaken a vast restocking of his cellar. Nell found time to slip upstairs and quickly dress Alice. She appeared among them, her face alight with joy at the sight of Jon. For a moment he swung her high, as he had always done, then set her down. "You're getting too big a girl to do that with anymore, eh, Kitten? Will you dance with your old brother instead?" For just a few steps they waltzed around the marble floor to the time of the piano, which had started again.

Alice's long golden hair flew outward like a veil; her movements were light and quick and perfectly in time. It was one of the moments when everything about Alice seemed to fall into place; she was normal and right, and magically alive.

"What a beautiful girl!" Thomas exclaimed, his tone faintly awed. Lally remembered it always as the first time a man had specifically referred to Alice as a girl, not a child.

"Yes," Lally agreed. "Yes, she is. Quite beautiful."

The guests, enchanted at the sight of the young officer and the golden-haired girl, pressed forward to exclaim and applaud. For a moment Alice was nonplussed; then she ran to Black Jack and hid her head in his vest. But Lally heard her delighted laughter, and saw her face turned sideways, as though she must make sure once again of Jon's reality. But Jon was back at Sandy West's side. He drew her toward his father and Alice. "Billings, I hope everyone has a full glass," he said. "Yourself included."

"Why . . . ? Yes, Master Jon. One moment, sir."

Billings hurriedly topped up a few glasses near him, and found a clean one for himself. The words had penetrated the noise of the crowd. A kind of expectant hush fell on them; someone must have told the person at the piano. The music stopped.

"Father . . . everyone. By now I hope I've introduced you all to Sandy West. But if not, you'll all meet her in the future. Sandy and I have some happy news to share with you. Most of all, with you, Father." He swung around. "And you, Lally. With my darling sister, Alice." He placed his hand in Sandy's. "Please raise your glasses, everyone. Sandy has, just this afternoon, agreed to marry me. We expect to be married before I return to France."

For a moment there was absolute silence. Then the voices broke out. Exclamations of surprise, words of congratulation, an underground murmur that was not quite either thing. The marriage of Black Jack's only son was a matter of some importance to those who understood what went with such a marriage. The light from the chandelier shone fully on Sandy West, and none could find anything wanting in that bright, expectant face, which was now turned, brazenly some thought, to receive Jon's kiss.

Through it all Lally watched Black Jack's face. She had heard nothing after the moment Jon had said "marry me." She saw people's mouths move, saw the eager surge forward, the outstretched hands. She saw Jon place a kiss fully on Sandy's lips. She saw Black

Jack frozen for some moments, just as she was. Then, rather numbly, Black Jack propelled Alice ahead of him; she saw the father's hand clasped in his son's once again. And Alice was laughing again. And Sandy West had received the obligatory kiss on the cheek from her future father-in-law. But Lally knew that Black Jack, like herself, did not quite believe what he had heard. Lally found herself treading on some fragments of the plate she had broken when Jon had first appeared. She wished she could have dashed the champagne glass to the floor to join them. People were moving all around her, but they seemed to move as puppets, without sounds. "Marry me . . . marry me . . ." Jon had said. Until those words had been pronounced, she had hoped, even though the hope had been forlorn. Now the hope was gone. She could not bring herself to move forward, to join the group offering congratulations. She stood, rooted, even turned away to look at the fire, anywhere to escape the sight of those two, their arms entwined, accepting the good wishes. She did not want to see Black Jack try to compose his face, to wipe out the surprise, the shock. No doubt Black Jack would put a very good face on it. There was no reason to suppose that Sandy West would not make his beloved son a very good wife. But he had not been consulted. But then, Lally reminded herself, why should any man who had survived the trenches for almost a year consult about whom he should marry? His manhood was written plain; he had earned the right to choose. He had chosen. Black Jack must accept whomever that choice might be.

Then Lally felt Thomas's hand upon her elbow. His was the only voice that penetrated the silent clamor which hung around her. "Lally—Lally! You hear me? You've got to go and wish Jon well. You must! Come on now. For God's sake, Lally."

How had he known? Was it written so plain? She found herself propelled forward, Thomas's arm still firmly on her elbow. The champagne spilled a little; it didn't matter. "Jon . . ." she said as she kissed him.

"Dearest Lally." The kiss was returned. "I know Sandy and you will always be friends. You'll take care of her for me, won't you?"

Somehow, with Thomas still gripping her elbow, the pressure quite painful now, she kissed Sandy West's cheek. Her lips framed the words, "Happiness to you both. Good luck."

Then, back by the fire, in the comparative quiet with Thomas, he said, "Good girl! Now drink to me!"

There was little left in her glass. But Thomas had lifted a full bottle from the tray of them that Billings was opening. "Now drink to me, Lally. To yourself. We deserve it, too."

She drained the glass, and when he had refilled it, drained it again.

*   *   *

It was over at last—the final good nights, the good wishes for Christmas, the good wishes for "the happy couple." The last motor had reluctantly "caught," the horses' hoofs sounded sharply on the frosty hill, the fires were banked, the lights were out. Lally sat alone in her room and wept. She was ashamed of her weeping, and still could not stop it.

The last good night from Black Jack had been the hardest. He had switched out the light in the hall, and they had walked upstairs together, the last to do so. In the light from the landing Lally could see his expression plainly; he had dropped the pretense of excitement and pleasure. Lines of age she had hardly noticed before seemed deep.

"It isn't," he said without preamble, "that I think anything but good of Sandy West—though I wish I *knew* her. I wish she seemed a less obvious choice. A bright, very pretty young woman, but I can't see anything beyond that. Perhaps there isn't anything. I don't suppose I mind so much about Jon not confiding in me. He's more than earned the right to his own decisions. I mind about *you*, Lally."

"Me?" She had struggled desperately to keep her tone even. "What have I to do with it?"

"A great deal. I had always hoped that Jon would—well, that he would see what you are. That it would be you he chose."

"Oh, Father!" She made her voice sound annoyed, not bitter. "All Jon sees is his fat, good-natured sister. Do you expect him to fall in love with someone he's known all his life? And after all, why would he look at someone like me, when he can have someone like Sandy? Jon loves me. But he'll never be in love with me."

They had reached the landing. She made to move toward her room. Momentarily, Black Jack reached out and detained her. "But you would have liked him to be 'in love' with you, Lally?"

For once she had no answer for him; she turned away, and he was forced to let her go.

Her desperately striven-for calm lasted while she washed and got ready for bed. She brushed the long thick black hair furiously, cleaned her teeth as carefully as she always did, and was dismayed as

she looked for a final time in the mirror over the washstand to see
the first tears come sliding down her face. "Oh, shut up, you damn
fool," she said angrily to her own image. "Look at you! What did
you expect? He could have anyone. He deserves better than Sandy
West. Why should he want you?"

The tears did not stop. She switched out the light and pulled back
the curtains. A soft snow was falling, just as it had done on the only
other time she had seen Sandy West, the last time she had seen Jon
before this night. She dropped down on the window seat and watched
it, watched it in the blur of tears. Why weep? If it had not been
Sandy West it would have been someone else. It would never have
been Lally Leeds. Dimly she saw the few lights that showed below
her of the city she had come from, the nameless child who had been
spun under Black Jack's horses' hoofs. The memories came fast;
there had been little time to remember such things in these last,
wearying months. She thought of all the times with Jon, she thought
of him through the stages of his boyhood. Tonight he had stood before them as a man who has looked at death, faced it, and had not
been ashamed to say he had been afraid. He had returned, and had
claimed a woman as a warrior's right. The prize was his. She thought
of these things, and gradually the flow of tears was checked. It did no
good to weep. Pray for him to be happy; most of all, pray for him
not to die. *If I should die . . .* She had been unable to stop the
words coming back to mind. Oh, damn Rupert Brooke and his he-
roics! Damn all his fine sentiments which urged young men on to
their deaths. Damn all the poets and the orators! Damn all the
heroes!

She turned angrily from the window. She felt a gnawing hunger.
She hadn't, after all, eaten very much—just what Billings had forced
on her. There would be plenty left in the pantry. She blew her nose,
and wrapped her dressing gown more closely around her. It didn't
matter now how fat she was. She went downstairs on quiet feet.

*   *   *

She found Thomas pacing the corridor between the bedrooms
when she came back upstairs. He wore the standard-issue pajamas
and robe which the hospital handed out; all his own things had been
left behind in the general order to retreat. His limp seemed more
pronounced. "Thomas!" she whispered.

He turned. Only one dim light burned. His face looked tight and drawn. "Thomas—what's wrong?"

"Oh, nothing much, Lally. Just the usual you see at nights in the wards."

She nodded. Men in pain are wakeful. If they could walk, they often did, pacing the long corridors outside the wards. Sometimes the sister on duty would authorize an extra measure of drugs, but not often. All orders for medication were written in the charts, all doses administered were recorded. Very seldom, except in extreme cases, would anyone risk the wrath of the doctors by offering something extra. Lally always carried with her a small quantity of a fairly harmless prescription put up by the local chemist, the usual remedy against pain. Occasionally she offered it to patients, not hoping that it would give much relief, but just the thought of the drug itself, the offering of it, seemed to soothe them. She knew she risked instant dismissal if it were ever discovered. "I have something . . . it might help, a little."

He paused on the threshold of her room. "Oh, for God's sake," she said crossly, "don't be such a ninny. As if you don't know me well enough . . . as if this were any different from the hospital."

She filled her tooth glass with water and brought out the powder in a little white envelope. Thomas advanced slowly. "But it is different, Lally."

"Oh . . ." She was sick of the stupid game of manners. She closed the door behind him. "Take it, Thomas."

He spilled the white powder onto his tongue and swallowed the water, grimacing a little at the bitter taste. "I don't know if it'll help. I don't think you're ever quite going to be rid of the pain in that leg. That's what they tell me, at any rate. At times when you're cold or tired . . . or hungry."

He put his hand tentatively on her arm. "You, Lally . . . you. What about the times you're cold or tired . . . or hungry? What helps you?"

She was feeling immeasurably older than she had that morning. "They say God helps those who help themselves. That's all I can do, Thomas."

"Is it, Lally? Can't I help?"

"You?—what way? *You* help me?"

"Why not? Just a little . . ." She felt herself drawn into the unaccustomed, warm embrace of a man. "If you want to cry your eyes

out now, Lally, it's all right. There's no one to see. No one but me.
You love him, don't you?"

He was taller than she, so that her head fitted against the sharp,
tight line of his neck. In all the times she had bathed and fed and
tended men, she had never felt about their bodies as she felt now.
She had never known tenderness from a man except Black Jack; she
had known comradeship, laughter, bantering good humor, but never
tenderness. She had never felt the warmth of a man's body pressed
against hers. There was only some distant memory, like a dream, of a
time when a man had picked her up from the cobbles, clutched her
to him, and rubbed warmth and life back into her. "Thomas . . . do
you think they all knew? Do you think *he* knew?"

"*I* knew. Doesn't that say something, Lally?"

The warmth was all-embracing, as his arms were now. "Dear
Lally—let me help. It's just you and me. No one else. Cry if you want
to."

She raised her face to his. "No. Suddenly I'm finished with tears. I
don't want to cry. I want a man to love me."

"You're sure?"

"I'm sure."

In her bed they drew warmth and comfort from each other. She
had not thought how beautiful it would be when a man's hands ex-
plored her body, the beauty of his body against her. He buried his
face between her breasts. It did not matter any longer what she
looked like, the ample flesh was a reward to them both. Even when
he entered her the sharp pain held a joy. She uttered something softly
against his shoulder; she realized she was urging him on. "Please
. . . on. Oh, yes . . . yes."

They made love again before they slept, the young man's urgency,
his long deprivation matching her own need. Somewhere on the
snowy hill she heard the first sound of horses' hoofs against the frosty
ground before they slept in each other's arms. When she woke the
place beside her was empty, but his signet ring was on the bedside
table, and a note scrawled on the white paper which had held the
powder. *Keep it until I come back.*

* * *

She did not go down to breakfast, a fact which so surprised Cook
that she came to see Lally herself, bringing tea and toast on a tray,

which would have been an unheard-of breach of the household rules in the days before all the rules had to be broken.

"Why, Miss Lally . . . I've never known you to be off your food. Or lie in bed. Are you sick then, lass?"

Lally swallowed the tea, but somehow could not touch the toast. "No, Cook. Just a bit tired. Thought I'd lie in a bit." She had thrust the ring and the note under the pillow at the first knock.

"Well, then, there's no one'd deny you your right to that. Working them long hours. You've learned what it is to be standing on your feet all day. All of us lie in when we can. Take your time, lass . . . take your time. There's enough commotion with that yon fair-haired thing downstairs. I don't know whatever could have come over Master Jon, getting himself engaged like that, and never a word to a soul. Fair shook Mr. Pollock, I can tell you. Mr. Billings isn't quite himself this morning."

"Lieutenant Handley . . . ?" She thought he must be gone. The note had held a terrible finality.

"Oh, he's there, Miss. Quiet like. After all, all the attention's on that Miss Sandy and Master Jon, isn't it? Or should I be saying Captain Pollock now? Grown up, he is . . . and marrying. It's all so sudden-like."

She went, eventually, with more admonitions to rest, and Lally was left alone. Sudden-like. Yes, it was. Sudden-like she was a woman, had known a man's love, his tenderness. She had won something from the night of bitter defeat which she had not thought she could ever win. She felt fulfilled. Unhappy, but not despised. She moved cautiously, and felt the hurt of the night's lovemaking, the tender hurt. Against all the rules of wartime economy, she filled the bath and lay there a long time, watching the soft mound of her body as it seemed to waver under the water. Someone had found it desirable. Whether it had been from kindness or from love she did not know, and did not care; but she had not been despised.

She took extra care with dressing, arranged her hair so that it appeared to give her face more length, found the perfume she had saved from the London season. She also took out the pearls Black Jack had given her, not worn, she remembered, since that August day when their world had seemed to fly into pieces. Then she went downstairs to the drawing room, where they were all gathered having a prelunch sherry. Thomas sprang to his feet, wincing at the sudden shock to his leg.

"Well . . ." Black Jack said. "Look at this lie-a-bed! Will you have champagne, m'lady? Or will you settle for sherry? Here—Cook's made some pâté—Billings said it's probably made of rabbit's foot and goat's milk, but she's made it taste jolly good. Well, my darling, had a good rest?"

She smiled on them all. Smiled at Jon and Sandy, sitting together on the sofa. Smiled at Alice and Black Jack. Finally smiled, most lingeringly, at Thomas. "Yes, I've had the most wonderful night. I just thought I'd let you all get on with the wedding plans without any sisterly interference. Has it all been decided? Where? When? I hope I'll be able to get leave from the hospital. Surely they'll let Margaret come up?"

She spread the pâté on the toast, then smelled and finally sipped the pale, fine sherry. It seemed to have gathered into it all the warmth and dryness of the sun. "Well, when is it going to be? I suppose it will have to be pretty informal because the time is so short. But I'm sure we'll all help to make it a great occasion, won't we, Father?"

She found they all looked at her with surprise. It was not like Lally to dominate a conversation or a gathering; not like Lally to make suggestions, to ask questions. She stood with her back to the fire, and sipped the sherry again. "Oh, that's lovely. Just what I wanted." She turned and faced Sandy West, looked down on her where she sat close to Jon. "Now—tell me all the plans. Perhaps I can help . . ."

She had never known such confidence, nor had she ever known quite such pain as she did in seeing Jon sitting there with his hand twined in Sandy West's while she discussed their marriage.

"Oh, I forgot. It's Christmas Day, isn't it? Happy Christmas, everyone." She saw Thomas's lips part in a slight smile; did he nod at her approvingly?

Alice came over to her quietly, nestling her head against Lally's shoulder. "You look tall this morning, Lally. Like a giant, or something."

Lally fondled the golden hair. "Or something, pet . . ."

II

By special arrangement the wedding was five days later. Telegrams had been dispatched to brother officers whom Jon knew had leave.

Sandy had, in turn, summoned all the friends of her London season, and the friends she had made while working for the Red Cross. She wore her mother's bridal dress, and a long string of pearls of matchless quality which Black Jack had gotten from the London jeweler who had supplied the pearls for Margaret and Lally. There was also a large solitaire diamond, a marquise cut, which he gave to Jon to place on Sandy's finger; there had not been time for an engagement ring before the announcement. The wedding ring he let them find for themselves in one of the jewelers' shops in York. These days, the jewelers were accustomed to fitting wedding rings at short notice. It was simple, and cost very little. No one but Black Jack knew the cost or the carat weight of the enormous solitaire diamond which accompanied it. Even Sandy West's imperturbable blue eyes flickered a little when she saw it.

"This?—for *me?*" It was becomingly said, but she knew her worth —or was it her price, Lally thought, and acknowledged that she was being malicious. Sandy West knew every particle of her worth, or her price. She was more than pretty; even Lally in her most grudging moments had to admit that she was beautiful. She was well-born; her father was a baronet with an estate on the Yorkshire wolds, that gentle, swelling country that makes the north and west of Yorkshire seem so wild and desolate by comparison. In every sense she was a fitting bride for Jonathan Pollock—but perhaps, Lally thought, the Wests were thinking that Jon just might possibly be a fitting groom for their beloved, beautiful daughter. He had wealth, as they knew, from Black Jack; he was handsome, well-mannered; he was an officer. Therefore he was a gentleman. So they reasoned. So Alexandra West was permitted to marry Jonathan Pollock with her parents' blessing.

They were married under the soaring spires of York Minster—the standing of the West family in that part of the world demanded that. It seemed that a goodly portion of the lunch-hour crowd of the city came to gape at the bride. A trickle of officers had found their way from their homes all over the county to attend. Evidently Jon was popular, and many of them knew Richard West and the West sisters. Sandy's two sisters were her attendants and wore the white dresses in which they had been presented at Court, with little white ermine capes against the chill of the great medieval building. Some brother officers had turned out in full-dress uniform, but the predominant color was khaki.

Black Jack, Lally, and Alice had waited early that morning at

Leeds station; Margaret had telephoned the night before that she had managed to get leave, and was coming up. Jon had left for York the day before. "I'm not going to chance being late for my own wedding," he said. But as Black Jack came into the station and headed for the platform at which the London train would arrive, the station master, in his top hat, approached him. Most people in Leeds knew Black Jack, at least by sight.

"Morning, Mr. Pollock. Great day for your young lad. Please give him my best wishes. There's been a telephone message from Miss Margaret. Seems she's motoring up to York directly. So you're not to wait."

Black Jack was annoyed and troubled. "Silly girl. She's risking missing the whole thing. And where did she get a car from? God, I hope she takes care driving. It's a devilish long way."

Cook and Billings and Nell had gone ahead by train earlier that morning; they were waiting on the steps of the minster. "Have you seen Miss Margaret?" Black Jack demanded immediately. It was half an hour before the ceremony was to begin. The guests were arriving, the organist had begun to play, a crowd had gathered on the pavement. They waited another ten minutes, then filed into the places on the groom's side of the church. Lord and Lady Bletchley were already seated there; Lady Bletchley deemed the occasion had warranted throwing off wartime austerity. She wore purple velvet under her furs and many rows of pearls; a huge cluster of pearls and diamonds adorned her purple toque. "Don't approve of these wartime marriages myself," she hissed loudly at Black Jack. "But dear Jon's getting a fine gel. I've known her mother all my life." So the seal of the Bletchley approval was set on Sandy West.

They were surprised by the sudden appearance of the Marchioness, in response to a telephoned invitation from Black Jack. She shivered a little as she settled close to Lally. "The train was held up for hours—and there was nothing to eat. I felt unpatriotic traveling all this way for a wedding—and I had to cancel three committee meetings. But sometimes we just have to get together for some happy reason . . . or we'd go mad." She was wearing her Red Cross uniform, and looked severely smart and distinguished. She turned and looked at Lally closely. "And how are *you*, child?" The eyes were inquiring and kind, and too discerning, Lally thought. Did she guess what agony this hour was—and the hours to come? "A little tired, I think, aren't you? I suppose we all are." For an instant the gloved hand was laid on Lally's, and quickly removed, as if she feared to probe more deeply.

Five minutes before the ceremony was to begin Lally heard Margaret's excited whisper behind them.

"Just made it! We had to park *miles* away. Everyone in Yorkshire must have turned out. Look who's here."

Black Jack and Lally turned around fully, to see Brockton Weymouth at Margaret's side. "Hope you didn't mind my coming, sir. Margaret assured me it was going to be very informal, in the circumstances. And in any case, I knew you'd be nervous about her motoring all the way up here by herself."

"Brock supplied the car and the petrol," Margaret said. She squeezed past Black Jack to place a kiss on her grandmother's powdered cheek. "Granny, you look gorgeous!"

"*Where,*" Lady Bletchley demanded, "did you get that coat? Quite unsuitable for a young girl." It was a long coat of white ermine, the tall collar framing Margaret's exquisite, vixenish little face to perfection. She wore a tiny fur hat, and looked, Lally thought, like the Winter Princess from some Russian fairy tale.

"Brock borrowed it, darling. Isn't it heaven? I'll introduce you to Brock at—oh, here she comes!" The organist had broken off, and taken up the chords of the Mendelssohn wedding march.

Then Lally sat, chilled by more than the chill of the old stones about her, and watched Jon married to Alexandra West in York Minster.

*   *   *

At the reception at the Wests' house at Burton-in-the-Wolds, Lally found herself beside Brock Weymouth. "Miss Lally—you look delightful. You're still nursing, Margaret tells me."

"Yes," she said. "What are you doing over here? I thought you'd be in America."

"I do a bit of submarine dodging in the interest of selling things to the needy Allies."

"Then you'll need to sell a lot more. We're not achieving much at the rate we're going. If you mean to bring Jon back alive you'll have to hurry."

"My, Miss Lally—such serious sentiments for a happy occasion."

"I *am* serious, Mr. Weymouth. Would you bring me another champagne?" She looked over the throng; the long, often horsey

faces of the aristocracy, the ruddy faces of the farmers, the degrees
of ostentation in the dress of the women. As the wine was consumed,
the noise level rose. The young officers circulated among the young
girls—more girls than young men. The marquise diamond flashed on
Sandy West's—no, on Sandy Pollock's—hand. The speeches were
made, the toasts drunk. For an occasion that had been improvised in
a few days, it was impressive. Cook stood uncomfortably in her tight
boots, wedged between Billings and Nell, saying nothing, her eyes
fixed on Jon. Black Jack was being charming to Sandy's sisters, making them laugh at something he said. The shock of his son's sudden
marriage had receded; he was determined to enjoy the whole occasion. He could, like them all, only hope for the future.

Alice said, "Couldn't I have some champagne, Lally?" And then
she added, "Couldn't we go home? It's so noisy here. Who is the
lady Jon's with? Will he come home soon?"

Lally looked down at the perfect young face, a face now betraying
the first signs of discomfort at the strange scene. Alice always grew a
little frightened when too many people pressed about her, strange
people. She realized that Alice had not understood the marriage service, had seen the whole occasion as yet another party from which
Jon would return alone. "I don't see why you shouldn't have some
champagne, Alice. And yes, we shall soon go home."

Brock Weymouth brought two glasses of champagne, and Lally
gave one to Alice. "You'll have to get yourself another glass, Mr.
Weymouth. You can't let two ladies drink alone."

It was only on the long cold drive back, with Cook and Billings
and Nell huddled in the back seat, that Lally realized she had had
nothing to eat at the reception. She fought weariness and a slight sensation of dizziness, the effect, she thought, of too much champagne.
Perhaps it was that which loosened her tongue. As they approached
the outskirts of Leeds she said, "Now that it's over, Father—I mean
Christmas and the wedding—I thought I'd better tell you. I'm going
into real nursing. I'm going to apply for overseas service. I know I'm
under age, but they often turn a blind eye to that sort of lie. I know
they'll take me." Four days ago she hadn't known that she would
ever say those words. But they were said, and they seemed as inevitable as Jon marrying Sandy West.

The headlights flashed over the bare branches of the trees. The
road was empty, and had an ominous glint of ice on it. The Yorkshire winter was taking its grip on the countryside. Lally felt the car

slide a little as they rounded a tight bend; Black Jack struggled for control. When they had straightened and the road stretched smoothly ahead again he said, "I can't let you go, Lally."

"You must, Father. You must let me go as you let Jon and Margaret."

The response seemed dragged out of him. "Does that mean I've lost you all?"

She didn't try to answer, just huddled deeper into her coat, and watched the road ahead. Behind, Cook's snores rose even above the sound of the engine. And far behind them, so that only occasionally did they catch a glimpse of the headlights, Brock Weymouth and Margaret followed in the Hispano Suiza, where Alice lay almost cradled in the Marchioness' arms, asleep in the back seat, exhausted and a little overwrought by the day's events. They would all be spending the night at Grangewick. Lally knew that Black Jack was glad of Lady Ross's presence; she would accompany Margaret and Brock Weymouth on the drive back to London the next morning. She sensed that Black Jack, like herself, was rather puzzled by the way Brock Weymouth had quietly, rather mysteriously, become part of the group, almost a part of their lives.

❦ CHAPTER 8 ❦

I

The matron at the Infirmary was reluctant to let her go. "You can be of great use here, Miss Pollock. You could join the nursing service. Train to be a real nurse instead of a VAD. We have as great a need of women to nurse the convalescent as they have over there. Sometimes it is harder to nurse them back to a full life than to patch their wounds and send them back here. You could be a good nurse, Miss Pollock. I would like you on my staff." Lally realized she had won an accolade. She could stay here forever; she could nurse the wounded, help the convalescent. She could stay with Black Jack and Alice. She could be their dependable, loving, loyal Lally. "Matron, I would like to go."

The woman had nodded. "If you must, you must. I'll say nothing about the fact that I know you're under age."

Lally was posted to a military hospital, No. 4 London General Hospital, just across the river in South London. She found the accommodation for nurses sparse, and she shook a little with nerves before she reported for the first time for duty. The sister was rushed. She had only a few minutes to give to her newest recruit. "You've applied for overseas, I see. Well, you'll see enough of what comes off the troop trains here to get you ready for that." She glanced at the papers in her hand. "The matron at Leeds seems to think quite well of you, Miss Pollock. You'll be here for a few months. Then you'll be posted overseas." She looked sharply at Lally. "You go just

where you're sent. I hope you've not applied for overseas service because you're thinking of following someone to France?" Then another look at Lally seemed to dismiss the thought. "No—I suppose
not. Well, Miss Pollock, I hope you won't regret it. I've done some
time overseas. It's dirty and it's hard. But you've chosen it—so, good
luck. Now report to Staff Nurse Jeffries on Ward Four. Surgical."

The cases were generally worse than she had seen in Leeds. They
came directly off the troop trains, and many still wore the filthy rags
of uniforms that no one had had time to change; many of them died
there, having just made the haven of the English side of the Channel.
The discipline of the military hospital was strict; she found she was
put back to the humble duties of the VAD, allowed only to scrub
and clean, carry away soiled dressings, carry meals, light cigarettes,
and empty ashtrays. She was incredulous to find that at the daily inspection by the M.O. every man who could get out of bed stood
rigidly at attention at the foot of his bed, thermometer in his mouth.
There was a muddle over what VADs were called. They had not
earned the right to be called "Nurse," a privilege jealously guarded
by those who had earned it. "Sister" was an almost unimaginable
height above them. But "Nurse" and "Sister" were used indis-
criminately by the Tommies—though the frown on Sister's face would
check them if she heard the term used to any but her. Outside the
hospital everyone wearing a Red Cross of any sort usually got called
"Sister." "Miss" didn't seem right.

Lally wrote to Black Jack, *I feel such a fraud when someone calls
me "Sister" or "Nurse." But it's hard for the men to tell the
difference. If they're very ill they don't notice that Sister and Staff
Nurse wear a shoulder cape, and of course we don't. They say it's
more relaxed in France; the VADs do more because they're all so
rushed, and the lines get blurred. I'd like to do some dressings, but of
course I'm not trusted to do that. But if all I'm fated to do in this
war is scrub and fetch and carry, then that's what it will be. Someone
has to do it.*

On Lally's off-duty hours she met the Marchioness several times at
a Lyons Corner House near the office in which she worked. Over
weak tea they talked, and Lally felt she was suddenly much closer to
the Marchioness in age. The older woman, she thought, often looked
tired and strained. She headed a section of the Red Cross which attempted to trace men reported missing, most of them believed dead.
"It's depressing work. There's no chance, really, that many of them

can have survived, but it's terrible for the relatives just to be told 'missing.' How? Where? Who saw them last? To know that they're really dead must give a kind of peace—but when whole platoons just disappear, who is there to question? So many unburied, or in mass graves. After the war, we shall have to record and remember all of them. Names on tablets—that's about all we can do." The Marchioness always asked about Black Jack and Alice. "I never did get to Pellham Langley for the shooting. I used to be quite a good shot. Remember me to your father when you write." The lady who had seemed so formidable to Lally during her coming-out season had become almost a friend. They now shared experiences Lally had not imagined before.

Occasionally, when they could arrange their time off together, she met Margaret in London. They went one afternoon to the Savoy for tea. Margaret poked the remains of a cake she had barely touched with the butt of her cigarette. Outraged, Lally wanted to object to this waste of food in wartime, but she hesitated, afraid to make Margaret hostile or defensive. She cherished these few contacts, was reassured that the closeness of their growing up together had not been undermined by the changes in their lives.

"I hate to say it," Margaret confessed, "and I'd only say it to you, Lally, because I know you won't lecture me. But I'm *enjoying* the war. I'm having the time of my life. That's a terrible thing to say when so many are getting killed and injured. But I didn't start the war, did I? I can't do anything more than I'm doing now, which is driving old generals around, to end it. So why shouldn't I enjoy what there is to enjoy? If it had never started, I'd be stuck up there at Pellham Langley, waiting to be invited to other people's houses, and trying to find a chaperone. Thank God, all that's gone. Women are never going to be the same again, are they? After the war, who's going to tell us to go back to our places? They can't very well put us back on the shelf, can they?"

"The next thing," Lally said, "is that we'll have the vote. Have you thought about that?"

Margaret shrugged. "Oh, politics—the suffragette thing. It doesn't interest me much."

"It should, if you don't want to be put back on the shelf."

Margaret looked at her in surprise. "Why, Lally, what's come over you? I didn't think you'd have very strong views on that sort of thing."

"Neither did I. I'm finding out."

Margaret called for the bill. "I'm going on to have drinks at a house on Park Lane. Want to come? It's one of those things where it doesn't matter if you bring someone extra. I'm meeting someone there."

"I have to be back on duty at ten."

"Well—you have plenty of time."

Lally thought of the wards, generally quiet at night unless there was the unexpected arrival of a troop train; she thought of the sparse little cubicle she inhabited in the nurses' quarters. The thought of a few hours of gaiety was tempting. She was wearing her uniform. "Is it all right to come . . . like this?"

"Of course. Patriotic. Everyone does it. In fact, Lally, you look better in that uniform than in your own clothes. If you'd just lose a bit of weight you'd be . . . well, attractive."

Lally remembered the three cakes she had eaten, the sandwiches which had preceded them. "I think I was born fat." Then she laughed. "No, that isn't true, is it? I nearly starved before Father found me."

Margaret, unexpectedly, touched her hand. "Just as well for all of us he did. Now, come on . . . you'll enjoy it. It's quite the thing now. Just drinks, and then everyone goes off somewhere else for dinner. Easy way to entertain."

And so Lally attended her first cocktail party. She didn't know her hostess, and no one introduced them; no one seemed to care. There were, of course, a large number of military uniforms; people who appeared to be total strangers talked to each other with great animation. Lally cautiously sipped a gin and orange. Then close by her ear, above the level of the noise, a vaguely familiar voice. "Lally—why it's you! Never expected to find you at something like this."

Sandy West—no, Sandy Pollock—was smoking through a long cigarette holder. "Have you heard from Jon lately? He's not a very good correspondent, is he? But then, I'm not either. I've been so busy . . ."

Lally knew that Sandy's work with the Red Cross largely consisted of meeting troop trains—those with men returning on leave, and those bearing the wounded—at Victoria Station, and handing out cups of tea and cigarettes. Now that Lally had herself seen the new casualties from the troop trains she had given a reluctant respect to Sandy's fortitude. It took a kind of courage to be able to face some of those terrible wounds and not visibly flinch. Jon had returned to France just a week after they had been married. Sandy had rented a flat of her own in London. *I intend to have it ready just in case Jon gets a short leave,* she had written Black Jack. Black Jack had been a little puzzled at the arrangement, and then had shrugged and laughed. "I'm just old-fashioned, I suppose. I don't know why I should expect Jon's wife to come and live with us. After all, what would she do with herself? Better to keep occupied." Unspoken was the hope that she would be occupied with a pregnancy, but that had not happened. Lally, looking at her closely, thought she looked prettier than ever, but seemed to have lost a little weight. There were enchanting shadows, almost lines, under her cheekbones.

"You have met Harry Gaunt, haven't you? Harry got a bit of leave, and he's helping to cheer me up. I saw Margaret come in. How is . . . ? How is Mr. Pollock?" She had hesitated about what she should call Black Jack. They didn't know each other well enough to have decided such small but important things.

She neither listened to nor tried to hear Lally's reply. Already she was talking across her shoulder to someone else. Beside Lally, Captain Henry Gaunt said, "May I bring you another drink, Miss Pollock? You probably don't remember, but we met when you and Margaret had your coming-out ball. Great affair. Best of the season, I thought."

Lally looked up from her empty glass. The coming-out ball had been like all the others, and his was one of the forgotten, nameless line of faces. But it was a particularly good-looking face; the mouth was redeemed from severity by a rather sensuous tilt at the corners. "What do you hear from old Jon? By all accounts, he's a rotten correspondent."

"Not much," Lally admitted. She was staring at the ribbons on his chest. The Gallipoli campaign was one, and was one of the others a D.S.O.? If the war went on much longer they would all have their breasts lined with ribbons. "A drink, Miss Pollock?" he urged gently.

Perhaps it was because she hadn't heard recently from Jon and didn't expect to hear much in the future; perhaps it was because she found herself unable to put together a satisfactory reply to Thomas Handley's last letter, written from his convalescent hospital near Bristol; perhaps it was because she hated the thought of returning, alone, to duty in the hospital when the evening was just beginning for almost everyone else in the room that she handed over her empty glass. "Just a small one, please."

She was two minutes late on duty, and was reprimanded by Sister. And did she imagine that Sister's nose twitched just faintly? She turned away hurriedly, afraid she smelled of gin. The first man she approached to take a temperature grinned at her; he had been there almost a month, both legs riddled with shrapnel; he would never go back to the front. "Been out on the town, have you, Nurse? That's a girl. Live it up while you can, that's what I say."

She smiled back. They were forbidden such badinage with the patients, but it was a rule everyone broke when Sister was not present. "You know, Nurse, you've got gorgeous teeth, you have. All your own, are they?"

It was a very backhanded compliment, but Lally felt absurdly pleased.

Gradually, and rather grudgingly, she was allowed to assist with dressings. She received her innoculations for overseas service, and hoped it would be France, rather than a hospital in the Middle East, or a hospital ship. But you went, as Sister had warned, where you were sent.

There had been only one half day with Thomas Handley, and Lally had lied and said she was going to meet Lady Ross. Thomas had been discharged from the convalescent hospital, had spent five days at home with his family, and had taken the last two days of his leave to come to London. With only a few hours off duty before she had to be back in the nurses' quarters, she had gone to see Thomas. They had met at what was supposed to be a *thé dansant* at the Café Royal, but they didn't dance. Lally was forbidden to dance in uniform. She drank tea, and for once the cakes did not tempt her. There was no awkwardness in their silence, but there was pain. The day after tomorrow Thomas would return to France.

Gently she had tried to push his signet ring across the table. Quite firmly he pushed it back. "I meant it for you, Lally. I want you to keep it."

She remembered how he had restored her pride, made her feel desirable and wanted on that night when Jon had passed forever beyond her hope. She gazed at him there, and wondered why he bothered with her now. But his face was intent, earnest. "Remember how we drank that night to reunions, and no farewells. I meant it, Lally. I mean to come back. I mean to survive. I want to really live the life I talked about. *Do* something. Have you ever wanted to travel—I mean, really travel? Not art galleries. Places. Samarkand. Peking. Tibet, even. Mysterious places. Someday we'll have a journey together, Lally. I'll think of it when I'm back there. When it's very cold and my feet are in inches of filthy water, I'll think of the warmth of deserts. Great, untraveled deserts. I think you'd manage rather well with a camel, Lally."

Suddenly she burst into laughter. The tension was broken. "I'm afraid the porters—or whatever one has in the desert—might mistake me for the camel."

He threw back his head and laughed with her, so loudly that the people at the nearby tables turned to look at them. It was a familiar wartime scene, except that the girl in the VAD uniform was stout, and the young officer was romantically handsome. Thomas raised his arm to attract a waiter. "To hell with all this tea and cakes business, Lally. I want to drink champagne with you again. To drink to reunions and no farewells."

The waiter brought the champagne and glasses, and then said to Thomas quietly, "I'm sorry, sir. We have to go to the basement. There are zeppelins reported overhead."

"Right," Thomas said, and rose immediately. He thrust a five-pound note into the waiter's hand. "Then please be so good as to bring us another bottle of champagne. Might as well try to enjoy the time."

"Quite, sir." Officers at the end of their leave were often given to such extravagances.

They sat in the basement with all the other people. They heard no bombs fall, and the building didn't shake. But she and Thomas, off in an alcove where sacks of sugar were stored, drank to each other. "Lally, I wish it could have been something else. But you're not the sort of girl one takes to a hotel. That night . . . I can't ever forget it. It was the—"

She touched his hand. "Thomas—no more. Reunions, no farewells. And fill the glasses, you idiot. Now you've spent all this money . . ." She looked at him in the half-light, across the champagne carelessly poured and frothing too much. "Samarkand . . . Tibet . . . the hot desert. Whenever it's cold, I'll wish a desert for you, Thomas."

They talked, and finished the two bottles of champagne. They were allowed to go; the zeppelins had dropped some bombs in South London. Somehow Thomas found a taxi and came with her back to the hospital. She made him stop the taxi a long way down the street from the nurses' quarters. "We're not supposed to be alone with men, you know. I told Sister . . ."

His lips were on hers. "Keep the ring, Lally. I intend to come back to claim it." It was, she thought, perhaps the usual thing said on the eve of returning to France. She would be a memory of something warm and alive, something clean, even fragrant. She did not draw back from his kiss. The taxi driver was patient. She was handed out of the cab by Thomas, and she tottered a little as she went down the street. It was as well, she thought, that she didn't have night duty. The taxi drove slowly past her. She saw Thomas wave. Was it always like this when men were posted back overseas? She sat on her bed and rubbed the signet ring. Of course it would never happen. There would never be a fabled journey. There never would be Samarkand or Tibet. But one could think, and remember. Toast to reunions and no farewells.

"Pollock, it's lights-out in five minutes," one of the other VADs called out crossly. "I don't want you tripping around in the dark. I think you've had a bit to drink, my girl. Better forget whoever it was. He probably won't make it back."

* * *

Lally was given a three-day leave, and went to Grangewick. Black Jack was working long days, traveling between the mills and the mines, Leeds, Bradford, Sheffield, Port Talbot in Wales. Alice was lonely. On one dazzlingly bright winter day Lally took the pony and trap and drove Alice to Pellham Langley. The lawns were plowed under for vegetables, the hedges of the topiary garden unclipped. Alice was distressed because she could barely recognize Dog and Cat and Rabbit; she did not know any of the officers now convalescent in the big house, and they, not knowing that she belonged there, were indifferent to her presence. She wept in Lally's arms. "No one talks to me."

They returned to a tired Black Jack. Cook had prepared a special dinner, Billings offered the best wine. Alice looked lovely, but still distraught. "Everything's changed. No one talks to me," she repeated.

"It will all come right again, my darling," Black Jack said. For the first time Lally sensed that he wasn't quite sure that it would. "If only the Americans would come in," he said to Lally later, as they sat before the fire, both needing sleep, but neither wanting to break the thread of companionship.

"They will, when the German submarines have sunk enough of their ships."

She was only repeating what Brock Weymouth had said to her. He had impudently telephoned her at the hospital one afternoon, incurring Sister's wrath, and perhaps it was only his American accent which saved him and Lally from a formidable dressing-down. After all, who could expect Americans to know or respect the rigid rules which governed the nurses' lives. And as any intelligent person knew, the supply of American war materiel across the Atlantic was vital. Only in the spirit of goodwill was Lally permitted to speak to him for two minutes on the ward telephone, just long enough to agree to go to dinner with him. "It's your dear old American uncle, Lally . . ."

"Yes, Uncle," she said dutifully.

He waited outside the nurses' quarters, the Hispano Suiza drawing many of the nurses to the windows to see which of their number would emerge to be driven away in it. Lally wondered if the story about it being borrowed was true; it seemed always available. Who could ever know about Brock Weymouth? He seemed to be into everything, and yet he belonged nowhere. He lived in hotels in London and New York and Washington. He knew a lot of people. He never talked of them as friends.

He took her to dine at the Ritz. He was well-known, because he stayed there. Evidently he tipped well; the head waiter bowed to him, and fussed over Lally's comfort. Lally looked around at the splendor of the dining room, the fashionably dressed people, and said simply, "Why me?"

Brock looked up from the menu, which was not noticeably lavish compared to what it had once been, but which looked like a feast to Lally. "And why not? Margaret told me you're slaving over there in that hospital, and the food is uneatable. So . . ."

Lally found she was laughing. "I wish I looked as if I were starving, Brock."

He smiled briefly. "You're a good sort, Lally."

"Yes—I know. I often wish I weren't."

"What would you be if you weren't you?"

"Me?" She waited until he had tasted the wine which had just been poured. When her own glass was filled she tasted, and tasted again. It was wonderful—dry, pure, clean. "Why, I think I'd be slightly wicked, to start with. I wouldn't be good-natured at all. I'd be beautiful. I'd be slim and golden-haired, and I'd have golden eyes, like a cat's . . ." She broke off, sipping the wine again, hoping he hadn't noticed that she had very nearly described Margaret.

They dined at a leisurely pace, Lally relishing the attention lavished on her by the maître d'hôtel, the food, the sight of beautifully dressed women. It was possible to forget wartime London in that gilded room. Brock questioned her about nursing, about what she expected when she was posted overseas. "I expect nothing. We just do as we're told. I hope to help a bit. It was safer—and nicer—at Leeds. But I felt I was too far away from everything."

"Your father must miss you—and Alice must too."

"They must both miss Jon and Margaret. I can't always stay at home."

He said very little about what he was doing in England. She had the impression that he crossed the Atlantic frequently. That in itself was no small act of courage when ships were being torpedoed by German submarines in an effort to cut off the supply of goods and materiel to the Allies. But with Brock Weymouth it seemed that courage was of secondary importance to the fact that he was doing business. Whatever risks had to be run were all part of the game. And the rewards were for the quick and the daring. And he liked the rewards very much, Lally knew. He liked the world of this gilded room.

He drove her back across the river to the nurses' quarters with just ten minutes to spare before the curfew hour. She kept the carnation the maître d'hôtel had laid beside her plate. She craned to see herself in the small mirror on her cubicle wall, wearing the only "dressed up" dress she had brought with her, left over from her season, and already looking childish. Even that would be left behind when she was posted overseas. She put the carnation against her hair, white against its darkness, and for just a minute wondered what it would be like to be the person she had described to Brock Weymouth.

I I

Dear Father and Alice, I'm at the 34th General Hospital between Boulogne and Abbeville. She wasn't sure that the censor wouldn't strike the names of the two towns. *Things are rather different here.*

*The main hospital is an old abbey—cloisters and all. The refectory
and chapel and any other room big enough have been turned into
general wards. The monks' cells—that's what I suppose they were—
are side wards for the very seriously ill, and officers. Though sometimes they all get mixed up. The RAMC had taken over the gardens
and fields of the abbey to accommodate quarters for the doctors and
nursing staff, and for extra wards. Mostly the wards are just huts,
and the doctors live under half canvas. All the nursing staff at the
moment live in bell tents. All the washing and toilet facilities for us
are in one hut. There are duck boards laid between the huts and
tents, because they tell me when it rains, the ground turns into a bog.*
Lally pondered the few sentences she had written. "Things are rather
different here" was as much as she would permit herself to write,
thinking of the censor, and of the edict about writing home the dis-
couraging facts of the state of things in France. Things being
different meant that the military hospital in London, in memory, became a palace of efficiency and order. Gone were the great linen
cupboards, and the white covers on the beds. Gray and red blankets
and any makeshift arrangement for medical facilities had to suffice.
Sister's room was a structure of packing cases at the end of a ward.
The sterilizing unit boiled behind her. The linen was stored in packing cases, and they were lucky when there was enough of it. And the
distinction between real nurses and VADs had blurred to the point
that the VADs were pressed into doing whatever they could, and
calling Sister or Staff Nurse only when the condition of a patient was
beyond them. *I have a sense of being useful here,* she added cautiously.

She was remembering the strangeness of the first day. For the first
time she was leaving Victoria Station with the troops. She had telephoned Black Jack only the day before with the news that she was
posted, hoping he would not come, but he had come, and stood
there, waving to her as the train had pulled out. "I'll send parcels,
Lally. Ask for anything you want. Come home soon—safely, my darling." As if it were an afterthought, he added, "I think I'll telephone
Lady Ross. If I'm going to shed tears, it might as well be with someone else who loves you."

At Calais they had to wait for berthing, for the troops going back
to England, for the trains of wounded to pass. It took all night, and
she and three other VADs had to find their way to the 34th General
Hospital. They got there late the next afternoon, hungry, dirty, tired.

But the faces of the other nurses they saw looked even more tired. She was directed to the bell tent she was to share with another VAD. A neat little head raised itself off the pillow of a cot bed as she entered. "Oh, you 'ave arrived. Said you'd be here yesterday."

"We got delayed—"

Somehow Lally had known she was talking to a veteran. This young woman had been out here a long time—as time counted in a war two and a half years old. It could be seen in the wary wisdom of her eyes. They were gray-blue eyes behind fair lashes. She had a sharp Cockney accent; she had a pert, rather pretty little face under a mass of red hair; freckles sprinkled her fair skin. Her hands, late in March, still bore the chilblains of winter, the chilblains Lally came to know as part of the misery of those winters.

The sharpness in the voice softened. "Well, you just got 'ere in time for supper. I'm on night duty the next four weeks. I think you've got the same . . . the girl who was with me, Marjory, had to be sent home. Just got too run-down . . ."

Lally began to stow the regulation uniform, the dreadful underwear they were allowed, in two wooden crates. A sharp little wind blew under the edge of the bell tent. The young woman pushed back the blankets and rose from her cot. She offered her hand. "Barlow's my name. Susie Barlow."

"Lally Pollock." Lally found she was looking down on her companion. The neat little head was balanced by a small, neat body. The eyes were intelligent and observing.

"First time overseas, ain't it? Bet you lied about your age."

Lally nodded. "They don't seem to mind now. They used to be very strict about it. Now they need the help, and if you can get your parents to agree, they're glad to have you—lies and all. I've only got one parent—a father. He's not really my father, I'm adopted." Might as well get the story told, she thought. The relationship between her and the rest of the Pollock family could be confusing.

Swiftly, Susie Barlow was getting into the cumbersome, rather ugly uniform of the VADs. The skirt was only two inches from the ground, by regulation, and Lally was already aware of the dirt accumulated on hers. "Hope you brought lots of soap and flea bags. It's 'ard—hard—not to get lice. The men come in crawling with 'em."

The intimacy Lally had rather dreaded sharing with a stranger was made comfortable by the warm directness of Susie Barlow. She was willing, indeed seemed anxious, to share the hard-won knowledge of the eighteen months she had spent at the hospital. "I went in right away. After Mons, that was—'ad me brother killed at Mons. And a chap I knew—well, 'e was a mate of me brother's—'e and I 'ad sort of fixed up to get married. They were both in the Regular Army, see, so they got sent to Belgium right away. Remember the Kaiser called 'em 'a contemptible little army'? Well, the two of 'em, they were 'Old Contemptibles.' Both of 'em got the Mons Star." It was all said in a rush, as if she had to get it over with. "So that's why I'm 'ere. Couldn't stick it back there after they both got killed. It made me sort of mad inside to think of the Kaiser saying that about Bill and Jack. So I decided that there was going to be another Barlow to fill the place of the one that went. Though one of me young brothers 'as just turned eighteen, and *'e's* joined up. I told 'im 'e was mad. If 'e'd ever seen what it's like 'ere . . . well, 'e'll find out."

She wasn't, Lally realized, the usual type encountered among the VADs, who were almost always girls and women drawn from a comfortable middle-class background, most of them never having done a day's heavy work in their lives before they suddenly became scrubbers and cleaners, and part-time nurses. While Susie efficiently helped Lally stow the remainder of the few possessions she was allowed, the stream of talk went on. "I'm East End," she said, almost defiantly. "I was brought up in the Mile End Road. Some of them 'ere sort of look down their noses at me. I was in service, you see. Second parlor maid promoted from the kitchen because 'er Ladyship thought I could be trusted to dust the china without breaking it. 'ad a bloody awful old tyrant of a butler who made our lives 'ell. I stuck it a few years, and then went back home and started up a little dressmaking business in the front room—it wasn't ever used, in any case. 'andy with a needle, I am. 'er Ladyship wanted me for a personal maid, but I wasn't 'aving none of *that*. I'd 'ad enough of being ordered around."

"But you joined the VADs. *We* get ordered around."

A smile broke out on Susie's face; when she smiled she had a kind of saucy irreverence. "Yes, must be as mad as me brother. But I didn't 'ave a thing to lose, you see. Can always go back to dressmaking if I come through this business. Just couldn't get used to the idea of Bill and Jack going together, like that. Same company, you see. All wiped out. When the news come—came—" Lally noticed later that Susie strove to correct her own grammar, as she strove to add the "h's" to words. "I didn't even finish the dress I was working on.

Just marched straight out the door and, when I come to me senses, I was in the VADs. Nearly signed up as a Special Military Probationer, but that would've meant waiting a whole year before I could get overseas. So, 'ere I am. I suppose *you* were brought up posh. Sound like it."

"Susie, I—"

"Oh, don't worry. You're not like some of 'em. Good sort, I'd say. I'll steer you right—keep you on the good side of Sister, if I can. 'ere!—who are this lot?" She had picked up a framed snapshot Lally had taken, back in those early August days of 1914, of Black Jack and Alice perched on the rock above the waterfall, Margaret and Jon seated in the heather at their feet. "Your family? I thought so. Gorgeous looking, aren't they? All of them. And you're the odd one out. 'ere, I didn't mean to be offensive. Just—being adopted, and all." After only a fractional pause she added, "Well, 'urry up. You don't want to miss supper, do you? It ain't the Ritz, but it's all we got."

Susie became her mentor and guardian through the next weeks. "Watch this sister who's just coming back from leave. Proper old cow, she is. Thinks she's back in Blighty, the way she wants things done. Seems to think we 'ave proper things to do it with, too. Watch out if she ever lets you 'elp with a dressing. Whatever goes wrong, it's your fault."

But Susie Barlow had a touch with the men that even Sister had to respect. Lally followed her through the wards that were their responsibility. "Give us a fag, Nurse," was the usual plea from the men, while they grinned at her. When they were being less respectful, they called her "Ginger," or "Red." It was Susie who laid one restraining hand on Lally's arm before they entered a ward on Lally's second day at the hospital. "Better turn your nose off 'ere, Pollock. Gas gangrene. Most of them 'ave 'ad amputations, and it wasn't enough. Day or two, that's all they've got. Doctors can't cut away enough. Look cheerful, Pollock. Don't want their last sight on earth to be a down-in-the-mouth VAD, do you? Your dad'd be ashamed."

It was Susie who steadied Lally through those first weeks while she grew used to the sights and the sounds and the smells. She had a way of nodding toward the photo of Black Jack. "Your dad'd expect it, Pollock. Mind you, we're not seeing things as bad as they 'ave been. The French have been taking the big stick over at Verdun. Wouldn't doubt, though, we'll get some of it pretty soon. Seems to me these damn generals are always talking about some big push that's supposed to end it. Load of rubbish, if you ask me."

The cold spring gave way to the early days of summer. As Lally saw the stream of men who continued to come down the line from the forward dressing stations, the casualty clearing stations, often with only a field dressing slapped on their wounds, she began to wonder how much greater the numbers might be, and of Susie's dire prophecies. If there had been time to be frightened, appalled, dismayed, she would have been, but there was no time. The hours between duty were given over to the endless task of trying to keep clean. And sometimes when she fell exhausted into sleep would come the bugle for "Fall In," which meant another convoy of wounded had arrived, or was expected. Everything was short. They were short of beds, blankets, dressings, drugs—most of all, short of space. The old buildings of the abbey had stretched to accommodate all they could. The rows of crude huts which served as wards continued to grow. And still the wounded waited, laid out on stretchers in the cloisters, waiting for a doctor, a bed, an operating room. Sometimes they died there.

Lally kept most of this out of her letters to Black Jack. She told the story of Susie Barlow. *You'll have to meet her, Father. She's just about the best I've ever known. She's like one of those tough little London sparrows. Cheeky and resilient.*

Margaret wrote, *I'm rather jealous of your Susie Barlow. I didn't ever think you'd like anyone more than me.* But one day a parcel arrived from Margaret addressed to Susie.

Then there was the day Lally wrote, *I had a wonderful day last week with Jon! His battalion was stood down for rest, and he got two days' leave. Sister let me have a day's leave to meet him. I can't say where. He's well, but tired. They're all tired. He could have done with a good clean-up. We really had only a few hours together, and all we did was talk about all of you. He thought there might just be a chance of some real leave soon. But experienced officers and men are getting rather scarce.* Why say more? She saw them die every day, and she knew the casualty lists in the newspapers told the truth beyond her power. *He misses Sandy terribly.* It hurt to write that, but it would be expected. *Keep on sending him socks and as many parcels as the Red Cross will allow. There's always someone who needs every single thing in the parcel. Tell Alice to keep on knitting his scarf. He'll need it this winter. But perhaps after this big push we're expecting, it will all be over.* She no longer believed that, but she had to write something. She didn't mention the zeppelin raid which had damaged one corner of the main hospital building. Black Jack had enough to worry about. *Must end now. We've been put on alert to expect heavy casualties tomorrow. The hospital has been cleared of every patient except those too ill to be moved. So I'm writing this while there's still time.* The letter was dated June 30, 1916.

The generals had scheduled the beginning of the battle of the Somme for July 1. Both she and Jon had sensed that there was no real hope that he would get his leave in England. It had been a comforting lie to write it.

* * *

The dawn came early in that high summer. Lally lay awake listening to the boom of the great guns. For a whole week the most intensive barrage they had ever heard had been laid down on the German lines. They had expected the first attack to come at dawn, as was usual, but the nurses were at breakfast at seven-thirty when the first gigantic explosion came which signaled the beginning of the battle of the Somme. They learned later, from the lips of the wounded men they tended, from more official sources, from the newspapers, that there had been five huge land mines dug under the German lines. But the Germans had dug their own shelters deep into the chalky earth, and they had come through the barrage almost unscathed. The great artillery barrage of the past week, which had been intended to blow the trenches to pieces, to blast aside the barbed wire, had done very little. They also heard that the British infantry had been ordered to come out of the trenches and to advance at the ceremonial step of one yard per second burdened with equipment about one third of their own weight. The Scots troops came out to the sound of bagpipes, the Eighth East Surreys came out kicking footballs. It was as if, Lally thought, the generals were determined to play some obscene war game.

Later, when there was time to count, and the dispatches were filed, they knew it had been the bloodiest day in British history. With awe and shock they spoke of the figures—almost twenty thousand dead on that one day, and some thirty-seven thousand wounded, few prisoners. But this was later, when the facts were admitted, the figures actually given. On that day itself, and in the days and weeks following, all Lally knew was that the stream of casualties from the front was unending. She hardly remembered that she had worried about how well or how badly she would acquit herself, how she would stand up to it. What mattered was to remain standing on her feet. She grew used, and then almost hardened, to the sound of the moaning, sometimes screaming men; she saw them die while she tried desperately, and too often alone, to dress wounds. And if she was numbed by fatigue, she was aware that the doctors never seemed to leave their operating rooms. The medical orderlies ran with the stretchers. Lally saw the hospital chaplain, totally unqualified, administering crude anesthetics to have the patient ready when a table should become free. She found herself treating the less desperate cases, the ones that might hold a few hours until their turn came for the operating room. She knew that she did less well by them than they deserved, but there was no one else to do it. All the nurses were the same as she; no one stood still, no one had any time. She learned quickly, and by experience, and she was aware that it was often at the expense of the men she was tending. The beginning of the battle of the Somme was only the beginning.

III

Lally seemed to lose track of time after that. Hours on duty, hours off duty in which to fall into an exhausted sleep. But the "Fall In" bugle continued to sound remorselessly. The British advanced on a fifteen-mile front toward Bapaume; the French objective was Péronne.

A letter arrived from Black Jack. *For God's sake, Lally, how is it with you? I'm out of my mind with worry. You don't write. Neither does Jon. I'm sure he's in it. . . . If he's still alive, which hardly seems possible.* After that, she tried to find time to write short notes; it was selfish to leave him to worry, though she could say nothing to help him. How to say that she was alive, but that the hospital might be bombed? How not to let him know how frightful the conditions really were in which Jon was fighting, how dreadful the wounds?

The days passed into the nights; as she dated her notes to Black Jack she noticed that the days had slid into the weeks. The bright spark of Susie Barlow's energy did not seem to burn low. It sustained Lally, and she began to rely on it. Through July and August the battle went on, the Allies pushing forward, though with heartbreaking slowness. A letter came from Thomas. Lally realized that he must be in the sector where the fighting was fiercest. It could not have passed through a censor's hands, or someone had decided to let what he said go through. It might have been considered defeatist, even treasonable, by anyone who had not spent time in the front lines. *I beg you to get out. Get out by whatever means you can. It must be easier for a nurse. You don't have to shoot yourself in the foot. Why give your life uselessly?* In the little time she had to write an answer she pretended she had not understood his message.

She began to be convinced that they would all die. There was no way out. They would all die as she saw the men die, the ones who lived long enough to get to the dressing stations, to the operating tables, to the passage across the Channel to England, and who still died. Of those left on the field of battle, unburied, she tried not to think. She reached the point of fatigue when she ceased to look at every face with fear, lest it should be Jon or Thomas.

Death and dying had a sickening stench; it pervaded everything. Her uniforms, her underwear were soaked in it, dyed in it. She scrubbed her hands and nails cruelly, but still they smelled of death. Everything she touched carried the contagion. It wasn't long after the battle had begun that she woke one night in that hot, close bell tent; even in the warmth of the night there was the old smell of damp and of death, of foul air, air which was tainted. Her body, aching for rest, was the battered stick it had been when Black Jack had picked it up. The worst terror of those weeks and months was sleep itself, and the return to the place she had known before Black Jack brought her to light and warmth.

The awful smell touched the food, and she choked on it. She knew she had to eat because she had, literally, to be able to stand on her feet, but still she choked on her food, and pushed it aside.

" 'ere, ain't you going to eat that?" Susie demanded. "Your dad'd be awful worried if he knew you weren't eating." Susie fussed and clucked, and somehow found time to take tucks in Lally's uniforms, which she saw were trailing in the dirt. Her swift, clever hands transformed the shapeless garments. "No need to go around looking a disgrace."

Lally drank a lot of tea, and for the first time smoked a cigarette, and then more of them. She and Susie were sent to Le Havre for a few days' rest, and still Lally was unable to eat the meals some of the restaurants were able, amazingly, to produce. Officers talked to them in the restaurants, took them to places which still had a small reserve of Calvados. They were strictly forbidden contact with the opposite sex, as the regulations put it, but more than one regulation was broken in the chaos created by the battle of the Somme. They exchanged names and field addresses; some of the officers wrote when they returned to the trenches, some they never heard of again. The brief period of leave did no good for Lally. She dreaded sleep because of the dreams and the return to the dark place, and still she could force down only the smallest amount of food.

She barely noticed when summer turned to autumn and then advanced toward winter. One terrible, hopeless song was being sung. Lally hated and feared it; it brought only the picture of the lines of walking wounded, leading, helping each other, endlessly shuffling toward rescue and comfort that was never sufficient.

> *There's a long, long trail a-winding*
> *Into the land of my dreams . . .*

It rained, and it grew cold. That was the only way Lally knew the seasons had changed. She had stopped even looking for Jon and Thomas among the men who passed through the hospital. The nurses all went the rounds of the wards, looking at the lists of names, but by now it was routine. Sometimes they found a friend, someone known to them—or else another nurse recognized a name, and the word was passed. But Lally stopped looking; she carried on with her work and gained experience in the hardest and the cruelest way.

She had a note from Jon. His battalion had been sent back to the Ypres salient to recover, to rest, to absorb reinforcements. *There's hardly a soul of the original battalion left. They're sending us raw recruits who'll last only a few days.*

And in November the great battle of the Somme, which had been meant to finish the hostilities, petered out pitifully in mud and rain. It was reckoned in the newspapers that the Allies had gained one hundred and twenty-five square miles of territory, but had gained no target of prime strategic importance. The maximum advance had been about seven miles. And for this, Lally read, the British had lost more than four hundred thousand lives, the French almost two hundred thousand. No one was sure about the German losses, but some correspondents put them as high as half a million. It was as if the world, Lally thought, had blown itself apart in these few blood-sodden square miles. Could there be any young men left alive?

The great guns had now been reduced almost to a growling rumble. Why shell, she thought, what had already been shelled a thousand times? She read Black Jack's letters dully, and could not reply.

"Miss Pollock, you are to go on extended leave," Sister said. "We have no time to nurse you." Lally looked down wonderingly at her finger, which had turned septic from contact with any one of hundreds of festering wounds. Only Sister and Staff Nurse wore gloves for doing a dressing. But could such a little thing send her back? She felt stupid, foolish. The tone of Sister's voice somehow indicated that the whole, useless, senseless failure had been Lally's doing. A little more strength and the Allies would have broken through, and the Germans routed. Lack of strength was a terrible failing. Lally wondered how badly she had failed.

"Wish I'd 'alf your luck," Susie said cheerfully as she helped her pack. "Pity there isn't time to do something with that old uniform. But still, your dad'll see you nicely knitted up again. Get that finger well, my girl, or you'll lose it. And eat a little, will you?"

As Lally laced up her boots on the morning she went on leave she noticed for the first time that her feet seemed to slosh about in them, as if they'd been made for someone else. She hitched her skirt up with her belt, and it still trailed on the ground.

I V

Black Jack met her, not in Leeds, but in London. She saw his face through the sea of all the others at Victoria Station. Then the tears she had not wept through all the months started. She clung to him, saying nothing, unable to say anything. He himself said little, picked up her bag, and led her to the taxi he had somehow managed to get and to keep waiting. They drove to the Savoy.

How strange it all looked. How clean and ordinary—and somehow extraordinary. There was carpet underfoot, and bellboys—yes, still young boys. There were still young boys left in the world with faces untouched by battle. There were young boys and middle-aged and old men. And Black Jack was no longer black, but graying.

He led her into the sitting room of the suite he had, and once again his arms enfolded her. "Oh, Lally, love—what have they done to you?"

"To me? Nothing. I'm perfectly well. There are so many who

aren't well—never will be. Father, it was unbelievable. The wounded just kept coming and coming . . . and finally I suppose I didn't do very well, because they had to send me on leave. It isn't just this finger. The nurses get septic fingers all the time."

He turned her gently toward a mirror. "Lally," he repeated. "What did they do to you?"

She walked forward curiously. How long was it since she had taken time to look in the little mirror in the nurses' toilet hut? Now a long mirror reflected a stranger; who was this stranger in the almost ludicrously flapping clothes?—she wore only one glove because the other hand was bandaged. The reflection looked as if it belonged to some clown in a circus. Why hadn't she noticed that her clothes almost fell off her? She didn't recognize this person with the sharply etched cheekbones, and the eyes sunk in dark sockets. More than anything, as she stared into the big mirror, she thought she resembled nothing so much as a gaunt scarecrow in ludicrous rags. She burst out laughing.

"I do look a sight, don't I?"

* * *

She could not get used to it. When she lay in the huge bathtub, her bandaged hand propped on the side, she stared at her body, which seemed to waver gently under the water, and she did not know it. The very luxury of the place also seemed strange, even though it was what she had always known at Pellham Langley. She wrapped the bath sheet around her, and looked at the unfamiliar face again in a mirror. Hollows had appeared at her throat, her neck was longer. The black hair, piled high to keep it out of the water, made her seem inches taller. Black Jack had brought down some of her clothes from Grangewick, but nothing could be used except a dressing robe, which she gathered about her with a belt. It still trailed on the floor, as her uniform had. Dressed that way, she went into the sitting room to try to eat the lunch Black Jack had ordered. She warily sipped the wine, and poked at the salmon. Was it possible there were still things like this? She did not trust them. She ate very little, and then only to please Black Jack. The food had an odd taste. Not quite as bad as that she had tried to choke down at the hospital, but not good enough to want to make her eat more.

While she played with the food, Black Jack was on the telephone; he was making appointments for her with court dressmakers, milliners, shoemakers. She protested, and wondered how all these things could still be available in times of such shortage.

"There are always these things, Lally. They're mostly kept out of sight. But I haven't been dealing in cloth all my life and not found out who these people are, and what they will do for me. You can't go trailing around the way you are. And you've *earned* the lot!"

A doctor summoned by the hotel came to lance and dress her finger. "Soak it twice a day in a saline solution. I think you can probably manage to dress it rather better than I can." He looked at her sharply. "And get some rest."

Someone arrived with a coat and dress and hat, took some tucks by hand in it, just enough to enable her to get into a taxi, and to the dressmaker's establishment. Black Jack insisted on accompanying her. "My daughter needs everything," he said to the *directrice* who attended them. "Lingerie, dresses, coats, hats, shoes. At once. Tell all these people to bring the things here. She must have something to walk out of here in, and she must have a dress to wear tonight. The rest can wait until tomorrow."

"Impossible," the woman said. She spread her hands. "In a few hours? Impossible!"

Black Jack stared at her. "I'm sure, madame, you would not like suddenly to find that Brearley's in Bradford just couldn't supply you with that handsome velvet you rely on. And Kemply Brothers might find that bolts of a fine worsted had somehow been lost. Of course, if it's your French silk . . . well, even in wartime Lyons has a way of knowing what goes on in Yorkshire."

The woman's face tightened with anger. Then she signaled to the *vendeuse*. "Make sure that Mr. Pollock has everything. Everything that is available, that is."

Lally caught her glance as she left; she had looked at Black Jack with a kind of hatred, but also with respect.

* * *

Black Jack watched untiringly. With the permission of the ladies, he smoked, and he watched. Time and again Lally came out from behind the silk-faced screen to the long mirrors which showed front and back and sides. The gowns were lifted, pulled in, pinned. An elderly woman knelt on the floor, complaining that no one made clothes properly any more, pulled the hems into the right place, glaring up with loathing at the *vendeuse*. None of these gowns had been

meant for sale; they were for the models to wear, and for the ladies
to order from. But now they were taken from the rack and fitted for
Lally. And Lally fitted them.

She had always been quite tall, but few people had noticed because her height had been cloaked in flesh. The women became so
unconscious of Black Jack's presence that they talked before him
freely. "A corset?—no, no. Unnecessary. Things are different these
days. Mademoiselle has no need . . . oh, very well, the tiniest thing.
Perhaps just to lift the bosom up a little." The colors flashed by—
green and blue and a sort of peacock color. He insisted on the
brightest colors there were. Too long Lally had dressed in nonde-
script colors so that people would notice her less. Now he saw Lally
infinitely mirrored in dozens of angles. He wondered about this dark-
haired, pale-skinned young woman who had come back to him—a
woman with intense dark eyes almost too large for her face, with en-
trancing hollows under the cheekbones, a beautiful jawline, with lips
sensuously molded because the flesh had fallen away, revealing them.
Almost a beauty, but not quite in the conventional mode. The face
was slightly austere, except for the lips; it had an edge of wariness
about it, the look of knowledge which had taken away its youthful
bloom. But Lally had lived through how many nights since she had
gone to France? She had been older than her age when he had picked
her from under the horses' feet that night in Leeds; the time in
France had aged her in ways that were immeasurable.

And in the long time he sat, watching, smoking, pleased as the
milliner arrived, and hats were matched with coats, and the shoe-
maker clucked over various sizes and styles, Black Jack began to
remember other women he had loved. He remembered Latitia, who
wore clothes with immense confidence, and gave them added style;
he remembered Alice Trimble, who had bloomed from a quiet brown
hen to an elegant, lavender-clad lady. He remembered shining rows
of pearls, and radiant complexions—amber eyes, and soft brown eyes,
luxuriant hair. He remembered the scent of loved bodies.

"Father—we're ready now."

He started abruptly from his doze; ash was sprinkled down his
waistcoat. He looked up at her, and smiled at what he saw. "You are
beautiful, my darling."

She was dressed in green, with a hat which cast an alluring, dis-
tracting shadow across her face. The dark eyes were darker than he
had ever remembered, the color of the wild skies over the moors be-

fore a storm. He had summoned a taxi; she was quiet as they drove back to the Savoy, but she could not have failed to notice the heads which turned as they made their way through the foyer.

* * *

Margaret had permission to come up from Aldershot that evening, provided that her father gave his assurance she would be back by ten. She came bursting into the suite, and stopped short, as if an invisible cord had barred her way.

"Lally!—oh, my God!" She gazed at her sister, and then moved slowly, almost cautiously, across the room. She extended her hands, took one long, slender one in hers, avoiding the bandaged one. Then her arms went up in an embrace. "Oh, Lally! You're so beautiful! But *they* have done it to you. What you must have—" Her head was resting on Lally's shoulder. "I'm so happy you're back, dearest. Oh, dearest Lally. How I've missed you!" And then she drew back again. "So changed. But still . . . but still . . . Oh, damn, I'm crying. Father, why didn't you warn me?"

"Well, I wasn't quite sure myself. Have we truly got Lally back, Margaret? Or is this an apparition?"

"I'm back, Father—Margaret. Now stop all this. You make me embarrassed—nervous." The dark and gold heads were together again. "Margaret, I've missed you too. And Jon. And Alice. How do the men stand it? I couldn't take it for even these few months. I'm disgraced. It isn't just the finger. I couldn't take it. I've been sent home."

"Not forever, Lally. I wish you had been. Your Sister wrote to me. You must rest, and build up a little strength. And then they want you back. You're going back as soon as you're rested and your hand's healed. You're a very capable, experienced nurse. You're just like a soldier, Lally. You obey orders. It makes me feel so old—and inadequate. A father used to make the decisions once." He pulled a long face, and went to examine himself woefully in a mirror. "Well, do you think you two young beauties could escort your old father down to dinner?"

* * *

Sandy joined them, at Black Jack's invitation—almost a command, Lally guessed, for all the fact that he talked of being able to make no decisions—in the dining room of the hotel. She was brought to the table by the maître d'hôtel, smiling a little, pleased smile because she always knew that her entrance into any room was noticed and re-marked upon. "Father, darling." She kissed him on the cheek. She had, Lally realized, come to some arrangement as to what she should call him. She was the dutiful, loving daughter-in-law. "Margaret . . . you really are a wretch. You never get in touch. I know you're in London often enough . . . one hears." Then, almost reluctantly, she turned her gaze fully on Lally, who wore the gown of peacock silk. "Father warned me on the telephone. Seems you've been starving yourself to death. I do hope you'll eat up now you've got some de-cent food." She cocked her head slightly. "Though I must say, it's improved you. How do you feel? Not quite next to death's door, I hope. That finger's really only a scratch." She turned to the maître d'hôtel. "I'll have gin and a very little dry vermouth. Shaken. With ice. You do have ice?"

"Certainly, Mrs. Pollock."

She turned back to the three around the table. "Well, Lally, do tell me all about it. It must have been quite terrible. To judge by the way you look . . ."

* * *

They were back in the suite, drinking coffee, and Sandy was get-ting noticeably fidgety. She smoked constantly, and Lally was an-noyed to see that she, herself, smoked quite as much. She had eaten little dinner, had barely touched the beautiful wine Black Jack had ordered. She was feeling tired, she only half-heard the talk.

Then Sandy said, "So sorry, Lally. I didn't mention it before. It must have been so upsetting for you."

She hadn't been listening. "What?—what was upsetting?"

"Well . . . your friend. Your friend, Thomas Handley. I'm terri-bly sorry about his being killed. But nice for his family that he was mentioned in dispatches. He's been recommended for a decoration. Lally!—*Lally, stop it!*"

She never knew what caused her to strike Sandy West on the face. Just to shut that cruel mouth. Just to stop the words . . . The blow sent fiery prongs of pain through her poisoned finger, and up her arm. She crumpled to the carpet, not because she wanted to faint, but because it was the only thing that might relieve the weariness, the sadness. Far away she heard Sandy's outraged voice. "Well, for heaven's sake!—what did I say? Only what we all know. He's dead, isn't he?"

The carpet seemed a safe, warm haven. But even it had the smell of death.

*   *   *

Much later tears came, tears unlike the ones she had wept at the sight of Black Jack at Victoria. She wept quietly because Black Jack had fallen asleep in the chair beside her bed. When he woke, she asked the question, "Why didn't you tell me?"

His answer was nervous, strained. "I wanted you to get some rest first. I hoped all the things—the clothes—would distract you. But I never expected Sandy to come out with it like that. I doubted she'd even remember Thomas Handley. Of course she thought you must know. I'm sure she didn't mean to be cruel."

"When?"

"I don't know exactly when. His name was in the casualty lists two weeks ago. He died very bravely, Lally. So many names in the casualty lists. So many good lads . . . lads from around Leeds and a couple, even, from the village at Pellham. Names I remember—Jon's friends he brought to Pellham. I didn't know—I wasn't sure if Thomas was anything special to you. Was he?"

"I don't know, either. We wrote occasionally. That's all." But it had been much more than that; he had comforted her in the hurt of Jon's sudden marriage. He had made her seem desirable and loved. He had put her, in imagination, on the golden road to Samarkand. He had thought of her safety in that hell over there, and urged her to get out. There never had been a chance to discover if any of that feeling would survive the turmoil of war, whether kindness might have grown into something stronger. She turned her face into the pillow and wept.

*   *   *

Black Jack made her stay in bed the next day. He waited on her himself when the food was brought, and implored her to eat. She tried to do it to please him, and then found herself being violently sick. He held her as she retched emptily into the toilet bowl. The doctor, who was summoned again, left some pills to make her sleep; he cleaned and dressed her hand again. He could do nothing about her inner hurt. "Shock," he said to Black Jack. "Exhaustion. After all, we're seeing true cases of shell shock. It's not malingering, as some doctors claimed when the first cases came to them. Your daughter's been under severe strain. My advice is to take her back to the country. You say she used to ride . . ."

So they packed up and went to Pellham Langley, taking Alice with them to the little rooms over the stables.

She had no country clothes to fit. Black Jack searched in the attics, where their possessions had been stored when the house had been turned over to the military. He came down with things he had not believed it would be possible to see on another woman—Latitia's tweed skirts and jackets, a riding habit, a tweed cloak. Lally looked at them wonderingly. "You'd let me wear . . . these? These were *hers.*"

"Latitia would have given them to you, Lally. I know she would. I imagine they'll fit quite well."

They did, almost perfectly. How strange, Lally thought, to be wearing the clothes of a woman dead almost twenty years, clothes in the grand style of that age before the war, clothes of Black Jack's beloved wife. The tweeds were beautiful, the finest the Yorkshire mills could turn out. She even imagined that there was a faint trace of perfume left on them, or was that indeed pure imagination? She and Black Jack walked the moors, the cloak wrapped closely about her. She had assumed the mantle of another woman, Jon's mother. If only she could protect him, as a mother would. But she had not been able to protect Thomas. The December days were short, and the weather wild. It rained, and sometimes flurries of snow stung their eyes. Better to say it was rain and snow than let Black Jack see her tears.

* * *

Lally had scrambled up past the waterfall alone that day; Black Jack had had to go into Bradford, Alice had caught a cold. She sat by the fire in the stables with Nell, striving to get on with knitting the muffler for Jon. The time hung dully on Lally's hands; she could settle to reading none of the books Black Jack had bought for her in London. She had been ordered to take at least a month's leave. Her finger was beginning to heal. The last of the poisonous pus seemed to have been drawn from it. It was almost normal in size. Soon there would be no further excuse to stay. Along the edges of the beck ice lay. The great hope, the thing they all lived for, was that Jon might be given leave for Christmas; with the Somme offensive ground down, it was possible. Was it only a year since he had brought Sandy to Grangewick that Christmas Eve, and told them they would be married? Was it only—not quite—a year since she and Thomas had loved each other?

It was a clear day; a pale sun touched spots on the wide moors. There was no wind, and wrapped in Latitia's cloak, she felt warm. She turned the collar up around her ears, and settled on the broad outcrop of rock which was their usual seat. She gazed down into the valley where the tall chimneys of the mills sent their dark streams of smoke into the bright sky. Black Jack worried about their future. The German U-boats remorselessly sunk Allied shipping; the German government had warned America that henceforth armed merchantmen would be regarded as "cruisers." They never, Black Jack said, had more than a few weeks' supplies of wool and cotton to spin and weave. The great blast furnaces of Sheffield and Wales worked around the clock but the demand for steel could never be fully met. Black Jack had had a small hand in the development of a new weapon which had been used in the battle of the Somme—the tank; his steelworks had produced a prototype of Ernest Dunlop Swinton's invention. He had also poured capital into a factory to produce the new machine guns. "I don't know, Lally, if it's immoral to make munitions. All I know is that I'd rather Jon had a machine gun in his hand than an officer's service revolver."

Even in the still, clear air she heard nothing until a voice said, "Can I break into your thoughts, Lally?"

There was no other voice like that. She turned, already smiling. "Brock!" She jumped to her feet. For a second she hesitated about whether to offer him her hand, and then decided that was ridiculously formal. Instead she extended her arms, and was caught in his embrace.

"Well, I'm glad I'm welcome. Nell seemed doubtful about my coming after you, and she said, in any case, she didn't know where you'd gone. I made a guess. I always remember you and Black Jack sitting here. You seemed the most companionable people I'd ever seen."

"What a long time ago it seems. What are you doing in Engand—or is it so secret I shouldn't ask?"

They settled down on the rock. "What am I ever doing? I'm selling, Lally. I'm selling until the U.S. gets into the war, and then I guess I won't be doing it any more, because the government will take it all over." He took out his cigarette case, and offered it to her, and said nothing when she accepted, just lighted it, and then his own.

"You think America will come in soon?"

"Has to. Wilson got re-elected on the peace platform, but he's for war. Divided opinion about it in the States. Don't see why we should get messed up in Europe's quarrels—that sort of thing. But we'll be in." He waved his cigarette as if to dismiss the subject. "You're looking great, Lally. I had to be in Leeds, and I called at Grangewick in the hope of finding you and Black Jack"—he used the name quite unaffectedly—"there. And Billings sent me on here to Pellham. He was very woebegone. Sounded as if you were on your deathbed. And that's what Margaret said, just about. They're wrong. You're much tougher than that, Lally. Who wouldn't be a bit tired after listening to those damn guns for all those months and trying to patch up what came down the line? There ought to be medals for girls like you."

"You saw Margaret in London?"

"For a few hours. When I could drag her away from her colonels and generals, and all the lesser lights who flock around her. She's a very popular lady, Margaret—and she doesn't like staying in the barracks at night. I can tell some people think she's unpatriotic giving any time to a man like me not in uniform."

"Margaret enjoys a good time," Lally said, but not with resentment. "Why shouldn't she have it? There's enough of the other sort of time. I'm sick to death of women looking as if it's a sin to smile. Yes—I know. A lot of them have every reason to grieve, but they shouldn't begrudge people like Margaret their good times. The sight of her brightens up the place." She added, "You know, if I had my way, they'd take down some of those gloomy war posters and put up a few of girls like Margaret—smiling as hard as they can!"

"Lally—Lally, stop being so generous. You'd look all right on a poster yourself, you know. I always suspected there were beautiful bones under that baby fat. I don't agree with Margaret and Billings. I think you look gorgeous—dark and mysterious. Almost the *femme fatale*. Those slightly smoky smudges under your eyes are very alluring. I'm sorry about your hand, but Nell told me it's much better. I'm sorry, too, to see you've caught the habit of smoking the weed. Ruins the health, they tell me. Can't do a thing about it myself. I'm hooked. It's about the number one priority item being shipped to the Allies from the States. The British Tommy has to have his fag. God help them, sometimes that's all they have."

"Brock, you didn't come here to talk to me about cigarettes or President Wilson. Why did you come?"

Promises

171

"Well—I did say I was in Leeds on business. I'm fond of old Black Jack. Of you, Lally. And Alice."

"And Margaret?"

He waited, and smoked in silence, finishing the cigarette, lighting another from its stub. She thought he was not going to answer. "I'm in a bit of trouble. About Margaret."

Her first reaction was alarm. If Brock Weymouth had caused trouble for Margaret, she shouldn't be sitting here beside him.

"Yes, trouble," he continued. "I didn't think it would ever happen. I've always loved women. Used to get along just great with them, even when I was a kid. Used to be able to twist the matron at the orphan home around my little finger, as they say. And she was a big woman. I just love female company—the prettier the better. And as soon as I got some money I was happy to spend it on them—for whatever—as much as I had. And when I got even more money, the sky was the limit. I suppose that's what's wrong. I've always thought of women as pretty babies to be given presents. I thought that was all there was to it. I once was married—but I don't think I paid the right sort of attention to my wife. I turned around one day, and she'd left me. Probably wanted something different from presents—like my time, or something. Can't say I blame her. But now—now I've come a cropper. I've discovered there's one woman I really want. Just one. Margaret. And she doesn't know I exist. It's unthinkable, Lally. Here's hard-bitten old Brock Weymouth, and she treats me like some elderly uncle, nice to have around to take her out to dinner when there's no one else she'd rather be with. Every time I see her it's some new guy—a pal of Jon's, or Freddie's cousin, or Reggie's brother. I listen to it, and it's a lot of—" He searched for the cigarette case to offer her another; she shook her head. "Yep, Lally, here I am. A Grade A American male who knew the whole score. I think I'm in love with Margaret—and I don't quite believe it."

Lally sighed. "Believe it, Brock. When someone like you says he's in love, believe it. But don't look to Father or me to help you. You're too dangerous for Margaret. If you ever fell *out* of love with her, then heaven help her."

"Just give me the chance. I'd protect her and cherish her and love her as long as she lived. Goddamn it, what has the woman got? She's hardly more than a kid, and I'm a fool."

"She's got what her mother had. I never knew her mother, but

Black Jack adored her. That's enough, isn't it? You and Black Jack aren't so unalike."

He sat and finished his cigarette. The December day was drawing to a close. The shadows were already deep in the valleys. He got to his feet. "O.K., Lady in the Cloak—you look like something out of a picture gallery. And you're too damn smart, Lally. You know too much. Now, let's go down. Perhaps you'd be good enough to give me some supper. I brought a few things with me, like ham and eggs. Feel hungry?"

She didn't reply, just accepted his hand as he helped her down the track by the waterfall.

The lights were showing through the thin curtains of the stable block when they got back to Pellham Langley, and Black Jack's car was standing beside the Hispano Suiza.

* * *

Brock had brought more than ham and eggs. What he produced was more like a prewar hamper from Fortnum and Mason. Lally felt guilty as she unpacked it, as she had felt at the dressmaker's as the silk and velvet had been draped over her. She started to protest, but looking past Brock she saw Black Jack shake his head. Was she to spoil Alice's pleasure in the chocolates—or Nell's in the tin of biscuits —or even Black Jack's enjoyment of that half wheel of Wensleydale cheese, which should have been plentiful in Yorkshire but wasn't any more? There was butter and tea and coffee—treasures they were now. There were, incredibly, two bottles of the fabled Romanée Conti; she heard Black Jack's gasp of disbelief as he read the label. "My God, Brock, where on earth did you get this?"

"Better not ask, Mr. Pollock. We all have our ways, don't we?" Lally didn't like the way he appeared to lump Black Jack in with his own approach to securing things, whatever things they were. She had witnessed Black Jack's display of force at the dressmaker's, but Brock's, she sensed, was an instinct of much greater ruthlessness. His drive for possessions, and the power they conferred, was something Black Jack lacked—probably because he had always had possessions, and a measure of power. She didn't know who Brock had threatened or bribed to produce this lavish spread, but she felt uncomfortable with it. She wished she didn't have to cook the ham and eggs, drink the Romanée Conti. She remembered their talk as they had sat above the waterfall. If Brock Weymouth could not approach Margaret directly, did he plan his approach now through her and Black Jack? The spread of gifts on the table had ensured his presence there in this small and humble room, the intimacy of belonging to the Pollock family in a way few people had ever experienced. Alice had received many toys in her life, but nothing ever to equal "Madame Butterfly," as Brock had instantly christened her. The doll, which Lally thought could have been a museum piece, sat side by side with Teddy Rose, and Alice touched her with awe. The exquisite little oriental features were topped with a wig of real black hair, the silk gown was stiff with hand embroidery, the fan a small masterpiece of ivory. How had Brock known that something so unusual, so exotic, would capture Alice's imagination, make her face light up with joy? It had been a risk; it might have been so unusual she would have shunned it. And it fell exactly into the category of a present which could have been given either to a child or an adult, so that the child in Alice who had never grown up was not more stressed than the adult into which she was physically maturing. Clever, Lally thought—too damned clever, as Brock had said of her. He must have brought it from America—so this visit, as casual as it might seem, had been carefully planned. The only unexpected element was that she herself was present; he couldn't have known she would have leave. Surely he couldn't have known that?

* * *

Black Jack and Brock had made good inroads into the Wensleydale; they had reached the last half of the second bottle of wine, and Nell had put Alice to bed. Lally tried to hide from Black Jack how little she ate; while some enjoyment of food had returned, she found she had little capacity for it. During the meal the talk had ranged widely, but it was mostly, as it was bound to be, of the war. They talked of the useless slaughter of the Somme, they talked of when America would come in. "Wilson made a speech in October," Brock said. "What he said was something like 'I believe the business of neutrality is over. The nature of modern war leaves no state untouched.' I guess he means it."

Brock showed no signs of leaving; they would finish the second bottle. Lally refilled the coffee cups. They were settling closer to the range, and Black Jack had brought out the brandy when the knock came at the door. Black Jack glanced at Lally in surprise, and then went to open it. An orderly from the hospital stood there.

"Sorry. Mr. Pollock. Telephone call for you over at the house. The party wouldn't give a message. Said it was urgent. They're holding on."

Black Jack got his coat and was gone. A hideous fear clutched at Lally. She found herself unable to utter a word to Brock. He held his brandy glass to her lips. "Take a sip, Lally. Just a sip." He didn't try to reassure her.

Black Jack came back. They listened to his steps on the stairs, slow steps. No hurry—no need to hurry. Lally stood up, and faced the door. Black Jack entered; his face was a numb, shocked mask.

"Jon?" Lally said at once.

He sank down in a chair. "No, not Jon. I'm ashamed to say I'm thanking God it isn't Jon. It's Sandy."

"*Sandy?* What's wrong with Sandy?" The wild sense of relief sweeping through her made her less aware of Black Jack's anguish.

"Sandy's dead. Sandy's dead." He repeated it as if he did not himself believe it.

"How?" Brock's tone was very quiet; he did not seem intrusive now.

"That zeppelin raid on London last night. Not big, by most standards. But big enough for Sandy. A bomb hit the house where she had her flat. They got her out of the wreckage about midday. One of the tenants who survived identified her. Someone knew her home address up at Burton. And then the Wests got in touch with Margaret, since she was nearest. She was sent off duty and allowed to go up to London. The War Office have been in touch with Jon. He's allowed home on compassionate leave at once. I'll be going to London to meet him. That was Margaret on the phone now."

Lally could say nothing. She felt guilt and shame because she had been so sure it had been Jon, and she could not confess her relief. And then the realization of Jon's hurt came crowding in. He had loved Sandy. "Father . . . of course I'll go with you. Poor Sandy. Who would have thought . . . Jon will take it very hard, I think."

Black Jack looked up. "Yes, I think he will. And I'd like you to be with me. I'm just so grateful *you're* not still over there. I need you, Lally. I don't know how to face Jon."

"Jon couldn't blame you, Father. You can't blame yourself—"

"There's something Jon has to be told—or he'll find out—that'll make it much harder."

"Mr. Pollock, shall I leave? This is private, and I'm intruding . . ."

Black Jack looked around at Brock inquiringly, as if he had taken his presence for granted. "You, Brock? No, not intruding. Everyone will soon know." Now he stared at the heart of the fire which glowed behind the bars of the range. "Don't see how it's possible to keep it quiet. The newspapers always know about that sort of thing. Really, it's ordinary reporting. It will be in tomorrow's papers. I wish to God there was some way I could get to Jon before he reads it, but that doesn't seem possible."

"Know what? What else is there to know?"

"The raid wasn't until two in the morning. Harry Gaunt's body was also in the rubble with Sandy's. Identified from his military disks. Margaret said—Margaret said she was told they were both naked. Sandy and Harry Gaunt were in bed together. How do I face Jon with *that?*"

* * *

Lally wakened Nell and told her—just the bare facts of Sandy's death, nothing else. "Someone will come out from Grangewick tomorrow and fetch you and Alice back, Nell. Perhaps it's better not to tell her. Perhaps she doesn't remember Sandy."

"She remembers the wedding, miss. I don't know about the rest . . ."

Nell was helping Lally pack. In a few minutes she was back in the little sitting room. Black Jack was ready for the journey; Brock had his coat and gloves on.

"Brock is going to drive us. Useless to hope for a train at this time of night."

"Have we enough petrol?"

"I've a few spare cans, and Black Jack"—the name came out easily—"has stored a few down below. It's enough to make it, I think."

"It's a long way, at night."

"Well, let's not stand around then," he said curtly. "So what if it is a long way? We've got to get there, haven't we?"

Lally was settled in the back of the Hispano Suiza with the few pieces of luggage. The moon showed the dark face of Pellham Langley, and the bare branches of the trees which lined the drive. Brock Weymouth seemed to have taken control. Perhaps just as well, Lally thought. Black Jack stared ahead at the road where patches of ice glistened dangerously, stared, and said nothing, his profile rigid and frozen as Lally watched it. The long, weary, cold hours went by; they stopped only to refill the tank from the extra cans they carried. The big, beautiful car held the road magnificently, or else Brock was a magnificent driver. There was no traffic. Brock broke the blackout regulations by using his headlights on full, but they were not stopped. Finally, from the height of Hampstead, they saw the flush of light in the sky that even the blackout regulations could not hide. In the late winter dawn they drove into a London already stirring and on its way. And then the forecourt of the Savoy.

"We managed to find a suite for you, Mr. Pollock," an assistant manager said. "Two bedrooms. Luckily there was a cancellation. Miss Pollock is already there. I'll have the switchboard ring through to her, sir, while your bags are taken up." He paused. Lally saw that the morning newspapers had already arrived, and were being prepared for delivery to the guests' rooms. Sandy Pollock's death would not be a headline, but it would be there. And then there were always the death notices. Her name, and Captain Henry Gaunt's name, would be in that list. "Mr. Pollock, forgive me if I intrude on your personal loss. But we have known the family—both families—for a long time. My deepest condolences, sir, on behalf of the management, and, I'm sure, of the staff." Which families? Lally thought—the Pollocks and the Wests, or did the management also know the family of Captain Henry Gaunt, D.S.O.?

Black Jack managed to thank him, gruffly. They went up in the lift in silence. Brock had tried to disengage himself. "Nonsense, man," Black Jack had said, almost rudely. "Must have at least a cup of coffee. Driven all night . . ."

The assistant manager hastened to say, "Room service will attend to you at once, Mr. Pollock." Brock stayed.

The assistant manager first of all knocked, and then opened the door to the sitting room for them. As she passed him Lally found that his eyes, trained never to betray surprise at anything a guest did or asked for, were slightly widened. What was he staring at? As he helped her off with the tweed cloak, she realized that she still wore the tweed skirt and jacket, the blouse with its elaborate lace jabot, of the period when Lady Latitia Pollock had been at the height of fashion wearing it.

The door from one of the bedrooms was flung open. Margaret,

disheveled, wearing the ordinary, practical nightgown and robe she would have worn in barracks, flung herself toward them. Her eyes were swollen. "Oh, thank God you've come. I was so afraid Jon would manage to get here before you did. I didn't know how I would face him. What can we say . . . ?" She appealed to all three of them; her eyes did not seem to see the assistant manager, who was quietly bowing himself out. But Brock's presence was included, as if he were naturally part of the group.

* * *

Black Jack, Margaret, and Lally met Jon at Victoria. He had telegraphed Grangewick from Dover, and Billings had relayed the message to the Savoy. They found him amid the confusion of the disembarking men, the stretcher cases, the officious Red Cross ladies. They knew at once that whatever newspaper he had read, it had contained the news that the bodies of both Sandy and Harry Gaunt had been found in the ruins of the building. His face looked frozen, reflecting nothing. He embraced Margaret and Lally, and extended his hand to his father. He did not speak a word.

The silence continued all the way to the Savoy, until he had thrown off his coat, and Lally had put a glass of Scotch in his hand. He remained standing, leaning against the windowsill, staring out at the river and the Embankment.

"Son . . ." Black Jack began. And had nothing to add.

"I know," Jon replied. "You don't have to worry about trying to break it to me gently—and, of course, no one can keep it from me. Some reporter fellow met me at Dover. God knows how he found me. From one of the Fleet Street rags. Told me the whole thing. They were in bed together, weren't they? Newspapers are always there when the bodies are brought out. The serious ones don't report things like that, but the rags thrive on it. No slander, just the truth. They can always print the actual facts, and let the public surmise what it wants. Is it true that you can't libel the dead? Anyway, I'd be wasting my time trying to prove that the bodies of Sandy Pollock and Harry Gaunt weren't brought out of that building. And it's just too much damn coincidence to imagine that they could possibly have been in different flats. No matter how discreet some reporting is, those are the facts, and that is what everyone will know."

He turned around and looked at them all. "Now I've said my piece. I know about it. I don't want to talk about it. I don't want your sympathy. You'll tell me what the arrangements for the funeral are, and I'll attend, as the War Office has so kindly given me leave to do. I'll do what a husband should, even though I don't feel like it. And that will be the end of it. I don't want to talk about Sandy. You understand me, all of you? I don't want to talk about Sandy."

Margaret's face had grown more tense. "Don't you think you're being a bit melodramatic, Jon? You don't have to cut us out like this. What did we do?"

"Nothing—nothing at all. Perhaps that's what I can't stand. Perhaps I'd have liked one of you to start raving about what a slut she was. You're all so good—and quiet—and sympathetic. Poor Jon. How terrible. Bad enough that she was killed—but *this* way. Well, Sandy's dead. That's it!" He drained his glass, and went over and refilled it.

"While you're there, Jon," Lally said, "pour one for me too, will you?"

His head turned quickly, and an expression of surprise he couldn't check showed on his face. "That's my girl, Lally. I need someone to get quietly drunk with. I didn't know you'd taken up this vicious habit. Wish to God I didn't have to keep up the mournful attitude until after she's buried. . . . Have a drink, Father? A drink, Margaret? You're not going to let Lally and me drink alone." He was splashing whiskey recklessly into his glass.

"All right, son. All right." Black Jack rose and went over to him. For a moment Lally thought he was about to commit what would have been the unforgivable error, at this time, of touching him on the shoulder. But he did no such thing. He simply accepted the glass from his son's hand, and raised it gravely to him.

"Rotten welcome home, Jon, but there it is. We'll get through it."

Jon poured for Margaret, and she managed to flick a smile at him as she accepted it. It was a macabre occasion, Lally thought. They would spend the whole evening talking about anything else but Sandy. They were forbidden by Jon to do so. So, for the moment, they must play his desperate game. She went to the telephone and lifted the receiver. "We're not accepting any calls for the rest of the evening, thank you." And then she pressed the bell for the waiter.

"Father, we're going to have a slap-up dinner. The best they can manage to give us. The best wines. Everything. Just look at Jon. He needs a bath, and he certainly needs a new uniform. He needs a haircut. But first thing he's going to have a good meal. Let's arrange it."

Jon looked at her and nodded. "Don't know what the VAD did

for you, Lally—but it didn't do badly." He bent and kissed her. "Thanks, love. If it were any other evening but this, we'd be down there on the dance floor, showing the whole town what a beautiful woman you've become." There was a note of rising hysteria in his voice. Lally had heard it many times in the wards. She took the glass from his hand, and began to refill it. "I've never been drunk, Jon. What's it like?"

"We'll find out together, won't we, Lally?"

*   *   *

Jon was sober enough when they buried Sandy Pollock in the churchyard near her parents' home at Burton-in-the-Wolds. The church was packed for the service. More people than anyone could have expected had come, come from long distances. Were they, Lally wondered, trying to convey to the Wests, and to the Pollocks, that it didn't matter what stories went around about Sandy? Were they trying to give support to Jon and Richard West, who, in the numbed lull after the battle of the Somme, had also been given leave? A raw, cold Yorkshire wind whipped through the graveyard, but somehow the crowd hung on. Lally saw frail old ladies being helped along the path to the graveside. Lady Bletchley was there, her face pinched and white. It was madness, Lally thought. Some need to identify, if only by their numbers, with the families. Lally dared not look at Jon's face while the burial service was read. It was his father-in-law who let the few terrible pieces of earth fall on the coffin. Both Jon and Richard stood as if they were on parade, their eyes fixed rigidly ahead, their bodies erect. Black Jack touched Jon on the arm when it was time to leave. The crowd parted.

The Wests made a great effort, considering the shortages, to give food and drink to those who had come a long way. Jon remained ten minutes among them, his lips moving mechanically in response to their murmured words. Then he sought Lally. "Come on! Let's get away from here. Get your coat."

Outside was the Hispano Suiza, the key in it. "Trusting fellow, isn't he, for a Yank? What the devil is he doing here, anyway? Is he after Margaret?"

"I think so."

"Well, he won't mind us borrowing his car, will he? He has to court the family, too, doesn't he?" He turned up his collar. "Hold tight, Lally—it's going to be a fast drive."

"Where are we going?"

"To Pellham. On the way we'll pick up Alice at Grangewick. Let's have a little sanity with us, shall we? I'm sick of this kind of madness."

*   *   *

It was one of Alice's charms that her own mental confusion made her oblivious to any strangeness in the behavior of others. That was what Jon had meant when he said, "Let's have a little sanity with us, shall we?" Alice was eating her supper in the nursery with Nell when Jon appeared. She simply opened her arms to him, as she always did. She had not known that they were going to a burial, just that they would be away all day. And she did not question Jon's demand that they pack at once and go to Pellham Langley. "We'll have Christmas there, sweetheart. Would you like that?" Christmas was, Lally realized, only two days away. Billings hurriedly packed a hamper of food. "I don't know, Miss Lally, whatever Mr. Pollock will say about this. All of you crowded into those little rooms. It would be better if you stayed here."

She shook her head. "We must do as he wants, Billings. Just for the time being, we must do everything he wants."

Billings turned and seemed to hurry beyond his usual pace as he started up the stairs. "I'll just go and remind Nell, miss, that she's to take the Christmas presents for Miss Alice. The child—I beg your pardon, miss—Miss Alice looks forward to Christmas. She still enjoys her presents as much as when she was a little girl."

Black Jack joined them the next day. "Gave us a bit of a fright when you took off, Jon, but I knew if you had Lally with you, it'd be all right." He looked tired and strained. "Then I got to Grangewick and found you'd kidnaped Alice. I had to lend my car to Brock to get back to London. Don't know how I'll get it back again, or how he'll get the Hispano Suiza. He's due to sail on Boxing Day, and Margaret had to be back on duty."

*   *   *

For Alice's sake they decorated the little living room with holly and fir; on Christmas Day when they attended the service at the church in the village, Jon declined to go. But afterward they were invited to take Christmas dinner in the biggest of the wards which held the officers still confined to bed. With a shock, Lally realized that it was the dining room of Pellham Langley; now, except for the view from the windows, there seemed no resemblance. The matron had commanded their presence. "We want a man to carve, Mr. Pollock. And it does the patients good to see a family together." When Jon demurred, she turned a firm face on him. "I know you've had a great sorrow to bear, Captain Pollock, but it is your *duty* to think of others. I expect you to be there." And they were.

After the meal, the ambulatory officers all crowded into the hall, where the piano was now placed. For once Lally was glad of her bandaged hand, which excused her from playing the piano. Matron took on the task; Lally's firm, strong voice, though, led the singing. The doors to the dining room, the drawing room, and the billiard room were left open so the men in bed could join in. Someone there had a good, true tenor, and he found a key to join with Lally. The voices of the others died away. *Oh come, all ye faithful* . . . Suddenly Alice's voice was heard. She was pitched perfectly to a high soprano against Lally's deeper tone, and that of the man who sang from his bed. Alice stood on the lowest step of the stairs, clasping the newel post. She wore a light-blue velvet dress cut down from one of Margaret's; her wonderful golden hair fell on her shoulders. Her sweet clear voice seemed to soar to that high roof. Lally saw the heads of the men turn. She could have been—perhaps she was to some who watched her—a vision of a Christmas angel. It was one of her moments of perfect clarity and ease and joy. At such times there was no one more radiantly, more serenely beautiful than Alice. Her face seemed to declare that nothing ugly had ever touched her, nor ever would. To some of those sitting there watching and listening to her, the effort and the hideous sacrifice of the past two years might have seemed worthwhile as long as something as lovely and pure as Alice could remain unchanged.

* * *

The snow was only light, and on Boxing Day they walked a little way on the moors, all four of them. Alice skipped ahead, and then kept running back to tug at Jon's arm, to hurry him on. That night they shared their Christmas goose from the hamper which Billings had packed, at the table with Nell. It was surprising, Lally thought, how little the conventions of servant and master seemed to matter now. The war had changed all that, along with much else. Nell was part of their lives, of their family. Almost unconsciously she had assumed their ways. From the time Miss Garner had departed, Nell had striven to imitate the speech of the family, so that Alice should not absorb her accent. It came almost naturally to her now; perhaps only by the broadening of her vowels and the directness of her manner could anyone have told that she was Yorkshire-bred. Lally, guiltily, realized that she seldom thought about Nell, taking her too much for granted. She was still attractive, but she was no longer a young woman. Had she, Lally wondered, given up any chance of marriage to stay with Alice? Had there been a chance?

"Did you hear what I said, Lally?"

She turned to Jon. "What—what was that?"

"Father just said he thinks he could find enough petrol from the vans that deliver to the mills to get us to London. We'll return the stolen Hispano, shall we? Margaret seems to know the address of the mysterious friend who always lends it. We could have a few days there. Do the town a bit. Shake off the blues . . . Do us both good."

Black Jack was nodding. Lally knew he was breaking one of the cardinal rules that they, the family, must never appropriate anything that had been consigned to the mills as a wartime necessity. But this time he would do it. He would do anything if Jon might have some activity, some pleasure.

She forced a smile onto her face; she was a little afraid of Jon in this mood. He had not recovered from the reckless, seemingly uncaring way he had greeted the news that Sandy had taken Harry Gaunt as a lover. He had not permitted himself a display of either anger or grief. He had shrugged, as if it hardly mattered. For all the love she bore him, Lally was not sure she wanted his company alone while this mood still hung on him.

Black Jack said, "Go on, Lally. There's a chance to wear those nice things we got for you. Shame to waste them . . . Sorry I can't go with you. There's a devil of a lot to see to at the mills, and I ought to get over to Wales. You both deserve your leave . . ."

As always, she agreed to do what Black Jack wanted. It would never be possible for her to refuse him.

*   *   *

They drove down from the snowy landscape of Yorkshire through countryside where the snow gradually turned to slush, and then to cold rain as they approached London. They found that the Hispano was permanently garaged at the Ritz. When Jon handed over the keys to one of the managers, the man consulted his notes. "Ah, yes, Captain Pollock. Mr. Weymouth gave instructions before he left this time. He thought you might return the car, and want to spend some of your leave in London. He said if you should have difficulty finding accommodation elsewhere, you were perfectly at liberty to use his rooms here."

"His *rooms*? You mean Mr. Weymouth keeps a suite here permanently?"

The man looked slightly uncomfortable. "Well, not precisely that, sir. Mr. Weymouth has a friend who maintains a suite of rooms here. The car, also, I understand, belongs to his friend. Mr. Weymouth just uses them whenever he's here. It's quite a usual arrangement, sir."

Black Jack had telephoned the Savoy in the hope of getting rooms for them, but had been given the promise of them only if there was a cancellation. Lally had known Jon hadn't wanted to go there. It was still too close to the time he had faced them and told them he did not want to talk about Sandy.

"That's very kind of Mr. Weymouth—and Mr. Weymouth's friend, " Jon said promptly.

They were shown to a two-bedroom suite overlooking Green Park. "That is quite an arrangement our friend Brock has. And *his* mysterious friend is never named. I would bet you a lot, Lally, that the friend doesn't exist. It's simply an invention. There's an awful lot about Brock Weymouth that could be an invention—including, of course, his name."

"He never claimed that his name was a true one. He simply doesn't know his name," she answered. "Does it matter? I don't know *my* name."

Quickly, Jon turned to her. "Lally, I'm sorry. You've been—well, just Lally for so long. A part of us. I keep forgetting . . ." He moved toward her, and she thought he was about to clasp her in his arms, a return of the warm, affectionate man she had known before the two years in the trenches, before Sandy's death. But then there was a knock on the door, and after a discreet pause, one of the housekeepers entered. She carried a large arrangement of flowers.

"Good afternoon, Miss Pollock. Captain Pollock. Excuse me. Mr. Weymouth always likes flowers in his rooms. He would want you to have them also." She settled them in a place of her own choosing, slightly rearranged two stems to create a better effect, and then turned to Lally.

"I trust everything is to your satisfaction, Miss Pollock?"

"Oh . . . yes, of course." Lally had inspected nothing.

When she had gone, Lally pointed through the window which gave a sideways view onto Piccadilly. Dusk was falling, but it was still possible to see the many men in uniform among the crowd. "Look, Jon—look at them down there. Doesn't it make you feel a bit guilty? Most of the men down there couldn't afford the price of a cup of tea at the Ritz."

He grimaced. "Lally . . . Lally, this isn't the time to put the social ills of the world to rights. They've been promised a better deal, after the war. Things improve all the time. Pretty soon you'll be lecturing me on votes for women."

She suddenly felt angry. "Don't you think we've *earned* them yet?"

He had been taking off his greatcoat, but he shrugged it back onto his shoulders. "Lally, can we call a truce till after the war? I was going to settle down and have a nice, slow scotch—from Brock's very ample supply. But if I've got to listen to a tirade, I'll go elsewhere. You choose."

It was unfair, she thought; it had always been unfair. It probably would go on that way. "Take your coat off, Jon. I'll pour the scotch."

He smiled. "That's my girl. What shall we do tonight? I'll call down to the desk and see what tickets they can get us for a show, shall I? And then we'll go somewhere to dance."

"A show? Dancing? Do you think we ought?"

"What are you afraid of? Someone's going to be shocked to see Jon Pollock out enjoying himself a couple of days after he buried his wife? Let them be shocked. What shall it be, Lally? If you don't come with me, I'll ring up someone else. There's always someone free. I still have the address book from the time before I was married. Some of the girls are still in town."

She slightly bowed her head. She didn't at all recognize this bitter, brittle Jon; he seemed to smile, but did not smile. They would dine and dance tonight, and it would be a mechanical performance. She almost thought that he had planned it this way; he hoped he would run into acquaintances, even friends. He wanted to show them how little Sandy's betrayal had affected him. She suspected that he might get drunk tonight. "I'd love to go with you, Jon. Of course." Black Jack had sent her for that reason, hadn't he? With Lally, Jon was safe.

* * *

It was after two when they returned to the hotel. They had seen the variety show at the Palace; Lally couldn't remember a thing she had seen or heard. She had listened to the laughter all about her, had witnessed the almost frenetic striving among the audience to milk every moment of pleasure from the few hours there. In the two clubs where they had danced afterward there were many uniforms, and most of the women still managed to look extremely well-dressed. They were a leaner, harder lot than Lally could remember from her season—but then her season had never included dancing at late-night clubs. She had never seen heavy drinking, either. Perhaps this night she had drunk too much herself. When they entered the suite she felt warm, and something that had been frozen in her since the moment Sandy had blurted out the news of Thomas Handley's death relaxed and thawed. She could allow herself to hurt now, and the hurting would be bearable. Sandy's death had momentarily thrust Thomas into the background; it had been her private grief. It occurred to her, as she sat with Jon on the sofa, sipping a final scotch, that she and Jon, at this moment, were in a like situation. Both hurt, both empty, both facing the inevitable return to France.

She looked at him. "Jon, I wonder if we'll both die?"

He shrugged. "Possibly. It's all too probable that *I* will die. I feel cheated because it all seems for nothing. I know—I went off a schoolboy, with patriotism shining from my face. That's gone now. Now I simply do my duty as I watch other men die, because if I don't, they'll put me up against a wall and shoot *me*. They make heroes out of cowards, because the alternative is death too. There doesn't seem any way to escape it. I want to *live,* Lally. I want to survive. I don't want posthumous medals. I just want to get through it all. And I want to live tonight. *Now.* Do you understand me, Lally? *Now.*" He leaned over and kissed her fully on the lips. "You're not my sister. You're Lally Leeds, and I want you."

She put down her glass. "You're sure?"

He nodded. "Yes, yes, Lally. Now. I may die before I can see you again."

It was the unrefusable plea, and her heart and body had ached long enough for him. She had waited, almost without hope, and now he had come to her. She did not know for how long, but he was hers. No longer his sister, but a woman.

In her bed their bodies sought and found each other in a recognition of mutual need, and with a strange surprise that they should couple with so much ease. They used each other, and they both knew it. Thomas Handley had first given Lally assurance that she was desirable. She now sought comfort in Jon's body, though she knew she did not, or only temporarily, possess his heart. She knew that in her he sought to assuage the nearly mortal blow Sandy had dealt him. Perhaps he sought a kind of revenge on all women. And she was Lally, always available. If they found mutual comfort, she thought, it was something. They could offer little else. He did not say he loved her; she had not expected that. And she did not allow herself to utter the words. They would make him ashamed, drive him from her. She would never drive him away. Hadn't he said, "You're not my sister. You're Lally Leeds." She began to reach toward a new identity.

In the morning he faced her unashamedly across the breakfast table. She wore the new silk robe Black Jack had bought her, and poured the surprisingly good coffee with a steady hand.

"No regrets, Lally?"

She smiled. "None . . . none at all."

But he had come to her for the wrong reason. Turning to look at the park touched by a wan, winter sunlight, unbidden the words she had tried to banish, from a poem of Rupert Brooke's, came back: *And the worst friend and enemy is but Death.*

* * *

The precious days of the leave sped away. They danced and drank and laughed, but the laughter deceived neither of them, nor many of those who watched them. They were suddenly desperate for life. They held each other like children warding off the dark, the terrors which lay beyond their vision. And they finally parted on a platform of Victoria Station, kissing each other like brother and sister, which they were not.

Lally, who had two more weeks' leave, returned to Leeds and Black Jack. Her finger was almost healed, but to Black Jack she seemed even thinner than the day she had come on leave, the face graver and strangely beautiful, the shadowed lines under the cheekbones now almost etched there. He wondered what might have happened between her and Jon during the time they had spent in London, and did not dare ask. These children of his were no longer children. He thought of her returning to France, and the fear grew in him that he would lose both of them. The evenings by the fire, which should have been a comfort to them both, seemed strained; they did not recall the past, they dared not talk about the future. Black Jack's heart ached for the lost, lonely look on Lally's face. A gramophone record arrived in the post from Brock Weymouth. Black Jack eyed it dubiously as he wound up the gramophone. "It's this new thing—jazz —is it? I wonder if one's meant to dance to it? Don't see how one can, do you?"

But Lally executed some steps to a tune called "The Darktown Strutter's Ball," her body and feet light; her ankles, now revealed by the shorter skirts, were lovely. Her arms moved in rhythm. But when she was gone, after he had seen her off at Leeds on the first stage of her return to France, Black Jack sat alone in the drawing room at Grangewick and wished her back with him. On an impulse he wound up the gramophone and played a song everyone sang, but which seemed to embarrass Lally: *There's a Rose that grows in "No man's land," and it's wonderful to see* . . .

* * *

And on the other side of the Channel, Susie Barlow's chatter was momentarily halted. She had helped Lally unpack, had savored the soap and the flea powder, the hairpins, the hand balm. But she was silenced when Lally brought out the two new uniforms, and the regulation supply of underwear Black Jack had sent for her. VADs received no pay; Susie's uniforms were mended and patched, her underwear washed to thinness. She sat down on the cot like a child on Christmas morning, and pulled on the new boots. "They fit! You've got a sharp eye, Lally." Then she looked up and Lally was astonished to see that her eyes were bright, almost tearful. "Gawd! 'ow —how am I ever going to thank 'im? I can't pay, of course. But he knows that." She looked across at the photo back in its place beside Lally's cot. "I'll just have to take care of you for 'im, won't I?"

❧ CHAPTER 9 ❧

I

Lally moved along the row of beds; only the light from the lamp on the center table revealed the faces to her, but she knew them. They were the same faces, endlessly passing. Some turned restlessly on their pillows, some breathed heavily in sleep induced by drugs. But they were always the same men—young, some beautiful, some who swore when the pain grew worse, some who, under drugs, spoke poetry. They were all beautiful, and all tragic to her.

In the few moments where there was time, she read the newspapers that reached them. The submarine warfare had begun again, and American ships were its target and frequent victims, though British losses were worse. How much more, she wondered, would the Americans stand before they said they would come over and do what had to be done? How much longer before they would relieve the exhausted and now nearly demoralized troops of France and England and the colonies? Much longer, and it would be too late.

In the chill March dawn a man murmured something as she moved through the ward. She bent close to his lips. "Water, Sister . . . please."

She brought the water in a fresh glass. "Don't swallow—just rinse your mouth and then spit it out. I'll hold the basin." He did not know there was no stomach to receive the water; his entrails were bound up, while they waited for him to die. She saw his eyes fixed on the light which grew steadily through the blackout curtains. He was seeing his last dawn. The eyes had grown glazed, but she knew they could still distinguish light, so she put out the lamp and drew back the curtains on the window opposite. For a moment she held his wrist, and found the pulse barely there. Then her fingers slipped down and she held the soldier's hand. She knew he would not be there when she came on duty that evening. She leaned over him. "Can you hear the bird? It'll soon be spring."

But she doubted that he heard her voice. The oblong of light at the window must be growing dimmer, as his hand grew colder.

* * *

They did come in. On April 6, 1917, they came in—the Americans. The long-expected, hoped-for news gave Lally a rush of joy. They were not here yet, but they soon would be. She remembered all that Brock Weymouth had told her of the almost unawakened industrial might of the United States. "They hardly know what they have, Lally—but, by God, when they get going, it will bring this thing to an end."

Spring had come, as it always did, to the wasteland. Along the roads, the remains of hedgerows still put out their swelling buds, the birds still sang among the thorn bushes, and pecked a living from among the garbage piles of the vast and mired armies. That April, the British, after a huge bombardment and the use of gas, began an advance. The battle of Arras, they called it. But one lonely name on the map was marked down in fame and infamy; the Canadians took Vimy Ridge. The British made an advance of four miles, but no breakthrough. Lally noted that they now were recording the third battle of Champagne. How many times would they fight over those foul places, the places where the dead still lay unburied, just cloaked in mud?

As she sat down to an evening meal in the mess before going on duty, another nurse thrust an old newspaper in front of her. "Don't know if you've seen it. I'm weeks behind myself. Don't get any time to read—or I fall asleep as soon as I begin."

The Romanov dynasty had ended with the abdication of Czar Nicholas. The Russians were virtually defeated, and by the end of the year would fight no more. Some man, whose name she had never heard before, Lenin, had been sent across Europe by the Germans to undermine the new provisional government. But Russia was far away. The end of the fighting on the Eastern Front would mean Germany could turn all her attention and her troops toward the Western Front. More frightening than any news of Russia was the knowledge, seeping through now, that the French troops had mutinied after the cruel losses of the previous April and May at Verdun. Lally had a horrible vision of every soldier, British, Canadian, Australian, French, the lot, just deciding to lay down their guns. She saw the Germans walking unopposed across an eerily quiet no-man's-land.

" 'ere—ain't you going to eat that?" Susie, seated beside her, asked. "Honest to Gawd, Lally, you're more and more like a scarecrow." She cocked her head on one side. "Don't know that I didn't like you better when you was fat."

Lally pushed the plate toward her. It also seemed an unimaginably long time ago since the fat and innocent Lally had begun on this sickening adventure. She had almost forgotten that the war went on in other places—Italy, the Balkans, Turkey, the Middle East. Men died also in those other places, and nurses tried to help them. But her own horizon had narrowed down to these few square miles of Flanders' fields.

* * *

Over There, Over There, they sang,
Send the word, send the word Over There,
That the Yanks are coming . . .

They had come, with a sort of heartwarming freshness, with a little touch of arrogant swagger. There were too few of them in the beginning, but they were to be seen in the streets of Paris in the brief thirty-six-hour leave Lally managed to spend with Jon. She knew of the many medical corps they had sent, the ambulance units, men who had offered themselves long before their country asked it. Now she saw them—and loved them, in their new, fresh uniforms, their air of brisk innocence.

They sat at a cafe in Paris in the warm July afternoon, watching the people of that now faintly shabby capital go by; they drank something that was called coffee. It was a stolen meeting. Lally and Susie had been given leave together, but Susie had left the train at Rouen. "Don't want to butt in, Lally. It's *your* time with 'im. Forget the regulations." Did Susie suspect what her relationship was with Jon? If she did she said nothing.

"Do you think we could be near the end now?" Lally said.

Jon shrugged. "The generals have been telling us that for three years. I believe nothing now. I'm conscious of not being conspicuously brave or cheerful. I just do what I have to do."

She woke in the morning to find him awake beside her, staring at her. "I don't even know if I properly remember you when you were little, Lally. The time you came to us. You didn't say anything. Monkey." He used her old nickname. He reached over and drew her to him. Lally was achingly aware that the sun was bright outside, and already hot. Jon must get a train back at eleven o'clock. The small hotel they had found looked with an indifferent eye on their staying there together. The war had continued a wearyingly long time, and young people would not wait for love forever. So many of the things that had been the convention three years ago had been torn in shreds. Too many had died to expect the young in battle to forgo the joys they might never have again. Lally sensed the desperation in the way she and Jon made love—she because she might lose him, Jon because he was trying to wipe out the hurt of the woman who had betrayed him. And she was grateful he had never said, "I love you." Jon had never lied to her.

She saw him off at the station, and then went to the buffet to sit out the hour before her own train left. A captain in the Wiltshire Rifles took the seat beside her. "Have you come on leave?" he said hopefully.

"Just going back," she answered. She knew what the question implied. No one waited for introductions anymore, and the time was too precious to waste on the preambles.

He shrugged. "Hard luck on me. I've got forty-eight hours, and you're a striking-looking girl. It would have been nice to spend the time with you."

Could it have been the first time, Lally wondered, that a man had approached her not out of duty because he was a guest or Jon's or Margaret's friend? This man had never known the old Lally. And he desired her. She smiled at him. "I'm sorry, too," though she did not mean it. They talked and sipped the Calvados he bought her. He saw her to the train when the time came. "Do you mind if I kiss you?" he said, just before the train pulled out. "I can always pretend, when I go back, that I spent my leave with you." The kiss was lingering. "Every man in the station is envying me," he said. He held his hand in a rigid salute as the train drew her away from him.

II

"You 'ear all kinds of rumors, don't you?" Susie said. "Don't know what to make of it. 'ere, want a flea pad? Me mum sent six. Shove 'em in your knickers if the little buggers start to bite too hard." The wards were strangely quiet. All but the patients too seriously ill to move had been evacuated. That meant another offensive was to begin, and all possible beds had to be available. "Don't know 'ow it's possible," Susie went on. "Fought over this ruddy bit of ground Gawd knows 'ow many times. What'll they call this one?—the third bloody battle of Ypres. Seems more like the sixtieth to me. Wouldn't you think those stupid old men would make up their minds about something? Couldn't run a bloody railway, if you ask me, much less a war."

Lally finished washing her hair for the second time. That morning, she had found the dreaded lice in it. As she put the fine-tooth comb through it, examining it anxiously for evidence that they were still there, the sound of the guns started, that ominous, well-known rumble that set the earth under their huts trembling. The beginning of another offensive. She envisioned it as she had seen so many now—the stream of wounded and dying, the sickening mess of the operating rooms, the hurried jobs of surgery, the frantic efforts to patch and bind and hold together until the men could be passed on to the ports, and, with luck, make it back to England. She thought of the weeks, perhaps the months ahead when there would be little time to wash at the leisurely pace she and Susie now enjoyed. In a few hours they would start coming. She thought of the flea pads and the fine-tooth comb; she thought of the lice on the men's bodies.

"Damn it, Susie, I've had enough. If there's going to be much more of this, I'll be as comfortable as I can."

" 'ere, what are you doing? You can't do *that!*"

Lally had taken up her small sewing scissors, woefully inadequate for the task, but they would have to serve. She would have liked one of the sharp, surgical scissors they used in the wards, but that would have meant asking permission from Sister. There was nothing in the regulations which said a nurse had to have long hair. And hadn't she heard that all across the United States women had suddenly taken to cutting their hair short? It began to fall away. It slid onto her shoulders, and then to the ground, long, dark masses of it.

"Oh, my Gawd!" Susie breathed.

She kept on, cutting steadily, almost afraid to look in the tiny mirror. It felt strange. She shook her head, and it felt marvelously light and free. She dared to look, and saw the ragged line she had created. Straight, dark hair fell across her cheeks—and stopped. A new sort of face seemed to emerge, behind which the hair did not fill out the space between chin and shoulders. She turned away, half afraid.

"Well, I'll get a barber to even it up later."

"What will Sister say?"

"She doesn't have the right to say anything. Besides, what'll she see? It can all be tucked into the cap. Much easier than before. Come on. We'd better get to breakfast. They'll be sending the cases down the line pretty soon."

It was the beginning of the third battle of Ypres, which they later called Passchendaele. It was fought over the bitter, waterlogged, death-infested ground of the former battles. It began on that bright morning, the last day of July 1917 when Lally in despair and impatience cut her hair. It was the short dark days of November when it sank into nothing, the death roll of the great guns fading to near silence. Two hundred and fifty thousand British were casualties at the end of it, and they had gained four miles of territory. Lally had seen many of the faces of that battle, some died within her sight; others lived to be passed onto the trains at Calais and Le Havre and thence to England. They might live, but their spirits had died.

* * *

The hospital barber had trimmed her hair neatly. She was used to the freedom and ease of it. But she still wore her nursing cap pulled tightly down about her ears. Susie had studied her closely one night as they prepared to fall into bed; propped on her elbow, she said, "Dunno, if I don't go and do the same meself. Looks a bit—what do they call it?—seductive?" She rose and went to the mirror, catching her red hair up in both hands. "I dunno . . . if it ended there . . . then I wouldn't have to bother with all this nonsense of holding up the rest of it. Maybe I will." Her thoughts moved on. "It's all going to be different after the war, ain't it, Lally? I mean, it's got to be." She yawned, and sank back on the cot. "Gawd, 'ow me feet hurt. I suppose that's what I'll remember most. Me achin' feet."

* * *

The hospital grew quieter as Passchendaele petered out. There was a little more time to rest, to examine themselves, to write letters.

"Gawd, you look a wreck," Susie said.

"Look at yourself!" Lally replied.

Susie nodded. "I think you're right."

Then one day Susie came hurtling across the duck boards that linked, over the muddy ground, the various huts and wards. "Lally! It's your brother. Come over from St. Omer on a motorcycle. Sister says . . ."

Lally flew into his arms. "Jon . . . oh, Jon! I guessed you had to be all right, because they would have told me if you weren't. But you didn't write . . . just those few cards." Why did she reproach him? The little respite he must have gotten when his battalion was sent down the line should have been given to sleep.

He held her back from him. "Lally, what was there to say? You've been so close to it yourself. What one needed to do was to keep Father from worrying too much. But with a gentleman as shrewd as Black Jack Pollock, there's nothing he can't see through. Did you know he's been keeping a canteen going at Calais for the past two years? He funds it, and it's staffed by conscientious objectors and middle-aged men. He's kept it all quiet; I only got to hear about it in a round-about way. Met an ambulance driver who said he's sent over six fully fitted-up ambulances. Did you hear yet about Cambrai?—three hundred and eighty British tanks in the first offensive! And Black Jack Pollock was responsible in God knows how many ways for them being there. He's invested heavily in them, and he *believed* in them." He stopped, the first rush of words run out. He looked at her, frowning. "Lally . . . you *look* different. I don't just mean being thin. What's happened?"

She realized she had run out of the hut without her cap. "Nothing, Jon—nothing. I just did what you do every so often. I got a haircut."

He stood back from her for a few minutes silently. Then he smiled. "Damned if I don't like it! You look gorgeous." He folded her in his arms again. "Lally . . . Lally, it's so good to see you." In her rumpled uniform, smelling she knew as much of sweat as of iodoform, smelling, perhaps, of the flea pads, he embraced her tightly. She allowed herself a moment of this luxury, then she gently disengaged him. "Jon, that's more than they allow a brother . . ." She was aware of the interested eyes that watched them.

His arms fell to his sides. "Sorry. It's hard to remember. Can we go somewhere and talk?"

They paced in the cold of the old cloisters of the abbey. "I've had a letter from Father," he said. "We've been stood down for two days, but that's all. I can't get leave—there are too few officers at the moment. I borrowed the cycle and dashed over here the minute I read his letter. I wonder if you can get any leave? Father's beside himself. It's Margaret, you see. She's bound and determined to marry Grenfell. Immediately."

"Who?"

"Robert Grenfell. You remember the chap who was at Eton and Oxford with me. Nice chap . . . but well . . . He came to Pellham quite a few times. The family lives in Yorkshire. Pleasant to get on with. He's Viscount Grenfell now. He was the third son, but the two older ones were killed. He's the only one left now. The only child. Lord Gough's heir."

Lally remembered. The handsome, fair, though somewhat weak-faced son of the aristocracy. Yes, pleasant to get on with. That was about all she could remember of him. It was not enough. Not enough for Margaret.

"Father's dead against it. He thinks Margaret will walk all over him, and be bored out of her mind before a year is over. Of course, they haven't had a year. These leaves . . . everything is so intense. One says what one doesn't really mean." He and Sandy West had married on one of those leaves. Was he saying he hadn't meant it?

"What am I supposed to do?—even if I can get leave?"

"Talk to her, Lally. You have some influence with her. Father . . . well, she always did know she could twist Father around her little finger."

"And me no less." The November dusk was growing in the cloisters. His face looked worn, worn the way his uniform was, a kind of thin shabbiness. No one would ever be able to take from his face the look of terrible, tired experience now permanently stamped there. He had come through even this last horror of battle with only a minor leg wound, which kept him out of the trenches for two weeks. It had been of so little significance he had sent only a postcard about it. It had been as if he had not wanted to draw attention to it, as if he feared his luck would run out. One by one his school friends, the friends of the Oxford year, had gone. At Passchendaele his best friend, the Honorable Patrick Kimble, his cousin, had been killed.

"She admires you, Lally. You do know that? She always writes about you being over here. She knows she couldn't have done it herself. She'd have gone to pieces in a day. Not lack of courage, but she couldn't have helped showing what she felt. Soldiers don't want pity. They want help."

"But what difference will all this make—even if it were true? About her and Grenfell—if she really wants to marry him?"

"You're the last hope, Lally. She's got it planned for about four days from now. Grenfell got a piece of shrapnel in the leg. It'll keep him in England for about two months. She means to be married, and Father thinks it's madness. I agree with him. Couldn't you talk to Matron? Things are fairly quiet now, and you surely must be due for leave . . . ?"

She walked with him back to the mess. "Funny, I always thought Brock Weymouth would get her. I thought she'd give in in the end."

"Better if she had. I'm not sure about Weymouth, but at least he could stand up to her."

She gave him cocoa in the mess hut, and miraculously one of the nurses produced a tin of biscuits. She took him to be introduced to Sister, and then dared to take him to Matron. The lady greeted them graciously, removed her spectacles, and pressed her fingers lightly against her eyelids; she also looked tired, Lally thought. Matron listened in silence as Jon told his story. Lally could tell by her expression that she was not a great deal distressed by the story of a sister who was going to make a perfectly respectable match with Lord Gough's heir. Only she didn't know Margaret, and she didn't know Grenfell.

At last she said, "Well, Miss Pollock, I know you're due some leave. If it is your father's express wish . . . One is aware that parents also make sacrifices of daughters as well as sons." She drew paper toward her and wrote swiftly. "Take this to Sister Masterson. You have two weeks." She smiled faintly. "I hope your father isn't going to get as great a shock over you as over your sister."

Lally blinked. "Matron . . . ?"

"Your hair, Miss Pollock. Your hair."

Lally put her hand to her capless head. She was out of uniform in Matron's presence. "I'm sorry, Matron . . . about not wearing my cap. My hair . . . it's just so much easier to keep clean this way."

The woman nodded. "I know. But if that's the only change for women, we may not have achieved very much for ourselves during this war." She held her hand out to Jon. "Safe journey back, Captain."

Susie waylaid them on the way out. "One of the girls just unearthed a 'alf bottle of Calvados, Captain." They gathered around the end of a table in the mess hut, drinking it in mugs in case Sister should appear. "'elp keep you warm on the journey back, Captain." En masse, they saw him off on the borrowed motorcycle back to St. Omer. They pressed their good wishes on him; Lally felt cheated of those last, precious moments with him. But then, they were not supposed to be lovers, just brother and sister. All of them knew the story of his wife's death; he was young and fair and eligible. He bore the charm of one who has survived three years of war, and three terrible, bitter, bloody campaigns. They touched him, as if for luck. The motorcycle sped off into the darkness. "I say, Lally, invite me home when it's all over, will you?" someone said. "I'd like to know your brother better."

"Get in line," another voice answered. "Whose brandy was it, anyrate?"

* * *

In the pitching, tossing vessel crossing the Channel she read more fully about the battle of Cambrai, the battle now famous because of the first mass use of tanks. The British had launched a surprise attack of nearly four hundred tanks, and penetrated the German lines in three places. It had been planned as a limited attack; no one had expected the breakthrough. Lally's heart sang with pride as she thought of Black Jack's involvement, however remote, in that action. And then she felt the now familiar disillusionment as she read that the action had not been followed up. What that meant was that no one on the General Staff had expected the success, and there hadn't been sufficient reserves available.

"Sister . . . Sister . . . I wonder. Well, me mate here . . . 'e's started bleeding again. And the nurses with the men all 'ave their hands full. Could you take a look . . . ? Sorry, Sister, I know you're probably going on leave . . ." The soldier swayed uneasily with the ship's roll, balancing on crutches and one foot. But his mate was a stretcher case, with a leg gone. She saw the hemorrhaging, and went for a doctor, who could not come at once. She took dressings and tried to stem the hemorrhage, holding a light tourniquet on the stump. Now, in the hospital, they were able, when they got a suitable donor, to give a transfusion, using the method which prevented the donor's blood from clotting. This had been introduced by the American Harvard Unit when they came to the Camp Hospital at Camiers. It had been as long ago as 1915. But the facilities and knowledge were seldom available, and certainly not here on the boat. The doctor, when he came, was hardly able to do more than she had herself. He looked grim as he felt the pulse. "Thank you, Nurse. We'll just keep him quiet and comfortable, and in a few hours we'll have him safely in the hospital." He smiled at the soldier. "Just hold tight, lad."

Lally saw him taken off by stretcher as she left the ship. His face was deathly pale, his eyelids closed. She wondered if he would ever open them again on a hospital ward.

III

The face that came toward her in the gloom of the early December evening at Victoria Station was not Black Jack's. A familiar face in an unexpected place. "Brock!"

He saluted her before permitting himself to put his arms about her. He was wearing the uniform of a major in the United States Army. "You see, Lally, they caught me, after all. Didn't think they'd ever get old Brock to do anything so uncharacteristic as joining up— but here I am. Well, really, it's nothing to do with being patriotic. It's just that the U. S. Government had taken over the distribution of just about everything, so there was nothing left for me to do but come over and see that they did it as efficiently as possible."

She stood back and looked at him in the murky, yellow light in which tendrils of fog trailed. "I never expected . . ."

He took her arm, and her bag. "To hell with the rule that says an officer can't be seen carrying anything. Come on, my girl. I've got a staff car waiting. Black Jack's got the rooms at the Ritz. And they've given me a broom closet to sleep in for the time being."

They were out in the forecourt of the station. A driver raced to take the bag, and then to get the door of the car open. "I don't understand. You're here in London. Do you have leave? And how did you know . . . ?"

The car slid out into the traffic. "Leave? My dear, in a sense, I'm always on leave. I'm always in London, that is. You wouldn't think I'd be stupid enough to get myself sent to France, would you? People get killed in France. No, Lally . . . the hero bit isn't for me. I've always been in the business of supply—supplying whatever anyone wanted wherever they wanted it. I just do it for the Army now. Quartermaster Corps. I requisition things, I get them across the Atlantic, to France, or the Balkans, or wherever. It's the same thing I've always been doing. The only thing that's different is that now I do it officially for the U. S. Army. Oh, there's another small difference. I only get U. S. Army pay."

"I suppose that's why you sleep in a broom cupboard at the Ritz? But your friend is still lending you the suite my father is using? I suppose the Hispano has been sent back to your friend because you have a staff car now?"

He offered her a cigarette, lighted it, and leaned back. "Lally . . . Lally, what are friends for?"

She smoked in silence as they moved slowly through the blacked-out streets. The sense of the fog was now more pervasive; it caught in her throat. She found herself remembering the still, white face of the young soldier. He would probably die. She would be escorted into the warmth of the Ritz and he would never remember anything but the cold of the trenches.

"Friends, Brock? Yes . . . friends. Have you tried to stop Margaret marrying Grenfell? Father's right—it isn't a good thing."

His voice was cool. "Perhaps you might try to tell that to Margaret yourself. After all, who am I? All I can do is lend a few things, like hotel rooms and cars. Margaret never needed any of those things —she's always had them. Now Grenfell's got himself a war wound, a romantic sort of limp, and Margaret has turned around and says she's wildly in love with him. What's to stop them marrying? Beauty and rank and money on both sides. Perfect. *Me* stop Margaret? If Black Jack can't stop her . . ."

"He could. She's still under age."

"Can you imagine that? That he'd go to that length—and drive her away from him forever? Not Black Jack."

"Then why am *I* here? What am I supposed to do?" She was suddenly angry. She was remembering the soldier again, thinking she could have done more with her time, thinking, perhaps greedily, that with a few days' leave, she could have met Jon.

"What are you to do, Lally? Well, I suppose you're here to help Black Jack get through it. I suppose you're here to be Margaret's bridesmaid."

"And you'll stand by, and watch it?"

In the darkness, his hand reached hers, touched it briefly. It could have been an accidental encounter. Brock Weymouth was not the sort to seek comfort from a woman's hand, unless he desired her. "Watch it? What else? Margaret doesn't know I exist. Oh, by the way—Grenfell, to the disgust of his parents, has asked me to be best man. None of his chums is on leave at the moment. I guess they must have killed off an awful lot of them. He's really scraping the bottom of the barrel."

* * *

Margaret faced Black Jack rather than Lally. "Can you *please* tell me why I shouldn't marry him? What's wrong with Bobby? Is he insane—or a coward? We're in love, and it's war. And we're going to marry."

"Can't you wait just a little longer, Margaret?" Black Jack urged. "Now the Americans have come in, it can't last much longer. It'll be peace again, and you'll have time to think. I hate to see you rush . . ."

Margaret sank down on a chair. She covered her face with her hands. The sitting room at the Ritz was very quiet, the sound of the traffic muffled by the thick curtains and the veil of fog. Brock had excused himself and gone. They had eaten there, rather than the dining room. The food had been beautifully presented, but was not as lavish or exotic as Lally remembered. Even here, the war was taking hold.

At last Margaret raised her head. "What's there to wait for? All of them—I've seen almost every one of them go. All Jon's friends, all the ones we met during the season. Most of them are dead, or hopelessly maimed. There aren't many of the first ones left, Father. And you ask me to wait?"

"Are you marrying Bobby because he's all that's left?"

She wiped the tears furiously from her cheeks. "*You!* You dare say that to me? Don't you think I know the stories. You and Mother were married barely a month after you met each other. You didn't wait!"

"That was different—"

"Everything is different! Every case is different. Shall I wait to see if Bobby survives? Shall I tell him I have to wait to see if he comes back alive or in a coffin—if they can find a body? Shall I be cautious and cool? Or shall I take my chance with the rest of them? Women take chances, too, Father. If Bobby's all that's left, then I'll take what's left." She turned an agonized, imploring gaze on Lally. "Lally —you tell him. You've *seen* men die. I never have. You know what it's like to see them all go. One after the other." She turned back to her father. "I've crossed off their names in the casualty lists. And Bobby's alive, and there's a good chance he won't be sent back to France. I might have a normal life. I have the *right,* don't I?"

Black Jack sighed, and got to his feet. He took his hat and coat from the stand beside the door. Then he crossed to Margaret, and touched his hand to her cheek. "Just so long as you're sure you want to marry him, my love. Just so long as you're sure." He put on his hat and coat. "I think I'll just take a little walk. Get some air . . ."

"*Air?*" Lally said. "It's fog outside."

He shrugged. "Oh, well, perhaps I can get hold of Brock. We might go for a drink somewhere. . . . He seems to know all the places."

After the door had closed Margaret looked at Lally. "Does that mean it's all right? He's not going to stand in the way anymore? I didn't want to hurt him, Lally, but I *know* what I want. Maybe I did say Bobby's all that's left. What's wrong with that? Maybe he was meant to live so that we could find each other. When there are so many, it's hard for any one of them to stick out. You're not sure, are you? Well, *I'm* not sure, either. Who ever can be? We just take our chances." She wiped swiftly at the moisture left on her cheeks. "Oh, hell, Lally, let's celebrate!" She went and pressed the bell for the floor waiter. "Let's see if they've got any champagne left in this place. There's a lot to celebrate. We're alive. You and I and Jon and Father. And Alice. Bobby's alive. He'll be a good husband, Lally. Don't you think he'll be a good husband . . . ?"

As they drank the champagne, which the hotel still could produce from its cellar for Mr. Brockton Weymouth's guests, and talked of how the wedding would be arranged, Lally thought that, to her credit, Margaret had never once mentioned the things that Brock thought made Robert Grenfell a desirable match in her eyes. Beauty and rank and money, Brock had said. But in the wilderness of death which surrounded them, the most attractive thing to Margaret about Robert Grenfell seemed to be that he was there, alive. Like Jon, he had survived.

*   *   *

They were married a week later in the parish church of Pellham Langley. Once again the wardrobe of Lady Latitia Pollock had been combed, this time to bring forth the clothes for the bride. Margaret wore her mother's wedding gown of lace, once white, now cream-colored with age, and a long white ermine cloak, which had been her mother's ball cloak, and not seen since she had died. It had to be worn against the chill of the church, which had not been heated for the past year. Robert, Viscount Grenfell, stood beside her; for the period of the ceremony he had passed the walking cane he used to Brock Weymouth. Lally thought he seemed more handsome than she remembered; illness had caused him to lose weight, and he had assumed that interesting air of fragility which some invalids wear. Until he spoke, he might seem to be a poet. But Bobby Grenfell was still the same, amiable, rather weak-seeming young man Lally remembered. But he looked at Margaret with adoring eyes. She could not forget the way he had repeated the words of the marriage service. *With my body, I thee worship* . . . It seemed not to matter either to him or to Margaret that what followed was, *with all my wordly goods I thee endow.* Why should it? They were fair children of fortune, Lally thought. Brock handed back Bobby his cane for the walk up the aisle. He hardly needed it. Margaret's arm was under his. Perhaps, Lally thought, after all, Black Jack—and she—had been wrong. Perhaps there was a true sense in Margaret to support the man she had married. To support and cherish him, as she had promised, so long as they both should live.

* * *

They were not able to manage as good a reception as had been arranged in that wartime wedding of two years ago by Sandy West's parents. Most of the food laid out had been brought as gifts by tenants and friends of Black Jack. And his seemingly inexhaustible cellars were robbed to provide the wine. The matron at Pellham Langley had begged Black Jack to have the wedding in the village and the reception at the house, rather than Grangewick, which would have been more convenient. "It's the patients, you see, Mr. Pollock. They would enjoy it so much. They love to think that someone is getting married in the face of all this."

So there were many in the blue suits of the convalescent among the friends and tenants who met to toast Miss Margaret, now Lady

Grenfell, on her wedding day. "Damn me, Brock," Bobby Grenfell said, with something Lally thought were near-tears in his eyes. "Damn me if I don't like it better this way. Spontaneous, friendly . . . not like the stuffy big do's before the war. I *know* Margaret means this—and I'm a damn lucky man."

"Just so long as you remember it, Bobby."

Grenfell blinked and considered the remark; he had never been quick, Lally thought. But there seemed no harm in him. Was that the best she could think of this almost brother-in-law of hers, that there was no harm in him?

"I'll remember—of course I'll remember. Damn good of you to stand up with me, Brock. Parents can't quite understand it, you know. A bit old-fashioned. Hardly ever met an American before. But they're learning." Lally wondered how they had taken the news that their only surviving child, and heir, had invited a nameless, unknown man, hardly an acquaintance, much less a friend, to be his best man. The suggestion had probably come from Margaret, and in the absence of another ready choice, Bobby Grenfell had agreed. Anything to please Margaret. The major was presentable enough, wearing his uniform as if he had been born to it, doing all the correct things. His presence had seemed a heartening indication of the new Anglo-American alliance which soon would win the war. Perhaps Bobby Grenfell was being credited with a burst of imaginative inspiration, quite apart from the fact that none of his real friends were available, all either in France, or dead. No one wanted to remember the dead at a wedding, so Major Brockton Weymouth, with that splendidly upper-class name whose origin only a few knew, stood in admirably. How many, Lally wondered, would guess how much the best man had wanted to stand in the place of the groom?

She and Alice had been Margaret's bridesmaids, she wearing the court dress, drastically and clumsily recut by the village dressmaker; one of Lady Latitia's white dresses had been sacrificed to make a dress for Alice. They both wore borrowed furs. Lady Bletchley had come to Witfell to witness the marriage of her granddaughter; she wore the same grand purple as at Jon's wedding two years ago, the same diamonds. She nodded approvingly at the whole proceeding. This was a match she could be pleased about. She examined the pearl earrings which were Bobby Grenfell's gifts to the bridesmaids. They were not matching pairs; Lally's had a small surround of diamonds. "From the Gough jewels, no doubt," Lady Bletchley said. "There wouldn't have been time . . . They make a handsome couple, don't they? I'm thankful dear Margaret is safely married off." She accepted champagne from Brock Weymouth with a hand that trembled slightly; she looked noticeably older, Lally thought, than she had two years ago. Five of her grandsons, including the Honorable Patrick, had died in those years. "I worried about Margaret . . . This war, so unsettling. And she's a great deal like Latitia. I didn't know where her fancy might light. But now she's safely settled . . ."

The Marchioness had come up from London. "How long will it last?" she commented to Lally. "Grenfell's a fool. I hope *you* won't rush into something, Lally. Keep your head, child. Black Jack's obviously going to be leaning heavily on you—I suppose he's always done that. But he's aged. Working too hard, I suppose. Who's this Brock Weymouth? Handsome devil, but I don't think I quite trust him . . . Here. Alice, let me look at your earrings. Lovely . . . lovely. You look lovely, child." When Alice wandered off she said, "But the trouble is she isn't a child. As beautiful as that, and too innocent to know how men will look at her . . . and want her. Black Jack will have to be very careful of her. Come, Lally—let's get over to the fire. That church chilled me to the bone." She was wearing a long sable coat, a relic of the time when her husband had lavished money on her, and on the gaming tables. "I hope when it's your turn, Lally, it will be in peacetime, and we'll be able to do it properly. I want Black Jack to put everything in my hands, and give me carte blanche with money, as he did with your season. It will be a beautiful wedding. I'll show everyone that that season wasn't a sham. I'll be godmother to your first child."

As they approached the fire a young officer, wearing the blue convalescent suit, thrust forward two chairs eagerly. "And who," Lally asked, "have you got in mind for the groom?"

"You'll be sensible, Lally. You'll wait. And then you'll have your pick. Look around you, girl. All these young men, and their eyes are devouring you, even with that outlandish hair. Don't lose your head, Lally. Black Jack's money is always there in the background. When you were fat you would never have forgotten that. But now . . ." She turned to the nearest officer. "Young man, are you blind? Can't you see our glasses are empty? And I've had nothing to eat."

Within minutes they were being supplied with plates of ham and illegally shot grouse; there was a small crowd of officers around them; Billings had had a bottle of champagne lifted from his tray so that their glasses should never be empty. "You see what I mean, Lally? You're not used to it. Keep your head."

The reception grew loud and cheerful as the drink circulated. Someone played the piano; the matron beamed on the whole scene. Black Jack's face had relaxed from the knot of tension that had twisted it all through the ceremony. In the midst of the crowd, the Marchioness had studied Brock with qualified approval. "Someone told me he's very clever, and he seems to be rich. But no one knows who he is."

"He doesn't know himself."

"Rubbish! I've never seen anyone who was more sure of what he is—even if he doesn't know *who* he is. That man wants the world. The one part of it he didn't get today was Margaret."

"You *know?*"

"I'm not a fool, Lally. When everyone else was watching the bride during the ceremony, I was watching *him*. He may be in love for the first time in his life, and he doesn't know how to deal with it. But he lost, didn't he? He's not used to losing. I wish Bobby Grenfell wasn't such a fool . . . It's such a temptation for a clever man to move in." She pointed suddenly. "Margaret's going upstairs. God knows where —perhaps the matron's office—to change. You'd better be there at the bottom of the stairs when she throws her bouquet."

Reluctantly, Lally went forward. There weren't many young, unmarried women to compete for the bouquet. Travel was too difficult. In the new climate of freedom between the classes, some of the girls from the village were present, and the daughters of the tenant farmers. It was a wartime wedding, and a popular one. Margaret paused halfway up the stairs. These were the stairs she had used all her life, only temporarily lent out. She belonged there. Lally thought her beautiful, but not quite as radiant a bride as she might have been expected to appear. Margaret waited a dramatic moment before she tossed the bouquet.

A slight young figure seemed to leap off the floor. The bouquet fell into Alice's eager hands. A silence descended on the group. Everyone knew Alice should never marry. She looked around, expecting

applause, dismayed by the silence. Suddenly the piano was ham-
mered. The song Lally most hated was thumped out, voices took up
the words.

> *Keep the home fires burning,*
> *While our hearts are yearning . . .*

❧ CHAPTER 10 ❧

I

A sense of weariness fell on Lally. On the return trip to France, for the first time she felt seasick. She looked at the men around her, and she knew the feeling of dread and hopelessness they experienced. What they faced was to be endured; they knew nothing else.

Then, on the dock at Calais she saw a full battalion of American troops being debarked. She saw the fresh young faces, the clean, well-fed air they exuded. There had been no time for disillusionment with them. She saw the gantries swinging the loads of materiel onto the dock. In that, as much as in these fresh young men, was the hope. She had listened to Black Jack talking about the appalling losses of British shipping. But the blockade imposed by the British had hit hard into the German economy, and some actually said they were starving. Would it finally come to that? No victory won, just two weary giants fighting to a senseless standstill, toppling into the mud over a nonexistent victory line? Sometime during the days when they had prepared for Margaret's wedding she could remember Brock saying to Black Jack, "I've bought a lot of sugar . . . everything that's scarce makes money." Did he think no other way? She supposed it was possible to be in the U. S. Army and still be running some sort of business back in the States. What sort of business was it? He never said. It changed with the changing needs.

"Well?" Susie said, "what are you looking so down in the mouth about? Your sister got married, didn't she? And to a lord! So then, cheer up. After all, the Yanks are here, aren't they? It has to be over soon. Nothing can keep on like this forever."

Why did she keep remembering Brock, and what he had said as they had sat over the fire at Grangewick after the wedding? "The economy of the Allies has turned around. When the war began, England and France had a lot of money invested in America. Well, all that's changed. They have used up all their credit, and now they're deeply in debt. We keep supplying materiel, and keep lending money. O.K.—so we're saving ourselves, but we're also getting rich. The balance of money has tipped in our favor. Until this war we didn't know how much we had to sell."

Black Jack had gloomily sipped his brandy. "I shouldn't complain . . . I shouldn't. I've made a deal of money out of this war because I prepared for it. But they say this year income tax will go to thirty percent. Can you imagine it?—*thirty percent*. It will finish a lot of people—especially the landowners. Land doesn't return that kind of money. Bletchley was telling me he was finding the going hard. He's never been a businessman, of course. Just lived off the estate. Naturally, his idea of hard going is rather different from most people's." Then he leaned forward. "Brock, can you put me in touch with anyone who has woolen yarn . . . or even raw wool? Our stocks are very low. So much shipping which was supplying us has been sunk. You think a consignment's coming, and then you hear it's at the bottom of the Atlantic." He sat back. "I'm sorry. That sounds crass. The men on those ships are also at the bottom of the Atlantic. And my son is alive."

Brock scribbled in a small notebook. "I'll make some inquiries. Maybe I have a friend or two . . ."

Like the friend, Lally wondered, who always supplied the suite at the Ritz? Who were Brock's friends? And then she realized that there he was, sitting by their fire at Grangewick, after all hope of winning Margaret had gone, and she thought he now had to be counted among their friends. Brock would go on making his notes, and his "friends," his connections would supply most of what was needed. Would he trade off sugar for yarn? And what would the fee be? She was certain he did nothing which did not turn a profit for himself. Or was she certain? He was sitting here at the fire. What did he gain from that? Then Brock looked directly at her. "You should be in bed, Lally. I'm driving down to London tomorrow. I could drive you to Dover if you wanted."

"The petrol?"

"Didn't I tell you I was in the Quartermaster Corps? That's Aladdin's cave, Lally."

"Well—if you just drop me in London, that'll be very convenient. I promised Lady Ross I'd spend a night with her before going back."

"Yes . . . Lady Ross," Brock said, rather musingly. "She's very fond of you, Lally."

"Fond? How do you know?"

"I have two eyes."

Black Jack drained his brandy. "Brock, I'll take that ride down with you. Since you're going and using the petrol in any case."

Was it the fact that she would be seeing the Marchioness which caused Black Jack to make his sudden decision? In London he took Lally and Lady Ross both to dinner, and then saw Lally off at Victoria the next morning. He barely mentioned the Marchioness, but neither had he said when he would be returning to Yorkshire.

She was roused from her reverie by Susie's words. "Try to put a smile back on your face before you go into the wards, Lally. You've just 'ad leave—and a wedding. The lads like to see a smile."

Lally glanced along the length of the cold, damp hut where they ate; she looked at her cracked, chapped hands, which two weeks of warm houses and lanolin had not healed. She found herself fixing on the smile Susie had wanted. "Right. Come on—let's brew up some cocoa. I'm passing round the biscuits Brock gave me. *American* biscuits, Susie."

* * *

In the raw cold of a January morning Susie came racing into the mess hut, waving a newspaper. All the nurses turned from their food to look at her. " 'ere! Why didn't you tell us. Military Cross, 'e's got. 'e's a bloody 'ero, and you didn't even tell us."

She thrust the newspaper under Lally's eyes. There it was, among the list of decorations awarded. *Captain Jonathan James Pollock, First Yorkshire Light Infantry. Military Cross.*

"Must have done something special in that third bloody battle of Ypres. Didn't he say something—or write something about it?"

"No—no, nothing. Nor my father. Perhaps he didn't tell him."

"Well, girls . . ." Susie looked around at the other nurses, who were already taking the paper from her hands, verifying what she said. "Well, there 'e was. Handsome as a god. *And* a 'ero. And we let him go!"

"We've had plenty of heroes through our hands, Susie. It's just that they don't all get medals." Lally shivered, more from fear than the rawness of the morning. What had Jon said? "They make heroes of us in spite of ourselves. For cowardice they put you up against a wall and shoot you." Jon would never think of himself as a hero. "I just want to live," he had said.

II

It was everywhere about them—the sense that it soon must end, but waiting through the days of winter, Lally began to think that the spring would never come. The spring would have to signal something —the opening of a new offensive, the strengthening of the American forces, the vital strengthening of hope they brought. To her, when she saw them, the fresh young faces still looked fresh, not the exhausted, battered, demoralized faces of the British and French. It was a false spring of hope. From March until early April the Germans launched a new offensive. The Allies had to wait until early June before the United States Second and Third Divisions, together with the French, stopped a sustained German attack; the U. S. Marines captured and held Belleau Wood north of Château-Thierry against repeated German attempts to dislodge them. Word was beginning to leak through of crisis and near-riots in Germany; there was talk of starvation. The German submarine fleets could no longer fend off the wave of goods and materiel crossing the Atlantic, and the British fleet was increasingly liberated to enforce the blockade of Germany. It was, Lally thought, a strange way to win a modern war. The guns still shook the ground under their feet, and overhead, increasingly, they witnessed the battle in the sky. There were stories of air aces, on both sides. "Seems so clean up there, don't it, Nurse," one corporal whose dressing she was changing said. "Seems so nice and clean. None of this muck and filth we've got down 'ere. They tell me the best job is a mechanic back there with the flying blokes. All you 'ave to do is keep them planes properly looked after. If I ever get back to Blighty, I'm going to study to be a mechanic. Seems to me the damn lorries and ambulances and such are always breaking down. Should be a job for a mechanic after it's over. That is, if I get back."

"You will," Lally said. It was an automatic response. There was a sense of the tide turning, but it was infinitely slow. It was as if she watched a long, dimly lighted strand, with the sea a pale gray; an inch, a foot perhaps, of mud-colored sand was exposed. Then the sea would come rushing back. Had anything been gained?

"Miss Pollock, are you dreaming?" Sister's voice beside her was chilly with reproach.

"Ah, no, Sister—just chatting, we was," the corporal said cheerfully. He was not intimidated by Sister. He had been wounded twice before. He wore a decoration, and knew how to use its authority to defend the nurses he liked.

Sister's tone was icy: "Miss Pollock, finish the dressing and see the corporal comfortable. Then you may go to the mess. You have a visitor."

Lally spun around. "A visitor? Captain Pollock?"

"Finish the dressing, Miss Pollock."

"'elp!" the corporal said, in mock pain. "Yer killin' me, Nurse. I've 'ad better 'andling at a dressing station." Then he winked at her. "Go on, luv. Yer brother, is it?"

Lally deliberately slowed the pace of her movements. "Corporal, I promise not to kill you. Not just yet." Methodically she finished the dressing, taking extra care with it. She straightened the bedclothes, plumped up the corporal's pillows. She found the cigarettes he had mislaid. "Go on, luv," he urged her again. "I know yer dyin' to get away. . . . Fond of 'im, I can see."

She nodded. "Yes—I'm very fond of him."

But it was an American staff car which waited outside the mess hut, and Brock Weymouth who stood up to salute her. "Brock!" She tried to keep the disappointment from her voice. "You—here in France?"

He removed his cap, and bent to kiss her cheek. "Well, I decided I couldn't go back to the old U.S. of A. without being able to say I'd seen this side of the Channel. Could be handy, you know. Impresses people. Of course, I'll never be a hero, like Jon. No medals or anything. For medals you have to get near the fighting. That isn't my style."

"But what are you *doing?*"

"Doing . . . ?" He shrugged, deliberately vague. "There's always a general who needs a few things supplied. I shift a few trucks around. Mostly I make sure my generals are comfortably housed and fed, so that they can get on with the business of winning the war. We have our uses, guys like me."

"Brock, you're an impossible cynic. And what's all this?"

He was unloading a cardboard box—tins of peaches, cakes of soap, tinned butter, jam, boxes of biscuits, chocolate, toothpaste, lanolin, anchovy paste, real coffee, Lally saw. "Spread it around. I guess you girls get as short of these things as the men do."

"I couldn't take all that."

"Then you might stop being so selfish and think of the other nurses. Will they love you for nobly handing it back? None of my generals will miss it for a moment."

She shook her head. "You never change, Brock. Whether it's cars or hotel rooms—"

"How's Margaret?" he said abruptly, cutting her short. "I've sort of lost touch since I've been in France. Used to see her quite a bit in London. She didn't seem to be settling too well into the role of married woman. The guys don't flock around the way they used to. Scared of compromising her, I suppose."

"But you weren't."

He shrugged again. "Me? Well, you know me. I'm not an English gentleman. I break the rules. But have you heard from her?"

"Not lately. She never was much of a letter writer. Father says she's well, though. Still driving. Bobby hasn't had any leave since he was posted back here. Yes, I think she probably does get a little bored."

"And you, Lally? What about you?"

"What's there to say? I just get through the day. And the week. Afraid most of the time. We fall into bed and sleep, and get up and begin all over again. The patients move on, and more come down from the casualty clearing stations. You generally don't get to know the men very well—they're either dead, or moved to a hospital farther away from the lines, or sent back to England. Brock . . . when will it end? You must hear talk . . . you're around the General Staff all the time."

"Lally, honey, the General Staff don't talk to lowly guys like me. They want clean sheets on their beds, and fires in their rooms. I've begun to think that if I didn't already have a few irons in the fire, I'd go into the hotel business when it's all over." His face grew more serious. "Just try to remember that gradually we're pulling ahead of the Germans in this blockade business. The level of the tonnage of shipping we're producing is passing the level of tonnage they sink. Their alliances are in a mess. They're hungry, Lally. That's what will do it in the end."

"But *how*—how do they keep on finding the reserves and the ammunition? The guns still hammer away. They still mount offensives."

He touched her hand. "Lally, I've got three hours, and I'd rather talk of other things than the war. I told Sister I was here at the request of your father. She's given you time off. No great deal, I imagine. She said you were just due to come off duty. I've lined up a little dinner at a place down the road a piece. They have duck and some decent wine, unimaginable as it may seem. So take off your apron, there's a girl, and come to the feast."

"How did you get permission from Sister?"

"I have my ways, Lally. Like a dozen bottles of whiskey. I always heard that good nurses like to have a bottle around to give the fellows a nip when the going's rough. I tried a few bottles on her—she didn't turn them down."

It was true. Sister was a strict disciplinarian with her nurses; with the men she was compassionate while still being professional. Sometimes the reward for enduring a particularly painful dressing was a tot of whiskey. It was a prized luxury.

When Lally went to change she saw that the apron she took off had been flecked with bloodstains. She took out her cloak, and went back to the mess hut. Brock was there, surrounded by the other nurses who had just come off duty, and they were exclaiming over the contents of the box he had unpacked. Then another one was hauled onto the table. Unbelievably, it contained bottles of whiskey and brandy.

"Brock! We can't take that!" Lally protested.

Susie was one of the ones who turned around to stare at her. "Who asked *you*? The major just made a gift to the mess. Don't you think we deserve a tot now and again? The word's already around that he gave the same to Sister for the men. We're not taking anything from them." She turned her pert little face toward Brock. "Never refuse a gift from an ally. The generals don't . . . whiskey or guns."

"Well . . ." Brock replaced his cap. "Let's just say it's an early Christmas box. That's if Sister asks. You'd better celebrate it early, ladies, because if things go right, you won't be here for Christmas."

Susie said briskly, "All right, girls. Let's start organizing Christmas, and get all this stuff out of Sister's way."

* * *

They dined at a village almost untouched by the shelling. There were the red tabs of the General Staff sprinkled through the diners, who were mainly military. Lally looked around carefully, and saw that the majority were American officers. "I can hardly believe it. Perhaps it's true, after all. Perhaps it will end, finally. Do you really think before Christmas, Brock?"

"Lally, honey, I just said that because I could hardly bear to look at those faces. Those girls are short of everything a woman seems to need. Perhaps it was right . . . perhaps not. But the General Staff would prefer us to spread a cheery word. Now, don't look for a menu, because there isn't one. But there's a pâté, and there's duck, and Madame has just picked some strawberries."

"Strawberries . . . that seems a world away. Last time I had strawberries—"

"Last time you had strawberries, Lally, it *was* a world away. Someone told me you were a fat little deb, and you gobbled everything in sight on the supper tables. But the young men always wanted to talk to you because you were the brightest girl around, and Margaret was the most beautiful. Now that's some powerful combination." He nodded as the waiter brought a discreetly covered bottle to the table and poured. *"Vin ordinaire,* of course, Lally. But we used to call it Puilly Fumé."

The June sunlight streamed through the long windows which gave a view of a garden only slightly neglected. Beyond the roses on the trellis there, Lally guessed, would be the kitchen garden that grew the strawberries and other such delicacies; there would be the yard where the ducks and chickens pecked, no doubt watched over by someone with a gun. The bread on the table was white and fresh, the table linen was starched. There were such oases as these left? From the road the house had looked modest, and had borne no sign to indicate that it was a restaurant. And yet it was packed. But the staff cars had discreetly driven off; the drivers would wait until the meal ended.

"Lally, if you're going to sit there and look guilty, I'm taking you straight back to the hospital. Goddamn it, enjoy yourself! What difference can one decent meal make?—you can't take it to them in the trenches."

"I'm sorry—I shouldn't spoil—"

"No, you shouldn't. And don't spoil the fun for the girls back at the hospital. You could turn into a real bore, Lally."

"And Margaret wouldn't?"

"You're damn right! Margaret wouldn't. She'd enjoy every minute of it, and she'd let every man who laid eyes on her know she was enjoying it. They're looking at you, Lally. The officers who haven't had the luck to have a woman with them are turning round to look at you. Enjoy it! Drink your wine, and eat your food, and damn well enjoy it! You're not a fat little deb anymore. You're a woman—a very desirable woman."

"Are you . . . ? What do they call it? Making a pass at me?"

"No, I'm not. I'm just telling you what's what. Next time I get a few hours near here, I'll take out that little red-headed piece with the cute nose. *She* wouldn't make any objections to duck and Puilly Fumé."

She held up her hand. "I solemnly promise to enjoy every minute and every mouthful."

"Well, that's better. Only don't be solemn about it."

They ate, and talked, and the brief time sped away. Lally tried not to keep bringing Jon into the conversation; she noticed how many times Brock clamped his lips on Margaret's name. On that long June evening the sun had barely begun its decline as they sipped their coffee and cognac. Very soon they must start back. Brock had still not said what his final destination was that night. She was realizing how very circumspect he was in not actually naming the people he served; but then he had never said anything about what interests he had served before the war had placed him in uniform. There was still no background to Brock Weymouth.

Perhaps the wine and cognac had made her reckless, or the ever-present sense they all had these days that the time was short, and things might be said which would never have been uttered before. "You still think a lot about Margaret, don't you, Brock? You were best man at her wedding, but you still don't quite believe that she's gone. You've lost her, Brock."

"Yes, I stood there at a wedding. That was all. Afterward I saw a woman in London who didn't realize she'd been married."

His face seemed blank; he could have been reciting a railway timetable, something not to be disputed. "We'll have to be on our way, Lally. I've a piece to travel tonight."

He escorted her through the tables. And yes, there were, she saw, some glances which went to her, and lingered. She dismissed them; women were scarce on the ground here.

At the main gate of the hospital it was she who brushed Brock's lips with a kiss. "I really *did* enjoy it. Thank you for telling me I'm turning into a sourpuss. I'll enjoy every single thing that comes my way in the future. There will be a future, won't there, Brock?"

"There'll be a future, honey. You bet there'll be a future. I, Uncle Brock, personally guarantee it."

The staff car roared away into the still-light June evening. "Phew!" Susie exclaimed when Lally came in. "You don't 'alf smell! Full of good wine, are you?" She rolled over on the cot. "Wish *I'd* 'ad him for a few hours. Well, never mind . . . Tell me, what did you have to eat?"

* * *

Afterward Lally always thought of that dinner with Brock as a turning point; it marked for her a spark of hope rekindled in the awful weariness of the months and the years of bloody stalemate.

After the American forces had made their mark at Château-Thierry fortune swung toward them—toward them and the fresh young men and the superior force of their equipment. In July, when Ludendorff threw his forces once again against the Allies in the second battle of the Marne, they made little progress against the Americans and the French. Nine American divisions were committed to the battle and they forced the Germans back across the Marne; the French retook Soissons. August had dawned with hope. Lally could feel the sense of excitement through the wards and the huts as the news came of the battle of Amiens. The British plans had been careful and well-concealed, and they hurled four hundred and fifty tanks into the struggle and gained eight miles on the first day. Eight miles in that wilderness of mud and ruin where thousands of men had died to gain a few feet. "Gawd!" Susie said. "I can't believe it. Do you think it's the truth this time, Lally?"

Swiftly, that August and September, the news came that could not have been invented or exaggerated. In the second battle of the Somme and of Arras the British and the French took back the old, death-ridden landmarks—Roye, Bapaume, Noyon, and Péronne. The

Germans fell back to the Hindenburg line. The Americans took St. Mihiel. In September and October, Argonne and Ypres were fought over yet again; the Americans got through part of the Argonne, and the British took St. Quentin and Armentières. The rumor ran that the German and Austro-Hungarian governments had appealed to President Wilson for an armistice, accepting his Fourteen Peace Points. Sometimes Lally would wake from sleep, aware that she was struggling for breath, her heart pounding. All she could think of as she performed the tasks that had now almost become routine was that Jon had fought in two of the latest battles and was regularly being returned, after being sent down with his battalion, to the front lines. He would stay in it to the end, and it seemed too much to hope, after this endless time, that he could survive to the end. She dared not hope.

"Why are you looking so down-in-the-mouth?" Susie asked. "We're winning. Finally, we're winning!" Lally had no reply. She did not want to speak Jon's name, as if doing so might direct the attention of the gods of war toward him. It would be the cruelest blow if he should not live out these final days.

They were the final days, though very few were sure of that. During October the British and Americans continued their advance; the Germans began to withdraw rapidly. By November 10 the Americans were at Sedan. They were where it had begun, almost, Lally thought. They later learned that on November 3 mutiny had broken out in the German fleet at Kiel; the mutiny spread to Hamburg, Bremen, and Lübeck. The whole of northwestern Germany was involved, and there was no way the German government could contain the news. Then revolution broke out in Munich.

Kaiser Wilhelm II abdicated, and fled to Holland. The Socialist leader, Scheidemann, proclaimed a German Republic.

In a railway coach at Compiègne the German representatives accepted from Foch the demands of the Allies. They were designed to make the Germans helpless, and they were agreed to.

The directives went out. At 11 A.M. on November 11, the great guns of the Western Front fell silent. There was a dazed sense of disbelief, a quiet moment of somber skepticism before the hysteria of joy and relief broke. Lally found herself comforting a sobbing soldier, a man who had borne his frightful wound with stoic bravery.

"I made it, Nurse." He clasped her hand so tightly it hurt. "By God, I made it! I've beaten that old bugger!"

"Beaten—*who?*"

He looked up at her, the tears still streaming down his face. "I'm alive, aren't I?"

Lally came off duty to find Susie lying on her cot, her shoulders heaving, her eyes puffed; she blew vigorously into a handkerchief— Susie, whom she had never seen break before. "Well?—ain't I entitled to a cry, too? Everyone else is doing it."

Jon, Lally thought . . . there had been no news of Jon for two weeks. Men had died in the last, the very last hours. Was Jon alive? Nothing in her heart made her certain.

That night, as the men in the hospital beds sang the ribald songs they had learned in the trenches, and no one checked them—as everyone greeted everyone else with smiles, Brock Weymouth fought his way through the rejoicing crowds, along the roads clogged with vehicles which had no particular destination and which madly blew their horns, to the nurses' mess at the abbey. This time no one tried to conceal the case of whiskey. The RAMC men, doctors and orderlies, ambulance drivers, invaded the mess hut. Nurses slipped back to the wards with bottles.

"Lally, you O.K.?" Brock said.

"I wonder about Jon," was all she could answer.

The party continued until the early hours. No one cared about sleep; the regulations for the moment were abandoned. They wheeled in a battered piano, and someone bashed at it constantly. Brock was surrounded by nurses; even the sisters thawed toward him. There was another American in the hut, but it was for Brock they sang "Over There." They forgave him the smart, uncreased uniform; they even forgave the fact that he could find the whiskey with which to be generous. They weren't going actually to say that the Americans had won the war—that would be to deny too many of their own dead. But they knew that they would not have stood and bellowed out the songs that night without them. One captain, more than a little drunk, pounded Brock on the back.

"Make you honorary member King's Own Wiltshire Rifles, old chap. Welcome to the regiment."

"Thanks . . . I appreciate it." Brock fought his way to Lally's side. He found her sitting, watching the celebration in a rather detached fashion. The tin mug of whiskey beside her was almost untouched. "Stop thinking of Jon, he's all right. Look, I'll get on to it first thing in the morning. Communications are going to be chaotic for a while. Everyone will want to be demobilized tomorrow, and everyone will want to pack up and go back home. We can't—we have a bit of mopping up to do."

She turned to him. "I've just begun to realize that. It can't go back tomorrow to what it was. In fact, it can't ever be the same again, can it? In the moments when I haven't been thinking about Jon, I've just remembered that if I really was born this month—this is the month we decided we'd fix as my birthday—the day Father found me outside the Corn Exchange in Leeds, then I'm twenty-one, Brock. I turned twenty-one somewhere along the way, and didn't know it."

He leaned forward and kissed her. "November eleventh is your birthday, Lally. Happy birthday."

"Did they ever give *you* a birthday, Brock?"

He grinned. "Why, sure. They gave me the birthday every red-blooded American boy would want. I was supposed to have been born on the Fourth of July. Brockton Weymouth is the original Yankee Doodle Dandy."

She found herself returning his kiss, warmly, a sense of affection and kinship flowing through her. He had come as a stranger into their midst; now she knew him as a dear friend.

"Then we won't ever forget each other's birthdays, will we?"

II

The days passed, and there was no telegram from Black Jack, and Lally began to feel some certainty. Jon was not killed, more than likely not even wounded. She could wait now. She went the round of her duties. It was painful to see those who had survived the war but did not inherit the peace. Many still died. Hardest to see were those who came in, released from the trenches, but delirious with the infection which had been named "the Spanish influenza." These cases they tried to isolate, but whole wards still caught the infection. Lally saw many of them die. She watched a doctor write out a death certificate. Sister stood by his side.

"The figures are beginning to be published, Sister. They say it's the worse pandemic since the Black Death in the fourteenth century. In fact—" He ceased writing and looked up at both of them. "You'll probably be run off your feet for a good while longer. They're beginning to say that the death figures may even be worse than all we've suffered through the war. It's spread everywhere. Try to see that your nurses get enough rest, Sister. God knows, I'd like to see them get enough decent food, but I might as well whistle for that."

* * *

The telephone call came as Lally was washing before going to bed. A VAD came rushing to the hut. "Pollock, it's your brother. Run! God knows how long he can hold the line. Everyone in the world seems to be trying to telephone at the same time."

Jon's voice sounded faded and distant. The line crackled with static. "I'm at Dunkirk, Lally. I caught one—second last day. Nothing much. Just in the hand."

"Jon!" A hand injury could not be so serious. "Are you all right?"

"Great! But they think I should be tidied up a bit, so they're sending me back home. I'm going to Chelsea Royal, I think. Looks as if I won't be coming back to France."

"Thank God!"

"Is that all you can say? You're not sorry I'm leaving?"

"You'll be safe and well. You're going home. That's all that matters."

"Well, then, will you do something for me, Lally?"

What could she do for him? "Anything," she answered.

"Get down on your bended knees and beg for a forty-eight-hour leave to see your wounded brother. Brock is laying on transport. And he's going to be best man."

Sweat broke out on her hands. "Whose wedding?"

"Ours—yours and mine, Lally. Unless you have someone else in mind. Lally! Are you still there?"

"Yes . . . yes, I'm here."

"You don't sound very enthusiastic."

"I . . . I . . ."

"Does that mean you're coming? Is there going to be a marriage? I've got the padre lined up. He's known me for a few years, but it took a lot of convincing to make him believe that I *can* marry you. I don't have Sandy's death certificate, and he always thought Lillian Pollock was my sister. He accepts Sandy's death. The colonel vouched for that. He just never thought of anyone asking to marry his sister. Oh, and since it's France, I think we've got to go through a civil ceremony, too."

"I don't know if I'm *allowed* to marry, Jon. You're sure? You don't have to . . ."

"Stop it, Lally. Just stop it. I've grown up since the days of Sandy. I know what I want, and I'm not wearing romantic blinders. What I have to be sure about is you. I always wondered if you didn't just feel sorry for me. They say a lot of women do. You know the story. Soldier headed back for the trenches. Compassion, pity. Might be his last time, that sort of thing. Was that it, Lally?"

The crackle on the line was worse. "What? What did you say?"

"You weren't just sorry for me? Lally, can you hear me?"

"No, I wasn't sorry for you. It wasn't that—oh, God, it's impossible trying to talk about this. Shouting through a telephone. I think there are a couple of dozen people who can hear me."

"Me too. But it only needs an answer. We don't have to discuss it. Will you, Lally? Will you come? After all, once it's done, what can they do to you? Just kick you out. And the war's over. You've done your stint. I have to have an answer, Lally. Are you coming?"

"Yes! Somehow I'll get there. Even if I have to desert. I'd hate just to walk out, because we have a lot of sick men here. They need—"

"I'm sick, too, Lally." She found no reply to that. His voice came, thin and tense, through the crackling wire. "Be outside the abbey at eight A.M. Thursday. Brock has a convoy of U. S. Army lorries coming through. The officer in charge has been told to look out for you. You'll get a ride all the way here."

"Brock, how does he do it?" Thursday was the day after tomorrow—in fact, nearly tomorrow already.

"Don't ask questions. Just be there. Can I tell him you'll be there?"

"Yes." Abruptly the line went dead.

She paced the cloisters in the cold darkness trying to make sense of the telephone call. There it was—just a telephone call, but all the hope of her life had been answered in it. But had it been answered? Jon had said nothing about loving her. There had never been a courtship; there had been the one, ultimate act of love between them. She had no doubt that what she felt for him was love, but what had he said? The words came back: "I'm not wearing romantic blinders." Was that enough? She listened to the echo of her own footsteps in the empty cloisters. If he married her from pity, because he felt he ought, the marriage would fail. The dream would be dead, as surely as if he had died. And yet, why should the dream die? Sudden anger and scorn for herself flooded her mind. Why didn't she believe what had happened?—why didn't she let herself believe what Brock had told her?—that in the eyes of men she was desirable. Believe she had been able to inspire passion in Jon. Don't even let herself think he had turned to her to escape the hurt of Sandy. If she didn't have Jon wholeheartedly now, she would win him. Grasp the chance. If she left it for time and conjecture, she might lose him. A man had escaped almost four years of hell and death; he wanted life, not anguished conjecture. He had asked her to be outside the hospital, waiting for the American convoy. She would be there, and let the future settle itself.

* * *

Quivering with excitement, fear, and hope, she went to Sister and explained that her brother had been wounded, and was being sent back to England. Could she have leave?

Sister eyed her steadily. "Your brother seems to be in no danger, Miss Pollock. It's unlikely, now that hostilities have ceased, that he'll ever be sent back to France. He wasn't Regular Army, was he?"

"No, Sister."

"Well, then, he'll probably get an early discharge, once he's better. I imagine you can wait to see him."

"No, Sister, I can't."

"You know the state we're in with this influenza. We need all the help we can get."

"Forty-eight hours, Sister. That's all."

"Well, Miss Pollock, you've worked hard, no doubt of that. You're more than due leave. But then, so are we all. Well, since it's just forty-eight hours . . ." She picked up her pen and began writing. Lally felt herself sag with relief. "Miss Pollock," Sister said, as she handed over the slip, "have you thought of taking up nursing professionally when you're no longer required here? I think you are the caliber of woman we need. I myself will be returning to St. Thomas's hospital in London. I am hoping to bring a small cadre of young women with me from here. The nursing profession is a very honorable one, Miss Pollock—and this war has made a great difference in the standing of women. They even say . . ." Her usually severe face twisted in a wry smile. "They have promised us the vote. I hope you'll consider my proposal, Miss Pollock."

"Yes, Sister. Thank you." She clutched the precious slip of paper. She had accepted Jon's proposal.

* * *

She passed the next day in a fever of hope and recurring doubts. She thought she had grown a little light-headed; she noticed her hands trembled a little as she worked. Chills of nervous excitement shook her body. She seemed unusually clumsy with the dressings; a thermometer slipped from her fingers and shattered. At supper she found it difficult to swallow. Susie eyed what she was unable to eat. "You're not going to finish that, Lally?" Without waiting for a reply, she reached over and helped herself from Lally's plate. "Never seen you so het up. But still . . . it's wonderful he's come through it all, and only that leg wound and now this bit of a scratch. Can't be many been that long in the trenches and got away with that little. Though, mind you, it might turn out to be a bit more than a scratch when they're sending him back to England. Still, if he was able to talk to you, he's all right. Lucky Sister let you go . . . well, why not? You've earned it."

Lally folded her clothes into a suitcase while Susie watched. It contained nothing that could remotely be described as bridal wear. She looked at the plain, serviceable underwear, and longed for just the touch of silk. And then she realized that underwear didn't matter. As she tossed restlessly on her pillow she remembered the Marchioness's promise that she would organize her wedding. It would have been a grand wedding. She drifted off into an uneasy sleep, feeling her cheeks burning even in the chill of the tent; her cheeks burned, and still she shivered.

It was Susie who woke her, not the alarm clock. "Is it time already?" she croaked. "I mustn't be late. At the gate. Eight o'clock."

Susie's hand was on her forehead, and then went swiftly to her pulse. "Sorry, Lally, I don't think you'll be keeping your appointment. I think you've got it—the bloody Spanish flu. Look, I'll just go and tell the night Sister. And see if we can find a doctor."

"No—no!" Lally struggled to rise. The candle Susie had lighted swum before her, a dim ragged light which seemed to leap about, and could not be focused. "I've got to go, Susie." She struggled to her feet, and then fell back on the cot. "Got to!"

"There's no 'got to,' luv. You were raving in your sleep. About Jon. And you're burning like fire." She thrust Lally back into the cot,

and began covering her with extra blankets taken from her own bed.
"You couldn't walk out of here if you tried. Shame, I know . . . I'll
see if I can just find Sister. Awful thing is we can't do anything for
it—just let it run its course."

When she was gone, Lally tried once more to get to her feet, and
found herself crashing back onto the cot. Then she reached frantically for the blankets to try to ward off the icy chill. It felt as if cold
hands touched her spine; her skull seemed to pound through the pillow. "Jon . . . Jon . . ." Despairingly, she knew the convoy would
pass the hospital, and she would not join it.

*   *   *

It was two weeks before she was on her feet again, shaky, weak,
experiencing the most profound depression of her life. She had been
moved from the tent into a hut where there was a stove. Susie had
done most of the nursing, taking a few minutes from her ward duties
to look in on her, and all her off-duty time sitting with her. "A few
aspirin, that's all we could do. Thought you were a goner, once,
Lally. Your temperature went so 'igh—and you were raving. Sister almost sent for your dad to come over. Then your temperature
dropped suddenly, and it was over. You know some right good swear
words, I'll say that. Never thought a nicely brought-up young lady
like you would ever 'ave 'eard them."

Swear words—no, she hadn't heard them very often. Just sometimes in the wards when one of the men had been delirious. But she
suspected that words of that sort had come from the black, cold
room of her memory. She had been back in the old nightmare, with
the smell of sickness and poverty, the aching cold, the curses, the
blows. Her body ached from the blows.

She crept along in a weak December sunlight to the mess hut, and
found herself unable to eat. "Better shove it into yourself, Lally.
You've got to be able to walk. They're shipping you back home. But
you 'ave to wait until you can walk. They're not putting you on a
stretcher. 'ere, feel up to reading your post? There's masses of
it . . ."

She sat wrapped in a blanket in front of the iron stove and read
the letters. Most were from Jon, in an awkward handwriting she did
not recognize. *It was rotten luck for you. They let me telephone
every day—when I was able. I was pretty frantic. Sister told me you
nearly died. We didn't tell Father until it was over. Dear Lally—get*

well, and come back quickly. I need you . . . The words trailed off the end of the page, a strange scrawl. *Brock and I didn't know what to make of it when you didn't show up with the convoy. Thought we'd risk telephoning. Brock in his best military manner. Said I was being shipped back. When we knew what had happened, we just sat there and got drunk. You would have liked your wedding, Lally. Brock got a cake—an iced cake, can you imagine? And champagne. It was going to be in the ward, where everyone could see it. Brock even borrowed a veil.* . . . *Just come home quickly, Lally. We were supposed to cut the cake with a sword* . . .

She snatched at the next letter, with the same scrawled handwriting; uncontrollable tears were streaming down her cheeks. It wasn't fair. She had missed her own wedding. There would never be another iced cake. *Sorry about the handwriting, Lally. I hope you can understand it. I'm not used yet to writing with my left hand. The right one's in bandages. Got a touch of gangrene out there in France. That's why they sent me back here. As you can see, I'm at the Royal Chelsea. They tidied it up very well. I only lost two fingers, and they say it's healing nicely. Of course that means I won't ever play cricket for Yorkshire now—but I think I can bear that. I'll just dream of sitting watching cricket again, the way we always did. Somehow it always seemed to be sunny before the war, though I can distinctly remember games being rained out. And girls always wore white dresses. Promise me you'll always wear a white dress when we go to the cricket matches, Lally.* There were other letters. *Father's here in London, and Margaret comes in every day. They're letting me out tomorrow—they need the bed. I'll be coming in for dressings. Half of London seems to have the flu. Brock's offered us the rooms at the Ritz. Lady Ross wants us to stay with her. I feel so pampered, and still so deprived. You're not here. Make it quickly, Lally. Send a telegram when you know you can come. Be well, my love.* My love . . . my love . . . He had called her his love. They were not love letters, but he had, at last, called her his love. It was enough, she would make it enough. She wiped the tears from her face, and moved slowly back to the table, which had not yet been cleared. There was bread left, the coarse black bread they had grown used to. And a tin of strawberry jam. She spread the jam on the bread, and poured a mug of tepid, substitute coffee. She would eat, and she would be well. She was going home to England, and there would be a wedding. He had called her his love.

* * *

Boxes were delivered to the mess hut from Brock. "Where on earth did 'e get calves'-foot jelly?" Susie wondered. " 'e really *must* 'ave thought you were dying. And look!—'am. Ham," she corrected herself. "Now listen, you're supposed to eat all this, and get well. They won't let you go until you look as if you can make the journey. I expect you'll get a long leave. You probably won't come back. I suppose . . . I suppose we won't ever see each other again."

"Susie! That's a bad joke. You'll come up to Yorkshire. My father's dying to meet you."

The small shoulders shrugged. "I don't know. Might be a bit out of place among you people."

Suddenly Lally had the strength to shake those small, tough shoulders. "I'll start swearing at you again, and you wouldn't like that. You've been so delicately brought up, remember?"

The sharp, wise little face tightened in a grin. "Yes—I'll 'ave to remember."

III

The Marchioness did not have her wish. She had pleaded with Lally in letters to have the wedding in London. *After all, you would wish your friends to attend, and Yorkshire is not very convenient.*

I have pointed out to her, Lally dear, Margaret wrote, *that we don't have so many friends left now. Most of the ones who would have come are dead. What's the use of asking just the parents of our friends? It's too painful for them. We're all so delighted about you and Jon, but it's hard on the others, the girls we came out with whose fiancés were killed, and all the men who aren't ever going to ask any girl to marry them because they're afraid of pity. We're lucky, you and I, Lally. I've got Bobby, who's alive, and only got that slight limp, and Jon, who's only lost a couple of fingers. It's almost hard to look at Father's face. He can hardly believe he's got Jon back, and his favorite girl is going to marry him. Mind you, it's causing a bit of gossip. The papers are starting to remind people that you really aren't Jon's sister.*

Lally could hardly see Jon for the crowd who came to Victoria to meet her. There was even Brock's face—how had he gotten here? "I was stood up as best man once," he said as he hugged her. "Do you think I'm going to be cheated again?"

Jon had one arm in a sling; the other he put clumsily about her. She had the fleeting feel of his lips on hers. Then Black Jack's arms were enfolding her. "Oh, Lally, you're like a shadow. Darling, girl, we nearly lost you." Jon was still mute. Her eyes went to his hand again, then she scrutinized his face; it was very thin, the lines which these four years had given it prematurely were there forever, lines which curved downward from his mouth, which radiated from the corners of his eyes, as if he would be eternally gazing from a firing step toward a horizon, straining to see an invisible enemy. Then suddenly the mouth curved upward in a smile; it was to Lally as if light had poured through the murky gloom of that December day. Margaret had snatched her from Black Jack's arms. "Oh, Lally, what would I have done if I'd lost you?" And there were the Marchioness's cool lips lightly on her cheek. "Dear child," was all she said. Bobby Grenfell gave her a swift peck which passed as a kiss. "They ought to have medals for you girls—at very least campaign ribbons."

They went back to Brock's rooms at the Ritz. The place was assuming an almost painful familiarity to Lally. Night had descended on Green Park, and drinks were being served. "Are you sleeping in the broom cupboard again, Brock?"

"Well, no—they found something a little bigger. Jon and I are sharing." Lally sipped her drink and looked around her. She loved them all—and yes, in a way she had to include Brock Weymouth in that feeling, but when would there be time alone with Jon? Had not Jon insisted on it? He sat silently, looking at her from time to time; their eyes met, but they said nothing. About them, the talk flowed.

"You're going to wear Mother's wedding dress, just as I did—you're only an inch taller, and no one will be looking at your feet. And the ermine cape. Alice has grown out of the dress she had for my wedding, but we found one of mine which almost fits her. It's to be in the village church, just like my wedding. We can't use Pellham for the reception—it should have started to empty out by now, but it's this awful flu. They've more men than ever—full to the attics. And of course they want to try to keep them isolated. So it's the village hall, Lally. But you'll be delighted to know that just about every single person in the village has contributed a little sugar so you're going to have an iced cake. It'll be so wonderful. All together at last—and at Christmas!" Margaret hurried on, perhaps aware that she had reminded them all of Jon and Sandy's wedding at Christmas. "We've telephoned invitations all around. The trains are being met at Leeds for anyone who wants to come. But it's really going to be a lovely local affair."

"And when," Lally said slowly, "is it to be?"

Margaret's face froze. "Why, darling—it's the day after tomorrow. Didn't anyone tell you?"

Lally shook her head, and unaccountably tears began to stream down her face. At once the Marchioness was on her feet. "Lally is still weak, and we're all shouting things at her. Come, everyone. Jon, you can order dinner here. I believe Major Weymouth has organized something for us in the dining room. Come, everyone," she repeated.

They left, and silence fell. Slowly Jon came toward her, and his arm went around her. "Sorry, Lally. It hasn't been what I hoped. But soon we'll have peace. We'll have time. We'll have all the time in the world now. It's going to be you and me from now on. It's like starting to live again. I hope I'll soon stop feeling like an old man. I hope I soon can stop feeling guilty because I'm alive, and just about everyone I ever knew is not. Come, Lally . . . drink up. And we *will* send for dinner. You have to eat. You look so pale and thin, and you *did* almost die. I couldn't believe it. The war had ended, and there was no more shelling. I thought nothing could touch you and me anymore. I was the one who was expected to die." Gently he turned her face with his good hand until she was looking out of the windows. "Look, love, the lights are on. The lights, Lally. It's the beginning of life again."

*   *   *

Unbelievable as it seemed to Lally, they were indeed married two days later, in the parish church of Pellham Langley. She moved automatically through the preparations. There had been some further grumblings from the Marchioness about the inconvenience of the arrangement. They all, somehow, managed to squeeze into Grangewick. "The very least Jack should have done was arrange for the ceremony to be here in Leeds. All the guests have to make their way out to Pellham, and what do they have at the end of it? A village church and, I've no doubt, a drafty little hall."

"Yes," Margaret admitted. "That's about what it will be. But, darling Lady Ross, don't you see? It's Lally's home. *And* Jon's. It wouldn't seem right in any other place. They've both come back from the war, and everyone wants to see them there, where they belong. There've been so many boys from the village killed, and some of them back there for life, crippled. It's something we owe them."

A little smile played around the Marchioness's lips. "You are about the last person, Margaret, I would have expected to be afflicted with a sense of *noblesse oblige*. But you're right."

"I didn't," Margaret confessed, "see it that way until Father said so. And *he* is right."

"I've observed your father very often is. Is that how you feel, Lally, child?"

Lally just nodded. Together they were pinning and taking tucks in Lady Latitia's cream-lace wedding gown. Was it possible that she was even more slender than that figure in the portrait? She had promised Jon that she would eat, but the smallest amount of food now seemed too much. "It's all that disgusting muck you had to eat over there, Lally," Margaret said. "We'll manage better here. Surely things will start to be available soon. Things will be better . . ."

Suddenly she whirled away from Lally, who was standing on a stool. "Oh, I intend to have the time of my life! I'm going to make up for every single party we missed. Bobby's promised we can have a house in London, and we can spend a fair amount of time there. I intend to have a party every night."

"That sounds extremely tedious, Margaret, dear," Lady Ross said. Margaret flashed her a look that was almost one of pity, as the young do toward those they feel have grown old and unadventurous. Lally, looking down at the Marchioness, saw that these war years had left their traces on her also, but she was still the handsome, somewhat imperious figure she had always been to Lally.

Standing by the fire, Alice clapped her hands. "Can I come to the party, Margaret? And Teddy Rose, and Madame Butterfly? We'll sing for the guests."

Margaret brushed a kiss carelessly on Alice's forehead. "Of course you can, my pet. It will be one long party, I promise you."

Lady Ross's face was suddenly stern. "Margaret, don't make rash promises. It isn't fair." The reference was obviously to Alice, but Margaret ignored it.

"Oh, but I intend it will be just that—one long party."

* * *

The party in the village hall was not what Margaret had been thinking of, but it was a party. Lally felt warmth and a sense of affection flow from the people who lived there, and the guests who had

made a long journey were gathered into it. They mingled, as before
the war it would not have been possible; now men who had shared
the trenches, privates and officers, saluted each other in the cama-
raderie of those who have been under fire, and survived. For once,
rank had no place. Lally, as she circulated among the guests, heard
Lady Bletchley, who had become rather deaf, say in a loud voice, "I
don't think it's quite *decent* . . . She's almost his sister!" Lady
Bletchley wore the same purple velvet she had worn to Sandy and
Jon's wedding, and to Margaret's, but this time she wore no diamonds. It wasn't, Lally thought, that she had had to sell the diamonds—it was simply that the purple velvet had survived the years of
shortages, and there was no need to wear diamonds to the wedding
of a nameless girl, even though she was marrying her grandson. Lally
thought then of Black Jack's second wife, Alice Trimble. Had she
been regarded in this light? As she looked at Black Jack she could
remember the night, after Alice Trimble's death, when she had
climbed into the chair with him, and made a promise to look after
the new young baby, and to look after Margaret. She had walked
down the aisle on Black Jack's arm and he had given her in marriage
to his only son. In many ways, the promise grew more important,
loomed larger. She was summoned to the cutting of the cake.

Everyone gathered close. She looked at the faces of those she had
lived with for many years; she looked at the faces of the villagers,
which were familiar and trusted. With Jon's hand on hers, she put a
slight weight on the sword, and the sugary crust broke. It had been
quite thin, and there was not much substance within. But everyone
cheered and clapped. Someone else—Billings, of course—had begun
to cut the cake into appropriate slices, and to pass it around. Black
Jack's cellar had been scraped almost to the bottom. The glasses
were raised, again and again. The talk grew loud, almost boisterous.
The ill-tuned piano began to sound. They sang all the old songs,
thankful that they no longer needed them. Lally didn't mind those
songs now; she just wanted everyone to sing. She moved around the
hall, which had felt chilly when they had entered but had now become overwarm. People greeted her by name. "So glad, Miss Lally—
he's got the best of the lot." "Thank you . . . thank you."

Then one thin, almost skeletal hand, emerging from a black sleeve,
was placed on hers. "You wouldn't recognize your mother, Lily, but
here I am, at your wedding. And proud as a peacock."

She stared at the gaunt, lined face under a beaten black hat. The eyes she saw were as dark as hers; in some ways, that thin face could have been an older version of the face she saw in the mirror these days, with the high cheekbones, the dark, arched eyebrows. Afraid, she drew away.

"Well, I couldn't blame you, dear. It's a shock. But I just had to come to see my own daughter married. Haven't I been watching you all these years, proud of you, and all? And here, married into the gentry. Well, Lily, it's something you've managed. And wasn't I right? If I'd kept you with me, why sure you'd be dead—good afternoon, sir. Lovely wedding, it's been. Oh, yes. Just lovely."

Black Jack's hand was on her elbow. "Lally—it's time to go."

"Oh, yes, sir. And didn't she make the most beautiful bride? Never could have thought it, sir. Not that time . . . long ago." A quiet chuckle came from those thin lips.

Lally looked from Black Jack back to the woman. She realized that it was not the first time they had met. The hand on her elbow was protective; then her other hand was joined in Jon's. With a hail of good wishes and loud applause, she was led into one of Black Jack's old carriages; there were shouts of farewell. In the fading afternoon light, all she could see and remember was Black Jack's face, clouded, troubled. Even Jon's arm about her, their drawing close under the carriage robe, did not dispel the fear aroused by the woman in black, with dark eyes which were so much like her own.

* * *

Lally changed at Grangewick, and there was the familiar small crowd to see them off at Leeds station—Margaret and Bobby Grenfell, Black Jack, and Lady Ross, who had accepted Black Jack's invitation to stay at Grangewick for a few days. There was Alice, still in her bridesmaid's dress, clutching Madame Butterfly. It was frightening to see this beautiful young woman holding the doll as a child would. But no one tried to take it away from her, or suggest she should leave it aside. No one could bear to upset or hurt Alice. She kissed Lally, and clung to her. "You'll be back soon, Lally. You and I and Jon will be doing things together . . ."

It seemed to Lally that Alice thought it perfectly natural that Lally and Jon should be together always, as they had been since Alice could remember. They were still her brother and her sister, but they now were married. Lally wondered if Alice could even remember the wedding of Sandy West. The untouched face betrayed nothing but pleasure. Black Jack had explained to her that this great war was over. Everything would now be as it once had been. They would all be together, and there would be no more separations.

Only Brock was missing. He had taken an earlier train to London, and tomorrow would be leaving by troop transport for New York. "Things to arrange," he had said briefly. "It'll take me a few months to wriggle out of the Army, but I've some things that need attention, and I've persuaded my general that I'm urgently needed back home. Have to organize transport to get our boys back home. And on the side I've a little organization of my own to do. The word is that Congress will ratify the Eighteenth Amendment."

Lally had shaken her head in puzzlement. "Prohibition, Lally. There's going to be a law to prohibit the manufacture and sale of alcohol in the States. Can you imagine the stupidity of it? It's a law made for breaking. And the ones who can supply the means are going to make a killing."

Lally had shuddered at the word "killing"; she wondered how much longer Brock would figure in their lives. He had been best man at both weddings, but his function seemed now to be finished. He would return to America. They might see him occasionally. He would be the friend who had supplied so many gifts during these hard years. He would be remembered with gratitude, but he would diminish in importance to them. But he had been insistent right to the end.

"My friend would be very upset if you didn't use the rooms at the Ritz for your honeymoon. He hates them to be empty." When Jon had tried to protest, Brock had cut him short. "For God's sake, Jon, you're not thinking of going to Scarborough or some such end-of-the-world place for a honeymoon! You both need bright lights, and warmth, and a few laughs. Go to theaters and nightclubs. Dance your legs off."

So they entered the familiar suite at the Ritz. Jon surveyed the masses of flowers, the champagne cooling in the silver bucket, the unbelievable delicacy of caviar, which the waiter had brought as soon as they had been shown into the suite. "Mr. Weymouth's compliments, Captain."

"I wonder which Russian general Brock knows," Jon murmured.

The same housekeeper Lally remembered appeared. "I hope everything is satisfactory, madam? Captain Pollock?" As was her habit, she touched the flowers just slightly, and made sure the curtains were tightly closed against the night. "It is a great pleasure to welcome you back again, madam—sir. And may I express my best wishes for your happiness. Such a terrible ordeal you both have been through—serving all these years. I'm sure you deserve great happiness."

She was remembering, of course, Lally thought, the time she and Jon had come to these rooms after Sandy West's funeral. They had been Miss Pollock and Captain Pollock then. It was the first time Lally had been addressed as madam. Somehow she had not believed herself married until that had happened. All the world had changed.

"Mr. Weymouth was most anxious that you should have everything we could provide for your comfort. You will call me, madam, if there is anything I may do for you? If you should wish a ladies' maid . . . we are still short of staff, but we can manage a little extra here and there."

"You said Mr. Weymouth was anxious for us to be comfortable," Lally said. "What about Mr. Weymouth's friend, whose rooms these are?"

The housekeeper smiled a faint, professional smile. "Well, madam, Mr. Weymouth's friend very seldom comes here. He usually leaves all such instructions to Mr. Weymouth." She was backing toward the door. "You will ring, madam, if there is anything . . ."

When she was gone, Jon went at once to open the curtains. He switched off the lights in the room so that they could look down along the length of Green Park and Piccadilly. A glow of light came back to them. He poured the champagne by it. "Look, Lally—there are even more than there were just a few days ago. More lights. More traffic. You were so tired then, Lally—weeping. And I—I was afraid. I was afraid of the peace. I was afraid for you. I wanted to make you happy, but I wondered if either of us could ever be happy again. After what we've seen. I wondered if there would be nightmares forever. I don't feel like that now. Somehow it's right that we're back in Brock's rooms. In an odd sort of way he helped it all happen."

He put his arm about her shoulders, and lifted his glass to the lights which lined the edge of the park and of Piccadilly. "Our lights, Lally. We'll never be in the dark again."

* * *

But when he lay sleeping in her arms, Lally relived her own nightmare, now more hideously real. In the safe, warm comfort of their wide bed, filled with Jon's love, she woke from the nightmare. It was there again, the smell, the taint of that damp, dark room. But now there was a hand reaching out to her, gripping her with fingers which were like claws. "You wouldn't recognize your mother, Lily . . ." She saw the beaten hat, the gaunt face. Was that woman her mother? The past threatened to claw her back.

I V

They did as Brock had ordered, went to theaters and night-clubs, made love, and let the Ritz serve them whatever could be provided. "It's almost sinful," Lally said. "I should still be there in France . . . suddenly I don't care."

Jon drew her close. "I feel that my bones should be there in France. Is this me living here, Lally? Safe and warm and clean. Making love to you." He buried his head in her breasts. "God, how wonderful you smell. A woman's smell. Sometimes I wake at night, and I smell the trenches. Putrid, foul. Then I roll over beside you. Clean, beautiful, warm." The words were a constant theme with him. "Perhaps I did die, and this is heaven."

"I always suspected I was an angel." She kissed him. "Are we going to get up today?"

He pondered the question. "I don't know. I used to imagine what it would be like to lie in a warm bed all day. Sometimes I used to want to get wounded just so I'd escape from the front lines and wake up to find myself in a bed in a hospital. Just think, I can push this button here, and a waiter will rush through the door and give us breakfast. Yes, I must have died and gone to heaven. I don't deserve it, but that is the only thing that can explain what's happened."

But they stayed, in the end, less than a week at the Ritz. "Can't impose on Brock forever, and there's no chance I can get a bill from them at the desk. At any rate, I rather fancy being back at home. It'll have to be Grangewick for a time. I'd like to be back at Pellham, but we'll have to wait for that."

They were back for Christmas. Lally was surprised to find that Lady Ross had remained there. "I've been invited to the family Christmas," she said simply. Never before had Lally thought that this stately, handsome woman might be hiding loneliness behind her calm facade. She seemed at times almost to be presiding over Black Jack's household. She had only one sister, "living, my dear Lally, in one of those terrible icy castles in Scotland. Married to a laird with no money, and they have *five* girls to try to marry off. The older ones are past it, I'm sure. Two went to France to nurse. Worthy girls, but plain and dull, I'm afraid. Sometimes they stay with me in London. It's rather a trial."

It was as much as Lady Ross had ever told Lally of her personal life. From Black Jack Lally had heard the story of the Marquis of Ross, her husband, who had madly and compulsively gambled away his fortune, and had shot himself when he had to declare bankruptcy. That had still been a raw wound the summer Lady Ross had presented her at Court. She never spoke of her husband.

And Lally had noticed that during the time they were all at Grangewick, Black Jack was never absent for an evening. What, she wondered, had happened to Mrs. Campion, the lady they all knew about but never spoke of? In all the time Lally had been away, perhaps Mrs. Campion had faded from Black Jack's life—or was he merely observing the convention of politeness to his guest, or savoring the presence of his children?

Among them they began the preparations for Christmas. It would be a simple Christmas. Food was still very short, but Cook had sprouted a kind of genius for improvisation. "Had to, Miss Lally. Couldn't get white flour or butter. No sugar. Sometimes I was driven to despair to think of something to put on Mr. Pollock's plate. All the nice little bits . . . they came from that Mr. Weymouth. Well, and now here's another package. Don't know how he does it. But it's a bit of Christmas cheer, Miss Lally, and I won't question as how he came by it."

So Brock was evidenced at their Christmas table almost as clearly as if he had been physically present. They had white sauce on their brussels sprouts, they ate pudding made with the fruit he sent, had liqueur-filled chocolates in silver dishes. "Absent friends," Black Jack murmured as he raised his glass before they ate. "And I thank God for peace at last, and that you all are gathered with me around this table, well, and safe." His gaze took in all of them, Jon, Margaret, Lally, and Alice. He smiled at Bobby Grenfell, and bowed slightly toward Lady Ross, seated on his right.

"Amen," Bobby Grenfell answered with great emphasis, and did not, as he usually did, look confused when all eyes turned on him. So profound was Black Jack's relief that all his children had survived the war that he seemed prepared to relax his opposition to Bobby Grenfell. Perhaps he now found himself more understanding of Margaret's urge to marry—to marry a man who had survived, no matter that he was not the ideal man for her. Black Jack had had time to assess the effect of the war on the young women of Margaret's and Lally's generation. Very many of them would never marry because the men of their generation had been swept away, lost to the maw of the trenches and the shell holes, the poison gas and the gangrene. He might now be grateful for a son-in-law who could make a normal life for Margaret, give her children, give him grandchildren. "Yes . . . absent friends," Bobby Grenfell echoed. For a moment before all of them appeared the vision of the casualty lists, the names of the ones who would never come back.

Margaret, hating the spell of morbidity which threatened to engulf the table, said brightly, "And especially Brock, for all the goodies. I don't care now how he gets them. Now that no ships are being torpedoed. We must visit America, Bobby, don't you think? But we must go before they bring in this prohibition. It would be too deadly never to be able to have a drink."

"I don't think," Jon said, "that there's any fear of that. People like Brock seem determined to get around that law. He pointed out that huge border with Canada. Plenty of places to cross it. He mentioned something about Cuba and the American Virgin Islands. There'll be quite a bit of rum-running, it seems."

"It all sounds rather dangerous," Lady Ross observed. "But how terribly naïve of the Americans to think one can legislate a vice or a pleasure out of existence if people are bound and determined to have it."

There was no Boxing Day hunt that year near them. The local master had had to give up the hounds because he could not feed them, and his whippers-in had both joined up. "It couldn't matter less to me," Jon said. "Even when I'm able to ride again, I don't think I'll ever want to ride to hounds. I think I've seen rather enough of blood."

"Exactly my opinion, old boy," Bobby muttered, staring into his brandy as they sat over the fire. "Don't intend to take it up again."

"Your father, Bobby, will be furious!" Margaret gasped. Lord Gough had been master of his own hunt, the Wold, and had welcomed the idea that the return of his only surviving son would mean someone to take over from him.

"Can't help it, Margaret." Bobby yawned slightly. "Just don't care for the thing. Feel rather like old Jon here."

"Well!" Margaret said. "*I* intend to hunt, once the hunts get going again. Don't expect me to be cooped up in the country all winter with no amusement." Her face had clouded. They were about to take up residence at Neatherby, the dower house of Lord Gough's estate. Margaret didn't attempt to hide her dismay at the thought of being there permanently. She was prodding Bobby into buying the London house he had promised. The money, however, had to come from Lord Gough, and he was, at the moment, reluctant to see his heir with too many distractions from what would be his principal business of running the estate. Lord Gough had strong feelings about absentee landowners, and matched Black Jack's opinion that Yorkshire was the only place on earth worth living in.

Bobby looked up. "Well, if you feel strongly about it, darling . . . of course. I'll tag along with you." He nodded toward Black Jack. "Can't have her racing all over the field by herself, can we, sir? She's a bit wild with a horse, I do remember. Goes at fences any sensible man would have second thoughts about."

Lally stiffened, as did Black Jack. He had condoned all his children riding to hounds, because he could not bear to see them deprived of the social life the hunt afforded. But the death of Lady Latitia had made every moment while they were on the hunting field an agony of suspense for him.

"I'd be grateful, dear fellow, if you *would* keep an eye on her," he managed to say. "And after all, she's your responsibility now."

Margaret rounded on them. "You two! Talking just as if there hadn't been any war! Women are responsible for themselves now. You're both so old-fashioned."

Lally had begun to think Black Jack might have more in common with his son-in-law than he had imagined. They seemed to be entering a conspiracy of appearing to let Margaret have her head, and still watching over and guarding her. Bobby had, perhaps, taken over part of the task Lally thought was hers, was sharing the promise she had given to Black Jack. Bobby might not be the brilliant husband Margaret might have been expected to marry, but he seemed to understand the task he had undertaken. Black Jack glanced at Bobby with a look which might have been interpreted as one of gratitude, even of affection. Lally slumped back in her chair, feeling as if some

weight had lifted from her. It could almost be as Lady Bletchley had
said: Margaret was safely settled now.

At the piano Lady Ross was trying out some music from sheets
which Brock had sent. *I'm always chasing rainbows* . . . she sang
softly, fingering the notes. "Why, it's pure theft! That's from Chopin!
Here, Alice—" Alice was seated on the long piano bench beside her.
"Sing it with me." Alice could not read music, and took a long time
spelling out simple words, but she had a quick ear to repeat what was
sung to her, what notes were played. They got through the song with
only a few stumbles. Everyone applauded. Around one of the legs of
the piano were grouped Alice's most beloved playmates, Teddy
Rose, fur worn in places, and Madame Butterfly, whose beautiful
gown was beginning to show the strain of constant carrying around;
they had a new friend, a strange, rather forlorn but appealing little
creature, a rag doll. *Her name is Raggedy Ann,* Brock had written
in his Christmas card to Alice. Like everything Brock had given her,
in Alice's eyes, this was a prized possession. She had held the new
doll on her lap through Christmas dinner, while Teddy Rose and
Madame Butterfly sat on their own chair.

When the song was finished, before Alice could ask for more,
Margaret said, "Let's roll back the rug and put on some of the jazz
records Brock sent." Margaret's slim, beautiful body in its silk
sheath, uncorseted, began to girate to the rhythm. "Oh, Bobby, don't
you *long* to go to America?"

Jon put his bandaged hand around Lally and they also swayed to
the rhythm, though not as passionately as Margaret did. Then
through the music he said quietly, "Let's go to Pellham. We can use
the stable block—keep away from the house. I want some air, Lally.
And quiet. We'll walk on the moors. I want to be quiet with you,
Lally. And alone."

A sense of hope raced through Lally. Jon was seeking aloneness
with her, as lovers do. "I'd like that. We'll go tomorrow. As soon as
you've had your hand dressed . . ." Her thoughts were racing ahead.
Food to be begged from Cook, who would give it gladly; Billings
would unlock the wine cellar. Black Jack would provide a horse and
trap. It would be the simple honeymoon her heart had longed for—
and Jon had said he wanted to be alone with her. The music's blar-
ing sound suddenly seemed too harsh. They would have the peace of
a place they had always known, but that peace would be changed because they now knew it in a different way. Their bodies had been

buffeted by the fire storm of Flanders, their senses battered. They both knew they craved the quiet, but their bodies, close as they danced, also craved the full expression of their acknowledged sensuality. They would lie and listen to the wind shriek across the moors, swoop down to touch Pellham Langley, and they would know each other fully. The promise was there in Jon's embrace, in his eyes. Lally's hope grew stronger. The last memory of Lally as a sister would drop away. They would be lovers, and in love.

*   *   *

Lally was up early the next morning, anxious to talk to Cook about the food they would need to take with them. She hummed as she started down the stairs. An unseasonably bright sun shone on the frost-rimmed garden. She and Jon would . . . Abruptly she halted, and withdrew around the bend of the staircase. Black Jack was down there in the hall, and with him was the black-clad figure who had appeared, like some evil fairy of a nightmare, at her wedding.

"You're very good, Mr. Pollock. I'll not forget it." The tone was ingratiating, hateful to Lally. "You may be sure I'll keep out of her way. I wouldn't want to spoil anything for her . . . you understand." Lally listened, but could make out nothing Black Jack said. There was the sound of the door opening, and the woman's voice again. "I'll not be troubling you, sir, count on that." The door closed.

Lally came around the bend of the stairs and faced Black Jack. "It was she—that woman! The one at my wedding. What did she want? Who is she?"

Black Jack gestured to her. "Come down. I wish you hadn't seen her. Before, she's always been discreet. She's never come near the house." He drew her close to the fire. "Perhaps she grew bold after she got into the reception in the village hall."

"Before! When before? Who does she say she is?" She could hear the shrill pitch of fear in her own voice.

He placed both hands on her shoulders. "Steady, dear Lally. That woman claims she is your mother."

She felt her body sag, as if she might faint. "The wedding wasn't the first time you'd seen her. I knew it."

"She's appeared a number of times—over the years. But then so have other women. I have sent them all away. I have given them a little money, and sent them away. None has ever come back. Perhaps they understood that I might, the next time, have called the police.

Perhaps charged them with trying to extort money. But this one—she has been back."

"Why? Why is she different from the others?"

"Perhaps because I half-believed her."

"She had proof?" Lally said weakly. The smell of the damp dark room was with her again; she felt the blows, heard the cries and the curses.

"Nothing on paper. No marriage lines. No registration of your birth. But she knew one thing, or perhaps it was a lucky guess. She knew about the piece of paper on that blanket. She knew you were called Lily. Not Lillian, which is your adopted name. She knew you were called Lily."

She put her hand on the mantel to steady herself; she saw that it trembled violently, out of control, as if it belonged to some other person. "*That* woman—my mother! How could she have known I was brought to Pellham? How did she trace me to you? I was abandoned—I could have died that night. How did she know I was still alive?"

"More than one person knows *where* I found you, Lally. She claims she stayed to watch. She was there, outside the Corn Exchange. She thought someone would surely take you. She saw the accident. It wasn't too difficult to find out who owned the carriage."

"If—if it's true, why did she abandon me?"

"She says the man she was living with was beating you both. A drunkard. She had to get away from him. She once had been a mill operative in Bradford. She had a chance of a job with Mallham's. But she would have to live with all the other women operatives. There was no place for a child. So she . . . that's what she says, Lally."

"My father?"

He shook his head. "She doesn't know who your father is. He might not have been the man she was living with."

Her head went down. "I can't believe it. I *won't* believe it. I'm Lally Leeds. Lillian Pollock. I don't belong to that woman."

"Believe nothing," he said.

"But *you*—you're not sure. You give her money, don't you? That's what she comes for."

"Yes—I do that. I can't seem to help myself." He lifted her face, so that she was forced to look at him. "Try to understand what I feel. If that woman truly is your mother, then I owe to her one of the most precious things in my life. I owe you to her. Can I turn her away when she says she has no money?"

She clung still to the edge of the mantel, her body flooded with fear and fury. "I can't answer that. I wish she'd died, as I almost did. I don't want to belong to her. I don't want . . ." Her voice was rising again.

"Hush, Lally! It need never concern you. Forget that woman. You don't belong to anyone. Only to Jon. Live for him. Forget her. Now come—you're pale as death. Come and eat some breakfast."

With pride Billings produced a full breakfast of bacon and eggs, but she waved the plate away. The single mouthful of toast caught in her throat. The smell of poverty and death was there, more strongly than ever before. Worse than the smell of the wards, worse than the most vile, gangrenous wounds she had ever tended. The coffee Billings poured had come from Brock, real coffee. She did not taste it; all she wanted was its warmth. Her chair was near the brightly burning fire, and still she shivered.

*   *   *

She went with Jon while he had his hand dressed; the wound had been a mangling one, and two of his remaining fingers would always be stiff. But it was healing. Somehow the sight of that healing wound helped to relieve the shock of seeing the woman who claimed to be her mother. Black Jack had told her to say nothing to Jon. "It's not his concern. It is probably not the truth." She packed extra dressings to take with them to Pellham Langley, and she was almost happy by the time they started out. A cold, sleet-laden wind blew, and it was nearly dusk when they arrived at the stable block. Black Jack had telephoned ahead, and one of the gamekeepers, who had turned to farming during the war, had been in and lighted a fire; they saw its glow through the curtains. She helped Jon rub down the horse and feed and water it. They carried the hampers of food and wine Billings had given them up the stairs. She realized that this would be the first meal she had ever prepared for Jon. They had eaten at the same table most of their lives, but she had barely poured a cup of tea for him.

"Why, Lally—what is it? You're crying!"

"Can't help it. *This* is the real beginning, Jon. The wedding, the Ritz, Christmas at Grangewick. That all belongs back in time somewhere. We'd done it before, in other times. This is where it begins.

You and I. I'll have you forever, Jon, won't I? We've been through worse things than we could ever have imagined. And we've come out on the other side. We paid in advance. Life owes us something, Jon. It's going to be all right from now on."

He kissed her on the lips. "It's going to be bloody marvelous! How can it be otherwise? We're survivors, you and I, Lally. You know—" He drew back a little from her. "You know, I think we should have lots of kids just to make up for some of the chaps who went. Maybe we could fill Pellham. Better—we could fill our own house. Shall we forget the food, and go to bed?"

She laughed. "We won't forget the food—and we will go to bed."

* * *

The days that followed were of healing peace. They did not go near the wards of Pellham Langley, where the flu still ravaged the patients, and some died. The newspapers were beginning to give the worldwide count of those who had died of the Spanish flu; it seemed it might be higher than the millions who had died during the war. Lally once had seen a hearse at the front steps of the house, and she had hurriedly drawn Jon away. They breathed the cold, clean air of the moors, huddled together when the snow flurries flayed their faces, went eagerly back to the fire in the rooms over the stable, and to their bed, warm and deep. The silence fell on them like some delayed blessing. In that silence and warmth they came to know each other's bodies with ever-growing intimacy; their response to each other seemed endless, and of endless variety. Lally felt almost drugged with love, though her senses grew keener. They knew they had never needed the luxurious trappings of the Ritz, the food, the music. They listened to the wind, and drank their wine before the fire. Lally dressed Jon's hand and cooked their food. They saw few people, and those, watching them walk hand in hand, left them alone.

Gradually her dreams ceased to be tormented by the vision of the woman with the lined, gaunt face. At times she could almost forget that the woman's eyes had been disturbingly like her own. Gradually the smell began to retreat; with Jon's coaxing she ate reasonable amounts of food, though often she did not want it. Whenever she woke from a dream of that woman, Jon's arms were about her. She let herself believe what Black Jack had told her. "Live for Jon. Forget her." But the eyes had indeed been very much like her own.

Only one thing would have given Lally the total happiness she craved, but was beginning to think might never be hers. She and Jon grew steadily in the physical experience of love; he was a good lover, and she found her response eager and whole. She heard his whispered endearments; he seemed happy in her company—seemed to want no other distraction. But she was never certain that he had not turned to her instinctively as a healer, as someone to salve all the hurts of war, all the misery of Sandy's death and the knowledge of her infidelity. She waited, hoped, longed for the moment when Jon would seem to recognize her as someone other than the Lally he had always known. It was possible, it was all too possible, that he had turned to her in his first pain, and at the end of the war had turned again to her because she symbolized all that was safe and secure and known, someone who would love him, and never betray him. He was safe with Lally. He turned to her again and again, offered endearments. She did not dare ask to hear him say "I love you." Suppose, she thought, she had demanded that, and he could not say it, or said it only to please and placate her? Be still, she told herself; be still and wait. Hadn't Jon said they had all the time in the world?

❧ CHAPTER 11 ❧

I

They returned to Grangewick. The house was quiet, in a way Lally had never known it. Margaret had gone back to Neatherby with Bobby. Black Jack spent a great deal of time at the mills. "Of course we'd always been at full capacity during the war. Now I'll have to send my sales managers hustling to find business. Our woolens and worsteds will sell, I believe, anywhere in the world, but we'll have a harder time with steel. The Americans have learned to compete very admirably. We may not find our old markets quite so ready to buy British without question. We'll have to stir ourselves. I was thinking of going to America. Have a look at their mills—steel and textiles. I could look up Brock."

"I wondered . . ." Jon began.

Black Jack looked at them eagerly. "Why don't you? I mean, why don't you both come? Margaret says she's dying to go to America. Perhaps we all could go?"

Jon smiled. "Father, I'm still in the Army. Officially, Lally is still a VAD. No, what I was thinking . . . Of course I'll get my discharge soon. They can't keep a man in the Army with a couple of fingers missing. There won't be any trouble about Lally getting out. I was thinking . . ."

"Yes?" Lally was aware of an edge of suspense in Black Jack's tone. They had never dared until now to talk of Jon's future.

"Well, I thought perhaps I ought to get my degree from Oxford.

I'd like to *finish*—you know, just to have gone through it. To know I could do it." Black Jack was nodding. "Then, if you'll have me, I'd like to start at the mills. I know I'm pretty old to be an apprentice, but then, I'd have a pretty good teacher."

For a moment Lally thought Black Jack might break down and weep. He suddenly decided that the fire needed poking, and he busied himself with that. Then he straightened. "Any time you are ready, son. It's a different, and probably a more difficult, world you're going into than anything I ever knew, but the business of being in business is nothing to be scoffed at. Strange, though . . ."

"What's strange?" Lally said.

"I was suddenly thinking of Jon's grandfather. When he made his money, and built Pellham, I think he had some vision—very unlike a Yorkshireman—that his heirs would somehow wash the muck of business off their hands. They would be landowners, of a sort—that's why he bought Pellham. And by virtue of that, they'd be gentry. I wonder what he would have thought of a grandson who had been to Eton and Oxford volunteering to go back to the mills?"

"He couldn't have imagined a grandson who fought in what turned out not to be a gentleman's war. I suspect, Father, that the world of gentlemen is almost washed away, though some of the remnants are going to hang on for a while. But that's yet to be proven." He turned to Lally. "Well, shall we scout around for something to rent in Oxford? Are you ready for the mills when I've finished there? It's not Margaret's idea of an exciting life."

"I've had just about enough excitement," Lally replied. "And one can take only so much of dancing at the Savoy. We'll go and visit Margaret from time to time in London—country cousins. We'll be able to be gentleman farmers Saturdays and Sundays at Pellham. I don't at all mind the smoke of Leeds for the rest of the time. After all, it was where I was born." Saying those words aloud, she found that she was able, also, to face the existence of the woman who said she was her mother. These few weeks of marriage, the hope that they would build on them to a relationship which was unassailable, had given her confidence to say the words, to acknowledge that she had been born in an unknown place, of an unknown father. She turned and looked at the city below her. "Will we be staying here when Jon is finished at Oxford? It's the most convenient for getting to the mills in Bradford, and down to Sheffield." She was amazed at the calmness of her tone. They were deciding their future, and it sounded routine, ordinary. The very ordinariness of it seemed now a luxury.

"I think I'd better talk to the agents for this house, then," Black Jack said. "It was only rented to me on a five-year lease. I didn't expect to need it that length of time. Would you be willing to stay *here?* I thought you'd want something in the country. And a place in London, like Margaret. If I bought this . . ." He gazed around the room, up at the ceiling, as if he were reviewing the whole house from attic to cellar. "It could stand some money being spent on it. Bathrooms, there aren't nearly enough bathrooms." He looked slightly offended when they both started to laugh. "What is it?"

"Don't you know, Father, that Pellham is famous for having more bathrooms than any house in England? Any old house can have a hundred bedrooms, but Pellham is distinguished by having more bathrooms than the Ritz. Everyone suspects you have some money invested in sanitary ware."

"Laugh, my children. You'll find there'll come a day when you can't sell a house that hasn't got a bathroom for every bedroom, or thereabouts. And the first to do it will be the Americans."

II

So they scouted and found a small flat in Oxford even before Jon's discharge was final. He had been accepted back by his old college, Magdalen, which was prepared to tolerate married undergraduates who had served in the war, provided they dined regularly in Hall. "It's only a matter of time before I'm discharged," he told his old tutor. His hand was now in a light bandage, and he was working constantly to make writing with his left hand legible. They bought the prescribed textbooks in the Oxford bookshops.

"Is it going to be boring for you, Lally? There'll be nothing much to do. It's a pity you couldn't start a course, but then they'd never let a married woman into a college."

She smiled at him. "Let's have no more talk about being bored when we eat three good meals a day, and are warm and dry. Are you forgetting already?"

He shook his head. "No, just not quite believing it." The figures were beginning to be counted, the losses totaled. An unbelievable ten million dead, twenty million wounded. The Paris Peace Conference had opened in Versailles, and had resolved to create a League of Nations. Rhetoric was high and proud and hopeful. But in Russia the Third International was sworn to attaining worldwide revolution and the overthrow of the capitalist system. The struggle for Russia itself had not ended; the Bolshevik Red Army waged war on the White Russian Army, with the Allies supporting the White Russians. Lally found it hard to believe that there were still British Army troops fighting in a war and a country few of them could understand. She read the papers as carefully as she always had, but now with a sense of weariness, almost disinterest. Let them fight, but let it not touch Jon or her. She began to be glad of the missing fingers. They would never have him again. Let them fight their wars, physical and ideological; leave her and Jon to have their peace. Her world was growing smaller, selfish, self-centered. She was pregnant.

She waited until they were at home for a weekend in the newly vacated Pellham Langley with Black Jack and Alice to make the announcement. Black Jack had brought some mail which had been accumulating at Grangewick for them both. "Something official for you, Lally, it looks like."

She read the notice. There might be some sort of campaign ribbons, just as Bobby Grenfell said there should. "It seems I'm officially out of the Voluntary Aid Detachments. Just as well. I could hardly nurse a baby with one hand and pass out bedpans with the other."

She saw the shock register on both Jon's and Black Jack's faces. Perhaps she had been afraid to tell Jon alone—but why afraid? She had been certain of Black Jack's joy, but less certain of Jon's. Hadn't he said he wanted to fill Pellham Langley with a brood of children? He had said that, but would he now see this child as something that even more tangibly tied him to her? Why did she think he would not wish that? The child was only evidence of their love, wasn't it? Anxiously she watched Jon's face. It changed from the first shock to a brilliant smile. He came and sat on the sofa beside her, his arm about her, rocking her a little.

"What do you think of that? A baby! Well, Father, there you are. You're going to be a grandfather. Isn't Lally a wonder? Was there ever a better girl?"

"No—never," Black Jack said. His eyes had seemed, for a moment, to mist. "Darling, Lally, promise me you'll take great care. Promise me you'll *eat!*"

"Oh, I'll see to that," Jon chortled. "If I have to stuff it down her throat. We're going to have lots of kids, Father—Lally and I." His eyes ranged around the big drawing room; his gesture indicated the whole house. "We'll populate it for you, Father. All those bathrooms are going to be used." He hugged Lally again. "You're going to be *well,* you understand, Monkey. It's going to be the healthiest baby there ever was."

"Healthy, yes . . ." she said faintly. He took it so matter-of-factly. Of course Lally would produce children, the way she did everything else. "Couldn't we wish it to be a bit intelligent, too?"

Alice came in. Jon got up and caught her around the waist, waltzing her around the room. Her expression was bewildered, but joyous. "Lally's going to have a baby, Alice! You're going to be an aunt!"

Alice looked at Madame Butterfly, tucked under her arm. "A real baby, Lally? A true one?"

"Yes, my darling," Black Jack answered. "A true one."

Black Jack insisted on telephoning Margaret that evening with the news. Margaret had used her allowance from Black Jack to rent a small but fashionable house in London. Lord Gough couldn't prevent her doing that, though he didn't approve of it. "Oh, Father, what a bore! Now you'll have grandchildren all over the place. I'm going to have a baby—sometime in November, the doctor says."

"Margaret!"

"Well—I'm supposed to produce an heir, aren't I? The Grenfell line has to go on. There's only Bobby left, and his father *expects* sons to inherit the title. God help the poor little soul if it's a girl. In fact, I only hope to get the money out of Lord Gough to buy a house here by saying I need to be near *very* good doctors. I need a lot of pampering and hand-holding. The fact is, I'm healthy as a horse. It's Lally we have to take care of. I hope she'll start to eat now."

"We'll make her." Black Jack sounded flustered. Suddenly his family was multiplying; he might have hoped, even longed for such a thing, but it was happening very quickly. They were to find it was common throughout the country. There was an urge among those who had returned, who had survived, to replace those who had gone. The older people looked toward children with hope. They represented some kind of future, the reward for a battle fought and won.

Black Jack immediately abandoned any plans for going to America. "It can all wait." When Alice heard the news she crushed

Teddy Rose and Madame Butterfly and Raggedy Ann close to her full young breasts.

"How am I going to hold them all?" she wailed. "So many!"

"One at a time, darling," Black Jack said. "One at a time."

* * *

Jon had one term at Oxford. The summer came, and they returned to Pellham Langley. Grangewick was undergoing its conversion at Black Jack's orders, and was not habitable. Most of Pellham Langley had been redecorated, and the furnishings returned to their places; Lady Latitia's portrait hung over the drawing-room mantel again. Jon walked Lally on the gentler stretches of the moors, took her on sedate picnics in his father's Rolls, driving at hardly more than ten miles an hour. He played tennis once more, when he could get a partner; he tried cricket, and found that the missing fingers along with the stiffened ones affected his grip on the bat, and his bowling was wild. "Well," he admitted, "I always told myself I'd be quite content just to watch cricket if I ever got back. I can't ask for more."

Lally exchanged letters with Susie. She had come out of the VAD and had a job at Harrods—*Until something more interesting comes up.* She had refused a visit to Pellham Langley. *I can't ask for a holiday just yet. The job isn't much—selling dress lengths. But there's a lot of others who would like it. I think I only got it because Sister wrote me such a cracking reference. Would you believe it? She asked me if I wanted to nurse at St. Thomas's. But I just couldn't stand the thought of going back to being a probationer.*

In August Margaret and Bobby came from Neatherby, where they had gone at the end of the London season. Black Jack had arranged some shooting, but it in no way resembled the vast, organized sporting occasions before the war. The game was sparse, having lacked the attention and protection of the gamekeepers during the war. Starvation and poaching had made inroads on the bird population. Men were now applying eagerly for jobs as gamekeepers and beaters, but mostly they were young and untrained. It would take years to get the shooting moors back to the state Black Jack had once gloried in. "Well, it's still enough sport for us," he said. "Perhaps it never will come back. Perhaps that's part of what's gone."

He would not allow Margaret or Lally to follow the guns unless they could safely do so by car. "What if a storm blows up? Suppose you two get drenched?" He fussed over them more than the doctors did. Lally wondered if it was a sense of guilt which lingered from Alice Trimble's death in childbirth. Some men, she read, felt that way. So she and Margaret lazed away the August days, their bodies already thickening and heavy.

"We must look ridiculous," Margaret said one day when a favorite dress would no longer accommodate her swelling belly. "Two bloated, overfed women, with everyone clucking around as if we were the only women in the world who ever had babies. *Everyone* is having a baby now. I'm dying for it to be time when I can really have an excuse for getting back to London. At least having a baby won't be the only topic of conversation."

"The air here is good for you, darling," Bobby said soothingly. "And we must spend a little more time at Neatherby. The parents expect it. They really do expect me to take an interest in the estate. Of course they understand about you having to be in London with your doctors. But it's their first grandchild, you know. They can hardly believe it's happening. You know how it is . . . They're getting on a bit, and having lost David and Guy, well, I suppose they didn't really think there was a hope of grandchildren."

Margaret shrugged, a little petulantly. "If only they didn't *fuss* so much." Then her manner became more gracious; she still had hopes that Lord Gough would make them a gift of a house in London. "Of course, darling, I understand. But I do have to have the baby in London. I wouldn't feel safe stuck away there in the country . . ."

"They're a shade disappointed that the baby won't be born at Dentdale." Dentdale was the sixteenth-century Elizabethan mansion of the Grenfell family, the house of which, on Lord Gough's death, Margaret would be mistress. "But they understand that you want to be with your own doctors. Anything so long as you and the baby are well."

Lally knew that Black Jack had tentatively suggested that he should buy a London house for Margaret and Bobby, and Bobby's pride had been stung. "Margaret has enough from you, sir, I think. Won't do her any harm to wait a bit for her own house in London. She has a perfectly good one at Neatherby." Black Jack had repeated this to Lally, hardly able to keep the satisfaction out of his voice. "Don't know as I don't agree with that old stick, Gough. Wouldn't hurt her at all to spend most of her time at Neatherby. *We* never needed a house in London. It would be good for their children to know where they belong. Damned if I don't think Bobby mightn't turn out to be not such a bad husband for her, after all."

So Margaret and Bobby, toward the end of August, returned to Neatherby, and Jon suddenly announced that he did not want to return to Oxford. "I'm too old," he said. "I just can't get back the feeling I had. It's a hard slog without any real meaning to it. I just can't see the relevance of Greek and Latin after the trenches. I see the eighteen-year-olds who've just come up, and I feel like an old man. Of course there are plenty of chaps in my situation—but I suspect most of them feel just about as I do. I never was a scholar, but I seem to have lost whatever little feel I ever had for it. Better chuck it than make an ass of myself by failing completely. It was part of being young, I suppose—being at Oxford. I think I'd better begin my stint at the mills and the mines."

If Black Jack was either elated or disappointed, he said nothing. Perhaps he remembered that he also had failed to finish his appointed time at Oxford. From one day to the other the running of the mills and the mines had fallen to him. Jon would have a gentler time, being eased in more gradually. "As you wish, son. Take your time. There was an education in the trenches none of my generation ever had."

In early September Susie Barlow arrived at Pellham Langley, in the company of Black Jack, who had been to London. "Your dad wouldn't take no for an answer." Lally noticed that now Susie hardly hesitated before placing "h's" where they should be. "To tell the truth I was getting a bit bored with selling dress lengths." Her small face puckered with laughter. "Ever so fancy. And the *time* it takes some of those ladies to decide on a few yards of material to make a petticoat. I've got half the shop on the counter, and they're still asking to see more." She leaned closer to Lally. "Your dad's really something, isn't he? Said it was to be a surprise for you. Went to the general manager and made him promise I could have a job back anytime. Said it was a patriotic duty owed to our gallant nurses. Lot of rubbish, of course—but he made him promise. Said his daughter was having her first child—she was a gallant nurse, too—I'll tell you, the place was swimming in heroines. Said she needed the companionship and help of an experienced nurse. I didn't like to point out that we didn't have much call for midwives in our section. But that point was too delicate for men to go into. I let it be. Your dad . . ." She looked down at her hands, the practical, hard-working hands that now looked considerably softer and smoother than Lally could ever remember. Susie was wearing a skirt and jacket which were simple but conspicuously smart; her neat little figure looked neater than ever. "Your dad insisted that I accept the same wage I was getting from Harrods. I didn't like to accept—I have my pride too. But I can't afford not to work. I help my mum and dad a bit with money to make up a little for the years of the war when I didn't earn a penny. So your dad's really paying me just to sit here and put my feet up. I think that's exactly what I'll do. Gawd, Lally, this is a *house,* isn't it? Biggest place I ever saw in my life. It'll take me a while to find my way to the kitchen."

Lally hugged her in delight. "Oh, dear, Susie! Be careful. You can't put your foot into the kitchen without Cook's permission. And tread carefully with Billings. He's getting on a bit, and a bit crotchety, too. He can't understand why things haven't gone back to what they used to be. He's only got two footmen now. I think there used to be five, and a sort of pantry boy. And Cook's only got one scullery maid. There're only three chambermaids and two parlor maids. Cook and Billings put up with it cheerfully enough during the war—but they didn't have to run a house this size. What they can't get used to is that everyone has to be trained. Before the war the little girls started about fourteen . . . there were any number of them."

Susie said, "Don't I know? I was one of them, remember? But who wants to go into service now? You're expected to bib and bob and curtsy, and 'yes'm' all the time. No wonder I took to selling dress lengths at Harrods. At least when the shop closes, it closes. You're there on time the next morning and no one asks any questions. I wouldn't go back into service if my life depended on it. But don't worry. I know how touchy butlers and cooks are. I won't step over the line. I just know my way around it. I made it my business to inform your Mr. Billings that I'd been in service. Didn't want him to think I was trying to pull the wool over anyone's eyes. So we understand each other. I'd never, Lally, do anything to let down such a lovely man as your dad." She gazed around the great drawing room, looked a long time at the portrait of Lady Latitia. "You've got everything, Lally. A real gentleman for a dad. A gorgeous husband." She winked with wicked glee. "And didn't even have to leave home to get him. I'll tell you, Lally, it caused a stir in the mess when the news came you'd got married. Couldn't figure it out. Sister had to come and explain that it was all quite—what did she say?—quite *proper.* He wasn't really your brother." She giggled. "Sounded a bit naughty. Had a bit of a time explaining it to my own dad and mum. Did you know your dad went down to see them in the Mile End Road? Very correct. Just to say I was coming on an 'extended visit' to you. 'Course they knew all about you." She languished back in her chair. "I know I'm supposed to sit up proper like a lady." Then real laughter broke through. "Hell, Lally, it's a long way from the time when we used to share the same basin to soak our feet in. When I saw that marble edifice they call a *bathroom* here . . . don't know as if I won't drown in that bath. Lovely way to die. If me mum and dad could just see me. Listen, Lally, do everything the doctor tells you, and have a healthy kid. You owe it to these people."

III

Susie stayed with Lally all through the deadening months when she felt almost too swollen and heavy to move. It was Susie who insisted on the walks every day in the garden, though she wouldn't let Lally venture onto the moors. "No, you don't! Twist your ankle and fall . . . Your dad'd never forgive me." She sent for books on midwifery, and studied them seriously. "I intend to know what happens when it happens . . ."

There were frequent telephone calls from Margaret. The births would be within a few weeks of each other. "If I'd *known* I'd never have allowed myself to get pregnant. It's awful! I can't go out anywhere, but lots of people come here. To tea and drinks. I lie on a sofa and try to cover up this *huge* belly. I'll tell you, Lally, I can't wait for the day I'll be able to see my own feet again. Bobby's being an angel, but I can't help thinking he's a tiny bit bored, too. He'd really like to be back at Neatherby, learning the ropes of the estate with the steward. He talks about Jon going to the mills every day. Rather envies him, I think. Though, honestly, I can't imagine Bobby in a mill or a mine."

The alterations to Grangewick were completed by October, and Black Jack insisted everyone move there. Vaguely, Lally perceived his agitation, his worry; he was afraid, she thought, that history might repeat itself. She could remember the morning of Alice's birth, the deep snow shrouding the moors, the winding uphill road to Pellham Langley. The village doctor had arrived, but the specialist from

Leeds, whose help had been needed, had been unable to make the journey. This time, Lally sensed, Black Jack could tolerate no such risk.

They settled into Grangewick, and the house was crowded. Lady Ross had come up from London. "I'm told these last weeks are very tedious, so I thought I might be able to help them pass. Margaret is full of complaints, but she has plenty of company. Too much company, I think. Bobby is afraid she wears herself out. But no one can make her stop, and Bobby hates to cross her. I'm afraid she is being horribly spoiled by that husband of hers. But he does adore her . . . and his parents are so overjoyed at the thought of a grandchild, they can deny her nothing. Lord Gough has bought them a charming house just off Belgrave Square. Not large, but big enough for Margaret to give her parties. It's being redecorated, and it's supposed to be ready soon after the baby's born."

"Poor little baby," Susie said. "If it's a girl I feel sorry for her."

Lady Ross nodded to her. She had taken a strong fancy to Susie. "She has the spirit to go with her red hair," she once said to Lally. "And lots of intelligence that is only beginning to find a way to be used. She's so utterly wasted as a shopgirl."

The Marchioness was still working for the Red Cross. "It's heartbreaking, at times, Lally. We still don't know where and when so many of them died. Did I tell you I've been invited to sit on the War Graves Commission?"

* * *

They heard the telephone ringing on a dark November morning. Black Jack was up, and downstairs answering it before Billings could struggle into his dressing gown. Margaret was in labor almost three weeks before her time. Lally and Jon and Susie clustered at the head of the stairs, and listened to Black Jack's side of the brief conversation. When he hung up he mounted the stairs, his face strained with worry. "Lally, go back to bed at once. Having one of you in trouble is enough."

"Trouble?"

"Bobby says the doctor and midwife are with her, and he won't let the doctor leave—not for anything. Margaret's screaming with the pain."

"Margaret would scream," Lady Ross said. "It's her nature." She was wrapped in a dressing gown, and a long plait of hair fell over one shoulder. Some of the austere handsomeness was gone. She looked, Lally thought, soft and womanly. The dressing gown, trimmed with rich red silk, was a little frayed at the cuffs.

"I think," Black Jack said, "maybe I should go to London. I could get the seven o'clock train. Might help old Bobby. He sounded pretty shaken."

"Would you like me to go with you, Jack?" Lady Ross said.

He looked at her with gratitude; at the same time he shook his head. "Oh, I couldn't let you do that. Besides, there's Lally . . ."

"Lally," Susie said, "has me and Jon. And the doctor and midwife aren't five minutes away. Do you think we'd let anything happen to her? And *Lally* isn't going to be screaming. Got more nerve and sense. She'll save her strength for the baby. Lady Ross, shall I come and help you pack a few things? I'm sure Mr. Pollock would like some company. Lally, you do as your dad says and go back to bed this minute. And you, miss"—she pointed at Alice, who had now appeared—"what are you doing out of bed?" It was said in a tone of mock severity; Susie had immediately given Alice her heart. "Go back, like a good girl. As soon as we have Lady Ross and your dad organized I'll be in to you and the others, and we'll all have some cocoa." It was understood that by "the others" she meant Teddy Rose and Madame Butterfly and Raggedy Ann. She had fallen exactly into the family's way of treating Alice as both a child and an adult. She clapped her hands, and Alice ran off, giggling.

Lally huddled back into bed. Jon followed after a few words with his father. "All the same," she said to him, "Margaret and I are being preposterously spoiled and pampered. There are millions of women having babies every day . . . some of them by themselves, alone and probably scared stiff."

"It's no use, Lally. You can't change the world just because you think you have too much. The fact is, my girl, you are bearing the much-wanted child of Jon Pollock, and the much-desired grandchild of Black Jack Pollock. Which may be far more important in the eyes of the world, but not in mine." In the darkness he turned to her and placed his hand on her belly. "Lally, love, be well. I know what Father's afraid of. I'm afraid, too. I don't want to lose you, Lally. There isn't a child in the world who could compensate for that." She felt the warmth of his hand, heard the tone of his voice. He was almost hers, more surely, closer. Once the baby was born . . . She resolved that he would hear no screams from her.

*   *   *

They learned that Margaret had had cause to scream. It was more than two days of agonized labor before she gave birth to a tiny, pale, but perfectly formed infant, a boy. Black Jack described on the telephone the way she had gazed at her son with exhausted eyes, and managed a smile. "What a lot of trouble you've caused, you tiny little thing. Here, let me kiss you, you bald little monkey. You nearly killed me, and I love you. Isn't it crazy, Bobby? I thought I'd hate whoever was causing me all that trouble. Now he's here . . . well, I'll just tell you now he's going to be spoiled. I love him."

"Hush, darling. Don't talk any more. Just sleep."

She had nodded. "He's the image of you, don't you think, Bobby? Your father will be pleased . . ." She smiled again, and let the drugs take over. "Yes, I'll sleep . . ."

Lord and Lady Gough had shared the vigil with Black Jack and Lady Ross. They had stared with relief and gratitude at their first grandchild. "Can't say I see anything of the family in him," Lord Gough said. "But he's a fine little chap."

"Rubbish, Percy," his wife had snapped, leaning over the baby, held by the nurse. "Those are exactly Bobby's eyes!" And indeed, Black Jack had to acknowledge, the baby's rather protuberant blue eyes did have much of the kindly, indolent, vaguely stupid look of his father, Viscount Grenfell.

* * *

When Lally's turn came she woke Jon quietly. "Just tell Susie," she said. "The waters have broken. It's not urgent, but perhaps I'd better be in a dry bed."

He started out of sleep in alarm. "Lally—Lally, you're all right. Does it hurt?"

"Not yet. Just tell Susie."

When the contractions started coming Susie was with her, with everything she had read about, the instruments that might be needed, sterilized and wrapped in clean towels. "Gawd, got enough here for a bloody lying-in hospital. But then, you never know. Bloody doctors don't know what they're doing half the time." The midwife arrived, and immediately wanted to expel Susie. Susie had put on her starched but worn VAD apron. "Just give me one good reason why I should go? Seen more than you have—never in a lifetime will you see what I've seen. Lally and me. She wants me here. Mr. Pollock *ordered* it." That seemed to answer any doubts. What Mr. Pollock wanted was instantly done. The doctor came, but he spent most of his time downstairs with Jon. They played protracted chess games as they waited, and Susie meticulously timed the contractions. Every hour Black Jack rang from London. "Don't worry, Mr. Pollock, everything's going beautifully. Just as you'd expect with Lally." The doctor seemed rather bored by this routine confinement.

It was, Lally thought, exactly as everyone had expected. After about ten hours, during which time the doctor was hardly needed, and the specialist who was on call was not summoned, she gave birth to a son. It wasn't that the birth hadn't cost her pain, but it was over soon, and it went as calmly and efficiently as Susie had predicted. "Gawd, ain't he beautiful? Seven pounds ten ounces. All right, Captain Pollock, you can come and look now. If you don't say that's the most beautiful baby—and Lally is the best damn mum . . ."

He laughed at Susie, but he went directly to Lally, not stopping to look at his son. "She always was the best—in everything."

"You'd better go on thinking that, Captain Pollock, or I'll come and kill you myself, personally." Jon kissed Lally's forehead, took both her hands in his. She had had Susie bathe her and give her clean nightwear before she would let Jon come in; she smelled of cologne. She had splashed it on herself to drive away the other smell—the smell of sickness and pain, the smell of poverty. It had returned violently in the final hour before the birth. She had hardly been aware that her child had been born; what she wanted was to be rid of the haunting smell, the smell and the fear. The touch of Jon's hand drove it out.

"It's all right, Lally, love . . . all right now, my love." "My love" he had said. "Rest. Susie tells me we have a beautiful son." She felt his kiss. "I've been so afraid, Lally. I thought I'd known the worst kind of cowardice when I was under fire. But this was something different. I felt as if I'd put you there—and I was running out on all the pain. I was the reason for it, and I couldn't do anything."

"*We* were the reason for it. Aren't you glad?"

He listened to the healthy squalls of the child in the beribboned cradle. "I'm not sure. I'm not sure if I'm brave enough to go through it again."

"Fool," she said. "Of course we'll both go through it again. They say it gets easier. It'll be a familiar story before you're very much older. Didn't we say we'd populate . . ." She felt herself drifting off toward sleep; this was like no tiredness she could remember.

*   *   *

She woke and found the room transformed by flowers. "Your dad has robbed every hothouse of every friend he has," Susie said. "And look, here's something from Lady Bletchley. A spray of orchids. Came to see the baby herself. Stiff old dame. But there's something about a baby that brings out the soft stuff in everyone. Your dad's arrived from London. She had tea with him—the old lady. All decked in diamonds she was."

Lally looked at the orchids. They were, she thought, probably the best that the Witfell conservatories, much depleted by the wartime heating restrictions, could yield. Her marriage to Jon had brought forth the purple velvet, but not the diamonds. The birth of a great-grandson had been deemed worthy of the diamonds. The baby was given to Lally to feed; she had insisted that she would feed the baby herself, and no one now dared oppose her. So Lady Bletchley had come, and worn diamonds. There was a dynastic stirring still in the old lady; she also looked to the replacements of the grandsons dead in the war. Lally fed her son, who seemed beautiful to her, and looked forward to seeing Black Jack. But after she had given the baby back to Susie, she unaccountably fell asleep.

When she woke again, the nurse, who had replaced the midwife, was fussing about the room. She hummed a little as she moved about. The room smelled only of cologne and fresh flowers. "Ah, there you are, Mrs. Pollock. Such a good, nice sleep you've had. Your father looked in, but didn't want to wake you. He's downstairs. Just as soon as you've had something to eat, I'll tell him he can come up and sit with you awhile. Ever so pleased, he is. Just fancy—two grandsons almost within a few days of each other. Look at the flowers, will you, Mrs. Pollock? Did you ever see such a lot—and in the middle of winter? Even local people sending them—not the sort of people you'd ever expect. I was just crossing the hall myself when this—well, this woman came to the door. The *front* door, Mrs. Pollock. I could see Mr. Billings didn't know what to say. Upset him a bit, it did. Well, she just brought a little posy. So I said just put it on the tray and I'd see you got it. Must have been sent by someone else, because she didn't look the sort who could afford such things. Freesias, aren't they? Have to be hothouse, at this time of year. Here, here's the card."

Lally deciphered the labored hand. *Good luck, Lily*. The strong perfume of the freesias was suddenly vile. She held them, squeezing the flesh of their stems between her clenched fingers. The nurse approached with the tray. "Now you'll have a little something to eat, Mrs. Pollock, and you'll feel stronger. Got to eat to be able to feed Baby—"

With all her strength Lally hurled the hated flowers from her, and thrust a clenched fist under the tray. It was wrenched from the nurse's hands, and the contents went flying into the air. There was a sound of breaking china. Beef soup and hot tea and thin slices of bread and butter bespattered the carpet.

For almost a minute the nurse dabbed at her soiled apron with the white linen napkin which had been laid on the tray. When she spoke her tone was deadly cold. "Well, Mrs. Pollock, I've seen childbirth affect women in many ways. But I've *never* seen such a display of vulgarity. They told me about you. Warned me. No lady, they said. Just something dredged off the street. Well, now you've proved it. You don't deserve that marvelous husband you have. Or your beautiful baby."

Slowly she began to remove the apron, and just as slowly folded it. "Well, Mrs. Pollock, I'll take my leave of you. Your *friend,* Miss Barlow, is, no doubt, quite capable of taking care of you and Baby. Birds of a feather, you are. The same class. I just hate to think of that little innocent being brought up by the likes of you."

Lally didn't hear what else was said. She turned over on the pillow and had not the strength or the will either to apologize or to weep. The flowers were from the woman who claimed to be her mother. The smell was rotten, rancid; the room was cold and damp.

* * *

The nurse was replaced by the woman who would become the baby's nanny. Later Lally wrote a note of apology to the nurse, but she knew it would never wipe out the memory of that outburst, nor could she possibly explain its reason. Only Black Jack, who had heard from Billings of the arrival of the freesias, could comfort her. "There are some things we can't help, Lally. You and Jon have a beautiful son . . . only think about that."

"That woman . . . ?"

"She won't trouble you again."

She didn't know how he could be sure, but she accepted what he said. She turned her attention to the things around her, thrusting away the memories of a dark and troubled place. She allowed herself to be petted and pampered for a few days, and then, with Susie's help, she was up and dressed, and came downstairs to dinner. "Darling child—" Black Jack sprang to his feet when she entered the drawing room, where he and Jon and Lady Ross were drinking sherry. Alice sat with them. "Should you be down?"

"Oh, Mr. Pollock," Susie exclaimed. "That's all old-fashioned rubbish. Lie in bed and you get weak. Lally's fit as a flea, and it's good for her to move around. Baby's with the nanny, so we don't have to worry about him. Don't you think, Mr. Pollock," she said pointedly, "that it's time Lally shared in the celebrations? You've all been toasting Baby in champagne. What about Lally?"

As if he had been summoned, Billings entered. He had assumed a place in the household no one could quite define, nor one he would ever be denied. The champagne bottles were wrapped in white damask, the glasses chilled. He had been told by Nell that Lally was dressing to come down and had acted on his own initiative. "I just hope, sir, that France has a good wine harvest next year. We seem to be getting perilously close to the bottom of the cellar."

"Unthinkable, Billings," Jon said. "How could you ever let it happen?" He embraced Lally, stood off to admire her in the emerald gown which had served her during her pregnancy as an evening dress. Its loose folds flapped about her now; she was miserably conscious that her waist was still thick, but she reveled in a refound sense of lightness.

"No one, sir, ever expected the hostilities to continue as long as they did. I laid in what I thought would withstand a siege . . ."

"Mr. Pollock expected a siege," Lady Ross observed quietly. "But he didn't want to tell any of you. He hoped he would be wrong."

"I wish he had been, m'lady. Now, sir, if I may be permitted the liberty . . ." Billings had, of course, brought a glass for himself. "May I propose a toast to the new generation, and let us forget all the old things of war?"

They murmured a repetition of his words. "May I ask, sir, what the baby is to be called? Everyone wants to know."

Jon drew Lally closer to him on the sofa. "We never talked of it before. We just wanted the baby born safely."

Black Jack cleared his throat rather nervously. "Well . . . Margaret was on the telephone today. She says if you call the baby Jonathan, they will call theirs David. That also happens to be the name of the eldest Gough son who was killed. Margaret's talking of being well enough to come up here for Christmas. We'll all have Christmas at Pellham. And the babies will be christened in the village church. David and Jonathan."

"Wonderful!" Jon said.

Within his enfolding arm Lally could not repress a shiver. The biblical text of David and Jonathan came back to her. *O Jonathan, thou wast slain in thine high places. I am distressed for thee, my brother, Jonathan: very pleasant hast thou been unto me: thy love to me was wonderful* . . . She shook off the thought. There was the other text. *The soul of Jonathan was knit with the soul of David.* Yes, that was it. They would be brothers of the soul. "Yes, Jonathan," she agreed.

"Two babies," Alice said joyfully. "Two babies here. True ones." Black Jack handed her his champagne glass. "I do think, Billings, that Miss Alice might have been included in the celebrations."

For once Billings looked flustered. "Why, of course, sir. How forgetful of me. Excuse me, Miss Alice. I'll just go and get another glass . . ."

None of them knew how to cross the barrier between Alice as a child and as a young woman, or how far they dared cross it.

* * *

In the end Black Jack's dream of a christening ceremony in the homely intimacy of the village church of Pellham Langley was doomed. The two children, in long lace robes, many generations old, were to be baptized in the grand and ancient setting of York Minster. The Goughs had insisted on it, and were backed up in this by the Bletchleys. The clear implication was that Pellham Langley might be all right for children of the gentry, but when it came to grandchildren and great-grandchildren of the aristocracy, something much more significant was demanded. Black Jack gave in on this point, because he won another which was, to him, even more significant. He had cabled Brock Weymouth as soon as both children were safely delivered, and Brock Weymouth stood there, dressed in meticulously tailored morning dress, on that day before Christmas as godfather to each of them. He had crossed in the roughest Atlantic weather the Cunard Line could remember, and was there just in time. Lady Bletchley was outraged. "Why, the man's a nothing! Patrick will be godfather . . ." She had forgotten that Patrick Kimble, Jon's friend at Eton and Oxford, had been killed. There were so many killed she had lost count, even of her own grandchildren. Lord Bletchley, nearly blind, and leaning heavily on a cane, had nodded, acquiescing to Black Jack's judgment, though a trifle unwillingly. "Jack's right . . . Jack's right. The Yanks are the coming lot. Our lot's wiped out. They tell me he's rich, this fella. Damn well better be. Won't be too many rich around in England much longer, with income tax as it is. Yes, better make alliances where you can. Blood doesn't seem to count anymore. Money talks."

Lady Bletchley wore new gray velvet, and her prewar furs. Her toque, copied exactly from those worn by Queen Mary, quivered with osprey feathers. Her throat was roped in pearls, and diamonds blazed on her age-spotted hands, and on the toque. Lally stood, wrapped in a fur coat, and watched as her son was christened immediately after Margaret's. In the name of each of them, Brock, as godfather, and Lady Ross, as godmother, promised to renounce the devil and all his works. Brock appeared to know the form of the service perfectly—but then, Lally thought, he would have taken care to do so, as he took care with everything. And he would never be a token godfather. One could be sure he would be all the things he promised, at least in the material sense. With Brock, the things of the spirit were the unknown.

The great organ pealed out, the choir sang. The ordinary citizens of York, beginning to gather for evensong in the minster on the day before Christmas, were given an especially sumptuous feast of music. Lally was reminded strongly of the day of Sandy's and Jon's marriage, when all had seemed so joyful, and her own heart had been like lead. She looked across at Margaret, pale and lovely, to whom motherhood had seemed to give an added beauty. She remembered on that day that Margaret had worn a white ermine coat and hat which she said Brock had borrowed for her. The one she wore now was not borrowed; Lord Gough had given her the choice of what was on display at Harrods. "Arctic fox," she had whispered to Lally. Her face, framed by that upstanding fur, had seemed indeed as if the two belonged together; the vixen eyes had gleamed. "Thank God," she had added to Lally, "that's one baby out of the way. The Goughs will expect more, which is a bore. Poor darling Bobby wants another right away, but he's terrified I'm going to die. Bobby's beginning to be a bit of a bore too, poor love, but then, he can't help it. Isn't Brock distinguished-looking, Lally? Who would have supposed Father would have had such a brilliant idea? He won't be like the old fuddy-duddy godfathers most children get." Had there been, Lally wondered, just an echo of Lord Bletchley's sentiment? "He'll put *real* silver spoons in their mouths."

The service came to an end. People began to rise and gather up their belongings. The choir was finishing an anthem. The dean signaled them all to wait.

"Now, dearly beloved, I have been asked to solemnize the marriage of Edith, Marchioness of Ross, to Mr. John James Pollock. The banns of this marriage have been duly posted these past three weeks, though I realize this comes as a happy surprise to most of you. This is a joyful occasion for all of us. For long, terrible years, our nation was in dire peril. Now we celebrate births and baptisms, and new marriages. Will the witnesses come forward please?"

Billings, who obviously had known in advance, produced a bouquet for Lady Ross, and another for Susie Barlow. Susie had made a dress of stunning beauty and simplicity for the christenings, and she wore a fur coat Brock had brought with him from London, which he said was borrowed. Now Brock took his place beside Black Jack. Lally knew there would be no fumbling for the ring when the time came. "Do you, Edith, take this man, John . . ." In a stunned sense of happiness and near disbelief, Lally listened to the exchange of vows. "With this ring, I thee wed. With all my worldly goods, I thee endow." The ring had been passed smoothly from Brock to Black Jack. Black Jack, the man Lally called her father, had married for the third time.

While the organ played, and the guests who had assembled for two christenings and had witnessed a marriage as well, murmured among themselves, Black Jack and the woman who would now be known as Mrs. Pollock went off to the vestry, followed by Brockton Weymouth, of New York, and Susan Barlow, of the Borough of Hackney, London, who would place their signatures, with the many thousands of others, on the registry of one of the greatest cathedrals in England.

Margaret turned to Lally in laughing disbelief. "Oh, darling, isn't it wonderful! She frightens me a little, because I always think she expects better things of me. But it's the best possible thing for Father."

Lally managed a smile. She wondered if what she was experiencing, apart from surprise, wasn't also jealousy. All her life Black Jack had told her he needed her, the family needed her. She had promised to take care of Jon and Margaret and Alice. In one stroke she seemed now no longer needed. The stately lady whom she had revered now would take over those tasks.

"What's the matter, Lally? Aren't you feeling well?" Jon whispered urgently in her ear. "This place is freezing. Neither you nor Margaret should have come."

"Of course we should!" She brought herself swiftly to attention. "Could we have missed this! Father will be happy, and so will Lady Ross."

Beside her Margaret whispered, "What will we call her, do you think? She's not Lady Ross anymore. But we can't call her 'Mother,' can we? I didn't even know her name was Edith . . ."

The wedding party emerged from the vestry. Edith Pollock's regal posture was nearly matched by Susie's. Brock Weymouth looked as if he was thoroughly accustomed to acting as best man and witness to such solemn occasions. Some things, Lally thought, were learned swiftly by those who wished to learn them.

The congregation, gathering beyond the rood screen in the great cathedral, was startled by a thunderous rendition of Wagner's wedding march. They had known a baptism was taking place beyond their sight, but none of them had expected the recession to be headed by a middle-aged bride and groom.

* * *

Black Jack had laid on a special train to take the guests from York to Leeds. There was a surprising number of them—some had not attended the ceremony in York Minster, but had come to toast the christenings at Grangewick, and the more hardy of them seemed determined to see in another Christmas morning there. The Bletchleys had departed for Witfell, an expression of utter disgust clamping Lady Bletchley's face rigid; Lord Bletchley, Lally guessed, would have liked to join the celebrations, but did not dare cross his wife. The combination of Brock Weymouth being godfather to both children, and then Black Jack marrying for the third time, had been too much for Lady Bletchley. "Well, I suppose one can only say for her that at least she's better than that Trimble woman," Lally heard Lady

Bletchley say to her husband in what she might have supposed to be a mutter. "Oh, well, I suppose the consolation is that she's too old to have children." There was, Lally realized, just as much awareness of the force of Black Jack's money and its ultimate destination in this aristocratic lady as there would have been in the most hard-nosed mill owner.

At Grangewick the babies were fussed over before being taken upstairs by the two nannies, but the only talking point was the surprise marriage. "Well, thee's played that close to thy chest, lad," one coalmining magnate said to Black Jack.

"Oh, that was just to save you the expense of a wedding present as well as two christening presents, Tommy," Black Jack replied. And shouts of laughter followed the remark. Yorkshire dearly loved an occasion like this. And, they remarked to one another, the Pollock family had done well for themselves. Twice now Black Jack had married aristocracy—never mind that the former Marchioness, now plain Mrs. Pollock, had no money. That mistake of his, that little governess in between, could now be forgotten. And there was his daughter married to Lord Gough's heir. Only Jon had married that nameless girl he had grown up with. *She* brought nothing with her, most of them thought, not even looks—though some of the younger men declared her dark and intense features, now she had lost all the fat, "interesting." The older ones said they preferred a good handful of woman, not these skinny young modern things. But then the feeling was that Jon had settled for the closest thing to hand once the war was over. Yes, they agreed among themselves, as they drank Black Jack's champagne, and ate his food, that girl they called Lally Leeds was a safe choice. There would be no trouble from her. *She* knew which side her bread was buttered on. And she had produced a son, in right smart order, just as she should.

Upstairs, where they had gone to take off their coats, Lally and the Marchioness—Lally as yet had no other name for her—exchanged smiles. "It *was* rather sly of you," Lally said.

"We didn't know if you'd let us do it—so we just went ahead." The Marchioness unpinned her hat and took it off. "Lally, are you pleased?"

Lally nodded. "It's marvelous. For him—for all of us. We always wondered if he'd ever marry again, but we never thought . . ." No one for a long time had mentioned the lady Black Jack had supported in Leeds. Somewhere, during the war years, while Lally and

Margaret and John had been away, she had seemed to slip out of sight and mind. No one had ever really acknowledged her existence, so no one needed to ask about her disappearance. All at once Lally had the vision of the calm and stately presence of the Marchioness presiding permanently over Pellham Langley. Black Jack would never be alone again. She began to share Margaret's pleasure.

But there was more than that. "I love him, you know, Lally. I began to love him that first summer—your coming-out. I saw how he loved you. You had everything Margaret had, and he would have given you more if that had been possible. And his love for Alice. Yes, Lally, I fell in love. I felt it dreadfully during the war years, when he would come and see me, talk about you all, his business difficulties, as if I were some elderly counselor. I wanted him to see me as a woman, but he seemed determined to keep me on some sort of pedestal. Very slowly he began to see me in the way I wanted, but it was too slow for me. In the end I asked him to marry me. It shocked him a little. I even had to *persuade* him. He had been thinking I was totally wrapped up in the Red Cross work, and would never move permanently to Yorkshire with him. I think it was the arrival of the two grandchildren that finally pushed me—and him—to it. The sudden realization that we were not getting younger. We arranged it all very quietly. People tend to laugh at these late marriages. We decided that we'd let them laugh after the fact. It's done now." She fluffed up her hair. "We're returning with Brockton on the next sailing. It'll be a honeymoon. Brockton has arranged a house in Palm Beach, Florida, for us. Some friend of his owns it. I'll take Jack out of this atrocious Yorkshire winter. He'll have the rest he's deserved, and it will give Jon a chance to try himself at the business without his father hovering. Yes, I know, it hasn't been easy for Jon to settle in. He'll have a better chance without Black Jack. You won't mind, Lally, having Alice with you for a time? Jack does need a change . . ." She pulled the belt on her slender waist even more tightly, and patted her flat stomach. "I don't look too bad, do I, Lally?" Her gaze met Lally's in the long mirror. "Oh, yes, I do have my little vanities. And I do love him."

* * *

Downstairs the party was growing noisier. The carol singers had come, sung their carols, taken some wine and mince pies, and departed with a handsome contribution from the best man and godfather. Billings, perspiring but beaming, was trying to direct the two young footmen and several waiters hired for the occasion. "Don't know what we should have done for champagne, Miss Lally, if Mr. Brockton hadn't arranged for some from London. A friend of his in the trade, he said. Very hard to get now through our regular suppliers. Not in any quantity. Major Weymouth, I must say, has *very* good connections—whoever they are." Billings seemed totally bewildered by Brock's identity. He had no background Billings could recognize, but then there was no way of telling with these Americans. He had sources of supply which in an English gentleman might be suspect. "I didn't know a thing about the marriage until this morning, Miss Lally. Not till they gave me the bouquets to hide. I had to give them to Nell to carry in a basket. At first I thought it was a joke. But Mr. Brockton isn't one for joking about such things." Lally noticed that Billings, despite his occasional reference to Major Weymouth, was falling into the habit of calling Brock "Mr. Brockton," just as he continued to call Jon "Mr. Jon." One of the family— more and more one of the family. Lally wondered if the Marchioness would ever discover the identity of the friend who had lent his house at Palm Beach. It would be stocked with wine and food and servants as discreet as any at the Ritz. Lally imagined a pale beach at its doorstep, and sea water warmer than any of them had ever known. Black Jack and the Marchioness . . . lovers. How long had they been lovers? she wondered. They could not have stumbled innocently, headlong, into this marriage. Both were too sophisticated for that. But they had told only Brock and, at the very last minute, probably, Susie. But already the house was waiting at Palm Beach.

Brock had given the usual silver gifts to the two babies. There were silver gifts from Susie, too, which Lally thought Brock had surely paid for—Susie could not have afforded them, and somehow he had managed to get around her great pride and make her accept them. "There's just a bit of a rotter in that man that I like," Susie had confessed. "He doesn't pretend to be what he isn't."

"But what *is* he?"

Susie shrugged. "With a man like Brock Weymouth it doesn't matter. But watch out. He's after Margaret, and he hasn't given up."

The icy cold of York Minster had not affected Lally as much as the cold that struck her at Susie's words. "What do you mean?"

"You know very well. Bobby's a fool—a nice man, but a fool.

Margaret will begin to look around, and guess who'll be there? Mr. Brockton Weymouth."

"How . . . ?"

"Lally, didn't you read there were over three thousand divorces in England last year? Wake up! Brock—he's a fast mover."

As if to bear out her words, beside them Brock was talking to a group of local millowners and the Lord Mayor of Leeds, of his rushed journey across the Atlantic. "I'll be glad when I can fly it. It'll save so much time." The statement was greeted with gales of well-intentioned laughter. These people knew that Mr. Brockton Weymouth was a very "warm" man, a man of some wealth, all self-made, therefore he could not be a fool. But to think of flying the Atlantic—it could only be a joke. Oh, yes, they'd all read about those madmen, Alcock and Brown, who'd managed the feat, and had ended ingloriously in an Irish bog.

"Air Mail services started between New York and Washington this year," Brock said, once the laughter had subsided.

"God love us—you Yanks," someone remarked. "Such mad schemes."

"Damn Yanks—claim they won the war for us," a voice growled in the background.

"Mayhap they did, lad," Lally heard in reply.

IV

Black Jack and the woman they all now stumblingly learned to call Edith stayed only until the morning of Boxing Day. Then they traveled south with Brock, and took a Cunard liner in Southampton. A strange silence seemed to fall on Grangewick. "Well," Margaret said, "what do we do now? The house in London isn't ready, and I don't want to go to Neatherby. But I suppose I'd better. Well, there'll be some New Year parties, I suppose, to liven things up . . ."

She appeared strangely tense. "Oh, it's just having got all the birth thing over. Those months seemed so endless. But I thought when it was over I'd feel so wonderful. Suddenly, from time to time I just feel like sitting down and crying."

"They're starting to call it 'postnatal depression,'" Susie said. "I read about it."

Margaret looked at her sharply. "What are *you* going to do now?"

Her tone was almost unfriendly. In an odd way she seemed to resent Susie's closeness to Lally. Never before had a woman friend stood between Margaret and Lally. Lally had always been hers. Sometimes Lally was faintly amused to witness the tiny sense of rivalry which had grown up between them. She was unused to being fought over.

"Oh, I expect I'll go back to selling dress lengths at Harrods."

"Rubbish!" Margaret said. All the generosity of her nature suddenly opened. She might know that in Susie she had a rival for Lally's affection, but she was not capable of being petty. "You're far too intelligent for that. There must be something else for you to do." No one mentioned marriage, as they would automatically have done before the war; for Susie, as well as for Margaret and Lally, the choices, the prospect of husbands had been cruelly narrowed almost to the vanishing point by the attrition of the trenches.

"Something'll turn up," Susie said. "Can't really see dress lengths being my life's work, so to speak."

"Then what do you see?" Jon said quietly. He was mostly quiet. He liked to sit near Lally, sometimes to touch her hand. He liked to visit his son in the nursery at odd hours, which upset Nanny. Parents were supposed to visit at prescribed times, and fathers were generally not openly affectionate. But a lot of things had changed with the war. And even nannies now had to bend the rules. The young parents didn't always hold with the values of the old. Nanny herself liked things the old way, and she complained in the servants' hall that things were not what they used to be. The young just didn't want to work, Nanny decided. All this, Susie had heard from her, and not repeated. But she knew of Jon's quiet visits to the nursery. She had seen the sense of wonder in his face as he had looked at his son. The child represented a peace Jon had not expected to experience; he was part of the miracle of having survived. Everyone noticed how quiet Jon was, as if he could never have enough of sitting by the fire, a book unread on his lap. "I like the warmth," he said, as if to excuse himself. "Got a touch of rheumatism from wading through the bloody water in the trenches. Never getting dried out." It was a common complaint. At Pellham, though, he endlessly walked the moors, halting to listen to the cries of the birds, the clacking of the grouse among the heather. The silence around Jon seemed full of noises he had never expected to hear again. The cries of his son were new noises to him. He listened.

"What, Susie, do you think you'd like to do? I mean—given a bit of backing. Given the chance."

"Oh . . . I dunno." Susie shrugged. "I spent my lunchtime walking all those posh streets around Harrods. Lots of little shops. Lots of people passing by. It's full of dressmakers, and such. But they've always got to make something in a real hurry. I've always thought it'd be a lot cheaper, and easier on labor, if we had things ready made-up. You know—a couple of sizes of a few styles. Could make an alteration in them in a jiffy. Little bit on the waist, little bit on the hem. The lady's got a new dress. Now the war's over, and things are easier, women are getting hungry for new clothes. They like to come into London from the suburbs. But they can't pay the prices of the classy dressmakers. Well, there ought to be a midway thing. Shops they can walk into without being scared out of their wits. Dresses they can try on, and see how they suited, and then have a few tucks and such taken here and there. Well . . ." She shrugged again, as if to dismiss her own suggestion. "It's just an idea. But I think the ladies would come. Not everyone can afford the top prices, and not everyone is ready to settle for the little woman around the corner who's only got styles in magazines to show, and to try to copy from. The lady's got no real idea how it'll turn out, or whether it'll suit her."

"Would you," Jon said, "be prepared to go into it as a real business? I mean—do this ready-made thing, to try it out? Perhaps you could begin to supply other places, make it bigger. After all, we've got the mills here in Yorkshire and Lancashire. We have to sell our cloth in any place we can. Perhaps it's time we started to think in terms of the end product. A good, ready-made product for everyone."

Bobby's mouth fell open. "I say, dear chap. You mean, no more Savile Row? Not custom-made?"

Susie snorted. "Custom-made? That's what makes them too expensive for the ordinary woman. She has to make her own at home, whether she's any good at it or not. Frumps, that's what most of them look like because they haven't a notion of style or, Gawd help them, a notion of how to put the bloody dress together. They buy the material and go home, and if they haven't got a little woman around the corner, they make a right mess of it. There should be something in the middle."

"Yes," Margaret said. "That's exactly right! I've often wanted that sort of dress myself. Perhaps I'm bored with what I've got and want a new one for a party. Perhaps I've outrun my allowance." She glanced at Bobby. "I've often thought it would be fun to try on a dress without feeling I had to give an order, and have seven fittings, and all the nonsense. Jon, what are you proposing?"

"I'm proposing that you and I, Margaret, for once in our lives, do something without Father putting up the money for it." He turned to Susie. "Margaret and I have a bit . . . a small trust fund set up by Grandfather Bletchley which we came into when we each turned twenty-one. It's not a lot—just something he did for each of his grandchildren as they came along. But it would, I think, start you. Set you up."

"I dunno, Jon. It's a risk, isn't it? I haven't any experience of business, just that bit of dressmaking I did before the war."

"Did you make that dress, Susie?" Margaret asked. "Could you teach other women how to cut from a pattern—enough copies so that the cost would come down?"

"Yes, I made it. Figured out how to make the pattern before I cut it. Maybe I'd have to make all the patterns myself until I got good trained help. But Gawd, if I went bust I don't know how I'd pay you back your money."

"That would be our risk, Susie. We'd share the profits when you make them. It isn't charity. After all, our grandfather and our father took risks. That's how money's made."

"I *say* . . ." Bobby's tone was both doubtful and awed. "Do you think it's wise, Margaret?"

She laughed. "It may not be wise, but it could be fun. It'd be a lot more exciting than getting three percent on stocks. I'd talk the place up for you, Susie. I know a lot of women my age who'd be glad to find a shop where they could get style without too much expense . . ."

"It would have to be more than that," Jon said. "Otherwise Susie'd just be running another dressmaking establishment. She'd have to sell to other outlets. It would have to go into volume business. One of a kind is no good, as Susie pointed out. You'd have to have a fairly big staff and salespeople out on the road. Not too ambitious to begin with, but enough volume to make it worthwhile. I've gotten to know a few of the people who come to the mills to buy for the fashion trade. I could try the idea on them. Maybe they could suggest some sales representatives, perhaps some outlets through the provinces. Not every woman can get to London to buy."

They spent the rest of the afternoon beginning to work out the details. The look of tense boredom had gone from Margaret's face; Susie's expression changed back and forth from excitement to fear. Jon got pencil and paper and started jotting down numbers. For the first time Lally saw the inheritance from Black Jack and James Pollock at work in him. She suddenly knew that Jon would make a success of his work at the mills and the mines when the time came; he would be able to pick up from Black Jack, and he would never despise his work. As swiftly as he worked on his figures, Susie's hands were busy with her own pad and pencil. Sketches began to flow. Margaret studied all of them. "Darling, Susie! That's hardly what you'd sell to middle-aged ladies."

"They wouldn't all be like that. But don't you see—everything's changed. We don't want all the clutter and frills anymore. Women are getting out of corsets. They want free and easy things, well-cut. They're not all trying to look like Queen Mary."

"Susie, I love you!" Margaret said. "You'll be my exclusive designer from now on. I'll wear the simplest and best dresses in London. I'll make it chic to buy off the rack!"

"I say, darling," Bobby protested. "Mustn't get too excited. Tire yourself out. It'd be Susie's business, you know—"

"And it'd be my business to sell." Suddenly Margaret put out her hand to Susie. "Are we partners?"

For just a moment Susie hesitated. Then the word seemed expelled from her: "Right!"

Margaret, who two hours before had been ready to quarrel with Susie, now leaned over and kissed her cheek. "Let's get it all down on paper, Jon. Let's get to the solicitors, and have it all signed and sealed before Father knows a thing about it. For once, we'll do something by ourselves. It's our money, after all. If Father were here he'd want to throw money at us, and we'd be swamped. This way, we'll have to do it on a shoestring—or Susie will. But it will be ours."

"I wouldn't be so sure Father *would* do that. Perhaps it's just the sort of thing he's been hoping we'd do for ourselves. We've been taking from him all our lives. It's time we broke out . . ."

Lally felt in some sense excluded. There had been no trust fund set up for her, and she was suddenly aware that she had never in her life earned any money. She had none to gamble with, as these two did. Nor did Bobby. His allowance still came from his father, as if he were still a small boy at prep school. None of the Gough acres could be sold to provide seed capital for such a business. He lived by his father's goodwill; only Margaret and Jon had this small independence to play with. The gamble obviously excited her.

* * *

It was Billings who, on New Year's Day, knocked on the door of Lally and Jon's room. The later winter dawn had not yet broken. It was just past seven o'clock. "Billings here, Mr. Jon. May I come in?"

Jon lifted his head from the pillow. "Come in." The old man wore his dressing gown. He held a copy of *The Times* in his hand.

"Sorry if I woke you, sir. It's been rather a shock." Lally saw that his hand trembled, so that the paper rattled.

"For God's sake, Billings, what's happened?"

Billings seemed to stumble toward the light Jon had switched on. "Here, sir. The New Year Honor's list. Your father—Mr. Pollock, sir. Your father receives a baronetcy. Services to the war industry, it says. For King and Country, you might say. Oh, Mr. Jon . . ." Now Billings' voice shook as well as his hands. "So richly deserved. He worked so hard. Those tanks . . . that was a huge risk. He could easily have just made money out of the mills and risked nothing. Just think . . . Sir John Pollock. But he never said a word, sir. Not a word, even to me."

"No one is supposed to, you know, Billings. It's supposed to be entirely confidential until it's announced. He certainly didn't say anything to *me!*"

"You're sure, sir?"

"I swear it, Billings. He said nothing, did he, Lally?"

The old man was mollified. "Well, he wouldn't, would he? I wonder if Lady Ross—I beg your pardon, Mrs. Pollock—knew?"

Lally remembered the conversation when the Marchioness had told her, after the wedding, that she had made the proposal to Black Jack. It did not seem the action of a woman who had striven for social or financial gain. Black Jack had met too many of them. Lally heard her words again. "I do love him . . ."

"I'm absolutely certain Mrs. Pollock didn't know," Lally said. "It would have made no difference, in any case."

"You're right, madam. It would have made no difference to that lady." He looked at Jon. "Forgive me for disturbing you this way, sir. But I was so pleased . . ." He stood back, as if to look at Jon properly. "You realize, sir, that a baronetcy is hereditary. Not like a knighthood. One day—may it be a long time from now, sir—you will inherit the title from your father. You will be Sir Jonathan Pollock. And your son after you." He retreated toward the door. "Well, sir— madam . . . a great day. We must send a telegram to Sir John and Lady Pollock. That Florida place . . . Oh, no—not yet. They will just have arrived at the Plaza Hotel in New York City. Guests of Mr. Brockton, I believe."

"No doubt," Lally said, "he has a friend who happens to keep a suite there."

Billings looked slightly taken aback. "That is exactly what he said, madam."

When Billings had gone, Jon dived back under the bedclothes. "Lally, what do you think? Marvelous for Father, and he deserves it. But you're going to be Lady Pollock someday."

She drew his body close to hers, cradling him with her arms. "It seems to me, my love, that we're becoming awash in titles. We'll have to have some children who will inherit absolutely nothing." She sighed as she held him. "Why didn't they make it a knighthood? It would have served Father just as well. And you and I would have got nothing from it. I really don't fancy being Lady Pollock."

"It is, as Billings said, a long way off."

❦ CHAPTER 12 ❧

I

It seemed to Lally a long time before Black Jack and Edith returned. The Yorkshire winter closed in; there were letters and postcards, but they came so slowly. "That air mail service Brock was talking about would be useful," Jon said, viewing the highly colored vista of a palm-lined road in Florida. Jon, however, appeared glad of his father's absence. "I'm sure he did it deliberately. He knows I have to find my way with the rest of the management, and make my mistakes. It's easier for everyone if he isn't on hand. I'm mostly fumbling and bumbling around, Lally. There's a hell of a lot to learn . . ."

Pollock textile mills and coal mines and steel mills were still a wholly owned concern. Black Jack, even at the height of his borrowing before the outbreak of the war, had never considered forming a company and allowing anyone else a say in their running. Some banks he had gone to had turned him down, demanding equity in the properties in return for lending money. Black Jack had politely thanked them and gone elsewhere. Those who backed him had backed his experience, and something they could not quite define—a flair, was the best they would say of it. "A nose in the wind," a few said. They had charged high interest rates, and Black Jack had paid. The properties were now totally unencumbered, and Jon was the only natural heir to them. "I've got to do it, Lally. I've started late, but there's no one else he can hand them over to."

"The delay," she said dryly, "was hardly of your making, Jon. Four years went out of everyone's life. Father's just too thankful to have you back with him to complain that you haven't gained much experience in running the mills."

But he and Lally were in an ambiguous position. Jon earned a salary from the mills—a little larger than a junior manager would have gotten. But there were many things they did not have to pay for. They lived at Grangewick rent-free; there had been the gift of a car from Black Jack, who also paid the wages of a chauffeur-handyman. Jon insisted on driving the car himself, and the chauffeur, Barnsley, sat beside him, waiting to drive the car back to Grangewick after Mr. Jon had gone into the mills in case Mrs. Pollock should want to drive somewhere, or, what pleased him better, to be driven. There were only, Lally thought, so many days one could go shopping, and she was not yet quite used to the custom of visiting for afternoon tea. After the years of work in France, she now seemed ridiculously idle. There was Nanny, Mrs. Dunstable, to take care of Jonathan, there was a parlor maid, and a chamber maid, and a cook who consulted her religiously every morning with the suggested menus, but really didn't need her. There was no need for a butler; for the few dinner parties they gave, Billings came readily from Pellham Langley to supervise the parlor maid. "Should have a footman, madam—but they seem to be going out of fashion with the young people these days."

Lally smiled at him. "Billings, we're not nearly grand enough to have a footman." But she was conscious that Black Jack paid the wages of all these people, and the money Jon earned went on food, and wine, and clothes for them both. It was hard to get used to. "Jon, there's so much left over . . . at our age, we're *saving*. It's as if we're already old. We should stop Father doing all this. We should try living on what you earn. I could look after Jonathan easily . . ."

He spread his hands. "It's no use. He'd only raise my salary until it was totally out of line with everyone else's at the mills. My salary now would pay for a semidetached house, and a cook-general, and you'd never stop toiling all day. Don't you think you've earned the right to put your feet up for a while? I seem to remember you complained about how swollen they were after a day on the wards."

Lally made no more protests. She learned to return the calls that were paid on her by other ladies with as little to do as she had. She pecked at cucumber sandwiches for tea, and went to the mills to collect Jon when they were invited to the new social institution, the cocktail party. She met the same people over and over, all determined to forget the war, all, it seemed, determined to put her back in the place she had left to go to France. "One would never suspect we have Lady Astor in Parliament, never mind the vote," she told Jon. "I almost begin to understand why Margaret wants to be in London all the time. I suppose one does see different faces there."

"You're not hankering after a London house, are you?"

She shook her head. "It wouldn't do, Jon. Father's going to need you here. I hope, in a way, he'll still need me. Even though he has Edith."

She was aware that in Leeds her social position was also ambiguous. She was Jon Pollock's wife, but she was still the child who had had no name until Black Jack had given her one. In Leeds and Bradford and Sheffield the name of Pollock had power; one day, no matter how far off, she would be Lady Pollock. She was aware, as she ate the cucumber sandwiches and sipped the sherry or the cocktails, that there were still plenty who, out of her hearing, called her Lally Leeds. She was almost thankful when, in March, Black Jack and Edith's return made an excuse for a trip to Southampton and London. Jon and Alice went with her. Billings insisted on being one of the party. "I've always seen to his clothes, though, strictly speaking, I'm not supposed to be his valet."

It was, Lally realized, the longest time she could remember that Billings had ever been parted from Black Jack. He was going to claim him back as eagerly as a father would his son. Edith would have her own battles with Billings' possessiveness, his sense of being the supreme authority. That part of the struggle Lally was happy to leave to Edith.

They spent a day with Susie before going down to Southampton. She had found the shop she wanted, just across Hans Place from Harrods. "I'll get 'em coming and going. They'll either see the prices in *our* window, and not go any further, or they'll see them when they come out, and be sorry about what they paid." It was a neat little establishment, made to look bigger by the extreme elegance and sparseness of the furnishings. "Dove gray . . . carpet, velvet curtains, chairs," Susie said with pride. "Margaret gave me the idea. Everything plain, and the clothes show off that much better. Any color looks good with this background, and there's just the faintest touch of pink in the lights to make some pasty-faced old dame think she's suddenly ten years younger in whatever we put on her. But, mind you—there's value."

She showed them the alterations room above, with its three seamstresses. "Tried to make them a bit comfortable. Decent lighting, a proper loo and washbasin. Proper lunch hour. No eating at the sewing tables. I've got a boy to run errands and make deliveries—that is, when we have deliveries to make." She took them down to the East End to see the workroom she had taken a lease on. "It's all just hope and blue sky. I've got to sell some designs in quantity before we'll need it. But Margaret's talking her head off about the place. She swears the press will come to the opening. I've got mannequins to walk around. Don't know how we'll all squeeze in. But Margaret insists there has to be champagne. She says she's going to drag in her mother-in-law, Lady Gough. Gawd, won't I be pleased when it's all over. Just imagine me, Susie Barlow, running my own business. Me mum and dad can't get over it. Of course they think I'll be a flop. And I'll lose all your money, Jon . . . Give my love to your dad, Lally. I still can't believe they asked me to be bridesmaid. Like a fairy tale. *Me*—with the likes of them!"

"In a few years they're going to be boasting they knew you before you were famous."

Margaret was at Southampton with them when the Cunard liner docked. It was Alice who first pointed out the figure beside Black Jack and Edith at the rail. "Brock! It's Brock!"

"Brock . . ." Margaret echoed.

"What the devil . . ." Jon smothered the rest of his words.

They met when the three emerged from customs. Just for a moment, Lally saw, Margaret hesitated before she offered herself to Brock's embrace. "How good to see you." Black Jack's face was tanned. Lally thought he looked handsome and rested; it had been a long war, and it had taken its toll of him. There was Edith, the blush of the sun still on her, looking happy and confident. It was all right—everything was all right. Brock swung Alice high in the air, as if she were still a slight wisp of a child. Perhaps it was not what one should do with someone who looked like a young lady, but it was what Alice wanted and expected. "Brock . . . Brock . . . I'm glad. Glad . . ." Alice's happiness was always infectious. They all squeezed into one first-class carriage on the journey back to London by dint of Alice sitting on Brock's knees. They went to Margaret's new house off Belgrave Square for dinner. They admired the decoration, the smart new colors, the "chicness" of the new lines. While Billings served drinks, Margaret went downstairs to plead with her own butler, Taylor, to allow this interloper to take over his territory for the evening. "He's a family institution," Margaret explained. "He's so excited about my father coming home."

"Then, m'lady, I'd better take the evening off. There cannot ever be two butlers in one household. But then, as you say, he's an old man, have to feel a bit sorry for him, so to speak. Doesn't know when he's past it. Sir John ought to pension him off, be kinder, really."

Margaret told this indignantly to Lally after dinner. "Can you imagine? But then Taylor served during the war. He got mentioned in dispatches. He can't help thinking someone like Billings is over the hill. It would break Billings' heart if he heard."

Black Jack and Edith and Brock went up to see the Honorable David Grenfell sleeping in his cot. Margaret's face grew tender as she leaned over him. "He's beautiful, isn't he?" she whispered. "I'm afraid he'll be horribly spoiled. Bobby and I adore him. And the Goughs just think the sun rises on him."

"He'll not be spoiled," Nanny Williams said, "if you just kindly leave him in *my* hands, m'lady." She did not approve of nursery visits at unscheduled hours.

"How can you spoil someone who's only four months old?" Edith said. Her finger touched the child's cheek lightly. "Yes, he is beautiful."

"Wait till you see Jonathan," Jon said. "I'll tell you, it'll be a great shame if these two don't hit it off when they're older."

Black Jack and Edith stayed another day in London to see David in his waking hours, giving him the toys they had brought from America, toys he was far too young to comprehend. He reached for the soft white rabbit Brock had brought, but the Teddy was too much for him. He opened his mouth and wailed. Teddy went into the nursery cupboard. "Too many people, m'lady," Nanny said severely. "He'll get much too excited, and I won't be able to get him to settle down." Black Jack insisted, though, that it should be he and Edith who wheeled David to the park that afternoon in his big high baby carriage. Nanny gave way reluctantly. "It's the third bench from the bridge on the left-hand side of the Serpentine facing Kensington Palace, Sir John."

"What is, Nanny?"

"Why, my bench. The bench I always sit on. The other nannies keep the place reserved for me. Just tell them it's for Nanny Williams."

Margaret was helpless with laughter as she saw them off. "There's a strict pecking order among the nannies, I warn you. If your employer happens to be a duke, then you rank highest, and so on down through the titles. If you're plain Mrs. Smith, your nanny might find a place on a bench over near the Bayswater Road."

That night Margaret and Bobby gave a cocktail party for Black Jack and Edith. It seemed to be entirely on the spur of the moment. "Hardly anyone bothers with engraved invitations for cocktails these days. One just rings up a few people, and they drop in. More fun . . ."

It was a faster tempo than the still rather sedate parties Leeds boasted, Lally remarked to Jon. The gramophone blared the latest jazz records Brock had brought, martinis were mixed, served with either an olive or an onion, stirred or shaken, as requested. Other cocktails could be ordered. The talk was loud. Bobby did his duty as host, gradually seeing that Edith and Black Jack were introduced to each guest. The mention of Florida and Palm Beach seemed magical. Everyone wanted to know about it. Had the winter really been that warm? Had they really bathed every day in the ocean? Brock was besieged with questions about prohibition. Did it work?

He gave his half-smile. "It can never work. It's one thing to enact a law, another to enforce it. If half the country sees no harm in breaking it, it can't work."

"I say . . ." a man standing next to Lally shouted through the din, "is that man really . . . what do they call it? A bootlegger?"

"He's *not* a bootlegger." Margaret had joined them. "He's a Wall Street broker. Has an office in Wall Street. It's the same as being in the City. Freddy, you're a charming idiot. Brock's frightfully respectable. And you're a ridiculous snob."

"Sorry, darling, don't be so touchy. I hear he lent your father and stepmother the house they've been staying in. Is he rich?"

"Does it matter? Brock has *friends*. They lend him all sorts of things. And he lends them to other people."

Lally edged away, seeking the security of Jon among the throng. Then she reminded herself that husbands and wives weren't supposed to cling to each other at cocktail parties. "Goodness," a man said close to her. "Your glass is empty. May I bring you another? Was it a martini?"

"Yes . . ." Lally said faintly. She had no idea how many it was safe to drink.

"You're Margaret's sister, aren't you? You won't believe it, but I was at your coming-out party. You looked rather different then. Seems an age ago, doesn't it?" One side of his forehead was creased with a scar on which the skin had puckered. He had a dramatic streak of white through his dark hair. She realized how close he had once been to death. "You've become quite lovely—whatever happened? Just wait a minute. I'll get the drinks and be straight back. Now don't stir, will you?"

He was back sooner than she thought possible. A bar had been set up, and two hired waiters dispensed drinks, another assisted Margaret's butler, Taylor, to carry trays. Somehow Lally always thought of him as Margaret's butler, not Bobby's.

Lally moved with the eddies of the party, but the nameless man who had attended her coming-out ball stayed by her side. "You surely must come to London to visit Margaret?" he said. "Won't you telephone me next time? I hear old Jon's awfully immersed in his mills now. We could have dinner, perhaps. A theater . . . ?" She pretended not to hear.

Then Brock was urgently at her elbow. "Lally, let's you and me take Alice back to the hotel. Someone's given her a martini, or perhaps two. I don't like the way she looks. Just you and me, quietly, Lally. We don't want to make a fuss and attract attention. But I'd like to beat the daylights out of whatever so-called gentleman gave them to her." She was startled at the anger that transformed Brock's usually smooth and controlled expression. Lally realized that she had made the mistake of seeing his affection expressed in the gifts he gave; that he should care so deeply about the well-being of this beautiful, flawed girl should not have surprised her so much, but it did. Seeing the disturbance in his face, she felt vaguely ashamed that she might ever have supposed his affection for Alice was less than real.

"Yes, of course—at once." She found Alice in a group of six, all of whom seemed to be talking across her head; she looked bewildered, and yes, her eyes had a strangely glazed look. She laughed without reason at what was being said, and her body moved in rhythm to the music. Gently, Lally took the glass from her hand. "Darling, Brock wants to take us back."

"Brock?—oh yes. Where's Brock?" They should never have left her alone, Lally thought. Even in the same room, it was not safe to leave her alone. She was now out of her protected environment where people understood such things. Somehow, all of them, except Brock, had overlooked that.

His arm was around Alice's waist as they went downstairs. No one would know if she were not quite surefooted. Brock would see to that.

"Sweetheart, we're all going to go back to the hotel. We'll have a slap-up meal with Teddy Rose and Madame Butterfly and Raggedy Ann."

"But why?" Alice asked. Her tone was almost a wail. "The party's not over. Margaret promised I could come to all her parties."

"Why?—well, sweetheart, it's because your old Uncle Brock's feeling damned tired, and just wants to sit down with you. Don't like these parties where everyone stands up. It's much more fun sitting down at a meal with you."

"Oh, well . . ." Alice looked at him with pure adoration. "Of course if you're tired . . . Brock's tired, Lally." Lally slipped a cloak around her. The chill air of the March night hit them, and Alice staggered a little on the doorstep. Brock whistled a cab from Belgrave Square. "Steady on, sweetheart. Soon be there." He never relaxed his grip on her waist until they were through the hotel foyer and in the suite. He placed her in a chair and brought her dolls to her. Then he rang for a waiter. "Hot soup as soon as possible," he said. "Then we'll have steak, medium rare. Potatoes and whatever else . . . Just bring it quickly."

"Certainly, sir. Any cocktails or wine, sir?"

"No," Brock said.

They were almost finished eating when Margaret telephoned. "Why did you disappear? We were all supposed to have dinner together when the mob had gone."

"Mob's right, Margaret," Brock answered. "I'll tell you tomorrow, and you'd better listen." He hung up; the anger had returned to his face.

*   *   *   *

Brock traveled up to Yorkshire with them. Lally noticed that now no one seemed to question his presence. He was not invited as if he were outside the family; he simply said whether he would come or not. "I said I meant to be a godfather, didn't I? I take the job seriously. I have to measure whether Jonathan's bigger than David. Besides I just want to hang around a bit. I want to be here when it becomes official that Black Jack has become Sir John. The news went down well in Palm Beach, I'll tell you. Though people were a bit disappointed he hadn't been made a duke." All the way up to Yorkshire he seemed to keep up a rattling pace of talk, and, as usual, said little of any consequence. Nothing about himself. He had spent only two days in Palm Beach, making sure that Black Jack and Edith were comfortable, and had then returned to New York. Black Jack had confirmed that there was an investment firm of Brockton Weymouth and Partners. No one seemed to know who the partners were. Brock lived in an anonymous suite at the Plaza Hotel; the only personal effects there were a few pictures of his own. He had, he said, a small place he rented on Long Island during the summer. He entertained regularly, he was invited to dinner parties; the talk was mostly of business when the ladies were not present. He seemed to have no particular friends.

"I really don't know why he's chosen *us,*" Black Jack said to Lally and Jon. "But he seems to want a family, and we come ready-made. And damned if I don't like the man, though I can't say exactly why. He's almost like a younger brother . . ." Then he smiled at Jon. "Or a much older son. He's very shrewd. Clever. It's hard to believe he started with nothing. Some people say he's all front. Spending every penny he earns. If that's so, he's good at disguising it. He seems . . . assured. He can talk tea from China and tin from Bolivia. Quote you the very latest price on them all, as if he just bought and sold that afternoon. Some of the people he knows are . . . well, are quite impressive. Big names. Big in business, that is. Society, as such, doesn't seem to interest Brock, or else he knows he won't be admitted to it, and he doesn't try. He has no intention of being snubbed."

"Do you think there's any truth in that story people repeat about him being a bootlegger?"

Black Jack shrugged. "Honestly, I don't know. I can't see Brock personally arranging the details of shipments of booze over the border or from Rum Row. But before he went back to New York, he took that new regular aeroplane service to Cuba. Says he's still in sugar."

"And sugar is rum," Jon said.

"Do you think," Edith observed, "that it's quite fair to be discussing Brock this way? After all, we did ask him to be our best man. He is godfather to the two babies. If he was acceptable then—"

"It's our fault," Jon said. "We're such stick-in-the-muds. We've all grown up knowing exactly who everyone around us was. Brock stays a mystery . . . and so we talk about him."

It was amazing, Lally thought, how often they forgot that no one knew who she was, either.

Brock, who with Alice, was permitted an unscheduled visit to the nursery to see his godson, returned to join them. "You could almost say he is more beautiful than David. He gave me the biggest god-damned smile you ever saw!"

"It was probably wind," Lally said.

"No, it wasn't! He knows what's what, this kid. He grabbed for my watch chain quick as a monkey." He nodded in acceptance of the whiskey Black Jack offered, and settled himself before the fire. "I'll tell you, Jon, I wish you'd let me have him for a bit while he's still a kid. Before your public schools beat all the initiative out of him. He could be a real wheeler-dealer, this one. If he were mine, I'd bet he'd be reading the ticker tape before they started to bash all that Greek into his head."

"An interesting education," Black Jack said. "We ought to think about it. Two godsons to be sent to the Wall Street runners every summer. That's how they do it in America. After all, we can hardly put them into the mills."

"But if we do that," Jon demurred, but he was also laughing, "when will they learn to play cricket?"

II

The year moved on its predictable course. Superficially, some things seemed to revert to the familiar. The lawn at Pellham Langley was resown, and was no longer a vegetable patch. The topiary animals were clipped, and there, to Alice's delight, were the distinguishable forms of Rabbit and Dog and Cat. Horses were in the stables, but they were for riding only. Black Jack permanently laid up the last of his carriages. Horses were still more reliable than motors, but motors were faster. There was much talk that wireless would become a thing for everyone, not just the amateur with the crystal set and earphones.

The mills and the mines were now running at less than full capacity. Black Jack and Jon went carefully through the order books, and sent the salesmen far and wide. "We still have the Empire to sell to," Black Jack said, "but it's not the certain thing it used to be." He began to pull back a little on the steel mill in Wales; the stockpiles of coal were already too high at the Yorkshire mines. It was inevitable that men would be laid off. A delegation of miners came to the mills in Bradford to see Black Jack, and went away dissatisfied. "I can't give jobs I haven't got," Black Jack had to tell them. "This country has war debts to pay."

"Aye, Mr. Pollock, but *you* don't have war debts," one of the union organizers said. "You cleaned up nicely out of the war, and don't say you didn't. And don't tell us about the shareholders having to be paid—because in this case, *you're* the only shareholder."

"I pay my taxes," Black Jack said shortly. He went home to Pellham Langley miserable and depressed. That night a stone shattered one of the front windows at Grangewick. One of the housemaids had hysterics when she found a dead cat on the doorstep next morning, and promptly packed her bags and left.

"Don't let Nanny take Jonathan out for a walk for a while yet," Jon told Lally. "It'll quieten down in time. But I wish I could see the solution. We expanded to meet the war demands. There just isn't the business now. Perhaps Brock is right. We've become too tired as a nation—and there just isn't the capital to build the sort of new plant we need. If I could persuade Father to go ahead with the plans for the new steel mills he'd *have* to go public. No private individual can finance things on that scale anymore. Myself, I think he's perhaps too much in love with the thought that no outsider owns a piece of Pollock's. Several of the textile mills could stand rebuilding, but it needs more capital than I think Father has. The new looms are quicker and more efficient—"

"And need fewer operatives," Lally said. "It doesn't solve the problem of jobs."

"Sometimes I think we'll *never* solve the problem of jobs. If Father would let me—oh, what's the use? I can't tell him I think some of his ideas are old-fashioned. It would be like telling him he's too old for the job itself. But he takes far too much on himself. Things ran all right for those months when he was away in Florida. I think he rather looked forward to finding things in a bit of a shambles when he got back. But that wasn't the case. I wish he'd delegate a bit more, or clear out some of the old fogies who've been doing the same job the same way for fifty years, and still talk about things being 'new-fangled' if they're less than a hundred years old."

"Can't you be patient for a while, Jon?" Lally said. "Try to remember that he and those old fogies ran the whole thing during the war, and worked at anything and everything for as many hours as they could stay awake. It's too soon to tell them they're past it. After all, remember Billings . . ."

Black Jack had told them of having called Billings to the library that year when talk began of organizing a modest shooting party for August. "Billings, don't you think we should be talking about your pension? I know there's been no formal arrangement, but of course I'll provide whatever we agree—"

"*Sir John!*" Billings straightened his shoulders. "Are you and Lady Pollock not receiving satisfactory service?"

"Why—of course. I just thought . . . I mean, a man of your age—"

"Sir John, age has *nothing* to do with running a household. If I could just get the decent, willing young men and girls we used to have before the war, there would be nothing I could not undertake. Lady Pollock oversees the menus, and Cook is able to provide whatever is required. She only needs a few girls to do the usual tasks. I trust I have restocked the wine cellar to your liking, sir? We have inferior help to what we used to have in the old days, but we make do, Sir John. I trust I have not allowed any falling off in standards?"

Black Jack found himself offering an almost incoherent apology. "I'm terribly sorry, Billings . . . I mean, the long hours . . . I was simply thinking of you. . . . We would hate to lose you, naturally. The place wouldn't be the same without you."

"I will take my pension, Sir John, when I think I can no longer be of use to you. Until then, pray allow this *old* man to serve the family in the usual way."

"Certainly, Billings. I leave everything in your hands, as always. I'll tell Lady Pollock you'll not be deserting us. I know she'll be enormously pleased."

Billings nodded. "Very good, sir." He was back in control again.

Margaret and Bobby, with young David, arrived a few days before the shooting would open on August 12. Too vividly Black Jack remembered the last time people had gathered for this occasion at Pellham Langley—the end of Margaret's and Lally's coming-out season, when Edith had been the Marchioness of Ross, when most people had refused to believe there could be a war, or that if there were, it would be a three-month affair to put the Germans in their place. It had been the time of his own great financial peril, when he had borrowed on everything he owned to stock his mills, and to pile coal at the pit heads. Sadly he remembered the beauty of the young people about him then, full of youth and enthusiasm to fight a war they did not comprehend. He found the guest book signed on that occasion, and not since used. There was the rollcall of those who had died. He could not quite see the faces to attach to many of the names. He just remembered the heat of that August, the languor of the white-clad figures on the grass, the sound of the tennis ball hitting the court, and there was Billings hurrying toward him with news of war. He closed the book as the noise and fuss of Margaret's arrival—she driving the car as she loved to do—claimed him. Margaret came first, calling to everyone; Bobby trailed her, as he usually did. Nanny came, swathed in a cloth driving coat and carrying David.

"Darlings . . ." Margaret called. Edith appeared on the steps and came hurying down. Billings was directing the footman to bring in the bags. Nanny Williams was going upstairs where she would share the nursery with Jonathan and Nanny Dunstable. It was strange for Black Jack to have the nurseries of Pellham Langley filled once more.

"We made it over from Neatherby in record time," Margaret exclaimed, kissing Black Jack and then her stepmother.

"Far too fast," Bobby said. "Sometimes Margaret scares me more in that car than I ever was in the trenches. How are you, Lady Pollock? . . . sir? How will the shooting be, do you think? My father's anxious to come over and join you. The shooting's very poor on our moors."

They all drifted into the drawing room for tea. Margaret talked about the season in London, which had just ended. "Things are starting up again. Lots of parties. They had the deb balls again. Poor things. Did we ever look quite as awful as that, Lally, do you think?"

"You always looked wonderful. *I* looked worse than awful."

"You both did your father credit," Edith said. "I was there, remember?"

"What I can't get used to," Margaret said, "is being referred to in the newspapers as a *matron*—even when they say a young matron. I forget there's David. There seem to be an awful lot of women around my age—and no men to match them. That's when it hits you.

How many are gone. People have trouble making up guest lists now." She paused and bent over a book Lally had left open on the sofa. "Oh, you got it, did you? I thought you'd be one of the first to read it." She picked up D. H. Lawrence's *Women in Love*. "Brock sent over something that's just the rage in America. It's this new writer, Scott Fitzgerald. Something called *This Side of Paradise*. I thought you'd like to read it. Oh, and I saw Susie just before we left town. She's doing quite well. No profits yet, but she's just about breaking even, which is more than we could have expected for such a short time. But then, her clothes are so *clever*—she seems just to have hit the right styles for now. Of course, the older women are still clinging to their corsets, and they don't much care for what Susie's doing, but the young ones love it."

"Some of us," Edith said, "feel we *have* to cling to our corsets, Margaret. We're not all twenty-two."

"But you have a divine figure, Edith. Susie's things would be wonderful for you. I wish you'd try one or two. It would give her such a lift, and be such good publicity. I did bully Evelyn Porter from *Vogue* to go around and have a look. She wrote it up, and it was quite useful. Susie's just starting to get some orders from provincial shops. Not big volume yet, but she's started a cutter and a few girls on the machines in the East End. It's a beginning. I wanted her to come up here, but she wouldn't. Said it wouldn't do if she was seen mixing with the people she was trying to sell clothes to. I told her that was all wrong. She *has* to mix with them to get known, and anyway, all *those* notions have gone. As long as you're original and amusing, you don't have to worry about your background."

"Let Susie take it in her own time, Margaret," Black Jack said. Lally peeled one piece of bread off the tiny watercress sandwich, and nibbled at it. She was remembering Susie's quick hands taking tucks in her uniforms as the pounds and inches had fallen away; she was remembering the sketches on the backs of envelopes of how Susie fancied the uniforms should have been designed in the first place. Lally had spent a week with Margaret in London in June. She had attended the parties and the theaters, the nightclubs that now were part of London life. She had bought three of Susie's dresses, which were straight off the rack, needing only the smallest alterations. Her skirts were now inches shorter than they had been at the beginning of the year. The short hair which she had adopted in desperation during the war was now commonplace. She smoked her cigarettes in a long holder, as almost everyone else did. She drank the new cocktails cautiously. New recipes for various ones were always coming across the Atlantic. Jazz was the thing to dance to. "You've always been light on your feet, even when you were fat," Margaret said bluntly. "Now we can see them, you've got divine legs." Was it really she Margaret was talking about? Lally wondered. She saw the fashionably thin figure in the mirror, with the loose uncorseted look which was now the style, and she still hardly recognized herself. On Black Jack's desk in the library were the pictures of her and Margaret in the court dresses, the three white feathers held in place with elaborate hairdos. Was that Lillian Pollock, presented by the Marchioness of Ross? Margaret looked no different, except perhaps more beautiful now, as if motherhood had given her an extra dimension . . . yes, more beautiful, and Bobby more hopelessly in love. Yes, and that was Jon Pollock, sitting across from her, her husband, father of her child. A wild dream . . . they had come through. They were starting a new life in a new age.

Edith was saying, "Was the report I read in *Tatler* true—about you both being at a weekend party where the Prince of Wales was also a guest? Did you like him?"

"Oh, he's a *dear* little man, Edith."

"Margaret, you impudent little minx! He's our future sovereign."

"Damned if I didn't think he was going to exercise the ancient royal prerogative," Bobby grumbled. "They say he's very partial to married ladies. He was very attentive to Margaret. I wondered if I'd ever get her away from him. Margaret's getting very used to being the belle of every party. I can almost guess at what stage of the party someone's going to say, 'Grenfell, you're a lucky man.' It's usually late, and they're a bit in their cups, and they've just danced with Margaret. I don't dare leave her alone in London all season. My father's getting a bit touchy about my being away so much. But what can I do?" He appealed to them all. "I can't just leave her alone, can I?—and she's entitled to some fun." He smiled his good-natured smile, but his tone was rueful. "Sometimes, I do confess, I'm half asleep myself, while she's dancing her legs off. Never seems to run out of energy."

Jon said, "Being neither your doting husband, nor your loving father, but only your old-fashioned brother, I'd say you could stand a little rest. Do I detect just the faintest shadows under your eyes? Seems you could use a bit of sleep and some country air."

Margaret stood up. "Dear Jon, what a bore you're getting to be. It's all this earnest hard work." She glanced at the clock, and then at her stepmother. "Edith, is it all right if I ring for Billings and ask for a cocktail? It's more than time."

Edith nodded. She recognized the restraint it required for Margaret to ask permission from anyone for anything in what had been her first home. "How can I deny anything to the lady the Prince of Wales admires? Of course, ring, Margaret."

"All the same," Black Jack said, before Billings could answer the bell, "I think Jon's more than half right. A little bit of sleep, dear child. Can't have it both ways, you know. Stay beautiful, and stay up all night."

Margaret turned back to them. "You know, Brock sent me another book. A book of poems. Oh, yes—laugh. All of you. You never think of silly, frivolous Margaret reading poems. Well, as usual, Brock knows just what might interest me. It's a collection by a woman. Edna St. Vincent Millay. I remember something particularly, and I like it. It says it so much better than I ever could. . . . I memorized it.

> *My candle burns at both ends;*
> *It will not last the night;*
> *But, ah, my foes, and oh, my friends—*
> *It gives a lovely light!*

A strange hush fell on the drawing room. It was broken only when Billings appeared. "Yes, m'lady . . . ?"

* * *

The guns sounded over the moors on August 12; the grouse fell. There were fewer than Black Jack could ever remember. Wartime poaching and the lack of gamekeepers had taken their toll. Beside him, Lord Gough grumbled. "Don't know how we're ever going to get things put to rights again. Young gamekeepers don't know their jobs . . . most of the ones who could've trained them are gone. Come to that, don't know how we're going to put the whole sorry country to rights again. People gettin' ideas about themselves. Factory jobs they want now. More time off. Young girls come to apply for domestic service, and the first thing they ask is how near is the bus into town. These moving pictures, boy friends. And the wages they expect. Damned if I know what'll come of it all."

Cocktails were served before dinner as well as sherry. Billings had been determined to learn how to make them. "Can't have anyone thinking we're old-fashioned here, Sir John. But I really can't approve, especially for the ladies."

After dinner they danced to jazz records. No one's skill at the piano was needed anymore. There were many fewer gathered around the dining table than at the last house party at Pellham Langley; there were plenty of women to invite, as Margaret had pointed out, but not the men to balance them. Sometimes, in the evenings, Black Jack filled in the gaps by inviting some of the younger, unmarried managers from the mills. They came, uncomfortable and stiff in evening clothes; some had broad Yorkshire accents. Those who didn't know the new jazz steps quickly learned them, and Black Jack noticed none were without partners. The young women were lonely.

"There you are," Lord Gough said, almost prodding Black Jack with his cigar as he observed the newcomers. "What did I tell you? Thin end of the wedge."

"I work in the mills, too," Black Jack said.

"You—you're different, Pollock. Money makes a difference. Always has."

III

The holiday time of August passed to the days of September, which held a touch of autumn. The heather on the moors, which in August was deep purple, began to darken toward the brown it would later assume. Jonathan and David, in the nurseries, were crawling, and making the first efforts to pull themselves upright, and still falling. Teeth began to come through, and Lally had a row with Nanny Dunstable about feeding Jonathan sugar to soothe him. "His teeth will rot away, Nanny, if he becomes too fond of sugar. He'll want nothing but sweets."

"In *my* nursery, Mrs. Pollock, children are only allowed sweets when I say they may have them. My children attend the dentist regularly, and no shirking."

Lally went away, defeated, helpless. She talked on the telephone to Margaret, who only laughed at the story. "Let her have her way, Lally. Nannies always get it, in the end. You're lucky to have one of the old-fashioned kind. I wouldn't dare cross Nanny Williams. She might leave, and God help me, I still can't change David's nappies. Nanny doesn't even think I should try. 'Might stick a pin in Baby' is what she says. And let's face it, Lally—I don't *want* to change nappies. Having babies is enough. I don't want to have to look after them." Margaret and Bobby had stayed on at Neatherby longer than Margaret had wanted. "But still, nothing much has started up in London, and I know dear Father Gough was just indulging me since David was born—giving us the house, and not making any fuss about my staying in London until the end of the season. So to keep him and Bobby happy I've said I'll stay at least until after the St. Leger." The St. Leger, one of the classic races of the year, held at Doncaster, was for Margaret a marvelous excuse for organizing a house party. "Promise me you and Jon will come, Lally. I've persuaded Lady Gough to put up some people at Dentdale, because of course we haven't room for many in this pokey little place. Father and Edith are going to stay with them." Margaret was openly uncaring of the charm of Neatherby, the dower house of Dentdale. It was locally famous as a small gem of Elizabethan domestic architecture, but Margaret found it dark and rambling and inconvenient; she complained that Lord Gough was unwilling to spend the money to have it completely modernized. "But he's coming round to the idea," she confided in Lally. "He thinks it might make me want to stay here more often. I keep telling him if we have any more children, we *must* have better facilities. And you know how he feels about having more grandchildren. But for the moment you and Jon will have to do with a room about the size of a broom cupboard. I'm afraid nothing nearly so grand as those broom cupboards Brock says they have at the Ritz."

Lally and Jon drove over to Neatherby two days before the St. Leger. They found they were the only guests staying there, all the rest being accommodated at Dentdale. "I've dumped the lot on Father Gough just to make him *realize* how inconvenient this place is. In any case, they've got masses of staff, and I've had to bring mine up from London. He's so awfully stingy with his money. It won't hurt him to spend a bit on my guests. They've decided to make a concession and have some of their own friends as well. There's a big dinner at Dentdale tonight, so get out the best of your Susie dresses, Lally."

Dentdale was two miles from Neatherby, in the same beautiful parkland grazed by the famous Gough herd of Angus cattle; they drove along a road lined with oaks to a house whose beauty made

Lally gasp—mellow, rosy brick with long mullioned windows. The great staircase hall was filled with guests, and footmen moved among them with trays. The Bletchleys had come over from Witfell for dinner; Lord Bletchley was almost totally blind now, and failing. Lady Bletchley resolutely ignored his frailty, as if ignoring it would cause it to go away. She wore lilac satin, and more diamonds than would have been thought possible for one woman to carry. The income tax which so burdened Lord Bletchley had not touched these assets. She surveyed the assembled guests—those who had come to dinner and the house guests who would stay with the Goughs for the St. Leger. "No doubt about it," she pronounced. "The *tone* is going down. There's at least one man here who owns some *shops*."

Jon took a glass of sherry from a tray for her. "Darling Grandmother, so do I—at least a small part of a shop. You must meet Susie Barlow, Grandmother. She's a wonderful girl."

"I do not care to meet Susie Barlow. I hope it will never be necessary."

During dinner Bobby was called to the telephone. He came back, smiling. "Sorry, Mother—they'd told him at Neatherby that we were all here. It was Brock Weymouth. He's just arrived in London. You remember Brock Weymouth, Mother . . ."

Lady Gough nodded stiffly, not looking pleased. Margaret was smiling. "Brock!—how lovely! Is he coming up?"

"Thought it'd please you, darling. Yes, I've persuaded him he just has to experience the St. Leger. So he's driving up tomorrow. I've told him we'd try to squeeze him into a broom cupboard at Neatherby."

"*That* man again!" Lady Bletchley trumpeted. "Very pushy."

Lord Gough leaned toward her. "They tell me he's rich. Makes a difference, you know."

* * *

Brock arrived the next afternoon driving a new Cadillac. "My friend has gotten rather tired of the Hispano. Asked me to bring him an American car to try out."

"Oh—it's *beautiful,* Brock." Margaret instantly demanded to sit in the driver's seat, trying out the latest refinements, the new gadgets. They all clustered around it, but it was Margaret who begged to be allowed to drive it. She drove it over to Dentdale, and insisted on her father-in-law coming out to inspect it. "It's glorious, Brock. Promise me you'll let me drive it to Doncaster tomorrow. It'll cause a sensation . . . oh, what a lovely car! It has everything. Bobby, *when* are we going to make a trip to America? I can't wait."

IV

Lord Gough's house party had made plans to split up after the St. Leger. The older members had all accepted invitations to dine informally at the house of one of Gough's friends near Doncaster. The younger ones were left either to return to Dentdale, where a buffet supper would be waiting, or to make their own arrangements.

"The man on the desk at the Ritz knew I was coming up to the St. Leger, and recommended a place called Seaton's," Brock said. "Seems it's nicely convenient on the journey back here. He made reservations for us—unless, of course, you'd rather go back to Dentdale . . ."

"I've always wanted to go to Seaton's," Margaret said. "They say it's the best place to dine in the whole of the North. I've never been able to get Bobby to take me there."

"Probably because it costs a fortune, and Bobby's got better use for his money," Jon said.

"Spoilsport. If Brock wants to treat us . . ."

"Brock does far too much treating." Bobby's slight resistance collapsed before the look he got from Margaret. "Oh, all right, darling. I suppose Dentdale's not much fun . . . and there seems to be hardly anyone going back there for supper. Thanks, Brock . . . appreciate it, old man. Anything to make her ladyship here happy."

The day of the St. Leger was calm and golden; they had moved among the sideshows and fairgrounds that always accompanied the famous race. Black Jack greeted old friends among the race crowd. Someone, whose lore of the race was profound, recalled that Black Jack's grandfather, "Gentleman Jack," had dropped dead on the racecourse after his hundred-to-one shot had come in first. "Don't see Black Jack betting much, though . . ."

"Just watch his daughter."

Lord Gough had a horse running in one of the lesser races. "Hasn't got a chance," Gough rumbled. "But we've always had a horse or two in training. Can't manage it much longer. Too damned expensive. Take my advice, Pollock. Don't put any money on it. I'm only running her because the trainer says she needs some experience." Black Jack looked at the odds, and decided that Gough was right. Then to the crowd's amazement, and the bookie's delight, the little filly, Flying Fish, outnosed the favorite at the post. Margaret tossed her handbag in the air, whooping.

"I won! I won!"

"You mean you *backed* it!"

"Certainly, I got a tip on it."

"A tip? Who from?" Gough glared around the crowd. Who had dared his horse to win a race she wasn't supposed to win?

"A friend." Margaret laughed. "Just a friend." She departed to collect her winnings from the bookmaker. She drank champagne happily with Brock and Lally while they waited for the great race itself. "You know I suspect I love to gamble. It's more exciting than anything I've ever done. We went over to Deauville this year. I went to the casino every night, and stayed till the sun was up."

"Did you win?"

She pulled a face. "Not really. At first, I won a lot, then I lost more than that. And then I kept trying to win it back. And I just lost more and more. I *know* I could have got it all back if Bobby just would have stayed a few more days. But he was worried about what I was losing. Sometimes . . . well, he's so *stuffy*. He almost seems old. Do you like to gamble, Brock?"

"That's all I ever do."

Her mouth fell open a little. "What?"

"The stock market, dear Margaret. That's the biggest gamble of all."

She shrugged. "It sounds dull."

"Not when you're watching the ticker tape and you've got a bundle on some stock. It's not dull then, I assure you."

Black Jack joined them. "Any tips?" he said.

"The stock market, or the race?"

"Either will do."

"Well, I don't know a damn about the horses, but I'll tell you one thing. Get out of sugar, if you're in it."

"*Sugar!*" Margaret exclaimed. "Why would Father be in sugar?"

"Only to make money," Brock replied. "I hear it's going to tumble."

"Excuse me," Margaret said. "I haven't placed my bet yet. There's only a few minutes."

"Let me do it for you," Brock offered. It wasn't usual for ladies to push through the crowds around the bookies.

"No, I always do it myself. For luck . . . I feel lucky today."

They watched the great race, and the second favorite beat the favorite by a length. There was both gloom and elation among the crowd. Some of Lord Gough's party had backed the winner. Champagne was ordered again. Beside Lally, Margaret tossed off a glass, and offered it to Brock to be refilled. "Damn," she said to Lally, "I lost!"

"So did I," Lally replied. But there was something shocked and desperate in Margaret's expression which told Lally that she had lost far more than the token amount Lally had bet. She watched as Margaret gulped at the champagne as if she needed it. "Damn this stuff. Tastes like sugar water." She tipped out the remains on the grass, and took a pocket hunting flask from her handbag and poured a large shot of whiskey into the empty glass. Slightly alarmed, Bobby watched. "I say . . . steady on, darling . . ." It was one thing for a lady to carry a hip flask to the hunting field to offset the chill of a long winter's afternoon, quite another to be seen pouring for herself in the middle of a fashionable crowd in the paddock at the St. Leger.

"Oh, shut up," Margaret replied. Her tone was ugly, and for an instant her face was also.

They stayed for the last race, which Margaret watched without interest. Then they went back to the cars, and joined the long line waiting to move out onto the road. Brock and Margaret and Bobby were several cars ahead of them. Margaret was once again driving the Cadillac; they could hear its horn sounding imperiously as pedestrians and some horse-drawn vehicles held up her progress. They had arranged to meet at Seaton's, where a private room had been reserved. "Something wrong with Margaret?" Jon inquired of Lally as they inched their way forward.

"Oh, she lost in the big race. And it's too bad, because I think she blames Brock."

"Why?—he wasn't tipping anything."

"No, he was talking about sugar. And she backed Sugar Baby."

The golden afternoon had turned chill. By the time they had cleared the local race traffic, Lally could see the clouds mounting in the west, and being pushed by a wind that was becoming strong. They drove steadily north, without catching sight of the Cadillac ahead. "Margaret must have been stepping on it a bit," Jon said. As they parked alongside Brock's car at Seaton's, the first rain drops were falling. "Well, it's the end of the St. Leger," Jon said. "All back to work tomorrow."

Seaton's dated from Jacobean times, and it had many rambling passages and small rooms for private parties. It was warm and chintz-clad, and a fire burned in the hugh fireplace in the bar when Lally and Jon passed by. They were led to an upstairs room where the others waited. Lally was glad to see that a fire burned there also. The autumn had truly come.

Margaret had been instructing the barman how to make a martini. She had sent the first one back, after taking a long sip. "It's foul. Far too much vermouth. You just *touch* the edge of the bottle to it. They don't have nearly enough ice," was her greeting to Lally and Jon as they entered.

"And Margaret's in a foul mood," Brock said cheerfully. "So watch out."

Margaret merely glared at him, and soon rang the bell for the barman again. "Make it a large one, this time. I could hardly *see* the last one. And don't swamp it with vermouth." While they studied the menu and ordered, she had another one. "What the hell," she said, carelessly. "Everyone's leaving in the morning, and I can sleep in."

"Mother's expecting us over to lunch tomorrow," Bobby said. "You promised you'd bring David."

Margaret lighted a cigarette. "Oh, damn. Well, you can take him, Bobby. She doesn't need to see me." She poked at the food that was served, but ate little. "I don't see why this place's got such a great reputation."

"That's not a very polite thing to say when Brock's the host," Jon said. "And if you'd *eat* some of the food then you might appreciate it a little. You've left half your meat."

"Don't know why I chose roast beef and Yorkshire pudding, I get it every Sunday." Then she smiled at Brock. "Yes, I am a real boor, aren't I? Just not very hungry. The wine's marvelous, though."

"Château Lafite usually is," Jon growled at her.

"Is that what it is?" She held her glass forward. "Always know a good thing. Let's have another bottle. I'll pay. I've got the last of my winnings. It can't cost more than that."

Brock rang and ordered the wine, although they had had almost two bottles. Margaret joked to the waiter about having a separate bill for it. "We won't take the last of your pin money, Margaret," Brock said.

"Pin money? That wasn't pin money. That was my housekeeping money. That was meant to pay the butcher and the wine merchant, and the bill from Fortnum's for all the little extras. Don't know how those extras add up so much. And Harrods have been sending less than friendly letters about my bills there." She held her glass forward for more wine. "I don't know. Susie's inexpensive little dresses really don't offset the bills for the shoes and the handbags and the hats. And the florist. And Taylor and Cook have been very patient about their wages. They expected I'd get everything straightened out when I came up here to Yorkshire. If your father didn't give it to me, Bobby, then my father surely would. I had planned to ask Father for an advance on next year's allowance. But it would have been much better if I'd been able to get it by myself. And I *would* have. I won a packet of money on your father's horse, Bobby. And then . . ." She turned to Brock. "Yes, you really owe me Château Lafite. I put almost every penny of the winnings on Sugar Baby. Blast sugar! Why did you have to talk about it? I always play my hunches. I could have cleared up every single debt I had if she had come home, and had a bit left over. Seems so easy, doesn't it? Hey, presto! No more troubles."

Bobby had sat very still as she had talked; Lally was troubled to see how white his face was. Could it be that at last Bobby was angry with his wife? His lips were pressed tightly together until he spoke.

"You mean to say . . . you really mean to say, Margaret, that you haven't paid the wages? Not even the *wages?*"

She shrugged. "Couldn't be helped. I gave them a bit on account. Oh, come, Bobby. Don't be such a wet blanket. You *know* I'll get the money. And I'll be careful in the future. I promise I'll be careful. I'll watch every penny."

"I trusted you," he said slowly. "You asked to be allowed to manage the household money, and I trusted you. But not even to pay the wages, Margaret. That's like stealing from those people. They can't afford it!"

"Then neither can we, I suppose," she answered lightly, but a flush had come to her face. "I didn't steal it. You're so old-fashioned, Bobby."

"Yes," he said. "And I'm going to be even more old-fashioned. From now on I'm going to tell you what we can afford and what we can't afford. We're going to sell that damned place in London. We're going to pay every penny you owe and we're going to close every single one of those blasted charge accounts. Cash only! We're going to live at Neatherby on the allowance *my* father gives us—which is what he always wanted us to do. I'm going to ask your father to invest money for you, not use it to clear up your debts. You're going to learn to be responsible, Margaret. If that's old-fashioned, that's too bad!"

"*I* have some money. My allowance—"

"I think your allowance should be a lot less than it is, and the rest invested for you until you get some sense. Don't you think your father has noticed, Margaret? But I don't believe he thinks it's as bad as it is. I have more than a suspicion that he'll back me in everything I'm going to do. He may spoil you, but I don't think he'd want to stand by and watch all of us being ruined. It's high time I took up the job I was meant to do, which is to help run the estate. For God's sake, Margaret, don't you understand—"

She stood up quickly, and the chair toppled behind her with a crash. "All I understand is that you're a stupid, weak, helpless idiot! All you want is to be back in your mother's lap. Hold daddy's hand. Be the good white-haired boy. Well, you can't make up for either of your brothers. They were twice the man you are! But you got your precious son and heir. Lord Gough has his grandson. I don't suppose you'll be mean enough to stand in the way of a divorce." She stood there, trembling; her fingers clutched the edge of the table and began to pull at the cloth.

Bobby rose. "Who said anything about a divorce? You're upset, Margaret. You're drunk. There'll be no divorce. In the morning—"

"In the morning I'm packing and going back to London. Do what you like about me. Evict me onto the street if it pleases you. You'll only make a further spectacle of yourself. Everyone knows what a fool you are. And what a fool I am. After all, I *married* you." She looked around the table. "That's what you all said, didn't you? You were all dead set against it, all of you, but Father most of all. You've got the satis . . ." Her voice wavered. "The satisfaction of being right. I won't oppose you on custody of David, Bobby. I suppose you're entitled to your son. Tell Lord Gough I'll settle for a decent alimony in return for my son. I know you'll take him from me in the end. Might as well be now."

"*Margaret!*" Jon's voice was choked with anger. "Bobby's right.

You're drunk and out of your mind. You're talking about your child!"

The tears were now streaming down her face. "I know who I'm talking about. I love my baby, but don't you take that holier-than-thou attitude, Jon. After all, you made a mistake, too. You married Sandy West. Oh, I know I'm not supposed to mention that name, but after Sandy you married for safety. And you're unbearably smug, you and Lally. You're getting just like Bobby. You'll stay at home in Yorkshire and run the mills, and he'll run his blasted estate. And you'll both grow to look just like a pair of your own sheep." She went to the rack beside the door and took down her coat and angrily thrust her arms into the sleeves. She swung her handbag at them all in a final gesture of defiance and rage. "Yes, just like sheep. Baa . . . baa. . . ." Her voice choked off as the tears welled again.

Bobby was beside her. "Margaret, take hold of yourself. Where are you going?"

"To Neatherby. To bloody Neatherby for the last time." She wrenched open the door and fled along the passage to the stairs. Bobby followed, not bothering about his coat. Jon sprang up.

"I'll have to go with them. Try to calm her down! God, what a mess." He fished in his pocket and brought out the car keys. "You follow with Lally, Brock. We'll be at Neatherby." He paused at the door. "Sorry, Brock. You've seen just about the worst of us now. She doesn't mean it, I know. . . . It's just . . ." He shook his head. "Oh, what the hell. They're *both* fools, she for acting as she does, and Bobby for not doing something about it before this." He turned and hurried after the others.

Brock rang urgently for the waiter. "The bill, at once, please. Quickly." It took several minutes.

"I'm afraid, sir, there are some items missing. I haven't had time . . . but I did observe the young lady leaving and I . . ."

"Yes," Brock said. "I'll bet you did." He was pulling notes from his wallet. "Will that cover it? The extra? Such as trying to keep your mouth closed about the young lady?"

The waiter's mouth opened slightly as he saw the pile of money on the table. "More than adequate, sir. Thank you very much, sir."

Brock put his arm under Lally's elbow as they went down the stairs. "Take it easy, Lally. We don't want anyone seeing two *more* people dashing out into the night. We've already had enough drama around here. Just take it easy."

But she pulled at him urgently. "It isn't that easy, Brock. Margaret still had the car keys. I was watching from the window and I saw Bobby and Jon just managing to pile in before she drove off."

The inn door closed behind them. There was only the single light over the door, and it illuminated little of the parking space, which was now almost deserted. The rain slanted down, splashing huge drops into the pools of water on the ground. It seemed to take an endless time before the motor caught. No one opened the door of the inn. The road, as they turned out, was slickly wet and deserted. It was the finish of the St. Leger race meeting, and everyone had gone home.

* * *

They were already within the park of Dentdale, just before the fork which led to Neatherby, when the headlamps picked it out. The great oaks, with which generations ago the Grenfells had lined their twisting drive, were massive and stately, and seemed to dwarf the twisted heap of wreckage at the base of one of them.

"God!" Lally felt the car skid slightly as Brock applied the brakes, but he rode out the skid and came to a halt beyond the other car. He flung himself out, and raced back. Lally gasped as the rain beat fully in her face, and she stumbled in a rut in the road. "Back up the car," Brock shouted. "We've got to have some light." She did as he told her.

In the light of the headlamps she could now see Margaret, in the rain, leaning against the trunk of the oak opposite the one the car had crashed into. Her clothes seemed to be plastered to her with water. She was staring at the wreck but remained motionless. Her stockings were torn, and she had lost a shoe. The rain seemed to have washed away whatever blood there might have been from a small cut over one eye. Lally touched her, and she responded by beginning to shiver violently.

"Couldn't help it. Jon kept trying to take the wheel from me. Trying to make me stop. I kept telling him to leave me alone. Bobby kept shouting at me! Wouldn't stop shouting . . . Go and help them, Lally. Make them come out. Tried to pull Jon out, but he wouldn't come. Selfish bastards, both of them. They're just doing it to make me afraid."

Slowly Lally went to where Brock squatted by the wreck. Something much worse than Margaret's fear pervaded her. She touched Brock on the shoulder. He turned. "Don't look, Lally! Don't look!"

But she had to look, didn't he know that? She had to look and see, and know the total sense of despair which engulfed her. Jon's chest had been crushed by the dashboard. Bobby's head had gone through the windshield, but the blood that had flowed from the severed throat had long ago stopped, and that the rain had washed away. His white shirt gleamed palely pink. She got down on her hands and knees and crawled into that mangled space until she could reach Jon, angrily shaking off Brock's restraining hands. Her lips closed on his pale, cold ones.

"I love you, Jon. I love you." It did not wake him. It never would.

Now she allowed herself to be dragged back by Brock. "We've got to get Margaret out of here. Quickly."

"Why hurry? They're dead. Dead, Brock. My beautiful Jon is dead. I love him . . . Oh, God, I love him."

He shook her. "There's no time for that. Come away." He started pulling her toward Margaret. "I've found her handbag. Take her back to the house, and try not to let any of the staff see her. No one was supposed to wait up, I think. And listen . . . This is what you're to do. Are you listening, Lally? Do you hear me?"

She nodded, but his voice seemed far away. "When you get her home, try to lock her up—or keep her away from everyone. Anything so that no one can reach her, or talk to her. Stand outside her door if you have to. Telephone for an ambulance, and for the police. And this is what you are to say. Are you listening, Lally? Are you remembering what you're to do?"

Helplessly, she nodded. "You and Margaret were in your car. I was driving—" He jerked his head over his shoulder at the crashed Cadillac. "I was driving that. You just found us." She watched, uncomprehendingly, as he got down on the ground and dragged himself along on the sodden grass. Then he put his hands on the shards of glass which still held on the rim of the windshield, to produce cuts and bleeding. Then she saw him take the flask from Margaret's handbag and drink the whiskey which remained, and even sprinkle some of it on his clothes. "I don't know if I can fool them. A bash on the head might look better, but I can't expect you to do that. If anyone sees her the way she is, we're in trouble."

Still without understanding, she watched him. All life had seemed to die for her when she had kissed Jon. "Trouble? What more trouble could we have?" She looked back at the Cadillac. "The worst has happened. Why do we have to do these things?"

"You know as well as I do, Lally. When you come to your senses, you'll know perfectly well. Margaret can't go to prison. She'd be out of her mind in a day. Margaret *can't* go to prison. It's possible she could be sent to prison, and I can't let her go. Now do as I say, Lally."

She stood for what seemed a long time. She felt the chill of the driving rain beginning to penetrate her clothes, but it was an alien body which felt it. Her own body seemed to have died back there with Jon.

"Lally, you must! *You must!* Think of Black Jack. Think of Alice . . . of Jonathan. You must!"

How could Brock, she wondered, ever have known of that night long ago, after Alice's mother had died, when she had crawled into the chair with Black Jack and offered a promise? Only she and Black Jack knew. But somehow Brock seemed to know. Did he know? It didn't matter. She had offered a promise which Black Jack had never appeared to accept, but which had always been implied in her behavior. She would take care of Alice. She would take care of Jon . . . and of Margaret. In some way, Brock knew.

"Quickly, please, Lally. I don't know how long it'll be before Lord Gough gets here. And Black Jack. I hope they were ahead of us, and needn't see this. Please hurry, Lally. *Please.*"

She turned and moved back to the car. The engine was still running. Vaguely she saw how Brock almost dragged Margaret toward the car, and pushed her into the passenger seat. "On your way now, Lally. You know what to do." She let in the clutch; the vehicle moved with surprising smoothness. Some other body than her own was working, under Brock's instructions, and under the terms of the promise she had given, unasked, to Black Jack. As Neatherby came into sight, before the headlights could wash the building, she remembered to cut them. As a member of the house party, she had her own key to the side door. Roughly she pulled Margaret from the car, both of them stumbling in the dark; finally her frozen fingers worked the key, and she bundled Margaret through the door. A few lights had been left on in the hall. She pushed Margaret before her up the stairs, and into her bedroom. And again remembering Brock's instructions as if he had written them, she locked the door.

Then she went back downstairs to the telephone.

Before she had finished the second call, Taylor—poor Taylor, whose wages Margaret had not even paid—was there, a gown over his pajamas. "Can I be of help, madam?"

She completed what she had to say to the police, hung up, and turned to Taylor. "Yes, you can. There's been an accident. Better get dressed. An ambulance is coming. The police will be here soon. Lady Grenfell is in her room, and must not be disturbed. You understand, Taylor? She must *not* be disturbed. She has just seen Lord Grenfell. He is dead."

"Madam!" And then: "Oh, my poor lady . . ."

She was halfway up the stairs. She turned back. "I'll see the police when they come. They will want a statement. My father and possibly Lord Gough will come. I don't know . . ." She shook her head, trying to remember what else she had to do.

He came to the foot of the staircase. "Mrs. Pollock? Mrs. Pollock— what else?"

She looked at his troubled face. "My husband," she said. "My beautiful Jon is dead." Then she walked up the rest of the stairs, turning the key to Margaret's room over and over in her palm, gripping it tightly, feeling it bite her flesh. Feel anything, she told herself, but do not scream. And what did she want to scream? "Murder . . . !"

V

Before dawn Lally sat with Black Jack in the dining room at Neatherby. She had changed her clothes, and taken away Margaret's wet ones. She had made a first, brief statement to the police. She said what Brock had told her to say. She had put Margaret to bed, and told her to stay there. "It didn't happen, Lally," Margaret had said. "I'm drunk and stupid, and it was a nightmare."

"Dream no more," Lally said. "Just sleep. It will be different when you sleep."

"There are some pills. In the bathroom cabinet. Sometimes when I can't sleep . . ."

Lally had waited until the pills began to take effect. Then she went downstairs to face Black Jack. Taylor, shocked and silent, had served them coffee.

She saw in Black Jack's face a mirror of her own desolation.

"Brock is with the police now," he said. "I don't know what to say
. . . what to think."

"We have to do what Brock told me to do. And we have to get
Margaret away from here. Back to Pellham, if we can. As far away
from people—especially from the newspapers—as possible. No one
must talk to her."

Black Jack's hands reached to enfold her. "We've both lost Jon.
We love him. Why all this . . . this concern for Margaret?" His
hands tightened on hers in a grip that was painful, but was welcome,
because she could feel it, when all the rest of her body seemed numb.
She was now acting as a kind of automaton; the feeling side of her
recognized this, as if she had become two personalities. She observed
herself acting out what Brock had directed. The other side, unacknowledged and helpless, was weeping.

She told him, because she had to. Without his help, she could
never get Margaret out of that room upstairs and safely to Pellham
Langley. There would be no purpose in what Brock was doing if
Margaret was not held safe.

"He will probably go to prison. That's what he thought about at
once. What he said was that Margaret could not go to prison. He
said . . . he said she wouldn't last a day. He knows. I think he
knows Margaret as well as we do. What will the charge be, do you
think? Manslaughter? How long do you have to go to prison for
that?"

His hands tightened once more on hers. "Lally . . . Lally, you're
not talking about yourself. You're not weeping. I know how you
loved Jon. And he's dead. You are telling me now that Margaret is
responsible. She was thrown from the car, but both Jon and Bobby
are dead. What do you feel? My darling . . ."

"Feel?"

She broke her hands from his, and began twisting them together.
"What I feel and what I do are different things. I have to protect
her, as Brock told me I must. Jon . . . Jon . . . I can't talk about
Jon. I can't let myself feel yet. If I did, I might want to kill her, instead of protect her. What would that achieve? Only more hurt for
you."

Suddenly she fell into his arms. "Father, help me to forgive her.
Help me." It was a prayer and a plea.

He held her; she breathed the damp smell of his suit. "Lally, nothing can give Jon back to us. We can only try to save Margaret . . ."

She waited for a denunciation, an outburst of rage. But it did not come. Black Jack loved all his children; he clung to those who were left to him.

VI

The next day was forever shadowed in Lally's memory. She was never quite sure how and when they got Margaret to Pellham—waking her from a deep sleep which left her too drugged to protest, and taking her forcibly. During the long drive to Pellham she said nothing, but the few hours which had lapsed had brought a sense of reality to her. In her room at Pellham she faced them. "I know I did it, Father. Can you ever forgive me? You and Lally?" She had turned her face away from them. "I can't expect you to answer. What will happen to me now? Will they put me in prison?" A shudder had gone through her body. Her face went down into her hands.

"That isn't going to happen, Margaret. Brock is saying *he* is responsible. He is telling the police that he was driving. You say nothing. Nothing but that you were in the car with Lally. I will try to keep the police away from you."

She looked up again. "We can't let him do that. *He* will go to prison."

"He seems prepared to do that, Margaret. I haven't talked with him yet, but I think I know Brock. You would do well to be quiet, as he says, and leave him to work out his own plan. It could be—it might be that he won't go to prison. He doesn't want you exposed . . ."

She looked from one to the other; her face seemed to grow whiter. "I can't be in his debt to that degree, Father. This isn't just Brock's presents, his generosity. This is owing him . . . it means owing him *everything*. This is a debt I can't ever pay off. We can't let it go on."

"Be quiet," Lally said sharply. "You've done enough. Talked enough. I have lied for you, lied to the police. Brock has lied. He is, if it comes down to it, going to go to prison for you. The very least you can do—the very least, Margaret—is do what you're told. If Brock chooses to do this, then you have no right to undermine him. Just be quiet. Think of your David. Think of Father. For once in your life, stop thinking about yourself."

"Where is David?"

"In the nursery here—with Jonathan."

"Lally . . . ?" Margaret's eyes beseeched her.

Lally turned away. "I have left two more of those pills. I have told everyone you must not be disturbed. Try to sleep. We have arrangements to make. We have funerals to attend."

"Lally . . . ?" Lally closed the door on that cry. For the first time in her life she did not let herself hear Margaret's wail of despair, her cry for help. For the moment, she had given as much as she could.

* * *

Downstairs, Brock was waiting. "They've given me bail. At Black Jack's insistence. They find it surprising that a man can be so magnanimous—after all, the death of his son and his son-in-law. But they acknowledge that I stand in a strange relationship to your family, Lally."

Lally's mind was running to the future, the statements that must be made. The possibility of a trial, even if Brock did plead guilty to whatever charge might be made. "The waiter at Seaton's?"

"Done," he said. "I tracked him down as soon as they let me go. A sum of money is guaranteed. When all the procedures are through —whatever turn they take, he will be paid, and later he will emigrate to America. There will be a job for him—more highly paid than he's ever imagined. And he will give no interviews to the press. He will speak to no one but the police when they get to him, and the magistrate or the judge or whoever will be handling the matter."

"And what will he say?"

"Exactly what I've told him. That I had quite a lot to drink. And he doesn't know who went in what car. It's not his business to worry about things like that. Why should he?"

"You sound very calm."

"I have to be. How is Margaret?"

"That's all you care about?"

"Margaret's alive, Lally. Jon and Bobby are dead. I *have* to care about her."

"Caring about her doesn't mean you have to do this. Go this far."

"You mean you don't want me to. You're thinking, aren't you, that for once she ought to suffer. Well, she'll suffer enough."

Then Lally began to understand what had been behind Margaret's cry of protest, a protest which, between them, she and Black Jack had stifled. From now on, Margaret would be Brock's creature. She would, as she had said, owe him everything. Finally, Brock had Margaret.

He was nodding. "Yes, you understand it all, don't you, Lally? *Now* you understand. Old Brock has stood by all this time and waited. I didn't cause that crash. I didn't want the lives of Jon or Bobby. No, not even poor old Bobby, who for the first time in his life was going to take a stand about something. I was prepared to wait around until Margaret let go herself. They were coming close to it. Oh, she might have done what Bobby said. For a while she might have been a good, obedient wife. But it wouldn't have lasted long. She would have cut loose, and I had every intention of being around when that happened. It just happened that I was around for the very worst thing. It's cruel on you and Black Jack. It's cruel on Bobby's parents. And on David and Jonathan. But it's cruel on Margaret, too. Can't we remember that? She made a bad mistake. Don't imagine she won't pay for it. If I have to serve a prison sentence for her, then I'll do it. I can take it. I grew up fighting for every damn thing. She wouldn't know how. You can't just toss Margaret into prison. You know that, Lally."

"You and Black Jack." She turned away from him, turned and saw the mist creeping in silently across the lawn, beginning to envelop the clipped hedges, the rose beds. The mist had a November feeling about it, as if the day were suddenly foreshortened, as if it might go on being November forever in her heart. The mist came too close, and she saw Jon's face in it, deathly and pale. They had boasted and laughed together too often. They had laughed and known delight because they had survived the holocaust of the Western Front. They had thought, as the young do, that they would live forever. Lally knew the November feeling would remain, and that she was no longer young. "You and Black Jack," she repeated without turning. "You will protect her from everything. Between you."

"Yes, Lally, and you will too."

She started to utter a protest, but closed her lips on it. What was the use of protest? The pale, dead face would not come alive.

The protest seemed stifled forever when Alice flung open the door of the library and raced into Brock's arms. "Oh, Brock! Father told me—about Jon and Bobby. Brock . . . ?"

"Yes, sweetheart. I'm here. Alice, can you understand? It was an accident. A very bad accident. Jon and Bobby have gone, my darling. We won't be seeing them anymore. But you've still got Father and

Lally and Margaret—and me, Alice. You've still got Brock. They're going to say some bad things about Brock, Alice, but you have to believe it was an accident. No one meant anything bad to happen. You know sometimes you just can't help things. You have to believe old Brock didn't mean anything bad to happen."

"You couldn't be bad, Brock. Never! Lally, that's true, isn't it?"

Lally had to turn and face them. The final commitment had to be given. "It's true, Alice. It was an accident. Brock couldn't be *bad*."

*   *   *

Margaret stood among them, frozen and mute, during the burial service for her husband, Robert Grenfell, and later, at Pellham Langley for her brother, Jonathan. Brock had retreated to London, where he would wait until the time when he would have to appear at the inquest. There had been a great deal of newspaper coverage of the accident, much speculation of the tragic event which had taken the lives of the only sons of two prominent Yorkshire families. There were photos of Margaret in her court gown, photos of her with Bobby after their marriage, even a photo of her with the Prince of Wales. There were photos of Lally and Jon. Brock did not emerge from his suite at the Ritz. The newspapers played up the fact that so little was known about him. "American businessman" was the most they could say. They unearthed the story of his upbringing in an orphanage. They found he had once been married; his wife had left him and was now married to an artist and living in San Francisco. She resolutely refused to talk to the press, and they looked elsewhere for copy. They wrote of the suite at the Ritz, the suite at the Plaza in New York. "The rich man without a home" they called him. The waiter at Seaton's talked to no one but the police.

In their turn Margaret and Lally were interviewed by the police. By this time Black Jack had thoroughly coached Margaret in what she was to say. Lally found that was one task she could not bring herself to do. Margaret answered questions tonelessly. She had an almost unearthly beauty in her black dress and pearls, the little pointed face sharp and tragic. The questions were brief; she said no more than she had to.

"One final question, Lady Grenfell. Wasn't it a rather strange arrangement that you and Mrs. Pollock were alone in the second car—that one of the gentlemen was not with you? In fact, was not driving you."

Margaret's face was perfectly composed. "I wanted it that way. Both of us drive—we're very good drivers. And Bobby—my husband —and I had had a quarrel over dinner. I had lost a lot of money that day at the races. Money I shouldn't have bet with. He was very angry with me. And I was angry with him because of what he had said to me. I asked Lally to drive me back to Neatherby. I—I'd had rather a lot to drink. I didn't quite trust myself, and I couldn't stand being with the men. They *all* took Bobby's side in the argument. But Lally —well, Lally and I have always been close. Lally has always taken my side." She added slowly, "Lally has always taken care of me."

These questions were repeated at the inquest. Margaret answered in almost exactly the same words. She avoided looking at Brock, and she left the coroner's court immediately after her evidence was given. A verdict of manslaughter was brought in, and Brockton Weymouth was sent for trial at Leeds Assizes. It created a further newspaper sensation when Sir John Pollock applied to have Brockton Weymouth released on bail on his surety. On hearing this, Lord Gough swept from the courtroom, a man mortally offended.

While they waited for Brock's case to come up, Margaret closed Neatherby and moved to Pellham Langley with David. Black Jack paid off her servants, except Nanny Williams, and paid her debts. The London house was put up for sale. "Give it all back to Lord Gough," Margaret had insisted. "I want none of it. It never belonged to Bobby and me."

Lord Gough had pleaded with her to stay at Neatherby. "We want David to grow up knowing what his inheritance is—in every sense. We need to see him, Margaret. He's our only grandchild." She had shaken her head.

"I can't live at Neatherby alone. David will come for visits."

Lally also resisted, but only for a short time, Black Jack's urging to return to Pellham Langley. But then the days and the nights grew too long, the silence too great. She thought of Jonathan alone in his nursery at Grangewick, and David alone in the nurseries of Pellham Langley. She crumbled, finally, the day Edith came to see her.

"I hope to take you home with me, Lally. Jack has told me—about Margaret. He's told me about what Brock's doing. I'm not such a fool that I didn't suspect that everything was not exactly as it was told. But what can the law do in the face of a man who insists he is guilty? Who insists on taking the blame? When there is no one to testify to the contrary? You are all bound up now, Lally, in the conspiracy of perjury. It isn't just silence—it is perjury. No one may speak now for fear of what it will bring upon all the others."

"And what has my going back to Pellham Langley to do with all this?" Lally felt the anger stir in her again; it was there all the time, the anger and the desolation. And the fear that she might lash out at Margaret to destroy her because Margaret had destroyed Jon. But in doing that she would also destroy Black Jack.

"Because I know what you have to try to live with. If you don't come to terms with Margaret's guilt—and her frailty—very soon, you never will succeed. And you will tear Jack apart. He loves you both. He is breaking his heart over Jon. And over you and Margaret. You are the only one who can make the overture of forgiveness, Lally. Come back and be with us at Pellham."

"I can't. I can't face her—day after day."

"Child!" It was spoken in the voice of the Marchioness, who had mercilessly drilled her for her Court presentation, who had never relented in her insistence that Lally attend every ball, which she had loathed, who had demanded that she be seen at Ascot and Henley with her beautiful sister, Margaret, because that was what Black Jack had wanted. And whose words, those well-remembered words, "Well done, child," had been among the sweetest of Lally's life. "Black Jack needs you, Lally."

Lally nodded, acceptance, resignation in her gesture. "I'll pack, and we'll close the house. There's nothing here—nothing at all, without Jon. What are Margaret and I going to look like to the world? I wonder. Two widows comforting each other. Loving daughters to our father, helping him bear his sorrow. Our children playing together. It's the perfect picture, isn't it? To outsiders we should appear to have only one enemy—Brock. But he's our best friend."

She turned to the older woman. "Edith, help me! I would do anything for Father. For him, I have to try to forgive Margaret. It won't happen in weeks. It may never happen. But it has to *seem* to have happened."

* * *

Margaret waited alone for her in the drawing room of Pellham Langley. She rose to her feet as Lally entered, took a hesitant step forward, and then halted. She twisted her hands together in a gesture of appeal.

"Thank you for coming, Lally."

"I came," Lally said stonily, "because Father wanted it. I have to try—"

Margaret took a few more steps toward her. "Will you try, Lally? I'd be so grateful. Father would be so grateful. I don't know how to ask for forgiveness. It's too big a thing to ask for. But if you could try . . . ?"

"Jon was everything—the whole world to me, Margaret. He's been taken away by your stupidity. My beautiful, my adored Jon. How can I . . . ?"

She saw the tears sliding down Margaret's face. Then she forced herself to take the necessary steps that still divided them. "I can only try. Because I promised."

She leaned forward to kiss Margaret's cheek. They stood close for a moment, two women in black, wearing the identical pearl necklaces Black Jack had given them on the day they were presented at Court. Lally's anger cooled, the bitterness receded a little. Margaret, too, was part of her life. She put out a hand tentatively and touched the other's shoulder. "I can only try."

* * *

Brockton Weymouth did not stand trial by jury at Leeds Assizes because he pleaded guilty to the charge of manslaughter. He was sentenced to one year's imprisonment. "The scoundrel should be hanged," Lord Gough declared, with a fine disregard of the law. *Millionaire American Goes to Prison* was the newspaper story. The brokerage firm of Brockton Weymouth and Partners continued to function in Wall Street, but the press could find no partners to make a statement about the matter.

Sir John Pollock would say nothing about the matter either. His two daughters and their children had returned to Pellham Langley to live with him. He hired extra men he called gamekeepers to patrol the park and discourage intruders, or those who asked questions.

When the first visiting day came around at the prison-outside of Hull, it was Lally, driving an inconspicuous car, who went to be admitted. She faced Brock through the grill.

"Well, Brock . . ."

"Well, Lally. We did it, didn't we?" He even wore the horribly cut prison garb with a certain air of insouciance. She remarked on it. "I grew up in the uniform of an orphan home, Lally. I know how to wear them."

* * *

Once a month she continued to visit him, bringing what addition
to the prison fare he was permitted. He grew a little leaner, if that
was possible, the features just that bit more pronounced, but he made
no complaints. "It's good for me. Quiet life—regular hours. I'm getting a lot of reading done. My man in London sends whatever they'll
let me have. His letters are a breakdown of all the important stories
in *The Wall Street Journal.*" The man in London took up the rest of
the allotted visiting time. He seemed to be some sort of employee of
Brock's, someone who kept in touch with the New York office. It
began to appear to Lally that Brock was fully running his Wall Street
firm from an English prison.

During each visit he asked carefully about Black Jack and Edith,
Alice and the two little boys. Always, last, he asked about Margaret.
"I'm glad she's there with you." He never asked for a visit from her.

"She'd write, but—"

"I don't want her to write," he said, almost harshly. "I don't want
her even to think of me here. Margaret must have no contact with a
place like this. I'll see her—in time. With time off for good behavior,
I'll be out by the summer."

* * *

So the months of the winter wore away, and the late Yorkshire
spring at last flooded the garden, and touched the moors with new
green. The November that Lally had known was in her heart remained. She saw the spring arriving with the eyes of a stranger.

The relationship between herself and Margaret experienced only
the slightest thaw, and that was mostly a facade put on for Black
Jack's benefit. They ate at the same table, played with their children
either in the nursery or the garden, and somehow remained separate.
Lally could not remember laughter being shared—but there was little
laughter at Pellham Langley. The few times they were in a room
alone, the silence grew tense and uncomfortable. They depended on
Alice to break that silence; through her, it was possible to talk, but
the talk was of little consequence. For Lally, the days and the weeks
dragged. There seemed little purpose in life except to watch, too
closely, Jonathan's progress. Nanny Dunstable performed all the
tasks which she wanted to do for him herself. She ached for some
task, something to tire and weary her, so that sleep would come easily, but there was none. Susie Barlow came to visit, and eyed her with
concern.

"Gawd, Lally, you look awful. Idleness doesn't suit you. Now, if I had you with me in London I could work you twelve hours a day."

"If I could just *be* with you in London. But I can't leave Father—not just yet."

Susie nodded. "Yes, I know what you mean. Margaret's a bit of a handful, isn't she? What's she trying to do—drink herself to death?"

The martini had now replaced the pre-lunch sherry, and Billings replenished the drinks tray almost as soon as tea was finished. The jazz records were played over and over, until the harsh melodies became hateful to Lally, a strident commentary on the hollowness of their lives. After dinner, Margaret sat across the fire from Black Jack, sharing his brandy, saying almost nothing. Susie surveyed the group and said to Lally, "One man isn't enough to cope with all you women."

"That's hardly my fault, is it?" Lally said.

She had known one moment of terror that winter. It was a bright day after a light fall of snow. A path on the high terrace of Pellham Langley had been swept clean so that the two nannies might walk there with their charges. Lally, plagued with restlessness, saw them passing the library window and decided to join them. By the time she had gotten her coat and scarf, the two figures with the high baby carriages had reached the far end of the terrace. And another figure had joined them. A woman, clad all in black, had halted them, and was bending over Jonathan's carriage, a hand outstretched to touch him. For an instant Lally felt again the hand that had clutched her as she had made her way through the guests at her wedding reception in the village hall. She felt a threat to her child she had never known before. She began to run. "No! No—get away. Get away from him!"

The woman straightened at the sound. She backed away a few steps, and then turned and walked rapidly away, going around the corner of the house toward the stable yard.

"Why, Mrs. Pollock," Nanny Dunstable said. "Whatever is the matter?"

"Who . . . who was that woman? What was she doing here?"

"That woman? Why, that's Mrs. Pickering. From the village. You must know her, surely. Sometimes she comes to give Cook a hand. Poor soul. Lost her two sons in the war. She just loves to come and see the babies. There's no harm in it, Mrs. Pollock. Why . . . I'm rather surprised at you. She's such a decent soul."

"Oh . . ." Lally said. Relief and shame flooded her. She knew

Mrs. Pickering. "Oh . . . I'm so sorry. I just thought . . . I'll apologize . . ."

"Well, don't worry, Mrs. Pollock," Nanny Williams said soothingly. "I'm sure she hasn't taken offense. We all understand what a hard time this is for you. And for the whole family, of course. A person's nerves can get a little out of order. Maybe you should see the doctor for a tonic."

"Yes, perhaps . . ." She turned abruptly and left them. Why did she fear her so much, that woman who said she was her mother? Why had she been so terribly afraid that some harm would come to Jonathan? She knew it for what it was—fear that the woman, the still nameless woman, was in some way going to lay claim to Jonathan as her grandchild, that she would shadow and cloud his young life as she had Lally's. But Black Jack had promised she would trouble Lally no more. There could not possibly be a threat to Jonathan. There would be no dark and evil-smelling rooms in his memory. Lally reasoned herself out of her fear, but still she had not the courage to go to Black Jack and ask him what had happened to that woman in black.

That winter there had been another loss. Nell had come to Lally one day to announce, shyly, that she had accepted a proposal of marriage from Captain Mortimer Crawford, formerly of the King's Own Somerset Rifles. "I got to know him, Miss Lally, when we used to come here during the war. He was here a long time—both legs amputated, and no family at home to care for him. We corresponded after that. Then last September, on my holiday, I went down to visit him. A place near Yeovil. I stayed at the local pub, and visited every day. He wanted me to see what it was like, you understand. He has a housekeeper with him, and a nurse who looks in every day to give a hand—you know, dressing and so on. He has a nice house—not big, a cottage, really. But he's built onto it so that he never has to go upstairs. A lovely garden, Miss Lally. He's become quite clever about taking care of it, though he does have to have help. He's got a long-handled thing he can root out the weeds with. He's tried to get about on artificial legs, Miss Lally, but they don't work very well. So most of the time he's in a wheelchair. It's just to keep from falling, you see. He's always going to need help. I expect that's why he asked me . . . well, you can't imagine a gentleman would want to marry someone like me, would you?"

Lally looked at that sweet face, remembering her from the earliest

days in the nursery. How old could she be? Not even forty yet, but
they had taken her so much for granted that her age had seemed
unimportant. The face, with its soft, unlined skin, seemed ageless. All
the years she had striven to help Alice had changed her voice and her
manner. All the times she had shared meals with them during the war
had taught her to observe their habits at table. She had read too
many books to Alice not to have absorbed, in a quiet fashion, an education of sorts. Every lesson hour Miss Garner had spent with Alice
had been a lesson for Nell also. She wrote a fair, clear hand. Lally
could remember the letters that had arrived in France. *Dear Miss
Lally, Miss Alice would like you to know* . . .

"Nell, do you care for him?"

She blushed. "I like him, Miss Lally."

"Enough to spend a lifetime taking care of him?"

She lifted her head, a trifle defiant. "It's a life, isn't it, Miss Lally?
I'd be married. Have my own house. Miss Alice doesn't need me
anymore, except for company. I don't mind looking after him. I saw
a lot of things much worse when Pellham was a hospital. I didn't expect anything like this, but it's come. I didn't accept right away. He
told me to go home and think about it, and talk to you. Well, just
after that, Mister Jon was killed. It wasn't the time for me to leave.
Now, I think it is."

It was another of the strange transformations that the war had
wrought. Looking at her in her wedding dress, which Susie had
insisted on supplying, Lally could hardly believe that this was the shy
little creature who had run from kitchen to nursery at Nanny's bid-
ding. Black Jack gave her away in the church at Pellham Langley,
and held her wedding reception at the house. Half of the village had
been invited, and Nell's relations, nearly all of them mill hands, from
Bradford. Margaret had looked around the dining room just after the
bride, helping her groom to balance on two artificial legs just for that
moment, had cut the cake with his sword. "Strange, isn't it, Lally?
Nell's having a rather grander wedding reception than either of us
did."

They had driven off, Nell wearing one of Susie's suits, in a
chauffeured car the groom had hired to be able to get to Yorkshire.
There would be no honeymoon. They would go back to the cottage
where they would spend the rest of their lives, and Nell would be
mistress of her own home. The faces of most of the villagers and the
Bradford relatives had registered incredulity.

Alice had wept when she realized Nell had truly gone. She moped for days, and after that took to spending most of her time in the nurseries with the two boys and the two nannies. "Where shall we ever find another Nell?" Black Jack lamented. "No wonder that Crawford man took her."

The two nannies were tolerant of Alice's presence, but they complained to Lally that she hindered rather than helped in the nursery. A young woman with some nursing experience was hired as a companion to Alice. She stayed only a month. "I'm sorry, Sir John. I just don't like the situation. This big house, out here all by itself. And everyone so sad. Your two daughters . . . those two little boys. And you're the only man in sight. Your Alice—she's a sweet girl. But I can't be expected to play dolls with her all the time, can I?"

* * *

Then the time came in late summer, a day warm even at that early hour, when Lally waited in the car outside the gates of the prison. The governor had granted Brock his freedom one day early so that he could avoid an onslaught by the newspapers. Lally had no idea why he had asked her to come, but then she had no idea why it had been she who had been selected to visit him through the months. Whatever Brock wanted was done. That was what Black Jack had decreed, and Lally had no reason to quarrel with that. She watched now as Brock slipped quietly through the small door in the huge prison gates. He slung his suitcase casually into the back of the car.

"Where now?" Lally asked, after she had received his light kiss on the cheek.

"Queen's Hotel, Leeds, please, Lally." It was the city's newest structure. As always, Brock knew the best place to go.

She stood with him as he registered under an assumed name; she was with him as he went to the suite reserved in that name. It was flower-filled. The man from London, Brock's man, was waiting there. He wore a dark, pinstriped suit, a bowler hat, and pearl-gray gloves lay on a table; he looked the typical City gentleman. "It's good to see you here, Mr. Weymouth," he said formally. He did not extend his hand until Brock had put forward his own; his role seemed to be that of some sort of superior servant. Brock introduced him as Samuel Parsons. "I have all the documents you requested, Mr. Weymouth." Brock had already picked up *The Financial Times* and was scanning the headlines. Then he called the floor waiter and ordered breakfast for three—a breakfast such as Lally, even in the days when she had eaten hugely, had never imagined. When it came, Brock could barely touch it. "I guess I just kind of lost the habit," he said.

By now the valet had arrived and unpacked two suitcases that Samuel Parsons had brought from London. The barber and a manicurist had been asked for. "May I suggest, sir," the valet said, "that I call a tailor? Some of these clothes, sir, seem—well, a trifle large for you. A little loss of weight recently, sir?" It was plain to Lally that the valet had recognized the man who had caused headlines in the local papers last year.

Breakfast thrust aside, and Brock now surrounded by those who had come to minister to him, Lally rose to go. Brock walked with her to the lift. "Thanks, Lally. Thanks for everything. I just wanted very much to see you waiting there this morning." As the lift doors opened, he once again kissed her briefly on the cheek. "Tell Margaret to telephone me, will you, Lally? I'll be waiting for her call."

The lift doors closed, blotting out his dark, laconic smile. It had not been a request, but a demand.

*   *   *

Five days later Margaret, Viscountess Grenfell, was married to Mr. Brockton Weymouth at the Leeds registrar's office. She had produced a certificate of her husband's death, Brock had produced a certificate of his divorce. It had all been carefully planned and smoothly executed, as if Brock had foreseen and provided for every contingency. Black Jack and Edith put their signatures in the registry as witnesses. Lally stood and, as Margaret signed, held the little spray of violets Margaret had carried. Brock, the marks of prison already gone, his morning suit now fitting his even leaner figure, had kissed his bride hardly more passionately than he had kissed Lally outside the prison. The action implied that, having waited so long, he now had no need for undue haste. Margaret, dressed in lavender, went through the ceremony almost woodenly, as if she had been told to play a role and was doing it; she exhibited neither pleasure nor displeasure. She smiled rather mechanically as the toasts were offered at the small luncheon party in a private room at the Queen's Hotel.

"I'm coming to America with you, aren't I, Brock?" Alice asked.

"Not this time, sweetheart. But very soon. Margaret and I have to get a home together there first. And old Brock's got some business to attend to. But you can come all next summer, Alice. There are lovely beaches for you to swim at there."

"But why are you taking Margaret and not me?"

"Because *I* am married to Brock," Margaret said tersely. "Can't you even understand that, Alice? You're not as stupid as that."

"I'm not stupid!" Alice cried. "Father told me I'm not stupid. You mustn't say it!" It was indeed one of Black Jack's real commands that Alice should never have her deficiencies pointed out to her. "You're horrible, Margaret. I hate you. Brock loves me best." Any sense of gaiety the luncheon party had had dissolved with Alice's tears.

Not even Brock could pay enough of the staff of the hotel to keep silent. As they emerged from the hotel to walk around to the railway station next door, a photographer from *The Yorkshire Post* was waiting. His colleagues in London were waiting as Brock and Margaret, with David and Nanny Williams, got off the train and took taxis to the Ritz. All of them refused to answer questions, but the pictures were front page in next day's newspapers, along with the story of the marriage at the Leeds' registrar's office. The tragedy of the two deaths the year before now became faintly touched with scandal. Viscountess Grenfell had married, within days of his release from prison, the man responsible for her husband's death. And the wedding had been attended by her father and her adopted sister, whose husband had also died in that car crash.

It was as plain Mrs. Weymouth that Margaret embarked on the Cunard liner the next day with her new husband and her young son.

Only with difficulty was Lord Gough dissuaded from attempting to get a court injunction to prevent his only grandchild from being taken from the country. Margaret's life, living in near seclusion in her father's house since Robert Grenfell's death, had been blameless. It was suggested to Lord Gough that he would have difficulty making a case against Margaret as an unfit mother, and it could only result in more unfavorable publicity. This was what Black Jack's solicitors told Lord Gough's solicitors. The two men did not communicate directly.

There was no picture of Brock and Margaret on deck as the Cunarder pulled out of Southampton. The couple had gone straight to their stateroom, and Viscount Grenfell was installed in the adjoining one with Nanny Williams.

But it was said by those who dined in the first-class dining room that first evening out that Mrs. Brockton Weymouth was surely one of the most beautiful women who had recently graced that room. Later in the voyage it was remarked that she drank quite a lot, and she danced with verve, and a kind of manic gaiety. "I don't blame her," someone observed. "I heard the whole family was living together up there in Yorkshire in a sort of mausoleum."

❧ PART III ❧

1925

❦ CHAPTER 13 ❦

I

The surf crashed on the beach in the aftermath of last night's storm, the sound almost covering the cry of the gulls. Lally liked it best as she now saw and heard it; the North Shore of Long Island in its placid moods, when the heat seemed to hang stickily in the air, did not attract her. This morning the wind blew fresh and strong from the Sound. The water, which touched her bare feet and sometimes surged to her knees, was cold. Perhaps last night's storm had been the first touch of the American autumn, "the fall," as Lally had learned to call it. She found a piece of driftwood, and flung it back into the surf. One of Brock's dogs, who had followed her from the house, ran eagerly to retrieve it.

She did not look backward to the house. The outline of its turrets and spires she knew by heart, as she knew the contours of the other houses which fronted on this bay. They had been coming here each summer since Margaret and Brock had married. It was, by now, a familiar landscape, but still one in which she did not feel quite at ease. There was an air of unreality about the massive roof lines, some boldly fronting the shore, as Brock's did, some withdrawn a little inland, behind a screen of trees. Like Pellham Langley, they spoke of wealth new-made, and myths and legends of wealth. If the money was there to afford one of these houses, the owners were spoken of with respect, sometimes awe, as a matter of course.

When they had first come to Long Island, she and Jonathan, Alice and Black Jack and Edith had stayed with Brock and Margaret at a somewhat humbler house, though still big by any standards. But it was back off the shore and, by comparison with some of its neighbors, hardly worth a glance. Brock had fumed with impatience at it. "Oh, something better's bound to turn up. This is just a cottage I used to use in the summer before—before we were married."

The next summer Brock had greeted them at the pier in Manhattan and driven them straight to this huge, though pleasing house. It had been built in the early years of the century by the magnate Arnold T. Brewster, of railroad fame, a thrusting, self-made man who had given his architect a brief for a "pleasant house, well-set, well-built," and then, unlike Black Jack's father, James Pollock, had left him alone. What he produced was Whytecliffe, almost a copy of a French château, not quite imperial in its size or splendor, but not modest. Its symmetry was a delight to the eye, but it stood strangely on that shore, its feet almost in the sea. It needed a placid river, or a reflecting lake, but it got Long Island Sound. Its owner, however, pronounced himself pleased, and it joined the ranks of the famous mansions which studded the shore. In the twenties, his wife dead, his only son estranged and gone to Texas drilling for oil, Brewster had put it up for rent. At least that was what Brock had told them. "It's only rented," he said. But Lally knew that at last he felt he had the setting for Margaret she deserved, the setting he had promised. They all suspected that the renting was like the friends whose suites at the Ritz and the Plaza he had "borrowed" and the house in Palm Beach to which Margaret went each winter—it was only a way of not admitting he owned it. Margaret had shrugged. "Oh, does it matter—so long as we have the use of it? I never ask Brock about any of his 'companies.' For all I know, I don't own the clothes on my own back. It doesn't make any difference, so long as I can wear them. Half of America's living on credit."

They had made the journey rather uncertainly the first year. During that summer when Margaret had been pregnant with his first child, Brock had almost begged for their presence. "She needs company—but she can't do the things she wants to do. With you here, she might be persuaded to rest."

"All very well, Brock," Black Jack had commented when he had arrived. "But what about my moors—my shooting? I've got gamekeepers raising grouse no one will ever eat."

"We'll come, Father," Margaret had promised. "Just as soon as we can. You'll give some house parties, won't you, Edith? Invite all the friends we have here. Just as soon as . . ." She had sighed in the heat of that August day in 1922. "Just as soon as this one gets born. It's such a bore. I can't go anywhere, and I weigh a ton. All the parties I'm missing . . ."

She seemed, Lally thought, to regard the bearing of Brock's child in much the way she had thought of Bobby's son, David. It was an obligation. Something to be paid for those months in prison.

The whole family, Lally discovered, presented something of a novelty among the rich of the North Shore. It wasn't that Brock could match the money of the older fortunes. He was regarded as something of an adventurer. His money lay in Wall Street, and was thought of, Black Jack guessed, as having somewhat dubious origins. "It's all on paper," Lally had overheard someone say late one night, seated on one of the terraces of Whytecliffe overlooking the Sound. "It could go down like a house of cards."

Two cigarettes glowed in the dark. "Couldn't care less. All I know is that he's got a good bootlegger. This whiskey is twelve-year-old scotch—even at the end of the party he serves that. And his wines are château-bottled."

"You could say the same about his wife—château-bottled."

"Strange guy. Damned if he doesn't remind me of the Boston Brahmins—long as a bean pole. D'you think it could have been one of their little indiscretions that was left on the doorstep of that orphanage? Might account for how he got his start. Perhaps one of those Boston stuffed shirts had an attack of conscience and gave him a handout."

"If that's the case, you'll never hear it from Brock Weymouth."

It was the mix of aristocracy and money in Margaret Weymouth's family that intrigued the Long Island set and gained admittance for her wherever she fancied to go, even admittance to the Piping Rock Club and the Meadowbrook Club, which Brock Weymouth on his own could never have achieved. She played golf and watched polo with the best families on Long Island's Gold Coast. It was well known that she was the granddaughter of a viscount, and she had been married to the heir to the earldom of Grenfell. Her son was Viscount Grenfell. Her father was a baronet, and was married to the former Marchioness of Ross. Her father's money might arise from such mundane things as textile mills and coal mines, but it was solid. It was the sort of money America understood very well, even though textiles and coal were now in a slump. Some of the Americans had visited Pellham Langley and pronounced it as being as big and splendid as anything the North Shore could boast—and was even a few years older than most mansions there. By American standards the Pollocks' money was "old money" and Margaret had an impeccable pedigree. Money and beauty and pedigree attacted the like. The North Shore took to her. In a sense, they admired Brock Weymouth for having been able to reverse the fashion begun before the turn of the century of American heiresses marrying into European aristocracy in exchange for their dollars. He had brought a beautiful English aristocrat into their society, a stylish, rather spoiled young woman who danced the best Charleston late at night, who wore her clothes with supreme elegance, and knew how to give a party without it seeming to be planned. They liked that.

Brock's dog had retrieved the wood and looked at Lally hopefully. She took it and threw it again, and the dog romped joyfully into the waves. It could only have been, Lally thought, the crowning piece for Margaret—perhaps for Brock, because Margaret regarded all such things as her right—when the Prince of Wales had come to visit last year. During the Prince's visit in 1924 every prominent hostess in America had longed to entertain him, but the word had gone out that His Royal Highness had written to Mrs. Weymouth that he was going to visit America and would like to pay a call. Margaret had replied that she would be delighted to see His Royal Highness whenever his schedule permitted.

It was one of the strangest occasions Long Island had ever known. Balls were being given at some of the grandest of the North Shore mansions for the Prince, but the "little party" given by Margaret Weymouth, when the Prince arrived in midafternoon, swam in the Sound with the family and dogs, and later sat down to a dinner with only twenty present, was the most sought-after invitation. A few extra guests were invited to dance after dinner, but the atmosphere was informal. Lally, who had never thought much about the personality of the man who would be the next king of England, was charmed and won over, when, after he had had the required first dance with his hostess, Margaret, he invited Alice onto the floor with him for a few minutes. Alice, who didn't know and couldn't understand who he was, responded with her greatest charm. She always responded to good manners, Lally observed. Margaret had told her that she must bob a curtsy, but beyond that, she simply enjoyed her-

self. Margaret might be beautiful, but Alice was beauty and innocence combined, and even a prince, for a moment, could be enchanted.

The story of Margaret's "little party" went around the North
Shore. All the grand balls seemed only what they were—grand. Hers
had been a family gathering. The Prince called her by her first name,
and relaxed as he was not permitted to do in most other places. The
little coterie of English had gathered around him and seemed to ex-
clude the rest of the world. Just enough people had been invited to
know this had happened, and they talked of it. Hostesses who until
now had resisted Brockton Weymouth and his wife hastened to culti-
vate them. They had the use of the private golf courses, the riding
trails which led from one estate to another.

"I don't know if I like it," Black Jack had said one day to Lally
and Edith. "I'm afraid it's all rather too much. Obviously Brock has
money, but *this* much money? I've a feeling he's overextended himself to give Margaret everything he thinks she should have."

Edith, who always used a parasol against the fierce summer sun,
tipped it toward her husband. "That, surely, is his own business.
Brock is very clever. And he seems very sure of himself. I don't detect any sign of nerves in him. And fortunes *are* made, Jack, on the
stock market. In fact, if you give people the chance, that's what
they'll end up talking about. Even the very rich are interested in
being richer. It's not considered bad form here, Jack, to talk about
money." She gestured about her—toward the stable block, the many
garages with their cars, the servants' wing, the enclosed and heated
pool, the outdoor swimming pool with its background of Grecian columns, the indoor tennis court, the vista of the Sound before them.
"Even if all this is rented, as he claims, Brock can hardly have nothing in the bank."

Black Jack had fanned himself with his panama. "I suppose you're
right, Edith. It's I who've become slow and old—not willing to take
risks anymore." Lally glanced at him sharply. It was not like him to
talk of age or slowness. He was now past sixty, the hair and mustache silver, but the eyebrows still that thick, startling black which
had first earned him his nickname. The summer sun he got at Whytecliffe tanned his dark skin to a rich color. He was still a strikingly
handsome man.

The dog barked at her heels, and she turned once again to hurl the
stick. He raced exuberantly into the surf, glorying in the wildness of

the waves. This was the reason, she told herself, that she came each summer with the others, obeying Margaret's summons to be with her. Black Jack's dark, tanned face was only one aspect. She saw her son, Jonathan, venturing into the water unafraid, his skin darkening with each passing week, his hair growing sun-bleached. He seemed to grow rapidly during those weeks of summer and sunshine. He played with his cousin, David, and the other children who gathered on the shore; he learned skills other than those he would have learned in England—in a sense, he learned another language. He became an accepted part of the group, joining the rough and tumble of the games, trying to hit with a baseball bat when his own inclination was for a cricket bat. On the pony Brock provided he rode the sandy trails of the big estates. She told herself she came for Jonathan's sake; she came because Black Jack wanted it. He might grumble about missing his shooting, but he came in June and often lingered past the sacred date of August 12 when the guns sounded on the moors. He liked to see his grandchildren play together. "It's good for Jonathan," he insisted. "Until he's ready to go to school, he has more company here than at Pellham. He's a lucky little boy—he's getting the best of both worlds."

Because of these visits Jonathan seemed to have escaped the shyness and self-centeredness of the only child, and the only child to inhabit a big house and command the attention of a grandfather perhaps too indulgent. He and David greeted each other enthusiastically each year, measuring in what ways the other had grown, what new skills acquired. They shared adjoining rooms with amiable give and take. Sometimes they talked of the day when they both would go to Eton in the same term—both had been enrolled since birth. At the moment, although it was mentioned, they really did not understand what that entailed. Margaret's decision to allow David to go was a concession to Lord Gough, and to David's future inheritance of the earldom and its estate. It was necessary that David should know what it was like to live in England, to be an Englishman. He would spend his holidays with each grandfather—some time at Pellham Langley, some time at Dentdale. And in the summers he would return here with Jonathan, and they would share the American experience. Each would grow up on both sides of the Atlantic. Perhaps Black Jack was right: it would be the best of both worlds.

As she turned to throw the stick once again for the imploring dog, she saw the figure on the shore, Margaret's figure. The walk was slow and labored. She was now pregnant with Brock's second child, who would be born in about five weeks' time. Lally stood still, and waited, letting Margaret come to her. She wore a long, filmy gown, and seemed careless that its hem was washed by the waves. She was, like Lally, barefooted.

"Lovely to feel this cool wind, isn't it?" she said as she came close. "It made me feel energetic. That was a wonderful storm last night, wasn't it? Did you ever see anything like the lightning? I sat by the window and watched it . . ."

She had the beauty some women are fortunate enough to gain with pregnancy. She had, Lally thought, only grown more beautiful as she matured. Margaret was now twenty-eight. Lally never quite accepted the shock of Margaret's beauty; each year, when she saw her once again, she was startled by it. The haunting curve of her lips grew a little fuller, more sensuous, as if experience had fashioned it; the short bob of her hair displayed the long neck and the faintly arrogant angle of her chin to perfection. She seemed utterly the woman of her time, the epitome of those who had embraced their age, trying never to turn backward to the war, enjoying their fast cars, their parties, the bootleg gin, their jazz. She seemed to suit America, its tempo and its style.

They fell into step, Lally slowing to accommodate Margaret's pace. Nearly always, when Lally was alone with Margaret, she felt dumb and speechless. In all the years which had passed since the night they had found Margaret under the oak at Neatherby, staring at the wrecked car with the bodies of her brother and husband, Lally had never been able to surmount the barrier which had risen between them. It was there still, unacknowledged in words, but there. Margaret made overtures, and Lally accepted them superficially. To outsiders, it seemed that they were still the friends they had once been. But there had never been again the easy pleasure in each other's company. There had never been, from Lally, the trust. All that belonged to the time before she had had the sight of Jon, dead, with the rain beating on his face through the shattered windshield. She had only to look at Margaret, her hair carefully arranged over the tiny scar that remained from that night, to have that scene recalled.

"Everything," Lally said, aware that she spoke for the sake of speaking, "seems bigger in America—especially the storms." Because there seemed nothing else to say, she bent and took the wood once again from the dog, and hurled it into the surf.

She glanced sideways at the other woman, knowing that she was fiercely envious of the swollen belly, the labored walk. Margaret would have another child. Another child whom Brock would love, and spoil a little—as he loved and spoiled Margaret. It wasn't fair, Lally thought. Margaret had too much, when she had taken so much.

She didn't let herself speculate whether Margaret was happy in her marriage to Brock. Margaret had all the things she wanted; her life was filled with people and entertainments, and the pursuit of what she called "a good time." Did she even, Lally wondered, know what happiness in marriage was? It didn't seem to matter. And Brock had what he had sought. He had Margaret, and soon he would have his second child. He could display Margaret in the setting he thought she deserved. At times she thought she almost detected a sense of self-satisfaction in Brock. Certainly he had not caused the accident which had taken Margaret's husband, but he had known, instantly and immediately, how to exploit the situation. He had been prepared for prison in order to have Margaret. She was only the most prized of his possessions. She was the mistress of his house, she wore his clothes and his jewels, she had her portrait painted with his son. She was the ornament he had desired more than any other, the peak of his spectacular achievements. And she was still the spoiled child of the nursery of Pellham Langley.

They rounded the point of land, all of it private beach but open to those who could claim the friendship of the owners. Across from them they could see the deep two-storied porch, with its great columns, of Land's End. It belonged to Bayard Swope, and people said Scott Fitzgerald had written parts of *The Great Gatsby* there. Margaret halted and surveyed the new bay, which opened before them. Here the wind blew more strongly. "I'm getting tired," she said. "We'd better go back." She turned, and the wind lifted the long thin gown outward before her, so that her bulging shape disappeared, and she was Margaret as Lally had always known her, like a wayward spirit of the storm.

The years since that night she remembered too well seemed cruelly empty to Lally, although they had been busy years. After Margaret's marriage she had stayed a while longer with Black Jack and Edith at Pellham Langley, and known the uselessness of her existence. In desperation Black Jack had urged her to visit London. "Go and see what Susie's up to. It's time you took off your widow's weeds, Lally. You can't mourn Jon all your life."

"Why not?" she had demanded. "Who will replace him?"

Black Jack had looked at her sadly. "I can't offer you a replacement. I just can't believe it's right to behave as if your life's over when it's hardly begun. You'll find someone else . . ."

Susie had shaken her head when Lally had repeated the conversation. "Not so easy. Look around you . . . where have the men gone?"

It was true, and they all recognized it. Lally did all the things Black Jack expected of her. She shed the black dresses, and took tea at the Ritz with the acquaintances of her debutante season, and girls she had met in the VAD, went to the cocktail parties they gave, gave some in return. But the men were missing. Sometimes Jon was momentarily forgotten as she found herself envying the marriage of someone else. The world went in twos.

She talked about it to Susie. The other woman nodded. "That's about it. I've stopped looking, myself. I do get about a bit among the designers. Queer lot, mostly, but nice. Nice—but not to marry. But you'd better watch out, Lally. You've got money. That's always a temptation to some men."

Lally mentally ran through the very few eligible men she had encountered. "After being married to Jon, there isn't much temptation for me."

"I was always," Susie confessed, "just a bit afraid about you and Jon. You always seemed to think you'd got everything in one stroke. The whole of your life wrapped up in one man. It scared me a bit."

Lally shrugged. "I *was* wrapped up in one man. Yes, I thought I'd got the lot. I couldn't believe my own luck, but I didn't expect it to change. I thought I'd won the prize forever." She flung out her hands. "What am I going to do with the rest of my life? I can bring up Jonathan—and probably spoil him because he's all I've got. And one day he'll be grown up, and he'll go, too."

Susie lighted a cigarette. They were sitting in her workroom. The desk in front of Susie was littered with papers—sketches, order forms, bills, an overflowing ashtray.

"There's one thing I can think of. You can come in with me. There's work enough, Gawd knows. I can't pay much of a wage, but then you don't need it. Besides, you've inherited Jon's share of the business. Why don't you come and take care of it?"

"What on earth would I do? I can't design. And I certainly can't sew."

Susie gestured at the desk. "Clear this up. Get out and sell. Generally make yourself useful. Organize. You've got contacts—the sort of contacts Margaret had. Use them. Drum up business. In fact, act like Black Jack's daughter."

It had worked, in the sense Susie had meant it to. Lally rented a flat in a mansion block in Knightsbridge. It was far too large for her needs, but she took it because it had a pleasant view over Hyde Park. She thought she might begin to entertain a little, have a few dinner parties, or more conveniently, cocktail parties. At cocktail parties, some of Susie's dresses could be shown off. The flat had a room for a live-in maid, but she didn't want anyone there permanently with her. After the long stay at Pellham Langley, she found she relished the privacy of her own flat. A daily cleaning woman took care of her needs, and when she gave her small parties, an agency provided the extra help.

She was within walking distance of Susie's shop, and she settled, rather thankfully, into the business of learning to be in business. As she grew more absorbed, she forgot about the plans she had made for an active social life. She called herself "the manageress" and Susie was known as the designer. Susie now more rarely descended from the workroom to talk to customers. "You know how to talk to them, Lally. You give the place a bit of class." The activity kept Lally going through the winter after Margaret had gone to America. Sometimes at night she found she actually was tired, and sleep came easily. But most nights the sleep was short and dream-haunted, and the same dreams recurred—the dream of Jon, laughing, sure of himself, sure of the future. From this dream she would wake, shuddering and alone, and forgiveness of Margaret seemed impossible. And there was always the old dream of the dark place, the place from which Black Jack had taken her.

At weekends she returned to Pellham Langley. Each week Jonathan seemed to have grown, acquired some new skill, a word or two. He looked forward to her coming. As much as Lally tried she could not resist the urge never to return to him empty-handed. There was always some new toy, until the nursery shelves were packed. "I don't approve of it, Mrs. Pollock," Nanny had said. "The child mustn't be led to expect some new thing every time you come. It makes him greedy."

She couldn't help it. It often seemed to her that she lived through the week with the expectation of seeing the small face, already quite disturbingly like Jon's, light up at her appearance, the arms go out, his treble voice calling, "Mummy!" What did it matter if he also put out his hand for "the surprise"? It was a game they played. No harm in it, she told herself.

Except in the most bitter weather, in that winter of 1921, she spent each weekend walking on the moors. She took short, gentle walks with Jonathan, for as long as his small legs would carry him. Then she walked alone, or with Alice, hard walks to tire her to the bone. That was a different tiredness from the one she knew at the end of the day in Susie's shop—the day that often didn't end until Susie put away her pencils, long after the bustle of the daytime traffic around Knightsbridge had slowed to its evening pace. "Right then— let's go and have something to eat."

There was a small French restaurant nearby, Armand's, which they used. "Don't remember food like this in France," Susie said. But often they ended up at Lyons Corner House. "Ever so respectable," Susie mocked. But it served its purpose. It was all right for two women to be there unaccompanied. It was middle-class, and safe, and predictably dull. Each week Lally gave the news of Pellham Langley, reported on Jonathan's growth, his cleverness, his charm. Susie was interested in the state of business in the mills and the mines. "Your kid's all right, Lally. You see him just enough so that you don't get on each other's nerves, or trip over each other. Now your dad—that's something else. Quite a slowdown in his business, isn't there? Lots out of work."

"Yes, and Father hasn't jobs for them. No one seems to have jobs for them."

They had begun to see the effects of the war debts in the lines of jobless. "They say America's booming," Susie said reflectively. "What happened?"

"We spent ourselves broke just keeping going," Lally answered. "The balance of wealth tipped from Europe to America, because America could supply what we needed to keep going. When the war began we had credit balances there that've all turned to debits. I think that's how Brock would explain it."

Susie nodded; she drew on her cigarette thoughtfully. "Sounds like Brock himself. I often wonder about him and Margaret. Somehow I never imagined him the sort to fall in love. If he has a weak spot, she found it. Without really trying, she found it."

Lally tried to forget about Margaret, even tried to forget Jon in the weeks and months when she attempted to build something upon the sometimes seemingly fragile foundation of Susie's talent. She learned to run the showroom as Edith ran her drawing room, gently, but with firmness. She learned to hide her irritation with customers who could not, or would not, be pleased. She learned to encourage the diffident and the timid, introducing women to colors they had never dared wear before, to the simpler, easy styles in which Susie excelled. Business was reasonably good, and was getting better. "We've still," she said to Susie one night as they finished dinner at Armand's, "got to get women away from the idea that they should, if possible, look as if they're rich. Away from the lace and frills and tucks. And those iron corsets. You'd think women would be glad to jump out of them, at last. But they cling to them."

"They have to, duckie," Susie said. "That's all the support most of them have. Can't expect them to turn into Isadora Duncan overnight. We have to do it gently—almost so they don't notice." She stirred her coffee slowly. "I'd love to be a real designer—you know, make clothes that make headlines. But the average woman's frightened of those sort of things until they've almost gone out of fashion. But my business isn't to make headlines. My business is to make a success of the business I've got."

The spring came, and the moors grew green again, the meadow pipits rose singing. Jonathan was growing. "Like a weed," Black Jack said fondly. "It's time he saw his cousin again, Lally. Margaret's asking for us to come and visit this summer." That had been in 1922 when Margaret had announced she was pregnant. She had planned to come to England, but her doctor had forbidden it. Lally thought it was more likely that Brock had told her doctor to forbid it.

"*All* of us? That's a bit of a houseful."

"I think Brock's household can cope. Margaret doesn't live in a cottage."

"That's what Brock called it."

"That's what it's fashionable to call it—a summer cottage on the North Shore of Long Island. It's like saying you have a little shooting place in Scotland when you have thirty thousand acres. I think we should go. You know how Margaret gets when she's pregnant. Bored and irritable. She needs company."

Lally's whole being had risen in revolt. She didn't want anymore to be the one to ease Margaret's boredom and irritability. She didn't want to look at Margaret's body, swollen with Brock's child, when Margaret had taken away from her the man whose child should be swelling her own belly.

"I can't go," she said. "I've got my job. It's a real job, even if it's a small one. And I won't go all summer without Jonathan. Before I know what's happened, he'll have grown out of sight, and he won't know me."

"Isn't that being a little selfish?" Black Jack had said gently. "A summer in that sun—on the beach there—would do Jonathan a world of good. The voyage itself. He'd like to see David again."

"Rubbish!" Lally retorted. "He can't even remember David. What do you think a child of two and a half is going to make of an ocean voyage? Dine at the captain's table? Or just be seasick all the way?"

She had flounced out of the house, and walked alone on the moors above Pellham Langley, brooding on its solid mass, aware of the mood she had left behind her. Black Jack would not ease his gentle but unmistakable pressure. Since Jon's death he had grown strongly possessive of his remaining children, Lally among them. His two grandchildren were a signal of continuing life to him. Margaret's present pregnancy was a joy, a new hope for the future. He and Edith and Alice would go to America, and Lally knew, one way or another, she would be persuaded to go also. She hunched on the rock at the top of the waterfall, the valley with the chimneys behind her, the valley which contained the little world of Pellham Langley and its village before her. She remembered the promises she had given, unasked, to Black Jack. "Do I have to keep them all?" she demanded of herself.

She talked to Susie about it when she returned to London. "Of course I told him I couldn't go. Why—it would be two months. Who'd run the shop?"

"Think you've become indispensable, do you?" Susie said. But she smiled as she said it. "Here, let's have a brandy and think about it." When the brandy arrived they waited to warm it in their hands. Armand himself had come to serve it. "Everything all right, ladies?" They now had their own special table at Armand's, a corner table from which they could either view the room or turn away from it. They were welcome customers, even though there was never a gentleman to accompany them. "This is really being *solidly* respectable," Susie had once said.

Now she said, "Course you ought to go. Do you and the kid a

world of good. Look, you've gone and got that pale London look. Been working too hard." She held up her hand. "No—don't tell me I work too hard. I was *meant* to. I love it. A few weeks away wouldn't hurt you. Business is slack in the summer. Everyone's got their clothes for the season. I've already got most of the sketches done for the autumn. And it's time I got back on the shop floor. Time I heard what the customer has to say, not what I think she should say. Go on, it'd do us both good. Besides—what are you going to do with yourself? Can't let the kid go by himself. He should have his mother with him. And you can't keep him all alone up there in Yorkshire. Bloody selfish, I call it." It was then that Lally knew Black Jack had talked to Susie by telephone, and an alliance against her had been formed.

"I'll think about it," Lally said crossly, and choked a little on the brandy. Armand was concerned. It was his very best brandy.

So that had been the first of the summers they had gone to Long Island, and they had been each summer since. They had been there when Brock's first child had been born a month prematurely. Once again Margaret had had an agonizing ordeal. When Brock was told that his child had at last been born, a son, small but healthy, he had almost brushed the news aside. "My wife?" he had demanded. "Is my wife all right?"

"Tired—but all right. She must rest."

Brock had gone to her, held her lightly in his arms, before he had gone to look at his son. Lally realized that she had not only envied Margaret her child, but now she felt a twist of jealousy about Brock's concern for her. She thrust the thought aside. She had wanted only Jon's love. Or had she come to envy any woman who possessed a man's love? She forced herself to kiss Margaret on the forehead.

"You did it again. Frightened us all half to death. But he's a lovely baby—worth the effort."

The baby was christened Daniel John. "Dan's a good Yankee name," Brock had said. "And if he could manage to grow up just a bit like Black Jack, I couldn't be more proud."

Because of the premature birth of the baby and Margaret's slow recovery, they stayed on in Long Island a few weeks longer than they had planned. Lally began to fret. "I must get back. It isn't fair to Susie."

But a cable had come from Susie. *Managing all right. Kiss the baby for me.* Lally began to imagine the cable Black Jack had sent to

Susie to elicit this response. She sat with Margaret on the deep-shaded porch of the rented house in the heat of an August afternoon and wondered what she was supposed to do with the rest of her life. Work with Susie seemed the only thing—it would have to be enough.

In a sand pit, hats on against the fierce summer sun, David and Jonathan played, joyously dumping buckets of sand over each other's heads, paying no attention to Nanny Dunstable's remonstrances. At the other end of the porch, Nanny Williams rocked the cradle which held the new baby, Dan. Alice sat beside her, just staring at the baby's face, occasionally leaning forward to touch the tiny fingers, to stroke the unbelievable smoothness of the cheek. Alice spent much time with David and Jonathan, and as much time holding the new baby as anyone would permit her. She gravitated between one and the other, the draw of the children seemingly irresistible.

"Lally?" Margaret's tone was gentle, tentative. She was stretched on a chaise, and Lally had thought her asleep. Lally turned.

"Lally, can you ever forgive me?"

"It's all over, Margaret. Let's not talk about it. You're not to distress yourself."

Amazingly, tears stood out in Margaret's eyes. Lally put them down to weakness after the birth. Margaret did not cry for other people. "I feel the anger in you all the time. Anger you shut away from other people. Lally, don't hate me. I need you."

"Need me? You don't need me. You have Brock—your children."

"I need you. I wish I could keep you here with me all the time. I would be better if you were here, Lally. You'd keep me—steadier. I do wild things at times. Mad things. And Brock lets me have my own way. As long as it isn't another man, he'd let me have anything in the world. Almost like Father. But you'd be tougher with me."

Lally thrust back her chair abruptly and rose. "You can't have me along with everything else. I can't be your keeper forever." And she had marched to the sand pit, unheeding Margaret's despairing, wailing cry behind her. The sun seemed to strike her head like an iron. She felt guilty and miserable, and it was too hot. She held out her hands to the two children. "Come, boys—we'll go for a walk to the beach." They scrambled to their feet, picking up buckets and spades. Alice was running across the lawn. Nanny Dunstable said, "You will have them back by teatime, Mrs. Pollock? You're sure you don't want me to come?"

"No, Nanny. It's too hot for you."

"I'm not sure it isn't too hot for us all. I'd rather the children rested all afternoon. And do keep their hats on, Mrs. Pollock."

Alice arrived, panting. "I can come too?" She grasped David's hand tightly and started to skip across the lawn to the path through the pines that led toward the beach.

"And *do* watch Miss Alice with the children, Mrs. Pollock," Nanny said. "She gets so excited just to be allowed to do something with them. Why just the other day when we went down to the shore she suddenly pulled them both out of my hands and *romped* into the water. All wet they got—all of them. They hadn't got their bathing costumes on, or anything. She stood there and laughed, and a wave came and rolled right over them. I had to wade in up to my own knees to get them out. Got soaked myself. It's easy to forget, Mrs. Pollock, that she isn't . . . well, she isn't quite responsible, is she? She loves them dearly, of course. At times I think she yearns for her own child. Poor lamb, that she'll never have."

Lally had walked the shore with the two children and Alice, Margaret's plea echoing with every beat of the waves on the sand. Forgiveness had been asked of her, but it came hard; she could attempt it only for Black Jack's sake. She watched the laughing boys, each with a hand trustingly in Alice's, saw the happiness in Alice's face, and knew how it would be reflected in Black Jack's when Alice related the simple pleasures of their walk, named those they had met on the beach, showed him the shells they had found. It would have been, as Black Jack said, selfish to hold these two children apart, to deny Alice the joyful experience of knowing both of them, of spending the days with the new baby. It would be selfish to deny Black Jack the consolation of knowing that she and Margaret were reconciled. She couldn't doubt that he missed Jon as much as she did, but he had had the grace to forgive Margaret, where she could only make a pretense of it. They turned back when the shadows started to lengthen, and a little coolness came to the air. Lights were starting to go on in the big house that Brock called a cottage; the baby had been taken to the nursery; Nanny Dunstable was waiting to take the boys to their supper and their bath. Black Jack and Edith were sitting with Margaret on the porch. The drink tray had been brought out by a manservant; Black Jack rose and came down the steps to meet them. He scooped up each little boy in turn and swung him high in the air. "Now, Sir John," came Nanny Dunstable's voice, "you shouldn't be exciting them just when I've got to get them calmed down for their baths and supper."

Yes, it would be selfish to deny them what they all wanted, Lally had thought. She bent over Margaret, who had straightened and sat up as she approached. She kissed her lightly on the forehead. "Hope you had a little nap while we were away." Black Jack smiled on her, and Margaret turned her face upward with a smile.

"No . . . but I'm sure I shall sleep tonight. Father, do give me a drink, will you? A nice dry martini."

Black Jack had mixed drinks for them all. They had sat in the growing dusk until the lights of Brock's car flashed among the trees along the drive. It was the signal for Black Jack to mix him a drink. Brock kissed Margaret first, then accepted the chilled glass from his father-in-law. "Well, and how are all my beautiful girls? And how are my boys?" He included his stepson, Lord Grenfell, with as much ease as he had responded to the birth of his own son. The heir to an earldom he might be, Brock's manner implied, but until he was grown he would be his, Brock's, responsibility, something gladly taken on because he was Margaret's son. He took a chair close to Margaret, touched her hand briefly, then took a slow sip of his drink. "Ah, well . . . that's another day done with. Hot as the hinges of hell in Manhattan today. Been looking forward to this moment since I got to the office this morning . . ."

He was a generous and welcoming host, Lally thought. He gave the endless parties Margaret demanded, because she loved to mix with people, to dance, to talk. He enjoyed the moments to show her off, but Lally knew that these moments for Brock were the best ones, when Margaret was quiet, and seemingly content. Darkness had fallen steadily. The cicadas sung. It was almost time to go up and dress for dinner. Turning, Lally found Brock's gaze on her, intently, almost questioningly. Was he, too, waiting for the break, the final gesture of forgiveness from her toward Margaret? She got up quickly. "I'll just look in on the boys before I change. See if there's anything—"

Brock rose also. "I'll go with you, Lally. Have to hug those guys good night. And my new little guy, if Nanny will permit it." He walked up the broad staircase, the half-finished drink still in his hand. They reached the nursery floor, and Brock's hand touched her lightly.

"Thanks for being here this summer, Lally. It's meant a lot to me.

It's made Margaret happy to have you here." Suddenly his arm
checked her walk; he turned her to face him. "You don't have to tell
me it wasn't easy for you to do what you've done for Margaret.
You're very dear to me, Lally." His hold was released. "Try to come
back next summer, will you? Even if it's just to please me."

They were leaving the next day. In every room the steamer trunks
stood, almost packed. The summer was over, Lally thought, and she
would be free.

"I'd do almost anything to please you, Brock," she said. "But I
don't know if I can give whole summers of my life . . . I have a
business to run, too."

He nodded. "I know. You and I, we'll always work, won't we?
But a little time to rest and have fun can't hurt."

She said, "I suppose I do take things too seriously. I don't quite
seem to know how to have fun, not in the way everyone here understands it." She added quickly, because after tomorrow she would not
see him for a long time, and it was suddenly important to say it,
"You're . . . you're very dear to me, too, Brock."

She was rewarded by his smile. They were at the door of the nursery. He opened it, and went directly to the big bathroom where the
two little boys were together in their bath. For the next fifteen minutes he industriously sailed boats with them, helped them dry themselves in the huge bath sheets, held pajama legs for them to step into.

"Listen, you guys," he said at the end of it. "You're going to have
to learn to do this for yourselves. You're not going to have me for a
valet much longer." David thought this very funny. He didn't understand what a valet was, but he liked Brock fussing over him. He liked
it that Brock had not gone immediately to the new baby. Brock had
become the father David couldn't remember. He took the children
into the simple white room that was the night nursery. This window
at the top of the house gave a view of the Sound; there were the riding lights of the yachts at anchor. Across the bay a house was lighted
up for a party. Very faintly, on a small night breeze, they heard the
first tentative sounds of a saxophone. Brock was suddenly in a hurry,
and gave the two boys over to Nanny's charge. He went briefly into
the room where his son slept, and looked down on him. Lally understood his sudden haste. It was the time of the evening when Margaret
grew restless. She would have heard that faraway sound of the saxophone on the summer night. Her still-weak body would have stirred,
and perhaps trembled. Brock had to be by her side.

Lally watched him go. She was glad that tomorrow they would leave. Sometimes it was uncomfortable to witness the intensity of Brock's feeling for Margaret, and to know Margaret's insatiable need for movement, for people, for music, and, sometimes, for drink. It was as if she, too, turned and turned endlessly, seeking distraction, seeking forgetfulness of that September night in the rain at Neatherby.

That first summer, three summers ago, had set the pattern for the years in between. Black Jack, Edith, and Alice set off early in June, taking Jonathan and Nanny Dunstable with them. Lally followed in July. They were usually back at Pellham Langley in August, though not always in time for the opening of the grouse-shooting season. Then it was Edith's task to return the hospitality they received with increasing lavishness on Long Island. The visit to Pellham Langley became, for some of the residents of those mansions along the North Shore, part of the summer or early autumn visit to Europe. When Brock had rented, as he persisted in saying, the Brewster house, Margaret had immediately started to give the larger parties the house permitted. For Lally it seemed there was scarcely a night when Margaret didn't entertain, or that they did not go to some other house to have dinner, later to dance to jazz records, or, if it were a real party, to dance to some big-name jazz band brought from Manhattan. Sometimes they drove into Manhattan to dance—the Cotton Club in Harlem was the favorite place. Lally wondered, as she saw Brock hurry from his car, sometimes to go immediately upstairs to change, how he stood the pace of his daily business life, and the parties that flowed one into the other. It was as if he lived his life to the ever-increasing beat of that syncopated rhythm. But he never seemed to flag or falter. Occasionally Black Jack begged a halt. "I'm getting on, Margaret. You forget. The old boy must have his rest."

"Oh, nonsense, Father. You have plenty of time for rest all winter at Pellham. Enjoy yourself."

"Perhaps we have different notions of enjoyment." But still he also struggled to keep up. He enjoyed, Lally thought, his summers in the sun, but in the weeks there he looked forward to the moment when he would climb above the waterfall at Pellham and look down on his world, breathing the cool, sweet air. He went to Whytecliffe because he needed the sight of Margaret and his two grandsons to reassure himself that all of life was not centered in Jonathan, as it tended to be when they were alone at Pellham Langley. He witnessed Brock's son, Dan, taking his first steps the summer after he was born. This, too, was a new life he rejoiced in. Alice looked forward to the annual trip eagerly. Once the snow left the Yorkshire moors she began to talk about the shore, the beach, the sun. She began to talk about the rides in Brock's big motor launch, which was anchored out in the Sound, about the exhilaration of sailing with Margaret in the little skiff, *Fancy,* which was Margaret's own, but which Brock feared and hated, and would have forbidden her to use if he. had thought she would have obeyed him. Alice found the quarrels about the skiff amusing. "Come, darling," Margaret would say to her. "We'll just go and show stuffy old Brock how easily we can handle it." And from the terrace of Whytecliffe Brock would watch, binoculars clamped to his eyes, their progress across the bay, the insouciance with which Margaret asserted the right of sail over power, and skimmed under the bows of the big yachts using their auxiliary power. Usually she knew the owners, and would wave gaily at them. Once, sitting on the terrace with Brock when Margaret had gone out sailing alone, Lally heard Brock mutter, "Little wretch. The way she waves at them she might as well thumb her nose. Of course they all think she's mad— and a delight. It's the same when she hunts. Always at the head of the field. They all know about the way her mother killed herself hunting. I sometimes suspect they're waiting for the same thing to happen to Margaret." He started frantically to gesture with his arm. "Come about, you fool," he shouted, although Margaret could not possibly have heard him. He watched in silence as the little craft went out toward the middle of the Sound. Only when, at last, she had put about, the gay red sail making a bright splash of color among the more sober yachts, did he lower the glasses. "I swear some night I'll go down and hole that boat, and sink it. She does it just to torment me. She knows I'm in a sweat every moment she's out there."

"Why don't you go with her?"

"She won't invite me. It's all part of the big joke, Lally. Old sober-sided Brock worrying his hair gray over his mad capricious wife cavorting all over the place. That's what they say, Lally. They say I'm too old for her. They say I'm not good enough for her. They say I'm a jumped-up nobody with an instinct for money, and the sense to know an object of value when he sees it. They wonder what happens to the hard-eyed man of business when he looks at his wife. They say I make a fool of myself over her—and they're right."

"You could never be a fool." Lally said it quite coldly. "You carry on to amuse her, and beneath it you know exactly what you're doing. And she's just that faintest bit afraid that the hard-eyed man of business will surface at any time—as I've seen him do. She's like a child, teasing you to see how far you'll let her go. And all the time wanting to know that the nursery is there, safe and sound, waiting to take her back to the quiet when she's tired of the games."

He turned on her. "And that makes me her nanny, does it? God-damn it, I'm her husband." He walked away from her, deliberately ignoring Margaret's progress back toward the jetty. He did not run down the steps to help her furl the sail as he always did when she returned. He turned and went back up the steps from the lower terrace to the house. The little red sail skipped merrily through the bigger vessels riding at anchor. Margaret had developed a considerable skill in handling her little craft, and loved to show it off. Resignedly, Lally started for the dock. Margaret was not likely to stow things tidily if she did not have help. Alice came flying out of the house and down the wide stairs. "Margaret went without me. She promised. And Brock's angry. What did Margaret do to make Brock angry with me?"

Lally took her hand and waited for the impudent little skiff to tack to the dock. "Nothing, Alice. You've done nothing. Brock could never be angry with you."

Alice looked up doubtfully to the open doorway through which Brock had vanished. "Sometimes I don't like Margaret," she said. "Sometimes she wants to laugh at me. And sometimes she laughs at Brock. No one should ever laugh at Brock. After Father, I love him best of all the men in the world."

Lally felt uneasy, wondering what thoughts stirred in Alice's only half-logical mind. "When people are married, Alice, they sometimes seem to quarrel, but they really don't. Margaret only likes to tease Brock a little. It's because she loves him and it's a sort of a game, you see. And she would never laugh at you, Alice. Margaret wouldn't do that. She loves you. Come with me now, darling. Let's go down and help Margaret with the sails."

Alice backed away. "No, I don't think I will. I don't think I'll help Margaret with anything today."

* * *

Each year, except the summer when Dan had been born, Margaret paid her yearly visit to the Goughs at Dentdale, and then came with relief to Pellham Langley. "I know I have to go there," she said to Lally. "They've a right to see their only grandchild. But I find it so dreadfully *mournful*. They're getting old, poor things, and he's the only interest in their lives—or it seems that way to me. They talk incessantly about him, question me about every single thing he does. And Nanny Williams. They have her down to the library and go through a real catalog of what he does every day, what he eats, what sort of children he plays with. Does he ride? Does he have proper supervision? I think she dreads it all as much as I do. They can hardly wait for him to be old enough to go to Eton. Then they'll have him every holiday except in summer. Poor David. He'll find it dreadfully hard. That gloomy big house and he the sole object of the attention of two old people. I can't stand it myself. I bought a Victrola and some records, and played them to myself in my room. Lady Gough came in one day and found me dancing by myself, and she nearly fainted when she saw the martini shaker. Oh, well . . . it's only two weeks a year. But I wish I didn't have to go through it. Sometimes I'm tempted to leave David there by himself and dash down to London, but that would be too cruel."

At the end of the visit to Dentdale and to Pellham Langley, she went to London, to the suite Brock still maintained at the Ritz. While Nanny Williams shopped for all the things that a properly brought up English boy should have, Margaret gave a series of lunches, cocktail parties, and dinner parties, went to theaters and nightclubs. All the old London contacts were renewed, and people, just back from shooting in Scotland, were glad to see her. She was in the papers, and written about in *Tatler*. She required Lally's presence at all these occasions, striving to introduce her to the few eligible men she knew. Lally now realized that half of Margaret's burden of guilt would be lifted if Lally should remarry. Lally found she could not conveniently fall in love to help Margaret.

Margaret suggested a visit to Deauville. Lally was unenthusiastic. "Somehow I didn't think you'd gamble again."

"Oh, for heaven's sake, Lally, don't start being stuffy with me. Brock's got loads of money for me to gamble with. And I don't lose so much. It isn't like poor Taylor's wages—" She stopped. "Oh, damn, can't I ever be free of that night? If only—Lally! Don't go! All right, we'll forget about Deauville. You can write and tell Brock what a good influence you are on me. Look, let's go and buy some clothes. Let's take Susie out to lunch first, and then we'll do a tour of the *couturiers*. She could fill her eyes. . . . Oh, yes, let's do that. We really don't have to *buy* anything."

Susie appeared for lunch at the Ritz in clothes that made almost every woman in the room look overdressed. The pert little face surveyed the room with amusement. "There's some great architect going around saying 'less is more.' Good idea, if you ask me. Yes, please," she said to the waiter. "I'll have a dry martini."

"Susie, you look wonderful," Margaret said. "And you're doing wonders. It's not just what Lally tells me. Father says so too, and he isn't given to over-praising. I think he thought it was all just a bit of a joke when Jon and I backed you. Now he's actually telling me that for once I showed a bit of business acumen. I don't dare tell him it was a dull, wet afternoon, and we all needed something to get excited about."

"*I* don't forget. I'm grateful to you, Margaret." Susie sipped her martini slowly, and nodded approval. "Don't often take lunch hour off, do we, Lally? Makes a nice change."

"You *work* too hard, both of you. If you hadn't dragged Lally in, Susie, I think I could get her to spend more time on Long Island. And a few weeks in Palm Beach in the winter would do everyone a world of good. I can't understand why Father and everyone else won't come and spend some time in Palm Beach."

Susie set her glass down. "You've got to understand, Margaret, that we can't all give up whatever it is that's our lives, and rush off to fritter away the time with you. Where would your dad be with his mills and his mines? He's a Yorkshireman, don't you see? If you kept him away from his Yorkshire, the mills and the mines as well as the moors, then he wouldn't be Black Jack Pollock. Just like me." She held out her neat, always skillful, hands. "I'm a working woman, Margaret. What you did gave me the chance. Now it's going well, and the two workrooms are going flat out, and we really have to have a third, you couldn't drag me away from it for all the tea in China. Or all the dresses in Paris."

Margaret's face lighted. "*That's* a good idea, Susie. We'll go to Paris. Have a good hard look at all the clothes. Brock would approve of that. We could look at the clothes, and have a good time. And Susie would come back with her head stuffed full of ideas."

"Well . . ." Susie said. "Might be a good idea. The fashion magazines only tell me so much. I'd like to be able to see the fabrics, and try to figure out how to reproduce them at a tenth of the price and

still not look cheap." She suddenly confessed. "I'd *love* to see the
Chanel collection. She designs the sort of clothes I'd like to see every
woman wearing."

Margaret said, "You know, Susie, I wish you'd *really* start up. I
mean . . . a salon in Mayfair. You'd make it, I know. Father and
Brock would back you. It wouldn't be just the little bit of money Jon
and I invested. I *know* they'd go for it."

Susie set down her glass. "Try to understand, Margaret. I'd like to
go to Paris with you and Lally. I'd like to look at the clothes, and try
to copy those I think can be copied for my sort of customer. But I
didn't start up to dress the rich. What I want to do is try to get some
ready-made, decently designed clothes into drapers' shops in the
High Streets all over England. We're beginning, Lally and I, to persuade some of the big shops in the provinces to take our line, to get
the customer into ready-made clothes instead of getting her little
dressmaker to try to copy some fashion out of a magazine that's just
too damn fancy, and won't work unless it's made in real silk. Margaret, if I'm ever going to make my million—oh, yes, I intend to
make a million—it'll be dressing the woman who can't afford to go to
Mayfair. The woman who's frightened to come to London to shop—
even if she has the money. There's millions of women out there just
dying for something with a little style that doesn't cost a fortune.
Lally knows. There's a lot of interest in what we're trying to do.
They're the sort of clothes I'd have loved to have had myself—oh,
ages ago. Before the war. Before women like me ever did anything
except go into domestic service, or, if we were lucky, get a job
behind a counter. I'm still one of those women, Margaret. I want to
see them well-dressed. And I think there's a fortune to be made in
it."

Margaret leaned back in her chair. Almost absentmindedly she
signaled the waiter for another drink. "You know, when you get
going, you remind me so much of Brock. It's that same sort of passion."

Susie pursed her lips, and her eyelid wrinkled in what might be
thought to be a wink. "Brock's ideas are much bigger than mine, but
I suppose we dream the same dreams." She raised her glass. "Well,
ladies, shall we go to Paris . . . ? Yes, I'd rather fancy a few days in
Paris stealing ideas."

They had their days in Paris. Susie sat demurely in the salons of
the *haute couture* while Margaret demanded to see many models,

and bought a few. There was a rush to do the fittings because Mrs. Weymouth had to return to America. The *directrice* threw up her hands and declared that no *couture* clothes could be made in a hurry; the *vendeuse* hissed that they would lose the sale. Margaret got her way. They all bought something from the Chanel boutique. Back in their hotel, Susie fell on the garments, examined them in detail. "You see," she cried, almost despairingly, "how can anyone compete? Look at this—every inch of it lined, so it'll hold its shape. Every seam bound. Wouldn't come apart in a million years."

"But we're not making clothes to last a million years," Lally said. "Just a few years. And to make a few thousand women happy. Not a bad ambition."

"I'm going," Margaret announced, "to talk seriously to Brock about all this. I'm sure he could arrange a much bigger investment in you, Susie. Much bigger money than Jon and I had. It would give you the workrooms you need—and sales people. Lally could take care of that end of it."

Susie looked doubtful. "We're just about breaking even now—that is, with paying back the loan. I'm not sure that I'm ready to take on something much bigger. Suppose I lost it all?"

Suddenly Lally was sure; she wouldn't allow Susie to waver. "Win or lose, I think Brock would be in there with you. And I'll speak to Father. It's got to be done right, if it's to be done at all. First, I think we have to close the shop to the public. We can't afford the time to look after that woman wandering in off the street. We'll have to have mannequins just for the buyers to see wearing the clothes. And hope we get volume orders."

"There goes my beautiful little shop," Susie moaned. "I felt so safe with that shop. Not too big, but just a bit grand." She looked from one woman to the other. "I wanted to stay small and quiet and be just a little bit successful."

"Brock isn't interested in being just a little bit successful, Susie. If you want to interest him, you'll have to expand."

Susie let the garment fall from her hands. "You've got me. I'll tell you—I'm shaking in my shoes, and I'm dying to plunge in. The 'Poor Woman's Chanel.' That's what I'd really like to be."

"Well, then," Lally said, "we'd better get back to London. You, Margaret, sail for New York on Thursday night. We'd better pick up your beautiful son, and get you back to your adoring husband."

"Lally, won't you—"

Lally cut off the plea. "You've told Susie she had to do it the big way. Well, she needs help. That means me." She shook her head. "Margaret, I can't come back with you."

Susie said quietly, "You can tell me it's none of my business, Margaret. But don't you think it's time you left Lally out of your life? Kind of—well, stood on your own feet?"

A fleeting shadow of panic crossed Margaret's face. "I don't see how I can leave Lally out of my life. At times, she's been all I had." Margaret bent and began to fold the dress Susie had let fall on the sofa. "It's something you don't understand, Susie. Lally's always . . ." The silk dress slipped from the sofa to the floor. Margaret turned and went to her bedroom at a pace which was almost a run.

Susie looked at Lally, bewildered. "What on earth . . . ?"

Lally carefully picked up the dress, her voice deliberately calm, though her hands shook a little. "It really is something you don't understand, Susie. However close you are to us both. It all began a long time ago . . ."

Yes, a long time ago. The nights in the nursery at Pellham Langley, the hot afternoons in Italy, the shared season in London, the shared fear during the war. It had reached its climax that night at Neatherby in the rain. Now she walked with Margaret on the beach at Whytecliffe, and very soon Brock's second child would be born. They were all gathered as they had been for the birth of Dan, who was now three years old. David and Jonathan were five and a half. David had started at a small private school on the North Shore last September, and at the same time a young man, Mark Shaw, had come to tutor Jonathan at Pellham Langley. Lally had reacted violently against the implied privilege of Jonathan having a teacher all to himself. "What's wrong," she asked Black Jack, "with the village school here at Pellham?"

"It's a fine and fair idea, my love, but we aren't yet a fine and fair society. You *know* where Jonathan belongs. It's not in the village school."

Lally had, with Black Jack, interviewed all the candidates who had answered the advertisement, and in the end had chosen someone Black Jack hadn't completely approved of. "I'd have liked a jollier person for Jonathan. They have to be together a lot."

Lally had chosen Mark Shaw because she sensed that he needed the job. He had taught for a time at a prep school, and had had to give up his post because his asthmatic condition did not permit him to partake in the rough and tumble of school life. Lally and he had paced the terrace of Pellham Langley while she strove to find the questions she should ask. Mark Shaw walked with a limp, though he easily kept up with her pace. They walked beyond the topiary garden to the gate that led to the moors. He had halted there, staring, listening. His eyes had gone to the path that led to the waterfall. "One almost imagines one hears Cathy—her voice on the wind. Calling to Heathcliff. Calling—" He had turned and his face had colored and his lips clamped down. "You must think me a romantic fool. I'll never be a Heathcliff, that's certain. Too weak even to be a schoolmaster. One small boy is all I'm capable of keeping up with."

Lally remembered that he had served during the war. "What was your war service, Mr. Shaw?"

"I was just old enough to serve for four months in 1918. A whiff of gas at the St. Quentin Canal, and then while I was trying to crawl away, a piece of shrapnel in the leg. They didn't send me back. *Your* husband won the M.C., Mrs. Pollock."

"Yes . . ." Why should she turn Jonathan over to this slightly embittered young man, a man who envied a dead hero, just because he was a hero, a man who seemed even to envy the fictional character of Heathcliff because he was the figure of a strong man? And yet something about the way he had looked longingly at the moors, had breathed the cold, wind-driven air, as if his lungs could not have enough of it, touched and moved her.

"Are you a good teacher, Mr. Shaw?"

"I can't say, Mrs. Pollock. I think of myself as a failure. That's not, I know, the thing to say to a prospective employer."

"Then do you like to walk? Would you like to walk here on the moors with Jonathan?"

He had looked once more directly at her, and a sort of passion had twisted those tense lips. "I'd like that more than anything I can express."

"Then you shall, Mr. Shaw. Be kind to my son. Teach him as well as you can. Let him enjoy the few years he's got before he must go to school."

Black Jack had demurred. "You really can't give a chap a job because you pity him."

"His qualifications are very good." She had been rereading his letter of application. "Too good to be a tutor just to a small boy. Let's hope Jonathan benefits. And the air here will do him good. After all, you couldn't expect a rugby halfback to lock himself up here."

Nanny Dunstable had handed Jonathan over to Mark Shaw's care reluctantly. "I would have liked to see a more *outgoing* type myself. But then, Mrs. Pollock's so softhearted," she said to Black Jack. She would go immediately into the employ of another family. "Of course, I'm the old-fashioned type of nanny. They say we're a dying race. Like Mr. Billings. Where would you find a butler like Mr. Billings?"

Billings still ruled at Pellham Langley, though he performed little more than token duties. He had three footmen under him, and he complained bitterly of the quality of the help which offered itself. "You'd think, wouldn't you, Miss Lally, that with so many out of work, we'd have our pick?" Even though he only supervised the serving of meals, he still kept the cellar books, still ordered Black Jack's cigars and cigarettes. The cook of Lally's childhood and growing-up years had retired. There was a new cook at Pellham Langley, and she conferred daily with Edith Pollock, but there never was a housekeeper.

"Good gracious," Edith had exclaimed, "aren't I capable of running my own household? And would I break Billings' heart? He still thinks he runs the place."

On Long Island Nanny Williams had sighed plaintively to Lally when she had arrived, a few weeks after the others, at Whytecliffe. "I do miss Mrs. Dunstable, Mrs. Pollock. I suppose Mr. Shaw's all right —though a bit moody for my taste. I always looked forward to Nanny Dunstable coming back. We used to talk about the old days . . ." For all her nostalgic reminiscences of England, Lally knew that Nanny Williams now thought of herself as being firmly located in America, and she enjoyed the greater comforts and higher salary offered to her there. With Dan only three years old, and another child on the way, she looked forward to years of employment with the Weymouths. As she had once said to Nanny Dunstable, and Nanny Dunstable had duly related to Lally, "Mrs. Weymouth . . . she's the sort to keep me on, even when the children don't need a nanny. Without Miss Lally, she leans on me. I'm part of home to her. Mr. Weymouth, I know, doesn't like her to be alone. I never say a word, of course. I just sit there knitting, or watching Master Daniel and his little playmates, and she just lies on the chaise, and either talks or doesn't talk, as the mood takes her. I can't help being fond of her. Sometimes I think she's still a little girl. Sometimes, too, she reminds me terribly of Miss Alice, even though they're only half sisters. Not quite responsible, if you understand what I mean. Mr. Weymouth, he looks to me to . . . well . . . protect her. As if I were her nanny, too."

For Brock she had only praise. She said forthrightly to Lally, "He's a fine father to Lord Grenfell, and Master Daniel, and such a kind husband to Mrs. Weymouth. Kind to me, too, Mrs. Pollock. Why, he's even taken my little bit of savings and invested it in the stock market for me. He looks after it personally. My port—portfolio, he calls it."

Nanny Williams had bridled a little when Lally had looked surprised. "Well, Mrs. Pollock, why not? Everyone's getting rich in America, aren't they? Even the little people like me. Mind you, Mr. Weymouth didn't want to take my savings and invest them. He wanted me to take a loan from him, and just leave my savings where they were. But I insisted. So he's put them in the most secure investments. He gave me the list, and I look them up every day in *The Wall Street Journal*. They're rising all the time. Some people make nasty remarks about how Mr. Weymouth made his money. And I say if there was anything wrong with Mr. Weymouth he wouldn't be in the position he is today. To me, he's a true gentleman."

By the time Lally reached Long Island that year Mark Shaw had cast aside the heavy tweeds he wore in Yorkshire and acquired some light clothes, which he wore with a certain air of unease, as if he didn't trust the warm weather to last another day. But his pale face had acquired a suntan, and he liked to swim. He looked almost relaxed, Lally thought, but he still said little when he was with the family. He had insisted on continuing lessons for Jonathan for several hours a day, and he included David in them. His concession to the holidays was that the lessons were often conducted on one of the terraces of Whytecliffe. He had been outraged to learn that David had not yet started on Latin and Greek. "They are both enrolled for Eton, Mr. Weymouth," he said coolly. "Do you want Lord Grenfell to go there looking a fool?"

"Never thought of him as a fool," Brock answered dryly. "But isn't five a little young to start worrying about Latin declensions?"

Mark Shaw's shrug indicated what he thought of American education. "Better start to worry, Mr. Weymouth, because at his prep school and Eton, they'll *beat* the Latin declensions into him."

Margaret's face was twisted with anxiety. "Oh, I wish he didn't have to go to that dreadful place."

"*Noblesse oblige,* Mrs. Weymouth," Mark Shaw said. "He will take his beatings as all the English aristocracy have. And if he survives Eton, he'll never have to survive anything tougher."

After that, on fine mornings at Whytecliffe, they could hear the treble voices of the two boys chanting, "*Amo . . . amas . . . amat.*" And then David bursting into laughter as Alice appeared and he rushed to accept her hug. "I *amo* you, Alice."

"Lord Grenfell," Mark Shaw said coldly, "not only is that incorrect, but Miss Pollock is not permitted to interrupt our lesson period."

"Miss Pollock . . . ? Miss Pollock . . . ?" David queried. "But it's only Alice. Alice can do anything she wants. Father and Mother say so. Grandfather says so. Everyone loves Alice. She's so beautiful, don't you think, Mr. Shaw? *Amo,* Alice . . ." And the laughter began again.

Mark Shaw had blushed painfully. He was the only one of the household not at ease with Alice, not knowing quite how to treat her. He was invariably courteous, but reserved. He did not take easily to a young woman of twenty-three whose great beauty would have made her outstanding in any situation but who was also, at times, quite embarrassingly childlike. He was almost the same age as Alice, and he seemed unable to accept the fact that she still carried about a battered creature, much mended by Susie's skillful fingers, whom she called Teddy Rose. And she still clutched dolls, Madame Butterfly, whose beautiful silk gown Susie had had to work long hours to try to restore, and Raggedy Ann, who lived up to her name. She sang to them, cradled them, talked to them.

"Shouldn't she," he once said to Lally, "have a . . . a companion?"

"You mean a nurse? A keeper, Mr. Shaw?"

"Well . . ."

"We think our love is sufficient, Mr. Shaw. We tried . . . a companion. Alice didn't like her. She sensed she was being watched, and not always lovingly. Once that woman locked her in, and if she hadn't been going of her own accord, Sir John would have dismissed her."

"I think you have all spoiled her. She could act much more sensibly if you had made her. She is everyone's pet, and no one must touch her—"

"No, Mr. Shaw. *No* one must touch her. And I really don't think that Miss Pollock is any part of your business. Beat Latin into the head of my son, if you must, and into the very unwilling head of Lord Grenfell, but pay no attention to Alice. She is very special to us —a child of nature."

"A child of nature . . ." He started to cough. The cough and a tendency to asthma were relics of the wartime gassing. Lally waited until the paroxysm passed. Finally Mark Shaw drew in a long deep breath, his eyes streaming. "Isn't that a rather dangerous idea, Mrs. Pollock?"

"I see no danger in what is beautiful and innocent."

But Lally noticed that Mark Shaw rarely addressed Alice directly, that he appeared to avoid being alone in her company. But he was, she had to admit, good with the boys, and was not pedantic in the way he taught them; he would ride with them in place of the groom, looking faintly displeased only when it was suggested that Alice join them. "I cannot be held responsible for Miss Pollock," he declared firmly.

"She will be no trouble," Black Jack assured him. "Alice, as you know, is good on a horse. She has no fear. She seems to have some natural rapport with animals. It gives her pleasure, Mr. Shaw. It gives her something to do. Unfortunately, filling time for Alice is not easy. She reads so slowly, and her concentration is so poor. But riding and walking and swimming . . . those she loves."

Mark Shaw thereafter reluctantly included Alice when he rode with David and Jonathan, or took them on long walks along the bridle paths of the North Shore, or along the beaches. He was a good amateur naturalist. He pointed out the birds, the differences between the species on that continent and in Europe; he directed their attention to the plants and the grasses, the bees that nosed among them. He shared their delight in the chipmunks and the squirrels. But he focused his attention solely on the boys, and let Alice trail along, picking up what she cared to learn. She followed eagerly, listening with absorbed attention, but seemed to remember little. But she strove to please. Lally and Mark Shaw sat one day on the lower terrace of Whytecliffe and watched Alice as she roamed the beach. The distant figure grew tiny, and Lally was about to go and bring her back when she turned and started toward the house. The wind blew her hair and her dress wildly. She climbed the steps of the terrace, her face flushed and shining, and she crooned a song whose words were blown with the wind. Her arms were filled with a wild assortment of foliage and grasses she had collected, a jumble of honeysuckle, marigolds, and daisies which she had plucked unthinkingly from the gardens around the boathouses, or beneath the sea walls of the great mansions; with them were mixed rank weeds. At the sight of her, Mark Shaw struggled to his feet.

"Ophelia!" he said. "As mad as Ophelia." It was said with such distaste that Lally turned to rebuke him. But he was already hurrying away, his limp exaggerated by his haste. Sadly Lally turned back to witness the disappointment in Alice's face. She opened her arms and the tangle of weeds and flowers fell to the stone floor. "Mark didn't like them," she said, her expression doleful. "I picked them for him."

Mark had then suffered an asthmatic attack and stayed in his room for the next week. David and Jonathan, delighted to be free of the Latin declensions and the botany lectures, had reveled in their freedom. The baby, Dan, took up most of Nanny Williams' time, and the two boys effectively escaped from her supervision, taking Alice with them as they rode and swam and walked the beach. There were so many activities among the young people along that stretch of shore, so much coming and going, so much gathering at stable yards and tennis courts, it was easy to lose sight of them. They both treated Alice as someone only slightly older than themselves, a grown playmate only too ready to be enticed into their minor escapades. "Let them be," Black Jack had counseled. "They really shouldn't have to do lessons during the holidays." They used Alice, Lally thought, with gleeful subtlety, always able to claim that they were in the care of an adult, but knowing that she would give in to any pleading of theirs. They often went to a neighboring estate where an indulgent parent had created a half-sized tennis court to instruct his young children; they were found, in Alice's company, on one of the big yachts anchored out in the Sound. "Alice said it was all right," they both said when they had taken Margaret's skiff and rowed out and invited themselves aboard. All along the North Shore the two were known, as the story of their fathers was known. There was, Lally thought, something almost unbearably poignant in the sight of them, both fair, both the same age, both having lost their fathers in the same accident. With their fair good looks and English manners, English accents, they were fussed over by the mothers of the children they

played with. And Alice, whose strange, nearly unearthly beauty had
an almost irresistible attraction even when she smiled with uncomprehending simplicity, was always welcome wherever she went.
Sometimes telephone calls would come from houses some miles
away. "Your adorable Alice is here, Margaret. Shall I run her back
home, or will you send a car for her?"

"Oh, do come yourself," Margaret would cry. "I'm dying to talk
to someone. How naughty of Alice."

"But she's so sweet. I'll be there right away." And the lady would
return with Alice, and there would be drinks on the terrace, or in the
huge conservatory which surrounded the indoor swimming pool. Everyone, Lally thought, seemed determined to make the last weeks of
Margaret's pregnancy "bearable," as she put it. And Alice was made
part of the conspiracy to spoil and indulge her; in Alice's name, almost anything could be done.

Lally and Margaret had now reached the steps of the stone boathouse belonging to the great mansion of the Harper family when they
saw Alice and the two boys in the distance. "She's slipped away with
them again," Margaret said with a faint trace of annoyance. "I don't
suppose anyone else is up yet. Oh, well, there's no harm in it, I suppose." She paused, and then sank down on the lowest step. "I'll have
to rest awhile. I walked farther than I should."

Lally looked at her in alarm. "You're all right, though? Should I
get someone to help? The Harpers . . . the Harpers would send a
chauffeur down here to drive you back to Whytecliffe. Or I could
telephone for one of Brock's cars. Brock would be furious—"

"Oh, it's nothing so serious as that. I always rely on you not to
fuss, Lally, but you're almost as bad as the others."

Lally sat down beside her. "I'm really not fussing. I'm just scared
stiff of what Brock would do to me if you suddenly started having the
baby in the Harper boathouse." She glanced back at the long, wide
porch behind them, the great fieldstone pillars that supported the
deck above which gave, she knew, a famous view of the Sound. Up
there couples danced on the warm summer nights; the room behind
them, with the long french windows opening onto the porch, could
comfortably hold a hundred people. "It wouldn't be such a bad place
to be born, at that."

Margaret sighed, and then shrugged. "You could have had it,
Lally. You really could have."

"Do you suppose I'd marry someone for a boathouse?"

"Oh, don't be stupid. It's the rest of it. All that goes with it. Gerry's not the eldest, but he's his father's favorite. Everyone knows that. And he's much smarter than Roddy. There isn't any doubt who'll get controlling interest in the business. You could have had it all, Lally."

"It just happens I didn't want it. I didn't want Gerry."

Margaret shrugged again. "Well, your choice, of course. But after the divorce he was ripe for the taking. He still hasn't remarried . . ."

"I don't think he's breaking his heart over me."

"He followed you back to London."

"He had business in London."

"He stayed much longer than he intended to. Old Man Harper knew all about it. He came to see me once. Alone. Asked a lot about you. Wanted to hear all about your nursing during the war. He went right back to when we were little girls together. I told him, Lally. I told him all that you did. How you—well, in ways—held us together. How we—I—depended on you. I told him how much Father loved you. He liked the story of Father bringing you back from Leeds that night. He liked the story of how you and the Marchioness got through the season. He said he couldn't imagine you being fat, because the only fault he could find with you now was that you were a bit too thin. I told him all about Susie and the business. He liked that. He said Gerry's wife had been a useless flibbertigibbet, and he'd be happy to see his son married to someone with some sound common sense. You know, *his* father came from just about nothing. Then he discovered that copper lode. Gerry's wife was high society, and he saw that didn't work. He wanted, he said, when Gerry married again, a girl—a woman—with her feet on the ground. He doesn't like Roddy's wife. Out of the same boat as Gerry's, he said. He wanted Gerry to marry you, Lally. He's in a hurry for grandsons. You could have married Gerry Harper, and been a copper princess."

"I didn't want the Harper copper unless I loved the man who owned it."

"He must have cared a lot about you. He's only in his thirties, and good-looking. He could have his pick. He wanted you."

Lally did not respond to Margaret's words. She let them blow away on the wind. Last summer Gerry Harper had courted her, wooed her. He had followed her, as Margaret had said, back to London. For a few brief weeks she had thought she was falling in love. Gerry Harper had charm as well as good looks. She began to look forward to the flowers which came daily, to their meeting each evening when he took her to dine and dance. He went with her to Pellham Langley at weekends. She could see that Black Jack was torn in his emotions. He wanted her to remarry, but he dreaded the separation which marriage to an American would mean. But he said nothing to discourage her or Gerry; he just smiled benignly on the courtship.

"Marry me, Lally," Gerry said, as she had known he would. And she had no answer ready. She hesitated because this in no way resembled the feeling she had had about Jon. Jon had been a consuming passion—her whole life and being. Gerry still seemed to be on the fringe of her emotions.

The question was put again, with the faintest touch of impatience. She wavered. "Don't you care about me?"

"Yes, I do." She cared about him, but she suspected that she cared because at last there was someone to fill the void of those empty nights, the hours after the dancing was over, the music had faded. Very briefly, in those weeks after the American summer was over, and the English autumn hung in misty shrouds about the trees, they became lovers. She told herself it was only what any mature woman would have done, what she must do because she still was not sure. They were good lovers; there was tenderness between them.

"Come back to the States with me, Lally. We'll marry and have kids." She did not hear what else he said. She had desperately wanted Jon's children; she could not begin to imagine the children of Gerry Harper. It was then she became sure.

"I'm sorry, Gerry. I can't marry you."

"You're only just finding out? You might have told me sooner I was wasting my time."

"I didn't know. I wasn't sure."

"I figure you're still in love with that husband of yours." She had seen how many times his gaze had gone to the photographs of Jon at various places about her flat, particularly the one on the table beside her bed. "Well, I can't say I care to spend my life trying to compete with a dead man. That just isn't my style. You're one hell of a woman, Lally, but if you're not completely mine, I won't settle for just a part of you. I'm not good at sharing."

"I'm sorry. I thought I could—"

"Forget it, honey. Better to find out now than later."

So he had left London, his last words a little soured. "Sure led me a pretty dance. There's gonna be a lot of laughing at ol' Gerry Harper back on Long Island. Didn't bring in the trout he'd been ticklin' so long. Well, good-bye, sweet. Probably see you around. Going to be coming to the North Shore next summer, I guess. Maybe you'll have found your guy by then. Maybe I'll have found my woman." He stooped to kiss her. "Well, honey, it's been great knowing you. Pity . . . pity. Good luck."

"Good-bye, Gerry," she had answered quietly. And he had gone, and the nights were lonely again, and through the hard-working days she had nothing to look forward to.

"You could have had him—and everything that goes with him," Susie said, over their dinner at Armand's. "Were you sure, Lally?"

"Yes, sure. He's not—"

"Don't tell me he's not Jon. We all know that." Then her face had wrinkled in her familiar grin. "Can't say I'm not relieved. Didn't want to say anything to spoil it. But I didn't know how I'd have managed without you."

"You would have. *You* would have, Susie."

But the capital that Black Jack and Brock had injected into the business was showing results, and the three workrooms were kept busy full-time. They were searching for a fourth. The buyers were coming from the provinces. "Women aren't as handy with their sewing machines as they used to be. They see the ready-made in the shops and they want it, right then," one buyer had remarked to Lally as she had filled out his order. She noted that it had increased by one third over the last season.

"Susie's things are doing well, aren't they? Our orders are up from everywhere."

"She's got the right idea, that's why. Keep it simple. It makes up well, in almost any material. The ladies aren't being frightened by something that's the latest fashion here, but hasn't reached Manchester yet."

One of the well-known *couturiers,* Julian, had come to see Susie's work because Margaret, who patronized him, had demanded it. He had come, his expression bored, and stayed because he was interested. Lally sat with him and observed his reaction. He had known Lally slightly before, though she had never bought any of his clothes, but watched Margaret order and be fitted; now he responded to her because he was interested. His usually languid tones were injected with enthusiasm. "She would have been great in *haute couture*. The thing is, Susie's a technician."

"A technician? Susie's a designer."

"There's a difference, darling. Susie's not one of your clever little girls who dash off a sketch and expect some poor wretch of a cutter to figure it out. She knows how clothes are *made*. She knows how material hangs. What will work and what won't. You can tell she's been making clothes ever since she was high enough to sit up to a sewing machine. She doesn't try for big effects that inevitably have to flop. And she knows her market."

"Then why do you say she'd be good in *haute couture?*"

"Because, if she were given the materials we work with, if she were given the endless fittings we allow for, for all the extra touches that make our damn dresses so expensive, she could really fly. You see, darling, she's a woman. She hasn't got any desire to make other women look ridiculous. That's why her clothes are a success in Bournemouth and Buxton and Bradford. Some of us know these things. It hurts us when some fat old cow comes into our salon and orders a dress that was meant for a slim young flapper. Susie's clothes manage to take the fat old cow into account."

Lally laughed. "You're very unkind—to fat old cows."

"Darling, if you had to put up with them as I have to, you'd be unkind too."

"Are you trying to seduce Susie into your salon, Julian?"

He drew on his cigarette, studying the model who walked and turned before him, displaying a dress of neat, unexceptional but flattering design. "No. Susie's not for me. She'd want to run the whole bloody show. We'd have a row within ten minutes, and start throwing the scissors at each other. Let her do what she's doing. She does it very well. With a bit of luck, she'll make a fortune while the rest of us hover on the edge of bankruptcy in our fancy salons. *Our* clients often forget to pay their bills . . ."

So, in the long, hard-working days the image of Gerry Harper faded. Lally ceased to look for the flowers he had always sent; she fell into bed tired and was not so acutely aware of its emptiness. For a little time she might have believed herself in love, but Gerry had not riveted and fixed her emotions, as Jon had. Even when he had been in London she had forgotten him for hours during the day as the business had pressed on her. She had welcomed his companionship, but when he was gone she found he had left only a shallow impression. She flung herself into the routine of business and the contrast of weekends at Pellham Langley, and the memory of Gerry Harper was almost erased, as the hillocks and depressions on the beach before her were gradually flattened with each succeeding wave.

"But still," Margaret said beside her, "it would have been so perfect to have you here, right with me—just a few minutes' drive away. I was hoping . . . Oh, well . . . no one ever imagined you'd turn down Gerry Harper."

"No, I suppose no one ever did," Lally answered dryly. But still, she reflected, it was pleasing to know that Old Man Harper, as everyone called him, would have welcomed her. She liked Old Man Harper. She hadn't encountered Gerry Harper this summer. "Out West," they said. And someone winked. "Checking up that all that copper's still in the ground." So the memory had faded a little more.

The dog had now recognized Alice and the two boys and had gone racing to meet them. The figures on the shore were near, and breaking into a run. They, the three of them, seemed to Lally in that instant to enshrine a miracle of beauty and grace: the young woman with her long blond hair flying in the wind, smiling, laughing, like an angel of light; the boys, fair and tousle-haired, bronzed from their weeks in the sun, running barefooted, leaping in and out of the edge of the waves. The barking of the dog was thrown back by the wind.

Margaret pressed her hands against the step and struggled to rise, and sank back. "Help me, Lally."

Lally stood and put both her hands into Margaret's, and pulled her to her feet. For a moment their hands lingered in each other's; their eyes met. "Thank you," Margaret said softly. Lally couldn't hear the words over the crash of a breaker, but she knew what they were.

II

By that evening the wind had dropped, and the languid heat was returning, but the huge swell of the surf, the aftermath of the storm, was only a little gentler. Brock came back from the city complaining that already the heat was building up again. "Had a few hours' relief this morning," he said, as he accepted his first drink from Black Jack, "but it'll be as bad as ever tomorrow." He bent to kiss Margaret. "And how are you, my lady? The next Weymouth not bothering you too much, I hope?"

Margaret moved fretfully on the chaise. "He kicks like hell," she said with ill-humor. She stared at the car in which Brock had come back from Manhattan being driven off by his chauffeur. "I do wish, Brock, if you have to have guards, that they looked a little less like thugs. And these men who keep popping out of the shrubbery, holding a rake as if they wished it were a pitchfork—couldn't you make them look a bit more like *real* gardeners?"

"Honey," Brock said patiently, "they only know how to do one thing—which is to look after you and the kids. Occasionally I do see them raking the grass, which is a help. But you really can't expect them to dress up in dungarees and straw hats, can you?"

She laughed. There was always the saving grace of her laugh when she knew she had sounded like a whining shrew. "Yes, darling—they would look even more out of place. I suppose it's really necessary to have them?"

Brock surveyed the group on the terrace; his gaze embraced them all—Margaret with her swollen belly, the two boys, David and Jonathan, who had reached the age when they were allowed to stay up for Brock's return; it swept over Lally and Black Jack, lingered on Alice. "Yes, my darling, I do think it's necessary." Then his features, which momentarily had become stern, relaxed. He also laughed. "Or if it isn't, then you must indulge the fond and probably foolish fears of a doting husband."

Margaret smiled, her petulance past. "I've asked Gertie and Bill over to dinner, Brock. They've got some friends staying with them who are coming too. Makes a little party."

The pleasure drained from his face once more. "Margaret, should you? I mean—doesn't it tire you?"

She spread her hands. "If you only understood how boring it is to be hardly able to move. Brock, dear, it won't be long. The baby's due in a few weeks. Once it's over, I'll be sweet-tempered—angelic—you'll see. Just help me over this last little bit."

He nodded, half-smiled, and sipped his drink. The lights were coming on all over the Sound; the riding lights of the yachts glimmered as the vessels moved on the still-roiled water; the lights of the great mansions began to appear, some showing boldly if they fronted the water, some faintly screened by trees. The North Shore was preparing for its evening entertainment.

Edith suddenly asserted her authority. "Boys, now it's past your bedtime. You'll have Nanny Williams coming to complain. Off you go . . ."

"I'll walk you upstairs, old chaps," Brock offered. "Got to go and shower and get the city dust off me. I'll look in and see that Dan's still alive and kicking, Margaret. And I'll be down in time for dinner. You won't make it too late tonight, will you, darling? I mean—you look marvelous, but I worry about you overdoing things." As the expression of petulance began to return to Margaret's face he held up his hands. "All right—whatever you like. Peace—anything for peace." He looked imploringly at Black Jack. "Could you have a monster-sized martini waiting when I get down? It's been that sort of day." He laid his empty glass on the parapet of the terrace and held his hands out to the boys. "Race you! Come on, you lazy devils!" They listened to the cries and the laughter as the three pounded up the grand staircase of the Brewster mansion.

Black Jack, his face almost lost in the darkness, turned to Margaret. "He's wonderful, Brock. Never forget it, Margaret."

The pitch of her voice rose almost to a wail. "As if I *can!* As if I can ever forget. Do you suppose there's a single day I don't remember what I owe him? If only I could forget, just sometimes—"

"Hush, my dear," Black Jack said. "You mustn't excite yourself. I didn't mean—"

"Jack," Edith interrupted hurriedly, "perhaps you'd better start getting Brock's martini ready."

Black Jack went to his task with relief, glad to be disentangled from Margaret's distress. Was there no way, Lally wondered, that any of them could be permitted to forget? At times she was close to pity for Margaret, burdened by the weight of her gratitude to Brock. She bore his children, and she was faithful to him. Lally had never heard her say she loved him.

Black Jack wielded the martini shaker with more enthusiasm than delicacy. It was, Lally thought, just another thing Brock did each evening; he suffered his father-in-law's martinis with good grace, as if it were he, and not the older man, who was the guest in this house. One waited for a chink to open in Brock's attitude of good humor and protectiveness; it was seldom there. There would never be, Lally reckoned, anything Margaret could legitimately complain about. Brock would make sure of that.

III

Gertie and Bill and their four guests came to dinner. Everyone seemed invigorated by the storm of the previous evening, and the resultant cooling of the temperature. The food, Lally thought, was, as always, very good—chilled melon balls, salmon mousse, tender roast beef, *sorbet* . . . the courses came and went, and she hardly touched them. Brock had enticed away a chef from one of Manhattan's best restaurants. He became aggrieved that his talents were not used, and Margaret delightedly obliged by regularly filling the table with guests, many at short notice, as this evening. They took their coffee and liqueurs on the high terrace, under the warm, star-filled sky. Last night's storm had cleared the air so that they were able to sit and gaze upward at stars that seemed to pulse.

Their desultory conversation was broken by the appearance of a man on the terrace; Lally vaguely recognized him. "Terry!" Margaret cried. "I didn't see you down on the beach." It was Terry North. The North estate, half a mile away, was almost another home to Margaret. She and Terry's wife, "Tiny" North, were friends and competitors in the hunting field, daring each other on to extremes of skill and madness. Tiny North, who was very tall, slim, and who dressed with an elegance which rivaled Margaret's, was almost as good-humoredly indulgent of her friend's whims and moods as Brock was. And she had formed an affection for Black Jack which had taken her three times to Pellham Langley. She was, Black Jack said, a good companion on a shoot. He could hardly have praised more highly. Now her smooth, bobbed head showed above the parapet. "Who's coming down to the beach? Buddy Rawlston has started a bonfire at their beach house. He says it's chilly for August." She laughed. She was wearing a dress of silk so fine that it appeared to cling to her as a second skin; under it, Lally thought, she was naked, and she didn't care who knew it.

Margaret heaved herself laboriously out of her chair and peered over the parapet. "Oh, yes—I see it. Let's go." The Rawlston place adjoined Whytecliffe, but in the fraternity of the rich whose houses skirted this shore the boundaries were never marked.

"Margaret—!" Brock and Black Jack uttered her name simultaneously. Both had the same restraining note. She reacted predictably.

An impatient shrug, a gesture to Gertie and Bill and the other four guests. Someone had started up a portable gramophone at the Rawlston beach house. *Yes, sir, that's my baby, No, sir, don't mean maybe* . . . Margaret had already started down the steps. Now all Brock could do was to hurry to her and support her as she went. "Margaret, let's not stay too late."

Surprisingly, she turned in view of the company and kissed him on the cheek. "I promise—not more than half an hour."

Alice had sighted the bonfire. "Oh, look . . . look!" She was flying down the stairs to the beach. Behind her Lally thought she heard Black Jack give a sigh. It would be another late night.

*   *   *

As these things had a habit of doing along the North Shore, the handful of people who gathered around the bonfire grew to something that came close to a crowd. The fire attracted the attention of those on the yachts as well as those whose terraces and gazebos overlooked that stretch of the beach. Small boats, either powered or rowed, began to put in at the Rawlston jetty. On the deck of the beach house someone energetically cranked the handle of the phonograph, and the music was almost louder than the slap of the waves against the sand. *Sometimes I'm happy, sometimes I'm blue* . . . Everyone sang the words, even if they couldn't hold the tune. Amazingly, among that crowd who must surely all have dined well, someone had produced frankfurters. There was a sizzling sound, the smell of pork and beef being cooked on spears over the bonfire; bread smeared with mustard was passed around. They ate it from their hands, with paper napkins, those people who had dined from fine china that evening. Inevitably the bottles of gin and scotch appeared. Glasses came from the Rawlston beach house. In the morning the servants would come down and clear away the debris of this impromptu party. There would be glasses left cradled in the sand, and many cigarette butts. People had their shoes off. One couple shuffled in the sand, their bodies outlined by the light of the fire, in a rhythm of the tango that almost managed to keep to the beat of "Jealousy." Others began to join in. It didn't matter that the sand impeded their movements; they seemed to enjoy the obstacle, delighted in overcoming it. Beside Lally, Margaret murmured, "Oh, Lord, I wish I could dance. I'm so tired of being *heavy*." Alice, who responded instinctively to music, danced by herself. These were not the strict steps of the tango; she was not capable of mastering them. But she danced, she leaned back, she swayed as if an invisible partner guided her. Here, on the edge of the foam, she was by far the most graceful among them. Her hair, which Nanny Williams had managed to persuade her should be worn each evening in a knot behind her head, had, as always, slipped into its shining, silken fall. Lally distinguished Mark Shaw's voice among those around her: "God! . . . Someone should . . ." Whatever someone should do was not done. The tango ended. Everyone applauded—the onlookers, the dancers. Alice was left, spellbound, in that last wild, innocently provocative gesture. Slowly her back straightened. Someone cranked the phonograph again. More people had scrambled to their feet, and were now dancing to "Dinah." Someone approached Alice and caught her hands. She did not accept a close embrace, but danced at a distance, not knowing what she was supposed to do, but always true to the rhythm. Lally heard her laugh, saw the golden hair flying. Anyone who did not know Alice, who did not know her history, might have imagined her a rather wild, impetuous young woman, unwilling to follow the set routine. The man she danced with kept trying to pull her to him, and she kept evading him, not as a deliberate provocation, but because her instinct urged her to remain free, as she had always been. Beside Lally on the sand, entrusted to her, were Teddy Rose, Madame Butterfly, and Raggedy Ann. Alice had brought them with her down from the terrace. It seemed impossible to associate these childish toys with the young woman silhouetted against the sheen of the night-dark water.

Lally had placed herself close to Margaret, a little withdrawn from the bonfire. Brock nursed a beer, and said little. Buddy Rawlston urged Lally to dance, and she did, just to one tune. Then she made an excuse to disengage herself. When she returned to Margaret's side she experienced a sense of weariness—no, it was not weariness, but *ennui*. They seemed to have done it all often, this crowd. They played at sport all day, and in the evenings they met to dance to jazz records. Were they all as tired of it as she was? The beat of the music might grow faster, at times it was more sophisticated, but could they ever leave behind the sense that it had all been done before? This whole group, her generation, were all still engaged in a fast tango to escape the memories of the war. Some of them had never experienced the war, and did not understand it, but nonetheless they obeyed a herd instinct that bade them enjoy themselves because it was they who had missed death, had missed destruction, mutilation. Glory in being young, and unmarked; glory in being alive in this, the best of all possible times. They were rich and favored, and the good times would never end. That was what the music said. Lally knew she was tired of the round of pleasure which appeared to demand such energetic application. Having an endless good time seemed such hard work. She turned and saw that Black Jack and Edith, after a word with Brock, had risen and were making their way along the beach to the steps of Whytecliffe. Close to her, Margaret said, "But I don't *want* to go, Brock. You know how hard it is for me to sleep now. Well, just a tiny gin, darling, and then we'll go."

Reluctantly, Brock got to his feet and went to the Rawlston beach house where a makeshift bar had been set up. His patience with Margaret, in these last weeks of her pregnancy, seemed as endless as the entertainments she demanded. He would humor and indulge her while the whole party, the party which seemed to have lasted for years, rolled on. Someone touched Lally's hand. She turned and the flickering light of the bonfire illuminated the features of Gerry Harper.

"Well, then," he said. "How're things, Lally? Miss me?"

"You knew I would."

He nodded. "Yes, I knew it. Damn stubborn little bitch. Changed your mind?"

"No, Gerry. I was just wishing I was back in London."

He groaned. "Oh, don't tell me. You're dying to be back in that dreary little business you and Susie run. For God's sake, Lally . . . a girl like you. There are better things for you to do."

"Like this? This evening—dancing all night, tennis at noon, nursing a hangover, waiting for the next party, which will be tomorrow night. You've been doing better things, Gerry." He looked hard and fit, his skin seemed dark and weathered.

"Yes, I suppose so. Haven't been dancing every night. Too damn tired. Great country out there, Lally. You'd like it. Can understand what my old grandpappy saw in it. My old man, too. But you can't live in a log cabin for three generations while Wall Street piles up the money for you. Guess my old man knows that that's where the real thing is, though. He'd have liked you to marry me, Lally." He touched her hand again. "*I'd* have liked you to marry me."

"Don't, Gerry—"

"No, I won't. One turndown is enough. But you're a hard girl to get out of mind. I've been trying damned hard. Lots of nice little girls around to try with. But none like Lally Pollock. Sorry—just give me your glass, and I'll cry into your gin."

"Just dump it out instead. I've had enough, and you're not the sort to cry, not over anyone."

"Damn right I'm not. Well, dance with me, then. It isn't the Ritz, but we'll make do."

She got to her feet. She didn't want to dance, but she was suddenly glad of Gerry Harper's presence, a note of realism in this make-believe party. She accepted his hand, and then she saw Brock circling the bonfire, a glass in each hand. At that moment he stopped dead, for a frozen second. Lally turned to see what had so transfixed him.

In the beginning very few had noticed. While Lally had talked with Gerry Harper, she had heard Margaret's low laughter beside her, a small chuckle which she had paid no attention to. Now she saw what was happening. Some of the dancers, those on the edge of the waves, trousers already soaked to the knees, the hems of the short dresses wet, had begun to shed their skimpy summer clothing. The first splash was hardly heard over the music and the slap of the waves; then someone rushed forward with a yell, naked except for undershorts, and hurled himself fully into the sea. A girl slipped off a silk dress and tossed it behind her; she wore a brassiere and silk pants. She joined the swimmer, who was now well ahead. There were cheers and applause. People began to drop clothes on the sand.

There was one who went further than all the others. Alice, in an ecstasy of excitement, pulled off her dress and her light underclothes; she poised, on tiptoe, as beautiful a sight as Lally had ever seen, the nude body braced, the arms outstretched. She seemed for a second to hover between the riding lights of the yachts and the light of the bonfire, a being of earth and sky. Then she ran, like an earthling unleashed, into the water.

Many others by now had seen her. That naked beauty was a sight to stir even those jaded senses. One man from the crowd gave a throaty cheer: "Good for you, my darling!"

Lally heard Mark Shaw's voice: "No! Shame!" Shame to whom? Lally thought.

The glasses fell from Brock's hands. He raced across the sand, not stopping to shake off his shoes at the water's edge before he plunged in. Lally saw that he struggled to get off his shirt, and held it as he waded into the waves, chest-high, toward Alice. Beside Lally, Gerry

Harper murmured, "Poor baby." Then he left Lally and went down to the water's edge, thrusting aside the others who were shedding their clothes and romping into the waves as if it were some novelty.

"Disgusting!" Mark Shaw said.

Lally turned on him. "You prig! Why aren't you helping, instead of standing there passing judgment?"

"Alice has plenty of strong men to help her."

Brock had reached her, and thrown his shirt around her. His arm around her waist, he struggled to bring her back to the beach. The shirt only barely covered her nakedness. She came out of the water, the wet shirt clinging to the outline of her body, her wet hair plastered down her face and back, laughing—a wild, manic laugh that rose above the sound of the crowd. A little hush fell upon them as Brock brought her from the surf and Gerry Harper went forward to drape his own shirt over Brock's wet one. The light of the bonfire danced upon the fair skin of her long legs and the golden fuzz of the pubic hair where the sun had never touched.

"Bathing belle of the year," someone shouted.

There was a swift cracking sound in that little stillness as Mark Shaw slammed his hand into the face of the man who had shouted.

"Why you . . . !" The tone was outraged. "Why you bloody damned little Limey cripple!"

Lally saw Mark Shaw topple back on the sand as the man thrust a fist hard up under his chin. He lay still, and the waves reached his head. In the silence they heard the struggle of breath; he pulled himself to his knees, and the asthmatic wheezing began.

Now Brock had brought Alice back to Lally. She was still laughing, the laughter of nerves and confusion, the beginning of distress, the note of hysteria. Lally folded her in her arms, shielding her from the gaze of the crowd. "There, darling . . . there. We'll just go back home now."

Unaided, Margaret had heaved herself first to her knees, and then to her feet. "No!" she cried. The phonograph record had come to an end, and her voice rang shrilly. "No, I've had enough! Enough of this babying nonsense. Alice is responsible, like anyone else. We've all indulged her too long. There's an end to it—now!"

With a gesture which evaded the swiftness of Brock's response, she had gathered up Alice's beloved friends. For just a moment Margaret stood with Teddy Rose, Madame Butterfly, and Raggedy Ann clutched to her body, so that the immense swelling of her belly was outlined. Then with deliberate strides she went to the bonfire. "An end to it. An end to all this babying nonsense!"

With one movement, as if she could not wait to be rid of them, the three toys were hurled onto the fire. The act silenced the last of the murmurs of the crowd, and that strange silence broke through to Alice's consciousness. She turned and looked.

Without uttering a sound, she was free of Lally's arms; the two shirts fell away from her as she raced to the fire. Only Margaret stood close enough to try to prevent her, and her weighted body was of little use against the strength of this maddened young woman. A collected gasp burst from the crowd as Alice thrust her hands into the bonfire, reaching for the melting and burning shapes. It was a cry of exultation rather than pain they heard as she grasped all three of them and turned back. Lally saw, with a further shock of fear, that the hot melted wax of Madame Butterfly's face ran down between Alice's naked breasts as she clutched the figures to her. Then, at last, Alice's cries turned to pain.

"Lally—Lally, I hurt!"

Lally raced to her and once more enfolded her in her arms. The wax had cooled, but it was still soft, and it stuck to Lally's dress; there was the smell of burned cloth from Teddy Rose and Raggedy Ann. Worse, there was the smell of burned flesh.

Now shirts came from half a dozen men. Feverishly, Brock wrapped the burned hands in cloth. The instant it was done, Gerry Harper caught Alice up and tossed her across his shoulder. It would be the easiest way to sustain the long run through the sand to Whytecliffe. Brock kept pace with him.

Despairingly, Margaret cried, "Alice . . . Alice, darling, I didn't mean it. I'll get you new ones, I promise. Tomorrow morning. Oh, wait! Brock, wait for me. Please wait for me." Brock didn't turn back.

It was Lally who walked with her, one arm supporting her. Behind them Lally could hear Mark Shaw's labored breathing. "Here, let me help, Mrs. Weymouth." Dumbly, she nodded. He, who touched no one if he could avoid it, put his arm about her waist to help support the weight of that burdened body. Behind them, they left absolute silence. It was one party on the North Shore which had come to an instant end.

IV

For a time Alice had whimpered in pain, until the morphine had begun to work, and then she drifted into an uneasy sleep. The hands, now expertly bandaged by the doctor, were laid over the light sheet which covered her, but in her sleep she plucked fretfully at them, as if to tear the bandages away. The doctor had shaken his head. "I've never known anything quite like it. What she felt for those . . . those little creatures"—he nodded toward the mutilated, charred figures of Alice's dolls—"was obviously more than the pain of the fire. Or, for those few moments, she didn't feel pain. A pity. She'll be badly scarred. They're starting to do something about burn victims now in the way of plastic surgery—they learned a lot during the war. But it's still experimental. A difficult and often painful process. Poor little girl."

"She's twenty-three, Doctor," Lally reminded him.

Dr. Morton sighed as he began to gather up his equipment. He was the doctor who regularly attended the Weymouth household, prescribed for any routine illness, assisted Margaret through her pregnancies. He had been present, along with the consultant specialist whom Brock had demanded, at the birth of her child. He would be present when the next child was born. He, by this time, knew Alice well. "Yes, I know. She's a young woman whom I, as a doctor, often make the mistake of treating as a child. Mentally, of course, she is a child. But she has the physical strength of a mature woman. How she must have loved those . . . those little things. She went, literally, through fire for them."

"Brock gave them to her, did you know?" Lally said. "Well, not Teddy—but he named him Teddy Rose." She realized that she was talking of Alice's toys as if they were the real people Alice believed them. "She's had dozens of other toys—dolls, rabbits, things like that. But these were always the special ones because Brock gave them to her. She's very . . . attached to Brock."

"Yes, I've noticed. And her attachments are fiercer than you would have with a . . . well, with a normal woman. She's had no opportunity of judging anyone by an adult standard, so she never sees their flaws, once she's given her love. Any failure on the part of those she loves and trusts is a calamity to her. One must excuse Mrs.

Weymouth. It was a strange situation, and in the last weeks of pregnancy a woman often becomes almost unbearably stressed and tired. She's highly strung, your sister, Mrs. Pollock."

"We know it," Lally said. "We're all aware of that."

"Yes, I'm sure you are." He snapped his bag closed. "Well, I'll be back during the morning. She should sleep now for a few hours, but if there's any problem, you must not hesitate to call me. I'll be in touch with a doctor—a man I know in Manhattan who's had a very wide experience of such burns. And there's someone else—an analyst, Mrs. Pollock, who might be able to help. If Alice could just talk to him . . . Of course, he couldn't help the brain damage—that's there forever—but he might be able to help Alice express what's in her mind at this moment. About her sister . . . and the dolls. Anyone who could help her to talk could be of benefit."

"I don't know," Lally said wearily. "How do we go back to the beginning with Alice? And could it do any good?" She turned back to the bed as Alice gave a little cry and the bandaged hands clawed at the sheets. "I was there the day she was born. Did you know her mother died then?—Black Jack's second wife? Her name was Alice, too. No one noticed for a long time that she wasn't developing as normal children do. She was so beautiful, and always so good, so docile. Everyone loved her. I suppose we—they—thought she was just a bit slow. No more than that."

"The accidents of nature none of us can help," the doctor said. He sounded mournful, as if he were personally responsible. Then he returned to a more professional manner. "Try to get some rest, Mrs. Pollock. I've given Mrs. Weymouth something to help her sleep. You must all try to be very gentle with her. She seems deeply sorry for what she did."

"Sorry?—yes, I know she is. We *will* be gentle with her, Doctor. It would hurt Brock—and Black Jack—too much if we weren't. We will tell the boys it was an accident. But we can't help what they'll hear outside this house."

He nodded. "There will be talk. Until the baby's born, let's try not to let any of it reach Mrs. Weymouth. Once the birth is over, she'll be better able to take what must come. I'll send a nurse for Alice first thing this morning."

"I'll stay with her. I wouldn't want her to wake and find herself alone."

When he was gone she wandered to the window. A pale slip of

light was growing in the east, along the water to where the Sound stretched out to touch the Atlantic. It was still too dark to see the curl of the waves against the beach. A murmur from Alice made her turn. Only one shaded light burned, and it fell softly on that beautiful face. The hands, swathed in their bandages, looked grotesque. The doctor had placed a dressing in the cleft between Alice's breasts where she had clasped the hot wax and burning rags to her. Then he had bound it in place by putting bandages around her whole body. They had slit a nightgown down the back to ease it onto her, to cover her shoulders, a white, lace-trimmed nightgown. If her face had not occasionally puckered with pain, she would have looked as beautiful as she had ever looked.

"Like an angel, isn't she, Mrs. Pollock?" Nanny Williams had entered quietly. "Why did the poor lamb do it? Why did Mrs. Weymouth— Oh, no, I mustn't start laying blame. She loves her little sister deeply, I know. She's just cried herself to sleep. Those pills the doctor gave were a help, but she'll be beside herself again when she wakes up. Poor Mr. Weymouth. He just sits there and holds her hand. If he weren't such a man, I think he'd cry too. And then there's Mr. Shaw. The doctor had to give him something to try to help *him* sleep. All that wheezing and gasping—he's wearing himself out. And Mr. Harper wouldn't go. He's fallen asleep in the library. I can't imagine what he thinks he can *do*."

"Just be here, I suppose. Well, you've got yourself a houseful of invalids, Nanny."

"That's what I'm here for, Mrs. Pollock. The family can always rely on me." Lally wished it hadn't been said with such professional zest. But people in Nanny Williams' position always needed to know they were needed. "Now, Mrs. Pollock, you go along and try to get some rest. The doctor spoke to me, and I said I'd sit with Alice. If she wakes she'll see a friendly face. And I'll come and get you at once."

"You're tired yourself, Nanny."

"Goodness gracious, I went to bed just a little after I saw Lord Grenfell and Master Jonathan safely asleep. I've had more rest than any of you. Please, Mrs. Pollock, just a few hours . . ." The need to be needed, Lally thought; the reassurance of being needed.

"All right, Nanny. Thank you. Come and wake me in two hours. I want to be with Alice when she wakes."

"That I'll do, Mrs. Pollock. Never fear."

Lally stood under the shower and let the water fall on her hair unheedingly, let it rinse from her body the smell of antiseptics and ointments. Her nostrils were not so easily freed. She roughly rubbed her body and hair dry, and opened the window wide. The streak of dawn had widened across the Sound, an angry red. "Sailor's warning," she said to herself, an automatic response to the sight. She fell onto the bed, and sleep came like a blow.

But then she was awake again. She saw that it was only an hour later. She had left the curtains open to let the breeze play about the room; it was now touched by the early morning light. For an instant she lay, puzzled, wondering why her hair was wet, why she wore no gown. Then she remembered Alice. She got up and put on a kimono and slippers. She padded softly to Alice's room.

There, the light was still burning, and Nanny Williams sat nodding, gently asleep, by the bed. The bed itself was empty.

She looked first, quietly, into the bathroom. Then, more swiftly, but still quietly, she went to Margaret's room. There also a light burned, and Brock lay crumpled in a chair by the bed, his hand locked in Margaret's. She listened outside Black Jack's room, and heard his reassuring snores. Perhaps Edith, beside him, was wakeful, but the night's events had brought their own exhaustion to Black Jack. She left them alone. She ran downstairs. The hall and all the main rooms were empty, except for the sprawled figure of Gerry Harper, who snored as loudly as Black Jack. The first maid had not arrived in the kitchen. If Brock's guards patrolled the grounds, she could see none. There was no movement she could see about the stable yards and the garages. It was yet too early, even for the horses. She went back upstairs. Before she woke Nanny Williams, she opened the door of the room where the two boys, David and Jonathan, slept. Those beds also were empty.

Then she raced downstairs. She shook Gerry awake. "For God's sake, Gerry! Alice and the boys are gone."

"Gone? Gone where?"

"How do I know? But I think . . . God, Gerry, I think the beach. The beach is always where she went."

He grasped her hand. "Don't wait for the others. We have to run, Lally. Run like hell."

* * *

Down on the beach they hesitated. "Which way?" Gerry demanded. "Would she have gone back to the fire?"

Lally thought. It was only twenty-four hours since Alice had followed her and Margaret—or had she tracked them?—in the opposite direction, around the point, to the Harper boathouse. "Yesterday morning she came with the two boys to your boathouse—Margaret and I walked over there."

"Right—she probably did it again. But you go the other way, just in case. She's probably feeling a bit dopey. Should have brought the glasses and looked from the terrace. But she could already be around the point. Perhaps we should have raised the others. Oh, well, let's you and I take a look first. If we don't find her—them—in a few minutes, we'll have to get everyone on the go. O.K., let's get going, Lally."

She turned from him, feeling no reassurance. Alice might have gone onto the beach, but equally she could have turned onto one of the riding trails between the estates. She could be anywhere. But it was only a little more than an hour, Lally kept reminding herself, since she had seen Alice sleeping, under the influence of morphine, in her bed. Was it possible that the two boys had gone alone? And Alice alone? Was Alice in some quiet corner of that vast house that Lally had not searched? Why hadn't she roused everyone? The self-questioning and self-accusations accompanied her as she ran along the beach and the light grew steadily stronger. She could imagine the panic and the outcry if she had run from room to room awakening the household. But that was what she and Gerry should have done. Was it time to turn back? Her breath was beginning to catch. Her body was bathed in perspiration; the muscles in her calves ached from running in the soft sand. The day would be stickily hot. It would . . . She was about to turn and go back. Then she stared hard. The early sun turned the waves to a million flashing mirrors, the light sometimes blinding, sometimes deceiving. Did she imagine three blond heads there among the waves, or did the light play tricks? No . . . yes—they rose and fell, as if dancing, bobbing with the movement of the surf. Three blond heads, just as she remembered them yesterday morning as they had come skipping and dancing along the shore. She started to run again. Yes, now she was sure. Three of them. She stopped and looked back for Gerry. She couldn't see him; it was probable that he was already around the point. But it didn't matter. She had found Alice and the boys.

As she grew near she knew that something was wrong. There was Alice, standing out breast-high among the waves, her hair plastered to her head, the remains of the nightgown hanging to her. And there were the two blond heads of the boys, but she was holding them fast, holding them at a depth where their feet could not touch the sand. Those two small blond heads were bobbing in the water, buffeted by the waves, as if they were unconscious of what was happening to them. The grotesquely bandaged hands were now like clubs; the two blond heads were pressed against Alice's sides, almost tucked under each arm.

"Alice!" Lally knew she screamed. The sound was washed away. "Alice!" She began wading into the surf. She knew the first real fear then. "Alice—let them go! Let them go." As the first big wave she breasted began to retreat she felt the horror of the undertow. To a strong swimmer it would have meant little, but she had never learned to swim as naturally as these Americans did, as naturally as Alice did, as the boys did. But the boys were not free. They were fixed in Alice's grip, fixed with a kind of maniacal strength. "Alice! Oh, God —Gerry!" Why hadn't Gerry come?

She waded out, taking the crash of the waves and the momentary confusion, almost panic, which they always brought to her. The salt water stung her eyes. She reached Alice, and tugged at her shoulder. "Let them go! Do you hear me? Let them go!"

The uncomprehending gaze was turned on her. With an effort which she knew she couldn't long sustain because she was nearly lifted off her feet by a wave, Lally struck the smiling face, possibly the first time that face had ever been struck. Now Alice seemed to recognize her. Above the noise of the surf Lally heard her cry out. She opened her arms and the heads of the two boys were free. Free for what? One drifted off, caught up in the curl of a wave, rolling, rolling. The other began to swim, panicked, but making for the beach, letting a wave carry him. Lally grasped for the one who had slipped away. She felt the waves suck and pull. She went down in a nightmare of foam and choking water, down and down, and then was tossed back again. The blond head was lost in a surge of green and white water. She couldn't see. She was slammed against something that was human. She grasped a limb, and rose to the surface, to see Alice's face. She stood on her feet, looking around her wildly. Where was the second blond head? There she thought she glimpsed it, in the green maze of water where now the sunlight glinted dazzlingly. But no, not there, or there. Where? She struggled back to Alice. "Where?" she shrieked. It was a useless question. Alice just stood there, taking the break of the waves over her, rising with them a little, coming back to place her feet on the soft sand as the waves receded. By now the slit nightgown had fallen off her. The waves were beginning to tear at the bandages; they had begun unraveling. The bandages around her breasts had broken with the force of her movements; the dressing had washed away. She was there, purity, and yet marked.

"Alice, help me. Help me find the other."

The blond head was shaken. She rose and went down with each wave. She seemed to enjoy it. She didn't hear what Lally said.

Lally tried to dive, and could not. She was lost in that green water, and each time she came up and tried to gasp some air, another wave came and she had to dive under it again. On and on it went; she saw nothing when she was under water. Alice stood there, glorying in the waves beating against her. Lally found herself caught in the suck of a bigger wave, carried under, knew the nightmare of drowning, and then the release as she was carried in the shocking aftermath of the wave toward the beach. She felt her face and teeth grind against the sand. She began to crawl up the beach out of the range of those merciless waves. Every limb was shaking and stressed as she pulled herself to her feet. One small boy stood there on the beach, wailing with dismay. It was not her son. Jonathan was the one who had gone beyond the waves.

* * *

Perhaps she stood for some time, and then a rage such as she had never known before overtook her. Her beautiful son, Jon's son, was there, in the roil of the green water. She stared at Alice's figure, still jumping as each wave hit her, and once more she waded out. At first Alice laughed when she saw her, and then, as if once again she had hit her, the look turned to apprehension and fear. Lally caught her arm, even in that moment of rage and pain not able to inflict the hurt that touching one of those burned hands would have given. She did not want to touch Alice, but she could not leave her in the surf alone. "Alice! Come!" Her voice was a shriek. Dumbly, docilely, Alice obeyed. They waded to the edge of the waves, where the sobbing little boy stood, his pajama jacket torn off him.

"Why did you do it, Alice?" he cried. "You said we'd just have a little swim. And then you held us!"

Alice shook her head. "I burned, David." She turned imploringly to Lally. "Lally—I hurt. I burned. The water was cool. The boys always come with me, but they didn't want to stay. I had to make them stay because I know I'm not supposed to be alone."

Lally tried to choke back her terror, the beginning of her grief. She was unable herself to go back into that green, white water. And she could leave neither of them here alone. She caught Alice's arm, and David's hand. "Run," she commanded.

"But where's Jonathan?" David cried.

"We'll find Jonathan," she answered. "Run!" They staggered along the beach, Alice naked, and, Lally realized with a shock, she herself was naked. The kimono had vanished in that struggle with the waves. "We'll find Jonathan," she said again, for the comfort of the child. Her legs were wobbling as she urged the other two on, trying to stay where the waves touched the shore and the sand was firmer. The rage and pain boiled within her. She recognized the figure running toward them, running strongly, with the ease of a man who had spent all summer out in the wilds, supervising the extraction of his copper from his mines, the man out of place on Wall Street.

"Lally—my God! Where's Jonathan?"

"There!" Wildly she jerked her head toward the ocean. "Why weren't you with me, Gerry? You could have saved him. *You could have saved him, but you went the other way!*"

V

It seemed that every small boat from every yacht in the Sound, every swimmer, began the search as the news was passed and telephoned around. The whole morning the Sound was alive with their activities, their noises. Lally heard them, and wondered what use it all was. But by noon they had brought back the body of her young son, unmarked by any fish or any other thing that swam in those waters. Black Jack came to tell her. Jonathan was laid on a bed in one of the grander guest rooms at Whytecliffe, terribly far from the intimacy of the room he had shared with David. They had combed his hair, which was still wet, and she could see traces of sand in it. They had put on a white shirt to cover his shoulders. The rest of his body lay under a sheet. Nanny Williams knelt weeping beside the bed.

"Oh, Mrs. Pollock, if you can ever forgive me . . . I fell asleep. I should never have left her alone. Who would imagine . . . ?"

Lally found herself unable to utter one word. She looked at the puffed swollen face of the woman, and she felt a kind of detached pity for the remorse which would haunt her. But she couldn't bring herself to say any words. They all seemed gone. Black Jack steered Nanny Williams from the room. Lally stood and looked at Jonathan —looked and looked, trying to photograph forever every small nuance of his features. He was bright and beautiful and young. And he was dead.

Edith came swiftly into the room. She touched Black Jack's hand. "Margaret's gone into labor."

Lally spoke, and was shocked to hear the violence in her own voice. "God!—can we have no peace!"

* * *

There was no peace that night at Whytecliffe. It was as hard a labor as Margaret had known with her two other children. She struggled—Lally saw she struggled during the times she went briefly to visit her—to hold back her cries, but at times they broke through, and that elegant room was ripped by screams as primitive as any peasant's dwelling had ever known. Dr. Morton had summoned the consultant gynecologist from Manhattan, and the two hovered in the room, or sat briefly on the terrace while the nurse remained with Margaret, timing her contractions. Another nurse sat by Alice. Alice was heavily sedated; they could not yet risk her arousal from the drugs to the experience of anguish and pain. Two women lay in agony that night in Whytecliffe, and Lally, as she listened to Margaret's cries, knew that she longed to scream also, longed to give tongue to pain and grief. But neither cries nor the relief of tears would come.

"Lally—oh, Lally!" Margaret cried. "Bring Lally."

When Lally bent over her she found her hand grasped with strength she hadn't known Margaret possessed. "Lally, I'm sorry. I'm sorry! If I hadn't burnt the toys, it would never have happened. Lally —if I could only give you back Jonathan. If only I could give you this baby."

"Bear down," Lally said roughly, knowing another contraction had begun. "Bear down. The sooner he's born the stronger you'll be. Brock wants you well and strong."

Margaret had refused all but a minimum of drugs. "I don't want the baby born drugged. I have so much to make up for."

"Make up? What have you to make up?"

"I have to try. I have to try to be . . . well, better. Lally, forgive me. I'll get through this if I know you forgive me."

Lally bent and kissed the forehead that was wet with sweat. "There's nothing to forgive. There never could be—not for Black Jack's daughter."

There it all was, as vivid as ever, the memory of that night she had curled up with Black Jack in his chair, the night Alice's mother had died, the night she had promised to take care of them all. She looked at Margaret's tortured, exhausted face. "Forget about it. Forget everything." She had said the words many times, and had not meant them. Somewhere from the depth of her own pain she found the beginning of truth. "Forget everything that's happened. Just get Brock's baby born. You owe me that. You owe me and Brock and Black Jack a fine, strong baby. That's all you have to do."

Margaret clamped her lips against another cry. When the contraction had passed she said faintly, "I'll do it. Leave me now, Lally. I'll get this thing over with."

She did not call for Lally again all through the hours of the night, and not until, in the hot afternoon hours of the next day, Brock's second son was born.

The baby was four weeks premature, but he was strong and well. Lally held him for a time, noting that everything about him was perfectly formed. He gazed at Lally unfocusedly, but the dark-blue eyes were Brock's, the slope of his forehead was Brock's; unlike his two brothers, his hair was dark, thick and dark. The face seemed to have no baby roundness about it, but a lean, hard adult look.

"I wish," Margaret whispered, "I could give him to you."

Lally managed to smile faintly. "No, this is Brock's child. I don't think there's a scrap of you in him. This is Brock's child to the fingertips. Look, Margaret—he's holding on to me already. Look how he's gripping me. He's going to be a doer, just like his father. He'll be as tough as Brock, and probably twice as clever—if you don't spoil him. If you let him turn into a brat, *then* I'll never forgive you."

"Then you'll keep coming to check on him—and me—won't you, Lally? To keep me to my promise." Tears of weakness came to her eyes.

Lally handed the baby back to the nurse. "Go to sleep. I'll keep coming."

Wearily she went downstairs to where Black Jack and Edith and Brock sat in silence on the terrace. A promise lasted forever, didn't it —renewed with each generation? She hadn't promised for any length of time, but forever. She thought of the young woman who had just given birth, and of the other young woman who lay in a deep sleep of morphine, the heavily bandaged hands strapped to the sides of the bed to stop her tearing at them. Forgiveness had to be extended to both now. She saw Black Jack lift his head expectantly; his look was almost pleading, the dark hooked brows raised.

"You have another beautiful grandson, Father." She looked from him to Brock. "Margaret has done you proud."

Brock rose, and took her arm and walked her gently along the terrace. He turned her away from the view over the Sound, turned her to the gardens, where the sprinklers worked against the burning afternoon heat; it was as if he wanted to blot out the sight of the water, the memory of yesterday morning. But over there, in the deep shade under one of the huge trees, she could make out the white-clad figure of Nanny Williams, the listless figure of David hunched on the seat beside her. The baby, Dan, recognized his father and came at a run across the grass.

"If I could have given the life of this new one for Jonathan's I would have, Lally—I mean it."

She watched as he swept up his son in his arms. "No. They're not exchangeable. Not at all. One doesn't equal the other. The new one— he's all yours, Brock. As Jonathan was all Jon's. That's what I mind so much. The last of Jon is gone. Everything of Black Jack must now continue through your and Margaret's sons, Brock. He'll go on that way. But there isn't any more of Jon."

* * *

The inquest was held, and a verdict of death by drowning returned. On Dr. Morton's evidence, and the evidence of a psychiatrist, Alice was deemed not fit to be questioned. Lally simply told the coroner that she had gone looking for the boys and Alice, and had seen, once she reached them, that her son was in difficulties in the water. She said nothing about Alice holding them both tightly to her at a distance from the shore where she could stand, but where the boys were out of their depth. She described her efforts to rescue her son. "Did Miss Pollock attempt to help you?"

"In a sense. As much as she could. She would still have been in great pain and under the influence of morphine. She didn't seem quite to understand what was happening. I had to bring her back to the beach myself."

Her evidence was accepted without further question. It had been her son who had drowned. The coroner expressed his sympathy. Black Jack held her arm tightly as he led her from the little courtroom.

* * *

Lally refused the suggestion of burial for Jonathan on Long Island. "No—I want him in his own place. With Jon."

So Black Jack and Mark Shaw traveled with her on the ship that sailed later that week, the casket containing Jonathan's body in the hold. Edith would stay until Alice was fit to travel. The days of the voyage passed in a trance-like state for Lally. She had food sent to her stateroom, and could not eat it. She found that, although she longed for fresh air, she could not bear the sight of the sea—the sea, endlessly the sea, all around her. She fancied too often she saw the sight of a bright blond head there where the white wake boiled. The need for exercise drove her onto the deck early one morning; Mark Shaw fell in beside her. They paced mainly in silence, around and around—a mile, two miles. As they approached the stern of the ship once again she tried to distract herself from the sight of the white water.

"What will you do now? It was thoughtless of me. I haven't asked."

"What will I do? I'm not certain. I can't go back to schoolmastering again. I'm considering an offer. An offer from Mr. Weymouth."

"What would you do for him?"

"He suggests I could be useful. As a sort of private secretary—a confidential secretary, he called it. And he would like me to continue to tutor Lord Grenfell. He wants him to be fully ready for Eton. The tutoring part of it I understand—although he's already going to school. I'm less sure about the secretary part. Wall Street isn't much my line, and I doubt how useful I could be. I would be there only one day a week—and mainly be responsible for the financial arrangements at Whytecliffe. I think . . . well, I suspect it's a

sort of invented position just to keep me around. A bit of England
for Lord Grenfell. Sometimes a companion to Mrs. Weymouth. It
sounds like a bit of a dog's-body job to me. Teach Dan his ABC's
and Lord Grenfell Virgil. But it could be . . . interesting. I'd live at
Whytecliffe."

Brock would never stop, Lally thought. He sought to draw all of
them, by any means, into his circle, to surround Margaret with re-
minders of home. She glanced at the strained, tired face of the young
man, remembering that she had not slowed her walk to accommodate
his limp, but he had kept up. He would be drawn by Brock. He
would give in. He would teach David Latin and Greek, and teach
Dan to name the grasses and the weeds, the birds that flew. He would
stay on and on, teaching the new, as yet unnamed baby when his turn
came, and he would be there at Margaret's side when she needed talk
more stimulating than Nanny Williams'. Yes, he would be a dog's-
body. She had given no thought to Mark Shaw since that night on the
beach when Alice had burned her hands. She realized she was as
guilty as any of them in regarding him as some sort of superior servant, someone cultured and educated enough to eat at the table with
them, but also someone to fetch and carry, to stay with the boys, to
collect Margaret's tennis rackets, or bring her her martini.

"I might even"—his laugh had no pretense of humor in it—"I
might even make some money on Wall Street. Everyone else seems
to be doing it."

"If you're going back, then why are you here—with us?"

"Did you think I could let you go alone? That I wouldn't share
this last thing with you? Jonathan was *my* responsibility. I blame myself that I wasn't up—awake—that morning. My room is next to the
boys'. But I'd asked the doctor for something to help me sleep. I was
having . . . having difficulty with my breathing. But I should have
heard."

"No one is to blame," Lally said firmly. "No one must be blamed.
We must never let ourselves blame Alice."

"And Alice must never be left alone again," Mark said as firmly.
"Have none of you learned yet? Do you all blind yourselves to the
danger she is to herself and others—because you love her? It *is*
blindness. You must protect others from her, and her from herself."

"It would break my father's heart to suggest some sort of . . . of
keeper for her."

"Then it must break. For myself, I hope I never see her again."

He left her abruptly, turning away and walking in the opposite direction. When he was tired his limp was more pronounced.

* * *

It was raining when they reached Southampton, and it rained during the whole journey back to Yorkshire. There was something fitting about the rain, Lally thought. Why shouldn't the whole world weep with her? It was raining as they buried Jonathan beside his father in the churchyard of Pellham Langley. The whole village seemed to be there, the crowd parting before them as Black Jack held her arm on the way back to the car. Billings looked old and stricken and bent. But he insisted on serving them when they returned to Pellham Langley. He brought the whiskey Black Jack had asked for, and glasses for her and Mark Shaw also. But he didn't speak of Jonathan.

"Why, I remember it as if it were just yesterday, Miss Lally. I remember the night Sir John brought you here and none of us thought you'd see the night out." He was remembering the survival of life, unwilling to speak of death.

"We've walked a long road since then, Billings," Black Jack said. He urged the whiskey on Lally. "Drink it. You look frozen."

"Frozen—but it's only August," she replied. "And you've missed the opening of the grouse-shooting season again."

"It seems, sir, that we've never had a proper grouse-shooting season since that one we missed when the Great War broke out. Things have never been the same since." Then he withdrew.

Black Jack turned suddenly from the fire. He seemed unaware of Mark Shaw's presence. "I wish you *had* married Gerry Harper," he said, his tone almost angry. "At least you'd have some sort of a life. Children. Something to build on."

Mark Shaw started to rise, embarrassed. She gestured impatiently for him to stay.

"One can't marry just to have children. Gerry's all right—but he can't ever be Jon."

"Jon won't come back. Nor will Jonathan," Black Jack said harshly, his pain evident. "Accept it, Lally. What will you do now?"

"What I've always done—work."

❦ CHAPTER 14 ❧

I

Lally was with Black Jack at Southampton when the Cunarder with Edith and Alice aboard docked. Lally was there because she knew she had to be. "Of course I'm coming," she had said when Black Jack had asked. Before this time he wouldn't have had to ask. Some almost buried part of her dreaded the sight of Alice. She had said that no one could, or must, blame Alice, but the nightmare that she fought most constantly now was the sight of Alice in the water, the two blond heads clasped against her, the strength imparted perhaps by drugs and pain enabling her to hold those two struggling figures just long enough to exhaust them. In her sleep, and in the long wakeful hours, she still fought to save Jonathan, and only a small voice of conscience questioned whether, if she had known in those panicked moments which boy was which, she would have first broken Jonathan lose and let David fight for himself? Until now she had never let herself ask how responsible Alice had been. She told herself that was another question she must not ask.

So she greeted Alice as always, and Alice flung herself into Lally's arms. "Oh, I've missed you." Then she thrust her hands forward. "Look, Lally—look! The marks won't go away. Every morning I look to see if they've gone, but they're always there."

Lally examined them carefully, as Alice expected her to do. Then she lifted them and kissed the still-livid scars. She had seen some burns like that during the war—sometimes the metal of the big guns had been dangerously hot and had been handled in haste. She thought of Alice's anguish when Margaret had thrown the dolls on the fire; the emotion must have been as great as any soldier had known to drive her to rescue them in spite of such pain. Then she looked from the marked hands to the beautiful, still-innocent face, and told herself that it never had been possible that Alice had known what she was doing that morning in the waves. She had sought the cooling comfort of the water, and she had taken the little boys. She had treated them as she treated her dolls, hugging them to her fiercely. Lally decided then that Alice had never truly known the line that divided those two little boys from the lifeless wax and rag images of her playthings. She had loved them with equal passion. She did not know she had destroyed one of them. Lally knew that that was what she, from now on, would believe. She would question no more. She would somehow find some peace.

"Darling," she said, "eventually they'll be better. We'll see if we can't make them better."

And Alice smiled. "I knew you would. I said, 'Lally will make them better,' didn't I? Lady Mama?"

Edith smiled wearily. "Yes, dear. You said that."

A woman in a severely styled coat and hat stepped forward. "Now, Miss Alice, we'll get our things and go ashore. You're going back home, dear. And I'm going to see this great big place with all the animals in the garden, aren't I?"

Alice's face took on a faintly cowed look. She glanced from Edith to her father, and back to the woman. "Yes, Barnes. We're going home."

Edith drew Lally aside as the small hand baggage was carried away. "Of course we had to get Barnes. Brock insisted on it. Alice can never be left alone again. We all thought, among us, we could do it. But one falls asleep—as Nanny Williams did. From now on Barnes will sleep in Alice's room. And we must have someone else, because Barnes cannot do it seven days a week, all day and night. But discreetly. Kindly. Alice must not be made afraid. It would break your father's heart." Then she put her hands on Lally's shoulders. "Remember what it was like, child? How splendidly you did that year? I always knew you would do wonderful things. *Your* heart has been broken. At the moment, you have nothing left. Help me to save what I can for Jack. Will you help me, Lally?"

"Always." Another promise given.

She went to Pellham Langley with them because Black Jack wanted it. They were met at Leeds by Billings and two chauffeured cars. "Welcome home, m'lady. Welcome home, Miss Alice."

At Pellham Langley Alice raced into the big hall. "Jonathan! Where are you? It's me. It's Alice. I'm home. I'm home. Jonathan, let's go and look at Rabbit and Cat and Dog. Jonathan . . . ?" She raced up the stairs. They heard her calling along the passage on the first floor. "Jonathan? You're hiding from me. Mark, bring Jonathan!"

Barnes started to go up what were to her unfamiliar stairs. Black Jack's hand restrained her. "She knows her way. She can come to no harm here." They heard her voice calling distantly on the nursery floor. Then she finally came down again. "Where are they?"

Lally took the scarred hands. "Mark has gone back to America, dear. To be with David, and Margaret—and Brock."

Alice seemed able to understand this information, but it was a long time before she asked the next question. "Jonathan? Where is Jonathan?"

"Jonathan . . ." Lally was not able to look into her face, so she grasped Alice and held her against her shoulder. "Jonathan is dead, Alice. Do you understand about someone being dead?"

Alice wrenched herself out of Lally's clasp. "Dead? Like Teddy Rose and Madame Butterfly and Raggedy Ann? Dead—like them? Did Margaret do it?"

"No, darling. Margaret didn't do it. It was . . . it was an accident, Alice."

She fled from them. They heard her scream as she ran up the stairs, "Jonathan? Teddy Rose? Not dead. Not dead!" This time, when Barnes ran to follow her, Black Jack did not restrain her.

I I

Autumn merged into winter, and Lally barely noticed the shortened days, the chill as the wind-blown rain hit her face. She no longer went regularly to Pellham Langley; not even her love for Black Jack could make her do that. There was no Jonathan to greet her, there were no "surprises" to find for him. Instead there was Alice's eager, still-questioning face. "Jonathan?" she still asked, but now only half-hopefully. When Lally walked on the moors Alice always begged to go with her. She had learned to ask permission from Barnes, and from another, a rather plump, more motherly soul called Shearing. Lally could never bear to refuse, mostly because it would have hurt Black Jack so much. So she and Alice walked where the three of them had walked so often before. Alice now was more silent. The great house at Pellham Langley was now without a child to warm and distract it. It grew in upon itself. Alice's silence perhaps reflected the silence of the house, the mourning, which she did not understand. Lally recognized a fear—a fear of beginning to blame Alice.

No one, on the advice of a London psychiatrist, had attempted to do anything about the burn marks on her hands. "The pain will be enormous," he had said, "and perhaps to no purpose, because it will be impossible to eradicate those burn marks. With the years, they will fade, somewhat. And by inflicting the pain and the terror of those operations, you may reawaken the emotions which caused them. Better that her hands should look as they do than that the poor puzzled girl should again begin to ask the questions. For the moment, let the mind and the hands try to heal themselves. Perhaps next year, when she is more stable . . . perhaps we will explore the mind a little. But have no false hopes, Sir John. At her age, brain damage from birth is not reversible. Should I awaken the spectacle?— the fears? She is docile now, and probably will be for the rest of her life, so long as no other terrible incident should trigger her anger and fear. You have made more of your Alice, Sir John, than anyone could have supposed. And you have done it only by love. Where you have been wise and loving, it would be presumption on the part of doctors to interfere."

Black Jack reported this to Lally, and took it as the last word; he returned to Pellham Langley. "Please try to come when you can, Lally. We miss you." He might have said, "We need you," but he did not.

Susie threw an increasing amount of work at her, as if trying to test how much she could absorb. To Lally's numbed, bemused mind, the work itself came easily. It was so much easier to fill the day with activities than to spend time alone, remembering. Susie herself was kind but blunt. "Lally, you've had a rotten deal. But look around you. There are a few million women who never had the chance to get married because their men went in the war. But you got Jon, and you got a child. You lost them. But once you *had* them. There has to be something in the memory of once having been loved. You once had a child. You think of the unmarried, childless women floating around this country . . . well, I'm one of them. You wouldn't want to be me, would you?"

Sometimes Lally thought she would have liked to be Susie. Susie saw the world now totally in terms of her work, and the work was paying off. The sharp, clever designs, never more advanced than the average woman in the provinces would venture to wear, were finding a market. The "Susie" label was beginning to be known through the trade, and asked for. It was not a name the average woman for whom Susie designed knew well, but the drapers in the High Streets did. "She's fiendishly clever," Julian said once to Lally. "The sheer simplicity of the things deceive the little woman in the street that she's not really very daring. But simplicity is the hardest of all things to get across successfully. Any fool can put frills and bows all over everything. If your father stays behind her, and Brock Weymouth, she'll probably make a fortune."

"I don't think Susie really cares about making a fortune. She just wants to be a success."

Julian raised his thin eyebrows. "How can you be one without the other?"

"Oh, I don't know. I think Susie gets more satisfaction from seeing one of her dresses worn on the street than by any of the money in the bank. She talks about being a millionaire, but she really hasn't any idea what that means."

"And you, darling, do. After all, coming from that rich family, you must understand money very well."

"Rich families have nothing much to do with understanding money, as a rule." She was suddenly remembering all the gilded youth of her childhood, the one long last summer before the war, the big hats, the pearls, the season of Margaret's triumph and her own anguish. She was remembering the long pleasure-seeking days on Long Island, the tempo that tried to go faster and faster as people seemed to lose the connection between the money they spent, and the way it was made. One generation removed from the roots and they seemed lost.

* * *

As if challenged by what Susie had said about the women who had never had the chance of husband or children, Lally made a deliberate effort to pull herself out of her mood of near despair, to banish self-pity, the sense of loneliness crowding her. Acquaintances she had barely remembered from her season, and the years after, suddenly emerged and tried to become friends. Parties and dinners became once more a ritual of her life. She found she welcomed them; they filled the empty hours between leaving the workroom, and the time when she sought sleep. Susie urged her to accept every invitation. "It'll do you good. People are trying to be kind . . . go at least half-way to meet them. You've been too wrapped up in Jonathan and the work here. Part of that's my fault, and I should have seen it before. Now I'd like to see you try to enjoy yourself a little. Accept every invitation that comes your way. It'll help, you'll see."

Lally was surprised to find it did help. A slow understanding of Margaret's restless activity began to dawn on her; was Margaret endlessly fleeing that one night of her life she could not forget? And now here was she, Lally, attempting the same thing, though not with Margaret's almost manic energy. An acquaintance of her coming-out year, Isobel Paynton, spoke what many people seemed to feel about her. "I'm so glad to see you making an effort, Lally. You remember, we all did try after Jon was killed, but you were so . . . so remote. And after that, so wrapped up in your business. Everyone would help, if you let them."

Lally blinked, and seemed to see Isobel Paynton, and others like her, for the first time. It was surprising how many people she knew, people who seemed to want her company, welcomed her to their circle. Some men had survived the war, after all; and the women lucky enough to have married them seemed as determined as any of Margaret's group to put the war behind them. Gradually Lally fell into the pattern of theaters and dinner and supper parties, and found she enjoyed organizing the return of the hospitality she received.

"My dear, it's good to see you breaking out," Julian said. "You were almost turning into a professional widow, and they're such bores." Julian was becoming omnipresent in her life now, as her escort, making up the extra place at her dinner table. She enjoyed his company; he was smooth and charming, and there was never any danger that there would be a romantic attachment between them. They were an agreeable convenience to each other.

It was at one of the cocktail parties she gave at her flat that Lally first thought she saw her. She always hired a butler and as many extra maids as were necessary from the same agency when she entertained. When necessary she hired a cook. The agency tried to send the same people, and Lally became familiar with most of them. They carried trays of cocktails and passed canapés. Afterward they left the kitchen immaculate, with dishes set out with cold meat and cheese and wine cooling for the few guests who remained. It was an efficient service, a useful adjunct to the woman, Mrs. Tracy, who came daily to do Lally's cleaning and food shopping. It was efficient and just about anonymous until she saw, under the frilled white cap the women always wore, the face she had first seen at her wedding. She saw the face sideways as the woman hovered by the elbow of a guest with a tray laden with drinks. Then the woman turned, and across the room their eyes met for a fraction of time—eyes which Lally had never forgotten. Then someone moved and blocked Lally's view. It wasn't true, she told herself. A passing resemblance—some half-remembered ghost from her past. But nevertheless, she managed to stay at that end of the room where the butler served drinks. As her gaze flickered across to the woman from time to time, the face coming and receding through the crowd, Lally grew less sure. The woman made no attempt to approach her. She seemed to spend most of her time in the kitchen; she mostly carried trays from which the butler served. The crowd began to thin; people said good-bye, and Lally was left with just four, Julian among them. They sat in the big bay window of the drawing room while the butler cleared the last of the empty glasses and the ashtrays.

The moment came when she had to go to the kitchen. To her relief there remained only Mrs. Tracy, washing and drying glasses, and the butler, Hopkins. "I hope everything was satisfactory, madam?"

"Yes, Hopkins—thank you." She gave him his tip. "Did I see a new waitress this evening?"

"Yes, madam. She's just joined the agency. I hope there wasn't anything wrong, madam? She said she had experience. I thought myself she did very well."

"No—everything was excellent, thank you. I just . . . well, I thought I knew her from somewhere."

"It's possible you've seen her at some other party, madam. Perhaps even in Yorkshire. I recall she said she had lived there for a time."

"Yes, that's possible." The fear that had first clutched Lally was growing. "She's gone?"

"Oh, yes, madam. There's just Mrs. Tracy and myself finishing up."

She had been mistaken, she told herself. It was just a passing resemblance. The woman had not stayed on, not waited until she knew Lally would have to come to the kitchen. But still Lally had Hopkins mix her another drink, and her hands were not quite steady as she accepted it. She returned to Julian and the other three guests. "Something wrong?" Julian asked. "You look quite pale."

"Nothing." She managed to smile. "It's just been rather a long day."

But later, when Julian carried trays into the dining room and they helped themselves to the food informally, Lally found as she raised the fork to her mouth that the old, fearful smell was back—the smell that accompanied the darkness of her dream. After that she pushed the food around on her plate, and made a pretense of eating it. She hardly heard the conversation; it seemed an endless time before they all left, but when they had gone the silence of the flat seemed unbearable because she now could hear the pounding of her own heart. She lay wakeful in bed, the old, terrible smell almost stifling her, and the remembered eyes bored through the darkness.

Gradually the fear receded. She thrust it away, would not permit herself to dwell on it. It was a coincidental resemblance to the woman who had claimed to be her mother. She would probably never see her again.

But she was there, the next time Lally gave a dinner party. It was Hopkins who served the soup, but Lally, from her place at the head of the table, with Julian at the opposite end, glanced toward the sideboard. There, reflected in the mirror above it, was the woman, wearing a black dress, a white frilled cap on her dark, silver-streaked hair. The familiar dark eyes now sought and held hers. For almost thirty seconds they gazed at each other's reflection in the mirror. This time Lally knew there was no coincidental resemblance. The woman staring at her was the one who had appeared at her wedding reception, the one who had talked with Black Jack in the hall at Grangewick. Lally laid down her spoon, and was not able to utter a word to the guests on either side of her. Hopkins came at last to clear the plates. "Are you finished, madam?" She nodded dumbly.

That night Julian carried the party for her. He covered her silence, exerted himself to entertain the six other guests, told stories with his slightly malicious wit, played the piano when coffee was served. The woman came and went, mostly carrying trays for Hopkins. She was deft and neat in her movements, Lally observed, and never again did she attempt to engage Lally's attention. But Lally was achingly, fearfully aware of her presence.

"Are you ill?" Julian said when they were alone. She had thrust another brandy on him, determined to make him stay, to make him outstay the help in the kitchen. She had called Hopkins to the hall to tip him, and gave him money for the cook and the waitress. She did not dare, herself, to venture into the kitchen.

"A headache, Julian."

He nodded sympathetically. "You're doing very well, Lally. People admire you for trying to get over the—the child's death. Not moping. Of course we all know it's hard. You're bound to get these spells from time to time."

She tried to thank him. "You're very good to me, Julian."

"My dear, what are friends for?" He was suave, urbane, and he had not realized that she almost shook with terror. She spun out her own brandy as long as she could to make him stay. The sounds in the kitchen had ceased. Everyone was gone. It was safe to let Julian go. He pecked her lightly on the cheek. "Off to bed now, like a good girl. Tell Susie I'll kill her if she's working you too hard."

When he was gone she wandered through the emptiness of the flat. It was after midnight. The sounds of the traffic had died, and silence pressed upon her. Once again the sound of her own heart was louder than anything else. She walked along the hall to her bedroom, and then stopped and looked back. A light still shone under the green baize-covered door. She crept back, placed her head against the door, and listened. There was no sound. Slowly she opened the door. Everything was as Hopkins always left it. All dishes washed and put away in the cupboards; her tea tray for the morning was ready. She was about to switch off the light when her gaze went to the door which led to the maid's bedroom and bathroom—a room not used except for storage because she had never had a live-in maid. It was slightly ajar, and as she stood there, her hand on the light switch, the door opened further. The woman stood there, wearing a plain black coat and gloves, a cloche hat pulled down on her dark hair, just the touch of a white scarf at her neck.

"Well—there you are, Lily. I've been waiting."

Lally grasped the doorframe. "You!"

"I've been wanting to come and see you for ever such a long time,

Lily. After your husband was killed. And then when I read in the papers about your little boy. That was sad, Lily. As your mother, I feel these things."

"*Mother!* You've been no mother to me! You're not my mother. You've only tricked Black Jack into thinking you *might* be. But you're not! You have no proof. Nothing at all. Just a clever guess."

That strangely harsh laugh she remembered sounded again. "Proof? What proof do I need? Every year older you get, the proof is stronger. Look, Lily—just look."

Almost tentatively the black gloved hand touched Lally's shoulder. Helplessly, as if her bones had turned to water, Lally found herself pivoting to face the green baize door. The slightest pressure from the woman's hand urged her nearer the mirror that hung there so that a manservant or maid could adjust their tie or cap before answering the summons of a bell. It was a narrow mirror, but the two faces could be seen there, and the light from the overhead lamp was bright.

Dark gray eyes looked at dark gray eyes; the eyebrows had the same dark curve, the same hollows appeared under the cheekbones. As Lally shifted slightly, seeking perhaps to deny what her own eyes told her, she saw the line of her jawbone exactly matched the other woman's. The woman pulled off the cloche hat, and her thick black hair, with its silver streaks, fell neatly in the same line across her cheeks as Lally's did. The face was older, gaunt, lined. It showed the years that separated them. Perhaps more, it showed the years of ill-nourishment, of poverty, of hardship. But it was still the face that Lally's eventually would become.

The compelling hand fell away from her. "You do see, don't you, Lily?"

"I see." For a few moments longer she gazed at that face, her own face grown old. Then she said, "What do you want? Is it money? More money?"

"Money isn't enough, Lily. I want my child. I want to have my child back."

"Your *child!*" Lally's tone rose in outrage. "You gave me away. Threw me away. Left me to die. You have no claim on me."

"I didn't leave you to die, Lily. You would have died within a day or two. That's how close we were to it. I'd seen plenty of others die. Other children. Some of them right there in that room where we lived. We hadn't enough food to keep body and soul together. I thought I could last the few days until the job I was promised began.

But you wouldn't have lasted. I couldn't take you with me to the mill. You had to go. So I left you where you might be picked up. At least that way there was a chance for you. The Corn Exchange was a good place. Some of those merchants are rich men. I never hoped for such luck as Black Jack Pollock."

Lally sank down on a chair. "What do you want?" she repeated.

"Not much. Just a chance to see you. I kept my promise to Mr. Pollock—Sir John. He's been paying me a little on a regular basis. I kept out of the way. Lived in a boardinghouse. Not fancy, but respectable. I haven't had to work. I did a bit of sewing and mending for ladies just to pass the time. No . . . no men, Lily. There haven't been any men."

"If you're my mother, someone has to have been my father."

"Don't judge me, Lily. A woman does what she has to. Sometimes there was only one way. I'd known better things when I was young. What I came to be was not the doing of one man—but it was a man who started it. I tell you I never went back to it. Not once there was Mr. Pollock—Sir John—to help me. I thought about you. I wanted to see my grandson—"

"Don't!" Lally clapped her hands over her ears. "Don't talk about Jonathan. I don't want to hear."

Slowly the woman replaced her hat. "All right, Lily. I'll go now. But I'll be back. I'll be back tomorrow evening. I'll come to the service entrance, of course."

"If it's money you want," Lally said, "I'll pay you more. Father needn't know."

"No, Lily, it isn't money. I'll be back."

The woman was gone. Lally listened to the soft closing of the kitchen door which led to the back stairs. The woman had been clean and neatly dressed. Her hair had a clean luster to it. But the room smelled. It was the old terrifying smell of poverty and death. Lally shivered violently with the cold that had suddenly invaded her body. The woman had needed to produce no proof. The proof was in the two faces which had confronted each other in the mirror.

The next day Susie had looked at her in alarm. "Gawd, Lally, you look terrible. Here, let me get you a cup of tea." When it was brewed she added a dash of brandy to it. "What is it?"

"Oh—just a bad night."

Susie held a light to her cigarette. "That wasn't just a bad night. It must have been a terrible night."

"Yes—it was."

Susie asked no more questions but hovered over her through the day. She insisted that they go to Armand's for dinner when she learned that Lally had no other engagement. She looked with concern at the small amount of food Lally ate. Outside the restaurant she said, "Here, let me walk you home."

A feeling of panic engulfed Lally. "No—I'm taking a taxi. Suddenly I feel like going to bed. I'll sleep. I'm sure I'll sleep tonight."

Susie saw her into a taxi, but once it was beyond her sight, Lally stopped it and paid off the driver. She started the walk along Knightsbridge, her footsteps dragging. At one moment she almost hailed another taxi to take her to King's Cross station, and the next train to Leeds, and to Black Jack. All these years, by threats and bribes, Black Jack had held the woman at bay. Now it was her, Lally's, turn to carry the load. She had not died that night outside the Corn Exchange. She had always sensed, unconsciously, that somehow, at some time, the gift of life would have to be paid for.

She half-expected the woman to be waiting for her, either outside the block of flats, or in the lobby. But the night porter greeted her cheerfully, and there was no message of anyone having called.

But she had barely taken off her coat when the service bell sounded at the kitchen door. She opened it, keeping the chain on the door. The woman stood there. Lally slid the chain off, and let it fall.

"I've been waiting, Lily. I've been out there on the stairs for hours. I came up while the day porter was on duty. They don't take any notice of people like me coming and going during the day. So long as you're respectably dressed, and look as if you belong. I waited up on the next landing until your Mrs. Tracy left. I wouldn't want to push my way in." She looked around the kitchen. "It's been a long wait, Lily. Can I make a cup of tea?"

Dumbly Lally nodded. She watched the neat movements of the woman, the careful way she set the cup and saucer. "Would you like a cup, Lily? You look done in." She did not argue when Lally shook her head, just went on and cut a piece of bread, and buttered it while she waited for the kettle to boil. "Do you mind if I sit down?"

Incredulously, Lally stared at her. This woman had to be her mother—or else the likeness was a cruel trick of nature onto which she had fastened. Her plain black dress with its white collar was severe. Her hands were bare, save for a slim gold band on her finger. Her body was thin, and she was of more than medium height. Susie,

Lally thought, might even have considered her stylish in her simplicity. But her face was ravaged and worn, and when she had smiled faintly she revealed missing and twisted teeth.

"Mrs. Brown I'm called. Rose Brown."

Rose—Lily. Was that the only gift she had had to bestow on her child? The name of a flower?

"Won't you sit down, Lily?"

Lally sank into a chair on the other side of the scrubbed table. "What do you *want?*" she whispered. "If not money—what then?"

"Just a little place here with you. Just a chance to see you. To look after you."

"*Look after me!* Now! After all these years. You must be mad. I wouldn't—"

"Wouldn't you, Lily? Wouldn't you do that?" The woman's head jerked toward the door to the maid's room. "I'd be so snug in there. I'd clean and cook for you. See to your clothes. I'm quite good at those sort of things. I'm not ignorant, you see. I've been in domestic service. I know how things are done. I didn't always work in a mill— or on the streets. You'd find me a help, Lily. It would be a pleasure to look after my own child. I never came near you so long as your little boy was alive. I never wanted him to guess who I was. I didn't want to shame him. But you're different, Lily. You were old enough to remember a little bit about how things were—how bad they were. Would you begrudge me this last bit of pleasure? Can't I ever show that I'm sorry for what I had to do all those years ago?"

Lally realized she was sinking beneath the weight of what was being imposed on her. Rage, compassion, pity . . . what was uppermost? Every emotion fought within her. The strongest of all was the old fear.

"I'd make sure no one ever suspected. I'd always wear a uniform, and keep my place. No one ever looks at people like me."

"Black Jack . . . ?" Lally whispered.

"Need never know. Ever since I came to London and found where you were living—and got myself a position with the agency you use—the landlady at the boardinghouse has been sending on the money Sir John sends through his solicitors. She keeps a few shillings for her trouble. You wouldn't want to worry Sir John, would you? It wouldn't do to worry him when he's been so good to us both. Of course, if you should marry again, I'd clear off. I wouldn't stand in your way. But just for a little while . . . let me, Lily. A mother is still a mother. I know what it's like to be a mother and lose a child. You know now, Lily."

Lally struggled for a few moments, twisting and turning within her own thoughts. "Why should I?" she said, a question almost for herself. "Why should I let you do this to me?"

"Because I've had nothing in my life. Nothing. You can give me something—for a while." The tone was quite smooth and even. She knew where her strength lay. Lally acknowledged a kind of emotional blackmail in what was being laid on her. Then she suddenly saw the way through the fear which had haunted her since the day Black Jack had scooped her up and taken her to a different life. Confront the fear, face it—and banish it.

"Yes," she said.

In the end it would be she, Lally, who would win, not the woman—she could not call her her mother. She was the woman, Mrs. Brown.

And so Mrs. Tracy was edged out of her life and Mrs. Brown took up residence. Sometimes Lally could not believe what she had done, had agreed to. Mrs. Brown was everything she had promised, and sometimes more. But there was an unreality in the situation against which Lally chafed. She found it almost impossible to accept that she sat while Mrs. Brown served her meals. Her cooking was plain, but good, and she took pride in its presentation. It was a shock to Lally when, on the first night Mrs. Brown occupied the maid's room, she came into her bedroom to find that her bed had been turned down, and her nightgown laid out. That happened at Pellham Langley, but never before in London. Her underwear was beautifully laundered, and when necessary, mended. Her dresses were inspected for sagging hems or stitches coming loose. A hundred little services were performed for her which were beyond anything an ordinary servant would have considered her duty. And yet she rarely saw Mrs. Brown. The door to the kitchen remained firmly closed unless she was wanted. When Lally entertained, Mrs. Brown took a subservient role to Hopkins, who thought that Mrs. Brown had somehow ingratiated herself with Mrs. Pollock and found steady employment. He made no comment to Lally on the situation. Lally, wary and still a little fearful, noticed that Mrs. Brown stayed away from her guests as much as possible, and when she had to carry trays or serve, she kept her eyes lowered, and her frilled white cap was pulled far forward on her forehead. She addressed Lally, even when they were alone, as "Mrs. Pollock." Only first thing in the morning, when she came to

Lally's bedside with tea did Lally hear the whisper, "Lily? Good morning, Lily."

Sometimes outrage rose in Lally's heart once again. She did not want to be served by her own mother. And yet if the woman was not her mother, then Lally was the victim of an unforgivable deception. Mrs. Brown stayed behind the green baize door of the kitchen, and offered little enlightenment about her past. She talked vaguely of having worked for the family of a vicar. "A big old rectory near Bath, Mrs. Pollock." She never volunteered any information on how she had come to move from the West Country to Yorkshire, and her accent was a strange mixture of a number of regions. She went no further back than the time of service in the rectory. It was as if existence had begun there; her parents were never mentioned, and Lally did not ask. It was enough, surely, to accept this woman as her mother; she did not have to accept unknown grandparents, perhaps aunts and uncles, cousins. There was a pact of silence established between them.

And yet Mrs. Brown, for all her discretion, seemed unable to restrain little gestures of possessiveness. If Lally were dressing to go out, she made some pretext to come into her room to see how she looked. "Oh, beautiful, Mrs. Pollock! I'll just set out the tray for cocktails now, shall I? Shall I leave a bite ready for you when you come in . . . some milk, perhaps? No? You don't eat much, Mrs. Pollock." She would telephone for a taxi for Lally, and see her to the lift. Lally came to dread the moment when she put her key in the door after an evening out, lest the green baize door should swing open. It never did. But she was constantly, endlessly aware of the presence on the other side of it.

And yet, she knew, she was slowly winning the struggle against the fear which had possessed her. The memory of the cold dark room would be there forever, but they had both survived it. Perhaps the interpretation Mrs. Brown put on her action in abandoning her child had some merit in it. Lally had been given, at least, a chance.

"What," she once asked Mrs. Brown, "are we to do if my father comes to visit? He comes to London from time to time. He never stays here, but he calls."

"He'd never know me, Mrs. Pollock. I would make certain of that. Who looks at someone like me? He'd probably never notice you'd made a change from Mrs. Tracy."

But he would, Lally thought. It was a tightrope she walked.

That winter, apart from the little sachets of lavender, hand-stitched, which appeared in the wardrobe, there were extra little posies of flowers in her room, quite apart from the flowers she herself ordered from the florist. Tiny pale roses, a bunch of violets, and then, sickeningly, the smell of freesias. She rang the bell. "Mrs. Brown, I don't care for freesias." Once again she saw herself hurling them from her on the day Jonathan had been born; fear and outrage rose again.

"I'm sorry. I'll never put them here again . . . Lily."

The use of her name was the only signal she had that Mrs. Brown had very well remembered the only other time she had bought freesias for Lally Leeds.

Somehow the first long winter passed, and in a strange way the tension created by Mrs. Brown's presence had distracted her from her grief over Jonathan. Had this woman, with an uncanny sense of kinship, known this? Lally suddenly realized, as she raised her eyes from the order forms and the work sheets of their four workrooms filled with seamstresses, that it was spring. There had been a very successful showing of Susie's dresses for spring, but that had been in November. There had only been the ritual presents to be bought for Christmas for Alice and Black Jack and Edith, but no stocking to fill for Jonathan. There had mostly been silence by the fires of Pellham Langley. Billings had had a mild heart attack, and now he presided only over dinner, and footmen carried trays for him. The moors had been white with snow that Christmas, but there had not been the joy of tobogganing with Jonathan. Lally did not play the piano for Alice anymore, or try to teach her the words of the popular songs. The gramophone had taken over completely; Alice now learned the words by listening over and over, and she sang them in her clear, beautiful voice as she went about the house. Lord and Lady Gough, in a gesture of reconciliation toward Black Jack, perhaps as a gesture of sympathy toward Lally, who had lost her son while they had retained their only, their treasured grandchild, came over to spend the night after Christmas at Pellham Langley. They were gathered before the fire in the big hall, splendid in full evening dress, when Alice came down the stairs. Her hair was bound up behind her head; she wore a blue dress, one of Susie's. With a jolt Lally was dragged back to that Christmas during the war when they had joined with the convalescent officers here in this hall, and Alice had sung a Christmas carol, and looked like an angel. Now, as she moved down the stairs, she swayed with unconscious provocation to the rhythm of what she sang.

> *Show me the way to go home.*
> *I'm tired and I want to go to bed.*
> *Oh I had a little drink about an hour ago,*
> *And it's gone right to my head . . .*

She seemed not at all to understand what she was singing, but the shock of the words registered plainly on the faces of Lord and Lady Gough.

* * *

So Lally gratefully accepted the spring, and went back to Yorkshire for a week. She walked the moors with Alice, breathed the air, slept, finally without the help of the drug her doctor had thrust on her. The ice thawed from the edges of the beck. As she and Alice climbed to the top of the waterfall, Lally thought she heard a meadow pipit sing.

"Oh, isn't it free, Lally!"

Lally turned and looked at Alice almost for the first time with pity. No one ever supposed she might resent those well-meaning keepers, Barnes and Shearing. Did Alice feel her privacy was violated? Did she realize that she was never, these days, alone? No one would ever know what went on in Alice's mind. Black Jack was still hesitant about committing Alice to the long ordeal of treatment by a psychiatrist, knowing it could do nothing to help the gaps of understanding she suffered, and fearing the pain and passion the experience could arouse. Who was to say Black Jack was wrong?

There were other things occupying Black Jack's attention that spring. "It's going to be terrible, Lally," he said. "Our price of coal is hopelessly uncompetitive against German and Polish coal. The mineowners are banding together, and I'll find it hard to stand out."

"What are they going to do?"

"There's talk of a lockout. I'll be forced to close the mines."

He said that on the only night he was at Pellham Langley during Lally's visit. He drove all over the Midlands and the North; the sessions with other mineowners lasted interminable hours. Edith had pleaded to come with him, but he had asked her to stay. "What sort of holiday will it be for Lally with no one here? And Alice will be lonely."

After Alice had been taken upstairs by Shearing, who made gentle, clucking sounds with her tongue, and uttered the words, "Come along now, my little lamb . . . come along . . ." Lally questioned Edith bluntly. "Do you find it lonely here, Edith? I mean, even when Father's with you? Having Alice on your hands all the time? People have always said Pellham was a lonely place—too far out of the world."

Edith sipped the brandy that Billings had ordered served to them. The household had been given strict instructions by Black Jack that Lally was to be tempted to eat and drink well, anything that would help her to sleep. "Lonely? No, not lonely." She took her gaze away from the fire. "I love Black Jack, Lally." She waved a hand impatiently. "I don't mean I'm fond of him—I *love* him. I told you that once. If he had asked me to come to live at the North Pole with him, I would have gone. I never think of Pellham being lonely. It is where Jack wants to be. That's all that matters to me."

Lally bowed her head. Why did one assume that all passion was preserved for the young? By the firelight she saw the intensity of Edith's expression. Was every woman close to him condemned to love Black Jack this way—as she herself did?

Black Jack came home with a drawn face, and bad news. "The mineowners have voted for a lockout. I can't stand alone against them, and I can't afford to run the mines at the price the miners say I must pay them. The miners are asking for a thirteen percent raise, and they still won't work the extra hour. With the price I'd have to charge for our coal, the mines would be broke in six months. They've *got* to see it. They've got to!" He sat huddled in his chair by the fire, his face strained and exhausted. Edith touched his arm, and gave him brandy. "There's a lot of sympathy for them," he went on. "Other unions are talking of joining them if they strike. It would be a general strike." Edith and Lally had heard it all by wireless, had read it in the newspapers, but they let him talk on. He seemed to need to do so. "How am I going to do it to them? Most of them have worked for me all their lives, and some of their fathers before them. But if they don't agree to the terms we can offer, the mines will close, and I may never be able to open them again. You know what happens to a mine when it's left idle. The pumps don't work, the water creeps in, the air gets foul and unsafe. You can't bury a mine like a piece of gold in the ground and then expect to find it bright and shiny when you want it again. And I don't want to bury the men!"

The mineowners began a lockout on May 1. By May 3, railwaymen, printing trade workers, dock workers, iron, steel, chemical, and power workers walked out in sympathy. Lally was back in London and Susie had her decision ready. "I'm keeping the workrooms open. I have to. The women who want to come to work will come. The others may have to be replaced. I can't let it all go now, Lally."

"You think they'll come?"

"They'll come because they have to. With the men out, or permanently out of work, the women have to earn. It takes a lot to make a woman go on strike."

"They're all from the East End," Lally said quietly.

"Don't tell me. Some of them are my mum's neighbors. I should be with them. In there, fighting with them. But times have changed, and Susie Barlow has changed with them. God knows how long the damn thing will go on, but I have to be operating and on top of it. I have to keep the business going." She thrust her cigarette furiously into the ashtray. "Oh, don't look at me like that. Yes, I'm selling out my own class. But I really don't belong there anymore. I'm not an idealist, Lally. I can't afford to be. Not on borrowed money. And what, by the way, did your father do?"

"He closed the mines."

"There! I knew it. He and Brock—and me. We're not sentimentalists. Blame the government. Blame Winston Churchill. But don't blame Susie Barlow for a general strike. Now you'd better go. I have work to do." She went to the drawing board; Lally watched the angry, slashing marks she made on the paper, marks without meaning. Then she realized that Susie's shoulders were shaking. She left quietly. There were times it was not wise to intrude further on Susie's prickly independence. The tug of loyalties was as great as Black Jack experienced, the anguish would be as deep, even though the difference in the number of workers involved was thousands against dozens. But for both of them it was their life.

It was over in such a few days, Lally thought, and most of the middle classes seemed to have made a sort of jamboree of it. Almost the whole of the student bodies of Oxford and Cambridge had turned out to drive buses and trains, some with more enthusiasm than skill. Lally could remember seeing one bus which bore the legend "This bus goes anywhere you like. No fares and kind treatment." Private cars took over the roads, stopped to give rides to workers who walked in great streams or patiently waited for a ride. Lally and Susie were out at six in the morning to pick up their seamstresses. Only two of the work force stayed away. "Unmarried," Susie said. "They can afford a bit of independence." She was tough and cheerful, and if she felt the strain of her divided loyalties she did not show it.

"Will you take them back?"

"Of course I will. They're just about the best cutters I've got. When they come asking I'll say, 'Yes.' "

Mrs. Brown went to help staff a canteen for the amateur train drivers at Waterloo. "I have to do my bit, Mrs. Pollock." Lally dropped her there before she went to pick up the first of the seamstresses in the morning. It was the last call on her way home at night. They exchanged hardly a word during those drives; Mrs. Brown insisted on their maintaining strictly the roles of mistress and servant. But Lally was becoming uneasily aware of a bond being formed.

Despite the air of gaiety which pervaded those days, there were moments of great tension. There was some violence. Buses were overturned, clashes took place between police and strikers, troops were even called in to protect food convoys. But there was no loss of life. And by May 12, it had all collapsed. All except the deadlock between the miners and the mineowners. The miners stuck to their slogan: *"Not a penny off the pay, not a minute on the day."* Black Jack was anguished and haggard when Lally next went to Pellham Langley. "I've had to buy German coal to keep the mills running. I can't have *them* closed too." He still smarted from the comment of Lord Birkenhead which became public: that the miners' leaders were the stupidest men in England, with the possible exception of the mineowners.

Because the mines remained closed, Black Jack refused to contemplate a visit to Long Island that summer. "I can't be on the other side of the Atlantic if a break should come. It isn't fair to the men. And it wouldn't *look* right." Lally was glad of the decision, although she didn't say so. It had not been her intention to go back to Long Island; the nightmare was still with her, the vision still too sharp. Alice begged to go, and Black Jack looked appealingly at Edith. "No, Jack, I'm staying with you." Silently, Lally applauded. Edith was a woman of great compassion, but she would let neither Alice's forlorn face, nor Margaret's increasingly agitated cables take her away from her husband. As the discussion went on by Atlantic cable and in the drawing room of Pellham Langley, Lally heard, with horror, Alice say, "I have to go. I know I'll find Jonathan there. You all keep him away from me." Suddenly she thrust out her scarred and puckered hands. "Look what I've done for him. I saved him from the fire. And you won't let me see him."

Edith rang for Shearing, and Alice, protesting, went upstairs. "I'm sorry, Lally," Edith said. "Some days she seems worse. More confused. She used always to seem so happy, even when she got things muddled up. Perhaps we should consult that man in London again . . ."

Black Jack said sharply, "I won't have Alice disturbed any more than she is. It's all very chancy, this psychiatry business. She'd have to be with him every day—live in London. Alice can't do that. She's *safe* only—only here."

So Margaret came to Europe earlier than was her usual custom. She came with her children, Nanny Williams, and a newly engaged nanny; Mark Shaw had fallen into the role Lally had foreseen for him. He acted as a sort of secretary, companion, occasional chauffeur, tutor to David; sometimes, when one of the nannies had time off, he acted almost as nursemaid to the children. He seemed worn and strained, and his look pleaded with Lally to judge nothing. They walked on the terrace as they had done the first day when she had interviewed him as a possible tutor for Jonathan. "It isn't so bad, Mrs. Pollock," he said. "I know what you think. But it's better than that. I handle all Mr. Weymouth's business concerning Whytecliffe, and I'm usually in Wall Street one day a week. It's a . . . well a wider world than most schoolmasters would ever experience."

He turned to her almost angrily. "I wish you didn't look that way, Mrs. Pollock. Do you think I enjoy most of what I do? To be a nursemaid? A lady's companion? But at least there on Wall Street I'm with men, and I like that. I like the rough and tumble. Does that surprise you? I've even taken my little bit of capital and put it into the market. And do you know what? I find I like the feeling of making money. I've invested my mother's money for her—some of it. She couldn't understand why I would want to take a job like that, but when I send her the stock-market pages from *The Wall Street Journal* with her stocks marked, and rising all the time, she is beginning to be—well, almost proud of me. Suddenly, in her mind, I've stopped being the son who couldn't even be a successful schoolmaster and turned into what she chooses to tell her friends is a *financier*. It's laughable, of course, but it's better than nothing."

Margaret stayed the obligatory two weeks with Lord and Lady Gough, and let them spoil David as much as their restrained natures would allow. Lally witnessed a strange tightness in David. He never spoke Jonathan's name, but he resolutely avoided the nursery rooms where he once had played with Jonathan, and which were now occupied by Dan and the new baby, who had been christened John Samuel but was called Sam. He preferred Mark Shaw's company to that of his half brothers. Lord Gough made a faintly damning comment on Mark Shaw. "At least he's an Englishman, and presumably a gentleman. David will be ready for Eton when the time comes."

Margaret endured her two weeks with the Goughs with the little patience she could muster, and came back gladly to Pellham. "Oh, thank God," she said to Lally, kicking off her shoes and curling up on a chaise. "They always make me feel as if I'm somehow on trial. And yet they're terrified that if they show disapproval I'll stop bringing David. You can't imagine the ceremony of mixing the martinis—their great concession to me. And they have bought a phonograph. For me, they say. They watch me dance with Mark, and they watch me trying to teach David some steps, and they just can't make sense of it.

"Oh, God, Lally, I can't imagine what's going to happen to David when he inherits. Will he cut himself off from us? I keep looking at Lord Gough and hoping his health holds up, but he's beginning to look a bit frail, poor dear. I suddenly have a vision of my little David sitting there at the head of that long table—all alone. He should have fun and playmates, and run on the sand . . . Oh, God, Lally, I'm sorry. I can't ever forget that David lived and Jonathan didn't. If I ever pray, Lally, I pray that you'll forgive that too. Yet, that was something *I* didn't have anything to do with." Her face twisted. "Yes, I did. I threw those stupid dolls on the fire. I don't forgive myself. Why should I expect anyone else to forgive me? I know . . . I'm foolish, frivolous Margaret. Most people like me, but no one respects me."

"Brock loves you."

"Does that mean something, Lally? That Brock loves me? That Father loves me? I wish you did."

It had been the first commandment of Lally's life. The first promise given, the first vow taken. "I love you, Margaret." And strangely, she thought, she really did. She looked at the lithe slim figure, the bobbed golden hair framing the pointed little vixen face. All beauty and grace. Let her laugh and dance as long as she could. Let her hold Brock's heart, and Black Jack's heart. The world had need of beauty and charm, and it was no crime to serve it.

Then Brock arrived, and in his wake a tide of guests from the various houses around Whytecliffe. The last guest bedroom at Pellham Langley was occupied. The big house resounded to the talk and the music and the clatter of plates and glasses. "I suppose," Black Jack said to Lally, "that this is what my father might have had vaguely in mind when he built the place." Then he laughed. "He could hardly have imagined the place filled with Americans, or music like this . . ." From the hall, the music blasted out into the still summer night to the terrace where they strolled together with Edith while Black Jack smoked his cigar. *In the meantime, in between time, Ain't we got fun!* They passed the open front door, and paused for a moment to watch the dancing. Margaret was in the middle of the group and, as always, outstandingly their leader as she moved in time to the music. "I wonder if she'll ever quieten down," Black Jack said.

Edith had discreetly hired a man who, for an enormous salary, was willing to call himself an underbutler to Billings, who could no longer cope with the influx of guests, but who insisted on giving lengthy and fussy orders, who presided majestically over dinner each night, who retired immediately afterward, leaving the younger man to attend to the needs of the guests, to respond to all the requests for cocktails whose recipes seemed beyond Billings' comprehension. "We're all growing a little old," Black Jack said, "but when I watch Margaret dancing—"

"When I watch Margaret dancing," Brock interrupted, "I feel exhausted." He had positioned himself on a stone bench on the terrace, smoking, watching the dancing inside. Then as Alice drifted by the open door, he sprang to his feet. "Come, sweetheart, dance with your old Brock." They went together onto the polished floor where Alice executed a very passable example of the Charleston, at which Margaret excelled.

Black Jack sighed. "How does Brock keep up with all of it? Margaret by herself is a handful—and yet the little boys have just as much of his attention. He loves David, I swear, as much as his own Dan and Sammy. I wish Gough could just watch him for an hour with the boys. He might think differently of him."

But the burden of the guilt Brock had assumed for Margaret could never be disclosed, nor Lord Gough's resentment and bitterness assuaged. So the two never met.

The guns sounded on the moors promptly on the twelfth of August that year as the grouse-shooting season opened. Black Jack had wanted to cancel it. "How can I be seen to have this kind of house party when the miners are still out? How does it look?"

"They'll not respect you any the more for not having your sport," Margaret said firmly. "It can make no difference, one way or the other—and besides, you've promised shooting to all these people."

So the shooting parties were organized; the beaters were hired, the gamekeepers wore their best tweeds and groomed their dogs with even more care, the big cars went on the moors loaded with picnic baskets. Billings had double-checked his cellar lists, but he wrote the wine menu with a shaky hand, and he grew irritable with the new man Edith had hired. Friends from London mixed with the arrivals from Long Island. Edith had begged Lally to take time off from her job. "I need your help, dear. Margaret is charming with the guests, but useless at organizing. When I most need her, she's somewhere else." Lally thought it an excuse to bring her to Yorkshire, because Edith had always run her household with supreme efficiency. But she fell in with Edith's wishes, because she knew they were Black Jack's. Did they guess how hard she sometimes found it to watch David walking with Mark Shaw?—David, when it should have been Jonathan. But she enjoyed Brock's company, and she couldn't withhold affection from the two little boys—Dan, who was golden and laughing, like Margaret, and the baby, Sam, just beginning to walk, and who was remarkably spare and lean, his dark looks an almost ridiculous reproduction, in so young a child, of his father's. Nanny Williams sighed over him. "He eats like a horse, Mrs. Pollock, and he looks as skinny as a rail. The doctor actually asked me if he gets enough to eat! Imagine! But then he'll be just like Mr. Weymouth—tall and thin. They say it's a real Yankee type, whatever that may mean. I like all my babies to be round and bonny."

"If he's just like his father, he'll be all right, Nanny."

On the shoots Lally hung back with Brock, who, although a fair enough shot, didn't seem to care whether he bagged any grouse or not. "Never did care for guns, if you recall, Lally. Remember the war—I used to put as much distance between them and me as possible."

"All I remember is that you got yourself transferred to France," Lally replied. "Brock . . . ?"

"What?"

They let the others move ahead of them. Although August, it was a gray, raw day on the moors. They had kept to the Pellham valley, so no sight of the chimney stacks of the mills disturbed the wild and lonely scene. The blast of the guns seemed an almost intolerable intrusion on the peace that should have reigned. "Do you ever think of it? The war, I mean? It's still just a few years ago, and yet it was another world. A whole other life. Sometimes I think I've been split in two, and I don't quite recognize the person back there in that time."

He nodded, gestured to an outcropping of rock among the heather. "Let's let them get on with it, shall we?" He gave her a cigarette, and lighted one for himself. "No one came out of it quite whole. In one piece. Not the English—or the French, though they seemed more pragmatic about it. The Americans, somehow, seemed to keep just a bit of innocence. Weren't in it long enough, and didn't suffer the casualties to make it much more than a big adventure to show Jerry just who was who."

"Is that all it was about?" They both turned as the voice intruded. "And there was I slogging away in the mud, and thinking I was making the world safe for democracy, as well as winning the war."

"Why Gerry Harper!" Brock said. "What the hell—" He got to his feet, holding out his hand. "Didn't expect *you*. Black Jack or Edith didn't say anything—"

"Well, let's say I kind of invited myself. Telephoned this morning and said I might sort of be dropping by. Lady Pollock, God bless her, said there'd be room, though I suspect the house is jammed to the rafters."

"You could always share the nursery with Dan and Sammy. They'd love it."

"Would Nanny Williams, I wonder."

"She'd get the thrill of her life, I expect," Lally said. She'd tried to keep her tone even and light, but the sight of Gerry had been a shock. Except for the inquest, she had not seen him since the morning on the beach, the morning she had sought, wrongly, to thrust the blame for Jonathan's death on him. She wondered if he had ever forgiven the unfairness of that outcry. But his presence here said he had —that, in fact, no forgiveness was required. He had simply known her anguish. He stretched out a hand to her now to help her to rise.

"You're looking good, Lally: It suits you—this place. Never thought of you as a Brontë character before, but if you just had a tweed cloak and a big dog . . ."

"That was where *I* came in, a long, long time before you, Gerry," Brock said. "Don't start thinking you're the only Heathcliff who ever walked these moors."

"Oh . . . ? Well, I had Mr. Rochester rather more in mind. Always fancied myself nearly riding down a beautiful lady, and falling in love, all with the mist swirling around just to give it a romantic flavor."

"Well, you're both quite out of character," Lally said crisply. "Neither of you is the romantic type. Now, let's go. My stomach tells me it's time for lunch, and the only place I ever feel really hungry is up here on the moors. I expect Edith has got a feast prepared, which will be passed off as a simple little picnic."

"I'm for that," Gerry said. "And I'm glad to hear you talking about food for a change. My father sent a message. He said, 'If you see that Lally girl, tell her to eat something. She's too damn skinny.'"

Lally laughed. "Kind of him to remember me. He's well, I hope . . ." They fell into what on the surface seemed comfortable gossip. But she was conscious of tension, and it had nothing to do with that last meeting on the shore.

Gerry stayed three nights, sharing a room with Mark Shaw. He seemed to enjoy the shooting during the day. He was an expert shot, and brought down, on the second day, the record bag of grouse. "Learned it all shootin' rabbits," he said laconically. With the vast Harper holdings out in the West, it was a gross understatement. Lally knew he had stalked deer through endless tracts of forest, had shot several bears. There was a stuffed mountain lion in Old Man Harper's study that people said Gerry had shot while it had been in the act of springing on him.

"I love your modesty, Gerry," she said. "But it doesn't become you. It doesn't seem right."

They were sitting in the library at Pellham, a room not much used at night by the other guests when the dancing went on in the hall. A fire still burned against the unseasonable chill of the evening, but it was getting low. The music might keep on until the last dancer had slumped into exhaustion, but soon the butler, the new one, would be on his last round to secure the windows, and ask if there was anything further they required.

"You're darn tootin' it isn't right. 'Ol Gerry Harper always was one for blowing his own horn. Now I'm suddenly getting all modest and shy."

"Why, Gerry?"

He dropped the faked drawl. "Because of you, Lally. Things have happened. I came to see you."

"What's happened?" She felt herself tighten.

"Well, hell, honey, don't get all tensed up. It's just that I asked Lady Pollock if I could come because I had to see you."

"Why just now?"

"Because now is it. This is the time. The Old Man wants to know, and so do I."

"Know what?"

"What's the only question I've ever asked you, Lally? I want to know if you'll marry me."

"I thought I answered that a long time ago."

"Things have changed. For both of us. A year ago you lost your child, the one thing that anchored you to this place—this sort of life, if you want to put it that way. And now, the Old Man has finally given up on Roddy. He made a horse's ass of himself just once too often, so he's been shunted sideways, into a safe place in the company where he can't do too much harm. I've become president—the Old Man's chairman. It means I've got to stick it out on Wall Street most of the time. It means I can't have whole summers out West anymore. Just enough to let the guys out there know I know what's going on, but not so long as to let the guys back in Wall Street think they can slack off. Roddy made a mess of things, and I have to straighten it out. I have to try to make sure it can't happen again."

"And what have I to do with all this? What's the difference?"

"Plenty. I asked you a long time ago. As you said, you answered me a long time ago. I've looked around since then, Lally. I don't mind admitting it. You're the only woman I've encountered who makes me think I could stick it out at a desk most of the year. In the old classic phrase, I feel like settling down. I've had enough of the old jazz and gin. The Old Man—"

"I wouldn't be marrying your father, Gerry."

"No, you wouldn't. You'd be marrying Gerry Harper, who thinks you're a swell girl. But it wouldn't hurt that the Old Man wants it.

Makes life easier after the mess of my first marriage. We could have kids, Lally. Not everything is gone because you lost your husband and Jonathan . . ."

She stood up.

"Wait, Lally. Just hear it out. Think a minute."

She gazed down into the dying fire. "I suppose you were planning to live there—in the house on the North Shore?"

He shrugged. "Is that so tough? It'd be . . . well, convenient. Of course we could always have our own place. Nearby. The Old Man would have it built overnight if you just said so. But he *likes* you, Lally. He feels comfortable with you. And he's an old man, all alone in that great barn of a place. He'd like to see you at his table. He'd like to see his grandchildren. And you'd be near Margaret. Our kids could grow up with hers and Brock's. . . . Just think about it. What's to keep you here now? Not that nickel and dime business you and Susie run. Think about it, Lally. Our kids. You've got plenty of time to have lots of kids if you want them."

She thought about it for a very short time. Just the time it took for one already red-hot piece of coal to burn so that it crumbled and fell through the grate. Kids. Another life. A different life. The ghosts of Jon and Jonathan left behind.

"We'd have trips out West, Lally. Take the kids. Get away from all that North Shore stuff. It could be good."

From the hall the phonograph blared:

> *The rich get rich and the poor get* . . . children.
> *In the meantime, in between time,*
> *Ain't we got fun!*

Had Gerry Harper, of all men, finally settled for safety? She was the right choice, the steady, sensible Lally. No more ragtime girls. No more social butterflies. His father wanted her. The finger of memory touched her again, prodded her. Wasn't that what Jon had done? Finding himself alive, against all expectations, at the end of the war, he had sought safety and peace, sought to bury the memory of Sandy West, sought, in the security of Lally's love, to forget the shells and the horror, to blanket the nightmares. Jon's father, too, had wanted the marriage. And all had taken her for granted. Why not? Why did she wait for something more dramatic, more compelling? Why must she always wait, and hope, for someone to say he loved her?

"It was 'no' before, Gerry. You can't afford a failure again. I can't afford to fail. Not for the sake of children, or your father—or for *me*. It has to be 'no.' That's the only thing I'm sure of."

"Goddamn it, Lally. You could *think* about it."

"If it was right, I wouldn't have to think about it."

She went to the door and opened it. The light from the hall, the music, flooded in. Gerry followed her. "Lally . . . ?"

She was out among the crowd. Billings' new assistant was passing around drinks while one of the footmen tended bar. The great Persian carpet had been rolled back for the dancers. Cigarette smoke hung in a haze under the high beams of that huge space. Alice danced in the middle of the crowd with a man Lally couldn't remember having seen before. Had the crowd become so big she couldn't remember all the guests, or didn't she care? From the landing Shearing watched, her eyes fixed on Alice. There would be no slipping out onto the terrace while Shearing or Barnes watched; there would be no visits to the boys' nursery.

Lally stood for a moment beside Black Jack's chair. "I think it's time I got back to London. The party's become too big."

And behind her, Gerry said to Edith, "I'll be taking myself off your hands tomorrow, Lady Pollock. There's a ship sailing on Wednesday I ought to be on."

In that instant Lally saw a light that might have been hope, was certainly expectation, fade from Black Jack's eyes. He seemed to disappear behind the smoke from his cigarette. "Sorry to see you go, Gerry. I hoped it would be a longer stay."

*   *   *

Lally woke to find Margaret sitting in the window seat of the tower corner, the seat that in the early days had seemed to Lally sometimes to look out onto fairylands, where the mists became creatures, the topiary changing and wavering, and the animals had life. Margaret was still wearing the dress of the night before. She hadn't been to bed.

She turned as Lally spoke her name. She rose and came toward her. Lally saw, in the dawn light, that her makeup was streaked, as if she had been weeping. "How could you do it?—again? You *knew* how it would have pleased Father if you'd married again. Gerry won't give you another chance, Lally. How could you do it?"

Lally sat up and looked at her directly. "Because for once I was thinking about what *I* wanted. I was thinking about what was right for me. Now go to bed, Margaret, and leave me alone." She lay down again, rolled on her side, and pulled the sheets up close to her ears. No further sound came except the quiet closing of the door.

* * *

During the week that Margaret and Brock and the children stayed in London, Mrs. Brown took a holiday. "I've arranged for someone from the agency to come. I promised you I'd never interfere in your life, that no one would ever find out about me. I'll take myself off, and then there's no risk."

She went, not saying where she was going. The maid's room off the kitchen was as neat and impersonal as if no one had ever occupied it. No trace of Rose Brown remained. Strangely, Lally found herself torn between relief at her absence, and missing the little touches, the ministrations which she had once found too possessive. She missed that whispered word in the morning. "Lily . . . good morning, Lily."

❦ CHAPTER 15 ❦

I

Susie's spring show was over in November, and so was the miners' strike. Lally insisted on taking Susie with her to Pellham Langley for Christmas. "Can't say as I'm not happy to be asked," Susie admitted. "Somehow, the general strike changed things. Not that Mum and Dad aren't proud of me, having got myself out of the Mile End Road and into the West End. But it isn't the same when I go there now. I drive the car there, and the neighbors see me, and they remember I helped break the strike. When I visit now, no one pops in, the way they used to. They see the car, and they stay away. I've left that world behind, Lally, and I haven't quite found my own. Maybe I never will. It's lonely—this ambition stuff. Yes, I'd like to see your dad again. He always did make me feel better about myself."

But the first evening, before dinner, she had smoked a cigarette as she watched Lally finish dressing. "Gawd," she said, "it's aged him, this strike."

"It hurt him to shut the mines, Susie. He has more of a social conscience than it's healthy for a mine- and a millowner to have. It was a long drain on his nerves. He had to stand with the other mineowners, but he didn't want to. He bought German coal to keep the mills going. There's a lot of bitterness here in Yorkshire. It'll take more than a year or two for them to start to forgive him." She wished Susie hadn't spoken about Black Jack. She had wanted to pretend what she saw—the face more gaunt and drawn, the hands and eyes nervous—did not actually exist, was just a twist of her own imagination about Black Jack. But Susie's candid stare faced down that pretense.

They exchanged gifts on Christmas morning, each of them glad of Susie's presence because she seemed to make enough noise to cover their own silence. At the last moment, before she left London, Mrs. Brown had thrust a small package into Lally's hand. Now she opened it to find a handmade, heavily embroidered silk petticoat. FOR MRS. POLLOCK—MERRY CHRISTMAS—ROSE BROWN. It represented many hours of work. Susie's experienced eye assessed it. "Beautiful," she said.

The post came, a shower of cards, and a cable from Margaret. HAPPY CHRISTMAS. NOW THAT THE SHOW'S OVER, WHAT ABOUT COMING TO PALM BEACH FOR SOME SUN? THE BOYS NEED YOU. I LOVE YOU.

"There you are," Susie said. "The show *is* over, Sir John. You've stood your ground. Stood with the other mineowners. You've been braver than most of them, because you cared more." She turned to Edith. "Lady Pollock, don't you think for once our golden girl is right? Wouldn't it do you all a world of good to go? Alice is quite pale and thin. You'd like to see the little boys, wouldn't you, Alice?" And then Susie's face colored. They all knew that Alice would never see the little boys again except in the presence of Barnes or Shearing. Edith covered Susie's embarrassment.

"I think it's a very good idea, Susie. I wouldn't mind some sun, I do confess. I'd rather like the sea voyage, too, even if it is midwinter."

Susie almost had their trunks packed for them by the time she and Lally left. "They do seem to need a bit of pushing. I had to do it. Your dad seems to have lost a bit of that . . . well, what do the Americans call it? Get up and go? He'll get a rest, and he'll be away from all the talk of the strike. He's had enough of that. He'll come back his old self."

Lally saw them off at Southampton with something like relief. It would mean a winter when she didn't go to Pellham Langley, a winter when the silence of the dining table and the library didn't oppress her. "We'll be back by March," Edith said. "The worst of the winter will be over." She added quietly, "And Jack will be better. Susie's quite right. He needs to hear something else talked about except the miners and the strike. He did what he thought he had to do, but he's been hurt."

"Yes," Lally said. "Take care of him. And Margaret. And Alice. Don't let Mark Shaw bully David into too much Latin and Greek. He's still a little boy." It was as yet impossible for her to separate them in her mind—David and Jonathan. In her mind there were always two figures on the shore, leaping and running, with Alice between them.

Instead of the usual cable from Black Jack and Edith when they reached New York there was, instead, a telephone call. Lally took it in Susie's office, and they stared in stunned disbelief as the operator told Lally it was a call from New York. The transatlantic telephone service had just begun between New York and London. Lally had never imagined hearing Black Jack's voice, familiar through the crackle, from three thousand miles away. "Is it really you?" Then Brock's voice. "I rigged it up just for you, Lally. My own personal line." Then Margaret. "Isn't it fabulous, darling? I'll be able to telephone you regularly."

"I hope she doesn't," Susie said. "You've got enough to do to cope with her at a distance."

But the message that came from Florida was by cable, from Margaret. COME AT ONCE. FATHER HAS HAD A HEART ATTACK. WE NEED YOU. It was immediately followed by a cable from Edith. JACK RECOVERING VERY WELL. NO NEED FOR ALARM. PLEASE DON'T COME UNLESS YOU WANT A HOLIDAY. Susie studied the two cables. "Well, that's Margaret, and that's Lady Pollock. I'd trust Lady Pollock's judgment. If you go, all in a rush like, you could frighten your dad. He'd think he's much worse than he is. I think that's what Lady Pollock wants you to know. But still, I hope he stays there a long time. All that nice warm sun."

For the first time when she returned that evening to her flat, Lally went directly to the kitchen. Mrs. Brown was there, vegetables for Lally's dinner spread on the table. She stopped slicing beans as Lally told her about the two cables. Before she spoke, Mrs. Brown went to the dining room and poured a small brandy for Lally.

"Go to him, Lily. No man was ever kinder to a child. He loves you. It will make him feel better just to see you."

But letters and more cables were exchanged across the Atlantic, and Edith's view prevailed. I THINK IT MIGHT DISTURB JACK IF HE THOUGHT YOU CAME BECAUSE WE WERE WORRIED ABOUT HIM. The March date for their return was postponed; April came, the daffodils bloomed in the London parks, but when Lally went to Pellham

Langley, mostly on Billings' insistence that she come to see that everything was still running perfectly, which she knew would be the case, there was still frost, and the tight buds of spring had not opened. "You'll tell Sir John that everything here is in order, Miss Lally? And might I be so bold as to suggest that you urge him not to return too soon? He was very anxious during the strike, and he got run-down. The change must do him good." Billings did not want to admit that Black Jack was mortal, so he dismissed the threat behind the heart attack. "It happens all the time, Miss Lally. Look at me. I'm sure there's many had me for dead—but, you see, I'm as good as ever."

"Of course you are, Billings."

* * *

Lally returned to her flat after that visit to Pellham Langley and the place seemed strangely quiet. Mrs. Brown had never made her presence obtrusive, but the silence now was different. Lally went to the kitchen; it was in order, and empty. "Mrs. Brown?" She had probably gone out to do some shopping. But still Lally moved toward the door of the maid's room, and knocked. There was no reply. "Mrs. Brown?" Carefully she opened the door a fraction. In the middle of the afternoon the curtains were still drawn, and the room was dark. She switched on the light.

The woman lay quite peacefully in the bed; there was no sign that there had been any struggle. Lally reached immediately to feel her pulse, but the hand was cold and almost rigid. There was hardly any need to place her ear against the thin chest wall. She guessed that at some time during the night the heart had stopped beating. *"Mother . . ."*

She folded the hands together, and went to telephone a doctor.

After Rose Brown's body had been taken away, Lally went carefully through the few possessions in the room. The underclothes were neat and clean, as carefully laundered as her own, but with no touch of lace. Her severe black dresses hung in the wardrobe; starched white collars and frilled caps were ready for use; two black coats; brilliantly polished shoes. There were only two pieces of paper. One was the address which Lally recognized as the firm of solicitors in Leeds who handled Black Jack's personal affairs, with the name of the senior partner, Mr. Aisgill, underlined. The second was an envelope simply marked LILY. She opened it.

The writing was stilted, as if it had taken Rose Brown a great deal of trouble to write what she did. *Dear Lily. If you ever read this, I will be gone. The doctor told me there was a bit of trouble with my heart. That was when I came to London looking for you. The little bit of work I did here was nothing. It never hurt me. And when I came here to stay I thought I was in heaven. I loved looking after you Lily. I loved to see what you made of yourself. It was a chance I took back there in Leeds all those years ago. I hope to see you marry again and have children. But I may not last that long. If I die here I will be happy. Respectfully. Rose Brown.* And then, as if it were an afterthought, something scribbled which was almost indecipherable. *Mother.*

"Mother . . ." Lally echoed.

She telephoned Mr. Aisgill in Leeds. "Yes, Mrs. Pollock, we have been sending a modest amount of money to a boardinghouse in Leeds for some years on Sir John's instructions. I'm afraid I don't understand how Mrs. Brown . . ." He listened as Lally related how Rose Brown had come to her. "I'm sorry, Mrs. Pollock. We had no idea. It was one of Sir John's firmest instructions that you must never be troubled by any contact with this woman. I'm deeply sorry, Mrs. Pollock. We should have been more vigilant. But we couldn't have known that Mrs. Brown would have the cooperation of the landlady in deceiving us."

"The deception was kindly meant, Mr. Aisgill. Perhaps when the landlady knew of her heart condition she agreed. You mustn't blame her. We must not blame either of them. Mrs. Brown came to me when she thought she hadn't much time left. We'll never know if she was truly my mother. There is still no proof on paper. I still know nothing about her. Her real name. Where she came from. I don't know who my father is, Mr. Aisgill. I don't know anything about Rose Brown. But I wish to bury her as if she had been my mother."

"Mrs. Pollock! But Sir John—"

"My father will not be disturbed. I will write to him when it is done. He will be glad to know that she—and I—are both at peace. So, Mr. Aisgill, may I ask for your presence at the church at Pellham Langley on the day after tomorrow? I would like you to be present. I am going to telephone the vicar at Pellham Langley and ask for the burial of Mrs. Brown in the churchyard. I will say she has Yorkshire connections—which must be true. He will know no more about her, nor will anyone else. None of us is *sure*, Mr. Aisgill. None of us is sure she was my mother."

But then he had not seen them side by side. He had not witnessed that confrontation at the mirror.

"If that is your wish, Mrs. Pollock, of course . . . but still . . ."

"The doubt remains, Mr. Aisgill. But Mrs. Brown is dead. We owe her a proper burial."

It was strange how the fact of death worked on even the most literal and legal minds. Perhaps they looked to their own deaths, and were properly in awe of the occasion.

"Of course, Mrs. Pollock. If you will telegraph which train you are coming on, I will meet you."

* * *

Two days later Lally and Mr. Aisgill were the only people by the graveside of the woman known as Rose Brown. Lally had carried freesias with her from London, and she dropped them on the coffin as it was lowered. She found she no longer hated their perfume. Later a headstone would record the name of Rose Brown. There could be no dates; there was no recorded history of this woman who could have been her mother.

That evening Lally began her letter to Black Jack. *Dearest Father, Today we buried the woman, Rose Brown, in the graveyard here at Pellham Langley. I did it because I thought she might have the right to be there.* She told him of Rose Brown's appearance in London, the role she had assumed in Lally's life. *I found I didn't hate her anymore. I didn't fear her. And I wonder why I was ever so afraid.*

She slept easily that night at Pellham Langley. And she realized it was now a long time since she had had the old dream of the dark and hated place. Confronting it, acknowledging the existence of Rose Brown, and the place she may have had in her life, had banished it. She knew she was finally free.

* * *

Black Jack and Edith and Alice lingered on in Florida until May, and then went to Long Island. *Father is well*, Margaret wrote. *He seems quite back to normal. But I'm hoping he'll stay through the summer—or at least until July. Then we can all go to Pellham together for August. But, Lally, he wants to see you. I know he does. He won't ask you to come over because that would be admitting that he felt, at one time, that he would never see you again. But he misses*

you. He's never been separated from you for so long since the war.
But he was younger then, and he hadn't been ill. I'm not asking for
myself for once. I'm asking for him.

Susie studied the letter. "And, for once, I think she's telling the truth. You should go, Lally. Your dad's more important than anything you've got here."

"You're pushing me, Susie."

"Yes, I'm pushing you. I know you never want to see that place again. You'll be thinking of Jonathan all the time. You'll see him there, in every corner. And there's Alice. You'd rather not see her there, would you? But until you face all those places you don't want to see again, you'll never get over it. All right—tell yourself it's because your dad would like a glimpse of you. Maybe he wants to know that you can face it all. Whatever the reason, you have to go."

Lally remembered the release that had come when she had stood beside the coffin of the woman who might have been her mother; there she had faced the possibility of her own past, and had been made free of it. Susie's shrewd intuition knew such things. "You always were bossy, Susie," Lally said, covering her sense of giving way to a wisdom that was only barely perceived.

"Yes—slum kids are, once they find their feet. And they're snobs. Just watch out. In a few years, I may not even know you."

So Lally went, and Brock was there to meet her at the pier on Fifty-seventh Street. "I managed to keep Margaret away," he said as they stowed her luggage in the car. That day he had dispensed with the service of a chauffeur, and Lally knew it was because he had wanted the space and the time to talk to her on the drive to the North Shore.

"It was a bit worse, I think, than Edith let you know," he said. "I went down to Florida and talked with the doctors. Then I got a man here to look at him. He seems well, but he's taking things quietly. The very fact that he does that makes me believe he's not as strong or as confident as he says. The doctors don't know much about the causes—except that the strain of the miners' strike could have brought it on sooner than it would otherwise have happened. Hard to believe it of Black Jack. He looks lean and fit, but I saw the change in his face when he arrived here in New York after Christmas. I knew, for once, that Margaret was right in dragging them down to Florida. But give him a few months, the doctors say. He could be as well as he ever was if he just had rest for a few months. Margaret has it all planned, and again, just for once, I think she's got it right. You all stay at Whytecliffe until the end of July, and then we'll all go to Pellham together. That's what Black Jack likes best of all—to have you all around him."

"Not just us, Brock. *We.* You're almost as much his son as Jon was. Sometimes I think he wishes you weren't so successful. Then he could invite you to come and help him run the mills and the mines."

"Oh, I don't think he needs me that badly, Lally. After all, he's got you to help him do those things."

She shook her head. "Women are a lot more independent than they used to be, but there's a world of difference between helping Susie run what everyone thinks of as a little dress business and sitting on a board of directors. Especially in Yorkshire. In London it might just be done, but Yorkshire and the whole North, I think, are still places where men make all the decisions—or are seen to. I could try it, but somehow I don't think he wants me to. He wants me to be free of all that. I suspect he thinks there's a better chance of my remarrying if I'm not all tied up with the muck that makes the brass."

Brock nodded. "You could be right. He wanted you to marry Gerry Harper. Might have worked, but if you thought it wouldn't, then I'd trust your judgment. Did you hear what happened to Gerry?"

"No." Why did she feel a sense of panic? Gerry Harper was no part of her life anymore. She had let him go—or had she supposed he was still there, hers for the taking?

"He got married. A girl from Denver. They say her family's sitting on about as much brown anthracite as the Harpers are sitting on copper. He's brought her to live on the North Shore, and they have an apartment on Park Avenue. She's only twenty, and this is really her first taste of the big time, even though the family have all that money. And she's taken to it like a duck to water. She can even beat Margaret when it comes to partying and dancing. Old Man Harper, they say, doesn't like it one bit. He's taken to coming over and visiting Black Jack. The two of them sit there on the terrace, looking over the Sound, not saying much, but I'd swear they're both thinking how much they'd have liked it if you had married Gerry."

"I can't help it," she said sharply. "I can't marry to please other people."

"You're damn right you can't. Never forget it. If I ever hear you're going to marry some guy, I'll take the liberty of reminding you of that."

"Do it, Brock. Do it."

Most of the rest of the drive passed in silence. She thought of the last time she had seen Gerry. Had she been a fool, after all? Were there many Gerry Harpers to be found? She savagely repressed the slight feeling of regret, and she almost cursed the kind of love she had felt for Jon because it seemed to make it impossible to put any other man in his place. It was rotten luck, she thought, to have fallen in love so long ago, and never to have been able to throw it off. There ought to be some release. In fairness, there ought.

Black Jack was there, on the high terrace, with Edith and Margaret and Alice, seated in the shade of an awning, as Lally came through the big doors from the main hall. He wore white flannels and a panama hat. He looked, as Brock had said, tanned and fit. Or was it just the tan? He saw her, rose, and lifted his hat. She was instantly aware that his shoulders seemed stooped—those shoulders which had always been so straight. His hair had turned quite white, though the eyebrows retained their startling black. A handsome man still, but, suddenly, an old man. She stepped into his outstretched arms. "Oh, Lally, it's good to see you."

Margaret had been right. She should have come a long time ago.

* * *

And as they sat there that May evening, as Brock mixed and served the drinks, the butler, forgetting all the aplomb that two years as a footman in an English ducal palace had taught him, came almost at a run with the news. "Mr. Weymouth—Madam! He's done it! You know—that Lindbergh guy who took off from Roosevelt Field yesterday to try to fly the Atlantic. He's made it! Nonstop to Paris. Just heard it on the radio. The news just came. Jeez—can you imagine it!"

They stared at him. Brock turned, the cocktail shaker still in his hand, the drink unpoured. The butler stiffened. "I'm sorry, sir. Didn't mean to intrude. I just thought you'd all like to know."

Brock began to shake the martini vigorously. It was a small task he had taken over from Black Jack; the results he achieved were much better. "Of course we wanted to know, Vickers. I think you'd better put some champagne on ice. And so long as it won't interfere with dinner, you should pass some around among the staff."

Vickers looked doubtful. "You mean *all* of them, sir? You mean

. . . well, the maids?—the sec—" He tried to cover his slip. "The gardeners and all, sir?" For a moment he looked agonized. "Sir, we have only *vintage* champagne."

"I hope so, Vickers, since that's what I paid for. Yes. Invite them all. The security men, even if we chose to call them gardeners. The maids. Just so long as I don't get the soup tipped over my shoulder."

"Sir!"

"All right, Vickers. A joke."

"Of course, sir. A joke." Vickers turned and started to walk back along the terrace. Then he paused. "Mr. Weymouth?"

"Yes?"

"When the news came from Paris—seems there was a big crowd to meet him at whatever airport he got to—they already put a name on him, this Lindbergh. Someone's called him 'The Lone Eagle.' Pretty good, isn't it, sir, that it was an American who did it first?"

"Pretty good, Vickers. Pretty good. Enjoy your party . . ."

After he had gone, Alice, who must have been puzzling over the stir of excitement, said, "An eagle? Who's an eagle?"

Mark Shaw started to explain. "An eagle—" he began.

But Margaret cut him short impatiently. "An eagle. Yes, they're right to call him that." She got up and went to the edge of the terrace, leaning on the parapet. "Just imagine what it must be like to fly. To be free of the ground. Free . . . flying . . . like skimming over the water, but up there, among the clouds."

"Not so silent—not nearly so free, I would think, Mrs. Weymouth," Mark Shaw said.

"You!—what do you know about it?" Had she resented the advisory, almost schoolmasterish tone of his voice? "Have *you* ever flown? You don't know much about *anything,* Mr. Shaw. You haven't lived!"

"Margaret!" The protest came simultaneously from Black Jack and Brock.

She came back from the parapet and slumped into her chair. She took up the martini glass and drained it. "I apologize, Mr. Shaw. That was wrong of me—and untrue." She raised the empty glass to him. "Am I forgiven?"

"Yes, Mrs. Weymouth." But his face had flushed and his lips folded in a line of resentment. Who would not, Lally thought, resent the implication that he had experienced nothing? It seemed to call his manhood into question. Some day he might be provoked into some

word or action just to prove that he was indeed a man. Margaret
played dangerously with his emotions.

Now Margaret put her head back, the lovely line of her neck silhouetted against the sky. "Well, Brock, where is the champagne?
When are we to toast our 'Lone Eagle'?"

"Eagle!" Alice echoed. "Eagle . . . eagle . . ."

"Oh, do be quiet unless you can talk sense," Margaret threw at
her, and ignored the wounded look that came to Alice's face. Carefully she did not look at her father to see the reproach registered
there. She held out her glass to Brock. "Another one, darling, please.
Just while we wait for the champagne."

Brock began at once to mix the martini and covered the chilled silence which settled on the group. "Time, don't you think, Black
Jack, to begin to investigate some airline stock? Maybe the manufacture of planes. It has to be the coming thing. A chance to get in at
the bottom . . ."

II

On the surface it was unchanged, the long, lazy days of the life at
Whytecliffe, but beneath the seeming calm, Lally recognized the tension, the underlying grating of the nerves, the suppression of what
she began to sense was almost hostility. Had Margaret begun to
resent and fear Alice? Had the worry over Black Jack's health laid a
strain on them which they could not acknowledge? The scene on the
terrace on the evening of Lally's arrival seemed symptomatic. The
days passed in swimming and playing tennis, riding, golf; the nights
in dancing. Everything was the same, and yet it was not. Black Jack
sat and observed it all; he did not move much, or speak much. Edith
sat always near him, striving to shield him from any source of aggra-
vation or distress, and knowing she could never do that fully. Slowly
Lally began to pinpoint the evidences of change, the differences
which two years had brought. This tightly knit little group was in
subtle ways beginning to break apart. David, at seven and a half, was
beginning to show a streak of independence, slipping away from
Mark Shaw's supervision whenever he could, meeting up with the
boys from the other houses along the Shore. He was involved, along
with some older boys, in an incident on the Harper place where the
windows of the indoor tennis court were smashed by stones they had

thrown. Brock hurried to have the damage repaired, and sent David to apologize to Old Man Harper. "You can't make me," David had shouted. "You're not my father!"

"Listen, sonny, for the moment I'm all the father you've got, so you'll just have to make do. Now get your ass on over there to Mr. Harper, or I'll make it feel pretty sore."

When he had gone, Margaret had stormed at Brock, "You're not to threaten him with physical punishment. I won't have it!"

"And I won't have some snot-nosed little kid messing up my patch. We live at peace with our neighbors, and if you can give me one good reason why he has to go smashing up other people's property, then I'm my mother's aunt."

Margaret had flounced off, and, in the face of a threatening storm, had sailed her little craft, *Fancy*, for miles along the Sound, knowing that by doing so she caused Brock an agony of apprehension. Edith and Lally met her on the jetty when she returned. While she and Lally helped stow the sails, Edith half-pleaded with her, half-threatened. "I know you did it to make Brock uncomfortable and anxious. But don't forget you make your father anxious too. And that I won't have, Margaret. Work out your quarrels with Brock whatever way you want, so long as you don't involve Jack. You have no *right* to upset him."

"Oh, damn!" Margaret said. "All this fuss over a few broken windows. David only did it because the others egged him on. They are older than he. He didn't want to seem a sissy. And where, I wonder, was Mark Shaw? Isn't he supposed to be David's tutor—isn't he supposed to be with him all the time?"

"Mr. Shaw was in Manhattan with Brock that afternoon," Edith said. "And you know it. Now stop being a silly, self-centered woman, and start thinking about your father. And stop insulting Mr. Shaw. At times I'm ashamed of you—the way you treat him."

"I get upset about David, and I take it out on Mark Shaw. David's never been the same, you know. Never—since Jonathan died. He seemed able to absorb it then, but ever since it's come out in dozens of ways." As Margaret spoke, Lally's thoughts went again to the biblical words. *The soul of Jonathan was knit with the soul of David.* It was true; even at so young an age, David had loved Jonathan.

"I know," Margaret continued, "Mark has a harder time handling him than I ever admitted. He's not doing very well at school, even with Mark to coach him. There've been a few spots of trouble I haven't told Brock about. I've smoothed them over myself. I've tried to keep all this to myself. But I see—I do *see* things. I don't know what to do about them. About David or about Alice."

She touched a point none of them wanted to recognize, much less talk about. Alice, in the hands of her two keepers, was a different entity. Perhaps she held to herself her own dreadful memories of that morning when Jonathan had died; perhaps she had forgotten all about it, and simply resented the close supervision she was now under. She had developed little tricks for escaping from them. She would sit with Black Jack and Edith, and then invent some excuse to walk by herself, offer to bring a lemonade, a glass of iced tea. She had made herself a favorite in the kitchen. Because she was Alice she broke all the rules that governed where she might cross the dividing line between servants and their masters. The famous chef Brock had hired had gone, deeming that he was not given enough scope for his talents; he had been replaced by a more ordinary but supremely capable woman. Alice would sit in the kitchen, eating the little cakes prepared for tea each day, chattering to Cook and Vickers, or listening to their own talk. "Well, who could refuse her anything?" Lally once heard Cook say to Vickers. "So beautiful she is. And those poor burned hands of hers. Isn't she better here with us, with some life going on about her, than with those two, Barnes and Shearing? I feel sorry for her. All that money—and no future. Only more of the same. Who could blame the child for what happened two years ago? But I reckon they do—even if they don't say so right out."

Was that the sense of breaking apart that Lally felt? Had the element of doubt entered all their minds about Alice? Margaret had kept on the second nurse she had engaged for the last trip to England. It was not, in that well-staffed house, and with Mark Shaw as David's companion and tutor, that Nanny Williams was overworked. Margaret feared, Lally thought, to leave either child alone.

Brock, too, seemed to have his fears. They were never expressed openly, and they seemed to be fears of some force threatening from outside. Margaret remarked on this morosely to Lally one day as they walked on the shore. They had resumed this practice, the walk without the others, the only time, Lally realized, when they really talked, not simply made conversation.

"I don't quite know what Brock means by it," Margaret said. "I don't know what he's afraid of. There used to be, I think, two security guards. Not so surprising—a lot of places have them. Keeps out unwelcome visitors—keeps the place private. But now I think there are about six. I never know. They change. He dresses them up as gardeners, or maybe an extra chauffeur. Someone's always and forever washing and polishing the cars, and keeping an eye on the house at the same time. Sometimes they're inside the house, pretending to mend a fuse, or change the washer on a tap. Since Jonathan—since the morning no one saw Alice take the little boys out, Brock's become afraid. But I don't know what exactly he's afraid of. Turn around slowly, Lally, and look. There'll be one of them following us now. Right back there—in the distance. Why do *we* have to be guarded? I once asked Brock outright. But you know how he can answer a question, and yet never answer it. He said the deals on Wall Street attracted a lot of public interest. The whole of America's crazy about watching Wall Street these days. Brock thinks I don't know how big some of these deals are. He knows I don't read *The Wall Street Journal*. But I do see the financial pages of *The New York Times*. I couldn't see myself what business deals have to do with protection. But those rumors still go on, you know, that Brock's been connected with some rather shady things. Perhaps he's been associated with some rather unsavory characters. Oh, not like Al Capone—not as bad as that. But all those sort of people have bodyguards. So that's what we have."

"It worries you . . ."

"Of course it worries me. I'd like our life freer—simpler. I never imagined it would get to this. Brock has a gun in his bedside drawer, and I think he keeps one locked in a drawer in the library. I'm pretty sure he carries a gun with him whenever he drives. I know for certain the chauffeurs all have them—I've seen them. How do you think it feels whenever I stay at the Plaza to do some shopping? There's a man in the room next to our suite who's there to follow me. And there's always someone hanging around in the corridor. Sometimes, I'm damned if I don't think Brock's got a couple of maids planted there—with the cooperation of the management, naturally. They'd rather Mrs. Brockton Weymouth be guarded than left to wander around on her own."

"He loves you, Margaret. If he's involved in something—something he thinks is dangerous, he wants to protect you."

"Then I wish he *weren't* in something dangerous. Why can't it all be straightforward? Father never needed—"

"Father's been involved in a long strike, and all the old bitterness against the millowners and the mineowners has surfaced again. They keep dragging up the past, when there was child labor in the mills and the mines—as if Father had been responsible for anything like that. No successful businessman is entirely free of the taint of having exploited or manipulated or—quite frankly—cheated some people in his time. Brock might be right to fear his enemies. He might be very right to want to protect you and the children."

"I should be grateful. I know he's trying to make sure nothing like what happened to Jonathan can ever happen again, for any reason. But it's too late for you, Lally. I know that thought nags at Brock. It does with all of us. We all were careless, and it seems we'll all pay for the rest of our lives."

Lally touched her arm. "Let's go back now."

Margaret turned obediently. "Yes, what need is there to talk? You know all there is to know." She raised her arm and pointed to the distant figure. "You see, he's turned too. He'll be just ahead of us by the time we get to the house. If we look closely we'll probably discover that he is the one who's going to be sweeping a corner of the terrace when we get there."

Lally wrote all these things to Susie—Black Jack's tiredness, Edith's watchfulness, David's increasing intransigence, Alice's growing moodiness, her attempts to escape her keepers. Susie wrote back, *I need you here but I can manage. Your job is to stay with them. They need you more.* So Lally passed the time in what she regarded as idleness, since she could do nothing that she considered was helpful. Until Brock spoke to her one night on the terrace when the others had gone to bed, even Margaret, for once, declaring for "an early night."

"Stick with it for a while, will you, Lally?" he said. "Just a little more. We'll be at Pellham in a few weeks. But I feel better with you here." Then he extended his cigarette case toward her. "A last cigarette before we turn in?" They smoked their cigarettes in silence, watching the riding lights of the vessels out in the Sound moving on a light swell, watching the stars become brighter as the lights of the great houses fronting the bay began to go out. Lally was acutely aware of Brock's closeness. She thought that, since the day he had climbed to the top of the waterfall above Pellham Langley, she had known only comfort in his presence, a sense of security. And yet, for certain things, he now depended on her. He almost spoke the words when he rose, crushed out his cigarette, and extended his hand to her. He bent and kissed her on the cheek. "Good night." He held her hand just fractionally longer. "Thank you, Lally." She didn't ask for what she was being thanked.

III

The July heat closed on the North Shore like a baffle; it seemed to Lally that the heat obscured even the solid lines of the buildings, so that they wavered and shimmered. All week long the temperature had climbed, and Brock, when he returned from Wall Street, seemed as close to terseness as Lally had ever known him. He had returned midafternoon on Friday, with Mark Shaw, from Manhattan, and had flung himself on a chaise in the shade, asking Vickers for iced coffee. "The market's in the doldrums. Everyone's taken off for the weekend. I didn't see why Mark and I should stick it out in the heat. Can't say I'll be sorry to get on that ship and head for Pellham. A good drenching in a good old chilly English August would suit me fine right now." Then he handed a paper over to Black Jack. "Thought you might be interested. I think I'll invest myself."

Margaret had appeared on the terrace, her face taut and strained. David followed reluctantly; in the doorway leading from the main hall a man in a policeman's uniform hesitated, and then came forward, directing his attention to Brock. On the way he put his hand on David's shoulder and propelled him along. "Glad to see you here, Mr. Weymouth. It's rightly something a man ought to handle."

Brock got to his feet. "What's wrong, Sergeant Willis?"

"It's the kid, Mr. Weymouth. There's been a bit of trouble over at the Hailey place. Bunch of kids—a cousin of the Haileys' with them— lit off some firecrackers in the stable yard. One of the horses just went crazy with fright. A thoroughbred, they said. Tried to jump right out of the loose box and injured itself pretty badly. In fact, Mr. Weymouth, it broke a leg and they've had to shoot it. Now how much your kid—or rather, Mrs. Weymouth's kid—had to do with the whole thing I'm not certain. Mr. Hailey's talking of prosecuting. It was a very valuable horse. Mr. Hailey says he's determined to get compensation from the parents. And he's not in the mood to be light with this one, even if he's only seven—and an English lord. I can't see what difference being an English lord makes to getting into trouble. Trouble's trouble to me, Mr. Weymouth. And I think you'd better get over to Mr. Hailey right away." He looked down at David. "I know about the other little boy two years ago, Mr. Weymouth, but it doesn't excuse this sort of crazy stuff. This boy knows horses. He rides ponies. He ought to have more sense. Well—I'll leave it with you. I'm not in the business of putting kids in jail. But there are juvenile offenders, Mr. Weymouth. Better take the boy in hand. I don't like to see these things begin to happen."

Brock had gone at once to smooth over the situation with Dalton Hailey. They knew each other, occasionally visited each other's houses—Dalton Hailey had an open admiration for Margaret, but it did not extend to forgiving her child for the loss of a favorite horse. Brock left behind a substantial check, and the commitment that David would be punished. There was no discussion about what the punishment would be.

The argument raged that evening, and through the next day. "I think it's time we turned him over to his Grandfather Gough for a spell. If he were in England he'd be at a prep school already."

"Turn him over to *me,* Brock," Black Jack said. "Gough's too old. Perhaps I'm too old, but I think he'd do better with us."

"No!" Margaret shouted the word. "I won't have him sent to one of those terrible schools. He's only a baby yet! It's bad enough that he has to go to Eton eventually. Can you imagine how he'd feel—sent to school across the Atlantic. Not able to get back for holidays."

"I've a feeling perhaps Brock's right, Margaret. Perhaps a little discipline . . ." Black Jack's tone was somber. "And, remember, he'd have Pellham to come to for holidays. And he would come here for the summer, of course."

"Pellham! *Pellham!* You must be crazy if you think I'd let David be alone at Pellham when Alice is there! Have you forgotten? You can't have forgotten? David saw Jonathan die! And Alice is responsible. If he makes trouble it's because he's seen that. He has nightmares about it. We all have nightmares about it, but David's only a child. You can't send him away. If you send him away then I tell you you better think of sending Alice away."

"No!" The high, shrill scream sounded through the huge drawing room. Alice had been sitting in one of the deep sofas. She had said nothing all evening, had addressed no word to any of them through dinner, and Lally realized that they had all thought she had gone upstairs with Barnes. She sprang up and ran down the length of the

room to where they all were grouped, ran to Black Jack. "I won't be
sent away. Father . . . Father . . . I have to stay with you."

Black Jack got to his feet and folded her in his arms. "There, my
darling. There . . . it's all right. No one will send you away. You'll
always be with me, my darling." He looked over her head, defen-
sively, at the rest of them. "She'll always be with me. You understand that."

* * *

The debate went on all through Saturday and into Sunday. David
kept to his room, and Mark Shaw stayed out of sight, and at mealtimes remained silent. Lally realized that his own future was being
weighed up with David's. If David was sent to school in England,
Mark Shaw's principal responsibility would be gone. He would still
have his function with Brock in the Manhattan office, but Lally
didn't know if he was needed there, or if the position was just a sop
Brock had thrown to save Mark Shaw's dignity. But the strain was
evident on everyone's face, in their actions and reactions to one another. Alice hardly let Black Jack out of her sight; she refused to go
for the usual walks with Barnes, just sitting docilely, listless and silent. Tension streaked between them all like forks of heat lightning.
Lally thought it was bad luck that Mrs. Shearing had chosen to take
this weekend off. Alice always seemed happier in her company than
with Barnes. She barely touched the food put before her at the table,
even though Black Jack begged her to eat. Except to refuse to go for
walks with Barnes, she said nothing for two days except to ask one
question: "Where's David?"

"David has been a naughty little boy," Margaret said. "He's staying in his room for a while."

"Are you going to send him away too?"

"No one is being sent anywhere, Alice," Margaret snapped. "Now
don't ask again."

After that, Alice's silence seemed to grip them all.

* * *

On Sunday evening they had all been invited to dinner with the
Harpers. It was not an occasion which helped any of them. Edith had
suggested begging off, but Margaret's refusal had been firm and
quick. "Oh, for God's sake let's not do that. It'll be a relief to be out
of this house for a while. We all need a break from one another. Be-

sides, if Lally doesn't go it will look as if she doesn't want to meet Gerry's wife."

She didn't, Lally thought, want to meet Gerry's wife, but she wasn't going to say so. So she washed and brushed her hair, dressed in her most becoming dress, and told herself she would not be jealous. She almost succeeded. She felt the warmth she had always felt for Gerry, but nothing more, and was relieved that it was so. She cast a detached eye on his bride, and agreed that she was very pretty; she had a light, bright manner, and the sparkle that only someone of twenty can produce. She talked eagerly of going to Europe, and Edith politely murmured something about coming to Pellham Langley for the shooting. "Oh, I don't think there would be time. We have so many places—Paris, Venice, Rome . . ." She was, Lally thought, just slightly in awe of Edith, having been told that she had been a marchioness, and she was not sure whether to call her Lady Edith or Lady Pollock. She said to Margaret, "And your little boy—he's a . . . a viscount? Is that right? Well, it's all very confusing."

"You'll have to forgive Carol," Old Man Harper said with a touch of waspishness. "She's something of an innocent still. She rides and shoots like a cowhand, and all the authorities tell me she dances a real mean Charleston. But don't expect too much from the child yet."

"I think it's time we left," Margaret said. She was tired of family rows. "Father isn't supposed to have late nights."

Old Man Harper gripped Brock's hand as he was leaving. "Heard the boy got into a bit of trouble. Be firm with him. That's the mistake I made with Roddy. Never was firm with him."

"David," Margaret said, "is *my* son."

"Then, little lady, you'd better take care of him."

"Rude old man," Margaret said when they were all settled in the car. "That poor girl Carol's going to have a hell of a life with him. Just as well you didn't take Gerry, Lally. You'd have had *him* to deal with."

"Lally," Brock said dryly, "had Old Man Harper in her back pocket. And she would have kept him there. But she wasn't going to marry *him* after all."

* * *

The number of lights on at Whytecliffe when they arrived told them something unusual had happened. But it wasn't until Brock had cut the engine that they heard the screams—the screams of pure hysteria. "Alice!" Brock said, and ran to the entrance door. Vickers had it open before he reached it.

"I had just telephoned the Harper residence, sir, and they said you'd left. It's Miss Alice, sir."

"I can hear that, man. What in God's name is the matter?"

Brock was already past him, and running toward the library. They all followed, Black Jack running more quickly than he should. "Jack, be careful . . ." Edith begged.

He was only seconds behind Lally; they both stopped at the library door.

Alice was there, on her knees, clutching the side of an armchair. She turned her head from side to side, shrieking, sobbing, then thrusting her face into the heavily upholstered side, as if to shut out the light, or some vision she had to escape. Mark Shaw was there, and so was Barnes. Barnes had evidently tried to place a hand on Alice's shoulder, and been swiftly shaken off. She looked as if she had been bitten. And Mark Shaw's face was bleeding from many small scratches. His shirt and his white flannels were smeared with dirt and what looked like blood.

"Mr. Weymouth—" Barnes began.

Black Jack silenced her by lifting his hand. Slowly he advanced toward Alice. With infinite care he knelt beside her, and placed a hand upon her head. "It's Father, my darling."

Momentarily the sobbing, the shrieks ceased. She flung herself into his arms, with an intensity which nearly threw him to the floor. "It's all right, my darling. I'm here, Alice. I'm here."

She raised her head and looked past his shoulder and saw them all grouped in the doorway. Then the shrieks began again. "Why haven't you telephoned for the doctor?" Brock demanded of Vickers.

"Well, sir . . . well, because I wasn't sure what you would want."

"Damn fool!" Brock exploded. "Whatever has happened, she needs the doctor."

Slowly Brock approached the two of them. And slowly Black Jack got to his feet and raised Alice with him. Then Brock took her arms, transferred the weight of her clinging body from Black Jack. "It's all right, sweetheart. It's your old Brock here." Now Alice clung to him, burying her face against him, much as she had in the armchair. "What is it, sweetheart? Tell old Brock."

"She doesn't have to tell you a thing, Mr. Weymouth," Barnes said harshly. "The girl's been raped, that's what's happened. And that man there, Shaw—did it."

Brock shifted Alice's body so that he faced the woman. "Are you certain of what you're saying?"

"Look at her. Is there anything else that can have happened?"

Brock forced Alice to relinquish her grasp, and he supported her at arm's length. They all saw the white nightgown that was torn in two, bloodstained. They saw her battered face, they saw the ferocious marks on her body and neck, as if she had been gripped by animal claws. There were earth stains on her gown also, and pieces of leaves in her hair. As Brock held her away from him, her hand slowly slid down her stomach; she rubbed the golden pubic hair, and they saw the dark shadow of blood caked between her thighs. "I hurt."

"God Almighty!" Brock said. With infinite gentleness he handed her back to Black Jack. Then he went to Mark Shaw and caught him by the front of his shirt. "True, is it? You've done this, you snotty little bastard."

"No—it wasn't that way! I tell you, it wasn't. I heard her screaming . . . outside. I came down. She was running from the bridle path. Screaming. All I did was bring her inside. I didn't touch her, except then."

Brock cursed and slapped him twice about the face with the back of his hand, powerful blows that snapped Mark's head back. In the midst of Alice's cries, they still could hear the asthmatic wheezing which immediately began. Mark Shaw was gasping for breath. "I didn't . . . I didn't . . ."

Brock dragged Mark Shaw back behind the big desk, his hand on his throat, forcing his head back so that the breath was even more choked. "Let me go . . ." The struggle for breath now was as great a noise as Alice's sobs.

"For God's sake, Brock!" Margaret started to go to him.

"Just stay out of it, Margaret. Alice, did this man hurt you? Alice, look at me. Did this man do it?"

She raised her face from Black Jack's shoulder. She looked at Mark Shaw as if she was trying to see him clearly. Her cries began once more. "I hurt! I hurt! The man hurt me!"

The report of the gun sounded loud even in that big, velvet-shrouded, book-lined room. A sound more shocking than Alice's cries. For a time Brock held Mark Shaw close to him, then he flung him away, as if he were something vile and disgusting. Something in the way Mark fell, the inert way she had seen so many bodies lie, told Lally he could be already dead. She raced to him.

"Don't touch the bugger, Lally. Don't put your hand on him."

But she knelt beside him, feeling swiftly for his pulse. The bright blood pumped from the place in his chest where Brock had shot him at such close range. For a few seconds Mark struggled to say something. She bent close to his lips, and the blood flowed over her dress, warm, full of life, life-shedding. "Didn't . . ." Was that what he had said? "Didn't . . ." Then the lips ceased to make their agonized sound. The face went slack. She saw the blood trickle briefly from his mouth, and then that also stopped. Beneath her, the pumping of the blood stopped as the life ran out of Mark Shaw.

She gently disengaged herself. His face looked peaceful enough, innocent enough, despite the scratches and the blood. It looked like the faces of many young men she had seen die. Many of those bodies, also, many of those hands she had held at the moment of death. A sigh, a whisper in the ward at night had alerted her. And they had died. But she had never seen anyone killed before her eyes. She looked at Brock in disbelief.

"He's dead. I'm sure he's dead."

"That's what I intended."

"Brock!" It was Edith's voice in protest, shock. "Sir—" Vickers was unsure what to do, what would be asked of him. "Fool, you should have—" Barnes didn't finish what she had begun to say.

"How . . . ?" Lally got up and moved close to Brock. He had dropped the handgun into an open drawer. How had none of them seen him take it out? They hadn't seen it because none of them had expected him to react in this way. And Mark Shaw had been defenseless. Lally stifled the thought. Alice had been defenseless too. "Give it to me, Brock. You may do someone else harm."

He slammed the drawer shut violently. "It's had its use. Don't touch it, Lally. No one but I will touch it." At that moment Lally remembered Margaret's talk of Brock keeping a gun in his bedside drawer, another in the library. And she had wondered if he always carried one with him in his car. None of them had seen him take a gun from the car, but he could have done so without them noticing. It could have been an instinctive reaction to the screams they had heard.

Margaret gave a little whimpering sound. "Brock . . ."

"Shut up!" he said roughly. "Just everyone shut up. Now don't let's mix this thing up. I shot the bastard. I killed him—if he's dead. He raped our Alice. *Raped* her! Do you understand what he did? That child doesn't know when she's in danger, and he knew it. He's always been slavering over her. Slavering—and at the same time, despising her. What did he think he was going to do? Rape her and kill her out there in the woods? Kill her so she couldn't tell anyone? God knows how he enticed her out there. Or did he follow her? Who the hell was taking care of her? Where were *you,* Barnes?" He cut through her attempted answer. "The man was mad if he thought he could get away with it. He was mad—in any case. A frustrated, cheated little cripple who finally blew his stack and had to prove he was a man. Look at her! He came damn close to killing her. Look at her neck. Who would have thought the little bastard was so strong? Well, I killed him . . ." The passion and the fury in his voice were running down. "Yes, I killed him. Poor, stupid ineffectual little bastard. Whatever I have to pay for it, I'll say I did the right thing . . ."

Then suddenly his head slumped forward. He put out a hand blindly toward Lally. "Oh, God, Lally, I didn't really want to kill him . . . Yes!—I did! I wanted to kill him. At that moment I wanted to kill him. I guess . . . I guess, though, death is too permanent a thing. I could just as well have thrashed him and let the law do the rest." His groping hand found Lally's shoulder. "But look at Alice. Look at what I saw. When a man does that to Alice, he doesn't deserve to live."

Lally held Brock, as she had held Mark Shaw. She heard the intake of his gasped breath, even over Alice's repeated screams. His weight seemed monumental, and all the others were frozen in attitudes which seemed to make them statues in a tableau. Why did everyone stand there? Shocked, frozen. She made her lips work, made the words come out in a tone of command:

"Vickers—call the police now, as well as the doctor."

* * *

All night—long after Alice's cries had been stilled by a hypodermic needle—the questioning went on. The dawn was breaking before Mark Shaw's body was finally taken away from Whytecliffe.

Sergeant Willis had long since been replaced by Detective Inspector Kane. The inspector had taken over the billiard room for his questioning. They all waited, as they had been told, in the drawing

room to be called to him. Cook had come down from her quarters
and supplied coffee and sandwiches. Those in the drawing room
remained untouched. Cook, whose rooms were at the back of the
building near the stable block, had had to be wakened by Vickers on
the house telephone. "I didn't hear a thing," she kept repeating to
anyone who would listen. The maids she had shaken out of bed said
the same thing. Individually the police squad came to the kitchen to
drink coffee, to eat her sandwiches and her pies, as did the photog-
raphers, the fingerprint men. Between them, they heard a lot about
the household at Whytecliffe. Most of it they already knew. Sergeant
Willis sat the longest, and he listened.

"Oh, there's those that say he was all mixed up with some big
bootleggers, but you didn't see none of it here. All very respectable,
it was. Except that we all knew those guards—those security guys—
carried guns. He didn't want Mrs. Weymouth involved in anything.
Too precious, she was. Precious spoiled. And if you ask me, that
poor thing, Alice, should have been locked up long ago. Didn't know
half the time what she was doing. For her own good—I mean. There
was nothing bad in her. Can't understand Mr. Shaw doing *that,*
though. Wouldn't have thought he had it in him. Most of the time he
wouldn't say boo to a goose. They say, don't they, that they're always the worst kind, when they get roused?" When finally Inspector
Kane called her to the billiard room she said the same things. She
had heard nothing, but she had plenty of opinions. "Can't say I'm
not sorry for Mr. Weymouth. He thought the world of that little
Alice."

And in the drawing room Barnes defended herself to the family.
"Well, there she was, fast asleep. So I went to the bathroom. I'm entitled to go to the bathroom, aren't I? And after that, I had a nice
long soak in the tub. I'm entitled to that, aren't I, after a hot day?
She was asleep in the next room—"

"You were hired to watch her," Black Jack said.

"And that, Sir John, is a twenty-four-hour-a-day job. After all, I
sleep in the same room with her. I can hardly do more than that.
And you expressly said she must never be locked in. Never. You said
she was terrified of being locked in. So unless Shearing is here, I
can't go to the toilet or have a bath? Is that what you're telling me,
Sir John? It's a bit late now."

From Vickers they heard what he had witnessed. "I was waiting
for you to return, Mr. Weymouth. To lock up and see that you had

everything you wanted. I was reading the paper. I guess I fell asleep. The screams woke me up, and I came running outside. I saw Mr. Shaw struggling with Miss Alice. There, where the bridle path goes into the woods. It looked to me as if he was trying to drag her inside the house and she was fighting him every step of the way. Tearing at him, scratching him. I didn't know what the hell—beg your pardon—had happened. There were supposed to be two security men on. When I went to get them I found one of them dead drunk. And I haven't set eyes on the other. That's some security Mr. Weymouth's paying for. Well, Barnes showed up and gave Miss Alice a belt across the face, and that shut her up for a while. Between us we got her inside, and then I telephoned the Harper place. They said you were on the way, so I waited. I thought you might not want to telephone the police—might have wanted to keep it all quiet . . ."

Lally listened to it all. The questions, the recriminations, the slight shifting of the facts each time the story was retold. Barnes, on the defensive, was ready to lay blame wherever she could. "You didn't have to react like that, Mr. Weymouth. Better let the law take care of such things. I know you were upset, but—"

"I'm not interested in your opinions."

"You don't have to talk to me like that, Mr. Weymouth. You killed a man you didn't have cause to."

"You accused him."

"What else would I think?—seeing the state she was in, and Mark Shaw all scratched up and with blood all over him? Anyone would have said the same thing. But there's a difference between accusing someone, and then going and shooting him. I would have waited to ask a few questions before I murdered someone. Alice never actually *said* he did it. She only said a man did it. That's all the doctor could say, either. That she'd been raped. That's a fact. They'll soon know if it was Mark Shaw. There are ways of telling . . ."

"You disgust me," Brock said. "Get out of here."

"Oh no, I won't, Mr. Weymouth. I'm staying right here until the inspector says I can go."

After they had all been individually interviewed, after all the servants had been questioned, and the security man was sober enough to confess he had heard nothing, they were summoned together to the billiard room. Detective Inspector Kane faced them all.

"There's no doubt that Mr. Weymouth shot Mark Shaw. He ad-

mits it. Many of you witnessed it. He shot him in a blind rage because his sister-in-law had been raped. There's no doubt about that,
either. The rape is a fact, according to the doctor, and the shooting is
a fact. Whether Mr. Weymouth shot the man who raped Miss Pollock is the matter that's open to question. We shall, from the lab reports, very soon know. You will come to the station with us, Mr.
Weymouth, and be arraigned in the morning. I understand your attor-
ney is on the way from Manhattan. I don't know what the charge will
be. Probably homicide. This was a deliberate killing, not an accidental one. It seems pretty obvious it was not premeditated. I just wish
you hadn't been in such a hurry. Because your security man, Paolo
Gambini, is missing, and unless he shows up here voluntarily within
the next few hours, we will have to put out a warrant for him. When
we pick him up we may charge him with rape. All of this will have to
wait on the time I'm able to question Miss Pollock."

"You won't question Alice," Brock said. "You will not question
her. Don't you understand? She's on the edge of madness. If this rape
has not tipped her over the edge, any process of questioning her
could."

"A judge will probably want to have a little talk with her—in
chambers."

"That's as far as it will ever go with Alice," Brock said. "Whoever
you charge with rape—whether you say it was Shaw or Gambini or
someone we don't even know about—you'll never get Alice into
court. No doctor would permit it—no judge would permit it. No court
of law would take her word as a witness because of diminished responsibility. I think that's why I shot Mark Shaw. Because on that
technicality he just might have gotten out of it all. No one can believe anything that child says. There would only be the lab tests. And
Shaw had the out of being able to say he had done it with her consent. Whether she had consented or not, no one would ever be able
to prove—because they probably could, if they wanted, prove she was
mad. You don't take the mentally unbalanced into court, Inspector,
and put them on the stand. Even our society is humane enough to
forbid that. As long as I live Alice will never appear in a courtroom.
I'll take this case as far as I have to in order to stop it. The best lawyers in the country will fight that. For as long as they have to."

"And you, Mr. Weymouth—will you fight appearing in court? Will
you defend that charge?"

"Hell, no. I've admitted that I shot Mark Shaw. I'll plead guilty. They'll put me in jail. I don't think I'll get the death sentence. I've been in prison before, Inspector. I survived."

* * *

Next morning before a judge Brock was charged with homicide. His lawyer argued for a charge of manslaughter, and lost. Brock pleaded guilty. It seemed evident that the sympathy of the judge was with him, because he was granted bail, which, however, was set at half a million dollars. A police hunt was started for Gambini when the lab tests showed that Alice had not been raped by Mark Shaw. The police also questioned every man on every estate for miles around—the owners of the North Shore mansions as well as their servants. The disappearance of Paolo Gambini could not be taken as proof of his guilt.

Whytecliffe became like a fortress. No one stirred on the terraces, no one walked on the beach, or used the bridle paths. The only place for exercise was the indoor swimming pool. A whole new team of twelve security guards appeared, and they patrolled the outside of the house. Only the police and the lawyers and the doctors came and went. Two of Brock's secretaries came from Manhattan to answer the telephones. Mostly they used only the same words: "Mr. Weymouth has no statement to make to the press." But the press made its own statements.

The whole saga of the Pollock family was recreated and redrawn. They wrote of Black Jack's three wives—the legendary Lady Latitia, the vague figure of Alice Trimble, who was the mother of the rape victim, the rather formidable figure of the former Marchioness of Ross. They wrote about Jon and his second marriage to a woman who might almost have been his sister, but most of all they wrote about Margaret and Brock. Their colleagues on the other side of the Atlantic combed the newspaper files for the story of the car crash in which Jon and Bobby had died, and for which Brock had gone to prison. They wrote of the marriage, three days after Brock's release from prison, to Bobby's widow. And this was all set against the background that the whole world seemed to want to know about—the background of wealth and privilege, titled people with long family trees, and of the two strangers in the midst of it, Brockton Weymouth and Lillian Pollock, who had no history and no real names. They told the story of a man who had come from nowhere, and made a fortune, and of a woman picked up from the streets of Leeds. They even used words like "war profiteer" about Black Jack.

One newspaper found someone who evidently did not care too much for Mr. Brockton Weymouth, and who was willing to recount the story of what had happened the night Buddy Rawlston had had a bonfire party on the beach. He described how Alice Pollock had stripped naked and gone into the water. He told about Mark Shaw getting into a fight over the incident. *If you ask me, that girl was asking for it. Whatever she got, she was asking for. Mad as a hatter, but the family treated her as a saint.* Sickened by this, they stopped reading the newspapers at Whytecliffe.

"We have to send the children away," Edith said. "We can't have them shut up here until Brock's case comes up."

"Where?" Margaret asked. "I won't have David sent to the Goughs. It would break his heart. Where can we send them that they won't think they're being punished for something?"

In the end it was Old Man Harper who solved the matter. He presented himself at Whytecliffe. "I've come to take the children," he said. "We'll get them out in a van, or something of the sort. None of the press will see. They'll only be half a mile away from you, Margaret. You can come every day. The press will only know you're visiting my house, but they won't know anything else. I've got my own security people, and I've personally promised that I'll knock the head off anyone who mentions the children to the press. I carry a checkbook and a big stick, and I can use both." Seeing him in the increasing frailty of his years, the idea of the big stick seemed ludicrous to Lally, but the checkbook was not. He knew how to use it.

So the children used the Harper place, the tennis courts, the swimming pool, but they did not ride or go to the beach. The press talked of them having been "spirited away." They all played a game with Dan and Sammy about having a holiday at the Harpers'; only David was not deceived. "It's all about Alice, isn't it?" he said. "It's because of the trouble. It's about Mr. Shaw? They say he didn't do anything to Alice."

"Who says?" Lally asked.

"Everyone. I listen. They think I'm a kid like Dan and Sammy. But I'm not a kid. I just listen. Sometimes I take one of the newspapers from the kitchen. They're writing about my mother and Brock. About my father—when he was killed with Uncle Jon. One of them said Brock was some sort of . . . of a gangster. Is that true, Lally?"

"No—not true. Not true at all."

The man Paolo Gambini had not been found, and the police could find no other suspect for the rape of Alice Pollock. Lally was afraid to look at Brock's face as the days passed, and the knowledge of a man innocently killed sank in; he never spoke Mark Shaw's name, but Lally sensed that he was never out of Brock's mind. Black Jack sat huddled in the drawing room, looking cold even in those warm summer days. Although the police had now unsealed the library, having gathered all their evidence, no one now ever went there, except the maids to dust and clean.

Each day doctors spent some time with Alice, mostly in the presence of Detective Inspector Kane. When they edged close to the subject of the rape, she either became mute or almost incoherent. "I went out," was the most she would say. "I went out. It was very hot. I wanted to swim."

Brock brought a team of the most famous psychiatrists in America to question her, to establish her unfitness to ever appear in court. Finally Black Jack stopped it. "What's the point? Alice isn't going into court. She is not part of the evidence of Brock having shot Mark Shaw. He's pleaded guilty to that—and there are plenty of other witnesses. If you find Gambini, you'll take her into court only over my dead body. The doctors, even your own, will never permit it. So leave her to whatever peace she can find."

"I agree with you absolutely, Sir John," Kane said. "There are parts of my work I find distasteful too. When we find Gambini, the case will have to be built on circumstantial evidence, and there will never be a question of Miss Pollock appearing in court. If you ask me about the chances of finding Gambini—"

"I didn't ask you, but I'd be interested to hear."

"My opinion is that we'll never see Gambini again. He could be nicely encased in cement in the East River now, or under a garbage dump in New Jersey. Mr. Brockton Weymouth's influence reaches very far in certain circles. He would never want Gambini brought to trial. Too much publicity. It is much better for him if Gambini just never appears again." By this time Inspector Kane was beginning to know the household and its members very well indeed.

"Mr. Weymouth is a very cool and very determined man. I would guess that about the only time he ever lost his head in his life was when he shot Mark Shaw."

Black Jack leaned forward on the cane he now carried. Lally, who had been with them during the interview, leaned forward also. "No, Inspector. I think there was another time Brock lost his head. It was when he met my daughter, Margaret. He's never quite recovered from that."

The months dragged by while they waited for Brock's case to come up on the crowded court calendar. "It isn't a trial," he kept insisting. "I've pleaded guilty. Even the lawyers won't persuade me to change that plea. They're not going to get any more from me. There will be no further stories for the newspapers."

He tried to send them all away. "For God's sake go back to Pellham. I'll be given a sentence. It won't be long. There's a lot of sympathy for a guy who kills someone he thinks has raped a defenseless girl. I'll get it over with. I don't *want* you there."

"You can't send us all away, Brock," Black Jack said. "I'm an old man, and I'm entitled to my stubbornness. And Margaret won't go. She told me so."

"If you think I'm going to let Margaret stay here while I'm in prison, you'll have to forget it. I've given orders that the house is to be closed. I still have a long lease from the Brewster estate, but that can always be disposed of. The office on Wall Street will continue. There are a few privileges they allow you in prison, especially on a light sentence. I don't think I'll be breaking stones. You have to take them all away, Black Jack, as soon as it's over. Pellham's the only place they can go. The reporters will soon get sick of slogging across the moors to follow them. The boys can ride . . . walk. . . . You'll get a tutor for them—" He stopped. "I suppose I'm never to use the word 'tutor' again. Since I murdered one. You may have a hard time filling that post. But we have to think of these things. Mark Shaw's mother—for one. I wrote to her. She refused any help. Don't blame her. But there are ways to do these things. A London banker will inform her that her son had investments through his bank, and they, in liquidating his estate, find that she will have a comfortable income. She will not question the source, since the bank is so eminently respectable. Of course she instructed her lawyers to sell all the shares of stock that Mark bought for her through our company. She is, I'm told, a woman with no understanding of investment. She will simply do what her local bank manager and lawyer in Buxton, Derbyshire, advise her. And they will advise her as I tell them."

"Is there no end to it, Brock?" Lally asked. "Are you ever going to stop arranging people's lives?"

"Not so long as I think they're being arranged foolishly."

She faced him. "And what you did to Mark? Wasn't that foolish?"

"That wasn't only foolish, Lally. That was stupid. I can't forgive stupidity. I will never forgive that act, no matter what I do for Mrs. Shaw, or how many years or months they send me to prison for it. It was stupid. I haven't often been stupid in my life. Very rarely. But the Pollock family seems to be my weak point." He had given up the elaborate ritual of mixing the martinis. He now drank his seventeen-year-old scotch neat. He drained his glass. "Damned if I know how you did it, Black Jack. To produce Margaret and Alice and make me love them both so much."

*   *   *

Lally experienced for the first time the magic and beauty and tragedy of the American autumn. She had never before seen trees of such brilliant color, not reds so red, nor gold so golden. The leaves swept sadly across the lawns of Whytecliffe, more quickly than the gardeners could rake them up. In the evenings there was the pungent smell of burning leaves still in the air. And then would come the wind, when the leaves swirled again, and the smell was again the smell of the sea, and the surf crashed on the shore. The children came back from the Harper place. The reporters had faded away. Brock's case was set for late October, and they could bide their time until then. Margaret was silent most of the time; she seemed to accept the days as they came. Only to Lally did she confess her restlessness. "It's coming around to hunting time again. I'd love to be out with the Meadowbrook, but of course I can't. I begin to understand Alice, Lally. I begin to understand why she ran out that night. If anyone shut me up, watched me day and night—I would have run out too. Anywhere. Even for a few minutes. It's terrible to think that I'm only just beginning to understand Alice. That she isn't a doll or a toy. She has feelings. We'll never understand exactly what they are, but I've only just begun to understand that they exist. And for her, Brock's going to be shut up himself. Just the way he was the other time . . . when I killed Jon and Bobby. I'm more in his debt than ever, Lally. He'll take it all, every bit of it. A sort of scapegoat for me. He'll arrange every last detail of it. We'll all be shipped off to Pellham the moment the sentence is passed. We'll be with Father and Edith and the boys. And we'll just wait until he tells us what to do next. And I'll do that. I'll just wait."

She slipped out occasionally to sail her skiff, *Fancy*. "Please, Brock, don't forbid it! I can't stay shut up in the house all the time. All the summer yachts are laid up. There's no one to see me. I feel free, for a little time."

"And so should *Fancy* be laid up. It's high time. It's not safe for you out there at this time of year."

"But I never go when there's a strong wind—hardly any wind at all. I don't want to worry you, Brock. Not give you any more worry than you have." And because the days and the nights were so quiet, because no visitors came to the house, and none were invited, because Margaret no longer played the phonograph, but sat for hours staring from the drawing-room windows across the Sound, and because she paid no attention to the drink he mixed for her before dinner, and mostly left it untouched, he could not refuse her this. Most of the times she went she took Alice with her, Alice who these days rarely spoke, and never laughed. "I pity her so," Margaret said to Lally. "She's still like someone in a trance. I never hear her sing now —I miss it. For an hour or so, when we're out there on *Fancy,* she seems free. Sometimes I hate to put back—as if we should go on sailing forever. Last time she said 'Thank you' to me, like a polite little girl. She almost smiled. I would give a lot now to see Alice smile."

But no one did see her smile. There were three new women with her now. Barnes had left Whytecliffe as soon as Inspector Kane had permitted her to go. Shearing reappeared only to pack her bags. "Can't be associated with something like this. No one would ever give me a job again." The three new women were all trained nurses, able to administer drugs if Alice should become unmanageable. A doctor from Manhattan came twice a week to see her; he tried various drugs but none seemed to elevate her mood, or lighten the depression which seemed permanently to shroud her.

"I shall be glad when you've gotten back to England," the doctor told Black Jack. "I think she associates this place with pain and fear. Back there, she may be happier. Perhaps you should consider a clinic . . ."

"Never," Black Jack said. "The only security Alice knows is here with us. And she adores Brock. I don't know what I'll tell her when he goes to prison. She won't understand."

"Keep reminding her she'll see him again. Don't try to explain prison to her. She believes she's already in one."

*   *   *

On November first Brock stood before a judge, pleaded guilty to the charge of homicide, and was sentenced to three years' imprisonment. He had refused to let any of them come to the court. "We all know the outcome. Why give the newspapers a field day?" The sentence was considered a light one.

So they had obeyed him, but Margaret had cried in despair when she had heard the sentence. "It's too long!"

"It's very light for that serious a crime, it could more likely have been ten years," Black Jack said. "It's because people can understand why he did it—and it wasn't premeditated. Myself, I think there's a lot of sympathy for him, but there's been so much publicity I think the judge was afraid to seem to be too lenient. But there will be time off for good behavior. Brock's too smart to forgo that. It won't be three years."

"Three years seems forever. The boys will be growing up not really knowing him. I'll be . . . I'll be growing old. Yes, I know it seems mad, but I *feel* old. Something so sad and sick inside me."

Before Lally's eyes in these last months of waiting Margaret had become a softer, gentler woman, a woman looking around her, as if for the first time, and seeing things she had never seen before. "I'll have to start on good works, or something." A wintry little smile broke her set lips. "Funny to think I might start to be exactly the person the Goughs would have loved for a daughter-in-law. I wonder will I be a better person when Brock comes out? I wonder if I could actually make something of myself?"

"Just love him. That's all he wants."

"Sometimes I think he would be better rid of me. I only mess up his life."

She looked around at the trunks already packed to go to the ship the next day. The chandeliers were being swathed in muslin, the furniture disappearing under dust sheets. The house had a melancholy air, as if already the shutters had been closed, an end written to this whole episode in their lives.

"I wish Brock would let me visit him in prison."

"He never would. He would never permit you to see him in a place like that."

"But he let *you* see him—when he was in prison."

"Oh, that was because he knew I wouldn't be shocked. I was—well, better used to things like that."

Margaret leaned forward and, surprisingly, brushed a kiss on her cheek. "I do try not to be jealous of you, Lally. I don't always succeed. Now, I'm going for a sail. The last chance I'll have. When I write to Brock I'll be able to tell him it was a beautiful fall day—the air almost still—calm, golden. The sun shone. I shall have to think of a lot of cheerful things to write to him about, Lally. I don't want to tell him that the last day here was terrible and sad. I want to tell him I went sailing with Alice, and it was beautiful. That we were calm . . . and free. That's what he wants to hear. Alice? . . . Alice . . . ? Just for an hour. Just you and me, darling. Alice . . . !" She had raced halfway up the stairs before Alice and her companion appeared at the head of them.

"You'd like to come sailing, darling? Come sailing for the last time with Margaret?"

Alice nodded. "Yes," she said. And then, as if it were an effort: "Thank you."

* * *

The air was, as Margaret had said, almost still. Scarcely a puff of wind flowed across the water. Lally watched the little red sail, now almost alone on the water of the Sound, tacking lazily, making little headway. Margaret must, Lally thought, have looked back at Whytecliffe from the sea, seen its splendor in the autumn sunshine, remembered all the things that had happened there, the births of two of her children, the dinners, the parties. She hoped Margaret did not think too much of Jonathan and Mark Shaw. But still she recognized that sail with Alice as a farewell gesture. It would be a long time, despite her good intentions, before Margaret learned to put the packing of trunks at the top of her list of priorities. Perhaps that was why Brock had so prized and loved her. He had grubbed and dug and worked for so much in his life. Unbidden to Lally's mind came the biblical quotation which may have explained why Brock had allowed Margaret all the indulgence, the liberty, the understanding he gave her. *Consider the lilies of the field, how they grow; they toil not, neither do they spin; And yet I say unto you, That even Solomon in all his glory was not arrayed like one of these.* Perhaps he had wanted one thing, beautiful and useless, in his life—a lily of the field.

But toward the end of the afternoon a November fog rolled in and blanketed the Sound. Lally anxiously paced the jetty until it became too dark to hope that she could see the red sail. The light on the jetty pulsed, but who could see it through the enveloping fog? The sea still was calm; the waves only gently smacked against the wooden piers.

She called the Coast Guard, and did not tell Black Jack, until it would have been time for Margaret to appear at dinner, that she had not returned. She wished she could have found some lie to comfort him when his face turned ashen. "They'll be all right, Father. It's so still and calm. Look, the fog has hardly moved. They're in no danger. It will just take the Coast Guard a while to find them."

*　*　*

The Coast Guard found *Fancy* the next morning, when the late November dawn broke, and a rising wind had lifted the last of the fog. The tiller was lashed, but the boom swung wildly. The current and the wind were now bearing the little craft on a course that might have carried her beyond the Sound, out toward Martha's Vineyard or Nantucket—or even, if *Fancy* had slipped past them by chance of wind or tide, out into the Atlantic.

Alice huddled alone in the skiff. She cried out when one of the coastguardsmen touched her. And then, as they wrapped her in blankets and tried to get her to drink hot coffee, she turned her face away from them. She was able to answer none of the questions they put to her.

Lally was driven immediately to the Coast Guard station. Alice's face lightened at the sight of her. "Lally . . . Lally!" The chief of the station watched their reunion, Lally's attempt to comfort Alice, with as much patience as he could muster. Then he broke in. "Mrs. Weymouth is missing, Mrs. Pollock. Can you get her—Miss Pollock—to tell us anything?"

"Where's Margaret, darling? Do you know where Margaret is?" Alice shook her head. "The big stick came around."

"Does she mean the boom?"

"It hit her. She went into the water. Just like Jonathan. She left me all alone."

"Do you think this young lady is telling all she knows? There was one oar missing . . ."

Automatically Lally came to Alice's defense. "She's telling as much as she can."

"I'm sorry, Mrs. Pollock. If Mrs. Weymouth went overboard, then we have very little hope of finding her alive. No one could be alive out there all night. We'll keep searching, though. It's just possible she managed to swim ashore somewhere."

"Do you remember, darling, when Margaret went into the water? Do you remember anything? Can you tell us, Alice?"

"No . . . she just went."

Lally folded the blankets more closely about Alice. She looked over Alice's shoulder at the chief.

He shook his head. "Bad as it is, it could have been worse. A few more hours, given this wind, and she could have gone helplessly out into the Atlantic, or died of exposure."

"But she's gone, hasn't she?" Alice suddenly asked, her tone almost pleading.

"Yes, darling. She's gone."

"There will be a lot of questions that will have to be asked if we get to the stage of an inquest."

"Alice is never to be questioned in a court. The doctors . . ."

"So I understand. They say she cannot be held responsible." He opened the door for them to leave.

* * *

In the car Lally told the chauffeur to roll up the glass screen between them, and give the maximum heat. She held Alice, still shivering, wrapped in the blankets, close to her. "It's all right, Alice. It's all right. . . . We'll soon be home with Father."

"She's gone, hasn't she?" Alice asked again. "She's gone. Like Jonathan and Jon. She sent Brock away. He's gone too. She told me Brock would be gone a long time. She burned Teddy Rose and Madame Butterfly and Raggedy Ann. She burned my hands. She was taking me away too. She said she was taking me away."

"What did she say, darling? What did Margaret say?"

"She said we were going for a very long sail, and we might never come back again. I didn't want her there anymore. I didn't want to be with her anymore. The big stick was there, and she went into the water . . ."

"Hush, my darling, hush. . . . We won't tell anyone what Margaret said. It will be our secret. You won't tell anyone else, will you, Alice?"

"I won't tell anyone. If you don't want me to tell. I love you,

Lally. You are not like her. You would never send me away. Father
said you never would."

"That's right. I never would send you away, Alice." A leaden
weight had descended on Lally.

*   *   *

They waited one full day, until the Coast Guard had called off its
search, before Lally made the long journey up the Hudson to Ossin-
ing, where the prison of Sing Sing stood. She knew that Brock had
never intended any of them to enter the place. The warden had
granted permission for a special visit. Lally had to sit across a barrier
from Brock, speak through glass, to give him the news that Margaret
was dead.

He sat a few minutes in silence. When he spoke his tone was quite
harsh, the lines of his face stern as he questioned her. "And why isn't
Black Jack here with you?"

"Well, Black Jack thought it better to stay with Alice. She's terribly upset."

"You're a rotten liar, Lally. Always have been. You've come here
to tell me Margaret's gone, and Alice may have had something to do
with her death . . . or was possibly an innocent victim of Margaret's
misguided sense of what was right to do. And Black Jack doesn't
come to help you say all this? What else is wrong?"

"I didn't tell Father about the rest of it. Only about Margaret
going. That was enough for him to bear. He's in hospital, Brock. He
had a heart attack this morning."

Something that seemed like rage colored Brock's face. His lips
came together, and she thought he never would speak. Finally he
said, "I've never felt helpless in my life before. I've always been able
to take some action. But here I am. Stuck in this place. I can do
nothing!" His hand slammed into the thick wooden table. She
thought for a moment that he might try to smash the glass. A guard
moved toward him. "Oh, leave me alone! I'm not going to break up
the place." He stood up. "Thanks for coming, Lally. Take them all
back to Pellham just as soon as you can. You'll have to take care of
David and Dan and Sammy. You'll have to help Edith take care of
Black Jack. You'll have to find some way of taking care of Alice."
He strode away from the barrier to the locked door. He did not look
back at Lally while he waited for it to be unlocked. The guard was
surprised. His experience was that men did not terminate interviews

before they were made to. "Look, Mr. Weymouth . . ." The use of his name told Lally that already Brock's connections had bought him a place of security and ease in the prison. "Look, you don't have to break it up just yet. The warden knows about your wife. Tough luck. He wouldn't want—"

"I've said all I have to say."

She called to him as the door swung open. "Brock!"

"What?"

She got up and leaned close to the glass, attempting to break this artificial barrier. "Almost the last thing she said before she went. Almost the very last. She said she loved you."

He shook his head. "Thank you for that gallant lie, Lally. The only person Margaret loved was herself."

❧ PART IV ❧

1929

❧ CHAPTER 16 ❧

Lally sat above the waterfall and turned her face toward the valley where the stacks of the mills rose. She preferred, these days, to look down on them rather than to look at Pellham Langley. Even though some of the chimney stacks no longer belched smoke, there still was more of an air of life there than breathed on Pellham.

She turned her back deliberately on all that waited down there for her. For just these minutes she listened only to the moan of the wind through the dead bracken, the heather stung by the first frost that had come in November. Soon she would no longer be able to climb up here; the icicles clinging to the rocks of the waterfall would defeat her, the snow drifts would push her back, the wind would make this vantage point a place eagerly looked forward to but unattainable again until the spring.

Down there, at Pellham Langley, the world had continued much as she had foreseen it when they had finally left America. The little boys had ceased to be little boys. David had begun at his prep school before going to Eton. He had become a tough and quarrelsome boy whom she knew would take his share of beatings and, when he finally arrived at the dignity and status of the sixth form at Eton, would be no more merciful to the young ones than his seniors had been to him. He did not have, as Jon had had, such a good friend as Patrick Kimble. Their friendship had made the school bearable. They had continued to laugh. But David, even at prep school, seldom laughed. He continued to visit his grandfather, Lord Gough, and he showed a polite interest in the estate. Polite interest only. He had already learned to turn a smooth, rather hard face to the world. He seldom talked to anyone at Pellham, other than the polite necessities, but he had learned to use its amenities to entertain his school friends, as he had learned to use Black Jack's generosity. He used Edith's skills as a hostess, with the sure knowledge that she would do anything in her power to make the school holidays at Pellham pleasant because that was Black Jack's wish. The cynicism that had been born on the day Jonathan died had hardened with his mother's death. It seemed to Lally that he could never allow himself to be vulnerable again; he was determined not to be hurt, so he did not permit himself to feel. The only man he had ever known as a father was still serving a jail sentence on the other side of the Atlantic. David, when with his friends, was careful to disclaim the connection with Brockton Weymouth, although his half brothers bore that name. "I just visited there for a while," Lally had once heard him say offhandedly. "I didn't really know him at all."

The two younger ones, Dan and Sammy, lived for the letters which came every month from the prison. Sammy had only the vaguest notion of the man who was his father, but he fed on every scrap that Dan could recount. Lally had often listened to a recital of the virtues of their father. "Father is very tall," Dan would begin. "And he was always fun. He used to come up to see us the minute he got home in the evening. He used to go to an office every day. Aunt Lally, will we go back someday to that place on the beach? I like that place. Would Father take us back there?"

"I'm not sure, Dan. But whatever he does, I'm sure you'll like it. Your father always made very good arrangements about everything. He is a very kind man."

Sometimes she wondered if he was. He was permitted only a limited number of letters, and the ones to her were usually only a transcription of verbal instructions given to his manager on the appointed visiting days at the prison. Checks arrived regularly for the maintenance of his sons, and for whatever David required, as well as his school fees. Black Jack had tried to object, but Lally had pleaded with him not to reject the money. "It's the only way Brock can let them know that he cares about them." She had never written that Lord Gough had adamantly refused any money from Brock on behalf of his grandson. "Do you think I'd let my boy's school fees be paid by a man who's twice a jailbird—and a murderer?" So Lally banked the money in David's name, and gave him a generous allowance during the holidays. David might reject the idea of Brockton Weymouth, but he accepted his money without comment.

There was a tutor at Pellham Langley for Dan and Sammy. "I don't want Dan sent to school yet," Black Jack said. "We must keep them together. We have to wait to hear what Brock wants to do when he gets out. He may—very probably he will—want to have them back in America."

"When Brock gets out" was a phrase very often on Black Jack's lips. He longed for his son-in-law's liberty, but he expected it to bring a separation from his grandchildren, and the thought saddened him. The convalescence from the heart attack he had suffered at the time of Margaret's death had been slow, and never fully complete. They had lingered a full two months at Whytecliffe, well into the bitter January weather. Then they had traveled to Florida to stay a further two months. So it had been well over a year that Black Jack and Edith had been absent from Pellham Langley. The Yorkshire spring had been late, and Black Jack had sat huddled over the fire, hardly seeming to care what went on in the world beyond his home, his particular valley. He seldom visited the mills, and he had never gone back to any of the mines. The managers and members of the boards came to Pellham Langley to report to him, but Lally had the impression that the journeys had become something of a sop to save the dignity of an aging and ill man. But there was always the knowledge that Black Jack was still the outright owner, and no decision of any weight could be taken without his consent.

Lally took to sitting with him during these meetings, and to reading the financial reports the managers produced. Black Jack smiled at her wryly one day. "I don't think you'll thank me, but with or without your permission, I have put you on the board of directors of the mills as my appointed director, as all of them were appointed in their time. It will, I think, take a bit longer to get the board of the mines to swallow a woman sitting with them. But in time, they'll accept you. They'll have to. I've been studying a plan for forming a family-owned company. The only shares would belong to us. They would not be for sale to the public. Only you and I, Lally, would have voting rights, until the boys came of age. You would have to administer trusts for David and Dan and Sammy, and exercise their voting rights. For Edith also." He was still clinging to his cherished independence by not going to the public for fresh capital. Lally was aware that both the mills and the mines needed fresh capital, but Black Jack would not let control of them pass from his hands. "When I'm dead, you'll have to do it all, Lally. You might as well begin to exercise some control now. It'll give all those solemn fatheads on the board a right good shaking-up to have a woman among them. They'll condescend to you for a while. They'll treat you as the little woman. But you'll shake them up. I can't take you away from Susie's and give you nothing in place of that."

"You didn't take me away from Susie's. I just decided I'd rather be here."

They both knew it was a kindly lie, and accepted it. She stayed in the saddened and lonely house because she was needed. She reluctantly, and at first diffidently, accepted the place on the boards to which Black Jack had appointed her, and encountered the prejudice and condescension which he had predicted. She began to read the financial reports more closely, to argue, in time, over points in them, and to struggle with the often, to her, difficult language of the financial journals. "This is a lot harder than running a little dress business," she confessed to Edith.

"Jack wants you to do it, my dear. You're young still. You have more freedom than a woman of my generation ever dreamed of. And you've got the responsibilities that go with it. Jack looks to you, Lally. In time, David will slip away altogether. He'll have the Gough estate, and the mills and the mines will be your responsibility. And, God knows, that's no pleasure in these bad times."

Lally, as she conscientiously studied the financial reports, thought, in a rather homesick fashion, of the days as Susie's manageress. There were now two women doing that job, and all she had were the visits by Susie to Pellham Langley. She seemed to blow a fresh wind of life and confidence through the house. Dan and Sammy adored "Aunt Susie"; David had pronounced her "a rather common little woman." "I hope your dad gets it all sewn up properly. Or that one," Susie said, referring to David, "will try to take over the lot. You'll just have to stick with it, Lally. Running our little business was a pastime by comparison with this. You have to do it, though. For your dad—for all of them. Gawd, I don't envy you. And, hell, how I miss you. Those two I've got are all right, but it doesn't run as smoothly as it used to. Most of all, I miss you when I've reached the time when I'm just about to throw the pencil at the wall in the evening, and I've got to go and have something to eat. I never realized how many problems we got sorted out while we ate. I almost hate to go to Armand's now. He always asks about you—and I'm just about on the point of blubbering, because I know you can't ever come back. He always sends his regards. I think he'd send his love if he didn't think it was disrespectful. Did I tell you he's thinking of opening another little restaurant? He's got his eye on a place in Jermyn Street. I think it could be something for us to invest a little in, Lally. Hard times and all—if it's the right food in the right place, there are going to be enough people who'll spend the money to eat out. I'm quite interested . . . I've got a bit saved . . ."

"Going to turn into an entrepreneur, Susie?"

Susie winked. "Why not? I have to keep up with you somehow, don't I?" Lally realized that she hungered for Susie's visits. It was Susie who now brought the "surprises" for the boys, who brought the news of a world that now seemed lost to Lally.

Edith listened to the talk, more and more often lying on a chaise in her room, staring at the view over the moors. Frequently, she was obliged to spend the whole day there; she had begun to suffer from arthritis of a hip joint, which made movement difficult. She persisted in her housekeeping role, but all directions were given from her room, and she was unable to oversee personally the way they were carried out. There were few guests at Pellham Langley these days, but Edith had an immense pride in seeing that it continued to run smoothly. "I owe at least that to Jack," she said to Lally, as she delegated the visits of inspection of the kitchen and the linen cupboards, the pantries and the storerooms. She made the effort, no matter how severe the pain, of dressing for dinner every night, and coming downstairs. She looked, Lally thought, as elegant as ever, but her face had begun to show the lines of pain. Black Jack had had a small lift installed for her. He took pleasure in her appearance and her company, and Lally saw that the best dressmakers from London came to attend to her wardrobe. Susie's simple little dresses were not for Edith.

Billings had almost completely withdrawn from the management of the household, only holding onto his right to order for the wine cellar. He lived his days in his own rooms, sometimes descending to share a bottle of Black Jack's best claret with Pickering, who had replaced him. Black Jack missed Billings, and was often curt with Pickering. It was Edith's task to try to soothe the relationship, realiz-

ing that after Billings' long service, his friendship, no one else would
ever completely satisfy Black Jack. The young boys were boisterous
and lively, and gave the house a superficial sense of gaiety. They
needed more than their tutor for companionship, and Lally tried to
supply that. Black Jack made no plans for them. There was always
the sense that their stay at Pellham Langley was temporary. Lally
dreaded the day when Brock would ask to have his sons back. Waiting for Brock was a state of mind for all of them. They waited for
decisions, for directions. "When Dad comes . . ." was a phrase as
often on Dan's lips as "When Brock gets out" was on Black Jack's.
They longed for him, and yet, in many ways, feared his coming. His
coming would mean change. He would take the boys away, and the
great house would fall silent.

The person who talked most of Brock was Alice. Every day she
asked if they expected him. Every day she asked Lally to write to
Brock for her, asked her to write that she missed him, and wanted to
know when they would go back to the house on the beach. Lally
never wrote that last question to Brock. The few short letters Alice
had received from Brock were almost in tatters from being opened
and refolded. Alice learned the words by heart from Lally.

Lally was uncertain what Brock thought of the reports brought to
him of Margaret's death. Her body had been washed up on a beach
along the Sound nearly a week after Alice had been found alone in
Fancy. The pathologist's report showed that she had injuries consis-
tent with having been struck across the back of the head by a heavy
object—such as the boom of the skiff, or an oar, but her death had
been caused by drowning. Alice had been questioned by doctors for
the police, and had either remained mute or had answered incoher-
ently. Once again it was ruled that she was incompetent to appear in
court. The coroner's court brought in a verdict of death by drowning.

So Alice lived out her days in her suite of rooms at Pellham
Langley, and she was never, at any time, alone. The three nurses
constituted a round-the-clock watch on her, and no one of the family
was ever with her unless the nurse was there also. Black Jack had
given explicit instructions that neither of the little boys was ever to
be alone in Alice's company. He did not explain his command, but
they all knew its reason. So Alice played her gramophone records,
she appeared at dinner each night, with whichever of the nurses was
on duty waiting in the hall, and said little, except for the daily demand for news of Brock. Lacking stimulation, her mental processes

seemed to grow more clouded and obscure. "It would be better if she were in a clinic," a doctor once again recommended. "She would have more company—people trained to interest her in other things."

"She will never go into an institution," Black Jack repeated. "You can call me a stubborn old man, but I believe—have always believed —that to stay at home was the best for Alice. I blame myself for the problem of her birth. I don't intend to see her punished for it."

Sometimes Alice walked on the moors with Lally, but Black Jack's insistence that one of the nurses always be present took away the silent companionship of the former years. Alice, Lally tought, was never alone, but existed in the lonely cage of her own mind, and no one ever knew the thoughts that were imprisoned with her there. Her face seemed to grow more blank with time; she no longer joyously welcomed the event of the few visitors to Pellham. When David brought his friends, she kept strictly to her rooms. It was as if, Lally thought, Alice had at last begun to suspect that there was something strange about herself, something of which David was ashamed. She made the ritual appearance at the dinner table, and then vanished almost immediately dinner was over. "My Aunt Alice isn't quite right in the head," Lally had heard David say as he studied his next shot at the billiard table, unaware that Alice had slipped into the room to watch the game. "You mustn't pay any attention to her. She's quite harmless."

Lally had held Alice that night as she had sobbed out her hurt and loneliness, had lain on the bed with her until she had fallen asleep. The nurse on duty had sighed. "If only she would talk, Mrs. Pollock. She's shutting away the past, and it might help if she would talk. . . . The doctors say it helps. But she says less and less every day, poor soul. It will be terrible for her when the boys go back to America. She seems to understand that eventually the boys will go to their father. But I daren't talk to her about it. I don't want her upset until that time comes. She does adore Mr. Weymouth."

"And he loves her," Lally said. But she was no longer certain of that. They had another year to go before Brock would send for Dan and Sammy, perhaps less. There might be months of his sentence remitted. And what then?

At one time it would have been possible to predict almost exactly what would have happened. Brock would have found a house for Dan and Sammy rather like Whytecliffe, in the kind of place where they could be expected to meet the right people. They would be sent to the right prep schools. They would have been destined for Harvard or Yale, with perhaps a further year at Oxford to strengthen their English connection. They would have lived the lives of the sons of a rich man.

But it was November, and only a few weeks since prices on the New York Stock Exchange had dropped with a thud that had shaken the world. Daily, Lally had read of the tumble in the prices, and had watched the London market and world markets respond. It was not just age and illness that caused Black Jack's hands to tremble as he opened *The Times* each morning. "It's gone like wildfire, Lally," he said. "I hardly dare to read about it. I never thought I might have to get used to the idea of being poor."

"Our country has been poor for quite a while, Father. We've been poor since the end of the war."

"We'll be poorer still, then," Black Jack responded. "Who'll buy our cloth and our coal? America will be offering them dirt cheap just to have a market at all. Do you believe these stories of stockbrokers killing themselves? They're reported—I know some of the names. Surely the press couldn't invent *that!*"

"Brock often said most of it was built on paper. The paper seems suddenly to have blown away."

"And Brock—what will he do? He was one of the fastest and the surest in manipulating the market. If it was all paper, then his paper has blown away too."

"Yes—I suppose so. I suppose he's . . . he's poor," Lally said.

"He well could be. In fact, I wouldn't doubt it. Why would he escape? Everything he had, I'm certain, was in the market." Suddenly his expression brightened. "He might . . . he might want to leave Dan and Sammy with us."

"I can't see that. If Brock had to dig ditches, he'd want his sons with him."

"But they're also Margaret's sons. He couldn't bear the thought that they would have anything but the best."

"Can we afford the best, Father? *Now?*"

"We'll manage. We'll manage somehow. The coal's still in the ground. The mills are still there. When the good times come back—they always do, Lally—the mills will be turning out the cloth. And people always need coal. In the meantime, I've a bit of cash that will see us through. It isn't like a bit of blown-away paper."

Somehow, perhaps because of the constant talk among the nurses and in the servants' quarters about what was happening in America, and the effect on the British market, Alice seemed to have caught the drift of sudden poverty. She came shyly one morning to the library, the nurse standing well in the background.

"Everyone says we're poor, Father. You can sell these. These will make us rich again." She proffered the three strands of pearls that were identical to the pearls Black Jack had given Margaret and Lally at the time of their presentation at Court. And then the pearl earrings which had been Bobby Grenfell's gift to the bridesmaids when he and Margaret had married.

"Oh, darling . . ." Black Jack had openly wept. Alice had waited, and had smiled—almost the radiant smile Lally could remember from what seemed times long ago. Then Black Jack said, "Of course, darling—they will make us rich again. No need to worry now."

But there had not yet been time to assess what the full effect of the stock market collapse would be. There had been some cancellation of orders to the mills, already working under capacity. The mines would fill the orders in hand, but no new ones had come. Lally had, with Black Jack, attended a full board meeting the day before. Black Jack had looked pale and shrunken as he had chaired the first board meeting since his return from America nearly two years ago. His tone was somber as he spoke, having heard the reports from the various divisions of his mills.

"We will continue to pay our hands and the miners for as long as we can. We will stockpile for a while with the hope that the collapse is only temporary. We will meet again before any decision is made to close any major part of our manufactories. We can only follow what the rest of the world does. We cannot create business where none exists. We must make as generous a provision as possible if we have to lay off workers. But that doesn't mean that we stop." He raised his head with a sudden return of his old spirit. "I still expect you to go out and look for business. It has never been Pollock's policy to huddle behind the barricades, and hope the whole thing will go away. Go out and make contacts, gentlemen. We will need all our friends."

Neither Black Jack nor anyone else in that room dared yet envisage the full extent of the slump of the next years. "We may just be glad, gentlemen"—he suddenly remembered Lally's presence—"and Mrs. Pollock, that we have no great outstanding debts. We are solvent, and we will survive."

Survive. Lally contemplated the idle smokestacks of the mills.

Many of them had been working at only half capacity since the boom days of the war. She knew herself the state of the order books, but it didn't seem possible that the fall of share prices in New York could halve the demand for the products of the woolen mills of Yorkshire, the cotton mills of Lancashire. They had always produced the best, hadn't they? People would go on needing clothes; people would go on needing coal; Sheffield would continue to produce the knives and forks and spoons for the world. They were still the center of an empire, weren't they?—they turned the raw material into the finished goods that that empire consumed. But supposing the empire decided to buy less, much less? Supposing it couldn't afford to buy? Suppose there wasn't really an empire at all, as some people were beginning to say. Suppose it had all ended in the utter and futile waste of those four years of war, along with the waste of the ten million lives. Supposing the empire had begun to collapse? As America had seemed to collapse in these last weeks. Suddenly she saw before her all the faces of the dead, the endless dead, the wasted dead. She heard the boom of the great guns once more. There had followed a decade in which everyone had tried to forget the dead, the waste, and the sorrow. The decade when they had danced to forget, the music had swelled ever louder and faster, and everyone was getting rich. ·

The guns had fallen silent. And now the music had stopped. Only the wind blew among the crags and the heather as it had always done.

"Happy birthday, Lally."

She could not bring herself to turn, fearing that all she heard was the sound of her own longing. But the familiar voice went on. "It's November eleventh."

She rose slowly and stumbled, almost unbelievingly, into his outstretched arms. "Oh, Brock! You've never forgotten. And I've never forgotten the Fourth of July."

She let herself stand, just holding him, smelling the smell of his tweeds, the faint smoke that lingered on them like peat in whiskey. The reality of his presence was stronger than ever. It was possible now to begin to believe . . . believe what? She didn't know.

"How?" she demanded. "How did you get out? It should have been another year."

Gently he detached her clinging arms. "Mind if we sit down for a bit, Lally? A couple of years in prison doesn't keep a man in good shape. They don't play tennis there. I found I was breathing rather hard coming up the waterfall. Of course, I'm old, you know. I celebrated my fiftieth Fourth of July in there."

She pulled him down on the rock beside her. "Tell me . . . tell me everything."

He was maddeningly slow as he lighted cigarettes for them both. She had a chance to study his face, his body. He was thinner, but Brock had always been thin. Were the shoulders beginning to seem a little stooped? And didn't they say men in prison were always pale? But his hair was well cut, his nails manicured. Yet the downward lines around his mouth had deepened, had almost hardened. He looked at her with those cool dark-brown eyes. Was it possible that they were cooler, almost cold?

"Telling you everything will take a couple of years, if you've time to listen. But I'll begin. I'm out, Lally, because I know how to behave myself in prison. I've had experience. They let me work in the library. Now that's a real cushy job in prison. I almost enjoyed it. Besides, it gave me plenty of time to read. I even began to advise the warden on his investments—on the quiet, of course. Wouldn't do for the warden to be seen consorting with known criminals. But if he ordered a few more books on economics than the librarian thought were strictly necessary, then it was the warden's business. I suppose I was the only one who read them. That and the second copy of *The Wall Street Journal* that came every day.

"So I kept my nose clean, and I always knew the parole board would be lenient. They're even letting me report to the British police because my two young sons are over here, and they agreed that a father would want to go to them. That, I think, is being real nice."

"Brock, you're fooling, as you've always done. How did you get here? Why didn't you tell us you were coming?"

"Not sure, Lally. Really not sure of my reception."

"What did you *think* your reception would be? We've waited and waited. We've waited each day with you. None of us knew what you thought about . . . about Margaret. What you thought about Alice. All the letters about finances. What the boys were to have . . . and so on. We didn't know a thing about *you*."

"Look, Lally, I killed a man. I killed a man, mistakenly, in blind rage. I've brought such trouble on your family. I'd lost Margaret. I was responsible for having that animal who mauled Alice on my property. How could I know how you all judged me? Oh, you were kind—all of you, in those months when we were waiting for the case to come up. You all said it was because I loved Alice, and couldn't bear to see her hurt—especially not to see her hurt that way, a way that would make her afraid of all men. But what did you really think? When I knew about Black Jack's heart attack, it was almost worse than knowing about Margaret."

"*Worse?*"

"Margaret was always on the knife's edge. People who were unkind said Alice was mad, but Margaret's was willful madness. It might have been madness which tipped her out of the boat that day. It might have been Alice. If you ask me, Alice had more right to live."

Lally drew back, shocked. "I don't believe you! You always adored Margaret."

"At one time—yes. It was the other madness of my life—that, and when I killed Mark Shaw. I made a mistake that night at Neatherby. Not that I wouldn't have done just the same, but I thought Margaret's acceptance of that situation implied a promise. But it was a promise Margaret never gave. No one ever asked her if she really *wanted* our marriage. I just assumed I had the right to it. Perhaps for all the years of our marriage she felt trapped, and she twisted and turned inside that trap. I should have let her go, but she might have gone to something worse. When I realized what I'd turned her into, I felt it was my job to protect her, in whatever way I could. So I loved Alice and I felt a duty to the wife I had once adored. Margaret understood the game we played. She was there to be protected and adored, the eternal plaything. If I had let her grow up, I might truly have loved her. Perhaps I loved Alice because she couldn't grow up. She was stuck there, eternally in childhood. And she gave me her love without asking, without hesitation. When I killed Mark Shaw I killed because I believed he had defiled the one pure and innocent love I had ever known. The man who hurt her had to die. That's what I felt then. I blew up, and I killed the wrong man.

"I got definite information while I was in prison that the man who hurt her really had died. He died rather nastily. The mobs don't approve of attacking or killing women or children. They wait until the boys are men, and they leave the women alone—unless they're whores."

"So you were connected with . . . with the mobs? There was always talk . . ."

"Yes, there was always talk. A lot of it was hot air. Some of it was true. I made far more money playing the market than I ever did in bootlegging whiskey. I was small-time, Lally, in the eyes of the mobs. But I acted with their permission. If they'd wanted me out of the way, they'd have eliminated me. I'd come up hard, Lally. I knew some of them in the days when I'd have been glad to shine their shoes. Old connections are useful. I helped steer some bootleg money into legitimate markets. They trusted me. But they knew where I had to draw the line. Someone like Margaret or Black Jack or Edith wasn't going to be connected with the mobs. They have their own protocol. That's why Gambini died nastily. He'd broken the code."

She sat for a time, trying to understand all he had said, the revelations, the cold hard tone of his voice. What had he said of Margaret? "If I had let her grow up, I might truly have loved her."

She said, "You saw the coroner's report? About Margaret? What did you think? Did you think our Alice could have done that? Was it an accident? Or did Margaret—"

"Choose anything you like, Lally. Any solution. It hardly matters to me. If Margaret chose to go, then it was her choice, but if that was so, then she nearly murdered Alice by leaving her in the boat alone. If—and it's quite an if—Alice was suddenly filled with a murderous rage, then perhaps Margaret had earned that rage. Perhaps Alice acted out of fear of that long sail Margaret said they were going to take. And if it was an accident . . . Well, they tell me there is such a thing—I really don't know if I should say a person—as God, who acts in mysterious and inscrutable ways. Whatever way, for Margaret, the long party had come to an end."

"You've got it all worked out, haven't you? Quite dispassionately."

"Yes—this time I have. There's a lot of time to think when you're in prison. When I was in prison here in England, I was consumed with a desire to possess something I knew any kind of money couldn't buy. That's where my judgment went astray. This time, there were long nights. I don't sleep very well in the smell of a prison. I did a lot of thinking, as well as reading financial reports."

"Then why have you come? Why have you come here? You could have sent for the boys. We always expected you would."

"I had to find my way back. I had to find my way back to something that was civilized, and someplace I could be at peace." He put out his hands and clutched her shoulders as if seeking strength from her. "Do you think it doesn't bother me that I killed Mark Shaw?

That poor, asthmatic, wheezing little guy, who probably had more courage than I'll ever understand. At least he went into the trenches. I would have turned and run like a coward. Remember . . . I *saw* what was coming out of the trenches, unlike the generals I served. I killed a decent man . . . I believe an honorable man. Yes, it bothers me a lot."

"You never wrote any of this. Not a word. I wrote to you. You never made any reply that even hinted of what you were thinking."

"Could I say anything? What words were there? Words on paper. I couldn't set down my feelings like a row of figures. I suspected that that was all you ever thought me capable of—adding up a row of figures. I did what I could for my boys, and I prepared for the time when they'd let me out."

"Now you're out—and you've seen your boys. What now?"

"No—I haven't seen my boys."

"You haven't—you haven't seen Dan and Sammy? You haven't seen Black Jack . . . or Edith? Why? How did you find me here?"

He almost stroked the cigarette as he drew on it. "I remember many things, Lally, as well as your birthday. I got the taxi from Leeds to drive me around to the stable yard. Then I sent a note up to Billings. Even if he's confined to his room, he knows where everyone in that house is . . . or should be. He's been the one who's really kept me in touch with this household. Long letters every other month. He hasn't left me with many questions to ask about what has been going on at Pellham. He knew where you were—or guessed. We both guessed. I came here. I found you."

"But why . . . why?"

"You first, Lally. The rest of the family I have in my heart, but you first."

"What do you want of me?"

"God, what a difficult way to put it. I want everything of you. I want us to be what we were always meant to be. You and I, Lally, have no names. We belong to no one. But perhaps we belong with each other. Didn't Black Jack give you a name—Lally Leeds? And some high hat at the orphanage gave me a name. Brockton Weymouth. That's all we know about ourselves. What we are, we made for ourselves. We aren't lost souls drifting together. We're people who've seen the lot. Do you smell it still, Lally? The smell of poverty?"

"How do you know?"

"Because I've smelled it myself. We're two of a kind. We had to wait to get the madness of our other loves out of our minds."

"Mine wasn't a mad love. I *loved* Jon."

"I know you loved him. I know how well. I envied him for that love. I can't ask you to love me that well, Lally. I just ask that you hold me in your heart, as you do the others."

She had always known it was true. She had always held him in her heart, rejoiced with him, sorrowed with him. He had always been there, from that first day.

He turned her face deliberately toward the mass of Pellham Langley, and then back toward the smokestacks of the mills. "Do you see it all? How much there is? How much responsibility?"

"How do you know I see it that way? You never wrote to me."

"I didn't dare write to you. You were beyond me. I couldn't attempt to influence you. You were Lally. Incorruptible. No money would buy you. No promise of good times. No sheltering. No holding. Why was I afraid of coming back to this family? Because of you."

"What are you saying?" She heard her voice sounding as cold as his had been.

"Will we marry, Lally? Will we consummate this as it might always have been meant to be? In the name of Lally Leeds and Brockton Weymouth—which are no names at all. Shall we make this a union?"

"Yes." The word was so simply said. It had been a long time coming.

He didn't even kiss her. Their kisses were meant for later, as they had always been. He drew her gently to her feet.

"Something else I wanted to tell you—but it wasn't nearly as important as what we've just agreed. At one time it wouldn't have mattered. You would have taken money for granted in a marriage to me. But now I have to tell you. I got out of the market about five months ago. I read so much in the bloody goddamned prison I knew the game was up for all of us. Or maybe it was just the prickling of my thumbs. Instinct—something every good gambler develops. I got out of the market. I sold everything I had. At the top of the market. So now all I have to offer you and Black Jack is a slice of capital, and some experience." He turned her to look directly at the chimney stacks. "I don't know when they'll all be smoking again. It might even take another war to get them going full blast. But it will be someday. In the meantime, I have a stash of whiskey legally in warehouses in Canada against the day Prohibition ends. And it will. That's for certain. And I'm buying real estate. Leases. Land. I'm buying back into the market at rock-bottom prices. I'm buying anything solid that will hold for the future."

"You'll never change, Brock. Always looking at the future. Always calculating . . ."

They were about to start climbing down the side of the waterfall. He held her back briefly.

"Yes, calculating, if you want to put it that way. But the calculations have changed. I came here first for you—then my boys. And this time I have no need to go back and prove anything to America. I couldn't take you all away from here. I couldn't leave Black Jack and Edith alone. Or Alice. David, Dan, and Sammy will grow up as Jonathan would have. Oh, yes, there'll be expeditions over there—raids, I suppose you might say. And I'll want you with me. But this will be home. Will Black Jack have me, do you think?"

"If you ask him—nicely."

He grinned. "Damn it, Lally. You know why I didn't write you—except those stupid letters about expenses, and so on? I thought if I wrote you'd start thinking you had to wait for me. Some sort of commitment. I wanted to find you—just like this. Hoping to God you still had some sort of place for me in your life. But not pinning you down as if it were some sort of promise. I didn't want you trying to make up . . . make up for everything. Do you understand, Lally? It isn't for the kids, or Black Jack or Alice. It isn't to help get the mills and the mines rolling. If it were just you and me here on top of the world, bare-assed, without a penny to our names—and always remember, neither of us *has* a name—I want it to be just for you and me. There won't be many surprises. Not much excitement. Is that O.K. with you, Lally?"

She nodded. "Yes."

Brock leading, they started down the rocks by the waterfall, rocks slippery with wind-driven spray. The recent rain had turned the falls into a torrent, and the noise pounded in Lally's ears. She put a foot down tentatively, and felt Brock's hands supporting her.

"Didn't you hear what I said?"

"What?" she shouted.

"About kids. We're going to have kids, Lally. Aren't we?"

She looked down at him, and beyond him to Pellham Langley, the huge mass of the house now almost lost in the evening shadow. The chimneys threw out smoke; the gardens had retreated behind their sheltering hedges. The world of Pellham Langley lay below her, and she saw it differently. She remembered that long-ago boast of Jon's that they would fill its rooms with children. Her senses quickened. It was Brock's face she looked at now, and no ghost of Jon came between them. They would be different, these children they promised each other. Not Black Jack's grandchildren, but Brock's children. Her children. The children of a new and uncertain age, and a father who would help to shape that age. These children's destinies would lie on both sides of the Atlantic, but would be centered here, the place that had first sheltered and cradled her, the place where she had been reborn. Perhaps only Brock, in all the world, understood what that meant.

She looked at him, and then jumped down to his level. They almost fell. Lally felt the spray of the waterfall on her face. She stretched up to put her arms about him.

"Yes, there'll be kids. And a lot more."

"I love you, Lally."